INDEPENDENCE PASS

*A possibly true story of blackmail, betrayal and bank robbery
set in the old Colorado west retold by an unreliable source*

PAUL W HARRIS

This is a work of fiction and not an historical document

ISBN: 0996657010
ISBN 13: 9780996657013
Library of Congress Control Number: 2015915636
Silver Queen Productions, Aspen, CO

Silver Queen Productions LLC, PO Box 938, Aspen, CO 81612
silverqueenproductions.com

To Tisha,
Hau 'oli la hanau!

This book could never have come to pass without the love and perseverance of my wife Caroline. Neither could it have come into literary being without the dedication and professionalism of my editor, Rebekah Williamson to whom I am enormously grateful. As my editor she taught me about writing. Nor could I have written this book without having a deep love and appreciation for all of the residents of Aspen both living and passed. It is from their stories and their history that this tale unfolds.

I hope you enjoy the adventure

Paul Harris

Chapter 1

Dublin, Ireland
1888

It wasn't raining hard. With the coming of the night it had eased into a brooding mist that wet the face, matted the hair, and made the footing treacherous. The splash of his misstep echoed off the walls of the narrow alley. One of the men ahead of him at the end of the alley turned back at the sound and looked his way. Daniel pushed his slight body into a notch in the wall, pressing his face against the mossy, wooden garden gate and prayed. Ages passed until he heard them move on. He dared a quick look to be certain and breathed again.

Slipping from alley to alley, shadow to shadow, he followed them all the way into the very center of the city, ignorant of their purpose. They dropped into a coal chute of a building across from the Bank of Dublin. Daniel crept forward. Suddenly, the head of a large man appeared from the hole and whistled. As if by magic, two men appeared out of the shadows and joined them in the hole. Daniel inched closer; enough that he could hear a man's voice.

"Where are the others, Clive?" the man hissed, his voice resonating in the small space.

"Dun'no, Paddy," said Clive. "Drank too much courage, I'd guess."

"Shit," answered Paddy. " Well, are we going to do this or not?"

"What if a police patrol comes?" Daniel heard a raspy, familiar voice ask.

"That's why we had the four lookouts," Paddy replied sharply, barely controlling his anger. "Look here, lads, we've got the dynamite and we've the opportunity here. Are you men or mice, eh? I say we go ahead. What say you?" There was no dissent.

Daniel was surprised by how much the voice commanded alliance. He all but stood up from his hiding place and rallied to the call.

"Alright then," Paddy's voice was decisive, "me and Patrick will set the charges and you two go down the block and watch. Whistle twice if you see anyone coming." Daniel hid as the two lookouts scurried off to opposite ends of the block and disappeared into the shadows.

Daniel dared a look and saw Paddy unwrapping a bundle. From his hiding place he listened, as best he could, as Patrick was instructed on how to safely insert the fuses into the explosives. Patrick was a quick learner and in five minutes, their chore was finished.

"Are you ready?" Paddy asked. Daniel had to duck back down quickly as Paddy stood up. "Come on then," he whispered.

The veils of shadows and wisps of fog cloaked them as they crept up to the bank, then they disappeared from Daniel's view. A match flared in the darkness and died. So intently was Daniel watching, he jumped when he felt a hand grab a hold of his shoulder. His heart stopped. Another match flared, he saw its reflection in the policeman's shiny buttons. The policeman roughly pulled Daniel closer, eyeing him suspiciously.

"What're you doing here, lad?" he barked, his face just inches from Daniel's. Whether it was fear for his own sake or for the other's he didn't know, but without consideration of the consequences, he jerked his knee up into the man's groin as hard as he could. The policeman released his grip and let out an "Ooff" sound, grasping his precious testicles with both hands. He looked at Daniel through tearing eyes filled with rage, but could do nothing to stop the brick in Daniel's hand from landing flat against the side of his head. He buckled at the knees and fell face forward. Daniel turned to run, but was held in place. The bobby's helmet had deflected the blow. He grasped Daniel's leg with a shackle-like grip.

The cop was stunned but not defeated. He fumbled for the whistle hanging on a lanyard around his neck and lifted himself unsteadily to his knees. He brought his whistle to his mouth and drew a breath to sound the alarm. Daniel felt anger rising in him. He slammed the brick a second time with all of his strength, hitting the policeman on the side of his head again. The cop was a tough product of the Dublin slums and though blood gushed from his temple, he reached again for his whistle. Daniel struck him with the brick again and again until the man fell limp at his feet.

His breath came in gasps; he fell back against the wall, still holding the bloody brick. His mind raced. He had done something unthinkable and he was in trouble so deep, it horrified him. Overwhelmed and shocked by his actions, he threw the bloody brick off into the night and dropped to his knees beside his fallen victim. The policeman lying inert beside him had seen his face. That was as good as a guilty verdict in a court of English law, followed by life in prison.

Daniel rose and stood over the fallen man, watching the blood, black as oil, seep over the rocks. The man at his feet stirred. Daniel came to his senses as if awakened from sleep. He wheeled and raced for the bank as fast as his legs would move him.

***

Patrick was mesmerized by his handiwork. He was intently watching the burning fuses, oblivious to the sound of running feet approaching, when his father pulled him back down into the recess. Patrick rose and saw Daniel running towards them, waving his arms. They looked at each other, mystified.

"Dud! Dud! Run, quick. There's a policeman coming," Daniel shouted. Paddy looked along the street seeing nothing, his anger rising. The two lookouts had also heard Daniel and were standing up, looking towards them.

"What the hell are you doing here, Daniel?" Paddy hissed when Daniel reached them. "I told you not to follow us. Ever!" Paddy raised his hand, but Daniel grabbed his arm.

"No, Dud. There's a cop over there. I just hit him over the head with a brick. Really, I did."

Paddy and Patrick looked at each other, then at the fuses rushing towards their explosive purpose. The shrill double octave of a police whistle split the night. They turned as one to see the injured cop stumbling towards them, blowing his whistle with all the breath he could summon.

"Oh, shit! Run, boys, run." Paddy gave the burning fuses one last look before he pushed his sons ahead of him. "Go, I say. Run like your lives depend on it." Daniel faltered, his father pushed him angrily. "Go, I say."

"What about him?" Daniel pointed at the approaching policeman and looked over at the sputtering fuses inching towards their destination.

"No matter, now. Get going! Now, I say!" It was too late for changes in plans.

Paddy was not the running man he was in his youth and began to fall behind, the police whistle gaining on them every second. The boys grasped him under the arms, pulling him along. Paddy stopped abruptly and looked back as if changing his mind.

It was dreamlike. Even before the sound of the explosion reached them, the policeman and his whistle left the ground in a giant flash of red and orange, his limbs flailing as he hurtled through the air like a rag doll tossed by an impatient child. Bricks and mortar clattered into the street, as smoke and dust mingled with misty air. In only one second, their world had changed.

Without another look back, they disappeared into the night, tight-jawed and scared, trailing the sounds of police whistles and the clanging of fire alarm bells.

⸎

Myra Shadlow woke with a start. She'd been fast asleep with her daughter Megan's head on her lap when her three men burst into the small stone cottage that was their home. Paddy didn't look at her as he lurched to the cupboard that held his whiskey bottle. She watched silently, her alarm rising as he drank thirstily. Her two sons stood sheepishly by the door, breathing hard, faces flushed. Myra Shadlow was no fool. She looked at them in turn until she rested her eyes on Daniel and raised an eyebrow.

"And what have you all been up to?" Daniel was no match for her gaze and dropped his eyes. Patrick did the same. She turned her head slowly and scrutinized her husband's face. Unbidden, her heart began to race. She sensed that something grave had happened.

"Myra, I think you'd better pack our things, quick like." Paddy said.

"Why?" Myra impaled Patrick with a look. Patrick, who by local reputation was the braver of her sons, stared at the floor and shuffled his feet nervously. Myra knew, as mothers do, that his courage withered when faced with the threat of her disappointment. "Patrick, look at me." She snapped at him, surprising them all.

"Dud blew up the bank of England, mum." Patrick blurted out.

"Oh, Paddy. You didn't. Not again?" Paddy was busy drinking and didn't meet her eyes. "Was anyone hurt?" she asked, and again looked from one guilty face to the other. Paddy finally looked at her and shrugged his shoulders, repeating a gesture that she'd seen all too often. The unspoken answer was as clear to her as if written on a blackboard.

"It was an accident, Myra. Really, it was. Wasn't it, lads?" Patrick and Daniel nodded like puppets.

"There'll be nowhere we can hide. They'll find us and we'll all go to prison. Where can we go?" she cried, certain that as poor as they were and as meager as their life was, it was by far preferable to spending years on a filthy prison barge on London's River Thames. Sedition against the British Empire was a treasonous offense and the monarchy's prosecution of offenders was relentless and notoriously without mercy. Megan began to sob and clung to her mother tightly.

"America!" Paddy shouted, startling them, "That's where we'll go." Paddy smiled brightly as if his sudden inspiration was an invitation for a family holiday. Silence greeted his enthusiasm, but Paddy was far from crestfallen. "Come on, everyone. Hurry, now. Pack your things. We'll leave tonight. I've friends that'll help us get on a ship." He bustled them off into their respective rooms as he issued orders, "Come on, me hearties. Hurry up and grab what you need. We'll be safe, but we've no time to lose."

Daniel and his family threw themselves into the whirlwind of escape. With their precious few belongings, they made a dash to the docks, where ships sailed for America almost daily. What was one more poor Irish family on a boat full of them?

⊲⊫

The foiled robbery was headline news the next morning, though if the truth were known, robbery was not the principle intention of the perpetrators. Politicians smirked privately, but assured the public that the police detectives were doing their jobs tirelessly. For the most part, that meant that they were making their rounds, beating any and all possible suspects in the vague hope of finding information. All over Dublin the police buzzed about like bees from a broken hive, searching and questioning people from all walks of life.

As is the danger with conspiracies, someone talked. Paddy and his son Patrick Shadlow became wanted criminals. Posters describing them sprouted all over Dublin, like weeds in the spring. Paddy's friends and fellow conspirators may have been stout of heart while drunk, but when sober, none was brave enough to take part in their escape, other than giving food for the voyage and wishing them well.

Paddy discreetly worked the docks and by calling in old favors, secured tickets on a merchant ship named the S.S. Orion, sailing for New York on the evening tide. Luck seemed to be with them; the dock was guarded by only a single policeman at the gate, looking bored and superior as he watched the impoverished emigrants and half-drunk well-wishers passing before him.

Myra clutched Paddy tightly as they approached the ship, which looked tired and rusty from many ocean crossings. Tenderly, he placed his arm around her, pulling her to him. He smiled his best smile and pulled them all closer to him.

"Alright, this is it, then. You're the Carrington family now." Paddy announced quietly. "Here are your tickets." Paddy handed each their tickets. "I suggest you try to be as English as you can." Myra saw that there were only four tickets.

"Paddy, where's your ticket?" Myra cried, grabbing his coat sleeves, forcing him look at her.

"Myra, you know me, I'm afraid of the sea." Paddy looked away, fighting tears.

"God Almighty, we're not swimming to America," Myra cried, "that there's a boat!" and she threw her arms about his neck, sobbing. "Paddy, you can't leave us!"

Daniel and Patrick looked at each other, confused. Daniel placed his arm around Megan's shoulder protectively as they watched the unraveling of their family. Paddy held his wife at arm's length and adored her.

"Look here, Myra," Paddy said, trying his best to sound reasonable. "All I could get was four tickets." It was a lie and Myra knew it.

Paddy just couldn't do it. He couldn't find the courage to leave the shore. Here he was, a grown man once proud and fearless, admitting to his family, and to himself for perhaps the first time, that he was unable to conquer his demons. Myra saw the truth in his eyes. "You have to come with us," she pleaded desperately.

"Come on now, Myra. You'll be alright." Paddy gathered Megan to him, enveloping his two women in his arms, fighting back tears. 'If ever there was a time to be strong, then it is now.' he told himself.

Paddy took a deep breath and steeled himself for the cruel lie he was about to tell.

"You all go on ahead and I'll follow as soon as I can get on another ship. I'll meet you in New York, soon. I promise." Silence engulfed them. Nobody seemed to be breathing.

"I'll stay with him, mum." Patrick said, placing his hand on her shoulder.

Myra stiffened and looked up at Paddy; fear in her eyes, her hand to her mouth. Patrick and his father had done everything together since he could walk. That he would leave his father here, in danger and alone, was inconceivable to him. Paddy smiled at his wife, love and sadness welling up jointly.

"There you go, Myra. See there? Patrick and me, we'll be on the next ship. Daniel can look after you all until we arrive. You'll do that for me, won't you Daniel?" Paddy drew Daniel to him looking deeply into his eyes. Daniel would always remember the smell of his father that night; a mixture of musky wet wool, sweet whiskey and sour fear.

"I, I, I will." Daniel said bravely, looking up at his father, realizing innately that he was being abruptly thrust into manhood. They held each other's gaze and each knew the other's mind as if they were one. Daniel saw there, in all of its cold clarity, that his father was leaving them, that he would not set foot on the next boat, or the next one, or any one.

Paddy knew it too, as he looked from one child to the other, comprehending that his sons would carry a share of the responsibility for his actions all of their lives. Never before had Paddy experienced such a crushing burden as the sadness he saw written on their innocent faces, knowing full well that it was he alone who should have to bear that weight.

The ship's steam whistle blew, shrill and deafening, startling them.

"All passengers aboard ship please. Last call for boarding passengers," announced the officer at the boarding plank. The time had come. Paddy breathed deeply, drawing courage from the Irish air.

"Now, listen up. Don't all go on together," Paddy advised, "Megan; I want you to stay with your mother." Megan's wide eyes answered, she nodded, unable to express her fears. "Here, Daniel. I want you take this, you'll need it. It's all the money I have." Paddy pushed a roll of notes into his son's hand. "Daniel, listen to me close. I'm trustin' you to keep safe all that I hold dear to me. Take good care of them. You'll be alright when you get to America. Someone will meet you. Now go on, and God bless all of you." It broke his heart to act so callously to the only woman he'd ever loved. He steeled himself to her tears and forced himself to smile.

"Myra, be strong. Please? For the children's sake."

"Why, Paddy?" she sobbed. "Why did you do this thing to me? To us?" she sobbed. Her desperate sadness cut Paddy's heart to ribbons. In his wildest dreams he would never have imagined that he would be forced to send his one true love away from his side.

He reluctantly pried his wife's hand from his. Daniel took his mother's arm as he led his little group into the line of passengers ascending to the ship's deck. Weeping, Myra turned back to wave at the only man she'd ever loved. This sudden division of her family was something she would not have considered if she had to live a thousand years. The ravages of her despair were draining her soul of the will to live by the minute.

"Come on, mum. We've got to go." Daniel urged his mother. "Dud'll find us. You know he will. You two go on ahead of me and I'll see you on board. Megan, take her arm and please try not to draw attention."

Daniel lagged behind and watched as the officer checking their tickets gave his mother and sister nothing more than a cursory glance. He watched them climb onto the ship and steeled himself for his own inspection as he approached the ship's officer.

'One more to go,' Paddy said to himself and crossed his fingers as he watched them board. He glanced sidelong at Patrick and placed his arm around Patrick's shoulder.

"Ticket sir," the officer asked Daniel. He handed the man his ticket and his heart stopped when he looked into Daniel's eyes as if reading him. "No luggage with you, sir?" he asked.

"I.I.I. g.g.guess I.I.I..f...forgot." Daniel stuttered.

"Daniel. Daniel," he heard over the crowd and saw his brother pushing through to the ramp, carrying his lone piece of luggage aloft. Smiling as if reprieved, Daniel waved to his brother as the cheap valise bound with one of his father's old belts was passed up to him. The officer watched the exchange with interest. Daniel was not the name on the ticket he held in his hand.

"Well, on you go then," said the officer. Daniel hurried up the ramp onto the main deck crowded with passengers and crew preparing for departure. Carrying his suitcase, he climbed the rusty steps to the top deck, one deck higher than his mother and sister. He found a space at the railing where he had a clear view of the dock below and made out his father and brother amongst the crowd. He waved, but they didn't see him. They weren't looking at him, but at his mother and sister.

As sailors began releasing mooring lines, the clear voice of an unknown tenor began singing 'Auld lang sine'. The crowd joined him and their voices rose to sing a lament to those who were leaving their homeland, heading off to a foreign land and to an uncertain future. Daniel felt his eyes stinging as the thought of leaving Ireland forever struck home.

Movement on the far edge of the crowd caught his attention. A black police wagon drawn by two black horses stopped at the gate to the dock, blocking it. Another appeared. From the back of the wagons spilled six policemen dragging a man bound in hand-cuffs whom Daniel instantly recognized. It was Clive, one of his father's friends and one of the lookouts the night they had blown up the bank. With mounting alarm, Daniel watched as Clive was joined by a well-dressed gentleman wearing a bowler hat and carrying a black umbrella. With an air of authority, the man in the bowler hat grabbed Clive by the collar, pushing Clive ahead of him into the crowd.

Daniel leaned out from the rail precariously, waving his arms to get his father's attention. He screamed their names, but they couldn't hear over the singing of the crowd. Danger was drawing closer. If only they would turn around, they might see the police moving through the crowd, but they didn't, focused as they were on his mother and sister. Relentlessly, the bowler hatted man moved closer and closer, still with a tight grip on Clive, who searched the faces in the crowd. Three more policemen followed them a few feet behind.

"Dud. Patrick...Dud." He yelled out, jumping up and down like a madman. The police had his father and brother surrounded and were closing in like a net being drawn shut. Again and again he screamed their names, yelled and waved his arms wildly, but still they didn't see him. The other passengers most certainly noticed him.

The ship's steam whistle screamed, crushing all other noise. Daniel, his hands to his ears, watched helplessly as the gangplank was pulled aboard and sailors cast off the last of the ship's mooring lines. Panic threatened to overwhelm him as the boat separated itself from the pier and the distance from the dock slowly grew.

Oblivious to those around him, Daniel continued waving his arms and screaming until his voice was just a rasping whisper. Finally he caught Patrick's attention, but Patrick couldn't hear his warnings over the noise of the crowd's chorus and waved back. Daniel emphatically pointed over their heads again and again.

"Behind you!" Daniel shouted, pointing behind them, silently mouthing the word 'Police' over and over until finally Patrick understood.

Patrick grabbed his father's arm and pointed at Daniel. He understood Daniel's warning. They turned and darted into the crowd.

Paddy hadn't gone but a few yards when he stopped abruptly, surprised to see his old friend Clive, but then he saw the dapper detective holding him by the neck. Clive stood still as a statue, surprised that Paddy had seen him first. There appeared to be a moment of indecision, and on Paddy's part disbelief, as they faced each other. With uncanny intuition, the crowd about them backed away and a space grew around them. The detective turned Clive towards their quarry.

"Is that the man?" he yelled, shoving Clive at Paddy. Clive, wide-eyed, pointed a damning finger at Paddy.

Paddy, realizing he'd been betrayed by his best friend, leapt for Clive's throat. Bowler hat saw and drew his pistol, but Paddy knocked it from his hand. The detective reached for his fallen weapon, and Paddy kicked it aside. They stood mere feet apart, glaring at one another, each with an urgent mission. Paddy let go his grip on Clive's throat and darted into the crowd, pushing Patrick ahead of him. The detective smiled at Clive as he bent and gathered up his pistol. He blew hard into his police whistle, directing his reinforcements after the fleeing pair, as the ship sent three short deafening blasts of its own into the air.

Along with his mother and sister, Daniel was forced to watch, horrified and helpless as the police descended upon their prey. Energetically using their truncheons with practiced skill, they viciously and cheerfully went about their duty of pummeling their quarry to the ground. Daniel couldn't imagine what his mother was going through watching this, or even if she could watch it, but he knew his sister would and she'd remember it all.

Tears blurred his vision and the lamplights along the dock haloed as he watched the police handcuff his father's arms and then his brother's behind their backs, and then drag their slack bodies away to the police wagon. He would forever remember the metallic taste of his anger as he watched his father and brother loaded like animal carcasses into the black Mariah.

Slowly, the reddish hue in his vision cleared. Only then did Daniel notice that the tall, well-dressed detective had separated from the group of policemen, and was walking purposefully towards the departing ship with Clive trailing him like a terrier. The man carried his rolled umbrella in military fashion, more as a sign of authority than protection from the elements. With Clive in tow, the detective walked along the dock, searching the crowded decks methodically. When their eyes met, though just momentarily, Daniel wanted to run and hide. His legs wouldn't obey. The man's eyes moved on, continuously searching. Daniel breathed again.

The S.S. Orion nosed into the channel. A hundred feet of oily water separated them but Daniel could feel the danger emanating from the man in the bowler hat, who was staring at the ship as if willing it to return to the dock.

Clive spotted Daniel. Smiling like a schoolboy, he tugged at the detective's sleeve, pointing. Daniel felt frozen in place, exposed. Like a hunter spotting his prey, the detective aimed his black umbrella directly at him and drew his finger across his throat. Those near him edged away. The detective's piercing stare held Daniel like an invisible rope that tied him to the shore.

As the distance between them grew, fog slowly enveloped the dock. Nothing was left of his beloved Ireland but the detective's eyes. It wasn't until the man had dissolved completely into the mist that Daniel could release the railing and say goodbye to his country and the loved ones it retained, wondering if he would ever see it, or them, again.

Chapter 2

New York

Daniel, Megan, and his mother stood elbow to elbow with the rest of the passengers as the S.S. Orion steamed up the East River into the New York Harbor. It was a gloomy morning, but still cheers rang out as they passed the Statue of Liberty, which appeared to have risen from the water cloaked in the early morning mist. The mood onboard was festive, with much backslapping and handshakes, as the passengers congratulated each other for having survived the rough weather of the Atlantic crossing. Gradually, a calm settled over the ship as the passengers prepared to disembark, each with his or her own dream of what the mighty statue mythically symbolized.

Myra had not fared well on the voyage. Weakened by worry and sea sickness, she looked pale and frail as they huddled together in the entrance to the cavernous hall of the Ellis Island Immigration Processing Center. From here they were herded like cattle by stern uniformed officials into lines that stretched the length of the building. Daniel noticed that officers were walking through the waiting crowd, examining some families closely. His worry increased when he overheard a rumor that they were sending sick immigrants back to Ireland. He jumped when he felt a tap on his shoulder from an elderly fellow passenger.

"They're looking for someone named Shadlow. Pass it on," the man whispered. Daniel's knees began to shake, but he did as he was told, despite the lump that had formed in his throat. The name Shadlow passed along the line.

It was the late afternoon when finally their turn came. Daniel stepped forward to present their papers to the official and prayed that the documents he'd forged on the boat would be enough. The official located their names on the ship's passenger list and glanced again at Daniel's forgeries. He gave Daniel a questioning look.

"It says here that there are supposed to be four Carringtons. There seems to be a Mr. Patrick Carrington missing from your party. Is he your father?" Daniel nodded dumbly. "Is your father not with you?"

"N.n.no." replied Daniel. "H.h.he's not coming." As soon as the words left his lips, a lump formed in his throat. "He died." Daniel blurted and heard his mother stifle a gasp.

"After he bought the tickets, I suppose?"

"Yes. It was sudden? Pneumonia." Daniel crossed his fingers behind his back. The official rocked back in his chair, considering them each in turn. He abruptly stood, scraping the chair legs on the floor. He was a thick set man, taller than expected and Daniel's pulse quickened as he came around the table and approached them. He offered his hand to Myra politely. She reached out her own trembling hand, which he took gently in his.

"May I extend my deepest condolences to you and your family, Mrs. Carrington," the official said sincerely. Myra attempted a smile and almost succeeded. He turned to face Daniel. "Stay here, Mr. Carrington," he instructed and walked to an office. Daniel watched him conferring with another immigration officer seated at a desk. They glanced at Daniel several times during their conversation, as if considering something unpleasant. He focused on helping Megan attend to his mother.

Several minutes passed before the two officials returned together. Their demeanor was professionally severe. Daniel prepared for the worst.

"Mr. Carrington, I want you and your family to go with this officer here," the officer said handing Daniel back his papers. "Welcome to America, Mr. Carrington. Good luck to you." He turned and resumed his seat at his table. "Next," he barked and gave no more notice to Daniel or his family.

The new official said nothing to them as he led them through a side door to a pier where a small cutter sat. He spoke quietly to the man at the helm and politely helped them aboard, placing their luggage inside the cabin. The two men cast off the lines and the little craft caught the wind and hurried away from the island. In the tiny cabin out of the wind, they huddled together for warmth and courage as they crossed the choppy grey water headed towards New York City.

The boat tied up at a largely deserted wharf, where the official helped them up the slippery wooden steps from the boat and escorted them down a long warehouse. At the far end a short, squat man dressed in a long plaid coat and wearing a short top hat stood, casually leaning against a wall, picking his teeth. At their approach, he pushed himself from the wall, straightening his coat. He looked at them each in turn, closely, as if he were buying them.

"May I call you Myra?" the man asked gently in an accent so familiar, Myra was taken aback. She didn't answer, but the strange looking man seemed to appreciate her condition, and smiled at her and at Megan. In a kindly manner, he came closer. Daniel could smell the whiskey on him. "And you're Daniel Shadlow, am I right, son?" he asked in a whisper. His manner was businesslike, but not discourteous. Daniel looked back at his mother, ashamed that they had been caught at the very doorstep of safety. Daniel nodded.

"Good," said the man, and clapped his hands together smiling a broad, if uneven smile, as if he'd won a sporting wager. "Stay put a moment." He walked a short distance away, guiding the official into a darkened corner. Daniel watched as the man handed the silent immigration official a thick envelope, which he opened. Smiling, he placed it into his coat pocket and without a word, touched his forefinger to the bill of his cap and walked back to his waiting boat.

"You'd all better come with me, quickly now." The man urged when he returned.

"Who are you, sir?" Daniel blurted out, confused and scared.

"Just say that a brave soldier like your father has many friends." At this, Myra stopped walking.

"Do you know Paddy?" she asked hopefully.

"Aye. We were friends." he smiled and gently took Myra's arm as he guided them towards the door. "Let's hurry before someone notices us." He led the way through a small door which opened onto a quiet side street where a horse and carriage awaited them. Myra stopped abruptly and faced the man.

"Who are you? And how did you know we were on that ship?" Myra inquired as the short Irishman helped her into the wagon after he had loaded the luggage.

"My name is Hogan. John Hogan. We've been expecting you," he said, encouraging Daniel and Megan to board the carriage. "And so have the authorities, by the look of it." Hogan added, handing her a folded paper. She opened it and held her hand to her mouth before passing it to Daniel with trembling fingers.

Daniel's eyes grew wide as he read. Written in bold letters on sturdy paper the words "Wanted for Treason" jumped out at him. "For treasonous acts and bank robbery, the sum of five thousand dollars is offered for the return to Great Britain of the terrorist named Daniel Shadlow." There followed an accurate description of Daniel which also contained the facts that he was traveling with his mother and his sister. It stated quite clearly that they were aboard the S.S. Orion and that they were all to be apprehended and placed on the same vessel for its return voyage. The guaranteed reward was to be paid by the Pinkerton Detective Agency at an address in New York City.

"That's a considerable sum they're offering for you, son. Enough for a frugal man to live out his days well. I should think there'd be many men wanting to get their hands on that reward."

Daniel closed his eyes. A tomblike silence swelled inside the carriage as it clip-clopped along the stones of the street. Slowly Daniel lifted his head and looked into the eyes of his mother and sister before he spoke what was on all of their minds at that moment.

"What can we do? Where can we go?" he asked the man, his voice low and desperate.

"For the time being, I know a safe place here in the city. It's filled with a million other Irish, so you won't stand out."

"I don't know how we can pay for this, Mr. Hogan. This is all the money we have." Daniel opened the leather wallet his father had given him.

Hogan looked at the money. "English money'll do you no good here, son."

"I'll get a job then," Daniel replied.

"I might be able to help you there," Hogan reassured them.

"Why are you helping us Mr. Hogan?" Myra asked.

"We're called the Fenians. We're a stout group of Republican Irishmen, bound and determined to repel the Protestants back to England." Hogan puffed out his chest and straightened his jacket. "Paddy Shadlow, your brave husband, was one of us."

The Fenians were a loose collection of Irish patriots who, with some regularity, hatched drunken conspiracies in pubs across the country, much to the annoyance of the English authorities.

Hogan placed his hand gently on Myra's shoulder and smiled. "That makes his family one of ours. You're not to worry yourselves. All will be well."

⊰⊱

Hogan's refuge was cold and damp and cramped. It was neither clean nor quiet, but it was shelter. They settled in with their few belongings and with the help of their new found friend, Hogan, Daniel found work running errands for Hogan's friends, mostly a scruffy, dirty lot involved in stealing and gambling. The small payments he received went directly into his mother's hands.

Megan cleaned and cooked in the communal kitchen and seemed to settle into their new surroundings, caring for her mother and making her as comfortable as was possible. Myra's health was also improving, but for a persistent cough. She barely saw Daniel anymore. He went out early and would return each night after dark to their small refuge, eat his dinner and collapse on his musty mattress.

John Hogan visited once a week, usually bearing a small package of meat or some other rare commodity. He always brought along news from Ireland and at least one ribald joke to tell them. Myra continuously asked for news of her husband and her son, but Hogan would say only that they were both still alive.

At the end of these evenings, before he left them, Daniel would hand Hogan money for the rent. Hogan would take it respectfully and touch his hand to the brim of his hat in return, as he said goodnight.

The weeks passed and the weather turned warmer. Daniel fell into rhythm of sorts and he'd all but forgotten his problem with the police when there was a knock at their door. It was Hogan and he was sweating.

"Can I come in?" he asked, as he pushed past Daniel.

"What's the matter, Mr. Hogan?" Myra asked. "You look like you've run a mile."

"I'm sorry Myra, but I have some bad news," he was looking at Daniel. "Son, I think it best if you pack some things. You have to leave here."

Daniel looked from Hogan to his mother to Megan.

"When? Why!" Daniel's voice trembled.

"Someone's been asking around about you. I can't be sure, but he sounds like he could be a Pinkerton man. They all dress alike. Black riding coats and black hats, it's like a uniform. I think he was one of them." He gripped Daniel's arm tightly. "You have to leave tonight. It's for your own good and the sake of your family, son." Hogan looked Daniel in the eye, his sincerity showing. "Look at me. You can't help them if you're in chains headed back to Ireland."

Daniel knelt down at his mother's feet. He looked up into her eyes. Myra's heart was breaking once again. He could see it clearly. There was nothing she could do.

"We'll make certain that your mother and sister are cared for, but you have to leave. It's not safe for you here, Daniel."

"You must go, Daniel." Myra drew her courage from some hidden wellspring and smiled bravely. "When, Mr. Hogan, will I be able to see my Daniel again?"

"It might be awhile. Do you know anyone in California?"

"My brother, Clancy Cody, he's in San Francisco." Myra said brightening. "He's made money there. He'll help us."

"That's good. I have a friend, a fellow Fenian, he can help you find where your Uncle Clancy is, I'm sure."

Daniel held his mother's hands tightly. "I'll work hard and send you money. I'll find Uncle Clancy and we'll send for you. I promise it won't be long. I promise." Daniel cried into his mother's lap.

Hogan was as polite as possible, but the urgency forced him to be brusque. "We need to hurry. I have a carriage waiting and a ticket on a train leaving tonight, but we'd best hurry, Daniel." Hogan placed his hand gently on Daniel's shoulder in a reassuring gesture. "I'll do my best to keep them safe until you can send for them."

Hogan accompanied them to the train and did all he could to keep their spirits up, but as the time of departure neared, the tension became unbearable. They approached the train in a small huddle and finally reached Daniel's car. Teary eyed and despondent, Myra clutched Daniel to her bosom. Megan bowed her head and wouldn't look Daniel in the eye.

His mother said, "I have something here for you, "so you won't forget us." She pressed the silver locket she wore into his hands. He opened it and saw the familiar portrait of her and his father facing each other, dressed for their wedding. There were also two locks of red hair tied, one for Megan, and one from her.

"I'll think about you both every day. I promise," Daniel sobbed into her shoulder.

Respectfully, Hogan tugged at Daniel's sleeve and walked him a few paces.

"Here is an address where you can send letters and money for their food and rent. I'll pass them along." Hogan handed Daniel his ticket and a worn leather wallet. "And here's a little money. It's probably not enough to get you all the way to California, but it'll get you part way. You're on your own from then on. There's an address in San Francisco in there that'll help." Hogan was a man who knew men well, and he knew Daniel was suffering. "Daniel Shadlow, look at me." Daniel looked up. "Daniel Shadlow, I promise you, I'll do my very best to keep your family safe." He held out his hand, and Daniel took it.

Though Daniel knew well enough that the Fenians were a shady lot, best known for their criminal elements, he had no choice but to trust them and this strange little man named John Hogan.

"Will we be seeing you again?" Myra asked tearfully.

"As soon as I can get enough money for your tickets," Daniel replied with as much conviction as he could manage, though his heart buckled under the weight of not knowing. Megan stoically stood by her mother's side, mute to her emotions. Daniel clutched them to his breaking heart.

Hogan looked from one sad face to the other with sympathy that only the Irish could take to an art form.

All too soon the conductor yelled, "All Aboard!"

"Don't worry about me," Daniel said to his mother. "I'll be alright." Myra's eyes were red from crying. She looked like such a pitiful creature compared to the beautiful young mother he used to know. "You'll be with me in California before you know it. I'll find Uncle Clancy and we'll send you money to join us there." He turned to Megan. "Take care of mum as best you can. One day, I'll find that swine Clive. Whether it be in this life or the next, there'll be a reckoning between us."

The train started moving and Hogan pulled at him to get aboard. Daniel broke away from his mother's embrace and climbed onto the steps of the moving train.

"One piece of advice," Hogan yelled. "Stay out of the cities. That's where the Pinkertons are." The train was picking up speed. Hogan ran alongside faster, he cupped his hands around his mouth. "I'm sorry to tell you, but your father died in prison. I didn't want your mother to know yet. She's too ill. I'm sorry, son. He was a brave man." Hogan was falling behind.

"What about my brother?" Daniel yelled over the puffing of the engine.

"I don't know." Daniel heard as the train gained speed, leaving behind his family, entrusted to a man he knew only as Hogan.

The whistle screamed again, reminding him of the dock in Ireland where he'd last seen his father and brother. Through his tears, Daniel waved back at his beloved mother and sister until the station disappeared and he could see them no more.

Chapter 3

The sheer size of America filled Daniel with awe in the same way as it must have affected everyone who crossed the vastness of the Great Plains. Lulled by the melody of the train rushing along its tracks, he lost count of the towns and cities that came and went as the endless horizons passed before his eyes and under his feet.

Occasionally, people working in the fields stopped to wave as the train passed them by. Daniel always waved back. It was reassuring to know that there were other friendly souls out there in this vast land.

When necessary, he'd stopped his westward journey and found work along the way. He had been a kitchen helper, a cook, and in Kansas he hired on with a desperate bunch of cowboys whose cook had taken off. After a time, he'd even made friends with them, in spite of their jokes about his cooking.

All things considered, the job had turned out well. Along the way, while traversing the cattle herds through Kansas, Oklahoma and Texas and then into Colorado, he'd learned to ride a horse, rope steers, and he'd even been offered a job to stay on with them permanently. Whenever they delivered their herds to the rail stations in the cities Daniel stayed with the horses while the rest of the cowboys drank and did whatever it was that cowboys did at the end of a cattle drive. When he finally said farewell, he was given a bonus from the owner of the herd along with a letter of reference. He kept some money for his immediate needs and sent the remainder of his hard earned wages back to his mother.

In Denver, to his surprise, he discovered that the completion of the trans-continental rail line was delayed.

"When will the train be going to California?" Daniel asked the man at the railway office.

"Could be later this year. Or it could be next year. Can't really tell. We gotta get the line through Glenwood Canyon first and it's costin' a man a mile, I hear."

Denver was a growing vibrant city. With the Rockies at its back, it was blessed with clear blue skies and broad horizons stretching back over the endless plains that Daniel had just crossed. Though it was rapidly growing both in size and sophistication, Denver was mostly considered a large cow town with a railroad. Continuous herds of cattle from Texas, Arizona, New Mexico, Wyoming and Montana were funneled into the cattle yards to be auctioned off and shipped to the hungry city dwellers in the east. Fortunes were being made because, cattle was big business.

Denver might've been adolescent, but it wasn't only about cattle. The new state capital boasted of its trolley system and shops full of the latest fashions from New York and Paris as proudly as it boasted of its saloons, dance halls and a popular theatre district that tended towards the risqué. For those with money to burn, Denver was the only place for eight hundred miles where any decadence could be procured. For the right price of course.

With the trail drives over and their cattle sold, the trail bosses and cattle owners could be seen drinking and smoking cigars at the Brown Palace Hotel, partaking of some of the city's more exotic and expensive diversions. The cowboys, as was their rite, typically got drunk and were, as often as not, ejected from the bars and brothels that were the second mainstay of the economy.

Denver abounded with wild tales from those who had recently come down from the high country. From what Daniel had heard, traveling in the mountains was dangerous even in the best conditions and the bad weather wasn't the only danger he would face. One old miner had told him about having his mine taken away from him in a swindle that had ended in gunfire. Only by abandoning his mine had he saved his life. Others, he said, weren't so lucky. They were just shot, buried and forgotten.

It seemed to Daniel that swindlers and murderers were the curse of all honest men up in the mountain towns. The reality was that criminals of every kind were the bane of all mining boomtowns. Lured by easy money, they preyed mercilessly on the bored, gullible miners whose only pleasures were drinking, gambling, and whoring.

Daniel had found lodging at a boarding house run by a widow named Mrs. Holland. She was kind and motherly to him, made sure that he was well fed, and did his laundry for him. He was made to feel comfortable and welcome in her house and he showed his gratitude by washing the dishes after each meal and chopping wood for the coming winter.

The Denver economy was booming and there was plenty of work at the cattle yards. When he applied for a job, he exaggerated his experience and was put to work with a man named Whitey, loading cattle onto trains bound for the markets on the East Coast. It was hot, dusty work and the stink of the cattle so clogged the air, it made breathing without a neckerchief over his mouth and nose impossible.

Daniel also found that working around trains was dangerous. He nearly got squashed between two rail cars on his first day of work. Luckily, Whitey grabbed him by the shirt and pulled him from between the two bumpers that would have crushed him paper-thin. They had made fun of him for almost having the briefest cowboy career ever known, but he learned quickly and after a couple of weeks of working shoulder to shoulder with them, pushing cattle around, he earned their respect.

If he was to continue hurrying to California then he needed enough money for a horse and supplies to get him over the Rocky Mountains before the winter set in. Another option was to stay where he was and send for his mother. Perhaps they could all settle in Denver. He doubted that the Pinkerton Detective Agency would have offices this far from New York.

He'd worked every day for a month, earnestly saving his money, when his boss, Whitey, invited him to come along with him and the other cowboys for a night on the town. They went to a restaurant where they ate the biggest steaks that Daniel had seen and afterwards, they took him to Maddy Silk's whorehouse on Market Street. It was the best-known brothel in Denver with supposedly the best-looking selection of ladies in four states. Some cowboys, he was told, would save their money for a year, just to spend it all at Maddy's.

Maddy Silk herself greeted them at the door and she embarrassed Daniel by making a big fuss over him since it was his first visit. While the cowboys made their rounds and selected their partners, Daniel sat at the bar listening to the piano player and sipping root beer.

He was watching the half-naked women in the mirror behind the bar when he noticed one of the ladies looking at him. He quickly looked away, but he saw her excuse herself from the conversation that she was having and head towards him. Daniel was so nervous, he couldn't look at her when she sat down on the stool next to him and placed her arm around his shoulder. She was wearing a black corset that plumped up her breasts and he thrilled at their softness when she pressed them against his arm.

"Thinking about a little company for the evening, cowboy?" she whispered in his ear and was rewarded when she felt him shiver. "You look a little tired. How about coming upstairs with me for a little lay down?" She laughed at her play on words. Daniel missed the joke.

"N..n..no, thank you. I already have a place to sleep," he stuttered.

She smiled and considered him more closely. "Don't you like me?" She blew in Daniel's ear and he shivered again; she could tell easily enough that he liked it, but then they all did. "I like you. What's your name, honey?"

"M-m-me name's D-D-Daniel," he answered. His eyes just wouldn't detach themselves from her exposed breasts. She found his accent and nervousness endearing. He was sweet and not at all like her regular customers. "It's nice to meet you, Daniel. My name's Agnes Day." She looked deeply into his eyes and slowly guided his hand to the soft, pale skin of her breast. He surprised her by pulling his hand back.

"What's the matter, Daniel, don't you like women?" She reached for his hand again and he let her take it. "Do you like boys more?" Daniel snatched his hand away, shocked at the thought. Agnes looked down at the floor, feigning disappointment.

"N-n-no…that's not it at all," he stammered. "I like girls, really I do." Agnes was a seasoned veteran at this business and suspected the reason for his reluctance. She also knew that opportunities like this came rarely in her professional career and they were moments to savor, for them both.

"Are you a virgin?" Agnes whispered. "If you are, I'll give you a freebie," she said softly, looking deeply into his eyes.

"What's a freebie?" Daniel asked.

"That's where I take you upstairs and show you all about the things that go on between a man and a woman. I'll show you things that'll make any woman fall in love with you. Come on, honey, let's go upstairs and have a little fun."

She took his hand in hers and coaxed him towards the stairs. It was all too much; he panicked. Whether he was afraid or whether it was his Catholic guilt he didn't know, he only knew that he had to get out of there. He pulled his hand from hers and darted for the door.

"Don't go," she yelled after him. "You'll never get another offer like this!" The girls watching laughed loudly as Daniel fled, almost knocking Maddy over in his rush.

"Do you think he'll be back?" Maddy asked sarcastically. Daniel heard the laughter; he was already through the door, walking away as quickly as he could, his embarrassment his only companion.

It was after midnight when he finally made it back home to Mrs. Holland's house. He found her sitting in the parlor knitting when he came in.

"Did you have a nice time with your friends?" He saw that she'd been worried about him and had been sitting there waiting for him to come home.

"Yes, Mrs. Holland. I had a fine time, thank you," he lied politely. She saw the red lip paint on his cheek, but said nothing about it. "Goodnight, Mrs. Holland," he said as he climbed the stairs to his tiny bedroom.

"Daniel," Mrs. Holland called to him. Daniel stopped. "Could I see you for a moment?"

Daniel came over and sat in a chair facing her. The windows were open and a gentle breeze moved the curtains.

"I was at the post office today and I saw this on the wall." She handed him a piece of paper. Daniel unfolded the paper and sucked in his breath. "The Pinkerton's regularly put these up to warn us about the criminals they are looking for. For some reason this caught my eye."

At the top of the page were the words, 'Wanted. $5,000 Reward.' Underneath was a description of Daniel. It was general in nature but surprisingly accurate. His age, seventeen, his height, hair color, Irish accent, recently arrived in America. It was him. And they were still looking for him.

"This is you isn't it?" Daniel looked up slowly. "I thought it might be," she said sadly. "You'll have to leave here Daniel. Head up into the mountains where they'll not look for you. You can have Marigold if you want." Mrs. Holland kept an old mare named Marigold that had belonged to her late husband.

The morning they left Denver, Mrs. Holland couldn't hide the tears that rolled down her cheeks as she waved goodbye.

"Here Daniel I have a little something for you." She gave him a twenty dollar gold coin and placed it into a small pouch on Marigold's saddle. "It's just in case you ever run out of money. It's not much but it might come in handy in an emergency."

Daniel held her hands in his and kissed her on her cheek. He mounted and waving goodbye, turned Marigold onto the road heading west towards the mountains. She'd grown fond of him and as she watched them go, she felt a surge of affection for him and fear that his youth and innocence would be his undoing.

Mrs. Holland stood at the open door long after they'd disappeared down the dusty road, her arms furled around herself as if holding onto their memory. She knew that she was going to worry about them.

⊨⊫

Daniel and Marigold headed up into the foothills west of Denver. Over the next several days, they passed through a multitude of small mining camps. The hastily erected towns were all similar with drab, flat-faced buildings, dank hotels and saloons by the dozen, an assay office or two, and a general store. Clusters of tiny, rough wood cabins that barely clung to the steep hillsides housed the mining families who had made it this far and had decided for whatever reason to go no further. Suspicious, hollow-eyed men stood in small huddles and watched him pass with looks that warned him not to tarry. Their thin, haggard women had the look of the damned, while their children played in the mud. Daniel was happier when he'd left these depressing places behind.

For a week of cloudless days, he rode through magnificent country. The higher into the mountains he climbed, the more spectacular the scenery became. The aspen trees were at the peak of their fall color, and the valleys vibrated with shimmering red and gold splendor at every puff of breeze. The nights were mild, so he cooked over a campfire and slept under an umbrella of twinkling stars. He woke to Marigold's impatient snuffling and bathed in the crystal-clear streams that rushed down from the surrounding peaks. The higher he went, the more snow he saw on the peaks. Though the weather remained mild, it had begun showing hints of the harshness to come. Winter was not far off. Neither was Leadville.

At ten thousand feet above sea level, the city of Leadville was the highest city in America and in spite of its prosperity, one of the ugliest. The Buena Vista Valley turns bleak and dreary as one approaches from the south, and what had once been a fertile valley of tall pines and swathes of aspen trees had been denuded for miles to satisfy the voracious needs of the mining industry. The valley was now a desolate plain that supported but a few shabby ranches with miserable-looking cattle and a scattering of listless, dirty sheep. To Daniel, on this chilly gray day, the valley looked mean.

When he passed people on the road, no one looked at him. Even when he'd politely asked directions, they had simply ignored him.

On a lopsided barn on the outskirts of the town hung a sign announcing that he had arrived at a place called Stringtown and according to the sign, the city of Leadville was somewhere up ahead in the smoky gloom. He pushed on and eventually came to a cluster of small cabins with tiny curtained windows and thick coal smoke curling up from their chimneys.

The day was all but gone by the time Daniel had boarded Marigold at the livery stable and then lugged his pack and bedroll to the small hotel on the main road that proclaimed itself to be the cheapest in town. For the princely sum of one half dollar he was shown a bunk and for two bits more, was given coffee and a bowl of watery stew made from gamy elk meat. The hotel proprietor, a bitter man named Bladgett, was far from friendly. Daniel ignored that the bread he was given was rock hard.

As it was, he was so tired and so cold he could barely get a spoonful of stew to his mouth without shaking most of it back into the bowl. Thin and meager as it was, it did the trick of warming his insides, but the hot food also made him sleepy and by the time that he'd finished eating, he could hardly keep his eyes open. Full, warm and tired, he dragged himself to the bunk he'd been assigned and fell asleep immediately.

Sometime during the night he awoke with a start, his heart racing, the room as dark as a coffin. He had been in the middle of a now familiar dream, being chased through alleyways by the policeman in the bowler hat, but the sound of muffled voices outside his door had jerked him awake. He lay very still, not breathing, listening for the voices again. Faint light leaked under the door and Daniel saw shadows moving on the other side. He heard the noises again and thought about getting his small pistol, but remembered that it was buried deep inside his pack. He took short breaths, and waited.

Two men came stumbling through the door, so drunk that they didn't see him in his bunk, until one of them sat on him.

"Hey. Get off me." Daniel yelled out. Whoever had sat on him was so surprised, he fell off the bed and onto the floor in a fit of laughter.

"Ssssshhh!!! Hey! Hey! Whad'ya want to do? Get us thrown out?" The one standing slurred

"OK. OK," the one on the floor said, trying to get to his feet and failing.

Daniel could see that his pack had been pulled to the edge of the bed. He was reaching for it when the man on the floor yanked the blanket away from him, spilling the contents of Daniel's pack onto the floor. Daniel sprang out of bed and gathered up his belongings. In the dark, he failed to see that the flailing drunk had kicked his wallet under the bed.

The door swung open, and Mr. Bladgett loomed in the doorway, a lantern in one hand and a pistol in the other.

"Alright fellers, you know the rules," Bladgett yelled. The room fell as silent as a church at midnight. "You don't come back here if it's after ten o'clock, and if you're gonna' come back here drunk, then don't come here at all." He pointed his pistol at the men on the floor. "I want you two out of here come dawn, or I'll shoot you both." The two drunks looked at each other and burst out laughing.

"Do you know who we are, old man?" said the drunker of the two. Bladgett paused and scratched his chin with the barrel of his pistol, as if trying to remember.

"No, I don't. And I don't much care since you'll be gone tomorrow morning, first thing. Won't you now?" Bladgett let his pistol roam between the two and they became very quiet. Satisfied that he'd made his point, he closed the door, taking the light with him.

"Before sunrise," they heard from the other side of the door.

The two drunks tried to be quiet, but as they fumbled around in the dark trying to find their bunks, they started laughing again, which got Daniel laughing too. The harder they tried not to laugh, the funnier it all became.

The door flew open again and Bladgett marched back in, gun in hand. They heard the hammer click back twice, and the laughing stopped instantly. Daniel looked down the barrel of a gun for the first time in his life.

"You too, young feller," the barrel stayed pointed at Daniel's head, "I want you out of here too. I don't much like the looks of you." Bladgett aimed the pistol at each of them in turn then slowly backed out of the room. "Before sunrise," he repeated before slamming the door closed.

When Daniel awoke, thin light seeped from around the blanket that covered the only window in the room; it barely registered on his brain that he was alone in the room. The incident that had happened in the middle of the night seemed like part of his dreams, since there was no trace of the two drunken cowboys and he didn't hear them leave. He was trying to clear his head when the door burst open, and he realized that it hadn't been a dream. The gun Bladgett was holding was real, and it was pointed at him.

"I thought I told you to be on your way, boy." Bladgett's voice was a low rumble, threatening like thunder.

Daniel hurriedly dressed and gathered his things under Bladgett's malevolent gaze. He grabbed his pack and bent down to look under his bunk, but could only manage a quick glance before he was grabbed by the collar of his coat and roughly pushed out of the room.

"Go on, get out," Bladgett screamed, pushing Daniel out into the street, slamming the door behind him.

The sun rose weakly, but it did little to brighten the town. Not even the fresh snow could cover the black soot that coated everything including, it seemed, the people themselves. At the stable, he found that Marigold had been fed and watered and looked reluctant to leave, but she was polite and took the bit without any fuss. Still in a daze and barely awake, he headed into town, happy to be putting the hotel and its belligerent owner behind him.

Though the sun had barely risen, Daniel was surprised to find that the city of Leadville was already awake and bustling with activity. The main street was crowded with wagons and carts loaded with coal and all manner of supplies going to and from the mines. Well-dressed men and women filled the sidewalks.

He found a small breakfast place, and after ordering bacon and scrambled eggs from the waitress, he absently looked into his pack for his wallet. A sudden, sick feeling overcame him. Frantically, he began spreading its contents on the table. Everything was there. Everything, but his wallet. Panic drained the blood from his face, his fingers tingled and the back of his neck felt clammy. He put his belongings back into his pack carefully, but again, the only thing missing was his wallet. Other customers in the restaurant were watching him. To make matters worse, the waitress brought him his breakfast.

"I'll be right back," he said to her as he grabbed up his pack and headed for the door. He'd only gone a few paces when he felt a tug on his sleeve.

"Hey, where do you think you're going?" The waitress spoke loudly enough so that everyone would hear. "You didn't pay for your breakfast." She had fire in her eyes and a good grip on his coat.

"I told you, I'll be right back." Daniel pleaded.

"Not without paying for your breakfast," she replied, keeping ahold of his coat.

Daniel saw the futility of explaining, just as clearly as he saw his wallet under his bed in the bunkhouse. He sighed, and in a gesture of futility, pretended to reach into his back pocket for his money. The waitress reluctantly let go her grip on his coat and as soon as she did, Daniel turned and dashed through the tables, knocking over chairs as he fled. He was already swinging up onto Marigold when the angry woman reached the door, the plate of food in her outstretched hand, the other on her hip.

"I'm going to tell the Sheriff," she yelled at him. People on the sidewalk were stopping to stare at them.

"I'll be back to pay you, I promise. Don't go anywhere." He yelled back over his shoulder as he wheeled Marigold around and spurred her through the traffic.

She watched him ride away and shrugged. "Where am I going?" she said to no one in particular and went back inside, picking at bacon from the plate.

He rode Marigold as fast as he dared back to the hotel in Stringtown and rushed into the bunkhouse only to find Mr. Bladgett standing in the room, broom in hand, smiling curiously.

"I thought I told you to get out'a here, kid." Bladgett yelled.

"I was looking for my wallet, sir.' Daniel said plaintively. "All of my money was in it." Daniel waited for Mr. Bladgett's reaction.

"Well, you can look for yourself, but it's not here." Bladgett declared.

Daniel dove under the bed and passed his hand over the rough boards all the way to the wall, but found nothing. He picked up the mattress and looked underneath it, ignoring the stains and the stuffing leaking from a dozen rips and holes. He sat on the edge of the bed with his head in his hands. Bladgett poked him with his broom. Daniel ignored him.

"As you can see boy, it's not here," he poked Daniel again, "Maybe them two fellers you was with last night took it." Bladgett was smiling, enjoying himself.

Daniel felt totally lost. Being stranded in a strange town with no money and no friends was not an enviable position to be in. Haunting memories of the hollow-eyed faces of the lost souls he'd seen in the other mining camps rose up in his mind like phantoms. Panic, fear, anger and a dozen other emotions pushed and pulled at him, forcing tears to well in his eyes "You best go after them fellers, son," His tormentor advised. "And tell the Sheriff about 'em, too. They didn't look like the type to be working in the mines, so I'd look in the saloons if I was you." Bladgett looked down at Daniel menacingly and poked him with the broom again, harder. "Well, what are you waiting for? You'd best get going, hadn't ya'?" Bladgett yelled and hit Daniel hard on the thigh with the broom handle. Daniel jumped to his feet, holding his leg, but Bladgett was ready for him and roughly pushed him across the room and out into the street, then slammed the door on his back.

From behind his dingy curtained window, Bladgett watched Daniel pace back and forth in front of his hotel, clenching and unclenching his fists in frustrated rage. Delighted with himself, he pulled out Daniel's wallet and counted the money. He laughed out loud. It was his first good laugh in years. He watched until Daniel was mounted and indeed leaving. "Tough luck, kid," he said with a chuckle, and returned to his chores.

⊲⊟⊳

Shaken, and in a somber mood, Daniel rode back into town considering his options. They were limited. He could keep going and try to make it as far as he could, or he could return to Denver. Or, he might even find work here in Leadville. He had a sudden thought. He remembered that he still had the twenty dollar gold piece that Mrs. Holland had given him as a farewell gift, though she said that he'd earned it. He reached into the secret pocket of his saddle and breathed a sigh of relief when his fingers felt the solid shape of the coin. All was not lost, at least now he could buy some breakfast.

Still in a daze, he rode into Leadville and eventually found himself outside the Sheriff's office. His mistrust of authority made the decision to seek help from the Sheriff difficult to make, but eventually he concluded that he had to do it if he was to ever see his wallet again. The lone deputy feigned interest and listened to Daniel's story with half an ear while making it perfectly obvious that he resented the interruption. Daniel could tell that he would be of little help.

When asked to describe the men who robbed him, Daniel found that he had only a thin recollection of either of them since they'd arrived in the dark and had left before he woke up. After listening to Daniel's story, the bored deputy wrote down some notes on a scrap of paper and suggested that Daniel look in the saloons around town for the men and come back to the office if he found them. He predicted that they would probably be drinking or gambling his money away in one of the saloons because that was what he'd be doing if he'd cleaned out this young fool. After pushing Daniel out of the office, the deputy crumpled the paper he'd written the notes on and threw it in the fire. He'd only pretended to be able to write, anyway.

Walking the length of Main Street, Daniel was surprised to find that almost all of the saloons were crowded even though it was early morning. He had left the Sheriff's office hoping that he could find the two men who robbed him, but by the time he'd passed a half dozen bars full of wild-eyed drunken miners, he'd begun to think differently. Even if he did find them, there would likely be more trouble since it would just be his word against theirs.

It slowly dawned on him that his world had changed. It was as if he'd gone to sleep in one place and woken up in another. Like a dousing of ice-cold water, he was startled to realize that he really was in the

Wild West, where men really did die in the street of gunshot wounds over gambling debts and false accusations. It was as if he'd suddenly stepped into a dime novel, and might not live to read the end of the story.

Whether it was from nerves or hunger, his stomach noisily demanded his attention. He took out the gold coin that had been given to him by Mrs. Holland, and absorbed its perpetual gleam as he held it in the palm of his hand. He had hoped that he could keep the coin as a reminder of her kindness and generosity, but what it represented to him now was a meal and the chance to get away from this ugly, dirty town. He felt sure that Mrs. Holland intended it for such a purpose and he held it tightly as he crossed the street heading for the bank.

The Bank of Leadville was a solid-looking building of red sandstone, four stories tall with a cupola on the roof. When Daniel entered he found it crowded with shopkeepers, townsfolk, and a collection of miners exchanging silver bars for paper money or depositing them into the trusted care of the bank.

As he waited in line for his turn at the teller's window, he couldn't help but notice the traffic in and out of the vault behind the tellers' cages. Pairs of armed men were carrying dozens of heavy boxes into the vault and carrying out large, canvas moneybags. A tall, heavyset man with a star on his chest leaned casually against the vault door. Beside him, a smaller man wearing glasses, probably the bank manager, stood and tallied the bags as they were carried out of the bank through the side door of the building. The moneybags were counted once more as they were loaded onto a wagon, this time by a large red haired man holding a shotgun in the crook of his arm. When Daniel looked back at the Sheriff again, their eyes locked.

Daniel became aware of harsh words passing between a stern, older man and a young, female teller. The older man's voice was rising and Daniel could see that the young teller was being embarrassed by the tirade.

"Can I help you, sir?" she asked when Daniel arrived at her counter.

Though not a small girl, she had graceful features, with dark brown hair that matched her eyes.

"Can you give me small change for this, please?" Daniel slid the coin towards her. She returned his smile.

"Come on then. Give the customer his change. We don't have all day you know, and neither does he." The old teller shot Daniel a brief, disapproving look then returned to his verbal assault on the young lady. "Come on, give him his money."

"Excuse me, sir," Daniel said, perhaps a little too loudly, but he did get the old teller's attention. "I think the young lady is doing the best she can."

The old teller pushed the girl aside. He looked over Daniel's shabby clothes with disdain. "And exactly what business is it of yours?" His eyes were too small for his face, like a rodent. "Do you think you know how to train someone to take account of all this money?" He paused for unnecessary emphasis. "Do you, boy?" The old teller pushed his face closer to the brass grill and Daniel recoiled, the man's breath smelled like urine, foul and bitter.

Daniel could hear people muttering behind him.

"Hey, what're you trying to do up there, fella, rob the damned bank?" a man in line yelled.

Daniel turned to answer, but found his view blocked by the bulk of a heavy leather coat bearing a large, silver-star with the word "Sheriff" written across it. A powerful hand the size of a small ham pushed on his chest, pinning him against the counter.

"What's the problem here, Wilbur?" the Sheriff rumbled, looking down his nose at Daniel. "Are you causin' trouble here, young feller?" He looked at the girl behind the counter. "This lout giving you problems, is he?"

"No, no, Daddy. Really, he was just trying to help, but Mr. Osgood took it the wrong way," she said bravely in his defense. "He wasn't causin' any trouble, Daddy. Really, he wasn't."

She smiled sweetly at her father, but the Sheriff was not one to be fooled. Without saying another word, he took Daniel by the shoulder in one of his massive hands and shoved him roughly past the people standing in line.

Outside in the street, the Sheriff spun him around and sent him sprawling backwards off the wooden sidewalk, into the mud. The

Sheriff's shadow fell on Daniel like a tower. "We don't like useless lit-tle troublemakers like you in this town. What was your business in the bank, anyway?"

"Sheriff, I was just over at your office," Daniel said as he struggled to his feet. "I was robbed last night. I wanted to see if you could help me find the two men who took my wallet."

"They took your wallet, you say? Well, if you was robbed by two men, then you should be able to give us a good description of them. Did my deputy write it all down?" he smiled, knowing that his deputy could neither read nor write.

"I really didn't get a good look at them because it was late and they—"

The Sheriff didn't let him finish. "Ahhhh…So you was drunk, and them fellers that you're talking about robbed you while you were all drunked up, eh?"

"No, sir, it wasn't like that at all."

"Well then, you must've been losing to them gamblin', and now you feel that they cheated you, is that it?"

"No, sir, I was asleep when they came in, and then this morn-ing they were gone and so was my wallet. You have to believe me. I wouldn't make any of this up." Daniel pleaded.

"Yeah, well, sounds fishy to me. Where do you say this robbery took place?"

"It was at a hotel in Stringtown, at a place on the main street."

The Sheriff noticed that Daniel was clutching something in his hand. "Can you tell me the name of this place or who owned it?"

"It sounded like Badger or something, I think." Daniel felt stupid.

The Sheriff knew the man he was referring to and had already guessed what had happened to the missing wallet. "Well, I can't do much about what goes on down there. They don't have any law in that shit-hole of theirs. They don't want us and we don't want them, either." He looked at Daniel's hand intently. "You never did tell me why you were in our bank. Since you was robbed of all your money and all." With amazing speed, the Sheriff grabbed Daniel's hand and twisted it, but Daniel kept a tight grip on his only remaining source of nourishment.

"I...I....I.. just wanted to cash in this gold piece so that I could get some breakfast," Daniel stammered. The Sheriff twisted Daniel's hand until it finally opened and smiled when he saw the glint of gold. Before Daniel could react, the Sheriff snatched the coin out of his hand and, after giving it a brief inspection, casually slipped it into his coat pocket. With a sneer, he pushed Daniel back down into the mud.

"Hey, Sheriff, that's mine! Give it back." Daniel struggled to climb out of the oozing quagmire he was sitting in. "I only went into the bank to get some money so that I could have some breakfast. It's mine, give it back!" Daniel's voice rose in frustration.

Noticing that they were drawing attention from people along the sidewalk, the Sheriff slammed his hand down onto Daniel's shoulder while smiling pleasantly to a pair of passing women. He proceeded to push Daniel into a narrow alley between two buildings, where they wouldn't be observed.

"Listen, you whiny little sonofa' bitch," The Sheriff's face was so close Daniel could smell the stale whiskey on his breath. "I don't know where you stole that gold piece from, but I'm confiscating it," the Sheriff's snarl twisted into a cruel smile, "as evidence of a robbery. I'll say I saw you take it from the bank and no one will dare to say otherwise. Do you understand me?" His big, florid face was only an inch from Daniel's. "Do you hear me, boy?" He lifted Daniel up by the collar of his coat until Daniel's feet were off the ground and pressed him up against the wall.

Daniel nodded. The Sheriff let him down. He smoothed Daniel's coat theatrically, then shoved him roughly back along the alley. Out in the street, he grabbed Daniel by the shoulder and turned him around so that they were face to face again.

"Son, let me give you a piece of advice. I really don't think this town is suited to the likes of you. So, since we're such good friends, I recommend that you just get on your horse, or whatever got you here, and get along out of my town." He gave Daniel another shove to emphasize his point.

Daniel stumbled into two men as he fell.

"Watch where you're fallin', son," one of the men said as they stepped around him. Daniel recognized the voice. He jumped up and grabbed the man by the coat.

"Where's my money?" he yelled. The man turned and looked at Daniel, his fists clenched, ready for a fight. Daniel noticed that his partner had slipped his hand inside the flap of his riding coat.

"Get away from me, you little asshole," the man said and pushed Daniel away with disdain. "I didn't steal your money. I've never seen you before in my life."

They turned to walk away, but Daniel launched himself at the man. The man deftly stepped to the side and pushed Daniel back down into the mud. With effort, Daniel pushed himself to his feet and lifted his muddy hands into a boxer's stance. The cowboy did nothing.

Suddenly, Daniel was lifted off his feet and slammed down onto the ground again. When Daniel looked up, the Sheriff stood over him, smiling. "What's going on here, boys? This little piece of shit botherin' you?" he said, looking down at Daniel sitting helplessly in the freezing, oozing mud.

"Howdy, Sheriff." Both men touched the brims of their hats in salute. "We were just heading for the train station and this little piece o'shit starts accusing us of stealing his money." The cowboy sounded more amused than angry.

Daniel tried to get back up to his feet, but the Sheriff's foot sent him sprawling again. "But it's them, Sheriff," Daniel cried from his knees. "They're the ones at the hotel last night. They're the ones that stole my wallet."

The older of the two, the one wearing a black homburg hat, smiled a big, pleasant smile at the Sheriff.

"Like we said, Sheriff, we ain't never seen this youngster before, and last night me and my friend here, well, we were just too drunk to be thinking about robbing anybody, even if we wanted to." They looked down at Daniel, then back to the Sheriff. "Well, you seem to have the whole situation underfoot, so to speak," the man in the homburg said. "Yes, sir," he said laughing to his friend, "this looks like one well-protected town."

"Yes, boys, it is. We've got a nice town here and there's a lot of money in that bank there and I don't plan on anybody embarrassing me by stealing any of it." He made a pistol of his thumb and index finger and pointed it down at Daniel. "Especially little snot-nosed weeds like you."

"You weren't really planning on robbing their bank, were you, son?" the one in the homburg asked.

"No, no, no," Daniel cried, holding his muddy hands open plaintively. The two men looked down at Daniel with new interest, then at each other.

"Honestly, he does look a bit like a bank robber." The good-looking one pulled back a bit. "If you was to look at him kinda' squinty like." They both squinted at the miserable figure in the mud and laughed at his discomfort.

"You know, Sheriff, I gotta compliment you on some fine police work, here." The one in the homburg touched his finger to the brim of his hat again. "Good day, Sheriff." They turned and headed towards the rail station.

They'd gone a little way when the one in the homburg turned to his friend. "Do you believe that kid was really thinking about robbing that bank?" They stopped a moment to look back at the miserable boy getting up from the mud.

"I don't know, Butch. He seems a mite young to be a bank robber, don't he?"

They took an appraising look at the bank as they walked past the building. "Nah...remember Billy the Kid? But you know what I do think?" the one called Butch said as they continued walking towards the rail station. "Here that fat Sheriff had the two most-wanted bank robbers in the whole state right there in front of him, and he gets his jollies pushing a kid around in the mud. I think that piece of shit Sheriff deserves to have his precious bank robbed. Take him down a notch."

They stopped once more to take a last look at the Bank of Leadville. The last thing they saw was the Sheriff kicking Daniel as he was getting to his feet. "Maybe we should think more on that."

Chapter 4

It had not been a particularly good night for Harry Rich, though it had started off well enough. He'd ridden into Leadville before dark and as usual had used some of his gambling money to buy himself a good meal. A big steak, well cooked, just the way he liked it, with fresh squash, green beans and potatoes that went untouched, apple pie with ice cream and coffee laced with whiskey. "That was a real meal," he had announced to all within hearing, then belched proudly and left without leaving the waitress a tip. She'd be content with just a smile anyway. Harry had a winning smile, or so he'd been told.

Harry sauntered to the men's room where he primped in front of the mirror, reassured that he did indeed look considerably younger than his thirty seven years. He smoothed back his thick and graying hair from his temples, stepped back a pace and gave his reflection a wink of approval. "Yes sir, Harry Rich. You are still a very handsome man," he said, agreeing with his reflection.

One by one, the other gamblers at the table had either gracefully re-tired or had painfully lost all that they could afford. Only Harry and a rheumy eyed, sick old man were left. A small crowd of spectators, mostly tired miners, filthy with coal dust, had gathered around them, drawn by the pile of money in the center of the table.

"I'll raise you a hundred," Harry said quietly, and placed the last of his money on the table, struggling to hide the fact that he finally had a decent hand.

Doc Holliday appeared to be asleep but definitely wasn't.

"D'you know what I think, Mr. Rich?" he paused and labored to take a full breath. "I think you're bluffing." The icy eyes that had stared down many a gambler and outlaw over the years were barely visible beneath the bushy gray eyebrows. Harry felt his world tilt awkwardly.

Doc reached out to place the bet, but stopped mid-movement and reconsidered Harry. "But, I don't think I've taken enough of your money yet, Mr. Harry Rich." He withdrew his hand and paused to take another deep, wheezing breath; he knew that Harry had no more money to bet with. "How about I raise you another fifty," he said, and reached into the pile of money in front of him, picked out another fifty dollars, and tossed it into the middle of the table.

Harry swallowed hard and tried to control the pulse that throbbed at his temple. He desperately needed to win this hand. He already owed Doc over three hundred dollars; a year's wages for a miner. Not paying the good doctor could be the death of him, literally. Harry cleared his throat noisily to hide his fear and pondered his lack of choices. He could grovel and beg and leave in disgrace, which could be bad for his reputation. Or, he could leave just plain dead, and leaving feet first would definitely be bad for his reputation. He had to play out his hand and he had to win it; it was his only chance.

"Now, Doc," Harry began in his most congenial tone. "I think that's very sporting of you, but I seem to be a little short of cash money at the present time. How about loaning me another fifty, at least so's we can make a gentleman's game of it? You're a gentleman, aren't ya' Doc?" Harry tried to keep from sounding desperate.

Doctor John Holliday looked long and hard at the man sitting across the table from him. He considered Harry a loudmouth, a mediocre hustler and a brazen fool and as an educated man, he did not tolerate fools very well, except when he was taking their money.

A wry smile grew on Doc's gray face like pale sunshine. In a sudden, fluid movement, he rocked forward in his chair, reached his arms out across the table and looked straight into Harry's eyes, holding them in a test of wills, his smile unchanging. He said nothing, but his silence was full of deadly foreboding. Harry knew he was in deep trouble.

Just as suddenly, Doc rocked back in his chair and mustered a croaky laugh. Deep liquid rumblings came from the shallow chest of the old gunfighter, and his body shook as the laugh turned into a violent coughing fit. His face turned reddish purple, and he held a stained handkerchief to his mouth as he endured the painful spasm.

"D'you know what I think?" he said, when the spasm finally passed, "I think that this'll be the last hand of the evening for us, Mr. Rich. So, unless you can beg or borrow some money from one of these good fellows here, I think that this game is over." Doc reached for the money on the table.

Harry looked around at the faces of the grubby spectators, and discretely displayed his cards hoping for help. Some conspicuously turned away; a few peered over his shoulders at his cards and shook their heads. They all knew that crossing Doc Holliday was not wise and, whether they won or lost money on Harry's hand, it was a sure bet that they would eventually lose one way or another.

Doc counted his winnings. "And now there's the little matter of the money you owe me." Doc Holliday's eyes were sparkling with an intensity that chilled Harry to the bone. "Isn't there, Mr. Rich?"

Harry was nothing if not resourceful, especially when faced with imminent death. "Now, Doc, you know I'm good for it, don't you?" Harry summoned his most winning smile and trusted that it would faithfully reinforce his absolute sincerity as it had so often done in the past. His not being shot depended on it.

Doc gave a rumbling laugh and spat a prodigious amount of phlegm into the spittoon at his feet. "Well, Mr. Rich, when it comes to gambling debts, you know how I feel. Don't you?" Doc dabbed at his chin with his handkerchief. "Don't play if you can't pay," he said and held up Harry's IOUs. Doc's hand was steady and unwavering, like his stare.

Leadville prided itself on being a modern, law abiding city. It didn't see as much gunplay as it used to in the old days before guns were banned within the city limits. Occasionally, a violent death did occur when men fought over a woman or gambling debts. Whenever that happened, the judge looked upon it as a personal matter between the two men involved, secretly pleased that they were taking care of their own business. That is, unless they happened to shoot some unlucky bystander.

Doc Holliday had always carried a pistol though officially illegal within the city's limits, and his aim was notoriously fearsome. Harry was acutely aware of the man's reputation and slowly rose from his chair and opened his coat to show that he was unarmed. The movement brought a twitch of Doc's hand.

"Now, Doc, you know I'll pay you." Harry's mind raced through a maze of possible life saving lies. "Hell, I'm a man of means. I have my own business in Aspen," Harry visibly swelled with self-importance. "I'll send you your money just as soon as I get back home." He paused. "Hell, Doc, I've got money in the bank," he announced proudly to the assembled gallery as if it should elicit a round of applause.

The silence was ominous. The men around the table backed away slowly as Harry edged closer to the door. He stopped and pointed his finger skyward as if in inspiration, "I know what I'll do. I'll go down to the bank right now and get them to loan me the money so that I can pay you right away." Harry turned to run but heard a deep, soft rumble that stopped him mid-stride.

"That would be a mistake, Harry Rich."

Harry turned around slowly, smiling broadly. He held his hands out in supplication, but kept backing towards the door. "C'mon, Doc? What's a few dollars between friends?" He tried to sound sincere. "I hear you're moving over to Glenwood Springs soon. You can stay at my place on the way and we can catch up on old times. I could pay you then, if you've a mind." He turned again to run, but stopped when he heard the scraping of a chair on the wooden floor. He turned back.

Doc stepped away from the table and walked towards Harry in a decidedly unfriendly manner. Harry saw the butt of a pistol as Doc casually pulled his coat aside and it alarmed him that Doc suddenly didn't look like a frail, old twig of a man anymore. He moved with the confidence and grace of a man much younger, and the menace in his eyes was chilling. Harry found it difficult to drag his eyes away from the gun reversed in the old man's belt. At any moment, Doc could reach across his waist, pull his gun and that would be the end of it.

Harry held his hands up defensively, palms outward, but kept backing towards the door. "Now hold on a minute there, Doc. Let's not be hasty. I've always paid my debts to you, haven't I?"

"No, Harry. You haven't always paid your debts to me. Just how many times have I let you off?" Doc's hand snapped up and Harry's heart stopped, but Doc only pointed his finger at him. "Not this time."

Out of the corner of his eye, Harry saw the bartender come from behind the bar and position himself at the door, blocking the only exit, a shotgun at the ready. "You owe me over five-hundred dollars, you no good lyin' scum. And I want my money now." Doc was only an arm's length away. Harry felt the sweat drip down the back of his neck.

Doc's eyes were aglow with a fervor that Harry had never seen before on any human being. Harry raised his hands defensively and joined them as if to pray. As he did, he felt the barrel of the pistol between his hands. Without thinking, he grabbed the barrel and bent it backwards, catching Doc's finger in the trigger guard and forcing him into the bartender. Seeing his chance for survival, Harry bolted through the door and ran full force into someone on the wooden sidewalk.

⊰⊱

Daniel didn't see it coming; he was still in shock and mumbling to himself in angry disbelief that he had been robbed twice and it wasn't even noon. To make matters worse, his pants were soaked and cold, muddy water leaked down the backs of his legs into his boots. He was brushing mud from his clothing when he was lifted off his feet and hurled from the wooden sidewalk landing face down in the muddy street again.

Coughing and spluttering, he climbed out of the mud wiping the muck from his face and out of his eyes. He was bending over to pick up his hat when he was grabbed from behind, spun around, and flung at an angry old man with a gun in his hand. The cadaverous old man pushed him away with a clear look of disgust. Abruptly, he was grabbed from behind again and held by someone gripping him tightly by the collar of his coat. No matter how much he twisted and turned, he couldn't get free from whomever it was that was holding him.

"Let me go!" Daniel yelled.

"Get out of the way, son, I have a gun here," demanded the old man with the gun.

"Stay right where you are," came the voice from behind him. "I've got a gun, too." Harry rammed his knuckle into Daniel's back. Daniel stopped resisting.

"I told you to get out of the way, son, and you will if you know what's good for you," said the old man.

It was like something out of one of the dime novels of the Wild West. It could have been thrilling, were it not for the fact that this was a real gunfight and there was a real pistol being pointed at Daniel

Whoever was behind him kept shoving him from side to side to keep him between the gun and its intended target. A crowd was forming around them, but Daniel was being thrown around like a doll and only saw them as a blur as he spun back and forth.

BOOM!

A gunshot boomed very close to his head. Everything stopped. Silence reigned.

A now familiar voice came from behind him.

"Hold it right there, all of you." The Sheriff holstered his pistol as he stepped in between Daniel and the old man. He placed both hands on the old man's shoulders in a kindly gesture. To Daniel, it appeared that his would-be murderer was a friend of the Sheriff's, and the possible consequences were unsettling.

"Now there, Doc, what's this all about?" The Sheriff looked down at the pistol in Doc's hand and gently pushed it back inside Doc's coat and out of sight.

Doc closed his eyes as if in prayer. With his increasing age and suffering the effects of the tuberculosis that were slowly claiming him, he wasn't the same man who used to easily control his destiny. An old lawman himself, he often longed for the old days when arguments were settled quickly, in the boom and smoke of a gunfight—where the undertaker took away the loser without fuss. Finished, over and done with, and usually no questions asked.

Slowly, John Holliday returned to the present. He could see Harry hiding behind this youngster, using him as a shield. They were a pathetic pair, both covered in mud, particularly the boy who, he noted with a smile, seemed to have muck all over him. Doc Holliday began laughing. Then the Sheriff began laughing too, and the people around them started laughing and pointing. Daniel looked down at himself. Covered in mud from head to toe and held up by the collar, he must have been a sight to behold; he had never felt so embarrassed. The laughter stopped when a loud, gurgling, cough cleaved the air, leaving silence in its wake.

"Harry, do you know.... what I'm thinkin'?" Doc's wheezy voice came in short bursts.

Harry peeked over behind Daniel's shoulder but kept a firm grip on his coat.

"I'm thinking you'd better not step foot in this town again. If ever you do.... you'd better have the money you owe me." Doc took a step towards them; his hand reaching into his coat. The Sheriff blocked his path and placed his hand gently on the old gunfighter's chest protectively. Undaunted, Doc leaned around the Sheriff and pointed a bony finger at Harry.

"Do you hear me, Harry Rich?.... And stop hiding back there behind that boy.... You're still a man, aren't you? Do you think that kid's going to protect you from me?"

"I told you that I'd pay you, didn't I?" Harry said loudly enough so that everyone could hear him. "And Harry Rich always pays his debts." Harry looked over the crowd. "Well, sometimes," he whispered in Daniel's ear.

Daniel felt the grip on his coat slacken and pulled himself free. His vision somewhat clearer, he noticed the Sheriff's daughter among the crowd that had gathered on the sidewalk. Drawn outside by the commotion in the street, she stood there with her hand to her mouth, her eyes silently questioning.

"Alright you fellers, that's it. I've had enough trouble out of you two," the Sheriff shouted vehemently. "I want you both out of my town, now." He grabbed Daniel by his coat and flung him at Harry, delighted that they both fell into the mud again. He leaned over and, using his finger as a dagger, turned his anger on Harry.

"And you, you good for nothing troublemaker, I want you to get back to that shithole of yours, and don't ever even think of setting foot in my town again. If I ever catch either one of you back in my town, I'll make sure that Doc here gets a chance to do what he's aching to do to you. And then I'll make sure that your miserable bodies never show up anyplace, anytime, ever. Do you understand me?" Harry nodded sheepishly, his humiliation complete. Doc walked back into the doorway of the saloon with his audience, thoroughly enjoying Harry's humiliation.

Daniel slipped into the crowd and headed for Marigold, standing patiently at the hitching rail in front of the bank, oblivious to his troubles. Unexpectedly, the Sheriff's daughter caught him by the arm as he was gathering the reins.

"I'm sorry about my father," she apologized intently. Daniel could feel the tightening in his throat and a familiar movement in his pants at the nearness of this beautiful young woman. Suddenly, he was clouted on the back of his head, knocking his hat off into the mud. As he bent over to pick it up, a savage kick from behind sent him sprawling into the mud again.

"Stop it, Daddy," the girl screamed. "You didn't have to do that to him!"

The Sheriff turned on his daughter. "You," he yelled, pointing his finger at his daughter. "You get back to work. I'll deal with you later when I get home."

With tears in her eyes, she turned and ran back inside the bank followed by the old teller. The Sheriff went to kick Daniel again, but Harry stepped in between them.

"Hey, Sheriff, he didn't do anything wrong. Leave him alone." Harry said reaching out a hand to help Daniel up.

"I don't ever want to see either of you again," he said, struggling to control his temper for the sake of those watching. "Either of you. Ever, in this town or anywhere else. Ever again." He lifted Daniel up by the coat for emphasis.

A group of riders escorting a pair of wagons was passing by; tough looking men carrying rifles. One of them reined his horse to a stop and waved the others to keep going. He was a big red-haired man with a full red beard. He looked down at the three of them standing in the street. Daniel remembered seeing him at the bank.

What Red Corcoran saw was a boy covered in mud from head to toe being held at the neck by the Sheriff. The poor lad looked helpless and frightened and it might have been amusing, were it not for the other man standing with him who was also covered in mud. He looked from the young man to the Sheriff and then to Harry and started laughing. "Harry, I shoulda' known that you'd be in the middle of this, whatever it is. How long've you been here anyway, one night?"

Harry shrugged and was about to speak but the Sheriff held up a finger in warning. Harry held his tongue.

The Sheriff spoke with renewed authority. "They've been disturbing the peace, Red. Do you know this lot?"

Red looked down at Harry and laughed again. "Well, Sheriff, I happen to know this one," he pointed at Harry, "but the young one I'm not familiar with. He could use some cleaning up though, by the looks of him. Who is he?"

"Don't rightly know that, but I don't rightly care either. He's just another young trouble-maker who don't belong here." Daniel flinched when he smoothed his collar. The Sheriff smiled broadly, pleased at Daniel's reaction. "If it's not too much trouble, I'd be much obliged to you if you could see your way clear to escort them back over the Pass since you're going that way, Red."

"You still got your horse, Harry?"

Harry nodded his head sheepishly.

"You got a horse, son?"

Daniel nodded and pointed to Marigold.

"You heading our way?"

"Absolutely, Red," the Sheriff answered for him. "He was just saying how much he'd like to get going, too. Isn't that what I heard you say, young feller?" The Sheriff pushed him towards his horse.

"Well, if you two're coming, you'd better get a move on. We've sixty miles to ride if we want to be back in Aspen by nightfall." Red touched the brim of his hat and the Sheriff did the same, giving each other the cowboy's salute.

While Harry lurched off to find his horse, Daniel climbed onto Marigold and turned to follow Red, grateful to be on his way. For the first time since dawn, he felt calm and almost happy as he rode out of Leadville; in his mind, never to return.

Red looked back once to see if Harry was coming and motioned to Daniel to follow as he nudged his horse up to a trot to catch up with his wagons and men. Satisfied that the boy could ride competently, Red settled his horse into a comfortable gait and smiled to himself, knowing there was more to be heard about what he'd witnessed. There always was when Harry was involved.

As they passed through Stringtown, Daniel caught sight of the owner peering from behind a dirty window looking directly at him. The man smiled and patted his vest pocket. It dawned on Daniel who had stolen his wallet. The look said it all.

The horses and wagons ahead of them gathered speed, and Daniel nudged Marigold gently to keep up. "It'll be good to get over those mountains," Daniel thought as they put Leadville further behind them.

Chapter 5

Daniel kept up with the others well. There was something exciting about riding with this bunch of obviously competent and well-armed men. They turned north off the main road at a desolate place called Balltown, then up a small hill into a spectacularly beautiful alpine vista. The valley that they rode into stretched for miles and tapered to a massive fortress of jagged, snow topped peaks that reflected off the calm surface of two lakes.

"How're you doin', son?" Daniel had been so taken with the view that he hadn't noticed that the big, red haired man had dropped back beside him. "What's your name?" he asked.

"Daniel Carrington, sir."

"My name's Red Corcoran, but you can call me Red. Or just about anything else. Just don't go calling me 'sir.' You got that?"

"Yes, sir. I mean, Mr. Corcoran." Red laughed and shook his head, impressed at the boy's manners. They rode along silently for a while, both men seemingly awed by the beauty all about them.

"Where do you hail from, Daniel Carrington?" Red asked.

"I'm originally from Ireland. But I'm from England if anyone asks." Daniel replied.

Red laughed out loud, a big belly laugh, it was a wonderful laugh befitting a man his size. "Me too," he said after a pause. "But I thought as much. I mean, picking a fight with the meanest sheriff in Colorado; you had to be either crazy or Irish." They rode on some more. "What're you doin' with that useless rascal back there, anyway?" Red pointed his thumb over his shoulder, and Daniel looked back at the hunched figure trailing behind them.

Daniel explained how he was on his way to California, but that he had been robbed in Stringtown. He told Red how the Sheriff had stolen his last twenty-dollar gold piece, and how Harry had knocked him into the mud and then had used him as a shield against the old man with the gun. Red showed little expression, but listened intently.

"Well, I wish you good luck getting your money back from any o' them thieving bastards," he said with a chuckle. "You're one unlucky feller, Mr. Carrington. Do you know that? But then it could've turned out worse, you know." Daniel had no response to the obvious. Red laughed his big laugh again. "Well, son, if it makes any difference, you nearly got yourself killed by one of the most famous gunfighters of the West. That was Doc Holliday who nearly perforated you back there. Ever heard of him?"

Daniel's mouth fell open. "Oh, yes. Sure I have. He and Wyatt Earp killed those men at the OK Corral, didn't they? I read a book about it."

"Yep, he's the one alright, and if he wanted to kill you, he would have. Just out of pure meanness. My guess is that you weren't the one he wanted to kill." Red motioned back over his shoulder at Harry. They rode silently for a while.

"Go get Harry and that old nag of his moving or we'll be leaving them both behind." Red laughed again. "It'd serve him right if we let him freeze to death on the Pass, but it wouldn't be fair to his horse." Red laughed and spurred his horse.

Daniel fell behind to wait for Harry, and the wagons picked up speed as Red joined up with them. Marigold was lunching contentedly on dry grass when Harry finally reached them.

"Red asked me to make sure you keep up. My name's Daniel Carrington. What's yours?"

Harry's drunk was wearing off and a hangover raged in full gale inside his head. His eyes hurt, his face hurt and his mouth tasted like dry leaves. "Harry. Harry Rich," he struggled to say, "and thanks for helping me out back there."

They picked up the pace and rode without talking, slowly catching up to the team ahead of them. On the side of the road, Daniel saw a small wooden sign which proclaimed that they were heading into Twin Lakes and that Ute City was another thirty miles further.

Someone had scratched grooves through the name Ute City and written Aspen under it.

Eventually they caught up to Red and the two wagons, each pulled by four Morgans. Daniel had seen draught horses before; plenty of them, pulling the coal wagons and brewery trucks back in Ireland, but the Morgans were very different. These were huge horses, at least a yard or more across their backs, but they were beautiful animals too, with chestnut brown coats and flowing white manes. They trotted along with graceful elegance as if the wagons were empty, though they were heavily laden with barrels and crates stacked higher than their sides.

"So what was that all about, Harry?" Red said, unable to curb his curiosity any longer. "It didn't have anything to do with you being a lousy gambler, did it?"

Harry's head fell onto his chest.

"Don't you tell me that you went and picked a fight with old Doc Holliday?" Red laughed, "Come on, Harry, please tell me you didn't do that." Red leaned forward in his saddle, but Harry kept his eyes averted. Daniel couldn't tell if Harry was laughing or crying. After a few moments, he lifted his head.

"Red, I swear, if you tell anyone, I'll kill you as soon as I can buy some bullets."

Red laughed louder. "You mean to tell me that you didn't even have the sense to load that little pistol of yours before you got into a poker game with the most famous gunfighter left alive?"

"I forgot to bring it."

Red laughed so hard, he almost fell out of his saddle. "I can't believe you sometimes, Harry. You must be the luckiest unlucky man still living."

"But Red, I really had them on the run for a while. I must've been up a couple of hundred dollars." Harry let out a deep sigh. "How was I supposed to know that Doc was going to show up and clean us all out?" Harry looked plaintively at Red. "D'you know what? I think he cheats."

"That would've just about sealed your fate, Harry. You know that calling Doc Holliday out for cheating is more than just stupid—it's suicide." They trotted on a little while before Red spoke again. "Tell me Harry, how much do you owe him? Fifty? A hundred dollars?"

"Five hundred or thereabouts," Harry mumbled.

"I don't think I heard you right. Did you say a hundred dollars?"

"No, Red. I owe him five hundred and then some."

Red shook his head in disbelief. "Damn it, Harry, no wonder Doc was heated. That's a lot of money. I'm afraid I can't help you there, my friend." They rode a while in silence before Red spoke again.

"I don't think you ought to go back there anytime soon, Harry. If you want to stay alive, that is." Red looked past Harry over at Daniel. "And you got this fine young lad here involved in a gambler's fight!" He looked hard at Harry, then at Daniel. "Maybe I ought to just let old Doc have his way with you. My life'd be a whole lot easier if I did." Red spurred his horse and yelled over his shoulder. "Come on, you two, we've got a lot of miles to cover if we want to get home today." Harry and Daniel nudged their horses into a canter and followed Red into a smattering of log buildings known as Twin Lakes.

Twin Lakes was barely a spot on the map and served mainly as a resting place for travelers heading over the Pass. It consisted of a guest Lodge for hunters, a general store, and scatter of small cabins. Across the road from the Lodge, Red had built a barn to store his equipment, a corral for his horses and a small bunkhouse for his men to use during the winter months.

While his men tended to their horses and unloaded various items, Red introduced Daniel to Frank and his wife Gloria, the owners of the Lodge who had come out to meet them.

Frank was a large, surly man with an unsmiling, unshaven face and mean eyes set wide apart. His wife Gloria, on the other hand, was a short, attractive woman with dark, lively eyes, long black shiny hair and a bountiful chest that Daniel couldn't help but notice. Gloria was comfortable around men, familiar with their desires from her previous profession and couldn't help but be flattered by Daniel's glances.

"It's nice to meet you, Daniel. Are you a friend of Red's?" she asked and held onto his hand with both of hers.

"No, ma'am, we just met." Daniel replied, embarrassed that she'd caught him looking at her breasts. Her hands were soft and warm and she moved closer to him as she spoke. Daniel was beginning to feel uncomfortable.

"He's adorable Red, can I keep him?" Daniel blushed. "Oh, I'm just kidding," she said and winked at Red, who shook his head knowingly.

"Come with me Daniel and I'll show you my puppies." Gloria led him around the building to the rear of the lodge.

Behind the Lodge was a large pen, fenced with barbed wire. As she approached, two big dogs bounded from their kennel to the door of the cage, wagging their tails. It took only a few more steps for Daniel to realize that they weren't dogs, but wolves.

Gloria felt Daniel hesitate. "Oh, don't worry yourself. They won't hurt you as long as you're with me." They seemed as docile and friendly as puppies when she reached in to pat them but when she brought Daniel closer, they snarled and growled and bared their teeth ferociously.

"Sit down!" she ordered. They sat, obediently. "These are my little darlings. Aren't you?" The wolves wagged their tails, watching Gloria expectantly. She kept a tight hold of Daniel's hand while he patted them so they could see that there was nothing for them to fear. They licked his hand through the wire, but unnervingly they growled and bared their teeth as if they tasted him for a future meal.

Daniel noticed Gloria's husband watching them from the back door of the Lodge. Frank glared at his wife before turning back inside. Gloria felt his concern and squeezed his hand.

"Oh, take no notice of him. He's the jealous sort, but he's harmless," she said calmly. Daniel reached out to pat the wolves again but they leapt at him, snapping and snarling viciously. Gloria quickly pulled him away and said something to them that Daniel couldn't hear. They looked at her intently, tilting their heads as if in conversation, then laid their ears back and obediently retreated to the far end of their pen.

"They don't like men," she said, "but they're gentle as puppies with me, and they're very protective. They'd probably eat Frank if they ever got the chance," she said with a smile to Red, as they walked back to the road.

Daniel was settling in his saddle when Gloria came over to him and placed something into his saddlebag. From his saddle, he had an excellent view down the front of Gloria's shirt.

"Here's a little jerky for the trip, honey. Why don't you come back and visit me some time?" she said, looking up. "Good luck over in Aspen and keep warm," she said with a wink.

The last sight Daniel had of Twin Lakes was of Gloria pushing forth, waving to him and blowing him a kiss. He couldn't help but notice that the men were laughing at him, but when he asked what they were laughing at, he got more laughter from them and Harry, too. Puzzled and embarrassed, he rode along in silence, enjoying the passing scenery.

Red dropped back after a while. "Say there, Daniel, I don't know how good you are with horses, but would you be of a mind to help Dutch and Pete with the wagons?"

"Well, I'm OK with the horses, but I don't know much about wagons." Memories of almost being squashed between two train cars at the cattle yards were still fresh in his mind. "I'm willing to learn if you want to teach me, though." Red looked over at Dutch, who nodded his approval but couldn't resist the opportunity to make a joke.

"I'm sure that Gloria would love to teach you a thing or two about hitching up her wagons," Dutch said with a broad smile, bending the creases in his leathery face.

"She was just showing me her wolves," Daniel protested in Gloria's defense. "Why are you all laughing? She was just being nice."

"Yeah, I'm sure she was," yelled Pete, the driver of the other wagon. "Did you notice how friendly those wolves of hers were to you? They're so jealous of her that when she and Frank get to doin' some cuddlin' at night, they nearly tear the cage down. Hell, you can hear 'em howling for miles up and down the valley whenever they go at it. I'm not lyin' either, am I Dutch?" he turned in his seat to look back at Dutch for confirmation.

Dutch added his weighty experience to the subject. "Hell, no. We've all heard 'em go at it at one time or another. Haven't we, boys?"

Everyone nodded, even Red. "My guess is that if you come this way again, you might get to hear them first-hand."

Ahead of them rose a wall of mountains like a solid ocean wave of impossible height, topped by a foaming crest of snow. This was the Great Divide, the spine of the Rocky Mountains, a range of peaks and valleys that stretched thousands of miles from Canada to Mexico, and cleaved America in two along its length.

Leaving the valley floor below them, the forests of aspens gradually disappeared and gave way to mountainsides covered with alternating cascades of hardy evergreens and barren avalanche chutes. The road cut a long traverse up the mountain face. The further they climbed, the harsher the terrain became.

Daniel was feeling the effects of the thinner air the higher they went. He noticed that the horses were also breathing hard too, exhaling clouds of steam from their nostrils with every step. He was amazed at the pace at which the Morgans were pulling the wagons up the long, steep incline, while Marigold's head bobbed up and down with the effort of keeping up with them.

For several miles, they crossed the face of the mountains along a narrow, roughly hewn road. They passed small cascades of snowmelt and precipitous drop-offs, where the smallest misstep could send them tumbling a thousand feet or more down to the valley floor. Each turn seemed to lead to a steeper section of the road.

Directly above his head and close enough to touch was the satin blue sky. The snowfields that spread out before him were like a white carpet to the heavens. Off to his right, he could look over the edge into the valley below, and just make out the thin ribbon of road along which they'd just come, wandering in and out of the trees several thousand feet below.

They'd climbed above the timberline and Daniel noticed the mood of the men had turned serious. The snow became deeper and the wagons began slipping sideways. The road had become a slushy, muddy track.

"They call this Independence Pass because it gives Aspen the independence to stay alive in the winter," Dutch explained. "We have to make this trip over the Pass twelve months a year, and when the winter comes, it's a dangerous proposition driving heavy wagons over this road. We've lost some wagons over the years and, I'm sorry to say, we've lost some fine men too." Just then, Pete's wagon lurched sideways towards the edge of the road. Marigold jumped out of the way.

"Whoa there, girl," Red said, as he reached out and caught Daniel's reins and pulled Marigold off to the uphill side of the road. The other riders took the same precaution in case the wagon slid backwards. Daniel was surprised at how deep the snow had become; it was almost up to Marigold's knees.

When the riders moved back onto the road, Pete turned to Red with a look of concern.

"Yeah, Pete, I know." Pete gave Red the thumbs up sign. Red continued, "We have a different setup for coming over this stretch of road in the winter. It's peaceful now, but these mountains are known for having a mean temper. It can get real dangerous up here in a hurry if a storm hits us. In bad winters it can reach forty, sixty feet deep, up here. The worst part is we have to clear the road after every storm or we lose it." Daniel tried to imagine the effort that it would take to shovel each foot of the road every time it snowed.

"Our job is pretty important to the town. If these supplies don't get through, the mines will close, and without work, a lot of families would most likely starve."

Up ahead, Daniel could see the next sharp turn and beyond that, what he assumed was the summit. Behind them, Harry's horse was plodding along. Harry looked asleep and was barely staying in the saddle.

"Hey, Harry, you awake?" Red yelled back at him.

"Yeah, I'm awake. Are we there yet?" he answered without opening his eyes.

As they were rounding the last corner, two grubby miners appeared from out on the mountainside. Red handed them boxes of dynamite and supplies. Daniel watched in amazement as they carried their boxes back along a narrow, snowy path and disappeared into a hole in the face of the mountain. The path to the entrance was barely a foot wide.

A slip would have sent them plummeting over a thousand feet, yet they walked along it with the casual confidence of mountain sheep.

"We bring them their supplies," Red answered Daniel's unspoken question.

"What are they doing all the way up here?" Daniel asked as Pete slapped his team with the reins to get them moving again.

"Oh, we get all sorts of madmen up here in these mountains. Those two work a gold seam out on that mountain there. I can't imagine how they do it up here all the year round." When they reached the summit, the wagon crews applied themselves to the serious business of preparing for the descent down the western side of the Pass. Daniel watched as the men unhitched the teams of Morgans, then reattached them to the rear of the wagons facing forward, and saw how the yokes at the front of the wagons were being fitted with a metal piece that looked like a farmer's plow blade. To Daniel, men and animals worked brilliantly in concert and the job was completed in just a few minutes.

After wishing each other good luck, the men took up their positions either at the front of the wagons where they steered them, or behind, where they controlled their speed. With the discipline of a military company, they waited for the order to move out, and both men and horses seemed anxious to get on with the journey. While he waited, Daniel turned a full circle and watched the clouds fly past as he admired the spectacular view of the Rockies from the highest pass in North America.

"Nice view, ain't it, son?" Red understated.

Daniel couldn't find the words to reply, he just nodded his head. Red followed his gaze, appreciating the circle of mountain peaks surrounding them at shoulder height.

"D'you know something?" He seemed to ask of the wind that tugged at their hats, "I never get tired of this view, it's different every time. Sometimes it seems so peaceful up here, like today. Other times, it can be as nasty and scary as anything the devil could conjure." Red looked at Harry, lying crumpled in a heap in a pile of snow. He shook his head in disgust.

"Why don't you get him up and put him in Pete's wagon? He's not going to be any help and I don't want him getting in the way." Red rode around the wagons, inspecting each one closely as Daniel pushed Harry's uncooperative form up into Pete's wagon.

Daniel gathered up the reins of the extra horses. Dutch gave him a wink and thumbs up as he headed to his wagon.

Each wagon team consisted of three men. A driver walking behind the wagon controlled the teams of horses by a series of whistles and tugs on the reins. Beside him, the brakeman walked, holding the ropes connected to the brake handles. The most dangerous job was done by the man in front, who steered the wagon.

Daniel could only imagine what would happen if a wagon ever got away from the brakeman and the horses were unable to hold it back. The consequences could be fatal if the man steering the team failed to get clear of the wagon's wheels or the horses' hooves. Daniel looked upon the men with new respect.

Red drove the lead wagon, Dutch the second, Pete the third, and Daniel rode behind with the horses in tow. Pete's brakeman was a quiet older man they called 'Dangerous'. Steering the wagon was a slightly built young man named Bolly who didn't seem at all comfortable being off his horse.

Ahead of them the road was snow-covered, and in the shadows Daniel could hear the snow turn from soft and slushy to hard and icy, crunching under the wheels of the wagons. Now he understood why it was important to Red to get over this part of the trip early in the day. It would be treacherous when the sun dropped behind the mountains and the road turned into a slick sheet of ice.

The road changed quickly from the gentle incline of the summit onto the steep face of the mountain. It was barely wide enough for the wagons. In several places, the edges of the road crumbled under their weight. Daniel was impressed by how both the men and horses seemed to know their respective jobs. When they came to a switchback in the road, the driver would give a shout or a whistle, and the brakeman would pull back on the ropes to the brake handles. The horses would take two more steps, then the horses would straighten their legs and brace against the weight of the wagon. When they had come to a stop, the man steering would step in front of the wagon and push or pull the yoke, which was attached to the axle, and pivot the front wheels in the direction they intended to go.

With the front wheels turned, the driver would give one or two whistles and one or two slaps with the reins, and the horses moved forward a measured number of steps. Then with military like precision, they would come to a stop and stand perfectly still as the brake was set and the angle of the front axle was shifted to a new position. Their potential fate was constant assurance that the men focused on the job at hand. The result was that the wagons swiveled around these impossibly sharp corners as if they were being pivoted.

Pete's wagon had traversed one switchback and had only two more to go to reach the valley floor when things started to go wrong.

The wagon in front of Pete's had gone a little too wide around the corner below them and was wedged into the cliff wall, blocking the road. Dutch was pulling hard on the reins, trying to get his team to back up while the man steering fought to turn the front axle back onto the road. With much shouting and effort from both man and beast, they succeeded and their wagon started moving again around the turn. Eventually, it would traverse the mountain in the opposite direction and pass directly below Pete's wagon.

Pete began to make his turn. He was most of the way around when Dangerous, his brakeman, stepped off the side of the road and lost the tension on the brakes. The heavily loaded wagon gathered speed.

Pete pulled back with all his strength, trying his best to keep the horses from moving forward, but they were into the steepest part of the turn, and the weight of the wagon was becoming too much for the team of horses to hold.

The Morgans strained and braced their legs, innately comprehending that if the wagon went over the cliff, they would go with it. They tossed their heads at the strain of holding back the massive weight slowly pulling them towards the edge. They snorted and whinnied in fear as their hooves slipped and the heavy wagon drew them closer to the brink.

Daniel jumped off his horse and ran to help Dangerous. Pete called out to Bolly, urgency in his voice.

"Turn the wheels into the hill! Turn them into the hill." Pete's voice was shrill. "Hurry, son, hurry, I can't hold them back. It's going to go. Dangerous, get the brakes. "

Pete's feet began to slip as the wagon picked up momentum. Daniel leapt down the slope past Dangerous, and hurried to help Bolly turn the wheels. The wagon was coming at them, and the weight on the yoke was driving it deep into the snow, gouging up dirt as it drove forward.

"Red! Red!" Real fear was now in Pete's voice. "We've got a runaway! Watch out below!" Pete was yelling at the top of his lungs. "I don't think I can hold 'em." Dangerous was back on the road. He was helping Pete with the team but they still had no brakes; the brake ropes had slipped under the wagon and were tangled in the legs of the horses. Dangerous struggled to reach the brake handle but couldn't. The wagon was pulling them off the side of the mountain. There was not one second to lose if the impending disaster was to be averted.

Pete was almost out of strength, pleading for help. Dangerous ran around Pete to the uphill side of the wagon and made another grab for the brake handle, but slipped and fell. He struggled to his feet and tried again.

"Hang on, Pete. I'm coming. Hang onto 'em," Red's voice was distant, but the fear in it was clear.

"I don't think I can hold 'em, Red. They're getting spooked." Pete felt his feet slipping more and more. "I can't hold 'em." The horses were tossing their heads wildly, their cleated hooves fighting for traction, their eyes wide with fear.

"Hold on, Pete!" Red yelled again. "Daniel, grab the axle and steer it into the hill with Bolly. Hurry!"

As the wagon continued to roll further around the turn, Daniel and Bolly heaved on the yoke. They pulled it out of the dirt and managed to turn the wheels enough that the yoke plowed itself into the cliff face. The wagon shuddered to a stop. The horses stamped their hooves and whinnied in relief.

Daniel found Pete sitting in the snow, exhausted from his efforts, his head in his hands. Recovering from his fright he struggled to catch his breath. He eventually looked up. "That was close, son. I can't thank you enough," he said, shaking Daniel's hand.

Red was still on the slope below them. "Are you men alright?" he yelled up to them. He'd stopped climbing, seeing that the emergency appeared to be over. He was out of breath from the exertion of running uphill through the snow, no mean feat for a man his age. He was no more than fifty yards downhill from them when Dangerous leaned on the wheel. Careless, as well as dangerous, his hand slipped off the slick surface of the wheel and he fell heavily against the brake handle, releasing it.

The horses had let the tension slacken from their yoke and the wagon lurched forward slightly, just an inch or two. The horses pulled back instinctively, their nostrils flaring, and the wagon stopped moving.

Pete was about to give Dangerous another piece of his mind and Dangerous was reaching for the brake to reset it when the wagon jumped forward again, then stopped. They all held their breaths, hoping. It lurched again. This time, a creaking shudder went through the wagon. The yoke, which was all that was holding the wagon back, snapped with a loud crack, breaking halfway down the shaft. They all jumped for the brake handles, but before anyone could reach them, the wagon started to roll down the hill. The horses snorted and tossed their heads in alarm, bracing their legs and stamping the ground.

It happened in slow motion. Pete was first to react and grabbed the reins to get the team under control. His back muscles screamed as he pulled with all of his might. The Morgans, sensing his desperation, braced their legs but slipped and slid as they fought against being dragged further and further down the slope. Their mighty muscles rippled and the sweat on their coats glistened in the sunlight.

Dangerous was reaching out to grab the brake handle when his feet slipped out from under him. He was pulled under the wagon and the heavy wagon rolled over him, crushing his left arm. His coat was caught between the wheel and the brake. If his coat wasn't released, his broken arm was going to be the least of his injuries. Dangerous didn't hear himself screaming.

Everyone else heard him.

Pete let go of the reins and rushed to help, but could only watch as the wagon pulled Dangerous down the mountain. He saw Bolly scrambling out of the way to avoid being crushed against the cliff and watched horrified as Bolly bravely made a lunge for the brake handle as the wagon trundled past him. He succeeded in freeing the coat and Dangerous rolled free but Bolly was pulled off his feet and barely escaped getting crushed, as the wheel rolled so close to his face, it grazed his cheek. The wagon began moving faster, with more determination. Pete and the giant, brave-hearted beasts were losing the battle.

"Get Harry out of there! Hurry, it's going to go!" Red shouted.

Daniel had forgotten about the drunk in the back of the wagon. He leapt onto the broken yoke, bucking and gouging a trough in the road, and climbed up onto the wagon. The yoke was digging into the road in stops and starts, becoming shorter by the second as pieces broke off in splinters.

Red was climbing up the hill below him, wading through the deep snow as fast as he could, but still too far away to be of any help. Daniel saw him waving him off, or so he thought. But Red was trying to get Daniel to turn the wagon over the side of the cliff. If it kept going straight down the road, it would collide with Dutch's wagon, which was still not completely around the next corner. Red had a vision of the mangled mess of horses and men all being driven over the edge of the road, cascading into the valley below.

Daniel was being tossed from side to side in the bouncing, lurching wagon. He grabbed Harry's coat and shook him violently. Harry was in no mood to wake up and slapped at Daniel's hand. "Harry, wake up!" Daniel yelled, as he was tossed about by the bucking wagon. Daniel shook him again. Harry lashed out with his arm, knocking Daniel onto his rear as the wagon twitched and rolled on.

"Hurry, son. Get him out, get him out." Red's voice sounded closer. The wagon was fast approaching him, dragging the terrified horses along with it. "Pete, clear the horses. Get them out of there now. Pete!

Can you hear me?" Red looked down the hill and saw that Dutch's wagon was around the turn, but not completely out of the way. It would be close. "Clear the horses, Pete. Let the wagon go," Red yelled again.

Pete dropped the reins and ran around his team of horses for the bolt that held them to the wagon. The horses panicked when he let go of the reins, thinking he had let them go to their deaths. From up on the wagon, Daniel looked directly into their bulging eyes. In them, he saw the purest fear and panic. These huge beasts were fighting with all of their massive strength. Their giant hearts were bursting with their desire to live.

"Bolly, grab the brake. Hurry, son, for God's sake, hurry," Pete yelled as he yanked at the bolt that connected the team to the wagon. Daniel stepped on the back of the wagon to help.

Desperately they struggled with the bolt while the horses fought, doing their best to hold the wagon back as it rolled steadily towards the edge. Bolly finally got a good grip on the brake handle and when he pulled back on it, the bolt came free. The wagon paused momentarily; the Morgans fell back and stood perfectly still.

Pete fell backwards with the bolt in his hand. The huge horses gracefully and magically avoided stepping on him. He had a moment of relief, but then watched impotently as the wagon broke free and began rolling again, gaining speed. What was left of the yoke splintered and was gone. In disbelief, Pete watched Daniel climb back into the wagon and scramble to the front. He managed to step on Harry's leg as he went.

"Get off me, you clumsy son of a bitch," Harry yelled, finally waking up. He sat up, facing backwards. He waved at Pete sitting in the middle of the road, then lay down again to go back to sleep. The wagon rolled on, gathering speed. Red tried to grab the brake handle as the runaway wagon passed him and was almost dragged under the rear wheels for his effort. "Get off it, kid! Get off," Daniel didn't seem to hear him. "Hurry, Harry, get up!" Red yelled as the wagon bounced past him.

The wagon was heading directly towards Dutch's wagon. Dutch and his brakeman started running to get out of the way. With all eyes on the runaway wagon, they watched in disbelief as Daniel scrambled over the driver's seat and leaned over the front of the wagon. At the risk of falling underneath the wagon, he reached down and grabbed the yoke and with all his strength, yanked it to the right. Nothing happened. He pulled again and again. On the third attempt, he succeeded in turning the wheels a fraction. With luck, they might just miss Dutch's wagon. He climbed back and kicked Harry hard.

"Get up, you stupid drunk," he yelled and turned to jump clear of the doomed wagon.

"Who you calling stupid?" Harry grabbed Daniel's foot as he jumped, twisting it violently. Daniel fell back into the wagon.

"Leave me alone you stupid man, and jump!" Daniel yelled, trying to break free of Harry's grasp.

Daniel took his hand back as far as it would go and landed a punch directly onto Harry's head. Harry's face was turned, so Daniel's gloved fist did little damage, but Harry released his grip. Daniel saw the edge of the road coming up only yards away.

"Come back here, you little bastard." Harry said as he tried to grab Daniel's leg. Daniel glanced back at Harry with disdain and jumped off into the deep snow on the downhill side. Full of indignant fury, Harry sat up, looking backwards at Daniel's receding body. Everyone was pointing at him, or past him, so he turned and looked over his shoulder.

"Oh. Shit. Oh. Shhiiit. Oh. Shhiiiiiiittttt."

The wagon left the road at an angle, accelerating rapidly and it careened down the slope to the lower road barely missing Dutch's wagon. It bounced violently when it hit the road, but its momentum carried it forward with enthusiasm and launched it airborne from the road.

It tumbled forward in graceful flight until the front wheels hit the slope below, where it vaulted high into the air immediately followed by the assorted muffled crashing sounds of the cargo as it distributed itself over the mountain side. A high pitched scream was the last they heard from Harry, or so they thought.

Chapter 6

Eventually, the sounds of the falling wagon and its contents ceased echoing in the narrow valley. Accounting for his men, Red saw the looks of shock and disbelief on their faces as they stood motionless and followed the fading sounds. Uphill, Pete was calming his team. Bolly was tending to Dangerous, who was crumpled over, holding his arm to his chest. With a sigh of relief, he saw that Dutch's wagon and team appeared to be intact.

"Harry! Daniel!" Red called out as he was joined by the others, all looking as bewildered as he felt.

"Looky there, Red!" Dutch was pointing at the hillside immediately below them. Something moved amongst the wreckage.

Red rushed over to the spot where Pete's wagon had left the road. He scanned the slope below relieved when the head of the young man who had just saved his business miraculously appeared from the snow. Red felt a wave of relief wash over him. "Are you alright, son?" he yelled down. "Are you hurt?"

Daniel lay back in the snow, breathing and watching the clouds sailing along in the bluest of skies. The events of the past few minutes were passing before his mind. There was a strange dreamlike feeling to it; as if he was an observer above it all, in one of those clouds, perhaps.

Someone was calling his name. He raised his right hand and felt sharp pains stab at various points on his body. After a quick inventory, he found to his surprise that there was no major damage. He took a deep breath and tried to stand, but his legs wouldn't support him. He fell back into the snow.

"Stay there, son. I'll come get you. See if you can find Harry." Red yelled to the men on the road below. He was sweating from the fear and the exertion. He stepped off the road and waded through the waist deep snow to where Daniel lay and sat down next to him.

Red patted him on the shoulder in gratitude and reassurance. "That was a very stupid thing you did up there, son." Red gave another of his deep rolling laughs. "Very brave; but very stupid. You saved some men's lives back there." Red turned serious. And, one of those lives more than likely, was mine. I'm in your debt." Red held out his hand. Daniel shook it.

"Is Harry dead?" Daniel asked when he found his voice.

Red shrugged. "Probably," Red sighed. "Too bad. He was a real character. A lousy gambler but, a real character. I'm going to miss him." Red stood with effort and helped Daniel to his feet. Together they made their way down to the lower road.

Red looked up at the sky. The day was waning and they still had many miles to travel if they hoped to get to Aspen before dark. He was considering the proposition when Daniel grabbed his sleeve and pointed down the mountain.

A pile of snow one hundred feet down the hill moved. A head appeared. The hatless, snow encrusted head turned and Harry waved weakly. "How y'all doin' up there?"

Red and Daniel looked at each other and burst out laughing. "He's alive, boys," Red announced to the men up the hill. Several moaned loudly in chorus.

A low rumble came from somewhere higher up in the valley. Red instantly scanned the slope above them. Over the years he'd learned that avalanches were unpredictable, deadly, and almost always came unannounced. Only after he'd studied the slopes above them and the ominous rumble had died away did he relax again.

"Let's see if we can get what's left of us down off this mountain, shall we?" Red looked up at the sun sinking towards the western horizon. His tone turned serious. "Still feel like lending us a hand?" Daniel nodded and Red held out his hand. Daniel took hold of it and felt the warmth and power of the man. "Thanks, son." As Red checked Dutch's rig, Daniel helped calm Pete's team of horses. Pete was still weak and exhausted for his battles and leaned against the wagon with his face hidden in his arms. It had been the worst day of Pete's career.

Though obviously in great pain, Dangerous had decided that walking behind the wagons was safer than riding in one. It wasn't long before he collapsed, clutching his arm to his side. Like a small family, they all helped load him into Dutch's wagon and made him as comfortable as they could. He groaned in pain as the wagon jolted down the bumpy, treacherous road. Red walked alongside the wagon and suffered at every bump, his friend's pain tore at his heart.

Harry had made it down the slope and sat sullenly in the snow, waiting for them. When the two remaining wagons finally reached him, he jumped up and grabbed Red by the coat and shook him roughly.

"You red-haired bastard," he yelled. "What were you trying to do, kill me?" Harry pulled back and tried to take a swing at Red, but Red casually pulled Harry's hat down over his eyes and spun him around.

Disoriented, Harry tore the hat off and immediately fell down on his hands and knees at Red's feet. Red was still laughing hard as he helped him up. Harry pivoted and took a swing at Daniel, but missed. Red grabbed him from behind.

"Harry, listen to me, will you?" Red lowered his voice but kept a tight hold of Harry. "This young fella' just saved your life. You owe him, Harry."

Harry looked over his shoulder at Red, then at Daniel. "Is that a fact?" His voice was full of doubt. "You saved my life? I was thinking you were just trying to kick my head in." Red let him go. "Well, thanks, I guess," Harry said sheepishly. "But you nearly killed me, you irresponsible little bastard."

"Stop it, Harry." Red was serious. "Shake hands, you two." Reluctantly, Harry shook Daniel's hand.

"I never thought you'd kill me this way, Red." Harry sounded deeply disappointed. "I always thought there'd be a woman involved, at least." Harry threw his arms around Red to give him a hug, but Red pushed him away, pointing his finger at him menacingly.

"Harry, I told you before," Red smiled. "Not in front of the men."

Harry threw his arms around Daniel instead. "Thanks friend." Harry said, engulfing Daniel in his noxious breath. "I guess this makes us friends for life, doesn't it? What's your name again?"

"Daniel Carrington." he replied, trying to detach himself from Harry's clutches.

"You've saved my life twice today and I can't even remember your damned name. I really am an ass." Harry still had a good grip on Daniel and showed no inclination to let go. "If it's none of my business, say so, but you gotta place to stay when you get to town?" Daniel shrugged. "Then it's settled. You're staying with me and that's that. It's the least I can do for saving my life." He loosened his grip and Daniel gratefully put a pace between them, gasping for clean air.

Harry made a transformation. He'd gone from cowardly vicious to masterfully magnanimous. His eyes seemed to be alight with fervor as he stood with his arms outstretched as if to encompass the valley. The side effects of Harry's sudden brush with mortality were only temporary. Abruptly, he spun around and slapped Daniel on the back, nearly knocking him off his feet.

"You can stay just as long as you want. We might just become partners one day." Harry babbled on enthusiastically. "I've told Red many times that I should get myself a bright young apprentice and teach him the business." He glanced sideways at Red. "Haven't I, Red?"

Red shook his head and watched as Harry gathered the reins of his horse and walked off down the road with Daniel in tow, as if they were old friends.

Red Corcoran was one of the most recognized people in Aspen, and not just because of his size, his full head of red hair, and the big beard he wore in the winter. He was often the first point of contact for miners and other travelers coming over Independence Pass to explore their fortunes in the Roaring Fork Valley. Most of these men had migrated from the smaller mining towns on the eastern slope and when the silver petered out, they moved restlessly higher into the mountains, usually westward. Aspen was the last chance for most of them to find the fabled fortunes that were the legend of Colorado.

He would often meet them trudging over the Pass, loaded down with their gear. He always greeted them with a smile and a tip of his big hat, saluting their determination. He knew the conditions these men would find in the mines and doubted that any would make more than meager wages for their efforts. Money they would invariably spend on women and strong drink for their slowly eroding souls. They'd also spend it on the cocaine and opium-laced medications that were the lifeblood of the mining communities.

The liquid cure-alls in the little blue glass bottles were sold at the drug store cheaply. When added to the miners' coffee, it got them going in the morning, kept them going all day, and relieved their headaches from cheap whiskey from the night before. It also took away the pain that they endured from the falling rocks that bruised and crushed their bones. Those injuries, no matter how painful, would never stop them going back into the mines, day after day. It was too bleak an existence for Red to comprehend.

At the base of the Pass, the road bisected the mining settlement of Independence, a collection of log cabins scattered on the valley floor and several mines that over the years had produced sporadic quantities of gold and silver.

At their approach, the miners gathered around. When Red told them about the accident, Jessup Bates, the mine foreman, agreed to send some of his men to see what they could salvage. Jessup's wife took a quick look at Dangerous and hurried back to her cabin to make a splint for his arm and to bring him some of the analgesic in the little blue bottle to ease his pain.

Harry, on the other hand, couldn't be contained. While Red's men turned the wagons around and reattached their teams, Harry loudly recounted his adventure, entertaining the small knot of miners that had gathered.

Jessup and Red walked a small distance away from the others. Red was deeply concerned. When Dangerous coughed, he moaned in pain. Red noted with alarm that a thin trickle of blood seeped from his mouth and his breath now came in gasps. Not only was Dangerous his employee, he was also his friend and he was hurting badly. Red suspected that the injuries were serious and though taking him to town was the quickest way to get treatment, Red was concerned that he might not survive the trip down to the hospital. Might it be better for him to stay overnight in Independence and have a doctor come up from town tomorrow? It was a difficult decision, but it had to be made quickly.

Jessup's wife had considerable experience with treating injuries of this sort and ministered to Dangerous with careful efficiency. She tied his arm to his body and after giving him what meager medications she had, she quietly informed Red that Dangerous most probably had broken ribs as well as a badly broken arm, and needed more care than she could provide. Together they decided it would be better to get him to the new hospital in Aspen, where a doctor could set his arm before an infection set in.

"Dutch, I'm going to ride on down and have someone come up and meet you with some lamps."

"Sounds good to me, Red," Dutch agreed.

"I'll send one of the boys to get the ambulance to meet you at the barn." The ambulance service was new and the city was as proud of it as they were of their seven volunteer fire departments. "I'll take Harry and the youngster with me for company. And Dutch, be careful. Even the horses are looking a mite tired."

Dutch waved off Red's concern. "We'll be alright. If the boys bring us up a bit of whiskey, they won't get any grief from me today. Just don't tell the boss, OK?" Red winked and touched his finger to his lips.

It was twilight when they arrived at Red's Stillwater Ranch. It was an organized place with a large barn, an assortment of wagons and neatly fenced fields, where knots of horses grazed lazily. Several ranch hands were standing around, awaiting the arrival of Red's wagons. They listened intently as Red gave them a brief account of the day's events. He dispatched one man off to town to get the ambulance. To the rest he issued orders and helped load the lanterns, fuel and blankets onto their wagon then hurried them on their way.

Satisfied he'd done all he could, he took his rifle from his saddle sling and led Harry and Daniel into the barn through a small side door. Daniel was surprised to find that the building was more spacious than it appeared from outside and thankfully it was warm. It had a large hayloft over half of the ceiling, and at the far end, an open space with a forge. The walls were lined with complicated leather harnesses and tack, all neatly strung, and space enough for a dozen stalls.

Daniel took it all in as they walked to the far corner of the building, where Red unhooked a small key on his gun belt to open the door to the office.

"Come on in boys. Take a seat," he said, striking a match and lighting the lamp on the desk.

Red collapsed in his big leather chair and let his head fall back. He took a slow, deep breath through his nose and let it out in a long, weary sigh. Harry was too tired and Daniel too polite to interrupt him. Red shook himself awake, and from a drawer, pulled out a full bottle of whiskey and three small glasses. He took a long look at the bottle; then filled the glasses.

"Here's to you, young feller. You saved us a lot more trouble than you caused today." Harry and Red tipped their heads back and downed the amber liquid with sighs of satisfaction. "What's the matter, lad, is whiskey not to your taste?" Red asked when he'd noticed that Daniel hadn't drunk his. Daniel looked down at the floor.

"I promised my mother that I'd not drink whiskey."

Harry and Red exchanged glances.

"I can respect that," Red said sincerely. "I wish I'd made a promise like that when I was your age." Red pointed his finger at Harry, "And you, Harry Rich. You might've even made something of yourself if you'd done the same thing too, and stuck to your Mormon ways."

Harry took Daniel's glass and drained it.

"I don't think so," Harry said, looking into the empty glass as if reading tea leaves. "There's too much fun to be had in this world, Red." Harry paused. "And whiskey seems to be a big part of it." He placed the glass back on the desk and his smile was wicked. "Hell, Red. There's plenty of time yet for the boy to find his vices." Red shook his head in despair.

"How are you off for money, son?" Red asked.

Daniel squirmed in his chair. "That Sheriff in Leadville took my last twenty dollars."

"You don't have any money then?" Harry asked incredulously.

"No sir." Daniel replied.

Harry grimaced.

"What're your plans then?" Red inquired gently.

Daniel shrugged. "I'm hoping to get to San Francisco before spring."

"Listen son, traveling across this part of the country's not easy in the winter, and winter'll be here real soon. It can be downright dangerous."

Harry helped himself to more whiskey, Red rocked in his chair, waiting for the boy to say more.

"I don't know what I'm going to do, Mr. Corcoran. If it wasn't for Harry here, I wouldn't even have a place to stay." Daniel looked at Harry plaintively. "I know if I get a job, I can save some money."

Red sighed and shook his head. "To be honest with you son, I'm not too sure about the wisdom of you two bunking up, but it couldn't hurt for a while, I guess. At least, 'till you can get enough money to be on your way again. That OK with you, Harry?"

Harry shrugged, as if it didn't matter to him one way or another.

"Come on Harry, do you think we can look after this young feller until he gets on his feet?" Harry's eyes were glazing over. The lack of sleep and the whiskey were starting to work on him like opium. "I'm talking to you, Harry." Red said loudly.

"OK. OK. But I need to eat something, Red," Harry was awake again, "and I'm sure the kid here's hungry too."

Red sighed, a long tired sound like a failing wind. "Well, I don't think they'll be down for an hour or two yet, so maybe we should eat while we can." Red stood and ushered them out of his office, locking the door again. Night had fallen as they headed for their horses. "The least I can do for the man who saved my ass is to make sure he has a decent meal." Harry shook his head trying to stay awake, he felt like throwing up. "What do you say to a big, juicy steak?"

"That sounds good to me, Red." Harry sprinted after them, suddenly revived.

"I don't want to be any trouble, Mr. Corcoran," Daniel said.

"No trouble at all, son. What did I tell you about calling me Mr. Corcoran?" Red slapped his hand on Daniel's shoulder. Together, they walked back through the barn and out to their horses. "I want you to leave your horse in No Problem Joe's stables," Red said, as they were untying their horses. "He's a friend of mine. Harry leaves his horse there too, don't you, Harry?" Harry grunted and turned his horse out onto the road. "Just tell No Problem that I'll take care of it."

They were standing between their horses preparing to mount when Red pulled out some money from his pocket, counted it and pushed it into Daniel's hand. He put his finger to his lips and nodded toward Harry.

"Thank you, Red. I can pay you back when I get a job," Daniel whispered.

"Not necessary son. I owe you for what you did today. I don't want to hear another word about it." Red made sure that Daniel saw him smiling before he tucked his chin down into his scarf again.

"Thank you, Red. I appreciate it."

"I know you do, son." In his mind's eye, he could see this young fellow working for him.

Ahead of them, a faint halo-like glow hung above the town, reflecting the yellow of the streetlamps and the furnaces of the smelters. Though Daniel had never been in this town before, excitement and anticipation rose in him.

They stopped outside the Ute City Livery and Stable. Red stuck his head inside the door.

"Joe, are you in there?"

There was no reply.

"We'll catch up with him at some point, I'm sure," Red said with certainty as he climbed back onto his horse.

Daniel was surprised to find that the town was busy even though it was after dark. He didn't expect that the streets would be full of horse drawn carriages bustling this way and that, and of noisy, friendly people—most of whom seemed to know Red.

They tied their horses together outside a brightly lit place called The Red Onion. For Daniel, it had been a long day with little to eat. As soon as they walked through the door, he was overwhelmed by the delicious smells. His stomach rumbled loudly and he clutched it to still the noise.

"Hungry, are you?" Red laughed. "Don't worry son, we'll get you fed."

A small, shiny man with a thin black moustache dressed in a fine black suit advanced on them flamboyantly. He shook Red's hand profusely, his thin-lipped smile betraying small dingy teeth.

"Vhat a pleasure it is to zee you again, M'sieur Corcoran." The shiny man said in a heavy, somewhere European accent.

"Antonio, I would like you to meet our new friend." Red paused, embarrassed. "I'm sorry son. I forgot your last name..."

Daniel held out his hand, "Daniel Carrington, sir." Antonio gave a slight bow and shook Daniel's hand limply.

Harry held out his hand too, but Antonio conspicuously ignored it. Harry tapped his hand on Antonio's arm. Antonio looked down at Harry's outstretched hand with a pained expression, as if it was a rotting fish.

"You, I already know," he said with a sneer.

"Your English is getting better, Antonio," Harry retorted. "I can almost understand you."

With a huff and raised chin, Antonio pivoted on his heels and eeled his way through the restaurant, finally stopping at a small table under an enormous rack of moose antlers. He handed menus to Red and Daniel, but held Harry's just out of reach, foiling Harry's repeated attempts to grab it.

"Gentlemen, I 'ope, zat you enjoy your meal." He dropped Harry's menu on the floor and slithered away, just avoiding Harry's grasp.

"Now Harry," Red warned, "be nice."

With a sigh, Harry picked his menu up off the floor. He was too tired to argue.

Daniel looked beyond the red velvet curtains into the formal dining room. It was ornately decorated and had an air of opulence well-suited to the fashionably dressed customers dining there. Mirrors about the walls created the illusion of expansiveness and intimacy, nothing at all like he would have expected in a mining town so far up in the mountains.

In a way, it reminded him of Maddy Silk's brothel in Denver. The women were attractively plump. The sparkle of their jewelry reflected flashes of light from the candles on the tables and the low chandeliers. Somber, well dressed men, wearing dark suits and string bow ties were gathered around the ornate bar, smoking large cigars.

A short, attractive waitress came over to their table and promptly sat on Red's lap and kissed his hairy cheek.

"Well then, aren't you a sight for sore eyes. Where the hell have you been? Don't you eat any more? Or maybe you're avoidin' me? What is it, Red? You can tell me the truth, you know." Red flushed under the barrage, but his face creased into a big smile.

"Now Beth, you know that you're the only one in my life; except for Harry, that is. Beth, I'd like you to meet our new friend, Daniel Carrington." Beth's smile was infectious; warm and friendly like a candle in a cold closet. Daniel was smitten.

"It's nice to meet you, Daniel," she said, leaning down to kiss him on the cheek. Daniel couldn't find the words to reply. Red cleared his throat loudly.

"Daniel, this here is my favorite waitress on the western slope," Red asserted proudly.

Beth stood abruptly and placed her hands on her hips in indignation.

"What do you mean; the western slope? D'you mean to tell me that you have other waitresses that you haven't told me about?" She held her hand to her breast and rested her arm on Red's shoulder as if she was about to faint. "You know what, Red? Sometimes I think you're just like all of the rest, with all your flatterin' talk and nice manners. To you I'm just another waitress, ain't I? I think I'm goin' to find me a real man." She turned and offered her hand to Daniel. As he stood, she looked up into his eyes. "Why, Red, he's not only cute, he's a real gentleman, too." Daniel smiled.

"He's quite a brave young man too, Beth. He saved Harry's life today. At least once, I'd say." Red poked Harry's shoulder, "Wouldn't you agree, Harry?" Harry slapped at Red's hand as if swatting at an annoying insect.

"Yeah, I guess." Harry sighed, and continued looking around the room as if searching for someone in particular. "Whose ass do I have to kiss around here to get a drink, anyway?" he said, and flicked the menu onto the table.

"Keep your pants on, Harry." Beth shot back, looking up into Daniel's blue eyes adoringly, still attached to his hand. "You'll get a drink when I'm good and ready."

"I hear that you're always good and ready, Beth," Harry sniped.

Beth took Daniel's hand and drew it around her waist, drawing him nearer to her. His hand felt the curve of her breast under her arm.

"Well Harry, I hear from reliable sources that you ain't so good and you're seldom ready. So there." She held her hand out to Red, "Can I keep him for a while? Please?" Daniel was embarrassed.

Red was enjoying Daniel's discomfort. "Well, I don't know about that. You see, Harry and me are trying to keep him around for a while, and I don't think he'll be much good to either of us if you get your hands on him. But, I'll give it some consideration if you'll bring us three thick steaks with all the trimmings."

"Drinks, too?"

"Young Daniel here's not a drinking man. Root beer OK, son? I'll have coffee and Harry would like water."

Harry looked up. "You know I don't drink water, Red."

Beth released Daniel and sailed off towards the kitchen. Daniel took his seat gratefully.

"I think she likes you, Daniel." Red smiled broadly.

"She likes everyone," Harry added.

"Now, now, Harry, be nice. We're trying to impress Daniel, here." Red sat back in his chair. "You never know. If he likes it here, maybe he'll stick around a while." He looked over at Daniel and considered him for a long moment. "I don't want to jump the gun, but I might be able to use someone. At least until Dangerous is back up on his feet. What do you think about joining my company, Daniel? You've pretty much seen the worst of what we do, and the pay's good." Red was smiling.

They heard a commotion at the front door, and turned to see Pete burst through the red curtains. He rushed over to their table, bumping into other diners in his haste.

"Red, you gotta come quick! Dangerous is taken real bad." Pete was out of breath. They could smell his sweat. "On the way down, he started spittin' up blood and then he went unconscious. They just took him over to the hospital."

Red got to his feet immediately and waved to Beth, signaling that he would be back. "Take care of the boy, Harry," Red said as he grabbed his coat and stuffed his hat on his head. "I'll catch up with you two later. Enjoy your meal." Red threw some money on the table and followed Pete through the restaurant.

"What happened?" Beth asked when she came over with their drinks.

"There was an accident on the Pass today. Dangerous got himself caught under one of the wagons." Harry relished the fact that he had the latest gossip; good or bad was of no concern to him. "Red's gone off to the hospital to see if he can help."

"What should I do with his dinner, then?" Beth asked as she put the drinks down on the table

"Just bring it along," Harry answered quickly, "he said he'd be back shortly. Didn't he, Daniel?" Harry kicked Daniel under the table. Daniel was watching two men looking through the large window, pointing at Harry. Harry slid over to Red's seat, putting his back to the window.

"I hope Dangerous'll be OK." Daniel said, sincerely concerned.

"Yeah, I'm sure he will." Harry said dismissively, "He's a tough old coot. He's had worse, I bet. He's another one of them that fought in the war. They're as tough as square nails. All of them old coots are. Just like No Problem Joe. Ah! Here's our food."

Beth placed the dinners on the table, and Harry attacked the food with a flurry of enthusiasm. Harry held his utensils as if he was doing battle with sword and spear and the outcome was somehow in doubt. Daniel stopped eating, awestruck.

Not surprisingly, Harry's din was drawing attention from the tables around them. Momentarily pausing his assault to take a breath, he noticed that Daniel and those at the next table were watching him.

"What are you looking at? Am I doing something wrong?" Harry said as he wiped his mouth with his sleeve.

"No." Daniel was embarrassed by his poor manners. "It's just that I've never seen anyone eat as fast as you do."

Harry looked down at his plate. What was left of his steak was shredded, and vegetables were scattered around the table as if they'd been dropped from the ceiling. "I had a lot of brothers and sisters, OK? When there was food on the table, whoever got through his food first got seconds. And seconds were rare."

Daniel began eating again, but kept a wary eye on Harry, who had resumed his assault with only slightly less noise, but no less vigor. Finished with his steak, he swapped his plate for Red's and without hesitation, plowed into the second steak with equal gusto. When Beth came by the table, she gave Harry a look of disgust.

"Aw, Harry. Don't you have no manners, at all?" Beth stood behind Harry with her hands on her hips, just out of range of the flying debris.

"What now?" Harry broke stride briefly. "What is this, the royal palace?" He quipped through a mouth full of food. Juice from the meat glistened on his chin. "Did you want me to let it get cold?" Harry shrugged and gripping the steak bone tightly in his grimy hands and like a good soldier, returned to the battle in front of him.

"Hell, we don't even know if he's coming back, Beth. We don't want to let a good steak go to waste now, do we?" Harry taunted her with a greasy smile.

Beth shook her head and gave Daniel a sympathetic smile. She leaned over and gently placed her hand against his cheek, lifting his face so that she could look into his eyes. "Don't pick up too many of his bad habits."

"I heard that," Harry shot back.

Harry had already finished the second steak. Everything was gone except for the bone and the potatoes. Surrounded by his field of destruction, Harry leaned back and patted his belly. Daniel kept a wary eye on him while he ate his own meal. The moment that Daniel finished, Harry stood, abruptly donned his coat and hat, scooped Red's money off the table and motioned Daniel to follow him quickly. They were almost to the door when they found their way blocked by Beth, hands on her hips, smiling at Harry as if this were a familiar game for them. She may have been small and stout, but she was intimidating. She glared at Harry.

"You wouldn't have forgotten anything, would you, Harry Rich?" Harry's only exit was blocked by her strategic presence.

"Harry, you know that Red is a very good tipper and he treats us quite handsomely. I'd be shocked if you were to treat me any differently—especially since he did buy you steak dinners with all the trimmings."

Harry swanned casually back to the table and, with his back to Beth, reached inside his coat and made a show of laying money on the table, under his plate.

"There," he said loudly, a theatrical performance of his generosity for those nearby, "don't ever let it be said that Harry Rich doesn't tip." Harry sneered at Beth and Antonio as he gathered Daniel by the arm and pushed him through the door.

"Let's get the hell out of here," Harry shouted. Daniel heard yelling coming from the restaurant. "The quicker, the better, if you get my meaning." Harry was already mounted and trying to dodge pedestrians when the door to the restaurant flew open. Beth stormed into the street, waving something in her hand.

"Harry, you cheap, miserable bastard," she yelled at Harry's back. Harry pretended not to hear. "Just wait till Big Shirley hears about this. You owe me, Harry Rich."

Harry turned and blew her a kiss. Beth shook her fist in reply and came over to Daniel. She gently stroked Marigold's neck and looked up at him.

"Daniel, you seem like a nice boy. I just want to warn you not to go spending too much time with the likes of Harry Rich. Bad can only rub off on good and not the other way 'round." Beth looked up the street at the departing Harry. She tapped Daniel on the leg to get his attention. "If you ever need someone to talk to, you can come along and talk to me. Anytime. Do you hear me?"

Daniel nodded, embarrassed by her intimacy.

"And Red Corcoran is as good a man as they come. If you want some advice, stick with him, not with the likes of that no-good, cheap, waste of manhood." She patted Marigold on the rump and winked at Daniel. "Now be off with you and take care of Harry before he gets into more trouble. And thanks for helping Harry and Red today. They're both special friends of mine."

"Thanks, Beth." Daniel said and turned to follow Harry.

"Watch out she doesn't get her hooks into you," Harry yelled. Beth raised her fist again and shook it at Harry. She smiled as she went back inside.

As they rode, they passed small groups of men heading either to or from their work in the mines. The procession criss-crossed and laced the face of the mountain with strings of twinkling lights that came from lamps called 'gads', that each miner carried. The miners hung them on the end of their pick or shovel and the light illuminated the ground for the man behind.

"When're you planning to be back in business?" A miner asked Harry.

"Real soon, fellers. Soon as I get the oven warmed up," Harry told them.

They came to Joe's stables, where the dozen sleepy horses in the corral showed little interest as they rode up. The barn was warm and clean, the smells were reassuring, and whoever No Problem Joe was, he was a man who took great pride in his stable and the care of the animals entrusted to him. Marigold would be well taken care of there.

"Joe, are you home?" Harry called out. He led his horse to a vacant stall and motioned Daniel to follow. Daniel followed Harry into the stall, where they removed the saddles and blankets and hung them over the short wall.

Harry showed Daniel where the feed was kept, and after exchanging the horses' halters for head-stalls, they gave their respective animals their well-earned feed buckets and made sure they had fresh water. As tired as he was, Daniel gave Marigold's coat a quick brushing, then did the same for Harry's horse, which jumped at the touch of the brush. Daniel looked for Harry and saw him at the end of the stable, peeking into a room at the back of the barn. He heard Harry talking softly to someone in the room, but Harry closed the door before he got there and placed a finger to his lips, motioning to Daniel that they should leave.

"We'll get acquainted tomorrow," Harry said, quietly.

Harry closed the door securely and Daniel hefted his pack and hurried to follow. They'd gone only a little way when Harry took a sudden turn off the road, then another. It seemed that he was disappearing into the trees and Daniel struggled to keep up. The night was moonless and the bushes and trees along the narrow track grabbed at his bag, and roots leapt out to trip him.

Suddenly, Harry stopped walking and Daniel, looking down trying to see the trail, bumped into him and fell backwards onto the ground. It was only then that Daniel saw the tiny cabin.

"Wait here while I get a light going," Harry said and disappeared inside, while Daniel got back up to his feet. A bloom of light flared as a match was struck. By its light, he could see Harry fiddling with a lamp. When it was sufficiently encouraged—it took four matches—Harry hung the lamp on a hook from the ceiling beam.

Daniel approached the doorway cautiously. Harry advanced on him with a surge of newfound goodwill. The new Harry was a generous and gracious host.

"Come on in, come on in. What're you waiting for?" Harry threw his arm around Daniel's shoulders and ushered him into the cabin with pride. "Well? What do you think of your new digs?"

As his eyes adjusted to the gloom of the smoking lamp, Daniel took another tentative step inside the cabin and bumped into a huge, black iron oven crouching on four stubby legs as if it were a matador's bull about to charge. With only some certainty, he could make out that the cabin was one small room. Everything there was to see was within two or three paces of where he stood. Two bunks against the walls, a small table with two chairs and the iron monster that consumed most of the space in the room.

"This is the kitchen," Harry said, pointing proudly to Daniel's left, spreading his arms wide for emphasis. Nailed to the wall was a bench that Harry had referred to as a kitchen and on it was a metal tub full of dirty dishes seemingly glued together by a dark, smelly, fungal substance. Daniel's mind went blank; his senses disrupted. On one hand, he was grateful to be inside and not out in the cold. But, on the other hand, he was feeling claustrophobic and nauseous, and he hadn't been in the cabin ten seconds.

"Someone must have stayed here while I was gone," Harry said in horror. "That'll teach me a lesson. You leave a friend in charge, then you come home to find this." Harry placed his arm around Daniel's shoulder, turning him from the disaster in his kitchen. Somehow, Harry avoided mentioning the large black object occupying the majority of the cabin's interior space.

"And this is the bedroom." Daniel only had to move slightly to his right to be standing in the 'bedroom'. "I know it's a little small with the oven in here and all, but you'll get used to it, believe me." Tattered army blankets were hung on rails attached to the ceiling and could be pulled around the beds to give a miniscule amount of privacy, but the bunks were so close that if both occupants got out of bed at the same time, they would surely collide.

As tired as Daniel was, he had no other choice but to be grateful. At least this night he had a full stomach and a warm place to sleep.

"What's that?" Daniel asked pointing at the giant iron oven.

"That's my business."

"Which is what?" Daniel's curiosity found a voice

"Potatoes! I cook potatoes for the miners in the winter and sometimes in the summer, too. In the summer it gets too hot in here with the oven going and I have to sleep outside, so I don't do it often—just when I need some extra money." Harry responded. "At least you won't have to worry about being cold this winter. This oven'll be going twenty-four hours a day from now till spring."

A loud banging on the door of the cabin startled them both.

"What do you want?" Harry yelled at the door. The door opened and a head peeked in.

"Hey, Harry. I saw there was a light on, so I thought that I'd stop in on the way down to Big Shirley's." The head looked around the cabin. "Hey! You've cleaned the place up." The disembodied head sounded surprised. "It looks real nice." Harry looked only slightly embarrassed.

Daniel cleared his throat.

"Willy Tomb, this is Daniel. He's going to be staying with me this winter." Harry clapped his arm on Daniel's shoulder. "He's my new partner." Harry took Daniel's look of shock for gratitude and carried on, "He's a fine-looking lad, isn't he?"

Willy came further into the cabin and took off his worn leather glove to shake Daniel's hand. Daniel couldn't help but notice that Willy's right hand had only three fingers. Willy looked down at his hand and put his glove back on.

"Don't mind that. A lot of us who work in the mines are missing fingers. It kinda comes with the job. Well, more like they go with the job." Willy's face opened up with a smile. He didn't look at either one of them directly as he spoke. "I guess you're the one that saved Harry's life up there on the Pass today."

It was Daniel's turn to look embarrassed. "Not really, I just helped a bit with the horses. I think Harry just got one of his lucky breaks."

"That's not what I heard. I heard Harry rode the wagon over the cliff. If Daniel here hadn't pulled you out, you'd be scattered all over that mountain like them boxes." Willy laughed. "From all of us that he owes money to, we're grateful." Willy shook Daniel's hand once again. "I bet old Doc Holliday would be more than a mite peeved to hear of your demise, Harry." Willy was looking in Harry's direction. "From what I hear, he'd really miss the money you owe him."

"How'd you hear that lie, Willy?" Harry snapped.

"You know how news travels in a small town," Willy laughed. "Still, I'd have given a week's wages to see you and that old gunslinger going at it." Willy looked down at the floor. "Will we be seeing you at Big Shirley's place later?"

Harry shrugged and winked. Willy started to leave, then stopped and turned back. "It's too bad about old Dangerous, eh?" Daniel and Harry looked at each other, then at Willy. "You didn't hear? He died just after they got him to the hospital. Sorry to give you the news. I guess there's goin' to be an opening for a new man with Red's company. Anyway, see y'all later." He left without looking at either of them.

Harry stood and headed for the door. "The place is yours. Make yourself at home. I'll be back later," he said as he left. He was gone but a few seconds when the door opened again and he stuck his head back in. "Thanks again for helping me out today. I really do owe you one. I'll see you in the morning." The door closed and Daniel was instantly asleep.

Chapter 7

Daniel came out of a deep sleep to a thumping sound coming through the wall next to his head. His brain cleared, and the torment of his dreams was replaced by the pain of sunlight streaming directly into his eyes. Surveying his surroundings, he saw that daylight did little to enhance them. In fact, it looked even smaller in the sloping light of the morning sun.

The persistent pounding was coming from the outside of a door behind the beast's tail, which even in the daylight resembled a charging bull, missing only a head and horns. As he reached for the door handle, the noise stopped. He waited a moment and listened. Behind him the front door suddenly crashed open, and a body toppled into the room.

Harry's visage was frightening, even worse when he took off his hat. His hair was matted, his bloodshot eyes were painful to look at and when he took off his coat, large, dark sweat stains showed under his armpits. Out of breath and flushed, he stank of whiskey and cheap perfume, and he needed a shave and a bath desperately.

"It's about time you woke up," Harry said as he wafted across the room. "I thought you were gone for good and we were going to have two funerals today." Pushing past Daniel as nimbly as his condition allowed, he grabbed the handle on the door and pulled. It didn't budge. Undaunted, he pulled again. It refused to budge.

"Can I help?" Daniel offered.

Harry held up his hand and addressed the door with even deeper grit. "No thank you, I can do this." He pulled again and failed again. Daniel stood aside patiently and waited for Harry to recover from the exertion.

"Here, give me a hand, will you?" Harry panted.

Daniel grabbed the upper handle and together they heaved. The door broke from the ice dam that had been holding it and swung open.

Just outside the door was the base of a pine tree with branches as thick as a man's leg. Harry stood back and with much pride said, "Well, what do you think? She's a beauty, isn't she?"

Daniel nodded in agreement, but had no idea why.

"Do you see my baby, here?" Harry affectionately patted the black monster which looked more like a small locomotive than an oven. "All I do is trim off the branches so that this tree'll fit through this hole in this door and then feed it into this oven a bit at a time."

The door indeed had a hole in it, covered by a flap made of leather strips. Daniel was impressed at the simplicity of the arrangement. Harry would never have to leave the cabin to get more wood and there were several more trees of similar size lying in a small clearing behind the cabin.

"Here, help me cut a few branches off and we'll get the oven going." Harry handed Daniel an axe. "Then how about we go out and get us a bit of breakfast? What d'you say to that, partner?" Daniel took the axe and began his first day of work as a possible business owner and cook's helper. The smaller branches came off easily and soon pine needles were crackling as they burst with heat in the cavernous belly of the oven. Harry filled a coffee pot and a bucket with water from the stream and put them on top of the oven to heat. The combination of the exercise and the smell of the coffee put Daniel in a wonderful mood.

The sun was high in the sky when they'd finished stripping the tree. Daniel watched with keen interest as Harry took a length of chain and looped it around the end of the log, seating it in the notches he'd cut into it. He then took the chain inside and attached it to a pulley system that hung from the center beam of the cabin.

When Daniel was clear, he pulled on the chain and with only a few tugs, the tree lifted off the ground slightly and slid forward. After some puffing and cussing, it poked its trunk into the cabin and Harry closed the door around it. As Daniel watched he reattached the chains to the log and smoothly pulled it forward into the oven.

With a self-satisfied smile, Harry collapsed into one of the two small chairs at the table and poured them both a cup of coffee. He added a liberal amount of whiskey from a bottle under the kitchen bench.

Harry stood back with a look of great pride admiring his ingenious arrangement. The fire was blazing and water in a bucket was heating on the top of the oven. Satisfied it was hot enough, he carried it into the adjoining storage room empty but for boards on the floor that kept the sacks of potatoes off the ground.

Ignoring Daniel, Harry stripped down to his long underwear and proceeded to wash using a sliver of cracked yellow soap that could've been an ancient artifact. Finished bathing, not a lengthy procedure, Harry dressed and rubbed salt on his teeth with his finger. Then, after pulling his hair flat with a gap-toothed comb, he appraised his appearance in the small mirror and winked at his reflection with obvious satisfaction.

"Well, partner. I'd say that's about enough work for us this morning. What say you and me head into town for a bite and I show you around? We have to go see No Problem and find out when they're going to bury Dangerous. Then we'll eat." He pushed Daniel out of the cabin and closed the door behind them.

In daylight, No Problem Joe's barn was bright and airy, sunlit from small windows set high in the walls.

"Hey, Joe? 'You around?" Harry barked. Joe's wrinkled face under a well-worn hat appeared from behind a stall. When he saw Harry, he returned to what he was doing. "How're things, Joe?" Harry asked loudly as he led the way down the barn.

"I'm not deaf, Harry." Joe said, straightening up painfully. Joe's head was large at the brow but narrow at the chin, and covered from crown to chin with thick, grey hair that formed a cocoon about his face. His face was not so much tanned as it was flushed red, as was his nose, which had more of a purple color to it. By contrast, Joe's pale, blue eyes were astonishingly clear. Their gaze was eerily penetrating.

"What do you want from me now, Harry Rich, you no-good, thieving bastard? Piss off." Joe's toothless face expanded and collapsed when he spoke. His f's and s's came out accompanied by small sprays of spit. Uncoiled to his straightest, Daniel could see that Joe had possibly been handsome at some previous stage in his life. He might even have been tall in his youth, but the years of hard work had taken a toll. Now he looked like a stunted piñon pine, gnarled by decades of wind and weather. He shook his head and continued raking the horse manure into a pile.

"Ah, Joe. You're such a kidder." Harry went to punch Joe playfully on the shoulder. Joe whipped the pitchfork around and held it like a spear to Harry's chest.

"Get away from me, Harry," Joe threatened.

"Well, I'm glad that I've found you in a good mood, Joe. I wanted to introduce you to my new partner." Harry remained undaunted. "This here is Daniel. Me an' Red met him yesterday on the way over from Leadville." There was no reaction from Joe. "Red said to stable his mare here and he'd take care of the feed bill."

Joe forced himself to stand as upright as he could manage and gave Daniel a look over. "Is that so?" He took Daniel's hand in a firm grip, as if testing his strength.

Daniel let his hand be pummeled.

"Nice to meet you, son," Joe's voice was croaky at best. "Red already told me all about you." Joe's handshake was becoming painful. Daniel was relieved when he finally let go and left them to check on Marigold. She turned her head and nibbled at his sleeve as he stroked her neck.

A tap on his shoulder surprised him. He turned to find No Problem Joe standing behind him looking squarely into Daniel's eyes. "Red told me you saved Harry's life yesterday. Is that true?"

"Not really. All I did was wake him up." Daniel smiled. "He had to do the jumping himself."

Joe laughed. "Well that's about the first thing Harry's done for himself since I've known him." Joe searched Daniel's face. "You can board your horse here as long as you want, son. She's a nice animal. What's her name?"

"Marigold, sir," Daniel replied.

"Well, I'll take good care of her. She's not young anymore, but she should see you to California. I'll see to it that she's kept warm and fed." He turned to walk away, but stopped. "I guess you heard about

Dangerous, then?" Daniel nodded. "He was a good man. I appreciate you trying to help him, but you can't save everyone. Just remember that." In his eyes was a look of deep sadness. "You still there, Harry?" There was no reply. "Oh well, I guess Harry's found my whiskey again. Come on, we'll find him in the back. Besides, Red gave me something to give to you."

Daniel followed Joe to a small room at the rear of the building. It was barely large enough for a cot and two small tables, one stacked high with old papers and dime novels, the other holding various dishes and two coffee cups, clean and neatly stacked. Around the walls hung assorted odds and ends of horse gear and faded framed photographs. The daguerreotypes were of men dressed in military uniforms, some grey, others in dark blue. A collection of military medals hung beneath a brown-tinted photograph of a seated Abraham Lincoln, surrounded by Union military officers in front of a tent.

"Mind if I have another one, Joe?" Harry held up a glass and a bottle of whiskey.

No Problem shrugged. "Might as well Harry, there's no stopping you when you're set on something." Harry poured himself another whiskey, half filling the glass, and drank it down in one gulp. "Harry, what was you doin' over there in Leadville? Not still trying to figger out how to rob that damn' bank over there, are ya'?"

Harry shook his head like a child caught planning mischief.

"Then I hope the reason wasn't just to go and piss off old Doc Holliday." Harry looked down at the glass in his hand. "I do believe that you'd make a better dead bank robber than a dead gambler." Joe slapped Daniel on his shoulder and cackled.

Harry remained unsmiling. He shuddered as the whiskey hit its mark and then let out a sigh of contentment. "Ah, that's better," he said with a big, broad smile. "I'll pay you back, Joe."

"That'll be the day," Joe said, taking the bottle from Harry

Harry made a place for the empty glass on the table, between the assorted papers and well-read dime novels. "You've been reading too many of these dime novels, if you ask me Joe," said Harry. "It can't be done, Joe. You and Red were right."

"That's right, Harry. Don't you forget it. Now, why don't you two git along and let me get on with my chores?" Joe pushed Harry from the room, but kept a gentle hold on Daniel's jacket to slow him. He closed the door on Harry's back and picked up an envelope from the table, slipping it into Daniel's coat pocket. "Red wanted me to give this to you," he said quietly. "It's just a little something to show his gratitude."

Harry stuck his head back into the room. "You comin'?"

"Keep your shirt on, Harry," Joe shot back, closing the door again. "Don't let Harry know about this." Daniel nodded as Joe opened the door onto Harry's pained expression.

"Come on, Daniel," Harry called out, impatiently walking off.

Joe caught Daniel's arm, pointing at Harry. "Make sure that you bring that piece of shit to the funeral service. It's at three o'clock at St. Mary's," he yelled, loud enough for Harry to hear.

⚑

The center of activity in town was a crowded corner between the bank, where the miners redeemed their work chits for money, and the two blocks of bars and brothels across the street from the bank, where they would lose it. Daniel heard Harry's name being called from one of the second-floor windows of a building across the street.

"Hey, Harry! Harry, baby," a woman called out.

Daniel was shocked to see that the woman was naked from the waist up. Her voluminous breasts jiggled as she waved. Harry blew her a kiss which she returned, smiling brightly. Suddenly, a hand came from behind the woman and pulled her back into the room. A man appeared at the window. He looked down, and seeing Harry in the middle of the street, closed the window sharply.

Most of the windows on the second floor had women in various stages of undress waving to men in the street, calling to some by name, inviting them to come upstairs to the brothel. Men stopped in the street to wave and shout to the women. Not even passing traffic appeared to be bothered by the inconvenience. Daniel didn't know whether to be shocked or thrilled. Never had he seen so much bare flesh and so many beautiful breasts paraded in public for all to see.

"We miss you, Harry," another girl called out. "Are you going to come up for a little fun? You're the best in town Harry, do you know that?" The other girls at the windows burst out laughing.

"Harry, don't their bosoms ever get cold?" Daniel asked.

Harry had to pull him out of the middle of the street to prevent him from being run over by one of the delivery wagons. "Son, with the amount of friction those tits see every night," Harry said laughing, "I'm amazed there's ever any snow on the roof."

"How come they're all hanging out of those windows?"

"You're joshing me, aren't you?" Harry stopped in disbelief and turned Daniel away from the bawdy scene. "This building here is the Ute City Bank. D'ya see all of these men standing around here? Well, they just got off work in the mines and they get paid with a chit at the end of every shift. They bring their chits down from the mines and cash them in for money here at the bank." Harry turned Daniel around to face the brothel across the street. "Then they immediately walk across the street and spend it all on whiskey and those women up there or down there."

Daniel saw a line of saloons from one end of the block to the other. Each and every one had women upstairs in the windows or standing in the doorways, soliciting customers.

"Do you see how the buildings get smaller the further down the block you go?" Indeed the buildings did get smaller. "The further you get from the bank, the cheaper the whiskey, and the cheaper the whores." Harry spoke loudly enough to elicit laughter from those men who'd heard.

"What's that place, Harry?"

"That's the Aspen Drug Store. That's where you go after you've finished drinkin' and whorin'. Ain't it boys?" Laughter followed. Harry continued to explain, in his world weary way, that the drug store was an important part of the town. It was where minor wounds were treated, headaches were mended, and the magic elixir of mining life in the small blue bottles was obtained most readily. Posters in the window advertised an assortment of elixirs for a multitude of morbid illnesses, portrayed in lurid drawings of unfortunate victims. The drug store was the purveyor of hope and dreams, and also the last resort of the prostitutes when they fell victim to their inevitable 'accidents'.

The wall of the building was plastered with large, garish posters advertising all sorts of products from cigars to moustache wax. They overlapped fanciful portraits of Wild Bill and Sitting Bull, touting the antics of Buffalo Bill's Wild West Show. The posters showed a reenactment of a wagon train being attacked by savage Indians on horseback, who were being defended by rifle wielding cowboys led, of course, by Wild Bill himself. Daniel was intrigued.

"Are there any Indians around here, Harry?"

"No, not any more. The Utes are just about all gone now, except for one or two. One of them's a good friend of mine. I'll tell you about him sometime." They strolled down the block past the saloons towards a grand building of rich, red sandstone. "And this here is the Wheeler Opera House," Harry announced as if he owned the building.

It stood alone like a tall man in a crowd of dwarfs. Three times larger than the smaller wooden buildings that slouched beside it, seeking credibility by their proximity. The ornate stone façade, the carved stone balustrade and leaded glass doors all made it a very impressive piece of architecture.

In vivid contrast to some of the other drab and surly towns Daniel had passed through, the town of Aspen seemed to be smiling at the world. The people were cordial to each other. Most of them greeted him with a pleasant, "Good morning," or a rumbling, "Howdy," even though they were strangers to him. Serious and purposeful businessmen mixed with knots of miners in various stages of intoxication, as easily as the professional women of the evening chatted with mothers with children in tow. Harry explained it away by saying it was the clean mountain air. Daniel thought it had more to do with the whiskey.

The White Kitchen was the opposite of Aspen. They found seats at the counter and were ignored by a hard looking waitress, who dropped mugs of ink-black coffee in front of them before they'd even sat, then busied herself delivering other customers their breakfasts.

She returned to stand directly in front of Harry with her hands on her hips, a snarl on her lips.

"Harry Rich, you should be ashamed of yourself. After what you did to Beth last night, this is the last cup of coffee you're ever getting from me," she snipped and walked away.

Harry held up his hands and leaned towards Daniel. "God, but news moves fast in this town. They all must be living in each other's underwear."

The waitress came storming back over. "I heard that, Harry. You'd better leave me a decent tip or you're not going to be welcome here again. Do you hear me?"

Harry nodded and looked away, rolling his eyes to the other customers, all of whom were enjoying his predicament. "Alright already, Hickory." He placed his hands together in supplication. "I don't even know why I come into this place."

"Because we're the only place in town that'll still serve you, that's why!" yelled the cook, a heavyset, gnarled old man with a grin uncluttered by too many teeth. He walked over with his greasy spatula, clenching a cigar that had an ash an inch long. "I heard about your trip over to Leadville." Daniel watched the ash closely, fascinated. The cook tapped Harry on the shoulder with the spatula. "I don't want no cranky, old gunfighter storming in here and shooting the place up. D'you hear me now, Harry Rich?" Daniel followed the ash, wondering when it was going to cease defying gravity. He became aware that he was being spoken to.

"The word around town is that you were pretty helpful to Red yesterday, son. Saved some lives, I heard," he said, without dislodging the ash. Daniel looked into his coffee cup, embarrassed by his sudden notoriety. "Harry, how did you ever run into a nice young feller like this one here?" The cook shook his head and smiled a gummy smile at Daniel. "Come in any time you want, kid—better if you're alone, though." He turned back to his grill and returned in seconds, bringing them their breakfasts himself. When Daniel looked up to thank him, he noticed the ash was no longer on the cigar. He glanced down at his eggs.

"Something wrong with your eggs?" the cook asked with one raised eyebrow.

Daniel forked a load of eggs into his mouth. "They're really great, thanks."

"Enjoy your breakfast," he said, smiling.

Daniel had hardly finished with his breakfast when he felt Harry tug on his sleeve and motion for him to follow.

"Harry Rich!" Hickory yelled in a voice that stopped all conversation. "Did you forget something?"

"I'll catch you next time, Hickory." Harry broadcast his biggest smile and pulled the linings out of his pockets.

"You said that last time." She pointed her finger at him like a pistol. Daniel reached into his coat pocket for the money that Red had given him, but pulled out the envelope Joe gave him by mistake. Curious, he opened the envelope. His eyes widened. Harry's eyes widened, too. He quickly covered the envelope with his hand and draped a protective arm around Daniel's shoulder.

"Don't mind her, Daniel. Me and Hickory, we're real good friends." Harry smiled conspiratorially as he hurried Daniel outside.

"I'll slip her a little something later...if you know what I mean," Harry said, never once taking his eyes off the envelope in Daniel's hand. "I thought you said that you didn't have any money," Harry said.

Daniel took a deep breath. He was not a good liar, not like his older brother, who had avoided a multitude of beatings from their heavy-handed father with clever and skillful abuse of the truth. His heart faltered, but the lie flowed forth smoothly anyway. "I found some that I forgot about."

Harry looked at him closely, then shrugged and turned as if to walk away. Daniel opened the envelope again and looked into it, shocked by the amount it held.

"Son, if I'd forgotten that much money, I'd be looking for it. You couldn't lend me some 'til tonight, could you?"

Daniel pulled out a ten-dollar note. Harry snapped it out of his hand and kissed it. "Thank you, my friend. I owe you one." Harry was once again complete.

Chapter 8

The streets were filled with people going about their business, conversing with friends or soaking up the warm autumn sun. Main Street ran east-west through town. At the corner of Mill Street and Main was a grand building under construction. Harry and Daniel stood across the street from it, watching the comings and goings of the workers lifting, carrying, plastering and painting the brand new edifice.

"This, my boy, is the Hotel Jerome. Jerome Wheeler is a good friend of mine," Harry proclaimed importantly. "He's the wealthiest man in town," Harry made a sweeping motion with his arms, "he owns most'a these mines around here. He's from back east money, you know." Harry added needlessly. "Makes a million dollars a month they say, selling silver to the U.S. government." Harry put his thumbs in his belt loops and rocked back on his heels. "Wants to put Aspen on the map, he says. Like Tabor did in Leadville. Tabor built an Opera House, Jerome built a bigger one. Tabor built a hotel, Wheeler built a bigger one, and Wheeler's hotel is going to be the first building in Colorado with electric lights, 'makes his own electricity somehow."

Wires were strung on poles along Main Street ending at the hotel and they watched the men working the pulleys on top of the building, hauling the thick wires up to the roof, to be ingested into the building by unseen hands.

"I think it's a dangerous notion myself." Harry confided. "Now don't get me wrong, I'm a forward lookin' man, but not all inventions are good, in my opinion. I'm a lamp man, myself. If it doesn't have a flame, it can't be trusted, I say."

Harry led them away from the noise and commotion of the construction site. As they walked, he pointed across the valley, showing

Daniel the gaping mouth of the Smuggler Mine. Tailings of waste rock from the huge mine spilled down the mountainside like lava.

"I didn't realize there was a train here, Harry." Below the mine, a train was pulling ore cars along a narrow gauge track.

"That just goes in a circle picking up the ore and taking it to the smelters. See down there? That's the new station for when the train gets here from Glenwood Springs. That'll change things. Everything we need here will come by train, right from Denver."

"What about Red? Won't the trains put him out of business?"

"Most probably." Harry walked away from the overlook and together, they headed back into the center of town. Opposite the Opera House, Harry came to an abrupt halt, pointing down at the ground.

"Directly under our feet are some of the largest silver veins in all of America. They've dug a cavern that's big enough to put the whole Opera House building in."

As they turned the corner, Harry nearly collided into a woman wearing expensive clothes and a large hat with many feathers, who was walking with a tall, muscular man.

"Harry Rich," she said with a smile, "just the man I want to see."

Harry gave Daniel a knowing wink.

"I've got a bone to pick with you, but it's going to have to wait. Right now, I need you to come with me; we have a problem." She grabbed Harry's arm and marched him across the street, with Daniel and the other man trailing a few paces behind.

They spoke quietly as they walked. When they reached the sidewalk in front of the Paragon Ballroom and Saloon, the woman stopped abruptly. Daniel, busy looking up at the girls waving and blowing kisses almost knocked her over. She looked him over critically. "Are you the boy who saved Harry's life yesterday?"

Daniel nodded stupidly.

"Shirley, this is Daniel." She extended her hand to shake Daniel's and in doing so, her shawl fell open, revealing her prodigious bosom, held hostage by gauzy lace. "They call me Big Shirley."

She wasn't what Daniel would call big in any specific measure other than the obvious, but she had an air of authority about her and a formidable grip. Daniel noticed a wonderful fragrance, like wisps of familiar flowers.

"Daniel. Daniel Carrington, ma'am. It's very nice to meet you."

"Red told me you did a really brave thing."

The muscular man went ahead and opened the door for Shirley, but let the door close on Harry.

"Come on, you two, our problem is upstairs." Shirley said and led them through the bar, crowded with miners drinking and playing cards. Some looked up and nodded to Shirley as she sailed through the room. One shook his fist at Harry and started to get out of his chair, but his friends pulled him back down. Harry quickened his pace, following Shirley up the narrow back stairs from the kitchen to the second floor.

Turning the corner in the staircase, Daniel was knocked backwards by a young girl carrying a bundle of linen. He put out his hands to stop her from falling, but he couldn't prevent the inevitable. They fell in a pile onto the lower landing. Fortunately, both Daniel's body and the pile of dirty linen softened her fall, still she pushed herself off him angrily and brushed her hair from her face.

She might have been fifteen, he guessed. As she straightened her dress and tucked her hair back into her cap, she accentuated the subtle curves of her young, narrow figure. Daniel couldn't help but smile foolishly. She flashed him a look of warning, a brief look, but one that a more experienced man would not have misunderstood.

Daniel clumsily bent down to help pick up the mass of bedding off the floor, but succeeded only in bumping heads with her. Hand to her forehead, she pulled away and looked him up and down with fully developed disdain.

"Stop standing there and get out of my way, now! Go on, git!"

"Are you coming?" Shirley's head appeared from above.

Several of the working girls came out of their rooms to see what the fuss was about. Shirley stormed back towards them. "All of you. Get inside your rooms and on your backs!" Shirley bellowed.

Harry lingered. "Any chance of a free one for me Maybelle?" Harry asked. She was a big woman with jiggling breasts and short legs.

"I'm too much woman for you and you know it, Harry."

"I'll be talking to you in just a minute," Shirley said, pointing her finger threateningly. Maybelle held her hand up over her mouth in mock fear. "Harry, you're such a pain," Shirley muttered, as she dragged him away like a reluctant child. They stopped outside a closed door at the very end of the hall. Holding one finger to her lips, she opened the door.

Red lay stretched out, face down on a bed, fully clothed, a whiskey bottle on the floor next to him, and another on the table next to the bed. Daniel saw vomit on the pillow. Harry gave Shirley a questioning look.

"Don't give me that look, Harry. I can't be a mother to every man in town. He was like this when I got here this morning. He has to give the eulogy at the funeral this afternoon."

Harry looked down at his friend, and picked up a gold pocket watch off the small table. He flicked open the cover and sighed—inside was a picture of Red's late wife and their baby son. "Damn it. I haven't seen him like this since his wife passed on. This is not good."

Shirley noticed Daniel looking uncomfortable.

"Daniel, it's important that we don't let Red be seen this way. Come on Harry let's get him cleaned up and moving."

Harry shook Red until he reluctantly opened one eye. "Hey, Red, wake up. We've got to get you up and out of here. Come on, you old rascal." They hoisted Red to a sitting position. "How'd he get here?" Harry asked.

Shirley came with a washcloth and a bowl of water from the dressing table. Daniel felt useless. "He was upset over Dangerous, so I fed him and told him that he could sleep here if he wanted." Shirley began to wipe the mess from Red's eyebrows and hair. Red was barely permitting it. "Hold on, Red. I'm trying to help you, here."

"I don't need your help," he snapped. "I killed another one." Red let his head fall into his hands. "And Dangerous of all people."

Shirley sat next to him, rubbing his shoulders tenderly.

Harry said, "Come on, Red, it wasn't your fault. It just was one of those things that happen. It could've been me that died." Red looked up and considered him.

"Don't take this too personally Harry, but I wish it was."

"Come on, Red, you don't mean that," Shirley said.

"Oh, yes I do."

"I know you don't, Red." Shirley looked into his bloodshot eyes. "Now come on and help us get you dressed for the funeral. You're supposed to tell everyone about what a good friend Dangerous was." Shirley's smile had the desired effect. She helped him up off the bed.

He briefly considered his reflection in the mirror. "God Almighty, what was I drinking anyway?" He picked up the bottle from the small table and looked for a label.

"Listen here, Red Corcoran," Shirley said, her finger an inch from Red's nose, "You promised me that you were never going to do this again."

Red sighed. "He was a good man, you know." He squeezed his eyes shut and limply dropped his head into his hands again, his shoulders heaved and shook. Shirley sat and looked at the others, waiting for the wave of emotion to pass. Red reassembled himself.

"You must think that I'm an old woman," he said, looking at Daniel apologetically.

"Come on, Red, you're as tough as steel. Why don't you go down to the bath house and we'll get you some of your nice duds. We'll give old Dangerous a decent sendoff and we'll all look nice doin' it, too." Shirley motioned for Harry and Daniel to pick up the rest of Red's things. "Harry, you're familiar with the back stairs here, aren't you?"

"I might've seen them once or twice over the years," Harry said, taking hold of Red's arm.

They half-carried Red down the alley. Harry knocked on a door. A young Chinese boy answered, looked them up and down, and let them in. "Please go tell your uncle that we have a special request," Harry said politely. "Will you do that, please?" The boy ran off through the door and disappeared. The room they were in was warm and already Daniel could feel the sweat starting to roll down his neck.

A door opened and one of the oldest men that Daniel had ever seen entered. He'd heard of mummies in Egypt that had been preserved so long, their skin was like leather. The old Chinaman in front of him was a walking mummy. But he was still very much alive, judging from the bursts of Chinese that came spurting out of him at seeing Harry. Obscenities, Daniel guessed.

"What you want now? You come make more trouble for old Chinese man, eh?" He slashed his finger at Harry like a knife.

"No, No, Mr. Chin. I want to ask you a favor. We'd like you to make a bath for our friend and make him well again."

The old man grabbed Red's hair and lifted the head. "He big Red man. I know him. What happen' him?"

The old Chinaman pointed to a door and they hauled Red into a small, hot room with a tub of steaming water in the middle and towels laid out on wooden benches. They had to help him undress and when Red was finally naked, Mr. Chin took a bucket of cold water and threw it on him. Red bellowed. Mr. Chin guided him into the tub of hot water.

Red opened his eyes, his head pounded like rocks into empty buckets. "Daniel, do you think that you could find my place?" Daniel nodded. "I'd like you to go and tell whoever is out there to bring in one of the wagons so we can carry old Dangerous out the way he'd want to be remembered. Then I want you to pick up some clothes for me. There's one good suit in a box on the shelf in the closet. Pick out a white shirt and a tie. It doesn't matter which one—they're all black anyway. Did I throw up on my boots, Harry?" Harry shook his head. Red's face slipped under the water up to his nose.

As Daniel left on his errand, the old Chinese man caught him by the arm.

"You the boy who save life of that Harry man in there?"

Daniel was not comfortable with being so well known. "Yes sir, I helped."

Old Man Chin looked deeply into Daniel's eyes and took his hand, turning it palm upwards. "Ah, so," he said, shaking his head from side to side.

Chapter 9

Joe was not at the stable when Daniel saddled up and hurriedly rode the several miles to Red's place. He found Pete and several others in the barn, hitching up a wagon. They had draped the giant tawny horses with dark blankets, and the mood of both the horses and the men was calm and reserved as they moved about with somber purpose.

Daniel explained the situation to Pete, who hurried about getting all of the necessary items—a crisp, clean shirt, a black and gray striped silk tie and a new black Stetson hat. Laying it all out on the bed, Pete drew a deep breath. "The last time he wore this suit, it was for his wife's funeral. I was hoping that I'd never have to see it again. I think Red hoped the next time he'd have it on, we'd be putting him in the ground next to her." He folded the clothes carefully and put them into a leather valise.

Daniel climbed on Marigold, tying the valise to the pommel of his saddle.

"Well, at least the wake should be interesting." Pete said, "Now get along there and I'll catch up."

<hr />

"That you, Harry?" Red sat on a bench, a towel draped over his head.

"Yeah, it's me. I brought you a little something to get rid of the cobwebs."

"It's not any of that God awful coffee that you make, I hope."

"Thanks for the compliments. Just see if you get any more free coffee again." Harry put the cup of coffee on the bench between them, took out a small blue glass bottle from his coat pocket and poured some of the liquid into the cup.

Red lifted the corner of the towel and watched. "I don't need any of that stuff, thank you very much."

Harry held out the cup. "If ever there was a day that you needed this, it's today. Come on, drink up, it'll get rid of your headache and you'll feel a whole lot better." He nudged Red with the cup. "You've got a speech to make and Dangerous expects the best stories you can think of." Harry persisted. "Come on, Red, take your medicine and let's get you ready. That young feller should be back with your fancy clothes any minute now."

Red pulled the towel off his head and took a cautious sip. Reluctantly, he drained the contents and shook his head. "By God, that's awful stuff."

Harry poured water into the cup from the jug on the table. "Here, drink this. It'll stop your mouth from freezing up."

Red drank all of the water and handed the cup back to Harry. Daniel opened the door. "Thanks, son. Any problems?"

Daniel shook his head, handing the bag to Harry. "Pete helped me find everything."

Red looked at Harry. "I guess there's going to have to be a wake after the funeral."

Harry nodded.

Mr. Chin shook his little, bony fist at Harry as they left.

❦

Red's wagon, draped with black cloth, waited outside the Church, its team of horses standing respectfully as friends of the deceased filed into the church. Red nodded to some and shook hands with others as he accepted their regrets and condolences before following the last of the mourners inside.

"I bet there'd be at least that many carriages at my funeral," Harry quipped as they walked up the steps.

"There'd be no funeral for you, Harry. You owe us too much money," said Red.

Several dozen people were already seated when they took their places next to Shirley. Red went forward to sit with the widow and her son and spoke quietly to them. She put her arms around him and Red held her as she sobbed quietly.

The service began and not soon enough for Daniel, the droning finally ended. Red escorted the widow and her son past the coffin where she paused briefly, her veiled head bowed, dabbing at her eyes with a small white handkerchief. Six men came forward to offer their condolences and then carried the casket out into the afternoon sunlight.

As the coffin was being placed in Red's wagon, a stout man dressed in expensive clothes approached. Respectfully, he removed his top hat and shook hands with Red, then with the widow and her son. In gentlemanly fashion, he helped both into a carriage that was by far the finest of the assembled conveyances and motioned the driver to follow the funeral procession. When the cortege had left, Red and the man spoke together, occasionally looking Daniel's way. The gentleman in the top hat squared his shoulders and walked towards Daniel with Red at his elbow.

"Daniel, I'd like to introduce you to Mr. Wheeler." Daniel took the man's hand and found his grip was every bit as powerful as Red's. He was impeccably dressed and wore a fashionable amount of facial hair that showed gray through what was previously dark brown.

"I've been hearing some good things about you, young man. Where do you hail from?" His voice was deep and suited him.

"Well, sir, I'm from England, but I lived for some time with my parents in Boston." Daniel was surprised how well the lie sounded.

"By the sound of things, I'd say that it was pretty fortunate that you two met." Wheeler turned to watch the departing funeral cortege. "From what you told me, Red, it could've been a whole lot worse, but for this young man here being quick thinking." Jerome appraised Daniel. "I think that I might be able to use a smart young man like you." Jerome raised one hairy eyebrow. "There's a lot of money under the ground where we're standing, and someone has to get rich on it." Wheeler took Daniel by the shoulders and held him at arm's length. "What do you say, young man? How about working for me?"

Daniel's head was swimming; he'd been inspected like a horse and now he was being traded away. "Well, sir, I really want to get to California as soon as I can."

Wheeler released his grip on Daniel. "California's finished, son. No possible use going there. All the gold's long gone and the rest of the state's just desert."

"Now wait a minute there, Jerome," Red interrupted. "I was hoping that if young Daniel here was going to stick around, he might think about coming to work for me—since I'm one man short on my team right now."

Daniel was overwhelmed. "I'd like to think on it if you don't mind, Mr. Wheeler. Thank you all the same. What is it that you do?"

Wheeler rocked back on his heels with his thumbs in the pockets of his vest and smiling broadly took Daniel and turned him to face across the valley where the last rays of the sun painted the mountain red.

"Do you see that big mine across the valley?" Daniel nodded. "Do you see that smelter down there belching smoke into this clean mountain air?" He turned Daniel completely around. "Do you see those mines up there with all that tailing shit covering the mountain?" Daniel nodded again. "Well, I own just about all of it. And the ground directly under our feet and all the damn silver that comes out of it. That's what I do around here. Most of the men you see around here work for me in some way or another—right, Red?" Red agreed. Wheeler nodded at Shirley as she and Harry approached.

"I know what you're trying to do, Mr. Wheeler," Harry said with a smile, "but it's too late. This here is my new partner." Harry placed his arm protectively around Daniel.

"Wait a minute." Daniel finally recognized the name. "Are you the Jerome B. Wheeler who owns that new hotel?"

"Yes, son. I happen to be that man indeed."

"And the Opera House?"

"And a lot of other things that make this town run." Jerome gently poked a finger into Shirley's side.

"You don't own everything, Jerome." Shirley pushed his hand away.

Wheeler's laugh came from the belly. "That's true enough, Shirley. There are some things that no man can ever own, nor has he a right to."

Wheeler tipped his hat to Shirley. "Well, I best be on my way. I just dropped by to offer my respects to the family." He shook Red's hand.

"Red, I know how much it hurts for you to lose a man like that. It never gets easier. Anyway, I must be off. Maybe I'll catch you all up at the wake if there's going to be one."

"We'll be over at The Paragon." Red shook Jerome's hand again. "And thanks again for letting the family use your carriage. That was a nice thing to do, Jerome. You needn't have done that."

"Hogwash! We've known each other for a good long time, Red. The only things in this world worth dying for are your friends and your family. You're both and so was Dangerous." Wheeler waved goodbye with his silver headed cane and jauntily strolled towards his hotel, but turned back after a few paces. "Don't forget about my offer, son! Come along and see me some time and we'll talk about your future."

As they watched him leave, Shirley spoke quietly with two women who handed her a small package tied with a bow of white satin. She pressed the small package into Red's hand. "Tell Honey this is a little something the girls put together for her. Let her know she can come work for me if she feels the need."

"I'm sure that it'll be appreciated." Red noticed the grip that Shirley had on Daniel's arm and smiled. "Are you going to be safe with that young feller escorting you through town? Or is he the one that needs protectin'?"

"Oh, I think I'll be just fine." Shirley looked Daniel over and gave his upper arm a squeeze. "Red, why don't you and Harry take my buggy to the cemetery? We'll go see that everything's ready for the wake. Won't we, Daniel?"

"Well Harry, let's go show Dangerous his new eternal resting place, shall we?" Harry joined him in the buggy as he snapped the reins and followed the wagon bearing Dangerous to the cemetery.

"I'm glad that's over." Shirley removed her hat and veil, tossing off the somber mood of the day. Her light auburn hair was held in a tight bun which showed off the graceful length of her neck. "What do you think of our little town so far, Daniel?"

"Well, Mrs. Big Shirley—" Shirley stopped and buckled over in laughter. "W.....well, what do I call you?" Daniel stammered.

"I'm not laughing at you, Daniel. It just sounded so funny the way you said it with your accent and all." Nudging him back into motion, "I think that Mrs. Doray would be best."

"I like the Opera house and the Hotel."

"And what do you think about the people you've met so far? What do you think about Red?"

"I don't know where I'd be now if he hadn't come along." Daniel's sincerity was undeniable.

"What was going on between Harry and Doc Holliday?"

"I can't tell you for sure, but it sounded like Harry lost some money to him. He was lucky to get out of there alive. If that old man had gotten his hands on him, I don't know what would've happened. He looked mean."

"Do you like Red, Daniel?" Shirley persisted.

"Yes, Ma'am. He's brave and the men like him and respect him. It seems like he really cares about his men and the horses, too. He treats his horses like they're his children."

Shirley laughed out loud, making Daniel smile. "You know, you're not the first person that's said that about him. I'm sorry for interrupting. What were you saying?"

"Where is his family?"

Shirley hesitated. "His wife and son died last year..... I'm afraid he hasn't been the same person since."

Daniel opened the door of the Paragon Saloon for Shirley with natural courtesy. Her smile was his reward as they entered. She strode into the room and handed her coat to Daniel, baring her dress which was demurely cut with a lace collar that graced the lines of her throat. As Daniel watched, enchanted, Shirley undid a series of buttons and bows. The portion of the dress that covered her shoulders was released at the neck by a final ribbon and in the wink of an eye, separated from the rest of the dress to reveal Shirley's most wonderful attributes. The bodice of her dress was a rich red and was cut low, trimmed with beautiful lacework guarding the overflow of her breasts. Her dress then angled steeply towards her waist, assisted by a whalebone corset, then gracefully curved out again over her hips.

In a moment that seemed to last minutes, he enjoyed the gentle movement of her daisy-white skin rising and falling like silk in the breeze. She looked at herself in the mirror over the bar, then back at Daniel. "If you don't mind, would you please be a dear and put these things in my office?" Shirley pointed to a door. "It's off the kitchen. Come on back and you can help me set up."

The office was intimate with a small red velvet-covered couch, a solid oak desk, and a shaded oil lamp spreading yellow glow across the desk. But for a few pieces of paper and a pen, it was neat and glossy from care and frequent polishing.

He turned to leave but found the cook blocking the doorway.

"What are you doing in here?" The cook carried a knife.

"Mrs. Doray asked me to put these things in here. My name is Daniel." He held out his hand.

The cook wiped his hand on his blood-smudged apron and shook Daniel's hand. "I don't ever remember seeing you around here before, you new in town?" Daniel nodded. "Are you related to Dangerous Bolon?"

"Oh, no," Daniel said emphatically. "I just met him a couple of days ago." Daniel turned to leave. "I came here with Harry Rich."

The cook's eyes took on a knowing look. "Then, I guess I'll be seeing you around here." He pointed towards the ceiling with his knife and returned to shaving meat off a side of beef on the cutting table. "Good luck," he said as Daniel walked out of the kitchen and back into the Saloon.

Chapter 10

Asmall knot of men were gathered around Shirley at the far end of the bar, so Daniel sat alone at a table quietly, watching her work her magic on their self-esteem. When Red and Harry pushed through the door, she eased herself away from her adoring crowd and joined them.

"I'll set out some sandwiches for everyone," Shirley said, taking Red's hand.

"That's very kind of you, Shirley. I insist on paying whatever the costs are tonight," Red said firmly.

"I won't hear of it," Shirley replied. "How was the funeral? Are Honey and her boy managing?"

"Well, the funeral was mercifully brief," Red said in his plain manner, "and, I think Honey will survive the loss somehow." A look passed between Red and Harry.

"Did you give her the gift from the girls?"

"Yes, I did." Red assured her and turned his attention to the somber crowd gathered at the bar. "Well… I guess we'd better start buying some whiskey, or people will think that old Dangerous was friendless."

Shirley caught him by the coat sleeve. "You'll be careful now, Red. Especially, after last night?"

"Don't worry; I'll fix it with the bartender." He winked at her. Forgetful Al placed two bottles of Shirley's best whiskey on the bar and Red filled a dozen shot glasses, handing them around. Solemnly, he raised his glass in the air. The small gathering stilled. "Alright, boys! Who'll drink a toast with me to the memory of our old friend, Stanley "Dangerous" Bolon?"

"We will," chorused Pete, Dutch, Bolly and the rest as they raised their glasses in the air and waited for Red to propose the toast.

Looking around at the circle of faces, Red could see that they needed something to dissipate the unspoken fear that bonded them all, that what happened yesterday to Dangerous could happen to any of them, at any time. He took a deep breath and gathered himself. "Here's to good old Dangerous," he said loudly, and immediately a lump formed in his throat. "May heaven have a special place for the clumsy." Laughter rippled through the small crowd.

"To Dangerous," they chorused and drank their whiskeys.

As the bottle made its rounds through the crowd, Pete, Dutch and the others began the ritual of entertaining with tall tales and jokes at the expense of the recently departed. Daniel sat with Harry and was content to listen and laugh along, but Dutch grabbed him by the arm and pulled him into the group gathered around Red.

"And here is the young feller who saved the day for us all...all except for Dangerous, that is." Dutch slapped Daniel on the back. Pete handed him a glass which Dutch filled with whiskey.

"No thanks," he said, trying to hand the glass back to Pete. "I don't drink whiskey."

"Oh, come on, son, be a man," said one of the men.

"It's a toast to old Dangerous," said another.

He looked down into the whiskey in his hand. The crowd stilled, sensing some conflict. He looked at the eager faces surrounding him, a border of sun-browned, rugged faces of the men who were members of this rare group of tough frontiersmen. He looked to Red and Harry for guidance.

Red reached through the crowd to stop Daniel from drinking, but a moment too late.

Daniel threw back the liquor and the men cheered as Daniel convulsed, coughing and spluttering, being slapped on the back from all sides.

Shirley pushed her way through the crowd and found Daniel on his knees, red-eyed and drooling from his coughing spell. She looked at the circle of guilty faces. "You should all be ashamed of yourselves. The lot of you!" She looked at Red reproachfully, though it was Harry who was laughing. "Are you alright, Daniel?"

He nodded, gasping for air. She grabbed him under the arms and helped him into a chair. He experimented with a deeper breath. "Really, I'm alright," he said when he could breathe again. "Thanks, Shirley."

Shirley helped him to his feet and he was rewarded by applause and more back slapping, which made him start coughing again. Pete and Dutch led him over to the food table at Shirley's suggestion.

"I'm holding you both personally responsible for that boy," she scolded.

"Shirley, it sounds like you're a bit taken with our young man," Red said, smiling at Shirley's rebuke.

"Yeah," added Harry, "we didn't get this kind of attention when we first got here."

"As I remember it, you found more than enough attention on your own when we first met, Harry." Shirley said, her hands on her hips.

"We'll try our best to keep an eye on him for you, Shirley. Won't we, Harry?" Red said.

"No problem. He's living with me in my cabin. Did I tell you that we're partners now?"

Shirley's hand shot up to her mouth in horror. "Oh my God, Red, how could you let this happen?"

"Shirley, I had nothing to do with it."

Shirley considered them both suspiciously. "Well, you both had better look out for him." She looked at Daniel again. "He could go somewhere in life," Shirley said, poking Harry in the chest. "And it will probably be to jail if he hangs around you long enough, Harry Rich."

"Yeah, yeah," Harry replied, wilted by the blast. "Come on, let's have us a drink," Harry said reaching for the bottle. "I hear some old fart's buying."

Encouraged by Pete and Dutch, Daniel was standing at the bar telling and retelling the story of the accident. When he noticed Red and Harry watching him, he lowered his voice self-consciously. Harry was not enjoying his celebrity.

Another bottle was opened and someone made another toast; this time Daniel was less inclined to resist. The whiskey burned going down his throat, filling him with a warm glow. It took only a few more for him to decide that he liked the sweet taste. He was enjoying himself and the attention.

"Daniel, this is Bob Hunter." Daniel heard Red say. He turned around to face a tall, good looking man with a shiny star on his coat. "This is the sheriff, son. He would like to hear about the accident. Would you mind telling the story again?"

"No problem, Sheriff," Daniel replied. Abruptly he lurched from the chair, holding his hand over his mouth. Harry thoughtfully grabbed a spittoon and held it under Daniel's head while he was noisily sick. The baritone sounds of his vomiting reverberating from the spittoon brought a chorus of cheers as if Daniel had achieved a tribal rite of passage. Finally, at the conclusion of the performance, Harry took their pale and pallid virtuoso under his arm and steered him towards the men's toilet amid a round of applause.

"I guess you have to learn sometime, don't you, Bob?" Red said with a smile.

"Yes, you do, Red. Yes, you do." Sheriff Hunter knew the feeling well. "Red, I'd still like to have a talk with this young feller. Could you have him come down to the office when he's feeling up to it?"

"Sure enough. And Bob, I do appreciate you coming over to pay your respects. I know you and Dangerous had some business over the years and it was awfully nice of you to send that condolence note to his wife. Thanks again."

"Not a problem Red, just common courtesy." He inclined his head towards Daniel. "Is that young feller working for you now?"

"I can't rightly say. I just met him and Harry's been talking as if they were partners. He's staying at Harry's cabin."

The sheriff smiled and shook Red's hand. "I hope it works out for him. He got what it takes to work the teams with you?"

"He's not real big yet, but he's quick on his feet and he thinks fast. No doubt I'd like to see him join us, but we'll just have to see. He's pretty new here still."

Red saw Shirley berating Harry as he came out of the bathroom. The sheriff knew to withdraw. "Good luck there, Red. See you around."

"Yeah; if I don't get killed first." The sheriff laughed and wisely exited through the ornate glass doors. "How's the boy?" Red asked when Harry sat down and poured himself another whiskey.

"I think he'll live," Harry answered and threw back his whiskey, "but I don't think that he actually wants to, if you know what I mean." They both saw Shirley charging in their direction holding a stack of towels to her chest.

"I want you both to go in there and clean that boy up and get him home." She pushed the towels into Harry's hands.

"Come on, Harry, I'll help you with the boy." Red held up his hands and stepped around Shirley, careful to stay beyond her reach.

They pushed open the door to the bathroom and looked down upon Daniel's crumpled body lying next to the commode, his face pressed to the cold tiles.

"He's a good looking young feller, isn't he?" Red observed.

"I think he used to be," Harry replied. They hoisted Daniel under the arms and lifted him into a sitting position on the toilet. Harry stood back and ventured an observation. "It's amazing to me how quickly they age at this altitude. He looks like he's aged ten years in the last couple'a days."

They wiped his face and hands and helped him to his feet. He smiled stupidly at them, tipped backwards, and would have hit his head squarely on the floor had they not caught him.

"Are you boys alright in there?" Shirley called through the door.

"Yeah. We'll be right out," Red yelled back.

"Do you think we looked like this the first time we got drunk?" Harry asked.

"We probably did." replied Red with a chuckle.

The door opened and Pete and Dutch came in. "Shirley sent us." Pete said, laughing when he saw what Harry and Red were dealing with. "We was wondering what happened to the life of the party. Here Pete, let's give our young hero a hand." It took all four of them to get Daniel vertical again and through the door.

Shirley was waiting for them. She put her hands on her hips and gave Red and Harry a searing look. "Well, what do you two have planned for him next?" Harry and Red looked at each other and burst into laughter. Shirley picked Daniel's chin up off his chest. "Go on. Take him upstairs," she ordered. "Put him in the end room, that way I can keep an eye on him. Come on you two, you both know the way," Shirley said, herding them through the kitchen and up the back staircase.

At the top of the stairs, Shirley dispersed the small knot of her girls waiting for customers. "Get out of the way, you lazy cows," she ordered.

"He's such a pretty boy," said one.

"You'll leave him alone, Kim Ellen. If I hear that anyone of you so much as touches him; I'll fire the lot of you."

"That's not fair, Shirley," Kim Ellen whined.

"As long as I pay you, you'll do what I say," Shirley said, encompassing the other girls who had come out of their rooms to investigate the commotion. "Get back to work, the lot of you," she yelled. Doors slammed up and down the hallway.

"Come on, let's get him to bed," Shirley said, entering the room where Red had been only hours before.

The room had been aired out, the bed had been made and there was a fresh pitcher of water on the nightstand with a clean glass on a piece of embroidered linen. They sat Daniel on the bed, but as soon as they let go of him, he faded backwards. His head hit the wall with a thump.

"God Almighty, you two. What are you trying to do, kill him?" Shirley grabbed Daniel's legs. "Help me with his boots, will you? That is, unless you're just going to stand around and watch?"

A pretty young woman, clad in a nightgown, stuck her head around the corner. "Is everything alright Shirley? I heard a thump on the wall." The girl paused and waited for them to see her logic. "Just one thump," she clarified. "You have to admit, Shirley, just one thump on the wall is a little unusual up here."

"We're fine, Lauralee. It's just a friend who had a little too much to drink. I think he'll live." Shirley said.

Lauralee was the oldest, and, it was said, the prettiest, most talented and popular of three sisters, all of whom worked as prostitutes for Shirley. Together and separately, they were Shirley's top moneymakers.

"He's cute, Shirley. Can we keep him?"

"All of you get out of here. You two you can come back in the morning and collect him," she said, hustling them from the room.

Out in the hall, Lauralee's door opened and the mass of Jerome Wheeler appeared, clad only in long underwear, clenching a cigar between his teeth. "Lauralee, are you coming back in here?" Jerome puffed on his cigar and smiled without a hint of embarrassment. "Hello there, Shirley. Hi, Red. Hi, Harry."

"Howdy, Jerome," Red and Harry said in turn as they passed him.

"Shirley, you still draw the finest clientele." Harry smiled.

"And I plan to keep it that way, Harry. I make my money by being discreet, so don't go blabbing this all about like you usually do." Shirley stopped and looked at Harry sternly.

"Ah, come on Shirley; everybody knows Wheeler spends more time up here than he does at his own house."

"Just nod your head, Harry," Red prompted.

Chapter 11

Daniel knew that something was wrong. His teeth felt furry, the pulse at his temples throbbed and when he tried to move, explosions of pain ricocheted through his head.

There were other sensations. Soft hands were stroking his hair. He smiled. It felt good. Comforting; like home or heaven. In his dream, an angel took his hand and he felt her place something extraordinarily soft and warm into it, guiding his hand over its roundness.

Foolishly, he opened his eyes for a split second and barely survived the wave of pain. He had never noticed how much morning sunlight could actually hurt. Somebody was definitely in the room with him; her shape was backlit by the pain blasting through the window. He focused on his hand again.

The door opened and Shirley walked into the room. In a single blur of movement, she placed the tray on the bedside table, grabbed his angel by the hair and hauled her to her feet.

Shirley's hand lashed out and slapped Kim Ellen's face. The slap was sharp and in the long, frozen moment that followed, both women looked at each other in silence. Daniel clutched the pillow to his chest, fully expecting to be the next one slapped, but Kim Ellen burst into tears and ran from the room.

"I'll be talking to you later, Kim Ellen," Shirley yelled at her back.

He was in trouble. He'd seen that same look on his mother's face. Surprisingly, Shirley calmly sat down on the edge of the bed and offered him the mug of coffee from the tray.

"I'm sorry about that, Daniel." Shirley smiled and handed him the coffee. "Do you know where you are?" He shook his head and winced in pain. "You're at my place in the same room that Red was in yesterday."

"Oh. Was that just yesterday?"

Shirley nodded and smiled. "Is it true that you don't usually drink whiskey?"

Daniel nodded and took a sip of coffee. "My father was a bit of a drunkard and I promised my mother that I wouldn't turn out like him. Did I get drunk last night?"

"Yes, I'm afraid you did," Shirley replied without accusation. She patted his hand reassuringly. Daniel reached for his coat and the envelope of money, but Shirley caught his hand. "It's not there, Daniel. Red has it and he'll give it back to you when you see him." Shirley stood up to leave. "Daniel, please don't take this the wrong way, but I hope I never see you up here again."

His boots were under the bed, but getting into them took several tries. Sitting on the bed waiting for the world to stop spinning, he tried to remember exactly when he got drunk. Toasting Dangerous he remembered, then being sick in the toilet, which would explain the sour taste in his mouth and the smell of whiskey on his clothes.

Getting sick in public and having to be put to bed in a strange place by unknown persons seemed sad, if not completely humiliating. He promised himself that he'd never get drunk again. As soon as he'd said it, he heard the echo of his father's voice promising the very same thing.

A light, clean layer of snow covered the streets, buildings, and lampposts. The sunlight shone through the thinning clouds and the air was full of ice crystals, giving the illusion that the air itself was full of diamonds. Daniel felt as if he'd grown somehow. Whereas yesterday he'd felt out of place, today the world seemed different; less intimidating. Pulling his collar up around his neck and his hat down further around his ears, he headed east to No Problem Joe's stable.

"How're you feeling there, tiger?" Harry asked him as soon as he'd entered. "Did those wenches give you any rest up there? I bet you're plum tuckered out."

"What're you making?" Daniel asked, hoping to avoid more of Harry's embarrassing questions.

"Well, since you and me are now in business together, I thought I'd get No Problem here to help me finish my new sled." Harry stepped back to admire his handiwork, though it was Joe doing all of the work. "Now I can double my output and double our profit." The sled was eight-feet long, with a basket meshed with woven leather straps and runners made of steel bent so that they joined at the front like the prow of a boat.

"What's it for?" Daniel asked dumbly.

"It's for our business, pardner." Harry said, proudly.

No Problem lifted his head for a brief moment.

"Exactly what kind of business is it that we're in, Harry?"

Harry stood up and stretched his back. "We're in the potato business. A profitable business it is too, ain't it, Joe?"

No Problem grunted.

"Pardon me, Harry, but what is it that we actually do?" Daniel was still unclear.

"You remember that big oven in my cabin, don't you?" Daniel nodded; the thing was unforgettable. "We cook potatoes in it and then we sell them to the miners. They use them to keep their hands warm on the way up the hill in the wintertime, then they eat them." He looked over to No Problem for corroboration, but getting none, he continued. "We get the potatoes cheap from the farmers down the valley and the Mormons in Utah. I have some connections over there. Almost pure profit and no real competition to speak of, is there, Joe?"

Joe grunted and kept working with the cinches in the webbing on the sled.

Daniel shrugged and walked over to Marigold and patted her flanks. Her skin twitched at his touch. "Feel like going out for a little ride, girl?" Marigold shook her head as if understanding the question. "Oh, come on now, it's a beautiful day out there. You'll love it." Daniel scratched her cheeks and she leaned her head to nuzzle him. He took the halter from the wall and gently looped it over her head and then placed the blanket and saddle on her back.

Harry came closer and cleared his throat. "If Red offers you a job, are you going to take it?" Harry casually reached out to pat his horse. It turned its head and tried to bite him. "By God, she reminds me of one of my wives. When you get back, we should take a ride down the valley and pick up our supplies." Harry looked at Daniel but kept a wary eye on his horse. "You are going to help me this winter, aren't you? I mean, if you don't want my hospitality and you want to move on, just go right ahead. I'm not the type to stop any man from going about his business."

"No, Harry, I really appreciate the opportunity and I said I'd stay. At least until I can get some savings together."

Harry relaxed. "Well, that's good to hear. I guess that makes us true partners then." Harry reached out his hand and Daniel shook it to seal their partnership.

Daniel headed out to Red's place, towards the Pass, over which he had come only three days before. The ride was pleasant, the day was warm. The mountains draped with a mantle of glistening new snow that dazzled the eyes, while scattered clumps of aspen trees that had not yet completely dropped their leaves were mottled crimson and gold. Their leaves quivered in the breeze as they hung on, seemingly fighting the end that gravity and winter had as their inevitable fate. Not for the last time would he think that this was one of the most beautiful places on earth.

Daniel was in a state of simple happiness. He had a warm place to sleep, food, a fine horse, and a new group of friends who seemed to like him. Though he hadn't been to church for some time, not a day went by that he didn't say a prayer for his mother, sister, and brother, and sometimes, when he was feeling particularly generous, for his father. They all got a prayer today as he and Marigold approached Red's barn.

Pete was working outside in the sunshine and he saw Daniel approaching. He laid down his tools and greeted him with a warm handshake and from his pocket produced a carrot for Marigold. He broke it in half and it held out to her on the palm of his hand to Marigold's delight, then put the rest in the side pocket of his coat, intentionally letting the leaves protrude. Marigold followed his every move until he came close enough for her to snatch the carrot out of his pocket.

"Good to see you, son," he said, patting Daniel on the shoulder. "How're you feeling today?"

"Still a bit wobbly, but I think I'll live. Who put me to bed, Pete?"

"Let's just say that it happened and you was no big problem to anyone. Now head on in there and see Red. Marigold and me, well, we'll see if we can't find us another carrot, won't we, girl?" Marigold noisily chewed her carrot and nuzzled around Pete's pockets hoping for more.

Daniel entered the barn through side door, helped himself to coffee and was looking up at the blocks and tackle suspended from a heavy beam when Red emerged from his office.

"That's what we use to work on the wagons," he said as he poured himself coffee. "It lifts them off the ground so we can change their wheels or their axles. When we're busy, we might have half a dozen wagons a day come limping in here with something broken. You'd think they'd at least make an attempt to stay on the damned road." Red was smiling. "Come on into my office, young man and get warm."

Daniel stood next to the small stove, rubbing his hands and enjoying the heat from the hot metal as Red went back behind his desk and closed the books and ledgers he'd been working on. He leaned back in his chair and clasped his hands behind his head, regarding Daniel.

"I've got something of yours here," he said, pulling the envelope out of a drawer and placing it on the desk. Daniel made no attempt to reach for it. "Go ahead, take it. It's yours, you earned it. I didn't want you to lose it, so I held onto it for you." Red felt no need to elaborate further.

Daniel took the envelope and pulled out the money. "There's fifty dollars in here, Red. I don't think what I did was worth that much."

Red reached for the envelope, took the money out and counted it. "Well, that's strange. I thought I put sixty dollars in there."

"I gave some to Harry." Daniel confessed. "He asked me for some money. He said he was a little short of funds." Daniel's stammer returned. "And, w...well, I am living with him as his guest and all. Was it a bad thing to do?"

"No, no, Daniel, it wasn't a bad thing." Red reassured him. Red leaned back in his chair, clasping his hands behind his head. "What do you think of Harry?" he asked. "What I mean is; do you think that he's a person that you should trust?"

Daniel considered the question carefully. "I only just met him a couple of days ago. I don't really know him well enough yet. Why?"

"That's not an easy question to answer." Red felt uncomfortable having put himself into the position where he had to justify his question. "There are friends, and then there are real friends. There's a difference. Do you know what I mean?" Red considered Daniel closely, "Look son, I know you're just a young man, but you must've run into someone that you would really like to trust, but something just doesn't let you trust them completely. Does that make sense?"

"I think I know what you mean."

Red smiled, feeling a genuine affection for the boy across from him. "Look, Daniel, all I'm trying to say is that you have to watch out for yourself. I gave you that money; it's yours to keep, so you can do whatever you like with it. I'd only like to say that I'd rather not see it go into Harry's pocket so he can just turn around and lose it to some other gambler. And let me tell you, they're all luckier than our friend Harry." Red pushed the money back across his desk.

"Thanks again, Red. I appreciate it very much. I'll try to keep it away from Harry." Daniel took it and put it into his coat pocket.

"Good lad, that's all I wanted to hear." Red was relieved that he'd made his point. "Now come along outside and we'll get us some fresh air."

"What're you going to do about the wagon you lost?" Daniel inquired as they walked from the office.

"Usually we'd just order up a new one, but we're running out of men to work with the teams. Most of them would rather slave in the mines or the smelter. Now don't get me wrong, I respect those fellers for going up inside that mountain day in and day out, working for a couple of dollars a day. That's a dangerous job to be sure, and there's no real future in it, is there?" They walked over to where Pete was checking the hooves of one of the Morgans, digging out dirt with a small tool. "Daniel, have you decided what you're going to do?" Red asked. "Are you going to stay the winter?"

Daniel put his hands in his pockets and shrugged. So much had happened to him in the last few days, he really hadn't had too much time to think the question through. On the one hand, with the fifty dollars in his pocket he could make it to Salt Lake, but then he'd be stuck there with the Mormons through the winter. The thought of being preached at for a whole winter held no attraction for him.

"You see, Pete here is my right-hand man. We're always on the lookout for a good man to join our outfit, aren't we, Pete?"

"Cain't never find good men when we need 'em, can we, Red? No matter how much we pay 'em." Pete looked up at Red with a sly smile.

"I wanted to see if you'd like to come and work for me. You're good with the animals and you don't scare easy. We thought you might like the chance to make some real good money over the winter. If you saved your money, you'd have enough to ride on that train all the way to California, come spring," Red paused before continuing. "And, we'd like to have you on our team. What do you say?"

Daniel didn't know how to answer. He knew for certain that this opportunity was neither offered often, nor lightly. It was an offer to be thought about at length.

Then there was the matter of Harry. He'd offered Daniel both his friendship and his cabin. Though the more he thought about his accommodations, the more he felt inclined towards Red's offer. Even if it meant sleeping in this barn, it might still have its advantages.

"What is it exactly that Harry wants you to be his partner in?" Red asked.

Daniel cleared his throat. "I don't really know for sure, but it has something to do with selling potatoes to the miners."

Pete laughed out loud.

"Look, Daniel, I don't want to throw cold water on what Harry's told you, but that little business of his is just one of many in this town." Red was trying not to dampen Daniel's enthusiasm. "Harry's never made any real money at selling potatoes. There's no reason he'll do any better this year than he did last year."

Pete tossed in. "Or the year before that, or the year before that."

"We're just trying to look out for you. This town could have some real possibilities for you if you make the right decisions. Even Jerome Wheeler, the man you met at the funeral yesterday, was asking what you were going to do here. He seemed very interested in talking to you about that sometime." Red placed his arm around Daniel's shoulders in a fatherly gesture.

Daniel looked at the ground and shuffled his feet, uncomfortable that he was going to have to disappoint Red. "Do you really think that I'd be able to do this kind of work? I've never seen a winter in the mountains. I wouldn't freeze to death like Pete said, would I?"

Red smiled a big, genuine smile. "Daniel, you'd be just fine. Between Pete and me, I believe you'd be in good hands. Not to say that there won't be some tense moments. I dare say we'll see our share this year as we do every year, but we always seem to make it through. That's why we don't have to hire men very often. Except for the winter, it's a pretty decent job. And it pays good money, too. Doesn't it, Pete?"

"You make about as much in a week as those miners make in a month," Pete confirmed. "Of course, you don't get to town very often and you're usually too tired to drink when you do. And, if you've got an ornery wife at home, like I do, it's almost the best job in the world."

Daniel drew his shoulders back and took a deep breath. He didn't want to disappoint either of them. "I really appreciate the offer, Red. But, I've already told Harry that I'd partner up with him and I couldn't go back on my word, especially after he's been so nice to me." Daniel didn't catch the look that passed between the two older men. "Thanks again for the money." Daniel shook Red's hand and felt the power in the man's arm. "Let me think about it."

"OK, son. Take as long as you want. Just let me be the first one you tell when you reach a decision. OK?" Red smiled, but his disappointment was real.

Daniel mounted and touched the brim of his hat as he gently turned Marigold towards town. Watching Daniel disappear down the road through the dappled shadows of the afternoon, Red was lost in thought. Pete had seen that look before.

"If you're thinking what I'm thinking Red, then stop it! He's a young man and if he's going to make a mistake in judgment, then better if he makes it early on. Better now than later on, when it can do some real damage."

Red sighed. "Yeah, Pete, you're right. It's just that sometimes you want to help these young fellers."

"All of them, or just this one in particular?"

"That's a good question, Pete. I might have to think on that a while."

Chapter 12

When Daniel returned to the cabin he found Harry with his bare feet on an upturned bucket by the fire, drinking coffee. He opened one eye and pointed to the coffee pot on the oven, so Daniel found a tin cup on one of the shelves and poured himself a cup. He took a sip and his head went back as if someone had stuck a pin in his tongue.

"What is this, Harry? It's awful." It was thick, strong, and about one-third whiskey.

"It's cowboy coffee, son. It'll put hair on your chest."

"Harry, I think this'd take it right off."

"You can drink it or not, but I guarantee that you'll regret not drinking it when you've been standing out in the cold for a couple'a hours."

Daniel tasted the steaming coffee again and confirmed that it could only be worse if it had dirt in it, but it was hot and sweet and it did seem to go right to his chilled bones.

"What happened to you last night?" Daniel asked as Harry fussed with the oven.

"You've got to keep an eye on the fire. If you don't watch it, you'll burn the lot and them miners get real ugly if you burn their lunches."

"What did you do all night?"

"What business is it of yours where I was or what I did?" Harry responded.

"I was just worried that something had happened to you." Daniel apologized hurriedly.

Harry sat back down at the table, holding his gaze on Daniel. "What I do with my own time is my own business. You're just a guest here, do you understand?"

Daniel was shocked by Harry's outburst of temper, but just as suddenly, Harry became his charming self again. "I'm sorry about that, Daniel. No hard feelings, are there?" Daniel shook his head, confused.

"Good," Harry said and proceeded to go about gathering things and putting them into the wagon. When the potatoes were done, they took them in buckets out to the wagon and covered them in heavy canvas. They pulled the small wagon to where the road began its one-thousand foot climb up to the mines.

For the most part, the miners were a simple lot, a trait which Harry and others constantly preyed upon. Poorly trained and mostly illiterate, they went into the mines daily to do battle with the mountain gods. Working ant-like in deplorable conditions, they received their pitiful wages daily, which they would usually spend drinking and gambling.

Few had money when they arrived in town and fewer ever worked their way out of the mines. Far fewer ever became rich. But man lives on dreams, so over the Pass came a constant stream of fresh victims who struggled with the elements and the ever-present danger to walk that cold walk into the mines daily.

The mines consumed men like firewood. But, so long as there was no shortage of willing men, the owners held the strong hand and the miners received no help if they were injured on the job. Painful injuries like crushed fingers or toes were considered superficial and for the most part ignored with the help of the little blue bottles.

It was still dark and cold when they started out for the mountain, but the exertion of pulling the wagon quickly warmed them, as did Harry's coffee. The place where Harry set up his stand was only minutes away, but when they arrived, two other stands were already doing business for the day. One was owned by a rough looking man who sold bread and small hunks of cheese, the other man, small and neat by comparison, sold dried jerked meat. Harry took the slats of his homemade trestle table and set it up closer to the road than the others.

"Harry," yelled the larger man, "what're you trying to do, take their lunch up to 'em?"

"The owners don't want us to interfere with the road, so sometimes they send some of their thugs over to cause trouble," Harry told Daniel and moved his table a few inches back from the road as the first group of miners approached them.

"Harry, you son of a bitch, I heard you got killed by old Doc Holliday over there in Leadville," said the first miner.

"Not so, Clint. I believe it was a standoff."

"What happened? Did he catch you cheating again?" Harry smiled through a clenched jaw. Clint continued, "Say Harry, these look like the same spuds you were peddling last year. I recognize this one." He pointed at the potatoes Harry had in front of him. "That one got more eyes than my whole family put together," he said as he took two.

Harry snatched the nickel out of Clint's hand. "Meet my new partner, Daniel."

Clint took his glove off to shake Daniel's hand. "See you two later if I don't get killed first," he said as he stuffed the potatoes in his pocket, gathered up his tools, bowed his head and began the climb.

Daniel was surprised by the number of miners who passed their stand. At times they were hard-pressed to keep up with the stream of men filing past. Invariably they insulted Harry, or the size of the potatoes, but soon the potatoes were all gone and the disappointed latecomers rushed past, muttering cuss words. Harry took care of the money, which Daniel didn't mind. It meant that he could keep his hands in his gloves while he handed out nice warm potatoes.

They were dismantling their table when a young miner in a strange cap and facemask approached them. The mask, which was held by a leather strap, had two hollow thimble-like metal tubes around the eyes and a hinged, spring lever on top that flipped covers down over the openings. The young miner and Harry spoke quietly together for a while, then Harry called Daniel over.

"Daniel, this is Ulysses."

"My dad wanted us to meet. You met him yesterday, at No Problem's. My dad's Shady Lane."

Daniel smiled and shook Ulysses' heavily gloved hand. He had a big smile, unusually good teeth and would have been handsome, but for his eyes being too small for his face. He was taller than Daniel and thinner in build, but it was his eyes that drew attention, for though they were small, they were exceptionally bright.

"Call me Leafy, everyone else does."

"Nice to meet you, Leafy Lane," said Daniel, smiling at the sound. "What is your hat for?"

"Oh, this?" Leafy said touching the goggles. "I'm a blaster. These things protect our eyes when the dynamite goes off." Leafy flipped the lever and the two eye pieces that cover the holes snapped down shut, then he flipped them open. "Well, I'd better get going or they'll be looking for me." He turned to leave, but turned back. "Are you doing anything tomorrow night?" Daniel shook his head and Leafy smiled. "I'll come by and we'll go out to the Saturday night fights."

"Sure. Thanks," Daniel replied.

Harry exclaimed, "As long as you have him back in time for his shift."

Leafy nodded and adjusted the pack on his back and waved to them as he left.

"Why don't we head into town and celebrate our first day as partners?" Harry shook the wooden cigar box that held the money. "I think we can afford a decent breakfast. How's about it, partner?" Daniel couldn't help but smile at the thought of a big, hot breakfast.

Back at the cabin, Harry busied himself counting the money while Daniel washed his face and hands in the wash-basin. They'd left a bucket of water on the oven, and it was steaming hot when they returned. Daniel was drying his face when he realized that Harry was sound asleep, snoring loudly. So much for having breakfast with his new partner?

Chapter 13

"Come on partner, time to get up." Harry was shaking him. "Time for us to go to work again." Daniel shook the cobwebs out of his head. He tried to stand, but his head hurt and he had to sit back down on the edge of the bunk.

"Here you go, drink this, you'll feel better. Trust me," Harry said, handing him a cup of steaming black coffee.

Daniel was falling into the pattern of their work, especially since it was three shifts every day. He would give the men their potatoes and Harry would take their money. He was told that the miners would put all of their lunches in a hole with a lamp for heat, then close the hole. Even those bringing their own meal would put theirs in too, so they could all have something hot to eat at mid-shift.

As was usual, Harry counted the money as soon as they came back to the cabin. He handed Daniel a couple of dollars, put some in his pocket, and the rest in a tin box that he slid under his bed. Daniel thought of asking Harry about the arrangement, but Harry was out the door and gone.

That evening, there was a knock at the door. When Daniel opened it, he was surprised to find Leafy standing there ready to take him out to the fights. Daniel grabbed his coat and hat, and together they headed into town.

"How'd you meet up with Harry?" Leafy asked as they walked.

Daniel told him the story about Harry and Doc Holliday in Leadville, then the trip over the Pass.

"And now we're partners and friends." Daniel finished his story.

"I don't think he's a good partner from all I've heard," Leafy stated plainly.

"Why do you say that?"

"Well, my dad doesn't trust him, for one thing." Leafy's tone brightened. "Have you ever been to a fight before?"

"You mean where they fight for money?"

Daniel shook his head and Leafy continued, "Each of the mine owners has a boxer or two. They challenge each other and the owners put up the prize money. The winner shares the money with the owner, then they drink the money away right there and then. You can never tell when one of the fighters will let the other man win."

"You mean the fights are fixed?" Daniel asked incredulously.

"Last week, there was this little Irish feller who took on this big Englishman and the Irish feller just knocked the stuffing out'a him." Leafy looked at Daniel. "It just looked fixed to me." Daniel smiled to himself, knowing that there most probably had been no fix in that particular bout.

Daniel paused as they passed Big Shirley's Paragon Ballroom. Through the window, he could see Shirley among a group of well-dressed men. "Do you mind if I just stop and say hello to Shirley?" Shirley saw them and met them at the door.

"What are you two handsome young boys up to this evening?" Shirley asked, smiling brightly. "Out to cause a little trouble?" She touched Daniel's cheek lightly. He blushed when he saw that men were watching them.

"Why don't you two go have your fun and come on back by here on your way home?"

He turned to leave, but Shirley caught him by the sleeve as they opened the door.

"How're things going with you and Harry?" Shirley asked, trying not to sound as if she was prying.

"OK, I guess," he said cautiously. "It's tiring feeding all of those miners with Harry, especially the midnight shift. I'm not used to the hours yet, but I should be soon."

"Come on back by here later. I've a message for you," she whispered in his ear as she pushed him through the door.

⚄

The fights were at a saloon named the Mother Lode. It was a crowded place and the air was clogged with tobacco smoke and the smell of unwashed men. Leafy found his friends gathered in a corner of the bar and did his best to introduce Daniel, but the crowd was noisy. Daniel felt a bump on his hip and someone pushed a whiskey bottle into his hands.

"Keep it low, so the barkeep don't see us," the stranger advised. No one was paying him any particular attention, so he faked drinking from the bottle and passed it back. The man had a gulp himself and handed it right back to Daniel. "Go ahead, have another. I'll hide ya'."

He'd never tasted anything so vile. It tasted like whale oil smelled. Leafy slapped him hard on the back and took the bottle.

"Pretty good stuff, ain't it?" Leafy took a big gulp from the bottle. A bell sounded and the crowd roared. Daniel saw two rugged looking men begin circling each other in the ring. The fighting was very stylized; the contestant's outfits seemed more theatrical than functional. Naked to the waist, they wore only shoes and colorful, high-waisted boxing pants with a belt of contrasting color.

Both fighters were bloodied, one more than the other, but neither seemed much worse for the wear. They circled each other like dancers and alternately one would reach out with a jab and lean back so that the opponent's return blow would fall short. Only occasionally would a punch reach its target, but when one did hit its mark, it was a solid blow and it brought loud cheers from the crowd.

Daniel was surprised to see women present. The more he looked, the more women he saw cheering and yelling alongside the men, some were even outdoing the men in bawdiness. Clinging to the ropes, they either taunted or flirted with the combatants between rounds and their comments and gestures were anything but genteel. The crowd loved it and the more outrageous the comments the more they were lauded.

There was a flurry of activity in the ring and the men in front of him rose up blocking his view. Daniel could only see one boxer still standing in the ring. No one seemed happy with the result and shouting matches raged all around him. The winner's hand was held aloft and he was escorted from the ring by his friends. He was immediately surrounded by both male and female admirers.

"That's Sparky. He's one of us." Leafy said, "He might not look like much, but he's good at this. He's the head blaster so he can take some punishment. Deaf as a post; but he's quick as a cat."

By the time Leafy's friends had collected their bets, another bout was under way and the crowd had surged to surround the ring once again. When their hero had dressed and joined them, they staggered off into one of the multitude of small saloons. When Sparky entered, he was greeted ceremoniously and given a seat of honor at the bar.

When the adoration had subsided, Leafy tapped Sparky on the shoulder. "Sparky, this is Daniel. He's staying at Harry Rich's place. He's the one that saved Dangerous up on the Pass." Sparky reached through the crowd and gripped Daniel's hand in a powerful handshake. Even though Sparky's eyes bugged out somewhat, he still had one of the most engaging smiles Daniel had seen.

"Have you had something to drink, son?"

"Yes, thank you, sir. I'm not much of a drinking man."

"Me either," he said. Three whiskeys magically appeared on the bar in front of him. Handing one to Daniel and the other to Leafy, he held his glass in the air. The room fell silent. Placing his arm around Daniel, Sparky held his drink in the air. "This here is the young feller who tried to save Dangerous Bolon from the curse of the Pass. Let's all drink to the memory of old Dangerous and to this young man's courage." The gaggle of men around the bar all raised their glasses.

"To Dangerous," they said as one.

At that moment Harry came through the door, shaking snow from his collar. He pushed through the crowd and angrily grabbed Daniel by the sleeve. "What're you doing with this bunch? Where were you? We had work to do." Harry pulled Daniel towards the door.

"Where are you dragging this boy, Harry?" Sparky's grip on Daniel's sleeve was unbreakable. "We're just getting to know each other." Sparky focused one of his eyes on Daniel, the other at Harry. "I think we should keep him here, don't you, boys?" A rousing drunken cheer rose around them.

"Listen here, you old rum bucket, you leave my partner alone." Harry leaned threateningly towards Sparky.

Daniel could sense the tension rising. He pulled free of Sparky's grip and shrugged. "I'm sorry but I have to go now. I forgot how late it was getting.

"Son, you just be careful of that feller." Sparky pointed his finger at Harry. "We'll be talking again sometime, Harry Rich."

Harry turned abruptly and headed for the door. Daniel had to run to catch up with him, but Harry was mute the rest of the way home.

When they returned to the cabin after the midnight shift, Daniel was hoping to hear that all was forgiven and forgotten. Harry sullenly counted the money and placed some of it in the small tin box that he kept under his bed.

"Don't you go touching that money under there," he warned as he headed for the door. "I know exactly how much is in there, so don't go getting any ideas," he said, slamming the door behind him. Daniel felt like he'd been punched in the stomach.

Chapter 14

Harry was still angry when he entered the bar at the Paragon. Shouldering the door open, Harry strode into the saloon smiling for the sake of appearance only. He hung his bearskin coat on the rack along with a dozen others, dripping snow into the brass catchall on the floor. Forgetful Al stood polishing glasses and scowling at him, so he avoided the bar and scanned the room.

Harry felt lucky tonight. Perhaps it was the flush of triumph that came from humiliating his young roommate, perhaps it was just the thought of the night of gambling that lay ahead. He perused the room and ambled over to a table where the competition seemed less formidable and slid into one of the available chairs. He ordered a round of drinks for the table, as was the custom, and settled in. Several of the players he'd gambled with before and knew their tolerances for loss and their reputation for paying their debts. It never paid off in the long term to win too much from someone who was unable to pay. Those situations could be dangerous in a town where every house had a firearm, no matter how humble its appearance.

Excusing herself from her customers, Shirley made her way through the crowded room to Harry's table. She placed her hand on Harry's shoulder, smiling and greeting everyone in a gesture that cast a warm glow over the players. She lightly tapped him on the shoulder and leaned closer, gaining his attention.

"Tell Daniel that Honey would like to see him to thank him," she said. Harry looked up, a smile creeping across his face. "It's not what you're thinking, Harry Rich. Get your mind out of the gutter. Be sure that you tell him." She shot him a resigned smile and headed for her office.

Shirley wanted to go home and reread the letter that had arrived today from Kate, her eldest daughter. It held both good news and not-so-good news, but she'd only had the chance to read it quickly. Her routine was to head home around midnight, when things had quieted down, and leave the place in the able hands of her manager, Dixon.

Dixon was a gruff character but an able manager and was universally referred to as Dix, since he came from Mississippi and spoke with a heavy southern accent. As was his custom he insisted on escorting her home and as usual, she didn't protest. She considered him one of her friends, though she knew that as long as he was her employee their relationship would never go any further. A fact she knew disappointed him considerably.

Maisie, Shirley's housekeeper, was asleep when she arrived home.

She threw her silk dressing gown over her nightdress and went back downstairs to sit quietly at her kitchen table with the letter. Enormously proud of her daughter, she smiled to herself that the address on the envelope was so elegantly written with such long, smooth strokes. *Mrs. Camille Doray, The Paragon Ballroom, Aspen, Colorado.* It was somewhat strange to see her name formally written, since so few people remembered her real name anymore.

When the kettle steamed, she poured the hot water into the little Chinese teapot that had been a Christmas gift from the Chin family. She was reading the letter for the third time when she heard the creaking board and the soft footsteps of her younger daughter, coming down the stairs. She looked up as Rachelle came into the kitchen and sat heavily in the chair next to her. Seeing her mother with her reading glasses on and the letter in front of her, she reached for the letter and Shirley let her take it. She didn't flinch when her petulant daughter threw the letter back down on the table.

"I knew she'd be back someday. I just didn't think it'd be so damned soon."

"Rachelle, that's no way to speak."

"At the whorehouse, you mean." Rachelle shot back. The insult was like cold water on Shirley's face, but it was nothing new.

"Either way, you're a young lady, and you're supposed to be respectful."

Rachelle slumped in her chair and pouted.

Shirley was tired and now was not the time to be drawn into this discussion, so she sipped her tea and waited for her daughter to break the ice wall that stood between them.

After a moment, Rachelle came to her mother with that little-girl, beguiling look of innocence that in the coming years would be the sword through many a man's heart. Shirley could see even from childhood that this girl had a killer, if not murderous instinct and if she so desired, Rachelle could be as successful as Shirley herself in the saloon business.

Tucking her hair behind her ear, Rachelle bent forward to kiss her mother goodnight.

Shirley followed the sound of her daughter's footsteps all the way up to her room, listening for the familiar creaking of the floorboards above her head. At times her daughter was temperamental to the point of being intolerable. Shirley sighed. She finished her tea and after rinsing out the cup and placing it on a clean towel, she followed her daughter upstairs. Pausing at the top of the stairs, she looked briefly at the closed door to the girls' room, then went into her bedroom, closing the door on the worries of her world.

Rachelle lay awake, thinking about her sister's return. She hoped that Kate had gotten pregnant and was coming home in disgrace. She knew all about sex from the women at the Paragon. It was no secret that her mother had been a whore when she'd first arrived in Aspen. Fact or not, it never stopped Rachelle from lashing out, sometimes with her fists, at anyone who would bring that to her attention.

Though at times it was hard to deny the fact, she was sure her mother never did those dirty things the other girls did.

Rachelle could easily see in her mind those filthy, dirty miners pawing and slobbering all over her sister. They wouldn't mind that she looked the way she did or walked the way she did. What did it matter? All they seemed to want from a woman was that she lay on her back while the men bumped and humped until something happened.

Occasionally, the doors to the working girls' rooms would be slightly ajar. Some of the things that she saw she wouldn't ever have believed unless she had seen it with her own eyes. She shuddered with revulsion.

Stranger still to her was that some of the girls actually seemed to enjoy their work. Kim Ellen in particular. She talked about it like she would do it even if she wasn't getting paid.

Her thoughts came back to her sister. Kate's bed was just as she had left it. Her mother always had Maisie change the sheets on both their beds at the same time. "Just in case she comes home suddenly," her mother would say. Hopefully, just a brief visit before running off to Australia or China and then crawling back home, penniless and ruined. The thought was pleasant enough to free her cares, and she floated into dreams of her sister's humiliation.

Chapter 15

"Harry, how do you mail a letter from here?"

They were relaxing after having just returned from selling to the afternoon shift. Harry didn't appear to have heard the question, but Daniel was patient.

"Give it to Red. He takes the mail to the post office in Leadville," Harry mumbled, as if it were painful to talk. It mystified Daniel how Harry could keep the hours that he did, sleeping only in snatches and staying out all night, every night. The one good thing about it was that he had the cabin to himself most of the time.

It was getting to be a cozy life and Daniel had plenty of food, although he had to do all of the cooking. Harry wasn't much help, though he always finished everything that Daniel cooked.

He was also becoming more comfortable with the town. People passing him on the street would nod or say howdy, and it made him feel happy and proud that he had the acquaintance of so many so soon.

His worst moments came when he thought about his family. At these times, when he considered the things that his foolishness had caused, he would see no end to his pain. His thoughts would turn darker, towards his brother rotting away in some British cell, being starved and suffering the beatings and humiliation that always befell the young in such places. English prisons were infamous places where the Irish were preyed upon and, being both young and Irish. Daniel could only imagine the suffering his brother had to endure both from the guards and the other prisoners.

Shaking off the anxiety and guilt that always accompanied these thoughts, he looked back down at the letter in his hand. Without thinking, he lifted the letter to his lips and kissed the place where he'd signed his name, "With much love, Daniel."

"You'd best be giving it to Red to mail for you in Leadville."

Daniel looked up, surprised to see that Harry was watching him. Embarrassed, he folded the letter and made an envelope of another piece of paper, which he sealed with glue from a bottle not much bigger than a thimble. Harry watched him as he carefully returned his writing materials to their leather pouch and put them all into his saddle bag.

"You know something, I don't know that much about you," Harry said casually. Daniel pushed his bag under his bed as far as it would go. They'd been roommates for nearly a month and Daniel had learned much about Harry Rich in that time. His instincts told him it would be prudent to tell Harry as little as possible.

"What do you want to know?" Daniel had listened to the tales that Harry routinely regaled him with after his nightly exploits. Harry seemed to know something embarrassing about everyone in Aspen. What was particularly alarming was Daniel's increasing awareness that when Harry drank, he talked.

"Where are you from, for instance?"

Daniel had prepared several stories which he'd hoped would provide plausible answers to this question, but now that he was being asked directly, he was confused with which lie he should go with. Harry took Daniel's hesitation for what it truly was, a sign of a person wanting to hide something.

"Hey! You don't have to tell me if you don't want to. We're just business partners and I *am* letting you share *my* house."

"I'm from England," he blurted out.

Harry stood as if to leave but hesitated, waiting. "Where in England?"

"Up north, near Scotland," Daniel threw out hurriedly.

Thankfully, there was a knock on the door. Daniel breathed a sigh of relief. Harry opened the door and found Red Corcoran, his giant frame blocking almost all of the light.

"Mind if I come in?" Red asked, smiling widely.

"Sure, Red. I haven't seen you in a while."

"Well Harry, that's one of the reasons that I stopped over." Red took off his hat as he entered and let his eyes roam over the room. "I have to say that your place looks real neat and tidy, Harry. If I didn't

know you better, I'd have to say that you got yourself a cleaning lady."
Harry smiled at the compliment. Red saw Daniel look up at the ceiling.

"Nice of you to notice, Red." Harry lounged with one arm over the
back of his chair and threw a casual approving look around the room,
basking in Red's compliment. "I've been a mite better of a housekeeper
since I developed a cabin mate."

"You mean to tell me that you do all of the cleaning, Harry?" Red
chuckled. "You'd rather buy a new tin cup than wash out the old one.
What've you done, turned over a new leaf?"

"I get a bit of help now and then." Harry winked at Daniel. Red
raised an eyebrow for Daniel's sake. "Want some coffee?"

"No offense, Harry," Red laughed, "but I'd rather be chased bare-
foot over the prairie by Indians than drink that stuff you call coffee. I
meant that in the nicest way."

Harry looked deflated, but poured himself some. "It is pretty awful
stuff, isn't it?" Harry admitted when he swallowed.

"The reason I came over is that when I was at Dangerous's place
looking in on his family, Honey said that Daniel never came over to
visit her, and she was a little hurt by that. Now, you don't seem like the
inconsiderate type, Daniel, so I asked Shirley if she'd mentioned it to
you. She said that she'd told Harry several times and knowing Harry
as I do, I wondered if you ever got the message."

Daniel was embarrassed. He'd felt strange about going over there
and had put it out of his mind. The truth of the matter was that the last
thing he wanted to do was make small talk with a grieving widow of
a man that he barely knew. But obviously he was going to have to pay
the widow Bolon a visit, whether he wanted to or not.

Red got up to leave but when he reached for the door handle, he
turned back and motioned for Daniel to follow him.

"Daniel, can I see you for a moment? I want to tell you how to get
to Honey's house." He nodded to Harry. "I'll see you around, Harry."
Daniel grabbed his coat and followed Red outside.

Harry watched them leave and as the door closed behind them, he
had a gut feeling that they were going to be talking about him. Harry
couldn't stop himself from going over to the window and carefully

pulling the curtain aside to watch them walk down the path to the road.

Red's horse was loosely tied to a tree and Red checked the belly strap out of habit. Daniel stroked the horse's neck and at his touches, the horse shivered. Red stood looking at him, resting his arm on the saddle.

"Look son, I hope you know that I think highly of you," Daniel nodded, but had an uneasy feeling in his stomach, "and I don't want to intrude on your life, but how're things going with you and Harry?"

Daniel shrugged and looked at the tapering wall of the mountain across the valley. "I thought that you and Harry were good friends." Daniel seemed to catch Red by surprise.

"We are, but I still don't really know the man as well as I should. He's a bit of a mystery to me in a lot of ways. I guess that's why I'm asking the question." Red switched to a lighter subject and clapped Daniel on the shoulder. "I hear that you and Leafy are going out to the bars and getting around town like two old-timers."

Daniel remained silent.

Red took a deep breath and stumbled into what he had been trying to say all along. "Look son, No Problem and I are a bit concerned that you're heading in the wrong direction." Red took another deep breath and squared his shoulders. "I mean, No Problem's heard that you've been drinking pretty regular. Is that true?"

"What business is that of yours?" Daniel snapped back.

Red held his hands up defensively, surprised at the sudden anger in Daniel's voice. "You're right, Daniel. It's really not any of my business. It's just that I think you have a lot of potential and I'd hate to see you waste it." Red was trying his best not to sound too paternal. "Son, I've been around these parts for a long time and I've seen this town consume men that I thought were stronger than me. There's something about this town that just draws a person in and sucks their good sense right out of them. They never notice it happening themselves, but those around them can see it happening. Then one day, they come to their senses and realize that their best years are behind them and their futures have melted away like snow." Red looked into Daniel's eyes and placed his hand on his shoulder to gather the boy's complete attention. "I just don't want to see it happen to you. OK?"

Red had given this conversation considerable thought, ever since he'd heard from No Problem Joe that Daniel had been seen drunk in town on more than one occasion. So far, the conversation was not going the way he'd hoped. There was an uncomfortable silence growing between them. When it became obvious that Daniel was not going to respond, Red smiled bravely and tried a different tack.

"Thought any more about coming on with me? Pete and Dutch were asking. I'm sure they'd be proud to have you come work with us." Daniel looked up and caught Red's smile. "Like I said, I want you to think about what I'm offering. It's a good job with good pay and you'll earn the respect of everyone on both sides of the Pass. And we're real popular with the ladies. So I'm told." Red smiled and let this last piece of information sink in. "So what do you say?"

"Red, please don't take this the wrong way. I know what you're trying to do, and I really do appreciate it, but I'm Harry's partner. I don't think it'd be right if I just got up and left him."

Red saw Daniel's point and realized that he'd been unfair to place him in such an awkward position. Though Red's intentions were of the highest order, he hadn't considered Daniel's sense of loyalty. He really liked this young man. Now if he could just save him from Harry.

Red had his foot in the stirrup and was about to swing up into the saddle when Harry came along down the path towards them. "You're not trying to steal my partner again, are you, you old snake?" he said. There was a chilly, uncomfortable silence as Red hoisted himself up into the saddle.

"Funny you should mention that, Harry. The fact of the matter is that's exactly what I was trying to do. You're a clever man on occasion, Harry. Now, if you could just put that talent into some real work instead of your poker game, you'd be as rich as Jerome Wheeler."

Harry placed his arm around Daniel's shoulder protectively. "No hard feelings, Red, but I need the lad. We're just about to expand the business and I really am counting on him." Harry smiled broadly at

Daniel. "If I'm right, we'll make a decent amount come spring, then you can have him."

This was the first Daniel had heard of Harry's new plans. Daniel slipped out of Harry's grasp.

"Listen here, Red; we were wondering if you had plans for Thanksgiving dinner yet. Weren't we, Daniel?" Daniel had no recollection of ever having discussed the subject. Harry continued on. "We were thinking that you and No Problem might like to come over and join us. I'll personally guarantee that you'll get fed well. What do you say?"

"That's awful nice of you, Harry. Sure, I'd be delighted to join you two fine gentlemen. Maybe all four of us bachelors can go out on the town, eh?" Red waved and gently spurred his horse forward.

Daniel remembered the letter in his pocket. "Red, Red, wait up!" he yelled, running to catch up. "Could you mail this letter for me when you go over to Leadville next?"

Red took the letter that Daniel handed him. "Gladly son, anything else you need from over there?"

"Could you find me some good writing paper?"

"I can do that. I know just where to get it." Red glanced at the address on the handmade envelope. "Going to New York, eh?"

"I wanted to let my mother know that I was OK." He realized he'd made another mistake. That was the second mistake today.

"This is addressed to Mrs. M. Hogan. I thought your name was Carrington. Did your mother get married again?" Red asked casually.

Daniel grabbed at Red's solution to cover his story. "M..m..my, father d..died," Daniel's stutter threatened to take over, but he fought it. "a..and she married a b..butcher from Boston and they moved to New York."

Red looked at the letter in his hand again before placing it into the inner pocket of his coat. He nodded to Daniel and turned away.

Harry and Daniel walked back to the cabin silently. When they were inside, an awkward silence enveloped the room that both of them ignored. Daniel lay on his tidy bunk, reading a dime novel. Harry sat at the table and considered his cabin-mate. He was becoming concerned; concerned that he still didn't have a handle on his young partner.

On the one hand, the boy was simple to read, with the normal and natural instincts of a young man. Harry could see some of himself in there at times. He seemed to like whiskey too, now that he'd gotten a taste for it. Perhaps Harry should be concerned about that but, hell, he was a man and that was his business.

But something else bothered him. The boy read his bible and silly dime novels. That of itself drew Harry's attention, being that Harry was only barely literate, he just couldn't see the point of reading for enjoyment. He had to admit, since Bill Cody had taken his Wild West Show on the road, there were thousands of people who wanted to read about the adventures of the frontier's famous lawmen and the infamous outlaws. Whether the books were truthful seemed of little consequence.

Another thing that intrigued Harry was the amount of time that Daniel spent writing. Daniel would sit for a half hour or more writing and return everything to his pack, carefully replacing it under his bed. He was becoming increasingly consumed by his need to know what was in Daniel's pack. It wasn't that he was insecure; he just had to know if there was something being written about him.

After some careful thought, Harry knew what needed to be done. He had to take a risk, a big risk. He had to show Daniel his deepest secret so that he could feel justified in robbing Daniel of his. He jumped up from the table, pulled his chair under the beam and grabbed the chains hanging from the roof.

Daniel looked up, shocked by the sudden movement and watched as Harry busied himself with the chains.

Harry stood on his chair and methodically repositioned the chains to the blocks hung from the center beam that ran the length of the cabin. Along the beam, several large eyebolts had been hammered or screwed in at various places, only one of which Daniel had seen used. Harry was unusually serious and conspiratorial, as if his mind was tossed about by indecision. Abruptly he looked down, as if arriving at a decision of great importance. Indeed for Harry, it was.

"Daniel, I know that I've had some moments lately when I was not myself. I'm usually the most pleasant man in the world, you can ask anyone." Harry hoped that Daniel would never feel the need to actually do that, since the result could cloud the matter at hand. "Sometimes I just don't think right and I know that I've taken it out on you. I'm sorry about that." The apology caught Daniel by surprise.

"No, no, Harry, it's alright."

Harry held up his hand to silence Daniel's protest and pressed on, secretly impressed by his acting abilities. "You know the money that I told you I'd keep for you from our business?" Harry motioned for Daniel to join him at the table. "That it was yours whenever you decided to ask for it?" Harry pinned Daniel with his most sincere gaze. "Well... I'm going to show you where it's kept." Pausing dramatically and seeing that Daniel was suitably impressed with his candor and sincerity, Harry drew closer. "You can't ever tell anyone about this. Do you promise me that?"

"You have my word." Daniel answered with the sincerity of someone used to guarding secrets. They shook hands.

Daniel's own life was filled with secrets and if the worst of them were to get out, it could land him in trouble too deep to imagine. His eyes went reflexively to the pack under his bunk. Harry cleared his throat.

"Daniel, I want you to know that I'm happy you came along as my partner. Even if I seem mad at you at times, it's not your fault." Daniel wanted to protest but Harry held up a hand. "No. I want you to know that I trust you. So, I decided to let you in on a little secret."

Daniel nodded, shifted in his seat nervously and waited for Harry to continue.

"Be a good lad and close the curtains for me, will you?"

Daniel went to the windows and closed the cut-up blankets that served as curtains. Harry disappeared into the store-room and returned with another length of iron chain. Satisfied that no one could see into the cabin, he pulled a chair under the main beam.

"Hand me that end of the chain, will you?"

Daniel handed him the chain and watched while Harry threaded the chains through the wheeled metal pulley, then around the front legs of the oven. He checked their lengths again, making sure that they were firmly secured. Daniel was intrigued with the operation and impressed by the speed at which Harry accomplished the task.

"Are you ready to be impressed?"

"Sure, Harry, impress me."

Harry walked behind the oven and pulled on the chain, hard. Both the oven and the iron plate that it stood on began to tilt backwards. Slowly, the oven and front of the base plate lifted from the floor. It must have weighed hundreds of pounds. Amazingly, Harry was lifting it with little effort. The log poking from the oven shifted, filling the room with smoke.

When the front of the iron plate which caught the ashes from the oven was a foot off the floor, Harry motioned for Daniel to look underneath. He saw that a hole had been dug into the rocky ground and a metal box sat in the center of the depression.

"No matter how hot the oven gets, this place stays cool. I can put paper money in there and it'll never burn. I've tried it with newspaper and it's as safe as your mother's breast. No offense meant."

"That's ingenious, Harry. I'm impressed that it came up so quickly."

Harry stood back, admiring his handiwork and enjoying Daniel's praise. "It occurred to me that if I had to leave in a hurry, it would be to my advantage to be able to get at my money quick." Harry pointed to the box. "Nobody but you and me know about this, so if I ever find anything missing, I'll know who took it." Daniel gave Harry a skeptical look as he reached for the tin box, but Harry stopped him. "Well there's nothing in there at the present time, but that'll change soon enough, my friend." A knock at the door startled both of them.

"Who is it?" Harry yelled.

"It's Leafy. Is Daniel there?"

"Just a minute, Leafy, I'll see if he's here." Harry and Daniel looked at each other. The cabin had but two rooms.

Harry leapt around the oven and careful not to make a sound, lowered it smoothly back into the notches in the floor. Pushing a stubby broom into Daniel's hands, he motioned for him to sweep the ashes and dirt back onto the front edges of the steel plate while he busied himself taking the chains from the ceiling, trying not to make any noise. Daniel swept around the edges of the oven as Harry went to the door and Daniel took the broom into the storage room. Harry took a deep breath and opened the door.

"Hey there, Leafy," Harry said smiling broadly. "What're you doin' lurking around my cabin? Come on in, son."

Leafy tentatively looked around the room before entering.

Daniel appeared carrying the broom. "Hi Leafy," Daniel said, acting surprised.

Leafy looked at them both suspiciously, then turned and looked over at their beds. Daniel's bed was made up neatly, but Harry's bed was a mess. The sheets were dirty, the pillow stained and the blankets were in disarray. They couldn't tell what Leafy was thinking, but there was a definite difference in the way he now considered them.

"Ah, come on Leafy, it's not what you're thinking. You just caught us in the middle of having an important discussion about the business. Say there, what can we do for you?" Harry said, taking charge.

Harry pulled out a chair and turned it so that it was facing away from the oven. When Leafy sat, he was now looking directly at Harry's bed. At the moment, Harry didn't care what Leafy thought about their living arrangement—something else had his attention. One of the chains was still looped around the leg of the oven and was clearly not supposed to be where it was. Harry stared at it in horror, then looked up at the ceiling, trying to hide his dismay.

Leafy noticed Daniel's puzzled expression and turned to see Harry motioning Daniel out of the cabin. Harry smiled in embarrassment, as did Leafy, who looked from one to the other and headed for the door. He didn't quite run, but he did cover the short distance to the door quickly.

Harry caught him by the arm as he reached for the door handle. "Say there Leafy, before you go bolting out of here, what did you come over here for anyway?" Harry smiled his most disarming smile.

"To ask Daniel if he wanted to go fishin' tomorrow," Leafy said, now unsure of the prudence of his offer.

Harry nodded to Daniel.

"That would be great, b.b.but I.I. don't have a fishing rod," Daniel stammered.

"You don't need one, just something to carry the fish back in."

"I guess you boys are going fishin' with Sparky then?" Harry said, forcing a laugh too loud to be natural.

"Yeah," Leafy replied, relaxing slightly.

"Well, good luck, Leafy, go catch us some big'uns." Harry put his arm around Leafy's shoulder to escort him outside, hoping that he hadn't yet noticed the chain wrapped around the leg of the oven.

Harry motioned for Daniel to follow Leafy. Daniel nodded and grabbed his coat.

Leafy turned back. "You might want to look out for that chain you've got wrapped around that stove of yours. So long, Harry." Leafy said to the closing door.

Harry collapsed heavily into a chair and looked malevolently at the innocent chain, shaking his head in disgust. All he had wanted to do was to convince Daniel of his cleverness; and now he'd jeopardized the whole plan.

His eyes wandered to the pack under Daniel's bunk and again he wondered if it might contain something that he could use.

The next thing he knew, he had the pack in his hand and was carrying it over to the table. It was heavier than he'd expected and made of good quality leather, well tooled and stitched. Its mystery drew Harry like a moth to a flame.

He was unhooking the strap when he thought he heard someone walking along the path outside the cabin. In a flurry of movement, he replaced the pack under the bed and scrambled back to the table and into his chair, just as Daniel opened the door. Harry's heart was pounding so hard, he was sure that Daniel could hear it. He would have to look some other time; perhaps tomorrow when they were fishing.

Chapter 16

It was a perfect day for fishing. Daniel and Leafy rode at the back of the group, listening as Sparky and the two men with him joked and laughed. One of Sparky's friends passed around a bottle of whiskey. When it came to Daniel, he looked at it, remembering the conversation he'd had with Red. Daniel pretended to take a big swallow and coughed violently as some of the fiery liquid made it into his throat.

"Don't drink all of it unless you've got some more," one of the men said. Daniel hurriedly passed the bottle to Leafy, who took a drink and handed the bottle forward.

"Who's that guy?" Daniel asked Leafy discreetly.

"That's Carter. He's one of the bosses at the Glory Hole mine. He works for Wheeler." They rode a while, enjoying the sound of the rushing river below them. It was several minutes until Leafy spoke again. "They say he hears the rock talking. Sometimes he makes us all stop workin' and when it gets quiet, he puts his ear to the rock and listens. If anyone makes a noise, he gets real mad. You only do it once, believe me. It gets creepy down there at times, especially when the rock starts moaning. I don't know what it is that the rock tells him, but whatever he hears, it works for us...we have a real safe mine. The guy with him is Boot Hill. Don't ask me how he got that name, but he's good with his fists and does some of the dirty work for Wheeler." In some ways, Leafy reminded Daniel of his brother; smart, gentle by nature and easy to be with.

"Where are we goin' fishin', Sparky?" Carter asked. Up in front of them, Sparky looked as if he had fallen asleep.

"Is he awake?" Boot Hill asked.

"Yeah, he's awake, aren't you, Sparky?"

"Down there would be good," Sparky mumbled. From where they stood, a spectacular view of the mountains to the south spread out before them. Seeing where Daniel was looking, Leafy named them.

"That one is called Pyramid Peak. It's nearly as tall as Pike's Peak, which is the tallest mountain in Colorado," he said proudly. "Over there are the Maroon Bells. That one over there is Mount Hayden, and over there to your right is Mount Sopris, it's about thirty miles away. That's a crazy mountain. It makes storms, or so the Indians say."

Daniel took it all in. He'd never seen a more beautiful range of mountains. As far as the eye could see, there were jagged peaks clawing the sky like fangs. Truly, he felt that something had brought him here by destiny. "Leafy, are there any Indians here?"

"Used to be. I haven't seen one in a while. There's an old Ute living out by the burial ground. Sometimes he and Shady go out huntin' together. I just think that it's an excuse for my dad to get away from my mother and get drunk, but they always manage to come back with deer or elk, somehow."

"Is he the only one in the whole valley? Where'd they all go?"

"I heard they didn't want to live with white men and went out into the desert." Leafy leaned towards Daniel. "I also heard they put a curse on the valley before they left."

"What kind of curse?"

"Oh, something about the valley breaking the hearts of everyone who tried to rob it of its 'spirit'. They meant the silver and gold inside the mountains."

Leafy led Daniel down a narrow path along the river bank where they found Sparky hunched over a piece of canvas. Daniel sat down on a log across from him, curious. He watched Sparky carefully cut sticks of dynamite into pieces, putting fuses into them.

"Ever been fishing with dynamite before?" Sparky said, pushing a fuse and detonating cap into one of the short red sticks. Daniel's father had done the same thing.

"No, sir."

"Here, I'll show you how we miners catch our supper on Sundays." Sparky turned one of his eyes towards Daniel.

"See, here. We dip the fuses into hot wax and that keeps them dry." He offered one of the short sticks of dynamite for Daniel to feel the wax, then stepping away from the small pile of explosives, he lit the fuse with a match from his pocket. Daniel watched intently as Sparky blew on the lit fuse and casually strolled the few yards to the edge of the river.

The fuse sputtered and hissed along its path with intermittent pauses. Daniel looked around at the others standing behind him, also watching. He was becoming impatient for Sparky to toss the damned thing into the stream. But Sparky just stood on the edge of the water, patiently, one eye on the dynamite and the other looking approximately at Daniel. Daniel couldn't be sure where Sparky was looking exactly; all he knew for certain was that the fuse was getting dangerously close to the noisy end.

Finally, Sparky took the dynamite from his left hand with his right, cocked his arm and turned to throw the dynamite out into the river. It slipped out of his hand. Daniel watched in horror as the fiery hissing thing landed at his feet and was already in full stride before it hit the ground. In two steps, he had launched himself at Sparky. The explosion came at the same instant they hit the water, but it was not the sound that he'd expected. Strangely, they were still alive and both had their legs attached, which would not have been the case had that much dynamite been under his boots. Sparky spluttered and fought to get up but couldn't, Daniel was laying on top of him.

Sparky stopped struggling and grinned. Daniel felt hands grab his coat and pull him back up onto the bank. To his dismay, he realized that they were all laughing. Sparky took a swig off the bottle and purposefully walked over to Daniel, who was still sitting on the ground, partly angry, partly confused. Sparky leaned down and handed him the bottle. Daniel wouldn't take it.

"Why did you try to blow me up?" Daniel asked.

"You'd better tell him, Sparky, or he'll just sit there all day and we'll never get any fishing done," said Boot Hill impatiently.

Sparky held out his hand and Daniel allowed him to pull him up to his feet. "Boys, I think this young man just tried to save my miserable life. Now ain't that a hoot?" He pushed the whiskey bottle at Daniel.

"Well, you dropped the dynamite, didn't you?" Daniel said, angrily pushing the bottle away.

"Daniel. Sparky didn't really drop the dynamite." Leafy bent down and picked up another of the dynamite sticks. "Look here, Daniel. Sparky pulled the fuse and the detonator out of the dynamite and that's what he threw at your feet." Leafy showed him exactly how it was done. "It's a trick these guys do to all the new men. When they did it to me, I just high-tailed it out of here. I thought they were all dead and I didn't want to go and pick up the pieces."

"He was halfway back to town, running as fast as his skinny legs would carry him before we caught up to him," Carter slapped Leafy on the back. Leafy colored with embarrassment.

Daniel felt a hand on his shoulder; it was Sparky.

"Son, you're the first one that we've ever pulled that trick on that didn't turn tail and run. You've got some balls there, jumpin' on me the way you did," Sparky said, sincerely.

Daniel took Sparky's outstretched hand and again felt the strange power of the man. "Now if you two men will stop holding hands," Boot Hill interrupted, slapping them both on the shoulder. "I'd like to do some fishing. Leafy? What say you and this young feller here get the net set up for us?" Boot Hill handed them a heavy bundle which held the net.

Leafy led Daniel, carrying the net a little way downstream to where the river narrowed enough for it to be stretched across. Holding one end of the net, Leafy stepped deftly from boulder to rock to the other side of the river and secured his end amid a chorus of directions.

"Ready to start fishing boys?" Sparky announced with a mischievous grin, lighting the fuse on one of the small sticks of dynamite. He waited until it had burned down almost to the very end and threw it underhand upstream into the pool, where it immediately disappeared under the water. They stood in silence for what seemed like minutes. Daniel thought that the fuse must've gone out. With a whoosh and a loud roar, a giant spout of water shot skyward, filling the air with acrobatic fish and spraying them with water and mud. The noise subsided in degrees as it reverberated in the narrow canyon. As the river regained its composure, Daniel was surprised to see that the surface was littered with dozens of stunned or dead fish, floating along in the current. Leafy punched him on the shoulder to get his attention.

"The net," Leafy yelled and dashed off. Daniel raced after him. When they reached the net, Leafy smiled broadly, pointing proudly at their fish trap which was filling with dozens of trout.

As Daniel laughed at the sight of the parade of stunned fish falling into the net, Leafy reached down to grab the end of the net. His foot slipped out from under him. As if pulled by an invisible hand, he twisted and toppled into the water with his left arm under his body. Even over the noise of the river, Daniel heard the sickening thud of Leafy's head hitting the rock. Frozen in horror, he watched as Leafy's body crumpled into the river and was immediately pulled downstream by the current.

"Help! Help!" Daniel cried. For an instant, he considered jumping in himself, but he was not a swimmer and Leafy was already twenty feet away, swiftly being dragged into the main current. Yelling for help and leaping from rock to rock, he slipped and fell, banging his knee on a rock and filling one boot with water so cold, it took his breath away. He saw Leafy lift one arm, gasping for air before disappearing downstream.

"Help! Help! Somebody help!" Daniel yelled as he raced through the trees and scrubby brush along the riverbank, trying to keep Leafy in sight. Around the next bend, the river widened and the current slowed somewhat.

Leafy saw Daniel running through the trees and weakly raised his arm for help with a look of panic on his face. Leafy tried several times to grab a big rock as he floated into an eddy, but the rock was slippery and his fingers were numb. The river cruelly tugged at his clothes, pulling him away from the rock, then swept him into a set of rolling rapids. Leafy was bounced from boulder to rock, and screamed in pain at each impact.

Daniel saw that the river was becoming narrower, causing it to pick up speed and Leafy was heading for a ledge where the water dropped off over a small cliff. He didn't want to think what would be waiting for Leafy at the bottom of the waterfall.

Leafy felt the increasing drag of the water and fought the current for all his life was worth. He went over the waterfall on his back, hitting the bottom hard enough to push all of the air out of his lungs. The river pulled him under instantly as it flooded his nose and tore at his eyelids, forcing them open. As if by magic, his head rose above the water. Just as suddenly, he was dragged back down.

Daniel pushed himself to his limit, his legs pumping as fast as his wet pants and water soaked boots would allow. What little trail there was to follow turned away from the river, so he threw himself headlong through the aspens, scrub oak and brambles that kept snagging his clothes. Breaking out of the trees, he caught a glimpse of Leafy. In a burst of speed, he raced across a rocky stretch of dry river bed and flung himself into the water, catching Leafy by the collar of his coat.

"Leafy, hang on. I gotcha! I gotcha," he screamed in his ear. Leafy weakly lifted an arm. Daniel kicked at the river with his feet, but the pull of the river took a hold of him. Leafy was a dead weight and the drag from his boots and clothing pulled them both back into the swirling river.

"Help! Help! We're down here!" Daniel screamed. On the edge of panic, he fought the impulse to let go of Leafy and to save himself and looked for something to grab onto.

They were speeding up again. He heard someone running through the water behind him and with the last of his strength Daniel threw his arm backwards and was shocked when another hand clutched his by the wrist. With renewed energy, he willed himself to kick harder. To his relief, he felt himself and Leafy swinging into shallower, calmer water. He thought he heard a voice telling him that he could let go; but his fingers wouldn't work.

"You can let *gou no*," a strangely accented voice repeated. Daniel saw a face he did not recognize, though the man's broad smile and twinkling eyes convinced him to let go of Leafy's coat. Another man appeared, also unknown to Daniel, and waded into the river. Together, they grabbed Daniel by his arms and dragged him to shore. Lying on his side retching water, he watched helplessly as the two men carried Leafy out of the river and laid him over a large boulder. One of them began slapping Leafy on the back. Nothing happened on the first two whacks on his back, but on the third, what seemed like gallons of water came gushing out of Leafy's mouth. He began coughing and retching. Leafy was alive. Daniel fell onto his back and tried to stop the shaking that rattled every bone in his body and made his teeth chatter.

Leafy was lying on his side, still retching and coughing, when the rest of the fishing party came crashing through the trees. They seemed to know the strangers and exchanged nods as Carter came over to where Daniel was sitting and placed his coat around Daniel's shoulders

"What happened, son?" he asked, crouching down and handing him the whiskey bottle. Daniel drank deeply and felt the life flowing back into him. He began to calm down.

"L.L.Leafy s.s.lipped and he f.f.ell and h.hit his h.head on a r.r.ock," Daniel struggled to say. "I c.called out for you, but I.I. had to run after him before he drowned."

"You did good son," Carter said, patting Daniel on the shoulder. "Now let's see about getting you two warm and dry." Carter stood and joined the two strangers talking with Boot Hill. After their consultation, the two strangers hoisted Leafy to his feet as Carter introduced Daniel to his rescuers.

"Daniel, these two fellers are Tomas and Bjorn. They're going to help us get you two thawed out." Daniel tried to look grateful, but the best he could muster was a spasm of uncontrollable shivering.

Neither of the men spoke, just nodded, turned and led them off down a path away from the river. They hurried as fast as the muddy trail would allow, taking turns carrying Leafy. After a while, one of the two strangers left the group and trotted on ahead.

"Where are we going?" Daniel managed to ask.

"Them Swedes have a cabin down here. Bjorn has gone on to get the fire going." Carter looked at the afternoon sky. "It's going to get real chilly here in a while, but I don't think we have far to go." Another spasm of shivering came over Daniel. The cold seemed to be stiffening the blood throughout his entire body. Just when he thought he couldn't walk on his frozen feet anymore, they came upon a large log cabin with a welcoming plume of smoke billowing from the chimney. Bjorn opened the door as they approached and ushered them in.

"Get dem out of deir clozes," said Tomas. They laid Leafy on a couch in front of the blazing fireplace. While they undressed Leafy, someone else tugged at Daniel's clothing. Daniel couldn't have resisted even if he'd wanted to. The piercing cold had sapped every ounce of energy in him. Naked and shivering, he was wrapped in warm blankets. Slowly, he felt the blood starting to flow in him again. Someone handed him a cup of hot coffee heavily laced with whiskey and he drank deeply, letting its warmth course through him.

Leafy was barely conscious and still looked only half alive. His feet were blue up to his ankles, and he had a nasty red and blue knot growing on his forehead just above his eye. Tomas and Bjorn came back in, closing the door quickly behind them.

"I t'ink it is hot enough for dem noo," Tomas said. They motioned for him to follow Tomas, but Daniel tensed when he reached the door. Tomas must have felt him shiver, because he patted him on the shoulder gently.

"Don't you vorry. You vill be varm soon. OK?" Daniel faced the door reluctantly. "You run kvickly. Yes? Come." Tomas pulled the door open and pointed to a small building several yards away. Daniel felt a push from behind and ran for the small building. Tomas pushed the wooden door open, closing it quickly behind them. Daniel had never seen such a place as this, nor had he ever been in a room so hot.

"Dis is sauna. Sit here and I go and get yur friend." He broke into a huge smile. "If you vant hotter you pour vater on rocks, see?" Tomas used an iron ladle to scoop some water from the bucket on the floor and poured it on the hot rocks, setting them sizzling, clouding the tiny room with steam. He smiled once more and was gone. Daniel was left alone with the heat, steam, and the flickering light of the lamp.

The wool blanket was rough and itchy, but he found to his surprise that he could take it away from his shoulders and not be cold. He was warmer than he'd felt in months, but he shuddered and started to tremble again, violently. Memories of the rushing water sucking him into its deadly grasp surged back through him. With effort, he willed them away and stretched out on the lower of the two benches. He was drifting off to sleep when the door opened. Leafy was ushered in, sporting a clean white bandage around his head.

"How do you feel?" Daniel made a place for him on the bench.

"I feel stupid and my head hurts." Leafy lifted his hand to his eye and touched it gently. He winced in pain and pulled his blanket closer around him. "Why's it so darned hot in here?" Daniel poured more water on the rocks and the sizzle of the steam made Leafy jump. The door opened and Bjorn handed them each a mug of steaming liquid.

"Here, drink zis and come in vhen you are ready. You clothes are drying and you friends are not in a hurry to leave just yet." He said before closing the door behind him. They were alone now; the only sounds that of the sizzling water on the rocks and their teeth chattering. Daniel sniffed at the drink and made a face, hoping to make Leafy laugh, but there was no response.

"Thanks, Daniel," Leafy said solemnly. "You saved my life back there and I don't know how to thank you." Daniel tried to protest but Leafy held up his hand. "No. I really gotta say this. I don't know what happened. I just reached out for the net and the next thing I knew, I was floating down the river. I saw you running along, then I couldn't see you anymore and that's when I got scared. That's when I thought I was going to die." Leafy poured a little water onto the fire and contemplated the steam rising, reliving the terror.

"I thought I saw you again, but then I must have gone into a dream. I knew it was my time to die, and it was so peaceful. Not like my other dreams from the mine. It was different." Leafy looked intently at Daniel. Daniel smiled nervously. He knew that they were both lucky men.

The homemade brew tasted of old milk, but they drained their cups and lay back, letting the heat soak into their bones. Not surprisingly, they both dozed and woke with a start when Bjorn opened the door and motioned them to follow him back inside the main log building. They found their clothes dry and still warm from the fire, so they dressed and joined the others sitting in front of the large fireplace. Daniel and Leafy thanked Tomas and Bjorn profusely, but the brothers were painfully modest.

Embarrassed, Daniel absently looked around the large room for the first time. The more he saw, the more impressive the cabin became. Whereas Harry's cabin was basic; the Swedes' cabin was a hotel. The overhead beams that supported the roof flowed with intricate carved designs of bear, elk, and mountain sheep. The upright support columns were tree-trunks, smoothed, polished and also decorated. The intricate faces of birds and strange looking animals were carved on the knobby protrusions where the branches had been cut off.

Off in the corner of the room were lengths of shaped polished wood, twice a man's height, lined up neatly against the wall. Smiling at Daniel's interest, Bjorn carried two of these pieces of wood into the center of the room and placed them on the floor. He then used leather thongs to strap himself onto them and walked a few short paces forward and backwards. Abruptly, he crouched down then jumped off the ground and landed back in a crouch, grinning like a child.

"Dees here, are Norvegian snow shoes," Bjorn announced proudly. "Ve use dem in our country to valk across the snow." Bjorn unlaced himself and invited Daniel to try them. Delighted, Daniel stepped onto the contraptions and promptly fell sideways.

"Ja. Ja. And it is even more difficult on the snow," Tomas laughed.

"Bjorn and Tomas are the best in the valley on these things," Carter said. "They use them to ski into town and on the weekends, they race each other up and down the mountain. They're a little bit crazy, but they're the best I've ever seen." Boot and Sparky nodded in agreement.

Tomas seemed quite used to the praise, but Bjorn looked down at the floor and shuffled his feet, as a younger brother would.

"Hey. I'll teach you," said Bjorn, looking at Daniel.

"And you too, Leafy Lane," said Tomas. "I'll teach you."

"Ah, I already know. My dad taught me."

"Ja, Ja, I know your fahzer. I'm the von vhat taught him, you know?"

Leafy looked at Tomas skeptically.

"OK. OK. So, I'll teach dis young feller to ski faster than you." Bjorn said mischievously. He took Daniel's hand and shook it vigorously. "You vant to learn, I vill teach you, ja?"

"Ja, I guess," Daniel replied, not sure of what he'd gotten himself into.

"Well, boys," Carter said, draining his mug and placing it on the table. "I think I've had just enough of this sour milk for one sitting. What say we head back to town before they send out a search party to find us?"

They parted company, glowing from the hospitality and whatever it was that the two Swedes had poured for them. It was a more somber group that headed back to town that afternoon. Daniel and Leafy were still recovering from the shock of their near demise and the rest were contentedly drunk. The subject of the lost fish came up towards the end of the trip and to everyone's surprise, Sparky pulled a fish out of a jute bag slung from his saddle. At least now they would have something to break the monotony of the elk stew.

When they came to the fork where they went their different ways, Sparky handed a bag of fish to Leafy and put two big trout into Daniel's saddlebag.

"That was a pretty brave thing you did today, son." Sparky said to Daniel. "I know I was a bit tough on you earlier, but I want to let you know that you can come work with me and Leafy down in the hole anytime. Now get yourselves home, you two." Sparky smiled and Carter and Boot Hill waved them on their way.

At Joe's stable, Daniel unsaddled Marigold and patted Harry's horse on the rear as he led Marigold into the stall. He was tired to the bone, but as always, he took the time to rub down his horse, then filled her feed bucket. He was bringing her fresh water when he was startled by someone standing in the shadows. Joe emerged with his hands in his pockets, looking a little drunk. He considered Daniel, his expression somber.

"That was a brave thing you did today, son," Joe said, slurring a little.

"What do you mean?"

"Fetching Leafy out of the river like you did."

Daniel shrugged and felt his face flush. Leafy could hardly be home and already old Joe knew what had happened.

"You both could've been killed. That's a mean little stretch of river down through there." Joe sounded genuinely concerned. "But, I'm glad you did it, son." Joe took Daniel's hand and held it with both of his. "Thanks," he said gravely and gave Daniel one of his best toothless grins.

"Thanks, Joe," Daniel said to his retreating back.

"No problem. Goodnight, son."

Chapter 17

There was light coming from the cabin and smoke rose from the chimney. Daniel's teeth were chattering uncontrollably as he approached. Thoughts of food and the welcoming warmth of the oven were the only things that propelled him forward. Thinking of the great black beast with fondness, he shouldered the door open and half fell into the cabin.

"Where the hell've you been?" Harry said, while making a show of pushing his plate away from him. "We're not going to be partners long if I have to be doin' all the work." Harry stood up defiantly, reaching for his hat and coat. "I'll leave you to do the midnight shift." Harry pushed past, but stopped when he saw the bag Daniel held. He snatched it out of Daniel's hand and looked inside it. "Is that all the fish you got?" he sneered, throwing the bag of fish on the table and slamming the cabin door behind him.

Numb, drained and disheartened, Daniel took off his hat and coat and sat at the table staring absently at the dirty tin plate and the other remnants of Harry's dinner. An overwhelming weariness swept through his body. When he closed his eyes, he began shivering with visions that he was still floundering in the river. His head fell backwards, shocking him awake.

He had a couple of hours before he had to put the potatoes into the oven, so he pulled himself over to his bed and fell onto it. He didn't even bother to take his boots off; just pulled the blankets up and drifted into a shivery sleep.

Harry was still fuming when he reached the Paragon. It was a quiet night by the look of it, just mainly the local scruffs and itinerant gamblers passing the time, hustling each other. Harry was festering alone at the bar when Carter and Boot Hill pushed through the heavy wooden doors and sat a few stools away. Carter nodded to Harry, who was looking at him in the mirror.

"Harry. You seen your partner this evening?" Carter asked.

"Yeah, I just left the lazy little shit. You all didn't seem to catch much fish. Did Sparky forget the dynamite again?" Harry laughed at his witty remark.

"So he didn't tell you?" asked Boot Hill.

"Tell me what?"

"That he jumped into the river and saved Leafy's Lane's life this afternoon."

"He did what now?" Harry recoiled as Shirley joined them.

"What's going on with you boys tonight?" she purred.

"We were just telling Harry here how his young partner saved Leafy Lane from drowning today."

"What happened?" Harry and Shirley asked together.

Carter and Boot Hill took turns telling the story. When they came to the part where Sparky threw the lit fuse at Daniel, Shirley reprimanded them about their childish pranks. She was fond of Sparky, but over the years had seen him degenerate. When they had finished telling the story of the day's adventures, Shirley sat back in her chair and let out a sigh of relief.

"My God," Shirley said. "How lucky for Leafy. I couldn't imagine being the one to break the news to Shady and his wife. Could you imagine how hard it would be for them to lose another son?" She had a brief moment of reflection. "Did Daniel seem alright to you?" She looked at Harry critically. "Did you make him something hot to eat?" She lowered her chin and looked at Harry. "Come on, Harry, you said you talked to him."

Harry avoided her gaze, picking at something imaginary on his sleeve.

Shirley stood, hovering over Harry. "Harry Rich, you're disgraceful. That boy saved your miserable life. You don't deserve to have a friend like that young man." Carter and Boot Hill nodded in agreement when Shirley looked at them. "You're not expecting him to go out again tonight and peddle those rotten old potatoes of yours in the freezing cold, are you?"

Harry shrugged, as if his logic was his defense.

"You get yourself home right now and make sure that that boy is fed. After what he did today, I think you should go out there tonight and let the poor boy sleep." Shirley pointed to the door.

Harry sat in sullen non-motion. Shirley reached down and pulled him to his feet, not at all minding that her fingernails were cutting into the meat of his ear. He reached up to grab her hand, but she slapped his hand down and held onto his ear until he was standing. Carter and Boot touched their glasses together and toasted Harry's predicament.

"Oh no," Shirley said in a moment of understanding, "you don't have any food at home for the poor boy, do you Harry?"

"Well, we did send him home with a couple' a fish," Carter said with a smirk.

"That's just about enough out of you two," Shirley barked.

Carter and Boot Hill looked down at their drinks.

"You stay right where you are, Harry Rich," Shirley said, releasing Harry's ear. "I'm going to make sure that you feed that boy something decent for a change." She held Harry immobile with a pointed finger. Having ascertained that Harry was indeed staying put, she stormed off towards the kitchen.

"Thanks, fellers, that was real helpful," Harry said, as he fell back into his chair. "God Almighty, what got into her bloomers tonight?"

"Don't rightly know," Carter said with a shrug, "but we're glad it's you that she's pissed off at and not us. At least we can sit here and drink tonight," he said laughing.

"Well, she's not my wife, so she can't go tellin' me what to do," Harry said, finishing his whiskey and heading for the door.

"Harry Rich, you stop right there." Harry froze in his tracks. Shirley's voice could rival the noon whistle when necessary. She handed him a basket laden with food. "Now you get straight home and take care of that boy. He's a hero, isn't he, boys?"

Carter and Boot nodded dutifully and were rewarded with a look of unbridled hatred from Harry that set them both laughing again.

"Now you get going Harry, before that soup gets cold," Shirley said, escorting Harry to the door. In a gesture that surprised him, she touched Harry lightly on the arm as she opened the door for him. "Harry, I want you to give Daniel a message from me. I want you to tell him that Honey still wants to thank him. It's important to her. Will you have him go and visit her tomorrow afternoon?"

"Anything else? You're starting to sound like my wife."

Shirley gave him a smile as she pushed him out the door. "Make sure you feed him."

"Yeah, I'll give him a massage too."

"That would be nice," Shirley said, closing the door behind him.

Daniel was asleep when Harry came home so he loaded the oven and considered his dilemma. The food he'd brought from Shirley's was for Daniel, but he was sound asleep. It wouldn't be right to disturb him just for some soup. Harry dared a peek into the basket and from that moment his stomach set a course from which there was no turning back.

⊟⊟

Daniel awoke with a start.

"Good morning," Harry said pleasantly. Daniel found it unnerving. Harry sounded not the slightest bit angry that Daniel had failed to do the midnight shift. "I'm sorry I yelled at you last night." They were sitting at the small table across from each other, waiting for the coffee to boil.

"I'm sorry that I was late," Daniel replied.

"I heard about you saving Leafy from drowning yesterday. I'm proud of you." Harry poured coffee into the two tin cups. "How's about a little eye opener?" Harry produced a bottle of whiskey from under the table.

Daniel held his cup out, realizing as he did that it had been some time since he'd had a day without an eye opener. Whether Harry was there or not, whiskey had become a part of his daily routine. The liquid fire coursed through his body.

"Shirley cornered me last night and made me promise that you would go over to visit with the widow Bolon. Maybe if you time it right, you'll get invited to stay for supper. I hear she's a good cook." Harry smiled.

"What're you smiling at, Harry?"

"Oh, nothing. I was just thinking that I bet she's over her mourning by now and would appreciate the company, that's all." Harry got up from the table and emptied his cup outside the door.

Daniel resigned himself to visit a widow that he'd not even met.

"Maybe you could take her one of the fish. I'm sure she'd appreciate it." Harry reached into his pocket and handed Daniel a dollar. "Buy her some candy, too. If she don't want it, I bet her son will."

"Thanks," was Daniel's half-hearted reply. "Harry..." Daniel began to stutter, "w..when do we actually divide up the money?"

"Well, um." Harry cleared his throat. "Whenever you want your share, just tell me. We'll sit down right here and have ourselves a little reckoning. That OK with you?" Harry stood up angrily. "What's that look for? Just you remember that if it wasn't for me, you wouldn't have a business and you wouldn't have this nice warm place to sleep, either." Harry loomed over Daniel, his finger pointed in recrimination. "For all you know, you could be slaving in one of the mines if I hadn't taken you in."

"No...No, Harry, that's not what I was thinking. I...I'm grateful, I...I really am." Daniel stammered, as he always did when he was unsure of himself. "I...I was just thinking that if I had to leave in a hurry, would I be able to get my money in a hurry, too?"

Harry eyed Daniel suspiciously. "Why? Are you plannin' on goin' someplace?" Had Daniel noticed that someone had been into his private things and had seen into his life and knew his secrets? Harry hung his head as if grievously hurt. Daniel had to trust him completely for the rest of his plan to work. Above anything else, he had to be completely sure. He tended the potatoes for a while before speaking again.

"What's the matter, don't you trust me?" He put his hands on his hips and leaned closer to Daniel, jaw clenched in aggravation. "Why did I go to all that trouble to show you my secret, then?" He turned his back to Daniel, hiding his smile, then wheeled around, pointing his finger into Daniel's chest. "And now you don't trust me? Sometimes I wonder if we really are friends." Harry sat down at the table and began drawing on a piece of butcher's paper. "Here's how to get to Honey's place." Harry folded the paper and pushed it across the table. "I'm sure you'll have a good old time," he said as he brushed past Daniel. "Oh, and by the way," Harry said as he opened the door, "you might ask Red if he's in need of a hand. I could do with a break from you."

With that, Harry was gone. Daniel's stomach turned over and he felt light headed. It was the same feeling that knotted his stomach when he felt the boat finally let go its last connection to the shore, casting them adrift, taking them away from their home. He collapsed back down into his chair and sat there, feeling lost and sad. How was it possible, when things were going so well, that he could've messed it all up in just a couple of minutes?

He was absently looking at the oven and wondering if he could remember the way Harry had arranged the chains when a thought struck him. In a panic, he fell onto his knees and searched under the bed. His pack was there, but something wasn't quite right.

He'd made a habit of always putting the pack back under his bunk with the buckles down on the floor. That way, the pack would have to be turned over so that the thief could undo the straps. It was something that he'd done since he'd been robbed in Leadville. Now the pack was on its back, buckles facing up. He fell on his bed and tried his best to overcome the fear and the panic.

⌘

Finished with his work and hungry, Daniel went to the White Kitchen for breakfast. Miss Hickory greeted him warmly and poured him coffee. The cook waved his cigar at him. Harry was there, sitting at a large round table with his back to him, talking and laughing with several miners.

"What's the matter, honey? Harry in a bad mood again?"

Daniel shrugged and looked into his coffee for consolation. "I think he's upset with me for something I did."

Hickory placed her hand lightly on Daniel's arm. "Forget about it. If I know Harry Rich, and I do definitely know Harry Rich, he'll get over it. He'll be over it in two whiskeys, I bet. Have you been over to see Honey yet? You should go over there. She's nice and she's been looking forward to meeting you. She's heard a lot about you and she's a good cook. Maybe she'll even feed you." Hickory was smiling in the same knowing way that others had smiled when talking about Mrs. Bolon.

"Harry said I should pick up some candy."

"That Harry," she said, looking over at Harry sitting at the other table, "he sure knows how to treat a lady. Someone over there will eat it, you can bet."

⊰⊱

It was quiet at Joe's stable. Only the shuffling of the horses could be heard. Marigold shook her head in greeting and rubbed against him as he fed her carrots, saddled her up and walked her outside into the brilliant sunshine. Following Harry's map, he crossed the river and climbed up a short hill where soon he was riding in the warm sunshine again. It was a glorious fall day and there was no need to hurry. After all; only a fool hurries to his execution.

Honey's place was closer to town than he'd thought. It was a well-made, solid, two story log cabin nestled in a thick patch of Aspen trees.

Tentatively, he knocked on the door, hoping that no one would be home. His feeling of dread rose as he heard footsteps approaching. To his surprise, the door was opened by a boy of eight or nine.

"Hello, my name is Daniel Carrington. I'm here to see Mrs. Bolon. Is she here?" Daniel asked politely.

The boy tilted his head and appraised Daniel. "I'll go get her," the boy replied and closed the door. Daniel was left on the doorstep, shuffling his feet. He heard more footsteps.

When the door opened again, Daniel was startled to see an attractive woman whose eyes were either the palest blue or the softest gray he'd ever seen. She was slender when compared to most of the women in town and instead of a dress she wore blue pants held in place with a belt of hammered silver discs. Her hair was pulled back and tied with a scarf that accentuated the long curve of her neck.

"My name is Daniel Carrington and I wanted to pay my respects to Mrs. Bolon. I was there when her husband was hurt."

"Please come on in," she said, closing the door behind him then leading the way into the living room. A warm, sweet aroma of bread baking filled the house.

He took a deep breath and cleared his throat to control his stutter. "Is Mrs. Bolon here?"

"Yes, she is," she said and smiled. "Please sit down and I'll get you some coffee." She turned and walked into the kitchen with a sway of her hips that captured all of his attention.

As he sat on a dark green velvet covered couch, the young boy, who Daniel imagined was her son, sat silently watching him.

"What's your name?" Daniel asked. The boy responded by looking down at the floor.

The boy's mother busied herself in the kitchen and as he watched her, he found himself smiling at nothing in particular, but became aware that his hands were caressing the smooth, carved wooden arms of the couch. She must be Mrs. Bolon's daughter, he thought, or some other relative come to help the old woman in these difficult days.

Smiling her strange smile, she came back into the living room carrying a tray which held a small coffee pot, cups and a bowl for sugar. She had taken off her head-scarf and her hair was pulled back. As she bent over to place the tray on the table, Daniel caught a hint of the curve of her breasts under her thin white camisole.

She looked up and caught him staring. Instead of being offended, she smiled at him.

"Thank you for the coffee, ma'am," Daniel said in his best Yankee accent, which prompted the boy to snigger behind his hand. "I just came by to pay my respects to Mrs. Bolon."

"You didn't really have to do that, Mr. Carrington," she said, as she walked back into the kitchen.

"Please call me Daniel."

"I just made some hard-timers, would you like one?" Daniel saw the boy nod his head enthusiastically as she returned to the kitchen.

"Yes, please. I don't know if I've ever had them before, but they smell delicious. Is Mrs. Bolon here? Because I can come back tomorrow if it's not a good time." Daniel felt his awkwardness returning, but it dissipated as soon as she appeared carrying a plate stacked with her freshly made cakes.

"No," she said, handing Daniel the plate of cakes so as to make space for them on the table. "This is a perfect time for you to visit Mrs. Bolon." She held out her hand formally for him to take. "I'm pleased to meet you, Mr. Carrington. I'm Honey Bolon." Daniel's mouth fell open as he took her hand and felt the warmth of her flesh. She smiled at his expression but did not pull her hand away.

"Momma, can I have one?" The boy interrupted, coming to her side and holding onto her hand.

"This is my son, Jackson. Jack, this is Mr. Carrington." The boy held out his hand and Daniel shook it as firmly as the young boy did.

"I'm pleased to meet you, sir," Jack said in a voice that matched his manly handshake.

"You can call me Daniel if you want. It's nice to meet you too, Jackson."

"You can call me Jack," he replied. "Can I have one now, please?" He begged his mother.

"Go ahead, but leave room for your dinner."

Jack placed one of the thick biscuits on a plate and the aroma of sweet dried fruits rose into the room. He carefully spooned strawberry jam onto each half of his cake before returning to his corner to devour his treat. Daniel was impressed with the boy's manners.

Honey prepared one of the cakes with butter and jam and handed it to Daniel on a small plate. He couldn't remember anyone ever having done that for him before.

"Dangerous taught me to make these. He told me they used to live on them during the war." As she spoke, she looked deeply into Daniel's eyes in a way that made him feel naked and vulnerable. Feeling his face blush, he dropped his eyes and involved himself with the cake in front of him.

After the first taste, he became as hungry as a bear. The sweet strawberry summer jam on top of the smoothness of the freshly churned butter created in him an eating monster with a voracious appetite. He ate enthusiastically, but eventually he slowed down and only then noticed that he'd eaten all but one of the cakes that had been on the plate. Suddenly embarrassed, he looked up and saw that Honey was smiling at him. When he looked over at Jackson, he saw that the boy was watching him with a look of amazement on his face.

"You must'a been really hungry Mister Daniel. I can barely eat one of them hard-timers and you just about finished off the whole plate of 'em."

"Mr. Carrington was with Dangerous when he had his accident, Jack." Honey refilled Daniel's cup. Jack stopped eating for a moment and considered Daniel anew before returning to his cake.

"Were you there when Dangerous saved all the men and the horses?" Jack asked when he'd finished eating.

Daniel noticed that Honey stiffened slightly. He knew what the boy expected to hear. Hadn't he also lionized his father when he was a boy?

"Yes, Jackson. He was very brave and he saved me from going over the cliff. Someone's probably told you the story already, I doubt you want to hear it all again."

"Oh yes, I do."

"Well, before I do, I almost forgot something." Daniel went outside and returned with a sack. "I brought you some fish." He held out the sack to Honey, who opened it and peeked inside.

"Look here Jackson, some nice, big trout." Jackson made a face and went back to the remnants of his biscuit. "He's not a big fish eater. Are you a fisherman?"

Daniel forced a smile at the thought of his fishing experience. "No, I just went along with some friends and they caught them in a net."

"Well, they look very nice. Thank you."

"And," Daniel added, reaching into his coat pocket, "I brought a little something, if anyone here likes candy." Jackson rushed over and reached for the bag.

Honey gently took his hand away. "Jackson," she said sternly, "you'll spoil your dinner." Jackson looked crestfallen and stuck out his lower lip. "OK, but just one," she said relenting.

Jackson gazed into the bag considering his choice and took out a toffee, then retreated to his chair and became involved in pulling the paper wrapper off. She offered the bag to Daniel who reluctantly took a toffee and ate it with similar gusto.

With Jackson at his feet, he told the story and hoped he was convincing for the sake of all concerned. The story, like the runaway wagon, gathered momentum. Daniel became enthusiastic, re-enacting the unfortunate accident. In his version of the events, Dangerous was the one who jumped onto the wagon while it was racing down the hill and was responsible for steering the wagon away from the others, saving their lives. He told how Dangerous climbed over all of the boxes to wake Harry Rich, and how he leapt off over the side so that he and Harry could save themselves.

Daniel sprinted on about how Dangerous had rushed to the aid of the other men. It was only when all of the men were attended to that he realized that he was hurt, too. It was a total fabrication of the real events, but Daniel hoped to construct a story plausible enough that Jackson would feel that his father was a hero.

Honey touched his arm and when he looked at her, he noticed the tear that slowly edged itself from the corner of her eye and made its way across her cheekbone.

The spell was broken when she took out a small white lace handkerchief, dabbed at her eyes then touched it to the tip of her chin. "Well, that was exciting," Honey said. "Would you like to stay for dinner?" she asked, brightening. "I'm sure you would be welcome to join us, wouldn't he, Jackson?"

Jackson smiled a sticky grin and nodded energetically at both Daniel and the bag on the table. Clever little devil, Daniel thought.

He remembered Harry and looked out of the window, noting the shadows that were falling across the town. It must be getting close to the time to start cooking the potatoes. "I'm sorry Mrs. Bolon, but I have to get back to work," he said and stood to leave.

Honey remained seated. "Well then, would you like to come to-morrow night?" she said, looking at her son. "Perhaps we'll have the fish." Jackson wrinkled his nose.

With a hopeful smile, she came around the table and linked her arm through Daniel's and walked him to the door. "What do you say to my invitation? Interested in having dinner with the widow Bolon and her son?" They'd stopped in the narrow hall and she reached out and took his hand in hers, looking up at him.

"Yes, thank you Mrs. Bolon. I've never had trout," he said.

"Call me Honey. Everyone else does," she said as she opened the door. Marigold was looking directly at him, jealous already. "Wait just a moment will you?" Honey walked back into the house and returned with a small bundle. "Here, take some more of these. You might get hungry on the way home." She handed him a bundle of warm biscuits tied in the scarf she'd been wearing earlier.

"I'll bring your scarf back tomorrow," Daniel said as he placed them carefully in his saddlebag.

"Make sure that you bring your appetite," she said, and waved as he turned Marigold down the hill.

Chapter 18

The cabin was hot but empty when Daniel arrived. The oven was bare and the wagon gone. He put the cakes into a biscuit tin, slid it under his bed and hurried to the mountain.

Harry was there already. He'd gone to work early and passed the time joking with the other food vendors. Harry was in a good mood. Now that there was snow on the ground, he could soon begin pulling their potatoes to the hill in the sleds. The new sled was almost finished and it was a big improvement over his old one. Joe had added metal strips on the runners and a stronger frame, making it much heavier. Strength was more important than weight, especially since he wasn't planning on being the one doing the pulling. It just had to get them over the Pass and back.

Daniel's heroism began to fester in Harry's mind. Whenever someone mentioned the bravery of his young partner, it fueled his anger. This young buck was new to Aspen and he was the one getting respect from the miners and from many others in town, also. When Daniel arrived, Harry made it a point to push him aside as he reached into the canvas bag for potatoes. "You finally decided to show up, did you?" Harry snapped.

Harry remained stubbornly silent for the rest of the morning. When the parade of miners ended, Daniel packed up their gear and as usual, Harry scooped up the money from the cigar box and put it all into his pocket.

"Did you go over to see Honey like I asked you to?" Harry said testily. Daniel nodded. "Good. You can take this stuff back to my cabin and we'll talk later." Harry's tone softened. "Look here Daniel, I'm not pissed off at you. It's just that we're not making as much money as I thought we would."

"All r.r.right, H.H.Harry, I'm sorry I'm letting you down. I'll go see Red tomorrow."

"Listen," Harry said, edging closer for sincerity's sake. "I just think that if you worked with him once in a while, it would be better. I'm not saying you should work for him full-time, but I'm sure that he's going to need some help over the next few weeks and I think you can help us both out."

"Sure." Daniel nodded.

Harry reached out to pat Daniel on the shoulder. Daniel flinched, expecting a blow.

"I'm not going to hurt you," Harry said, surprised by Daniel's reaction. "I'm trying to help you. You understand that, don't you?" Harry's voice had turned gently seductive. It worked as usual.

"Yeah, I understand." Daniel was relieved they'd avoided a fight in public and hurriedly finished loading the wooden slats onto their wagon.

"Don't wait up for me, OK?" Harry said as he strode off, headed into town. Daniel watched him leave, finished packing their things and headed home.

When he entered the cabin, he was surprised to find a basket of food sitting on the table. Attached was a note from Shady Lane and his wife saying how much they were indebted to him for saving their son's life and that he was welcome at their home at any time. Inside was a covered pot of stew and a loaf of fresh bread. Stew was the usual fare of the miner's diet. It was easy to cook, lasted well, and could be constantly fortified as new ingredients appeared. This smelled like no ordinary miner's stew.

He arranged the food around his chair and set himself a place at the table. Solemnly, he joined his hands together and said a prayer of gratitude. After three servings of stew, the sound of his spoon scraping the bottom of the tin plate signaled that he had done justice to Mrs. Lane's cooking.

When he could move again, he heated a pan of water on the oven top to wash the dishes. Without giving it another thought, he pulled Harry's bottle from under the counter and poured an inch or two of whiskey into a cup, filling it up to the rim with stale coffee.

As the whiskey warmed his body and soul, he reached back into the day and savored the warm excitement he felt when he thought about Honey. He just couldn't get her out of his mind, nor the embarrassment he felt when he realized that she was the widow of the late Dangerous Bolon. In particular, he remembered the shape of her neck and the pale color of the skin. He began to get aroused just thinking about her breasts.

If Harry didn't come home right away, he would be able to take care of his needs without interruption. He poured more whiskey into his cup, not bothering with the coffee and sipped the sweetly bitter liquid until the cup was empty.

He fumbled about the small kitchen, putting the remaining food on the edge of the oven. It would stay warm till morning when breakfast would be a repeat of dinner. After making a one-eyed perusal of the room, he rolled onto his bed and found himself laughing as he wrestled with his clothing. He realized that he was more than slightly drunk after he tried to take off his pants without first taking off his boots. When he tried to lean over to get them, he fell off the bed face-first onto the floor.

With difficulty, he pushed himself back onto the bed and pulled the curtain before he laid back with a smile and a dream of Honey's milky white breasts. He passed out with his problem well in hand.

He awoke before dawn and the two things he noticed when he pulled the curtain back were that Harry had not come home, and that his head pounded like an empty steel drum. Just lifting his head caused blinding pain behind his eyes. The thought of leaning down to pull on his boots sent a wave of nausea through his stomach.

Gritting his teeth in determination, he forced himself to stand, but had to sit back down quickly and hang onto the bed until the room stopped spinning. The bottle on the table was empty. He hoped that Harry had finished it, but knew in his heart that it was his own doing. Guilt came home to roost in him like an owl to its barn.

While he waited for the coffee to boil, he returned the empty whiskey bottle to its hiding place, almost throwing up as he did. He'd have to replace the whiskey and hope that Harry wouldn't notice what he'd done. With small painful movements, he went about winching more of the great log into the fire and was stacking the potatoes in the oven when the door burst open and Harry lurched through it, bringing half of the winter with him.

He fell back against the door, his head on his chest, eyes closed. Using maximum effort and gravity, Harry peeled himself away from the door and reached for the table but missed, knocking a chair over and hitting his head on the edge of the table as he fell. Harry's body convulsed as he put his hand over his mouth. He seemed oblivious as Daniel pulled him roughly outside and steadied him until the retching finally ended.

"I need some coffee," Harry mumbled as Daniel led him back inside.

Daniel poured him some then went to the door to sweep out the snow that Harry had dragged in with him. Harry reached for the bottle.

"Harry, you should eat something," Daniel said.

"Nah, I just want another drink. I'll be alright." Harry found the bottle and held it up close to his face. He looked from the empty bottle to Daniel and back to the empty bottle, the silence thick in the room.

"Ssshit," was all Harry said. "Whady'a say you do…" Harry paused and attempted to form a sentence. "Shit… morning… you do it and we'll call it even, OK?" Harry continued breathing deeply, eyes closed. Daniel helped him to his bed.

He was still asleep, snoring loudly, when Daniel returned from his shift. He moved about quietly so as not to wake Harry, grabbed the rest of the hard-timers, then headed to the stable.

"Shady dropped off some food last night. Did Harry eat it all?" Joe called out when he saw Daniel enter the stable.

"No, I ate it before he could."

"I guess he did some serious drinking again last night." Joe snickered.

"Well, he's looking pretty bad."

"That's Harry for ya'. Oh, well, no problem." Daniel saddled Marigold and led her outside while Harry's horse watched them with thinly veiled animal jealousy.

The ride out to Red's ranch was pleasant and relaxing, though Daniel had much to think about. The snow from the night before muffled the sound of the hooves. It was a dreamlike ride as the clouds thinned and the weak sunshine warmed the valley. He tied Marigold to the rail and headed for the side door, which creaked on its squeaky hinges when he opened it.

"Howdy there, young feller, how you been doin'?" Pete yelled when he saw it was Daniel entering the barn. Pete shook his hand roughly. "What're you doin' all the way out here? Get lost, did ya'? I thought you city fellers got skittish away from all them fine city women and all that easy livin'?"

"How's everything, Pete?"

"Well, if you ask me, things don't look too hot. They say they're almost all the way through Glenwood Canyon and there's talk of trains coming through by next spring. That would pretty much put us out'a business." Pete smiled bravely. "But till then, we're up to our necks in crap to load and crap to haul. 'You come out here looking for a job by any chance?" Pete asked casually.

"W.w.w.well, I was w.w.wondering...." Daniel began and was slapped heartily on the back by Pete before he could finish.

"Well, ain't that a bit of good news," Pete said, smiling broadly. "And I think it's about time, too. I always thought you should throw your lot in with us and try your luck at some adventure. Oh, yeah, I forgot. You've already seen some of that adventure part of the job, haven't you?" Pete laughed out loud, shaking Daniel's hand vigorously.

"Is Red here?" Daniel tried to keep his nervousness out of his voice.

"Sure he is. He's back there in his office, worrying how to keep us all in business. It looks like we'll be busy for the next month or so." Pete raised his finger to his lips. "Don't let on I told, will ya? It's supposed to be some kind of secret. Got something to do with Jerome Wheeler and his new fancy hotel, I hear. Next thing you know, he'll be naming the whole darned town Wheelerville."

"Come on son, let's see if Red remembers you," Pete said, steering Daniel to the back office. Pete slapped his hand on the wall. "Got time for a visitor, Red?" Red sat at his desk, spectacles resting on the edge of his nose and looked up from whatever it was that he was reading.

"Well, come on in here, young feller," he said, motioning Daniel to sit. "How're things in the potato business? Harry treating you decent?" Red nodded for Pete to leave.

"See you two later," Pete said, taking his cue.

"How about some coffee?" Without waiting for an answer, he followed Pete out of the office.

While Red was fetching the coffee, Daniel wandered around, looking at the photographs on the wall. He found himself standing in the doorway to Red's bedroom. One small window allowed the sun to stream into the room at a steep angle, lighting the dust particles floating in the air. The narrow single bed was neatly made. Next to it was a small, delicate table holding a lamp with an ornate lampshade patterned of cut colored glass and a framed picture of a woman holding a child. Daniel turned back to find Red already sitting back at his desk, seeming untroubled by Daniel's inspection of his personal life.

"So how're things going?" Red enquired. Daniel shrugged. "Things with Harry a bit tense, are they?"

"Well, he's not easy to live with, if that's what you mean. He wants me to see if I can work for you for a while."

Red leaned back in his chair and laced his hands behind his head, his eyes locked on the young man sitting across from him. "Did he say why he wanted you to work for me?"

Daniel shrugged again and looked at his hands. "He remembered that you offered me a job."

"Do you think you can handle working with us? The hours are long and sometimes you won't get back home for a couple of days if the weather turns bad. And it will, I can guarantee that. But I guess I don't need to tell you about the danger." Red laughed, "I seem to remember that you had some first-hand experience in that area."

Daniel relaxed and smiled.

"I pay pretty well and I make sure that my men are fed better than anyone in this valley," Red said proudly. "But I gotta be honest with you, I can't offer you much of a future here." Daniel noted a hint of sadness both in Red's voice and in his eyes. "The rail line is coming through next year. I believe that will more or less put us out of the business." Red forced a smile. "But until then, I could certainly use a reliable hand. What do you say to all of that, now that you've heard the worst? Still interested?"

"Thanks, Red," Daniel said gratefully. "I'll try to do my best."

Red stood and came around the table smiling broadly. "I know you will. So, when can you start? I have a special consignment for Jerome Wheeler coming over in the next few weeks and I'd like to have the same team of men escort it. By the way, do you know how to use a pistol?"

"No, I've never fired one."

"Well, don't worry about that. I'll show you how."

"Am I goin' to need to use one?"

"Never had to so far," Red knocked his knuckles on his wooden desk. "It's just a precaution. But it never hurts to look like you'll use it and know how. You do know what we carry, don't you?"

"No, not really. I thought you just carried the stuff that they sell in the stores here in town."

"Yes, we do that, but we have to make money both ways, so we take things from here over there, too. We take the silver that they mine here over to the bank in Leadville a couple of times a week. I can't imagine too many people being interested in trying to carry off a ton of silver between here and Leadville, but you never can be too sure about the dishonest mind. Someone might be thinking about how to do just that, right now." Red clapped Daniel on the back and steered him out the door into the cavernous space of the barn. "Hey, Pete, we've got a new recruit here. Do you want to teach him the ropes?"

Pete smiled broadly and touched his finger to the brim of his hat. "If I can teach Dutch, I'm sure I can teach this smart youngster."

"Say there, Daniel," Red said. "I was thinking that if you had the time and Harry wouldn't miss you too much, you could come over with us today. I could use the help. We'd be back sometime tomorrow. Are you interested?"

Honey had invited him to dinner. The thought of seeing Honey again was drawing him strongly, but this was an opportunity that he shouldn't miss. "Sure, Red. But Marigold doesn't have winter shoes."

Pete lifted Marigold's hoof. "Well, I do believe that someone has taken care of that for you already."

Daniel went over and looked down at the newly shod hoof. He hadn't noticed before, but she had new shoes complete with winter cleats. Pete was looking amused and quite pleased with himself.

"Someone must have shod her." The penny dropped into the slot in his mind. "Ooh...." he said, realizing what they'd done for him. "You knew that I was going to come out here and ask you for a job."

Red smiled. "Well, let's say that I was hoping that you'd come to your senses someday. I also had the vet look her over and he said that for her age, she was in good condition and would probably outlast both Pete and me."

Red put his arm heavily around Daniel's shoulder. Dutch strolled over and shook Daniel's hand, his big grin betraying his participation in the conspiracy.

"That was a pretty brave thing you did for Shady's boy the other day," Dutch said. "Pete and I heard about it and you know, we weren't that surprised that you'd do something like that, were we Pete?" Pete shook his head. "So are you throwing in with us then?"

Daniel looked around at each of them in turn. Red, Pete and Dutch had the same mischievous gleam in their eyes. He bit his lip as if in thought, though his decision had been made. He nodded and was instantly saluted in welcome by light punches on the shoulder.

He would recall this specific moment often in his future years and with it a wonderful feeling camaraderie; of being swept along in a river of risk and fate, of being invited to go on an adventure.

"Good then," Red said. "We all ready to head out, Pete?"

"We sure are, Red. The horses are saddled and waiting."

"Then let's get going before this day's wasted. You could've helped us by getting out here sooner, son."

"Did you really know I was coming out here?" Daniel asked.

Pete said nothing and headed out to the back of the barn, leaving Daniel to wonder. He came back a moment later and handed Daniel a gun belt. Both Red and Pete were strapping theirs on, so he did the same. He felt transformed into one of the characters from his dime novels. He began to pull the pistol out of its holster and immediately felt a powerful hand on his arm.

"Careful," said Pete. "It's loaded. We don't pull out our guns unless we're cleaning them or shooting them." Daniel took the admonishment as advice to be remembered.

Red looked up at the sky, reading the sun and the clouds with a knowing look. "It looks like the weather's going to hold, but we should get a move on."

The sunlight filtering through the naked branches was warm on their faces. Crossing the river at the Devil's Punchbowl, they rode single file along the narrow road that had been carved out of the cliff face. Daniel hugged the inner edge, nearest to the cliff wall.

"We usually give the horses a breather about here," Red announced for Daniel's sake when they came to a place where the road leveled out. Daniel was as glad as Marigold for the chance to rest. For lunch, they ate elk jerky and apples and Pete had brought enough apples to share with their horses.

"We're on the last flat piece of road here, so we'll ride a bit faster and when it gets steep again, we'll slow down. Are you sore yet?" Red asked Daniel.

"No, I'm fine so far." Daniel was feeling some soreness in his thighs, but kept it to himself. They rode together at a trot without speaking and after a few miles the road crossed a small stream and veered upwards. The trees were short and stunted here, and ahead of them, they stopped growing completely.

Passing through the town of Independence, they were hailed by several people who waved, but kept about their business. The road ascended steeply towards the summit and they passed scattered bits and pieces of the runaway wagon protruding through the snow. It was slow going and the horses' heads bobbed up and down with each step. The road flattened out as they neared the summit and the horses slowly increased their speed.

Red turned in his saddle. "Your horse handled that well, Daniel. She's a good one. What's her name?"

"Marigold was the name she came with, and I didn't see the point of confusing her with another one," he replied.

"Makes sense to me. We'll stop up here a'ways and give them a rest."

The sun came out from behind a scudding cloud and the reflection off the snow was so blindingly bright, Daniel had to hold his hands up over his eyes and look between his fingers. Just as suddenly as the clouds had parted, they again covered the sun. The pain in his eyes lessened, but the wind gathered the snow from the ground and swirled it around and into his eyes, stinging like sharp needles.

When they dismounted, both horses and riders stood leaning against each other as if neither had the will or the energy to move forward.

"Put these on son, they'll help." Red handed Daniel a pair of eye covers made of two wooden discs with slits cut into them. Stitched into a leather mask that covered his face down to the nose, they were then tied around the head with a thin leather strap. With his hat tied tightly under his chin and the scarf wrapped across his face, he almost disappeared from view.

They rode as fast as the conditions would allow. Though riding down-hill, at times both horse and rider had to heave together to push against the gale force wind which tore at Daniel's face, froze his fingers and forced its way into every gap in his clothing. When they gained the trees, the fury of the wind lessened. Looking about him, Daniel saw a breathtaking view. No matter which direction he looked, there were peaks lining the highest reaches, all enclosed by a layer of flossy clouds forming a canopy over the entire valley.

Both the horses and their riders reveled in the ease of their descent as the shadows stretched their long arms deeper and deeper into the valley below. Passing places he recognized, Daniel found himself struggling to place in order all the things that had happened since the first time he'd ridden along this road.

They came to the outcropping of hillock and fences where the reloading of the wagons happened, and Red stopped to check that all was in order. They let their horses drink from the stream and passed around some more of Pete's seemingly inexhaustible supply of elk jerky. Red pulled on the fences and checked into the small sheds and on his way back, he lined up several empty peach cans on the top rail of one of the fences.

"Let me see that pistol of yours, son," Red said, taking Daniel's pistol from him and spinning the cylinder to check that it was loaded. He turned and the pistol exploded with a report that shook Daniel's teeth. One of the cans jumped into the air and flew six feet.

"You still got it, Red," Pete said.

Red was stone faced as he deftly reversed the pistol and handed it to Daniel butt-first, pointed at the ground. Daniel took the pistol and placed his finger on the trigger. Red gripped his hand, vice-like. "First thing Daniel, always point it away from you. Ain't that right Pete?"

"Sure is, you only have to shoot yourself in the leg once to know why that's a good piece of advice." Pete rubbed his thigh.

"Here, son, this is how you hold it." Red walked behind Daniel and with his left hand on Daniel's left shoulder, gripped his right hand. The gun came up and fired. The noise and the recoil took him by surprise and he could feel his arm tingling. Another of the cans flew backwards. Daniel was as excited as he'd ever felt in his life as he let the heavy pistol pull his hand down by his side. He looked questioningly at them. "Look at the target, point the pistol at it and pull the trigger all in one movement. Go on now." Red stepped back a pace.

Daniel turned to face the cans and slowly lifted the barrel. He sighted along the barrel and fired. He missed.

"Not bad, but if someone was shooting at you, I don't think that you'd be alive to get another shot. Make the first one quick and don't bother aiming, just point the thing as quick as you can and pull the trigger. Just pick it up and fire it."

Daniel turned back to the cans and in a fluid movement, lifted the gun from his holster and pulled the trigger. The ground in front of him exploded.

"Try to get it all the way up next time."

A strange sensation came over him, like he was looking at himself from somewhere else. He watched himself snap the pistol up and fire. One of the cans spun up into the air. Pete and Red applauded.

"Now do the same thing to the rest of them," Pete yelled.

Daniel wheeled around, swinging the gun up, sending another can into the air. He repeated the same movement until the hammer clicked. "Weren't there supposed to be six in here; or didn't I count right?"

Red came over and opened his own pistol to show Daniel that one of the chambers was empty. "We keep the chamber under the hammer empty. On account of we don't want to accidentally shoot ourselves while we're riding. Do we, Pete?"

"I wish I'd met you sooner." Pete rubbed his thigh again.

"How did I do?"

Pete nodded and Red shook his hand. "Not bad for a beginner. Now, let's get going."

They mounted and headed down into the darker shadows of the valley evening. Daniel sat tall in his saddle, elated and proud.

Chapter 19

They reached Twin Lakes as the sun was spraying its final glow on the far end of the valley. Tired and hungry from the ride over the Pass, they unsaddled at Red's place, where a corral enclosed a barn and a small bunkhouse on the lakeside of the road across from a large hunting lodge.

Red pulled the saddle off of his horse and hefted it onto the top rail of the fence. "Pete, I want you and Daniel to turn out the horses and check the stock. See if we're ready to get out of here first thing tomorrow, then come on over to the Lodge. OK?"

"Sure 'nough. Say there, Red. Are we staying in the bunkhouse tonight?"

Red laughed and clapped Pete on the shoulder. "Well now Pete, I've been thinking about that and I reckon we should stay at the Lodge tonight." Pete smiled as Red knew he would. "No good scaring the young feller here with the accommodations in the bunkhouse on his first trip."

"Come on. Let's check the wagons. We've got valuable cargo to take back tomorrow." Pete looked sideways at Daniel and winked.

"What're we bringing back that's so valuable?"

"You'll see what I mean when the time comes," Pete said, a mysterious smile creasing his weathered face.

Daniel followed as Pete checked the wagons, making sure that the wheels were snug on their axles, greased and that the brakes were working. Next, he checked the yokes fore and aft of the wagons. Satisfied, he moved to the harness racks and methodically counted the groups of leather in tangles along the wall.

"This here is what we always do before we ever set them horses into one of these contraptions." The harnesses were complicated, but as he checked their condition, Pete patiently explained the purpose of each part in order. What seemed complicated at first was just a logical set of tack that kept the horses bound together. "It's a terrible thing to have one of these horses hurt just because we didn't do our job right. We need them to trust us. Now, let's get this gear put away and then we'll go eat."

⊲⊳

The Lodge was built of mortared river rocks and logs with three garret windows on the second floor that looked out over the road and the lakes. The cozy warmth and the smells of cooking hit them as soon as they walked in the door. They hung up their hats and coats and entered a large comfortable living area with a dining table and stuffed couches facing a blazing fireplace. Red was collapsed in a deep leather chair facing the fire. With effort, he lifted his head from the headrest at their approach. "Everything in order, Pete?"

"Yep. That Newly feller seems to be doing his job. The horses look good and the wagons are in good shape. I was thinkin' that we should use other horses to go to Leadville and save ours for the trip back. We might be pushing them a little hard if we take them both ways."

"That makes sense," Red said looking into the fire. "They're not as young as they used to be."

"Neither are we." Pete replied.

"How're you feeling, young feller?" Red asked Daniel.

"Hungry." Daniel rubbed the stiffness from his thighs.

"Well, we'll take care of that soon enough. I've ordered us some beefsteaks and then I recommend a good night's sleep. We've a long ride tomorrow. Pete, why don't you show the young feller which room is his so he can wash up?"

"It's the one at the end of the hall," said a smiling Gloria as she swanned into the room carrying four bottles of beer. She was as beautiful as Daniel remembered. "Well, well. If this isn't a nice surprise? I never thought I'd be setting my eyes on you again." Gloria seemed to float towards him. "Your name's Daniel, isn't it?"

Daniel nodded.

She placed the bottles of beer on the low table and when she bent over, Daniel couldn't help but watch her shape pushing against the bodice of her dress. Red and Pete exchanged knowing glances.

"It's nice to see you again, especially so soon." Gloria playfully pinched Daniel's cheek and winked at Red and Pete. "We don't get too many pretty boys in these parts much anymore."

"I would've thought that me and Pete would be enough for you in that department," Red said pointedly.

Pete poured two whiskeys, one for him and one for Daniel. Pete swallowed his in one gulp, but Daniel left his on the table.

"I got an idea." Gloria put her finger to her lips. "Why don't one of you handsome fellers come over here some night and just whisk me away?"

"What? And make you leave all of this?" said Red.

"For all you know, I'd just jump into your arms." She came down heavily in his lap, making Red groan. "You know I sleep downstairs you old fox?" She pulled Red's face into her bosom.

He pushed her away. "You're just too much woman for an old man like me, Gloria. Now, Pete here, he's always had a soft spot for you."

"The thought never crossed my mind, I swear," Pete lied.

Gloria inclined her head towards Daniel. "Is Red looking at my ass, Daniel? Don't lie to me now."

"Not anymore."

"I thought the old grouch had more spunk in him." She faced Daniel. "Maybe I need a young stud. What do you think, Daniel?"

Red sensed the boy's discomfort and came to his rescue. "Perhaps so, but you'd better not go setting your sights on young Daniel here. He's about to become one of my best men and I don't want him running off with you right now. I need him."

"OK," she pursed her lips, "we'll talk about it again in the spring. Why don't you boys go and get yourselves cleaned up and we'll all sit down and have ourselves a decent meal." Gloria squeezed Daniel's rear as she hustled them along. "Go on now. Go and get spruced up for me. I'll think about not poisoning y'all."

Heading for the stairs following Pete, Daniel stopped to admire the trophy animals and racks of antlers mounted along the walls. Above the fireplace was a moose head with antlers ten-feet across, staring across the room.

"Her husband's big on hunting." Pete was waiting for him on the stairs, "and he's a hell of a good shot with that long rifle of his." Leading Daniel down the narrow hallway, Pete stopped and lowered his voice to a whisper. "That son of a bitch would let you get a half-mile away before he'd drop you like that moose, and no one would be the wiser." Pete's words sounded very much like a warning. He pointed down the hall. "That'd be your room down there, son. I'll see you downstairs after you wash up." A board creaked under his weight as he walked down the hall.

Daniel's room was tiny, but it was clean and cozy and the windows were covered with white lace curtains. A blue and white washbasin stood on the nightstand and a clean towel lay on the bedspread that was neatly turned back from white cotton sheets and matching pillow covers. The room smelled fresh, as if a woman lived there.

He was pulling his undershirt over his head when Gloria entered, carrying a jug of hot water that she emptied into the basin. Daniel could see her looking at him in the mirror. She tested the water with her finger and turned and drew a line across his smooth chest, holding him frozen with her eyes. She gently stroked his cheek and let her eyes roam his young handsome face.

He'd had fantasies about just such a moment. The breath he'd been holding came out in a gush, making her smile. She stepped closer, took his face in her warm hands and drew his lips to hers. He drifted for a moment and came back to earth just in time to see her smile as she closed the door behind her.

There was a light knock at the door. He opened it, half hoping that it would be Gloria, but found Pete instead.

"You ready to eat?"

"Yep, I'm ready." Daniel stepped into the hall and followed Pete downstairs.

Red stood by the fire, warming his hands. "There you are. I was wondering if you fell asleep or if Gloria'd scared you both off."

"I heard that," Gloria said as she entered the room carrying a platter of sizzling steaks steaming with aroma. She placed the platter on the table and stood back with her hands on her hips. "Come on now. This is no time to be bashful, I don't get too many men to feed this time of year and I don't plan on missing any bit of it."

Red and Pete wandered over to the table set for five.

"Daniel," Gloria cooed and pulled out a chair for him to sit in, "you could sit here, next to me."

"Where's your husband?" Daniel asked innocently.

"God only knows," Gloria said. "Probably out back in the shed, gutting some poor animal." Gloria headed back into the kitchen and they heard her open a door and yell, "Frank! If you're goin' to eat, better do it now!" The door slammed and Gloria returned, carrying a basket of bread.

Daniel stood and pulled out the chair for Gloria. She looked up and smiled at him as she sat.

"Why thank you, Daniel. You are such a gentleman," she said, then took her knife and speared the top-most piece of meat. "Go on! Dig in, boys!"

They set upon their dinner like hungry wolves.

A door slammed and everyone ceased chewing, except Gloria. Heavy footsteps became louder and the room darkened as Frank entered and sat down, scraping his chair loudly on the wooden floor. Daniel didn't remember him being quite so big when he'd first seen him.

Gloria shot Frank a sideways look and put down her knife and fork. "Frank," she said, pointing at Franks dirty hands, "look at your hands, they're filthy. You could've at least washed up before you came to eat, you know."

Frank abruptly stood, knocking his chair over, and slapped Gloria across the face savagely. She covered her face protectively, expecting more. No one spoke or moved a muscle. Frank's rage was deadly silent and it engulfed them. The snapping of the burning logs in the fireplace sounded like rifle fire.

With considerable deliberation, he sat back down in his chair, stabbed a piece of meat with his knife and dropped it onto his plate.

Daniel looked at Gloria, his heart bursting with genuine compassion. She smiled at him, though her eyes were brimming with tears.

Gathering her composure, she placed her napkin on the table, excused herself and walked purposefully into the kitchen. Red's look held Daniel in place, nailed to the chair. Red motioned to his plate with a nod of his head and began eating as if nothing had happened.

For the rest of the meal, the conversation consisted of short questions from Frank and brief answers from Red. Frank finished his food and left the table. All three of them exhaled together as they heard the kitchen door slam.

Gloria returned to the table, smiled bravely and sat at her place. Her eyes were swollen and there was a reddened patch on her cheek. She picked at her food.

"Was it something we said?" Pete asked and they all laughed. Gloria threw her head back and laughed the loudest. The dark mood left from the room as abruptly as Frank had. Gloria dabbed at her eyes as she laughed and Daniel reached out and touched her arm lightly. She covered his hand with her own and smiled at him.

Together they rescued dinner, and soon relaxed as if nothing untoward had happened. Red and Pete did their share by describing the electric lighting at the Hotel Jerome and the new buildings sprouting like weeds. Gloria smiled in rapt attention, listening to tales of these new changes.

After dessert was done, they sat by the fire talking. Several times, Gloria reached over and touched his hand to emphasize some point in her conversation. Daniel resisted the urge to reciprocate. Facing the fireplace, he found it difficult to ignore the moose head above the mantle. It seemed to be staring directly at him, a warning look in its glassy eyes.

Red yawned and suggested that they turn in for the night. Gloria enticed them to stay up longer for more coffee and more whiskey, but to no avail. They thanked her for dinner and she assured them that she would have breakfast ready in the morning.

At the top of the stairs, Red touched Daniel lightly on the shoulder, turning him around. "Don't make too much about what happened down there. Them two've been married a while, and if she wanted to leave him, she would have by now."

"But how could she let him…" Daniel pleaded.

Red knew that at his age, Daniel could not be expected to understand the intricacies of marriage. He held his hands up in frustration and shrugged.

"Remember this well, Daniel," Red paused as if the statement he was about to make was a weighty one, "it's dangerous to get between a man and his wife."

Daniel found it difficult to fall asleep, but eventually his weariness took over. He drifted off amid visions of his head replacing that of the moose over the fireplace. Sometime in the middle of the night, the creaking of a board in the hallway startled him awake. He lay as still as a corpse, his breathing shallow, his muscles tense.

In the dim moonlight, he saw the door to his room open. He curled his legs up so as to spring out of bed at the first sign of the murderer. His pistol was on the chair by the door, too far away to be of any help. As quiet as death, someone slipped into his room.

"Who's there?" he whispered, as if to help his murderer commit his crime in silence.

The shape of Gloria came to him like an apparition. "Shh," she whispered and placed her finger to his lips as she sat down on the edge of his bed.

"What are you doing here?" he whispered, pulling the blankets up around his chin.

"I have a little something for you," she whispered into his ear.

Daniel felt his hand being taken from him, guided beneath her clothing. She cupped her ample bosom with his hand; warm and soft, it was the first breast he'd ever felt. He sighed in pleasure at the heaven in his hand. She guided his hand over the whole of her breast, eventually resting it so that her nipple lay exactly in the center of his palm; she squeezed his hand and let out a soft moan.

He sucked in his breath as he felt her hand slide under the covers and glide over the taut muscles of his thigh. Unable to control himself, he squeezed her breast more tightly, feeling the ecstasy of the weight. Gloria moaned again, this time more deeply, like a cat purring in his ear. Gloria reached out and skillfully caressed his erection. Each beat of his heart sent the pounding pulse of his blood swelling into his penis;

the rushing sound of his blood in his ears like a waterfall. He was over-whelmed with sensations and heard himself moan.

Shushing him again, he felt her face close to his. Her breath coming hotly, she brushed his cheek with her lips and he felt his mouth rising to find hers. He smelled her hair, sweet and fragrant as it brushed his face and chest. He was transported to the world of silken slavery that all young men have felt for all of history; surrendering himself as men have done to the inevitable forces of love and lust.

She pulled the covers off his body, then lowered her head to his stomach, taut as knotted rope. He felt her tongue run a course around and down his belly.

She had complete control of him in a way he'd never felt before. He tensed and moaned in ecstasy as her lips found the tip of his penis and slowly sucked him into her moist mouth.

Daniel felt that he was going to explode and reached down to pull her off him. She grabbed his hand and forced herself back onto him, fighting his strength with her hunger for him. He released her head in surrender and her mouth engulfed the length of him. An explosion that he felt all through his body made him shudder with the most in-describable release of physical and emotional pleasure.

His back arched, his head swayed from side to side, his breath came in bursts and he realized that he was gripping the bed with one hand and holding her hair tightly with the other, but she didn't seem to mind; she gulped his juices thirstily. As quickly as she had come to him, she was gone, leaving him with a flavorful kiss. The door closed soundlessly. A floor board creaked softly as she disappeared into the night.

He lay trembling, his pulse racing, his breathing uneven from the tension and the ecstasy. The room was silent and he was alone again.

Sleep overcame him quietly, just as she had done. He slept the sleep of sated youth; soundless and as motionless as a dead man.

A knocking on the door jolted him awake. It was still dark outside.

"Time to get up, son." It was Red's deep voice. "Grab your things and meet us downstairs. OK?"

"OK. I'm awake," he said, climbing out of his warm bed. Pete and Red were already seated at the table eating when he came downstairs. They nodded to him as he sat. The eggs and sausage were piled on a plate in the middle of the table so he helped himself. He wolfed down one plate and had helped himself to another before he noticed both Red and Pete staring at him.

"Do you eat like this all the time?" Red asked. "No wonder Harry wants you livin' with us." Red went back to eating his breakfast.

Footsteps approached from the kitchen. Daniel swallowed hard and looked up. Frank loomed into the room and dropped heavily into a chair directly across from him. Daniel applied more concentration to his eggs, but he could feel Frank looking at him. The skin on the back of his neck crawled and his mouth went dry. The only liquid close by was his coffee, and he tried to appear casual as he reached for his cup.

"I didn't get your young friend's name there, Red?"

Red looked up from his plate. "This is Daniel. You met him before, Frank." Daniel nodded politely and looked Frank straight in the eye.

"He's the one that saved our bacon the trip we lost Dangerous." Red looked hard at Frank, trying to get his attention. "He's working for me now."

"He don't look like much to me," Frank said sharply and glared across the table. "How do you like the elk sausage?" he asked Daniel.

"It's good, r-really g-good," Daniel answered, trying not to stutter but failing. He forked another piece of sausage into his mouth.

"I made it."

"It's very good," Daniel smiled, trying to look interested and not terrified.

"I killed it and gutted it myself." Frank was looking at Daniel, who slowed his eating. "And I skinned it too," he said, conveying a sense of pleasure. He hit the table with his fist, making Daniel jump. "I shot it from a half-mile away," he added.

Pete nudged Daniel. "You finished, son? We gotta get going." Pete stood and Daniel followed.

"Well, thanks for the food, Frank," Red said, as they donned their coats and grabbed their gear.

Hurrying across the road and heading for the barn, there was no talk. Newly was in the barn when they entered and he helped them with their horses while Red and Pete went over the day's chores. With scarves pulled up and hats pulled down tightly against the cold morning air, they walked their horses out to the road in the pale light of the sunrise.

"We should be back before noon, I guess," Red told Newly as they climbed into their saddles. "You'll be ready by then?"

Newly nodded.

They spurred their horses into a canter and kept up the pace until they came to where the road turned north towards Leadville. Unsurprisingly, considering the early hour, both the road itself and the Ball Town saloon were devoid of life. In the stillness of the dawn, they could hear the rushing of the Arkansas River making its way to the Mississippi. Red eased them down to a gentle walk to give the horses a breather, which also gave them a chance to warm their hands.

"Well, son," Red said, breaking the silence, "what do you think of Gloria?"

"She's a really nice lady and a good cook," Daniel replied, hoping his sincerity covered his nervousness.

"Did you get a good night's sleep?" Red asked casually.

"Yes." Daniel replied.

"The noise didn't wake you up, then?" Pete asked.

"What noise?" Daniel replied.

"The creaky boards," Pete said, smiling.

Red cleared his throat. "Frank really should get those floorboards fixed."

"What creaky floorboards?" Daniel asked innocently.

"The ones outside your room," Pete said.

"Didn't you hear those boards creaking in the middle of the night?" Red asked, smiling broadly.

"No," Daniel shot back defensively. "When?"

"Oh, I'd say it was about the time you got your little visit from Gloria." Pete looked over at Red for confirmation. Red nodded and he and Pete spurred their horses into a canter, leaving him to consider the implications.

"Hey, wait!" Daniel yelled.

Pete and Red had a good head start on him, and it was more than a mile before they let him catch up.

Red looked at him and it was all that he could do to stop from laughing. "Son, I hate to be the one to break the news to you, but you're not the first to have a midnight visit from Gloria." Red leaned over and patted Daniel on the shoulder. "Gloria's paid a visit to pretty much every one of my men over these years. Ain't that right, Pete?" Pete agreed. "So don't go thinking that you're something special. It's just one of the fringe benefits of the job." Daniel's expression made both men laugh out loud.

"But what about Frank?" Daniel bleated after a moment, his fear palpable. "Does he know she does this?"

"I'm pretty sure he does." Red turned in his saddle and looked Daniel in the eye. "He might be mean, but he's not stupid. That's what scares me." Red slapped Daniel on the back, startling him. "Now don't go feeling too bad about it," Red said brightly. "If it's any consolation, he must've liked you."

"What do you mean, he liked me?" Daniel's voice rose higher.

"Well, look at it this way. If he didn't like you; you'd be dead by now."

"What?" Daniel's breath came in short bursts.

"You remember that creaky board?"

Daniel nodded, remembering the sound as if it was his coffin lid closing.

"Well son, that board is right over their bedroom. Frank knows whenever Gloria takes one of her midnight strolls upstairs."

"True enough," added Pete. "Wakes him up as sure as if you hit him on the head with a shovel." Pete had to settle himself before he could continue. "She keeps nailing it down when he's out hunting," he started laughing again, "and he keeps loosening it when he comes home." Pete lifted his arms as if aiming a rifle.

"If he didn't like you, he'd have shot you in the back from a half-mile away. Call it an unfortunate hunting accident." Red said, seriously.

"How do you know that?"

"Well, son," Red paused. "So far I've lost three men to that son of a bitch."

"But why does she stay with him?" Daniel felt sick with fear and confusion. "Why doesn't she just pack up and leave?" he asked Red.

"Don't rightly know much about that particular subject," Red answered honestly. "As my mother used to say; 'There's nothing in this world as strange as the people God put on it.' And we've seen about most of it over the years, haven't we, Pete?"

"That's the God's-honest truth, Red." Pete shook his head sagely.

"You shouldn't worry yourself too much now, Daniel. He'd have to kill all three of us and that would've made his story look pretty weak if you ask me. I don't think he'll try anything as long as you're with us."

They rode in silence towards Leadville's murky fog.

Chapter 20

They rode towards Leadville at a steady pace. Daniel was glad for the silence, busy digesting the information that Red and Pete had given him. He found it difficult to shake the feeling of doom. The potential of a confrontation with Frank and thoughts of Gloria tormented him.

As they passed the boarding house in Stringtown where his adventure had begun, he looked for the owner. It would be good for him to see Daniel now with a gun on his hip. The windows of the house remained dark and mute. Red noticed Daniel's interest.

Though it was still early, the traffic into Leadville increased, as did the gloomy cloud of smoke and grime. Daniel thought of Ute City as his new home, where even the most humble of cabins was neater by far, in contrast to the cabins on the outskirts of Leadville.

The people, he noticed, were different too. Townspeople in Ute City were by and large friendly and cordial. In Leadville, the people they passed either looked at them with suspicion or averted their gaze.

They rode directly to the railhead to join up with Bolly and the wagon. Red signed for his shipments and followed the clerk into the back of the warehouse. When he returned, he was smiling broadly.

"What're you all smiling about there, Red?" asked Pete.

"We've got a couple of crates going back with us today, something for Jerome Wheeler by the look of it. I remember him telling me to expect something special, but you know how secretive the old bastard is." Pete nodded. "Pete, will you and Bolly load up the wagon, then come on over by the hotel? Give us about a half hour. And Pete," he winked for Pete's sake, "I'll take the youngster with me." Pete touched the brim of his hat as he urged Bolly and the wagon forward.

"What are we picking up at the hotel?" Daniel asked as they rode back into town.

"You'll see in due time." Red patted him on the shoulder. "Meanwhile, we still have to go by the bank. How do you feel about helping me with a couple of big old boxes of money?"

Daniel inwardly shuddered. Things hadn't gone well for him the last time he was in that bank.

They hitched their horses and walked up the metal steps to the side door of the bank. After a knock on the heavy door, it was opened by the old teller who gave them a grunt and led them inside. Red tapped on the frosted glass door with "Manager" etched into it. A shadow appeared at the door and to Daniel's surprise, it opened to reveal Prudence, the Sheriff's daughter.

"Oh, Mr. Corcoran, come in," she said, smiling as she ushered them into the office. "Mr. Ebest is in the vault, but he should be out in just a moment."

As Daniel passed her, she recognized him. "Oh! You're the boy my father threw out of town, aren't you?"

"And I couldn't be more grateful to him for doing so," Red replied cheerily. Prudence blushed. Red decided on having a little fun. "Well, Prudence, this here is Daniel. But you've already met, haven't you?"

"Not formally, no," she replied and blushed again. As they shook hands, the manager entered and she pulled her hand back hurriedly.

Mr. R. Ebest, the bank's manager, could have been a walking portrait of a banker. Short of stature, round in circumference, with wire-rimmed spectacles pushed forward on his nose. He nodded to his visitors as he rounded his desk.

"You must have something to do, Prudence," he said with a tone of dismissal. Prudence spun on her heels.

Ebest motioned for Red to close the door. "Have you seen today's paper?"

Red took the newspaper Mr. Ebest handed him.

'Butch Cassidy sighted in Buena Vista!' blared the headline.

"I'm having one of the Sheriff's deputies stay here in the bank at night." He looked up at Red, seeking empathy. "You can't be too careful. Especially with what happened down in Telluride." He paused. "Perhaps you fellers should be extra careful going back over the Pass."

"That's good advice. We'll be extra careful. Won't we, Daniel?"
Daniel nodded.

Mr. Ebest rose with effort. "OK, boys, let's go and get your cash."
He strode past them down the narrow hall to the vault. He swung the
giant steel door open with ease and led them into his vault, smiling in
satisfaction when he stepped over the threshold, as he always did.

The far walls were lined with boxes of silver and gold coins. On top
of those were stacks of heavy canvas bags marked in denominations of
the paper currency they held. It was these bags that caught Daniel's eye
because there were dozens of them, all stacked neatly one on top of the
other, almost to the ceiling.

"Constructed of one hundred percent English steel," he assured
them, perhaps for Daniel's sake. Satisfied that his guests were suitably
impressed, he led them out of the vault and took the manifest that Red
handed him. He called out to a man named Ben, who turned out to be
the old teller. "Ben, you take care of Red here." Ben seemed less than
happy at his chore.

"Now, if you'll excuse me. I have a widow to evict."

"I'll have my wagon over here in a bit," Red told the old teller as he
opened the side door that led into the alley. Mr. Ebest waved his hand
absently. "OK, young feller," he said to Daniel, "let's get along to the
Hotel and pick up our next treasure."

They walked briskly along the wooden sidewalk and crossed the
busy main street opposite the Hotel Leadville, nimbly dodging the
wagons and carriages that bumped along in the ruts where the mud
had been turned into frozen ridges.

Inside the Hotel, Red looked around the foyer, but didn't see
whatever it was that he was looking for. "Wait for me here Daniel,
I'll be back." Red left him and headed over to the reception desk.
Daniel looked around the palatial room with its thick carpets and
mahogany tables and chose a seat in one of the high-backed leather chairs by a window. It allowed him to keep an eye out for the
Sheriff.

He picked up a copy of the Leadville Times from the table and read
the front page story reminding the readers about the June robbery of

the bank in Telluride, another silver-rich boom town in the southwestern part of the state. Though he tried to concentrate on reading the story, something kept drawing his attention back to the artist's renditions of the faces of the robbers.

In a flash, it came to him. They were the men from the boarding house. The same ones that he'd accused of stealing his wallet. His heart fell. How could he have been so stupid? They were wanted men, bank robbers.

Daniel was so engrossed looking at the faces on the paper, he didn't notice Red approach, nor did he notice that Red had company. Red cleared his throat and Daniel pulled his eyes away from the paper.

"Daniel, I'd like you to meet someone."

Standing next to Red was the most beautiful creature he'd ever laid eyes on. Her eyes were the color of the earth, with browns and greens and flecks of gold, sparkling like light off gold dust. A bonnet covered her head, but Daniel could see wisps of dark blonde hair curling around her ears. She wore a pale blue dress of the latest fashion with a shawl of bright colors around her shoulders. Her smile was perfect. Her teeth shone white as snow, and she held her head in such a manner as to look regally born.

Red laughed. He'd guessed the effect she would have on Daniel. Not that he was any expert, but after two wives, he reckoned that he'd learned a thing or two about men and women.

Daniel leapt to his feet, dropping his hat and the paper as he did. It was only then, as he bent down to pick them up, that he noticed the walking stick. She saw his hesitation, but smiled gracefully at him.

"I just use it to get extra attention from men," she whispered to him with a laugh.

Red draped his arm around her shoulders, parentally. "Daniel, I'd like you to meet Kate. She's the special cargo that we've been sent to fetch. Kate Doray, this is Daniel Carrington. Kate here is one of Big Shirley's girls."

"It's very nice to meet you, Miss Kate," he finally managed to say without stuttering. He smiled at her in the triumph of his personal conquest.

Red cleared his throat. "Well Kate, we've a long trip ahead of us so I think we should get going. Not that you haven't had a long trip already, coming all the way from Chicago." Kate smiled and leaned on Red's arm.

"Daniel. Why don't you go and fetch Pete and the wagon?" Red tapped him on the arm and nodded his head in the direction of the front door.

"Oh, OK, Red." Daniel replied, tripping over the leg of the small table as he turned to go.

Kate smiled and watched him to the door. "Where did he come from?" she asked.

"I'm not quite sure," Red answered. "But he's a brave boy and I could use a few more just like him right now." Red looked around for Kate's luggage. "Where are your things?"

"I left them up in the room. I didn't know if you were going to bring me a horse or make me ride in that bumpy old wagon."

"I wasn't too sure of that myself, so, I thought that since you probably haven't been riding much, you could ride in the wagon out to Twin Lakes. Then if you felt up to it, you could take one of my horses and come riding back into Aspen like a conquering queen." Red became more serious. "Your mother can't wait to see you."

"How are they?"

"Your mother is just fine. You know how she is, too tough to die and too much of a woman for any man to live with. And your sister?" Red paused. "Well, she's just about as ornery as she ever was. I pity the man that she sets her sights on. He'll either be doing the laundry or pushing up daisies within a year of their marriage, I assure you."

Red watched as she took the stairs in an easy stride, using her cane expertly. He smiled and walked outside as his wagon pulled up in front of the hotel.

"Pete, I'm going to have Bolly go help Kate with her things." Pete nodded and Bolly climbed down off of the wagon. "We'll meet you over at the bank."

"Well, what do you think?" Red inquired of Daniel as they threaded their way back across the busy street.

"About what?" he replied.

"You know what I mean. About Kate?"

"She seems nice." Daniel replied shyly.

Red laughed loudly.

At the bank, Red signed for the four locked boxes and the five canvas bags. The wagon pulled up in the alley at the side door. Kate sat on the driver's seat next to Bolly, wearing an old hat and a heavy riding coat with the collar pulled up around her face. Her chin was tucked into her scarf and her hands were buried deep in her pockets. Without looking, Daniel could tell she was watching him.

From the side window of the bank, Prudence also watched him. Daniel was picking up the last of the money bags when Prudence came and stood in the doorway to the vault, blocking his exit. He tried to squeeze past, but Prudence wouldn't move for him.

"Howdy Red," came a familiar voice that drove an icy spike of fear into Daniel. Through the open door, he saw the Sheriff clearly.

"I'm sorry, but I really have to go. Now," he said in near panic. He pushed past her, but not before she grabbed him by the seat of his pants and squeezed his bottom.

Daniel was blushing bright red when he appeared and handed the last of the money bags to Pete.

Prudence watched him go. It didn't pass her attention that the young woman in the wagon also followed Daniel with her eyes. The woman in the wagon turned her head and looked directly at her. Prudence slid out of sight.

As if by magic, her father appeared at her side, startling her.

"How's my little girl today?" he asked, surly as usual. He was never one to smile and was generally considered to be in a good mood if he was not yelling. "I see that Red's got a new hand working for him," he said. "What do you think of him?" The Sheriff was intensely jealous where his daughter was concerned and every man in town knew it. She had resigned herself to the life of a spinster, knitting and quilting her life away. At least until her father dropped dead.

"Just another boy," she said, a knot of fear was growing in her stomach.

"Well, I don't want you talking to him. He's no good," he said, as if it were a proven fact.

"Why?" she asked flatly, knowing full well that she was walking a thin and dangerous line.

He turned, smiling for those watching. In a snake like movement, he reached through the bars and gripped her hand with such force she buckled at the knees with pain. "Because, I told you so. Is that clear?" Satisfied that he'd made his point, he let her hand go.

⊰⊱

It wasn't until they were passing the Stringtown Hotel that Daniel felt some of the dread lift from his shoulders. It so happened that as they were passing, the owner was in the process of tossing some poor soul's clothing into the mud. The hapless owner of the assorted gear was next. Daniel watched impotently as the hotel owner kicked the man as he crawled around in the mud, gathering his meager belongings. Daniel's instinct was to wheel his horse and help. Sensing this, Red grabbed Marigold's reins and held them tightly.

"Not the time, nor the place. Take it from me. Leadville is not a town that you'd want to get locked up in. Understand me?" Daniel nodded. Red patted him on the shoulder. "And right or wrong, there are some fights it just makes no sense to get involved in."

They had made good time and it was not yet noon when they pulled into Twin Lakes. Red escorted Kate over to the Lodge to change into her riding clothes while they helped Newly buckle the new team into place.

Daniel couldn't stop himself from repeatedly glancing over at the Lodge hoping to see Gloria, but she never appeared. Red came back with a pot of hot coffee and sandwiches. They were sitting on bales of hay, eating their lunches in the warm sun when Kate appeared from the Lodge. Daniel stopped chewing. He felt a slap on his back.

"Ready to go, pardner?" asked Pete loudly, then he lowered his voice conspiratorially, "I do believe that young Miss Kate there would like to ride. Why don't you go ask her?" Pete gave him a shove.

"Pete said you might want to ride back," Daniel said.

"I'd love to ride, if Red can spare me a horse."

"You could ride my horse, if you'd like. Her name is Marigold. She's a good horse." Daniel led her to where Marigold stood, tied to the railing fence. She stroked Marigold's flanks and blew her breath gently into Marigold's nose. She knew a lot about horses, he saw. Marigold smelled her and flared her nostrils in pleasure. Kate handed Daniel her coat and cane and reached up for the pommel to pull herself up into the saddle. Daniel reached out, but Kate pulled her arm away, the smile gone from her face.

"I don't need any help, thank you," she snapped. Her tone and the flash of anger that he saw in her eyes caught him by surprise. She smiled at him, embarrassed. "I'm sorry, Daniel. I didn't mean that. It's just that everyone wants to help me and I want to do things for myself."

"I understand," he said, still smarting from the rebuke.

"Thank you." In one fluid movement, she lifted herself into the saddle and sat as if she'd been born on horseback.

Daniel handed her the reins while he adjusted her stirrups. Marigold looked like she couldn't be happier as Kate rode expertly around the corral. Red, who had been watching, smiled and nodded at Pete.

"Are you ready, Pete?"

Pete nodded back.

"You all ready to go, Kate?"

"Ready if you are," she replied.

"Daniel, why don't you ride my horse and I'll drive the wagon?" Red climbed into the driver's seat of the wagon and drove out of the corral, leaving his wrangler to close the gate behind them. Daniel looked back one last time, hoping to catch a glimpse of Gloria.

He was somewhat surprised that Kate rode so expertly and showed no sign of her disability. When they passed the place where the accident had happened, Red pointed out the spot in the road where Daniel had jumped from the wagon and it had sailed off the cliff. Kate apparently knew Harry, and made a face at the mention of his name. She looked over at Daniel often as she listened to the story. Embarrassed by the attention, Daniel dropped behind. When they reached the valley floor, she slowed and waited for him to catch up.

"Red told me that you saved Leafy Lane from drowning."

"It was nothing really. I.I just jumped in and tried to help him is all," Daniel stuttered. "We were both drowning and s.s someone else had to s.save both of us."

"I still think it was a brave thing to do."

"Leafy fell in the river, and I fell in after him," he said simply.

"Oh, God. My mother was right. You men are all alike," she huffed, "I swear, Red, this boy is as bad as you are."

Red looked sidelong at her. "Now, Kate. Is that such a bad thing?" he smiled at her briefly and faced the road ahead.

There was no more talk from the group as they made their way into town, it was getting dark and they were tired.

Chapter 21

When they arrived at the Paragon, Shirley rushed out, scooped Kate up in her arms and hugged her fiercely, tears brimming in her eyes. "Oh Kate, you've grown so much," she cried, holding Kate at arm's length, savoring her as only a mother can.

"Only in the hips," Kate replied and twirled gracefully for her mother without using her cane.

"You look wonderful, doesn't she boys? I'm forgetting my manners. Come on in, you all must be exhausted."

"We can't tonight Shirley, but thanks for the invitation." Red nodded to the wagon where Pete and Bolly hunkered down against the cold. "We still have some work to do and we'd better get it done before we freeze our tails off. Daniel, why don't you get Kate's things for her?" Daniel carried Kate's luggage in from the wagon. She thanked him with a smile, and neither the gesture nor the effect it had on Daniel passed her mother's notice.

"Thanks again for bringing my baby back safe, Red. I owe you one."

"Come on you young colt," Red said, slapping Daniel on the back. "I happen to know where there's a decent place to eat that might even serve us."

They went directly to the bank and unloaded the cash into the waiting arms of the bank's manager. Then they went over to the Hotel Jerome and, with the help of several strong men, they unloaded the crates and pushed them inside the hotel.

After dinner at the Red Onion, Red, Pete and Bolly headed back to the barn at Stillwater. Daniel put Marigold into her stall at No Problem Joe's, then gave her a good brushing and went home, exhausted.

Daniel arrived to find a surly Harry lying on his bed.

"Where the hell've you been?" he asked.

He told Harry of his adventure over to Leadville and back. Harry absently listened to the story. His mood brightened only when he realized for the first time that Daniel's job with Red was the trump card in his plan. He picked up the Leadville newspaper that Daniel had brought and tried not to move his lips as he read about the robbery of the bank in Telluride.

Harry's mind was consumed by the potential of pulling off the biggest robbery in Colorado history; all others would pale in comparison. Butch Cassidy's fame would forever be overshadowed after Harry's devilishly executed robbery became known. On the other hand, if he became famous for committing the robbery, his new fame would almost certainly leave him rotting his life away in prison. Harry smiled to himself at the dilemma.

"Honey came by to see you," Harry said after a while.

"What did you tell her?"

"What could I tell her? I didn't know where you were." Harry was watching Daniel intently. He was taken by a feeling that strangely resembled compassion. It was more of his natural guile than anything relating to goodness that prompted his reply. "Let me tell you a little something about women."

Daniel looked up, hoping to see a lifeline uncurling towards him.

"When they're angry, all you have to do is distract them. Tell them they look nice, something like that. Most often, they just forget what it was that they were angry about in the first damned place."

Daniel sat waiting for the rest of the revelation.

"I told her that you saved Leafy when he went into the river."

Daniel understood what it was that he was hearing, but the importance was lost on him. "That was nice of you Harry, but why did you tell her that? We both nearly drowned."

"Well, for one reason, she didn't know who had saved Leafy's life, and she should know that it was you. After all, you did save his life, didn't you?"

"Why is that important to Honey?"

Harry paused to enjoy the moment. "Leafy is Honey's little brother."

"What?" Daniel's smile returned. "So, she's not angry with me anymore?"

⚔

Harry was considering the cards. His mind was not on the game as it should have been and he was losing his nickels at a regular pace.

Out in the street, he looked west. He pulled his scarf up around his chin and turned towards home.

In Harry's unsophisticated mind, robbing the bank was the easy part. All it took was just the right amount of dynamite and a match. Grab the money and run was the plan. He'd heard many a miner discuss it at length in the long winter nights over the years. They'd come up with many improbable ideas, culminating in lives of luxury and leisure, before they returned to the drudgery and danger of their real lives in the mines.

Even though the obstacles had not diminished one foot in distance or altitude, the plan that had slowly formed for him had more potential for success than any he'd heard. His plan depended mostly on his knowledge of the weather, luck, and a little help from his new found partner, Daniel. As was usual in these moments of reverie, Harry savored the potential fruits of his daring. The women, the fine clothes, the gaming tables laid out before him, the women again, but not wives, not ever again. He would stay as far away from Salt Lake City as money could take him. A shiver ran up his spine at the thought of the screaming, snotty children calling him Daddy or Pa.

With time on his hands, he stopped at the stable. The door groaned open on its hinges, prompting Joe's head to appear above the stalls at the far end of the barn.

"Hey there, Joe," Harry called out.

Harry was pleased to see that Joe was working on the sled. He was drunk as usual, but his fingers were working the leather strips with great skill, weaving them into the fabric of the basket of the sled.

Joe had been making sleds for the miners for dozens of years. Harry sat quietly and watched the gnarled old fingers twist and thread the leather thongs, dipping them in the warm water and stretching them over the frame.

He knew from his own experience that working with wet leather strips was like knitting worms, but Joe could do it blindfolded.

Harry paid attention to the detail of the lacings, knowing that his life and his stolen fortune would depend greatly on the strength of the sled and the woven basket that held it together. "I just thought I'd stop in and see how you're doin'," Harry said.

"You're a lyin' bastard, Harry. You came in to see if I was working on your sled."

"No, no, Joe, honest. I was just wandering home and thought I'd look you up is all," Harry said.

"As you can see, I'm working my fingers to the bone. Are you satisfied?" he said, looking down at his handiwork.

Harry turned to go. He stopped after a few paces, a thought entering his mind. "Say, do you have any plans for Thanksgiving yet?"

Joe looked up, surprised by the question. "Not that I know of."

"I was thinking that since I've got a new cabin mate, I'd cook us a turkey. You and Red could come over for dinner."

Joe looked at Harry suspiciously, then returned to his leatherwork. "No problem, Harry. That's a right nice offer. I'll be there."

"Great, Joe, we'll have ourselves a feast and maybe get ourselves a little drunk too."

"Sounds like a plan you've got there."

"I'll be seeing you then," Harry said and left Joe to his chore. Once outside in the cold, Harry wondered to himself why he'd made the offer to cook a turkey. He'd never made one before. Now he just had to win enough to buy one.

⚓

Shirley found it difficult to sleep, so she went downstairs to make herself some warm milk. Sitting at the table, she felt the presence of her daughter. The house was warm and silent, but a feeling of life breathed through it.

Perhaps in the great scheme of things it was good that Kate had the lame foot. It had seldom held her back and she was as popular as any child in school. Of course, some things were more difficult for her than the other children, but she was so well liked and considerate that the other children instinctively made small concessions for her though they were rarely necessary. Kate's infirmity had forced her to develop in ways that made her more self-reliant and considerate rather than the self-centered girl she could have become.

⁂

Harry was walking back down to town, hoping to win enough money for a turkey and a romp with a lady in one of the brothels. The Paragon appealed to him and he was reaching for the door handle when it suddenly opened and a large man backed out and slipped on the ice, nearly knocking him off his feet. They grasped each other as they struggled to find their balance. Harry reached down and picked up their hats.

"Here you go," said Harry, realizing only then that the person he'd bumped into was none other than Jerome Wheeler himself.

"Well, I have to thank you, sir," said Mr. Wheeler, brushing the snow from his expensive hat. Wheeler was inebriated and a little unsteady on his feet. Harry by reflex held him by the elbow as he cautiously placed his hat on his head. Satisfied that his accoutrement was safely where it should be, he turned to give his fellow pedestrian a decent look. "Oh, it's you; you're a friend of Red Corcoran, aren't you?"

"That's right, Mr. Wheeler. We've met before. My name is Harry, Harry Rich. I've been a friend of Red's for years." Harry was speaking in the most respectful tones, knowing all too well that Mr. Wheeler was the most prominent man in town and, by all reckoning, the richest.

"Well, Mr. Rich, how about having a nightcap before we turn in?"

Harry was taken by surprise by the offer and jumped at the opportunity to join him. Wheeler let himself lean slightly on Harry as he led him to the door of the Parlor Bar at The Paragon. Harry had little doubt that Wheeler had been upstairs in the brothel.

He was smiling broadly when they entered the warm, plush confines of the lounge. Glennis smiled sweetly at them, hurried over to take Mr. Wheeler's hat and coat, and even offered to take Harry's coat as well. Glennis took both without recoiling from the smell and feel of Harry's old bearskin. She deftly hung both on the gracefully curved coat rack and led them to the more secluded alcove near the rear of the bar.

Mr. Wheeler placed his order and Harry ordered a shot of the bar whiskey. Mr. Wheeler caught Glennis as she turned back to the bar to fill the order.

"Glennis, my dear, would you change Mr. Rich's order? I'd like him to try one of mine. You wouldn't mind tasting something different, would you, Harry? Do you mind if I call you Harry?"

"I would be honored, Mr. Wheeler. If you keep buying me drinks you can call me anything you damned well feel like calling me."

Wheeler let his head float back to rest for a moment on the high back of the chair, laughing his deep, resonant laugh.

"In that case, Harry, you'd better get into the habit of calling me Jerome. That is unless my wife is around. She doesn't like familiarity such as we do out here in the west." Wheeler laughed at his joke and Harry was again caught off guard at the deep richness of the sound and laughed along with him. The drinks arrived in the best cut glasses and Glennis gave Jerome the benefit of the view of her cleavage as well as a pleasant and genuine smile.

They sipped their drinks and Harry involuntarily let out a sigh of satisfaction as the liquor inked its way down. Rather than the harsh, caustic wash of his usual cheap whiskey, what he tasted now was full and flavorful. This was something he could get used to. He considered Jerome again with new appreciation for the advantages that the rich enjoyed. Harry confirmed in his mind that these types of pleasures would be his one day soon.

He copied the reclining pose of Jerome, knowing full well that other patrons were observing him, and reveled in the proximity to the unanointed king of Aspen. He was at the point of falling asleep when Jerome startled him.

"You're partnering with that new young man in town, Daniel Carrington, aren't you?"

Harry's head snapped upright; instantly back to being a mere pawn. How could Wheeler know Daniel, when he'd only been in town for a few months? Harry had lived in Aspen for a dozen years and this was the first time that they'd spoken or that he'd even acknowledged his presence.

"That's right, Jerome, I thought I'd give the young fellow a chance at making it big here in Aspen. What better way to get a jump on life than partnering up and being in business for yourself, I say. It is a new world out here you know." Harry hoped that Jerome would appreciate the wisdom and the generosity of his act of faith with Daniel.

"He saved your life I hear, up there on the Pass." Even though Jerome gave the impression of one who was taxed and tired, a second look into his ruddy face drew the casual watcher to the keenness of his gaze. And Jerome was gazing intently at Harry.

"Well, he did help a little bit up there, I suppose," Harry replied condescendingly.

Jerome said no more for a while, inviting Harry to fill in the silence.

"That's the reason I took the youngster under my wing. He showed good judgment and I'm the kind of man who can appreciate that." Harry babbled on, hoping to get himself into a better position for the deal that he hoped would come.

"That's the same thought I had, Harry. You know, you and I are similar in many ways I think." Jerome was as skillful a man as ever trod the earth when it came to playing on another man's ego. Flattery to Harry was like pollen to a bee, he lived on it and he lived for it.

"Did you know I got him a job working with Red?" Harry paused importantly. "I still need him for our business, but I thought that he would learn some important lessons working with Red once in a while." Harry was enjoying his own story and Jerome listened as he signaled Glennis for another round of drinks.

"Well, Harry, I'd be interested in talking with this Daniel, if you could see time to release him briefly from all of the important things that you have him involved in." Jerome was pleased to see that for just a split second, the lights went out of Harry's eyes.

"You want to talk to Daniel?" Harry said sullenly.

"If it doesn't inconvenience you," Jerome emphasized. "I know what an important job you do. Your hours are long and there's little glamour in it. But as you said, there are few better ways to gain wealth than owning your own business."

Not one to let a fish get off the hook, Jerome confirmed his request. "So, you'll ask Daniel to come over to my office at the Smuggler tomorrow or the next day, then?" Jerome was signaling Glennis for the bill.

Harry was confused at the abrupt change in his new friend's demeanor. "I can't say that he'll be there definitely, he is a busy boy you know, but I will tell him that you want to see him. He might have to go back over the Pass again."

"No, I don't think so. That won't be until next week," Jerome said with authority as he placed money on the tray that Glennis had brought.

Standing with some effort, Jerome shook Harry's hand firmly. "It's been nice to meet you. I hope that we have the opportunity to get together again sometime soon. No, don't get up," Jerome said as Harry tried to lift himself from the deep recess of his chair. "Sit there a while. I want you to have another one on me. It's all taken care of, isn't it, Glennis?" Glennis smiled sweetly and nodded to him and then to Harry. "So enjoy your evening and don't forget to tell your friend that I'll be looking forward to seeing him soon. OK?"

Harry nodded politely, confused.

"Harry, I hear that you play a little poker at times, for your entertainment only of course. Is that true?"

"Why, yes, I like the occasional game of chance. Rumors abounded that Jerome Wheeler was a lousy poker player but never blinked at paying his debts, no matter how large.

"We should get together sometime. I have a few friends and we get out on our wives on occasion and play a few hands just for fun. I'm sure you'll recognize some of them." Jerome gave Harry a theatrical wink. "I'll let you know and perhaps you might like to join us sometime."

Harry smiled as if he was already one of the inner circle, pleased to be numbered with the town's elite.

"Well, goodnight then."

Harry watched as Jerome wavered his way to where Glennis helped him with his coat and opened the door for him. Harry was not surprised to see Jerome lean forward and kiss Glennis lightly on the lips. She closed the door behind him and brought Harry another drink. Harry sat, trying the best he could to put all these strange pieces together.

Finishing his drink with total enjoyment, he decided that it might be time to go into the bar and see if he could strike up a game. And, if the gods were willing, perhaps he could parlay his meager stake into a quickie upstairs with one of the lovelies.

Chapter 22

As Daniel worked the morning shift change, he was reminded of how small the town really was. It seemed as though it didn't really need a newspaper at all; everyone just knew everyone else's business. Particularly troubling was how often it was mentioned that Harry had lost to someone he'd heard referred to only as "Duke." Daniel was familiar with some of the more flamboyant characters in town, but he'd noticed that whenever Duke's name came up, the conversation usually took on a more respectful tone.

Finished with his work, Daniel lugged his near-empty sled back to the cabin and found Harry partially awake and sitting at the table, deathly pale, gripping a mug of coffee. He looked close to tears.

"What's the matter, Harry?" Daniel asked with genuine concern.

"Shut up and mind your business." Harry's eyes were murky red. Daniel couldn't be sure, but he thought that Harry might have the beginnings of a black eye.

Daniel knew what was wise, so he walked outside and busied himself with the unloading of the sled. He squared his shoulders and took a deep breath before going back inside. Sitting at the table across from Harry, he poured himself some coffee and a liberal amount of whiskey.

"You don't look so good, Harry. Are you alright?"

"I'll be alright as soon as this coffee kicks in." There was definite bruising around Harry's left cheekbone. "I'm sorry that I snapped at you."

"Oh, it's OK."

"No, you were trying to be nice. I'm sorry." Harry nearly choked getting the words out of his mouth. "Thanks for doing the business for me this morning. I appreciate it. When are you going to be working for Red again?"

"I think he needs me to go next week. He's got some big thing that he needs a lot of help with."

"Got any idea what it might be?" he asked casually, betraying nothing.

"No. But it's heavy and it seems important. Maybe it's something to do with the electricity station that Mr. Wheeler's built."

"Could be." Harry slipped back into disinterest. "Oh, Wheeler wants to talk to you, said that you should come on by his office."

Daniel looked at Harry intently. "What do you think it's about?"

"Hell, I have no idea—maybe he wants you to marry his daughter or something." Harry smiled enough to remind himself that he had a hangover. Reaching up to hold his head, he touched the side of his face and winced. Feeling around, he discovered the welt on the side of his face near his eye. He got up out of his chair to look in the mirror, mystified by it.

"How did you get that?" Daniel asked innocently, already having a pretty good idea that it came as a result of last night's exploits.

"Must've fallen down," he said, and returned to the table. "I was pretty drunk last night. As a matter of fact, I was really drunk." Harry remembered meeting his new friend Jerome and having drinks with him, then he seemed to lose all memory of the rest of the evening.

Jerome Wheeler's office was modern with plush leather chairs, a big polished wooden desk, and afforded a view across the valley and east towards Independence Pass. Bread, sliced beef, and cheese had been laid on a table. Wheeler and Carter made straight for it.

Wheeler sat behind his massive desk, eating noisily and drinking coffee from a large white mug. There was no attempt at conversation while they ate. Daniel was relieved because he still didn't know the reason for this meeting. Finally, Wheeler called for his secretary, who came in and cleared the plates. Daniel rose to help, but was reprimanded by Wheeler in no uncertain terms. "It's her job to do that. That's what I pay her for," he said, with more than a hint of condescension. "Now, let's get down to business, shall we?"

Carter angled his chair, better to observe Daniel.

Wheeler sat back in his chair, rocking a little on the rear legs. He leaned forward suddenly, as if a decision had been made. "I'm always on the lookout for smart young men and you have something that I like in the men I hire. You're not afraid to take risks. Not that I want men to take risks that get themselves or other men hurt, you understand?" Assured, he continued. "I hear good things about you, Mr. Carrington, not just from Red Corcoran, but from Carter here, too." He steepled his fingers and considered Daniel. "So I'm going to offer you a job."

"But I've already got a job," Daniel replied instinctively.

"Mr. Carrington, may I call you Daniel? I know all about you and Harry Rich being partners." His tone was paternal. "Do you really think you're going to make your fortune selling a couple of dollars of potatoes a day? And for God's sake, son, look at the hours you have to put in." Wheeler's voice was rising. He adjusted his position in his chair. "Daniel, how much money have you made with your partner Harry Rich?"

The question caught Daniel by surprise. It was a question he'd wanted to ask Harry, too. His chin sank to his chest as he realized that whatever his answer, it was going to show him as a fool. Reluctantly, he answered. "I'm not sure."

"How is that? Doesn't he give it to you every week or every day?" Wheeler's voice was calm.

"Harry keeps track of the money. He said that he'd keep it safe for me," Daniel tried to inject confidence in Harry into his voice, "and I could have it any time I wanted."

"Does he keep it in the bank for you?" Daniel shook his head. "Then where does he keep it, buried under the floor?" Daniel looked up. "He wouldn't be that stupid, Daniel."

Daniel felt his face flush. "He's not stupid, Mr. Wheeler."

At the Durant mine, the owners had dug a few feet and found a little vein of silver which quickly petered out. Some owners gave up, some didn't. Some stuck it out and dug some more. Jerome Wheeler had been one of the ones who stayed.

When all of his other partners had quit and just he and Hyman were left, they kept digging, just the two of them, and that's when they hit it big. They uncovered solid silver nuggets as big as their heads.

They'd been there all the time, just under the trail they'd been walking over for months. It made Wheeler and Hyman their first fortune and it was still the richest mine in town.

Daniel sat silently.

Wheeler remembered how it had felt when he and his partner David Hyman had wheeled their first wagon filled with bright, gleaming nuggets down to the bank. Stubbornness was something to be valued when a man wanted treasure that was buried in the ground.

"I didn't mean to insult you or your partner, Daniel," Wheeler said after a while, "as a matter of fact, I had a talk with him just the other night and I found him to be quite a reasonable man. Did he mention that to you?"

"No, sir, he didn't."

"Daniel, I'm a wealthy man as you probably know. I've made some money and I want to make some more before I die." Wheeler paused and cast a sidelong look at Carter. "There's a new century coming and there are going to be great changes in this country when it gets here. I've built the electricity plant that will bring light and power to the town and all through my mines. Conditions will improve for the men and they will be more productive because of it. Isn't that right, Carter?"

Carter nodded enthusiastically.

"My hotel is going to be the first all electrically lighted building in Colorado and that's going to mark the beginning of a new age. Pretty soon, all of the houses and businesses in town are going to have electric light. Businesses won't have to shut down at sunset any more and there will be many, many new things using this power that we haven't yet thought of using it for. The Denver and Rio Grande railroad will be coming through Glenwood Springs soon. People will come here from all over the country and we'll have dozens of new businesses to cater to their needs." Wheeler paused to let Daniel grasp what he was saying. "Are you following me, son?"

"I think so, but where do I fit in?" Daniel replied.

"Perhaps I was getting a bit ahead of myself, I'm sorry." Wheeler looked down at his intertwined fingers on the desktop and began again. "What I'm looking for are some smart men, like Carter here, who are willing to learn how to run businesses in the new era. Yes, I know there are plenty that I could choose right here, but these new times are going to require a special type of man, a new type of businessman for a new age. Do you follow me now?"

Daniel's mind was opening slowly. "Why me?" he asked.

"If you're as smart as I think you are, you've noticed that only a few men in this town make all the money. Am I right?"

Daniel nodded his head, thinking about the grand homes in the sunniest part of town.

"The silver boom could go on indefinitely, but I think it has seen its best days. The reason that we're making money from the silver we're mining is that the government buys it all from us. As much as we can mine, they're buying. We're selling about three million dollars of silver a month to the Federal Government. David Hyman and I have sold them over thirty-million dollars of silver a year. It's called the Sherman Silver Purchase Act and it states that the Federal Government should own all the silver mined in the country so as to be the base of the money system."

Jerome pulled out his wallet, thick with money, and spread some of the bills on the desk in front of him. They were not all the same and they were of different sizes. He separated one from the rest and handed it to Daniel, who examined it carefully.

"See there, where it says that it can be redeemed for silver at any time? Well, that's good if the value of silver stays high. But, we're diggin' out so much silver that the government can't afford to be paying us in gold for the silver. And, we're not really stupid enough to be getting paid in this paper stuff. We don't know if it'll be worth anything tomorrow. The government is buying all of our silver and paying us in gold. Don't make a lot of sense, now does it?"

Daniel felt rather than saw that Wheeler was watching him intently.

"So, here's what I think is going to happen. I think that the Sherman Act is going to be revoked and the silver market is going to go bust. There's just too much silver in these hills for the government to be in the silver business. Gold, now that's a different matter altogether. Gold is going to be the base of money forever." Wheeler rocked back in his chair again and looked at the ceiling. "God, I wish I'd found a gold mine." Jerome sighed in his reverie and turned his attention back on the immediate matter at hand. "Now, Daniel, Red Corcoran holds you in high regard and Carter has told me how you jumped in the river to save Shady Lane's son, so I don't have to ask anyone else about your character. I'm offering you a job working here with us."

Daniel was overwhelmed.

"I don't want you to give me your answer now. I know you've a lot to think about and I wouldn't want you to make a rash decision that you might regret in the future. I just want you to think about it some. Will you do that for me?"

"Mr. Wheeler, I'm flattered that you offered me this job, I truly am, but I really don't know what it is that you want me to do for you." Wheeler got to his feet. "But I am going to think about it."

"Most men would jump at the offer, but I respect a man that has to look a gift horse in the mouth to see how many teeth it has." As Daniel got up to leave Wheeler came around his desk to shake his hand again. "You take as much time as you need and come on back to see me when you're ready to get to work."

After Daniel had left, Wheeler sat back down and looked over at Carter.

"Why don't you pour us a little taste there, John?" Carter went over to the sideboard and opened the sliding door, retrieving the bottle of Scotch whiskey. Pouring two glasses, he handed one to Wheeler and sipped his own.

"You think I'm making a mistake, don't you?" Wheeler held up his hand. "Even though you said that he had the balls of two men. Go ahead, spit it out. You're not going to be able to hold it in for long anyway, I know you too well."

"There's something that's bothering me about him. Not just that he's Harry Rich's partner and all, there's something else there too."

"Like what, may I ask?"

"Well, I can't put my finger on it yet, but there's something just not right about him."

"You're not jealous of him are you, John? If that's the case, I'd be disappointed. I'm looking at the future of my company, and you know that I trust you. I might even say that I trust you more than I trust my wife."

A moment passed before Wheeler let out a bellow of a laugh, Carter laughed along with him. Jerome's wife was renowned as being a more accurate source of rumor about Jerome and his business than either the *Aspen Times* or the *Diplomat* would ever be.

"See what you can find out about him, will you? I don't know that you're going to find out anything, but ask Leafy or whoever else he hangs around with."

Carter gathered up his coat to go. He looked back at Wheeler in his rich leather chair and winked with sly assurance. "I'll see what I can do, Mr. Wheeler."

Chapter 23

Walking up the path from the road, Daniel felt nervous but excited. The evening was filled with potential, not the least of which was the prospect of a fine home-cooked meal. There was no doubt that he was getting tired of the boiled anything that Harry cooked, and his personal cooking skills were no better.

Light shone invitingly through the lace curtains inside the front door of Honey's cabin. He'd hardly knocked when the door swung open.

"Come on in," Leafy said with a broad smile and drew Daniel inside. Honey's son came running across the room, holding his hand out formally. "Jackson, you remember Daniel, don't you?" Jackson gripped Daniel's hand, shaking it in his best manly fashion.

"That's quite a handshake you have there, Jackson."

"You can call me Jack if you want to." Jack released Daniel's hand, returned to his chair, and picked up his book, attempting to look as mature as possible.

He was hanging up his coat as Honey came out of the kitchen, taking off her apron. To Daniel, she looked beautiful. Her hair was pulled up behind her head, emphasizing her fine features and long neck. She wore a blue dress that had a collar of white lace. It was tight at the waist, drawing his attention to the hourglass silhouette of her figure.

"What're you two looking at?" she asked. She knew the effect she was having. The look she got from Daniel made all of the fussing worthwhile. Dinner plates and soup bowls were laid stylishly in front of each chair, and the mismatched silver cutlery reflected the glow of the lamp that hung above the table.

Honey brought a covered pot of soup to the table and started ladling it into their bowls. Surrounded by adoring men, Honey smiled at each of them. "Daniel, would you like to say grace for us?"

His prayer was brief but heartfelt and was as much a statement of his own personal feelings of gratitude for being in this tiny town as it was for the delicious meal to come. He finished the prayer and there was no snickering from either Leafy or Jackson, much to his relief. Honey passed warm bread in a basket covered with a crisp white linen napkin. Satisfied that all was ready, she invited her men to eat, and they did without further encouragement.

The soup was delicious. Daniel had to restrain himself from dipping his bread into the serving bowl to finish the last drops. He and Leafy were so hungry, they ate in silence, save for the slurping noises that Jackson was fond of making, much to the annoyance of his mother.

Leafy told Daniel of the troubles they had encountered bringing a large nugget out of the mine. It was too large to fit into the ore carts and when they tried to move it on a sled, the ropes wouldn't hold the weight and it crushed the sled that it was riding on. They eventually had to break it with more dynamite. When it reached the surface, it was in three pieces. The biggest piece was thought to weigh one ton, but they found later that the actual weight was a little over eighteen-hundred pounds. Still, it was an impressive find.

Honey brought in the main course; sliced elk roast in whiskey gravy and a platter of potatoes, turnips and carrots, all roasted to a wonderful brown. No invitation was needed as they dug in with an appetite that brought a smile to the cook.

"I hear Jerome Wheeler has some big shipments coming over the Pass. What's he got in those big crates?" Honey enquired.

Daniel looked at her, surprised at her interest. "I have no idea what's in them. We brought Shirley's daughter back with us this trip." Daniel added by way of conversation.

"And how is that little gimp these days?" Honey asked, with thinly veiled contempt.

"She looks very well and she's not really a gimp." Leafy gave him a warning look. Daniel noticed that Honey was glaring at Leafy. "This dessert is delicious, Honey. What's in it?" Daniel asked.

Honey's gaze fell away from her brother's and her face softened slightly.

Daniel saw the moment of transition where her mouth moved into her oddly crooked smile, but her eyes still held the flash of anger. It was unnerving.

Honey counted off the ingredients, reciting the recipe. She spoke of the difficulty of keeping the dried fruit away from her son, who seemed to have the inquisitiveness of a nine-year old and the appetite of a miner, especially when it came to sweets. Jackson delighted in being the focus of the conversation, with Leafy and Daniel taking turns telling stories and questioning him with riddles.

"Jackson, it's time for you to go to bed, so say goodnight to your uncle and Daniel and go get ready." She poured coffee for the three of them. "It's cold out there tonight and I don't want you two to freeze on the way home."

Jackson gave a hug to Leafy and a manly handshake to Daniel. After her son had gone upstairs, Honey reached up into a cabinet and pulled down a bottle of whiskey, placing it on the table between them.

"Better get fortified for the walk home," she said, and left the room to tuck her boy in for the night.

Leafy wasted no time opening the bottle and pouring a generous amount for himself and Daniel. "We'd best take advantage of her hospitality so we don't insult her," he said with a mischievous grin.

They drank their coffee and enjoyed the relaxing feeling that Daniel had come to expect from the whiskey. Presently, Honey returned and poured herself some coffee and whiskey.

It was pleasant sitting around the table, watching the fire in the grate and listening to the hiss of the pine resin leaking onto the coals. Honey took Daniel's hand, entwining her fingers in his. They sat for what seemed like hours to Daniel, just talking and holding hands.

"Well, I've got to get going, Honey," Leafy said and stood to leave, pulling a gold piece out of his pocket. "Old man Wheeler gave us a token of his appreciation today." He handed it to his sister who admired the shiny coin. "But we still have to be at work early so's we can dig some more silver out of the ground for him." Leafy took back the coin and walked over to the coat rack. "You comin'?"

Daniel reluctantly pushed his chair back and stood. He could see that Honey was disappointed. "I have to get up early tomorrow too, and help Harry. We're partners, you know." It sounded very much like an excuse, even to him.

Honey stood and placed her hands on her hips. "If you two really must go and leave this poor widow, I guess all I have to say is that you're just like the rest."

Daniel walked over to get his coat and hat. He felt Honey slip her hand in his. She looked up at Daniel, smiling.

"Thanks for dinner, Honey," Leafy said, closing the door behind him.

"Don't go just yet," she said to Daniel. "I've wrapped up a little something for you to take with you." She went back to the kitchen and returned with a thick waxed paper parcel tied with string. "This is for when you get hungry later." She leaned closer to whisper in his ear. "I've put a little something special in there for you when you have a quiet moment."

Daniel took the parcel. Feeling the weight, he smiled. "Are you sure you left something for Jackson to eat? I'd hate to think that I'd left the poor boy to starve."

"That'll be the day. No man of mine ever goes hungry." She took his cheeks in her hands and kissed him on the lips. "That's for saving my brother's life." She pushed him through the door and into the freezing night.

Daniel was surprised to find Leafy on the steps just below the porch, looking across the valley at Ajax Mountain. He was standing with his hands deep in his pocket and his chin buried in his scarf. Neither spoke.

Daniel felt awkward walking down the path and along the road heading back to town. There were so many things about Honey he wanted to know, and the only person with the answers was walking beside him. Certain things about her troubled him. Her dislike of Kate was one of them. It could be a dangerous subject and "dangerous" was a word that brought up another of the subjects that intrigued him. At no time during the meal did the subject of Dangerous come into conversation, which struck Daniel as strange.

"Your sister's a great cook," Daniel said.

"Yeah, I guess. When she puts her mind to it, she is."

"Jackson doesn't look much like Dangerous."

"That's because he's not his father."

Daniel stopped, but Leafy kept walking. "Who's his father?"

"Honey won't tell us who the father is. I really don't know if she knows."

Daniel waited for Leafy to tell him the rest of the story. They walked along in silence for several minutes, their feet crunching on the snow.

"Dangerous married her because he felt sorry for her and he wanted her boy to have a father."

"That was a nice thing for him to do," Daniel said sincerely.

"Honey was pretty wild when she was young. She ran away from home a lot, she used to get into trouble all of the time.….. When Shady found out she was pregnant, he kicked her out of the house. She went to stay with Big Shirley for a while and that didn't sit well with my parents. Shirley was good to her and put her to work in the kitchen. That's where she learned to cook."

"Why doesn't she talk about Dangerous? Didn't she love him?" Daniel was more than a little curious.

Leafy paused a moment, considering his answer. "I think she was grateful, but she never really showed it. She always expected that everyone should make her the center of attention. She can be a bitch sometimes, Daniel. Believe me."

"She doesn't seem to like Kate very much," Daniel said plainly.

They were nearing the small bridge that crossed the river. Leafy stopped where a narrow track faded into the dark, heading downstream. He nervously scuffed his feet, making small flat patches in the snow on the side of the road as he formed his thoughts.

"Because I want to marry her, that's why. Kate and I went to school together. I can't remember not loving her. When we were at school, the other kids used to make fun of her because of Shirley's business and her limp. I used to stick up for her. I haven't seen her since she came back from Chicago. How is she?" Leafy asked, with concern and hope in his voice.

"She's fine," Daniel said. "You should go and see her."

"I might do that." Leafy sounded less than confident. "Did she ask about me?" he asked.

Daniel didn't want to lead him on, yet he didn't want to see his new friend hurt. "I know that she was glad you didn't drown." It was the best he could do under the circumstances.

Leafy smiled at the glimmer of hope. "That's something, I suppose. Well, goodnight, Daniel."

They shook hands as much to break the tension as to reassure each other of their mutual respect. As he turned to go, Leafy spoke. "Daniel, I want to warn you about something and I don't really know how to say it."

Daniel hadn't walked but a few paces. He came back to face Leafy.

"I know you like Harry and that you're partners and all," he said with sincere concern, "but he's getting in pretty deep with some of the fellers that he's been gambling with. Not that it's anyone's business, but he owes a couple of them a lot of money. I'd hate to see your cabin burned down some night with you inside of it."

Daniel's heart skipped a beat. He was sure that if there was blood in his near frozen face, it would've drained to his feet. The thought of dying in a fire scared him deeply. In a town that showed a great capacity for tolerance, there was apparently a dangerous element that had old wild-west rules of justice.

"What should I do, Leafy?"

"I don't know. Probably nothing. But if I was you, I'd keep an eye on Harry."

"Should I warn him?"

"No, I don't think that would do any good and Harry would just deny it."

They parted company and Daniel headed home, deep in thought.

He'd heard others say that Aspen was like a mother; she knew her own instinctively and either you were welcome into her or you weren't. Daniel didn't know for certain whether or not he was one of her brood, but he was getting to feel that it was a place where he might just someday belong.

Chapter 24

Harry was only half awake. He'd burned the potatoes, given the wrong change more than once, been called a cheat and had mud thrown at him. Losing streaks he'd had before, but this one was notable, unusual and possibly disastrous. He was at a loss to understand what had changed.

Every night he'd feel the soft hand and gentle persuasion of lady luck enticing him. He'd head off with grand dreams of winning big pots of money. The problem must be that he was playing against better cheaters than he'd played with before. When he played with the usual bunch of losers he did acceptably well, but when he raised the stakes, things almost never panned out for him.

His usual method was to sit at the gaming tables and make jokes to put the other gamblers at their ease, but it had become more work than peddling potatoes. To make matters worse, he'd gotten in over his head. The players that he owed money to were not the type to take kindly to a gambler who failed to pay his debts.

Thoughts of gunplay and his demise crossed his mind. He'd also heard the rumor that Doc Holliday was planning to move to Glenwood Springs, soon. Should Doc Holliday catch up with him and he didn't have the money he owed, there would definitely be a showdown. Harry had no illusions as to who would have the advantage or what the outcome would be if it came to gunplay.

He was grateful that Daniel hadn't been around because he'd had to pull up the oven and borrow from their cash reserves twice in the last week.

Absently, he felt his paunch and was reminded of the fact that his belt had two more holes punched in it just to reach around his middle. He sucked in his belly. Running his hand over his cheek, he was shocked to feel the rough stubble of several days' growth. Looking in the mirror behind the bar, he got another shock. His beard had sprouted tinges of gray. The more he looked, the more gray hair he saw. His face was also gray and pasty, and there were bags under his eyes which were bloodshot with fatigue. He was a mess by any measure.

He was half inclined to head directly over to Mr. Chin's bath house but he caught sight of Clark and Cole at a table playing liar's poker.

"Howdy, boys. Mind if I sit with you for a bit?" he asked, seating himself before they answered.

"We're just passing the time here, Harry. Don't bother pulling out your cards."

"Not a problem, boys. I'll just be resting my bones, enjoying the pleasure of your company. Anyway, I'm not in a gamblin' mood to-night." Harry had tried his best to sound sincere, but for a man to whom sincerity was a foreign tongue, he missed his mark by a mile.

He was starting to relax and even beginning to enjoy himself, when he noticed that Cole and Clark had stopped talking and were looking at something over Harry's shoulder. Harry saw the reflection of the man they were looking at and saw the man behind him reach inside his coat.

Harry tried harder to remember where he'd seen this man before. He remembered the stiff black hat he wore because of the silver concho hat band on it. His mind was not working as well as it should in this situation.

It seemed that even the man in the black coat was waiting.

"I don't know I've seen you around here before, sir. Are you new to town?"

"Somewhat," was said in reply.

The man in the coat turned back and placed a black gloved hand heavily on Harry's shoulder. "You will be there tonight, won't you, Harry?" His tone was more an order than a question.

Harry cleared his throat, desperately trying to find his most mature voice.

"Maybe. If I feel lucky."

"You'll be unluckier if you don't make it." The man turned and walked away, his hands thrust deep in his pockets, his head down. He shouldered the doors open and they parted easily for him, seeming to know what was good for them.

"I think I've had enough for the evening," said Cole. Clark quickly agreed.

"Hey." They stopped putting on their coats. "Who was that? Do you know him?" Harry said.

Cole looked at Clark and they proceeded to put on their coats and button up. Clark was the first one to offer something.

"Seemes Luckett, I do believe. Not for certain, but he's big enough to be one of them. I heard he just got out of the jail in Canyon City."

"Hey, Harry." Harry looked up. "He's not the one that gave you the shiner, is he?"

Harry put his fingers to his eye reflexively, feeling the pain as he touched the skin under his eye. "Nah. I fell down." Harry lied as much to himself as to anyone else.

"You goin' to that game tonight?" Clark asked, his concern an odd element in his voice.

Harry hauled himself up to his full and unimpressive height. "If there's a game with fools bigger than me, then I owe it to them to go relieve them of some of their hard-earned money." He tugged at his pants, hiking them higher than they needed to be, just like the prize-fighters did. They were laughing loudly as they pushed the heavy door open and stepped out into the night.

He'd been set up and fleeced and because of his foolishness, every one of the top hats in town, including the Sheriff, now knew more about him than he would have ever wanted. "Daniel!" Harry said the name as if it were some revelation. "Now, there's a thought," he said aloud, stopping to appreciate the brilliance of his new plan. He had money and he didn't spend any of it. After all, it was Harry who bought all of the provisions. His mind was working at a feverish pace, justifying all of the potential possibilities.

He could get back to the game later that night with a small stake, say fifty dollars. Then he could stay in the game for a while to see how they played. If he was clever and lucky, he'd be back on top in a flash. Smiling for the first time in ages, he quickened his pace and fired himself up for his redemption.

Considering the number of times he'd been into Daniel's pack, he was certain he had more than fifty dollars. It was embarrassing that he would have to ask for a loan, but Daniel was more than a friend, he was his partner.

Daniel was sitting in his bunk, writing. He barely stirred when Harry entered. Harry mumbled a greeting and Daniel replied in similar fashion. He checked the oven and found that it was already stocked with potatoes for the midnight shift.

"Thanks for filling the oven, partner."

"It's the least I can do. We are still partners, aren't we?"

"Yes, we are. Of course we are. You weren't worried about that, were you?" Harry placed his hand on Daniel's shoulder reassuringly.

Daniel closed his writing book and put it back into his pack.

"When are you going back over to Leadville?"

"We're going tomorrow, should be back the next day."

"It might be wise to take some extra clothes and socks with you."

"Why?" Daniel asked. Harry was pouring whiskey into his coffee cup.

"There's a ring around the moon. It's going to snow tomorrow."

"How do you know that?" Daniel was skeptical.

"I learned it from an old Ute Indian named Spotted Horse. He used to mind that the miners respected the sacred ground and I used to help him run off some of the nastier elements. I respected him and he liked me. He told me some of the things that his people did to survive up here in the mountains before the whites pushed them out."

"Are there still any of them here? I'd like to meet one someday."

"Well, I think Spotted Horse is still alive. He usually camps near the hot springs down at the end of the valley. There's good hunting down there and he sells elk meat to the railway workers." Harry leaned back importantly. "Come spring, maybe we'll take a few days off and go visit with him. I think he might like you—he doesn't like many white men, though."

"How is it that he likes you, then?" Daniel smiled, his joke easing the tension.

Harry was only slightly offended. Daniel's demeanor towards him had changed since he'd started working with Red.

"Listen, Daniel." Harry paused to make his point more dramatically. "I've got a couple of favors to ask of you." Harry took a large swallow of his coffee. "None of them will get you into trouble." Harry watched as Daniel's mind went through the possibilities. "When you go to Leadville, do you ever go into the bank?"

Daniel nodded. "Sometimes. Why?"

"I want you to make me a map of the bank. How it looks inside, where exactly the door to the safe is, and how thick the walls are." Harry didn't intend to ask everything at once, but his excitement got the best of him.

"Why? Are you going to rob the bank?" Daniel heard the choir of voices of those who had warned him about Harry.

"Nah, someone else is interested, that's all." Harry winked theatrically.

"Who asked you?"

Harry sipped his coffee. "Never mind that. You'd be doing me a huge favor. Just see how thick the walls to the vault are and if you can measure them with the length of your arm or some string or something."

Harry saw the chance to switch the subject. He got up and busied himself, pulling potatoes out and placing them in the heavy canvas bags. Daniel came over to help.

"Daniel, could you loan me some money?" Harry said smoothly. "I'll pay you back, I promise."

Daniel slowed his pace, but continued tossing the spuds into the bag. Harry crossed his fingers behind his back. Daniel looked at him and shrugged his shoulders. "I guess so," Daniel replied. "What do you need it for?"

Harry had cleverly prepared for this exact question and adopted a contrite posture, shoulders slightly slumped and hands at this side. Not the stance of the totally defeated, but humble enough for someone of a forgiving nature to relate to. Harry took a deep breath and cast his eyes to the floor as he spoke.

"Well partner, I've been a little concerned about you and the business lately and I think I've been drinking a little too much." He glanced quickly at Daniel. Daniel looked down at the floor, sharing Harry's discomfort. Harry looked at the ceiling briefly and stifled the urge to laugh.

"Look here, Daniel." Harry grabbed the surprised Daniel by the shoulders and held him at arm's length, looking him squarely in the eyes. "You mean a lot to me. You know that, don't you?"

Daniel could only nod.

"I want you to help me stop gambling. Will you help me? If you help me pay off my gambling debts, I promise I'll never let it happen again."

Daniel was extremely uncomfortable being so close. "Alright Harry, how much do you need? Just let me go."

"Thanks, partner." Harry hugged him fervently.

Daniel patted Harry on the back twice in manly fashion. "How much do you need? Ten dollars?"

"Fifty dollars," Harry said.

"What?" Daniel barked.

"Come on, I know you must have some money saved," Harry pleaded. "I'll pay you back from the business. I'll be making most of the money now that you're working on the wagons so much."

Daniel went over to his bag, which was lying open, some of his meager possessions piled on the floor next to his bed. He was not so concerned that Harry knew where he kept his money, but about the other secrets that his bag held.

What surprised him was that Harry asked for the exact amount that he'd saved and had folded into his Bible. He opened his pack and pulled out his money. Daniel knew that he'd never see the money again, but somehow he felt that he owed it to Harry to trust him.

"Take it, it's yours." Harry hadn't made a move to take the money. "Go ahead, take it. I don't need it back," he said, looking at Harry's crestfallen expression. He had no doubt that he would go out and gamble it away. Daniel shook the money at him. Harry took it and counted it, Daniel noticed, before stuffing it in his pants pocket.

"Don't worry, partner, you'll get it back, I assure you." Harry shook Daniel's hand again and grabbed his coat from the back of the door. "Well, I'm off to work. Have a good trip over the Pass," Harry said. "You should take extra clothes like I said; it's likely to get real cold up there." Harry paused, "and thanks for the loan."

The door closed. Daniel was left to pack his things and turn in for the night; he had to be out at Red's place early. He was tired, but he tried finishing the letter to his mother, telling her about his jobs and the things he'd seen. He folded his letter and placed it next to the one he'd received from her. The Bible was thinner now that there was no money in it.

Chapter 25

It was still dark when Daniel awoke and dressed. Harry was not home. His bed was just as messy as it had been the previous night. Daniel made sure he'd placed his pack deeply under his bed. Though it was little defense against Harry, it was better than leaving it on the table.

He walked quickly down to the stables and found them to be as quiet as a church when he entered. He saddled Marigold, who seemed pleased to have some company. As he was backing Marigold out of her stall, he heard Joe coughing. Daniel was surprised to see him come out from his room fully dressed, as if he'd been awake for hours.

"Hi there, son." Joe waved tiredly. "You're gonna be late if you don't get a move on." He coughed again and this time there was a deep rumbling in his chest. Joe took a deep breath before continuing. "Pete was out of here ten minutes ago. He's probably wondering where the bejesus you've got to."

Joe would be someone to test the mettle of any woman. He gurgled up phlegm and spat it expertly into the flames of his small stove. What missed the flames sizzled on its hot iron belly. Joe stood in a trance, watching the different hues of the flames as they transformed his expectoration into light and steam.

"Can't do that at home, now can you?" Joe smiled. "You got enough warm clothes? It's about time we got a decent storm these next few days."

"Harry told me it's because of the ring around the moon."

"He said that, did he?"

"Yeah, he told me that an old Indian told him about the ring around the moon years ago."

"He told you that?" Joe smiled.

"Yes, sir, I can't wait to meet the old Indian."

"Well, you're looking at about the oldest Indian around these here parts, because I'm the one that told him that shit about the moon and the storms."

Daniel dropped his shoulders and let out a sigh.

"It's just Harry being Harry is all. No problem. Now go on and get out there and help Red get back alive one more time."

They walked outside together and Joe opened the gate. As Daniel passed through, Joe took hold of the reins. "Mind if I say something?"

Daniel climbed into the saddle. "Not at all, but I don't know if I can take any more information about Harry today."

Joe blew air through his lips. "Nah, nothing like that. I don't want'a get my nose into someone else's business, but if I were you, I'd be a mite careful of Honey. Not that she's a bad person, that ain't the case at all. It's just that she's lookin' hard for something and I would take my time being it, if I were a young man like you."

"I'm not sure I know what you mean," Daniel said.

"I'm just telling you to be careful there. Them women can be just plain bad luck. One day you'll see what I mean. You're a good boy, Daniel. Just be careful or they'll take everything you've got." He slapped Marigold on the rump and she started forward, glad to be moving in the cold air. "And another thing—"

Daniel reined his horse in and turned around to face Joe.

"If I were you, I'd be making a play for Kate. I hear she likes you." Daniel beamed. "And about that job with Wheeler? Think hard about it."

"Thanks, Joe," Daniel said, as he nudged Marigold into a trot.

"No problem," he heard Joe say.

⚍⚎

The ride over the Pass was uneventful, and they slept in Red's bunkhouse. Pete was the first up and when the others finally roused themselves, they found a pot of coffee bubbling on the stove. The room was warm but drafts came from all corners. They wasted no time climbing into their clothes. Some even wore their hats as they pulled on their pants.

Soon they were ready and set off at a good pace. The speed forced them to bury their faces into their collars and the cold air froze their nose hairs and made their breath freeze onto their beards and chins. Most of the men had beards or at least full moustaches and the benefit of this was apparent to Daniel. His face felt like it was going to fall off and his hands, clenched around the reins, were frozen after only the first mile.

They arrived at the bank as the manager, Mr. Ebest, was opening the back door for them. There was no deputy on duty, so Red had Daniel take a position by the door. Daniel watched as the manager opened the vault. He couldn't see the combination being dialed, but he did see the man stand up and turn the wheel several complete revolutions. The door must have weighed at least a ton, because it took both the manager and Red to pull it open, its hinges not making a sound. They emerged several minutes later with a cart piled high with bags of money which they wheeled to the door, where the men loaded it into crates that were then padlocked into the wagon.

"What're you doin' here, son?"

Daniel jumped as the voice startled him. He stood face to face with the Sheriff.

"R-R-Red told me to watch the door," Daniel stammered, looking away from the man's face, just inches from his own.

"Red, this little runt one of yours?" the Sheriff called out. Red came out of the vault with the manager close behind. Daniel was being held against the door by the weight of the Sheriff, who had lifted him up off the ground by a forearm across Daniel's chest and under his chin. Daniel was having difficulty breathing.

"Come on now, Sheriff, don't go scaring my men," Red said quietly.

"Haven't I seen this one before, Red?" he asked.

"Sheriff, I'm sure you've got other things to do. Come on, now." Red took a chance and gently pried his arm away from Daniel's throat. Red was close enough to smell the whiskey on his breath.

Daniel felt the weight on his chest lessen. With his feet on the floor again, his breath started coming in short gasps.

Hiking his pants up under his overhanging belly, the Sheriff turned back to Daniel, eyeing him carefully. "I don't want to see you here anymore, son. Is that clear, Red? I don't trust this little shit and I don't know how you could, either." The Sheriff's attention waned, drunken fatigue showing in his ruddy complexion and drooping eyes. "I'll be glad when that train puts you and your kind out'a business for good. We don't want any of you criminal types over here, stinking up our valley."

Red pushed Daniel through the door and closed it behind him, blocking the Sheriff's path. Pete, who had been silently watching the proceedings, motioned for Daniel to get on his horse quickly.

"I'd have to say that you got a real friend back there, Daniel," Red said to him and laughed. "He's just a mean bastard. Don't go taking it too personal, now." They rode briskly, heading as fast as possible away from the bank. "The next time you two meet, he probably won't even remember. He was drunk, you know."

"Yeah, I could smell it on his breath." Daniel rubbed his face, trying to rid himself of the taint.

"The whole town is scared of him. He keeps a tight rein, so the town fathers let him terrorize the poor miners and anyone else they decide not to like. His deputies are just as bad, especially his sons. As a matter of fact, one of them was the deputy at the bank yesterday. Did you see him? He was barely awake."

Daniel felt no better.

Chapter 26

D aniel woke lazily. He couldn't remember making it home, but he was in his bed and undressed, his clothes in a jumble on the floor. The cabin was warm and the smell of coffee and bacon lingered in the air. Daniel could hear Harry somewhere, but he tried to shut him out; his head hurt too much.

"Ah, you're awake finally." Harry filled a cup with coffee and whiskey and brought it over to Daniel. When he was slow to take the cup, Harry said, "Go on, take it. It's not like I make you breakfast in bed every day, is it?"

It was too early in the morning for Daniel to try to piece together these strange happenings, so he took the coffee and leaned back against the wall, trying to quiet the hammers inside of his head.

"There's bacon cooked over there, but you're going to have to make your own eggs." Harry reached into his pocket, pulled out a roll of money, peeled off some notes, and handed them to Daniel. "That's the money I borrowed from you. Go on, count it, there's fifty dollars there."

"You must've been lucky, Harry."

"You might say it was luck." He looked at Daniel with a smile. "I prefer to think of it as superior skill and daring. Oh, by the way, Honey came over to invite you to Thanksgiving dinner at her house. I told her that you were having dinner here with Red and Joe and me."

For whatever it was that Harry had planned for dinner, Daniel was grateful, but disappointed that he was going to miss out on Honey's cooking. Harry sipped his coffee, looking pleased with himself.

"I have to go and get more potatoes today. Can you help me?"

"Sure." Daniel got out of bed and dressed. He opened the door and had to shield his eyes. The glare of the sun reflecting off the new snow was painful. He waded through the new fallen snow and was surprised to find Willy shivering on the other side of the facility.

"Hey, Willy, how're you feeling?" asked Daniel.

"I got the trots."

Daniel felt for the poor man. It was hard enough having the runs in a warm toilet, but to have to sit in freezing temperatures with your buttocks sticking to the rough wooden bench was worthy of sympathy. Even the newspaper they used was frozen. The additional discomfort added insult to injury.

"Harry had better be careful." Willy mumbled.

"What do you mean? He won some money last night." Finished with his business, Daniel was in a hurry to get back to the cabin's warmth as quickly as possible.

"He won a lot, Daniel. But that's not the problem."

"What's the problem, then?"

"It's who he won it from that's the problem, and he's struttin' around bragging about it."

"Who was he gambling with?"

"I don't know for sure, but a guy they call "Duke" was one of them. He's a mean son of a bitch. If he was there, then the judge was probably there too. And if the judge was there, then possibly Wheeler was there, and then those lawyers what're tryin' to buy up all of town."

Daniel opened the door on his side to leave.

"You should watch out for the guy in the black hat and big bearskin coat," Willy added.

"Why?" Daniel asked.

"Because he doesn't like Harry and I think he's a friend of Doc Holliday."

"Thanks for the advice, Willy."

Daniel headed back to the cabin and found Harry packing the empty potato sacks onto the old sled. He decided not to say anything and helped Harry.

They pulled the sleds to the stable and set about saddling their horses. As they were heading out, they saw No Problem heading their way.

"How do you fellers feel today?" He looked from Harry to Daniel.

"I feel fine this day, Joe. How about you?" Harry replied.

"Well, I'm alive and that's generally a good thing. How're you son? Do you think you'll live?" No Problem was stroking Marigold's forelock.

"Not quite sure. How did I get home last night?"

Joe had a good laugh. "Red and Pete got you home and I took care of Marigold here. She seemed a little concerned that her owner could barely stand and was sick in her stall."

Daniel let his head fall forward in embarrassment.

"Don't worry, son, it's not like we haven't been there, have we, Harry?"

"Once or twice, Joe. Not that I'm proud of it."

"None of us are the day after, I reckon. But it happens." Joe checked the rigging of the sleds. "That's a pretty nifty setup you've got there. You could probably carry a cow over the Pass with it."

"That's not what I had in mind, but thanks for the help. We're about to test it out, go on down valley and pick up another load of spuds." Harry patted his side pocket. "That old rancher down there will be happy to see me today, I reckon. I'll be able to pay him in cash for a change."

"That'll make him happy, but how about me?"

Harry pulled out the roll of money, peeled off some bills and handed them to Joe.

"Looks like you've been cheating at poker again." Joe winked at Daniel.

"You know how it is, Joe. When you're hot, you're hot."

Joe counted the money twice and patted Harry on the leg. "Thanks, Harry. Let me know how the new sled works, will ya'?"

"No problem, we'll catch up with you later."

Harry gently nudged his horse to a walk and watched as the sled fell in behind his horse. The noon whistle blew, startling Daniel. As soon as they passed the new hotel, Harry kicked his horse into a trot and they headed out of town. The day was sunny, but the sun had little warmth and they felt the chill on their faces. They negotiated the narrow stretch of road, carved out of the shale bluffs overlooking the Roaring Fork, and came to the section of the valley that was used in the summer for growing potatoes and grazing the cattle.

They bought their potatoes from a farmer named Cerise who was reluctant to talk to Harry until he had shown him the wad of money he was carrying. The farmer then became as friendly as a lost brother and shared some of the whiskey Harry was carrying in his saddlebag. There was much backslapping and shaking of hands as they took their leave. The farmer even went into his house and came out with a freshly killed chicken and wished them a Happy Thanksgiving. Harry was a happy man as he rode back towards town.

Curious to see how well the sleds worked with weight in them, Harry kicked his horse into a run. Daniel followed. The horses handled the weight well. With the roads snow-covered, the sleds slid along behind them easily with little drag. Daniel was surprised at how fast the horses could cover the ground with all of the weight. Except for having to slow down through the curves, they rode as if there was nothing at all in the sleds.

They had been gone less than three hours before they were back at their cabin to unload the potatoes. As they were unsaddling their horses at the barn, Joe came in from outside, brushing off his coat and stamping his feet. "How'd it go?" he inquired.

"Couldn't be better, Joe. The new sled rode well and even the old sled rode straight as an arrow with the new harness." Harry walked back to the sleds outside with Joe. "Do you think I could rig up some long reins where I could sit on the sled and ride in it?"

Joe put his finger to his chin and thought for a while. "Why would you want to do that?"

"Oh, no reason. I just was wonderin', that's all." Harry hurried to explain.

"Well, if you ran the reins through the chest strap...of course, you'd have to put a couple of rings in the strap, but it could be done, I guess." Joe was intrigued by the challenge.

"Let's give it a try. Would you do it for me, Joe?" Harry was at his most charming.

"Sure, no problem."

"You'll be comin' for dinner on Thursday won't you, Joe? We'll be expecting you. We'll be having turkey," Harry said as he hoisted the chicken in the air.

"Sure, thanks, Harry. I'll be there." Joe watched them go, shaking his head.

❧

Daniel helped Harry sell the potatoes that evening. Afterwards, Daniel took the gear back to the cabin and Harry headed into town. There was food in the cabin and fresh bread, so Daniel ate well and finished his letter to his mother before he dropped off to sleep.

Daniel was not surprised when he woke that Harry was not home. It was not yet dawn.

Arriving at the Ranch, there was a fair share of joking at his expense about his falling down drunk again. It was gentle ribbing and in fact there was a lot of sympathy from them all. Red gave him a look, shook his head and "tut-tutted", then said nothing more about it.

The trip over to Leadville was uneventful. Daniel learned more about the horses and their skill, and the management of both the team and the wagon. At the railway station, there were more large heavy crates destined to go to Jerome Wheeler. Daniel drove that wagon to the stables with the cargo while Red, Pete and the others picked up the money from the bank. He had no contact with either the Sheriff or his daughter and that was quite alright with him.

At the end of the trip, Red paid them all in cash.

With cash in their pockets, they all headed for drinks at the Paragon Bar. Shirley welcomed them in and gave Red a kiss on the cheek to his embarrassment. To Daniel's disappointment, Kate was nowhere to be seen.

"How would you two like to come over to my place for Thanksgiving dinner?" Shirley had her arm through Red's, but was looking at Daniel.

"That's very kind," Daniel said, "but Harry is making dinner for us." Shirley frowned. "It wasn't my idea," said Daniel. He deeply regretted the fact that he would miss out on spending time with Kate.

"Well, I'm very disappointed. I'm sure Kate will be disappointed, too." Shirley leaned forward, kissed him lightly on the cheek and gave his hand a squeeze. "Off you go now. Go get some rest."

Daniel said goodnight to Red and Pete at Joe's stable. He was so tired, he could barely unsaddle Marigold. His arms were weak from driving the team; simply brushing Marigold was difficult. The brush felt as heavy as if it was made of lead. He noticed how well defined her muscles were becoming. Having fed and watered her, talked with her a little about Kate, he slapped her on the rump affectionately and headed home.

⊰⊱

Thanksgiving dinner was interesting, especially the way Harry interpreted it. He did the best he could to make the place look presentable. There was almost nothing to work with, being that there were only four tin plates, four forks and three knives. He bustled around in the kitchen, muttering to himself, and Daniel was glad when Red and Joe arrived, bearing cigars and a bottle of whiskey.

For the occasion Harry had borrowed two chairs so there was seating for everyone at the small table. There was no turkey, but plenty of chicken since Harry had bought another three. With his newfound wealth, Harry had also bought vegetables and to his credit, had made a respectable meal.

"Harry, what did you do, hire Honey to cook for you?" Red asked as he opened a bottle and looked in the cupboards for glasses. The whiskey splashed and the bottle gurgled as the amber liquid gained its release.

Harry had rescued an apron from somewhere, probably one of the local bartenders, and wiped his hands on it before taking the glass from Red.

"Here's to your generous invitation. Thank you, Harry." They clinked glasses and drained their whiskeys with sighs of satisfaction all around.

"What can we help you with there, Harry?" asked Joe, who looked far from competent with his ability to help in the kitchen.

"You know what, fellers, why don't you all just sit there and relax, because we'll be eating in just a few minutes."

Daniel was proud of what he and Harry had done. The counter was clean and cleared, they had made up their beds and the privacy curtains were pulled back, making the cramped space seem twice as roomy. The iron oven still dominated the room, but instead of seeming like an escapee from a foundry, it was welcome with the liberal amount of heat it dispensed.

Harry busied himself with setting the table with the bread and vegetables and when he reached into the oven, the smell that arose filled the room instantly. The chickens came out browned perfectly. Harry placed them on the top of the oven to drain while he made gravy. When all was done, Harry placed the chickens on the table and finally sat down with his guests.

Joe poured more whiskey. Daniel could already feel the warm glow coming from his stomach after the first shot.

"To our host and chef!" They toasted Harry. "A Happy Thanksgiving to us all."

Red took the initiative and said a short prayer of thanks to God for the abundance and another toast to thank Harry for the food he'd placed for them on the table. Daniel appreciated being among grown men who were longtime friends, and where there seemed to be no penalty for being the youngest person at the table.

"They're the smallest turkeys I've ever seen," said Joe, "but at least you had the sense to steal a flock of them." Joe watched Harry serve up the birds, holding his utensils at the ready.

"I'll save your favorite piece Joe, this little bit right over where it shits." Harry continued serving. They helped themselves to the potatoes, peeled and baked golden brown, with plenty of onions, carrots and yams steaming with the smell of butter and honey. The sound of metal utensils scraping the tin plates was loud and comical.

Daniel pulled back to watch this horde of three pillage the table. When he did, the first pang of guilt hit his chest like an anvil falling. He realized with shock that he hadn't even thought of his mother and sister all day; he couldn't even remember if he'd finished their letter.

"Are you alright, Daniel?" asked Red, sitting opposite. The scraping noises stopped as the others looked at him.

"I'm fine, I just thought of something I have to do."

"What's that, sneak over to see Shirley's daughter later?" Harry interrupted, chewing his food with his mouth open.

"No, that's not it at all." Daniel quietly went back to what was left of his meal. Red and Pete looked at each other, concerned for Daniel.

"I hear she's got your eye." Harry was intent on his food and noticed nothing, as usual. "And you've set your sights on her, I think." He went on with his eating. Red looked across at Daniel, but there was nothing to be read from his face.

"I just remembered that I haven't written to my family for a while and I guess I miss them. Not that this isn't great, but I miss them."

Harry pushed his chair away from the table. "He's a kid and he misses his mother."

"Harry, you don't have to be a kid to miss your family. Sometimes— even though I'm not as old as Joe here and my mother's been dead twenty years—sometimes I still miss her too," Red confessed.

"Don't you ever feel like that, Harry? Don't you have anyone you miss?" Joe asked. Harry ignored the question and continued eating.

"I pity you, Harry, I really do." Red said shaking his head. "That reminds me, Daniel, I've got something for you." He went to his coat hanging on the door hook and came back and handed Daniel a letter.

"I'm sorry I forgot to give it to you earlier. The postmaster in Leadville put it in my mail bag. He must've remembered your name from your letter I mailed for you. He's a pretty nosy feller."

Daniel took the letter, it was from his mother. His feelings of loneliness rose again but he pushed them back as he put the letter in his pocket.

"Aren't you going to read it even?" Harry asked.

"I'll read it later." Daniel tried to keep his voice level.

"Hey, don't get me wrong." Harry defended himself. "I've got a family, too." Harry got up and started putting more food on his plate. He was uncomfortable. "I've got some wives. Some kids too, out there in Utah, and don't you think I miss them?"

Red and Joe burst out laughing.

"Are you trying to josh us, Harry? You can't even remember half their names," Joe said, pouring more whiskey all around.

They drank more and the pie that Harry brought out from the oven for dessert was remarkable. It was filled with soft, hot pumpkin squash and sugar and had a dark golden skin on the top. It was spicy too, but had a lingering sweetness that Daniel had never tasted before.

"Did you see the ring around the moon last night?"

"Where did that come from, the old Indian again?" Joe asked, his mouth twisted in glee.

"I'll bet you ten dollars I can guess the weather in these here mountains better than you can Joe, you old bag of bones." Harry counted out money and threw it on the table in front of Joe.

"What's the interest in the weather all of a sudden?" Joe asked. "You still planning to rob the bank over there?"

"No! I just want you to put your money where your mouth is. I don't think you're as good at it as I am." Harry sat forward in his chair.

"No problem, Harry." Harry reached across the table and they shook hands. Joe sat back again and finished his whiskey.

"What's all this about robbing the bank of Leadville? Are you still on about that?" Red sat forward. "It can't be done. I've heard all the plans. Horses, the train, everything imaginable. There're only two roads out of town in the winter and you couldn't outrun the telegraph, no matter how fast you rode."

Harry sat back down in his chair, a self-satisfied smile on his face.

"How much money they got in that bank? What do you think, Red? You've been in that vault—how much money might be in there?" He sat up and poured the last of the whiskey around the table. "One million, two million?"

"Around there somewhere, I'd guess," Red said confidently. "But it can't be done, so why torment yourself Harry?" Red paused. "I hate to say this, but better men than you've tried over the years to come up with a plan to rob that bank."

"Coffee?" said Harry, jumping from his chair, reaching under the counter and coming up with another bottle of whiskey, almost full. "You're right there, Red, it can't be done." Harry intoned. "Not from here anyway, that's for sure. It's too far. What is it—about fifty miles each way?"

Joe and Red nodded.

"Close enough," Red said. "It could be a little more and that alone makes it impossible. No horse could go one-hundred miles in a day." He paused. "None of the horses from around here could do it, I guarantee that."

"And not over the Pass in the winter. You'd have to be crazy." Harry smiled into his drink. Joe and Red passed a look between them that Daniel saw.

"You'd freeze yourself to death on the Pass and I'd give serious thought to what could happen to you over there in that jail if you got caught. There's also the fact that as soon as Doc Holliday found out you were in jail there, he'd be having your meals made special, if you get what I mean. Not such a good place for you to end up, I think, Harry?" Red said.

"Oh, well. You can always dream, can't you?" Harry regretted having this conversation. "Don't go botherin' yourself over it, OK?" Harry started pulling bags of potatoes out from the storage and putting them into the oven. He gave the length of chain he was holding a tug and the log easily slid inside the oven another foot.

"That pulley still works, eh?" asked Joe somewhat surprised.

"Just like the day we put the damned thing up, I'd say." Harry poured coffee and more whiskey around and sat back down. "Just like that new sled we made, Joe. Built to last."

After the dinner and the whiskey they were all sleepy, except for Harry, who still had to go outside to feed the miners for the midnight shift. "Think you can give me a hand tonight, Daniel?"

"You stay here and I'll go do it." Daniel volunteered.

"That's awful nice of you, Daniel. I think I'll take you up on that kind offer." Harry sat back in his chair smoking his cigar.

⊰⊱

Daniel thought he knew the ropes about being a cabin mate with Harry. He was glad to have the chance to do something nice to avoid the friction that so often occurred between them. He got up and went about the business of retrieving the cooked potatoes from the oven and placing them into the heavy canvas bags that protected them. Harry did help by opening and closing the door.

"How's the boy workin' out with you, Red?" Harry asked trying to sound concerned.

"Why do you ask?"

"I was just wonderin' if you were planning to take him away from me is all."

"I think that old Jerome B. Wheeler's planning his future for him at the moment."

Harry looked like he'd been slapped in the face by a wet fish.

"Daniel didn't tell you that he had a meeting with Wheeler? He asked if Daniel wanted to work for him," Red said.

"You knew about this, didn't you, Joe?"

Joe nodded drunkenly.

"I wonder when he was planning to tell me."

"Well, we'd better be going. Thanks for the fine dinner, Harry. You're a man of constant surprises. Come on Joe. Let's get us home and to bed. Do you need a hand?"

Joe slapped at Red's offered hand. "I'm not a cripple yet. I can manage by myself." Joe instantly fell to his knees. Red helped him back to his feet as Harry looked on.

"Glad to see that you can still hold your liquor, Joe." Harry sniggered.

Red gave him a cross look as they made their way to the door. "We'll be seeing you, Harry. Thanks again." Harry closed the door behind them and when he knew they were gone, pulled out his money and counted it twice.

"Ahhh," he said, smelling the pile of cash. "Thanksgiving."

Harry fell onto his bed, the money clutched to his chest. It was the soundest sleep he'd had in months.

Out on the mountainside, Daniel was tooth-chattering cold. The miners came and went and the hot potatoes warmed his hands as he did his work. When he put his hands into his pockets, he would touch the envelope and be reminded. He could feel the heat coming from the letter. He knew she had to be sending him her love. He looked up at the full moon in the star-crowded sky and sent his thoughts and all of his love east, to his mother, his sister and whoever else in his family that was still alive.

Chapter 27

"Christmas'll be here soon," Daniel said pleasantly, walking the narrow line between Harry's moods. Harry's behavior had become more unpredictable than usual. Daniel was glad that he had another job which took him away from Aspen and Harry for days at a time.

"Are you going to work this morning," Harry asked, "or am I going to have to go do it again?"

"No, I'll do it. You look like you could use some rest."

"Are you saying that I need to get some sleep?"

Harry had aged in the weeks since Thanksgiving dinner. His face was more drawn, and noticeably he had deep dark circles under his eyes. He'd chosen to grow a beard, but though it was filling out, it looked like it belonged on someone else's face.

When he returned to the cabin, Harry was snoring loudly, the blanket pulled up to his chin, his hands crossed over his chest as if he were dead. Daniel pulled the curtain around the bed and set about tidying up the cabin. Daniel heard a soft knock on the door and opened it to find Honey and her son Jackson.

"Hello, Honey. Hello, Jack. Come on in," he said. He looked back over his shoulder at the mess inside.

"You don't have to invite us in if you don't want to, but I know how you men live, so I won't be shocked if it's messy." Honey smiled.

"No, no, please come in, but we have to be quiet, Harry's sleeping."

Honey made a quick appraisal before she sat down at the table. "I see you've been tidying up." She seemed impressed. "It's never been this clean." Jackson stayed near the door until Daniel pulled out a chair for him. He sat at the table like a little gentleman, back straight, hands in his lap.

"Would you like coffee? We don't have much else."

Honey smiled and shook her head. "No, thank you," she said as she opened her coat and removed her gloves. "You're probably wondering why we're here."

Daniel shrugged.

"You'll just think of me as a crazy old widow," she smiled impishly, "but I haven't seen you for some time now and I was wondering if you'd forgotten us."

"Oh, no. That's not true at all. I've been busy with Red. We've been bringing all of this stuff over for the new hotel and I'm a wagon driver now, so I'm hardly ever here."

Honey reached over and placed her warm soft hand on his. "Well, I know you're here tonight, so we were wondering if you'd like to come over and have dinner with us. We'd like that, wouldn't we, Jackson?" She squeezed Daniel's hand. Jackson nodded. Harry snored. They laughed at the interruption.

"How did you know I was here today?"

"I'm a woman. I have my ways." She laughed at Daniel's knitted brow. "No Problem, of course. He pretty much knows where everyone is." She patted his hand. "So you'll come, then?" Honey stood and Jackson made a dash for the door. She busied herself with the buttons on her coat, letting the moment grow between them. Stepping closer, waiting for his reply, her coat now buttoned to her chin, she took both of his hands in hers and looked up into his eyes. Honey intoxicated him.

"I'd like that."

"Good. Come over around dusk and bring your appetite." She kissed him lightly on the cheek. "You'd better get back to work," she said. "Come on, Jackson." They both waved back to him as they disappeared down the path.

Daniel had finished cleaning and was walking into town when two men on skis appeared racing towards him, swinging their arms and legs in big movements, the steam of their breath coming like puffs of smoke. There was an air of competition between them as they came closer, their arms pumping and their legs striding forward again and again, rhythmically. He could hear them yelling at each other and recognized the accented voices.

"Bjorn," he yelled as they shot past. Bjorn, the stockier of the two, glided to a halt. "It's me, Daniel. Do you remember? You and your brother saved us down on the river."

Bjorn took off his wooden ski goggles and pulled the scarf from his face. "Ja, ja. I do," he said. "You're the ones ve tried to saw out in our sauna. How are you doing? Hey, Tom, come here." He waited for Tom to maneuver himself back to where they were standing. "Zis is one of ze boys zat fell in the river zat day."

"You boys staying out of ze river?" Tom asked, laughing.

"I have, but I don't know about Leafy," he answered, admiring their skis. "I've never seen skiing. Is it difficult?"

"Not too much for someone young like yourself."

"Can I try?"

"Ja, sure vhy not? Ve vere hoping you vould vant to learn veren't ve, Tom?"

"If you like it, ve vill teach you to do it properly," Tom said enthusiastically.

They strapped Bjorn's skis onto Daniel's boots and Tom showed him how to walk, using the poles to help push. In a few minutes, he was skiing down the road at a fast walk while Tom ran beside him giving him advice. He was enjoying the feeling and rhythm of sliding on snow.

Gradually, he came to a stop and decided to turn around. His skis crossed and he fell in the snow bank. Bjorn and Tom were laughing as they helped him to his feet and out of the skis.

"Vell? Did you like it?" Daniel nodded enthusiastically. "Den we do it again soon ja?" Much to Daniel's regret, they strapped their skis on their feet again and said goodbye. Daniel watched them ski gracefully up the road until they disappeared.

<hr />

The streets were bustling with excitement, since Christmas was less than a week away. Every shop door had a wreath and strands of bright shiny ornaments hung in every window. Daniel peered into the shops and was heading nowhere in particular when he saw Shirley, Kate and another younger girl entering a fancy dress shop. He was peering through the window trying to see Kate when he felt a tap on his shoulder and heard Jerome Wheeler's booming voice.

"Merry Christmas to you, Mr. Carrington." He reached for Daniel's hand and shook it firmly. "How are you this fine day?" he said, brimming with good cheer. "What're you doin' outside my wife's dress shop? Not planning on wearing a dress, are you?" He looked around to be sure that his joke was well received. Carter and Boot Hill laughed appropriately. "Did I invite you to my Christmas Party at the Hotel, Mr. Carrington? If I didn't, please consider yourself invited."

"That's very kind of you, Mr. Wheeler. I'd be honored to come."

Shirley and her girls appeared from the store, carrying a dress box. Daniel smiled at Kate and she smiled at him in return. Shirley smiled at Wheeler. "Good morning, ladies." Wheeler tipped his hat politely and took Daniel by the elbow, steering him away. "Come with me, Mr. Carrington, I've something to show you." Daniel was escorted across Main Street and into the Hotel Jerome, where he found himself in the midst of a cyclone of construction activity.

Workmen were everywhere. The foyer, dining room and banquet rooms bustled with painters, plasterers, gilders and a variety of other workers.

The bar was nearly finished, almost to the point that it looked ready to serve customers. The walls were covered with expensive looking gold and red velvet-flocked wallpaper in a fleur-de-lis design and a large gilded mirror behind the ornately carved bar caught much of the light coming through the large windows and created a bright and genteel atmosphere. Wheeler puffed up and put his thumbs into his suspenders, gloating over his dream.

"And this is where Aspen's gentlemen will drink. Politely speaking, it's not going to be one of those nasty miner's dens, I assure you. It'll be known world-wide as a gentleman's bar, I promise you. Come on." Wheeler led the way. His mood turned progressively darker as they moved into the shambles that the dining room had become. Men were laying carpet under the ladders of the plasterers, who were trying to cover the miles of wiring snaking behind the walls and across the ceiling, pulling at the fresh plaster.

"Carter, get me the idiot who's supposed to be in charge here, will you please."

Carter came back with a small-shouldered man wearing a harried look and a hat that was too small for his head. Wheeler excused himself and when they were almost out of earshot, lit into the foreman, reducing him to splinters in moments.

"Just you make sure it's ready for Christmas, Mr. Kincaid, or so help me God, they'll be burying what's left of you in my basement. Do I make myself clear?" The foreman hurried away. The electric lights glowed for a few moments, flickered and then went dark.

"That's what has me most concerned, boys. The Hotel Jerome is very important to me. I want this building to be known as the first building in the state illuminated by electric lamps and I want it to happen on Christmas day." Noise and bedlam prevailed all around them. Daniel couldn't see how all could be in order for Wheeler's Grand Opening on Christmas night. "And by God, that's exactly what's going to happen. Right, Carter?"

"Yes, Mr. Wheeler."

"Get on with it, Carter. Make it all happen the way I want it to happen." Carter vanished from the room with Boot Hill in tow.

"Come with me, son," Wheeler said and led the way through the foyer and up the staircase, avoiding the obvious obstructions, careful not to get his clothes dirty. At the top of the stairs, they entered a large well-furnished room that overlooked the street.

"This will be my private salon. My 'sanctum sanctorum' as it were." Indeed it was going to be a grand salon, already decorated with some fine oil paintings. Wheeler strode around the room, looking out of the windows and admiring his views of the mountain and easterly towards Independence Pass. Daniel silently watched him parade around the room. "Close the door and sit down." He motioned to a high backed smoking chair, while he sat in a long red velvet couch and lit a cigar. Daniel closed the door and the noise of the workers diminished.

"Thought anymore about working for me?"

Daniel leaned forward, hoping that the pose would give the impression that he'd been giving it deep consideration. In fact, he'd hardly thought about it at all. "I've been busy going over to Leadville, Mr. Wheeler, but I have been giving it serious thought."

"That's good, son. I respect a man who thinks before he makes his decisions." He puffed some more toxins into the room. "You are coming to my party here on Christmas now, aren't you?"

"Oh, yes, I'd be delighted, sir."

"I want you to meet my family. You know, since you're going to be working for me soon," Wheeler gave Daniel a knowing wink. "I think it would be good for us all to get to know each other, don't you agree?"

Daniel nodded.

"Good. Then we'll look forward to seeing you." He stood looking down into the street and Daniel followed Jerome's gaze. Shirley was handing boxes to the girls in her buggy. They watched as she got in and drove it expertly around some construction debris, then headed towards her house. Daniel leaned forward, watching Kate. Wheeler turned him back into the room. "They're just prostitutes son. Use 'em, abuse 'em and lose 'em eh?" Wheeler let out a deep laugh at his own joke. "But I guess you know about all of that already."

"I'm not like that, sir," Daniel said, hoping that the conversation would end there. Wheeler swung around to face him.

"Do you mean you don't like women?"

"No, no, Mr. Wheeler. I just mean that I haven't met the right one yet."

"You're an interesting young man. Do you know that, Mr. Carrington?"

"No, sir. I'm not too different from most anyone else."

"Not true. There aren't many men like me out there and I guarantee you that there aren't many out there like you." Together they walked to the top of the stairs and looked down on the bedlam below. Wheeler seemed serene.

"Do give my offer some serious thought, Mr. Carrington." He patted Daniel on the shoulder with a gentle hand. "I'll be expecting you here, come Christmas. We're going to have the best party this little old mining town has ever seen."

"What should I wear?" Daniel had walked down several stairs already.

"Wear whatever you have clean and it wouldn't hurt to smell good. You know how the ladies like a sweet-smelling man." Wheeler laughed a rumbling laugh. "I've got someone special I want you to meet." Wheeler gave Daniel a knowing wink and returned to the room leaving Daniel to wind his way through the mob of workers.

⬦

"Daniel," Harry called. "Are you awake yet?"

"Yeah, I'm awake. What do you want?"

It was still dark. "Remember when I asked you to measure the thickness of the bank walls?"

"Yeah." The gears in Daniel's mind were slowly engaging.

"Were they more than a foot thick?"

Daniel remembered the confrontation with the Sheriff, the weight of the man's arm on his chest and his ugly face. "Oh, I guess so. Why?"

"I'm making a list of things we need and I just wanted to know how much dynamite to bring."

"What did you say?" Daniel flung back the curtain and leapt to his feet, wearing just his socks and long underwear.

Harry continued, not bothering to look up. "Oh, I was thinking that we should take the right amount of dynamite. All we'd do is piss them off if we only dented their precious bank and didn't even rob the damned thing." There was complete silence from Daniel. "But then, it wouldn't do to take too much of the stuff, that would be a waste, wouldn't it?"

"What the hell are you talking about, Harry? You're not really thinking about robbing that bank in Leadville, are you?"

"Yes I am, and I think that together, we can pull it off. What do you say, partner?" Daniel sat facing Harry, incredulous. Harry poured him some coffee.

"You can't be serious, Harry."

"As serious as a falling rock, son." Harry did look serious. The newest black eye that he'd been sporting these last few days only added to the madness in his eyes. Harry smiled an odd smile. "How much dynamite should I get? I would think a dozen sticks should do it, don't you?" Harry asked.

"But you heard Red, didn't you? It can't be done. It's too damned far for a man to ride a horse there and back in one day." Daniel was becoming increasingly agitated.

"That's where you come in." Harry spoke slowly, as if to a child.

"What do you mean 'that's where I come in'?"

"According to Dutch, you know the horses pretty well and Pete says that you know the road almost as well as he does. That will come in handy because we'll be going at night."

"But where would you stay during the day—they'd be looking for you, wouldn't they?" Daniel said, attempting to show Harry of the folly of his plan.

"Not if we come back the same night."

"You're talking like a madman, Harry. That's over a hundred miles in one night, in the middle of winter. Might even be more than a hundred, Joe said."

"Yeah, that's true, but I know how we can do it."

"How?" Daniel was intrigued, but he convinced himself that at no point would he allow himself to be talked into this fiasco, one that he was certain could have absolutely no good outcome.

"The sleds are the secret. Horses can run forever if they aren't carrying a man. We tie the sleds to the horses and they pull us over the Pass."

Harry concluded rightly that he had only one chance to make his case and that chance was slipping away. A change in tactics was called for. "Wait a minute, what am I doing telling you? You could just go on out and do the damned thing yourself." Harry raised an eyebrow, looking at Daniel suspiciously.

"That's not going to happen, Harry. I'm not going over that Pass again unless it's with a pistol on my belt and a half a dozen men with me to keep an eye out for that fat Sheriff."

"Look, I need you, Daniel. We're going to be using Red's horses. You know them and they know you, so we could get in and out of the corral without spooking them." Harry was trying his best to sound reasonable. "We'll leave our horses out there at Red's and if someone counts the horses, they'll count ours."

Daniel thought about it for a moment. It was possible. At night, their horses could be mistaken for two of Red's. "Why are you trying to do this? Are you in trouble again?" Daniel asked. "You have money in there." Daniel pointed at the oven and Harry's head slumped. "Don't tell me it's all gone." Harry nodded.

Daniel felt the same feeling of disgust that he'd felt the first time he'd seen Harry defeated by his own diversions. "If you need money, I can loan you some. I don't have much here, though. I'm having Red put my money in the bank for me. Not that I don't trust you, but at the bank they're giving me interest on my money. I think it's safer there than under the oven." Harry had fallen quiet again. With a deep sigh, Daniel pulled his pack out from under his bed and went to his Bible to search for the rest of his money.

"It's not there," said Harry.

"What do you mean it's not there? I put it there myself before I left. There was twenty-eight dollars there."

"I took it," said Harry softly.

Daniel slumped on the bed, his pack in his lap.

"I'm sorry Daniel, but I needed it. I thought I'd win it back, just like I did last time." Harry's voice sounded like that of a pleading child. "I'm really sorry."

"Well, I'll just have to go to Red and ask for my wages then." Daniel replied tiredly. "How much did you lose?"

"About five-hundred dollars, near enough." Daniel looked at him, horrified. "That's about as much as I would make this whole winter. If I didn't have to share it with my partner, that is."

"Where are you going to get five-hundred dollars?"

"By robbing a bank."

"And you want me to go over there with you at night and try to rob the biggest bank in Colorado and come back over the Pass all in one night? Just so you can pay off your gambling debts?"

"Yeah, it'll be easy—all you have to do is take care of the horses, then we can make it back before they know which way we went."

"And just how're we going to accomplish that?"

"We do it when there's a full moon and we get a good-sized storm. I think there's a full moon on Christmas; there was one around Thanksgiving, and that was about a month ago."

"Well, I can't this Christmas, Harry. I have other plans."

"Yeah? What are you doin'? Goin' over for some honey at Honey Bolon's?"

"No. I'm going to the Christmas party at the Hotel Jerome."

"Yeah, right," Harry said, unconvinced. "Did Shirley break down and ask you for a date? She's sweet on you, did you know that? Big Shirley's got you in her sights." Harry brought his hands up to resemble firing a rifle into Daniel's heart.

"Mr. Wheeler invited me to his Christmas party," Daniel said proudly. "Anyway, it's Kate that I'm interested in, not Shirley."

"Well, you're going to have your hands full there, my young man. For one thing, you don't have any money and everyone knows that Shirley is grooming Kate for someone better than the likes of you." Harry paused and rethought his argument. "So, if we can pick a night that isn't Christmas, you'll help me with the horses. That's all you have to do for me and I'll split the money with you."

"Harry, you're crazy. That bank is built like a fort and there're always people around it."

"Not if there's a storm. They'll all be indoors. They'll just think it was a mine explosion and go back to sleep."

"If there's a storm, how're we supposed to get back over the Pass? We'll just fall off the road somewhere, freeze to death, and they won't even find us until the spring comes."

"You've said it yourself. Those horses know the way so well, they could find their way back in a snow storm. You said that, didn't you?" Harry was trying to keep his frustration in check.

"Harry, it's just too dangerous and you aren't up to riding a hundred miles in a week, let alone a day."

"What do you mean? I can do anything that any man half my age can do." He looked in the mirror, smiling the winning smile that separated him from the rest of the pack.

"Harry, you're not up to the trip." Daniel paused, his mind elsewhere. "It's not possible. Even if I did think that it was possible, which it isn't, I wouldn't go with you. I don't want to get into any trouble."

"Like the trouble you're already in?" Harry watched him in the mirror.

Daniel's heart fell. He glanced at his pack. His Bible, papers, and all of his secrets were visible and unprotected. Harry returned to the table and waited patiently. There was an immediate and terminal difference in the way they looked at each other.

"What do you mean?"

"Daniel, your secret's safe with me. You can trust me. You know that, don't you?"

"Like I can trust you not to go looking in my personal gear?" Daniel was getting heated. "What gives you the right to read my personal stuff?"

Harry yawned. "I know you've got a chance to work with Jerome Wheeler. I certainly wouldn't want to put that opportunity in jeopardy." Harry laid his hands flat on the table. "And it wouldn't do to have Big Shirley finding out about your criminal past if you were actually interested in courting her daughter." Harry let the emphasis drain Daniel. "But then, on the plus side, you'd have plenty of money to make a life for you two. You could bring your mother and sister out here. That way they could be here for the wedding," Harry gloated smugly.

Daniel flew at Harry. Had Harry not anticipated it, it could have been painful. The coffee cups flew to the floor as Daniel tipped the table over, reaching for Harry.

"Settle down there, boy." Harry held his hands out in front of him defensively.

"Why are you doing this?" Daniel pleaded. He sat back down and let his head fall into his hands.

"I'm doing this because I need you to help me get over the Pass and back. And I know you can do it."

"I don't want to go help you rob the bank."

"You know that Pinkerton's can be reached by telegraph? I'm sure that they could have some of their boys out here in less than a week."

"What are you saying, Harry? You'd turn me in to the police? I thought we were partners."

"Look, here." Harry straightened the table and sat back down. "I'm not saying that I would do that. After all, we are partners. But we both know what would happen if you were taken back to England. We want to avoid that, don't we?"

Daniel was smoldering. His life was dissolving in front of him, complete with the dreams of marrying Kate and having a family. He could see the walls of his cell and smell the stench of decaying men. "What if we get over there and you decide that you can't rob the bank? Will you forget about what you know and let me leave?"

Harry adopted his most congenial attitude and smiled endearingly. "Of course. If you help me with this, I promise I'll never bring this subject up again. You can trust me on that." Harry wore his most sincere face.

"I don't want to do it." It was a test of wills. The tension in the room grew. Neither wanted to be the first to speak. Harry got up to fetch more coffee and poured some for both of them, topping up the cups with whiskey.

"I'll tell you what," Harry said, pulling a deck of cards out of his pocket. "We'll leave it to chance." Daniel was unmoved. "We'll each cut to a card and if you win, I promise that I'll never tell anyone about your secret. OK?"

"But...?" Daniel said. The word hung like a blade over his naked neck.

"But if you lose, you have to help me." Harry was at his theatrical best, pausing masterfully. "Then I'll give you some of the money, you can do what you like and we never need see each other again."

"And you promise that you'll never tell anyone what you know about my past?" Harry nodded. "That's not good enough, Harry. I want to hear you say that you'll never tell a soul, and I mean never."

"Alright then. I promise not to tell a soul that you're one of the famous Shadlow brothers who blew up the Bank of England." Harry was wondering if Daniel could see his crossed fingers under the table.

"Harry, I want that to be the last time you ever say that. OK?" Daniel looked at the deck of cards with both fear and fascination.

"Alright I promise, Goddamn it. You win. I promise I'll never say that again." Harry was in a hurry to close the deal. "Come on, we'll just cut the cards. The highest card wins." Harry shuffled the deck, squared them up, and placed them in the middle of the table.

"If I win, you'll never ask me to do this again."

"True," said Harry firmly.

"And if we do it and get away, then you'll give me half of the money and let me leave town whenever I want."

"Yes."

"Even if it's the next day?"

"Yes." Harry hoped that he wouldn't have to do any more lying.

"But if we do make it back and I do decide to stay here in Aspen, you won't ever mention it." Harry was drumming his fingers on the table impatiently, getting tired of Daniel's unwarranted suspicion.

"Yes. Is there anything else?" Harry's exasperation was showing.

"Yes, there is. If we make it back with the money, I don't want you going out and spending any of it until I leave town."

"What?" Harry was incredulous. "What do you mean not spend it? That's what I'm doing it for."

"If we've suddenly got money to burn, it's not going to take them long to figure it out."

"Yeah, that makes some sense." Harry contemplated the options. "They'll be off looking for someone else, maybe even Butch Cassidy." Harry was considering this new aspect of the robbery. "How long until you leave Aspen, do you think?"

"It could be till the end of winter. Or, I might just want to stay here in town a while longer."

"Well, that might be getting too far ahead of ourselves. You have to win here first for me to lose." Harry pushed the cards across the table.

"If I beat you, there's no way you can pull this off by yourself." Daniel reached for the cards confidently.

"But if I win, you'll help me get over there and back?" Harry's eyes were large and shining bright.

"Yes, Harry, I will." Daniel drew his card, a jack of hearts. Harry sighed as if his dream had lost its ability to fly. Harry's acting was

superb. He picked his card and with no change of expression looked
at it, pretending not to know what it was. He turned the card over.
Daniel's mind slowly registered the picture of the king of clubs. He
could feel the blood draining from his face. He let his head fall forward
till his chin rested on his chest and wished he were dead. He should
never have gambled with a gambler.

"Hey, will you just look at that?" Harry said loudly, slamming his
palm down on the table and startling Daniel. He placed his fists on the
table and leaned closer. "Soon you and me'll be rich and we won't have
to put up with this potato bullshit ever again. We'll be farting through
silk underwear soon, boy. You just watch."

Harry picked up the deck of marked cards and paced about the
room, his mind busily listing the things they would need for this adventure. He pulled out a piece of paper, licking the lead of his pencil.
"How do you spell dynamite?"

Daniel slowly climbed out of his chair, grabbed his coat and headed for the door. "Where you going? We got things to do, partner."

"I have to go for a walk." Daniel slammed the door as he left.

Chapter 28

Daniel sat alone in the back of the church with no idea how he'd gotten there. He generally gave religion a wide berth. As his brain came back from the abyss of his stupidity and the inevitable disaster of his decisions, he became aware of his surroundings. Up in front of him, women and young girls were decorating the altar for Christmas, talking softly as they worked. It was peaceful.

He was wrestling with the devils in his future when a priest stopped in front of him, not saying anything. Daniel nodded to the priest, who took it as an invitation to sit next to him. He sat silently, as if it were Daniel's choice to initiate a conversation. After a time, the priest spoke to him.

"You look troubled, my son," the priest said in gentle voice. "You know, you can come and talk to me anytime." Daniel stood and gave him a smile as he walked away.

He'd never felt so hopeless. Everything in his life, which only hours before held promise and joy, was dissolving like paper in a rainstorm. Hiding in a church held no resolution to his problems. He needed a drink, one at least. Whiskey might not be the solution to all of his woes, but it might deaden the pain and help him forget.

As he pulled open the church's heavy door, a girl with her arms full of decorations fell into him, knocking them both down. Her bonnet had fallen across her face. All Daniel could see was her ear. He noticed she had a very nice ear.

He tried to help her up, but her feet kept slipping on the ice. As she gained some purchase, her knee came up and connected with Daniel's groin. With a loud whoosh of breath, all thoughts of a future family left his mind. He pushed her away roughly and curled up into a fetal position, clutching at his injured area trying not to throw up.

"I'm so sorry! Are you alright?" Kate said, straightening her bonnet. "Daniel?"

Daniel opened his eyes and saw his attacker.

"I'm so sorry, Daniel. Where are you hurt?" She reached towards his hands, but he rolled away from her in pain and embarrassment. The priest had heard the ruckus and came to help, quickly realizing from Daniel's posture where his injury was located.

"What happened, Kate?" the priest asked, confused by the scene. He took Daniel's arm gently, and helped him to his feet.

"Father, it was my fault," Kate hurried to explain. "He opened the door as I was pushing it and I fell on top of him." She'd put down her bundle and bathed Daniel with her kindest smile. "I'm so sorry. Are you going to be alright?"

Daniel smiled as best he could manage.

The priest placed his hand on her shoulder, trying to reassure her. "I think he'll be alright, Kate. It seems that you two already know each other."

"We met coming over from Leadville," Daniel rasped.

"He works with Red Corcoran's company," Kate hurried on with no small amount of pride in her voice.

"Really? That's an interesting bunch of fellows you work with. Mr. Corcoran has been of great assistance to us building our humble church. We're very grateful to him." The priest turned to go back inside. He stopped and considered Daniel for a second, then patted him on the shoulder.

Kate reached out for Daniel's arm. This time, he allowed her to help him push himself away from the comfort of the wall. They were quite close to each other, she holding onto his arm, he savoring the wonderful intoxication of her perfume.

"Would you like to come to Mr. Wheeler's Christmas party with us? I'm sure he wouldn't mind." Daniel wondered if he'd ever ride a horse again. She took his pause for reluctance and squeezed his arm. "Please come?"

"Yes, I'll come, thank you for the invitation."

Kate smiled. The door to the church opened behind her.

"Kate, where are you?" said the girl at the door. "Oh!" she said, as she spotted Kate hanging onto Daniel's arm. The girl scowled at her and Daniel.

"That's just my sister Rachelle, don't mind her."

Daniel remembered where he'd seen her before. It was at Big Shirley's when he'd slept upstairs at the brothel. She'd seen him coming out of the room and must have assumed that he was visiting the women up there.

"I have to go now. I'll see you at the party." He didn't know, nor did he care what time it was—he needed a drink.

⚞⚟

The Red Onion had a crowd and there were men in there he recognized. It was the nature of his job working with Harry that he was known, at least by face, to almost every miner who worked this side of the valley. It didn't take long for him to find a place at the bar. The bartender slid a shot of whiskey in front of him as he sat down.

"Where did this come from?" The bartender nodded his head towards the other end of the bar. When Daniel turned to look, he saw no one he recognized. He looked at the bartender again who just shrugged and went about his job, polishing the glasses. As Daniel drank, his gaze caught the reflection of Sparky and Leafy in the mirror, trying their best to look inconspicuous.

Daniel got up and joined them at the end of the bar. They made room for him and patted him on the back. The association with other men seemed to be the medicine that he needed. With the whiskey warming him through, he felt the worries swirling about him drift away like clouds. Soon, only Leafy and Sparky were left of the group and they were all definitely drunk. They'd been drinking all afternoon and now it was dark outside.

"What are you doing for dinner, Daniel? My parents want to meet you," Leafy said.

"Thanks Leafy, but your sister already invited me to dinner," Daniel said, with a note of reluctance. He hoped he had disguised the fact that he was looking forward to seeing Honey again, especially if she was going to be as affectionate as last time.

Leafy smiled at him as they headed for the door and went their separate ways. Walking up an icy hill in his drunken condition was a daunting task. For every step he took forward, gravity would tug him back. He laughed every time he fell. He also thanked God that there were no other people on the road to see his clownish attempts to climb the hill.

The steepness of the slope and the ruts in the road were treacherous. He was sweaty and his pants legs were wet from falling by the time he made the top of the hill. He put his hands on his hips in triumph and surveyed the route of his ascent. He'd come uphill maybe fifty yards but he was sure that it'd taken him an age to do it. He shuddered at the thought that he would be navigating the hill downward on his way home.

His tongue was thick and he was thirsty from climbing up to Honey's house. He ate some snow, trying to force the moisture out of it by chewing on it, but it didn't help. He was preparing to knock when the door opened suddenly, surprising him. In front of him stood a large man dressed in black wearing a hat adorned with silver conchos.

Honey appeared surprised to see Daniel at her doorstep. "Oh, I didn't think you were coming," she said to Daniel as the man in black walked off down the path without acknowledging him. "Come in and sit down. You look a mess." She helped him out of his heavy coat. "Are you alright? You seem like you're hurt."

"I fell a couple of times coming up the hill." He winced again at the pain in his shoulder. His wrist was swelling and it was sore to the touch. Honey took his hand and led him into the dining room, where the table had already been used for a meal.

Jackson called from the top of the stairs. "Can I come down now?" he asked.

"Sure you can, just as long as you sit quietly while I fix dinner."

Dinner was brief. There was mostly a strained silence throughout the ordeal. She offered him no dessert, just some coffee, then made a point of saying that it was time for them to go to bed. Daniel was surprised to see it was almost ten o'clock.

"Jackson, say goodnight to Mr. Carrington and get ready for bed."

Her son gave Daniel a theatrical wink as he disappeared up the stairs. "I said go to bed," Honey yelled. He saw Jackson's feet sprint the rest of the way and heard his door close. "I'd like you to stay a while, but I think you should leave now."

She led Daniel by the hand into the small entryway, turning to close the curtain that served as a second line of defense against the encroachment of the winter chill. They were alone in the dim light and Honey was doing something to her dress at the neck. When she turned around in the soft light of the tiny room, Daniel's heart skipped a beat. He unconsciously let out a soft sigh.

Honey undid the buttons of her dress from her throat, down to the lace that covered her breasts. The expanse of her breasts was offered to his eyes. The indirect light shone over her pale skin, glimmering.

She took his injured hand, pressed it to her breast, cupped it with her own hand and guided it around the fullness of her bosom. She pulled his face down to kiss him gently on the lips. She had a mischievous grin as she reached for his coat and helped him into it. "Next time, don't come here drunk." She handed him his hat, then opened the door and pushed him out. He stood on her porch and watched the shades come down on all of the other windows around the house in a procession. Even drunk, he could read the signs to go home.

He pivoted to leave and smartly fell on his backside with a heavy, painful thud. He automatically reached down with his right wrist and yelped as pain shot up his arm. Grabbing his wrist, he struggled to his feet, looked across the valley at the lights of the town, and groaned at the thought of walking home drunk and tired.

The moon came out from behind the clouds. It was high in the sky behind the thin clouds and had a faint ring around it.

⊰⊱

"Where the hell have you been?" Harry barked as he entered the cabin.

Daniel was surprised to see that the cabin was draped with miles of leather straps, from one bunk to the other and back again.

"What's all this?" Daniel circled the room trying to find a place to sit, finally placing a chair on the backside of the oven.

"It's the harness for the sleds. I need you to tell me how big the necks of the Morgans are so that I can have enough room to fit them. How big do you think they are? This big?" Harry held up a loop of leather strap that was wider that his arms could spread.

"I think that's plenty big, Harry." Daniel had to harness the Morgans and remembered how hard it had been to get the harnesses on them. Their necks and chests were huge. It was impossible for a man of medium height to put his arms totally around their necks.

"We're going to try it out tomorrow."

"We're what?" Daniel said.

"We're going into the Christmas tree business. We're going to test out the harnesses on our horses by pulling trees around town and selling them. That way, we'll know how much money we can pull over the Pass without losing the sleds."

"I've got to go to bed, Harry. We can talk about it again tomorrow." He made his way to his bunk and fell into it, fully clothed. The dreams that awaited him would be of the soft warm breasts that he'd just held. "What's the rush for?" Daniel asked as he dozed off.

"Looks like a big storm coming and I thought we should be ready."

Daniel's dreams were dashed on the rocks of Harry's words. A soft moan came from deep inside of his chest, right from where his heart would have been, had it not sunk below the point of salvage.

"You're still with me on this, aren't you? You're not thinking of cutting out, are you?"

"No, Harry." The call of drunken sleep was overtaking him.

"Good, 'cause if you're thinking anything like that, it could end up being the worst thing you ever did…if you know what I mean." Harry waited for a reply, but it didn't come. Daniel was softly snoring.

Chapter 29

Daniel and Harry seemed to have struck some form of truce, but like all truces, it was fragile. Daniel had elected to do Harry's midnight shift and returned to find him sitting at the table in deep concentration. He ate some of the stew they'd been adding to for a week and sat on his bed to eat.

"How do you spell 'dynamite' again?" Harry asked. He was making a list; lines of concentration furrowed his brow.

Daniel repeated the spelling as he rested on his bed.

"What're you writing?" Daniel rubbed his wrist, which was troubling him, though the swelling had gone down some.

"Things we should bring with us."

"Bring with us where?"

"Over the Pass. Didn't you see the moon? Grab your coat and come with me."

Harry led Daniel outside and turned him to face east, where the moon had just risen. To Daniel's dismay, there was a broad silvery halo around the almost full moon.

"Isn't it beautiful?" Harry said joyously. "You know what this means, don't you?" Daniel didn't respond. "It means there's a storm coming soon, tomorrow, or the next night." Daniel's already sunken heart dove deeper into his boots. "Tomorrow might be the night we go over to Leadville because the mines are closed on Christmas. Those greedy mine owners give them poor bastards one day off a year and expect them to be grateful for it," Harry said bitterly. "It's the one day they won't be wanting potatoes, so we won't be missed." Daniel was too tired to care. The oblivion of sleep was comforting.

Harry was first awake, peering outside the door for considerably longer than usual.

"Close the door, you're letting the cold in."

Harry closed the door and put the coffee pot on the hottest place on the oven. He reached up and gave the chains a tug, pulling the log into the fire. Daniel was reluctant to get out of bed; the claws of his dream reaching out to his waking mind.

"What does the weather look like?" Daniel could only hope.

"Can't really tell. It's getting cloudy though. We'll have to wait and see."

"Wait till when, Harry?" The tension showed in his voice.

"Till I tell you we're going. We want the storm, but we want it at the right time. If it doesn't come and we rob the bank, then they can just follow our tracks back here. If it snows too much…" Harry shuddered as thoughts of his mortality floundered for purchase in his mind. "Well, if it snows too much, we might as well just stay here…" his voice trailed off as he sipped at his coffee.

Harry had been having his share of bad dreams too; mainly him being chased and cornered by his wives. The frightening part was that they were all there at the same time in his dreams and that scared him more than the Sheriff in Leadville or Doc Holliday, if the truth be known.

As the day progressed, Daniel could feel his heart being tugged downward by the lowering clouds. There was a clear and definite ring around the sun at noon and the air felt warmer and unusually damp. Most of the old time miners agreed that there was going to be a storm but what troubled Daniel was the general belief that the coming storm was going to be big.

He returned to the cabin after lunch to find no one there and a box sitting on the table. Inside it were over a dozen sticks of dynamite, fuse cord, blasting caps, coils of wire, a ball of twine, wire cutters and matches. He inspected the dynamite and checked the fuses for thin spots and holes. The blasting caps he rolled over in his hands and squeezed between his fingers as Sparky had shown him. They were all sound. He looked at the box on the table as if it would explode right then.

Harry burst in carrying a bundle of canvas.

"There's more in the sled." Harry pushed past. "Go fetch it, will ya'."

Daniel hesitated, tempted to run and throw himself on the mercy of the church, the law, anyone, it didn't matter, whoever would give him forgiveness for his terrible mistake and demand that he not go on this foolhardy venture.

"Come on, we don't have much time," Harry insisted.

"What do you mean, we don't have much time?" Daniel dreaded the answer.

"The storm's comin' and it's Christmas tomorrow. We'll never have a better chance. We're goin' over tonight."

The news blanched the color from Daniel's face.

"You're not quitting on me now, are you?" Harry stepped closer, his face only inches from Daniel's. "We've gotta go cut a few trees and try selling them around town. As soon as it gets dark, we're off." Harry placed his hand on Daniel's shoulder. "How's your hand?" His concern was selfish and undisguised. "It's not going to hold you up, is it?"

"It's not so bad," Daniel lied.

"Good. Better wear everything you own. It's goin' to get real cold up there." Daniel looked up at the sky. The clouds were skidding across the peaks, high up the valley. "You go get the horses and saddle them up and I'll get the sleds ready." Harry shoved him forcefully. "Come on, get going for Christ's sake, will you? If we're not ready to go by dark, we shouldn't be doing it at all." Hope glimmered in Daniel's heart. "But you will be ready, won't you, Daniel?" The air between them chilled.

"Yeah. I'll be ready." Daniel left the cabin and walked to the stable in a daze. The point of no return was fast approaching and he could feel the tightening in his stomach and the urge to vomit. Marigold was nervous too and fought the bit. "Come on, girl. I won't let anything happen to us."

"Goin' someplace?" No Problem Joe was standing behind him; Daniel had no idea how long he'd been there.

"Oh, hi there Joe. I didn't hear you come up. Yeah, we're goin' to sell some more trees." Here was a chance to tell Joe what Harry was dragging him into. Joe would protect him, wouldn't he?

"People still buyin', are they?"

"Well, we..." Daniel struggled to find the right lie. "Harry promised a tree to someone. So, we have to go get it for them." The small door swung open and in walked Harry carrying two whiskey bottles.

"Hi there, Joe. You're just the man I want to see." Harry announced, full of confidence and charm. "Come with me, you toothless old devil." Taking Joe by the shoulders he steered him towards the back of the stable, nodding his head for Daniel to take the horses outside. He walked Joe to his room and placed two bottles of good whiskey on the table.

"Merry Christmas," Harry said, opening a bottle and pouring the whiskey into two coffee cups. He handed Joe the fuller of the two and raised his cup for a toast. "A Merry Christmas to you Joe, and to all of us," Harry watched Joe drain his cup and by the time he left, five minutes later, Joe was well on his way to having a pleasantly drunken evening.

"Where were you?" Daniel asked anxiously.

"I was introducing Joe to one of his Christmas presents." Harry burped. "We'll have to check back in on him before we leave. I want to be sure that he sees us as late as possible." Harry climbed into the saddle. They rode a short way out of town to cut down the trees to drag around town in their sleds, wishing "Merry Christmas" to everyone Harry knew. The light had mostly gone from the sky though it was barely five o'clock and in Harry's mind, this would establish the fact that they'd never left town.

"I think we should get going as quick as we can. We're likely goin' to be running short of time as it is and we still have one more stop to make." Harry said. They stopped their horses in front of the Mother Lode and when Harry returned he was smiling broadly.

"Why did we stop there, Harry?"

Harry smiled back. "Another Christmas present for Joe. Now let's go pick up the dynamite."

They found Joe sitting in his rocking chair, his feet toward the potbellied stove. His eyes were closed, but he held a firm grip on his cup of whiskey, his breathing steady and soft. Harry reached out to touch him.

"What do you want now, Harry?" Joe's eyes didn't open; he remained in perfect repose. "You want your damned whiskey back, I suppose?"

"Nah, I just wanted to see if you were still in the land of the living."

"Well, get yourselves some women and leave me alone. Take 'em riding in your new sled, why don't ya?" The smaller stable door opened and one of the prostitutes from the Mother Lode entered smiling brightly.

"OK, Joe, have a Merry Christmas. I hope you enjoy your other Christmas present." Harry replied.

"Am I too early for you fellers?" The woman asked, smiling, somewhat drunkenly.

"No. Not at all." Harry said and motioned for Daniel to leave. "Joe, I'd like you to meet Elizabeth. She's going to be your companion tonight." Joe was smiling broadly at Harry. "It's on me, Joe."

"Well, ain't that a nice touch. Harry, I'm starting to think more kindly of you."

Elizabeth walked over, swaying slightly, and took Joe's hand. "Come, my sweetheart," she said, winking at Harry as she led Joe back into his small bedroom.

"Good night, you two. Merry Christmas," Joe said merrily, and closed the door to his room.

Outside, Daniel had been adjusting the harnesses.

"Well, that should take care of the old coot till morning." Harry took a deep breath and let it out in a whoosh and a puff of steam. "Here we go, partner. Tomorrow we'll be rich men." Daniel did not share Harry's confidence.

They rode out of town, ditching the trees by the side of the road and headed to Red's place where their venture could come to an early end if they were detected stealing his horses.

Only a glimmer of light shone from the barn windows as they approached the corral. The Morgans stood together in small knots, still as statues, difficult to see at night. Daniel opened the gate and led their horses inside, still saddled. He tied them to a tree, covering them with blankets and in the dark it was hard to tell they weren't Morgans.

Morgans, though huge, were just like children when it came to treats. They especially liked cooked potatoes, such as were in the bag that Harry handed to him. They came to him eagerly, nearly knocking him over trying to get at the potatoes as he led two of them out of the corral. Wearing head stalls, they were easy to lead and Harry busied himself fitting the harness on his horse, but Daniel's fingers were suddenly numb and he was having trouble with the harness.

"Hurry up. We gotta' get going." Harry whispered loudly.

Daniel knew with all the fibers in his soul that he was heading into certain disaster, but was unable to stop the momentum.

Harry roughly pushed him away from the horse and finished the process. He then stormed off and got into his sled and slapping the reins on the horse's wide back, guided his horse and sled out onto the road. Daniel followed him into the night, his mind awash in dread.

In his eagerness Harry disappeared into the night and it wasn't till they had ridden onto the only flat meadow for miles, that Daniel caught sight of him in the glim light of the rising moon.

The weather was holding for them as they passed through Independence, silent but for the sound of an accordion being played badly.

At the top of the Pass they stopped to rest and stood between their horses, out of the wind, drinking whiskey to warm and fortify themselves. Daniel couldn't speak for Harry, but he was glad the horses knew the way. The landscape at the summit was featureless and pale, illuminated only in flashes as the moonlight flitted and flickered through breaks in the fast-moving clouds.

After one more swig of whiskey, they mounted their sleds and headed off on the downhill leg. They were off the Pass in good time, judging from the position of the moon as they rounded the final corner and headed into Twin Lakes.

"How strong is your horse?" Harry asked. They'd dismounted and walked their horses up to the corral, watching the barn and bunkhouse for any movement. The horses in the corral stood quietly huddled together in the far corner with their tails towards the stiffening breeze.

"Why?" Daniel's face was frozen.

"I was thinking we could just keep the ones we got. What do you think?" Harry was serious. "Do you think they can make it?"

"I don't know. They're looking good now, but if they get tired and decide to stop, they'll just stop." Daniel glanced over at the corral. "Harry, we're going to rob a bank. I don't think that we should be lazy about trying to get away. Do you?"

"That makes sense."

Carefully and quietly they led the grateful Morgans into the corral. The other horses came over to sniff at them and get the gossip. They went about their business as quietly as possible, though it mattered little, since the rising wind blew all noises off into the night. As they were placing the chest straps on their fresh horses they heard the door to the bunkhouse open. The light from inside silhouetted a man relieving himself into the snow off the porch. Daniel recognized Red's stable hand, Newly. He stood for a minute looking over at the Lodge, then went back inside. The door closed and the night became the night again. Twin Lakes seemed peaceful.

Silently, they led their horses out onto the road past the Lodge and up the small hill overlooking the lakes and the Lodge. Harry came close and pulled Daniel's collar up tighter around his face.

"Are you ready partner?" Daniel nodded. He hadn't realized that he had been holding his breath. "Let's go rob a bank."

The wind and snow came in tandem and the moonlight reflecting off the frozen lakes came and went in bursts of glimmer. The footfalls of the horses' hooves were rhythmical and soothing. Daniel drifted off. Kate was in his thoughts, and so were his mother and sister. There was laughter and tears and a wonderful feeling of contentment, something that had so far eluded him.

He was smiling when his horse slowed and he awoke. Harry was walking towards him, pulling up his collar against the rising wind. They had made it to Balltown, where a single light shone weakly from the small saloon. Daniel stood with difficulty and stretched his cramped legs. Looking up into the sky, he saw the moon almost at its zenith. Harry looked up at the sky also.

"I'm wondering if the storm's going to come."

"That's not what I wanted to hear, Harry."

"What do you think?"

"Goddamn it, Harry. You're the one that has Indians as friends; you're supposed to be the expert. What do you think?"

"Oh, forget about what you think, let's just go and do it." Harry said, as he climbed back into the sled and slapped his horse into motion.

They stopped once more after leaving the canyon that led north. Harry had Daniel climb the telegraph pole to cut the wire with his wire cutters.

"Now, let's go and cut it again at the next pole," he directed.

"Why twice?" Daniel inquired.

"So that it takes them twice as long to repair it, of course," Harry said, as he gave Daniel a hoist up the pole. Daniel's hands were frozen and he lost his grip on the pliers which fell into the snow. After several minutes of looking for them in the blackness and the blowing snow, they gave up.

"Good thing I brought two of them cutters," Harry said smugly, full of his own brilliance as he threw away the fallen telegraph wire.

In less than an hour, they had passed through Stringtown. It was cold and wintery and the rising wind whipped snow about them and the few people they saw paid them little attention. They approached Leadville along the side streets down-hill from the Bank and tied up to a post adjacent to a deserted building several blocks away, where the moon-shadow of the building hid their horses.

"Let's go scout out the bank before we take the horses any closer," Harry yelled over the wind.

They approached the bank cautiously, slipping from one shadow to the next. From the side alley, there was nothing to discover. Only a dim glow came from the window adjacent to the side door. Everything looked quiet and in order as they walked up to the main street and casually looked around the corner, past the bank and down the street. Nothing moved. The main street was mostly deserted, except for the rare soul scurrying from one bar to another, trying to escape the cold or the loneliness of the night before Christmas.

Harry nudged Daniel and together they stepped onto the wooden sidewalk. Regrettably the boards under their feet creaked and the sound of their footsteps resonated loudly. Stealthy and silent, they were not.

Nearing the bank's front door, Harry slowed and pointed to the footprints left in the new snow. He held his finger to his lips and pointed again at the ones going inside the bank; they were of a large man.

"Keep walking. If there's someone in there, they might've seen us standing here at the door." They hurried along the sidewalk and the door opened as they turned right at the corner of the block. Harry risked a quick look back.

"Well, now we know there's someone in there. It's probably one of the deputies. I can't see that fat Sheriff sitting guard on Christmas Eve. Let's check out the barn and then we'll see who's in the bank."

The stable was dark and the doors were secured with chain and a heavy padlock. Harry pulled gently on the doors and smiled to himself. "I'll wire these shut so they can't get their horses; that should give us a head start on them. Come on, we don't have much time. Let's see who we're going to surprise in the bank." It was snowing more heavily now, the flakes big and flat were piling up on the ground quickly. Daniel looked behind them and saw that the footprints they'd made coming over to the barn were covered almost completely.

The alley window of the bank was too high for them to see through. Daniel found a box and held it steady for Harry to climb up on. Harry took off his hat and slowly raised his head over the sill.

"What do you see?" Daniel asked anxiously. Harry climbed down and sat heavily on the box. "Harry, what did you see?"

"We might as well just go back home."

"What do you mean?"

Daniel pushed Harry aside, climbed up on the box and, taking off his hat as he'd seen Harry do, he peeked over the edge of the sill. The view he had was from an angle that looked into the corridor that led to the vault from the main area. A portion of a wall obstructed his view, but he could see to the front door. A large shadow moved across the room. Someone was walking towards him, and immediately he recognized the rotund silhouette. The Sheriff turned and looked directly at him.

Daniel ducked his head and slid down the wall. He caught Harry by his coat as he was trying to slink away. "Where do you think you're going?"

Harry turned, looking small and frightened. "Did you see who's in there?"

"Harry, did we come here to rob a bank or not? What does it matter who's in there if they can't get out, like you said? You did say that, didn't you?"

"Well, yeah, I did say that." Harry sounded uncertain.

"Then let's get on with it and get out of here," Daniel said.

Harry took a long deep breath. "Let's go and get the stuff then," he said.

They ran down the hill to the horses and Harry unhitched one of them from its sled. "We don't want anyone to know we used the sleds. We can have the horse pull the money boxes downhill. If they follow us they'll think we were on horseback." They led the horse up the hill and tied it to a fencepost before lugging their tools the two blocks up to the bank.

"Do you know how to fuse the dynamite?"

Daniel nodded.

"I'll go and make sure that the stable doors are wired shut," Harry whispered unnecessarily.

"How much dynamite should we use?" Daniel was whispering also.

"Why not use all of it?" Harry said seriously.

"Are you sure?"

"Why not? We don't want to take it back with us, do we?" Harry thought his logic was sound. "I'll be back." Harry dashed off into the night with the coils of wire over his shoulder.

At the stables, Harry tied the front and side doors with lengths of wire. He twisted the ends of the wire around themselves so that the wire couldn't possibly be untangled by hand. The rear door was a little more difficult, but he completed the task in good time and had a small amount of wire left over with which to secure the front door of the bank. His task finished, he raced back to the bank and found Daniel putting the fuses into the dynamite he'd tied into two bundles with twine.

"I think we should put them on this side of the building," Harry suggested.

"I think we should put them on *both* sides of the building," Daniel replied.

"Why?" Harry sounded irritated.

"Because that's the weakest point of the vault, the corner of the building, and there's less chance for it to fall down on us."

"The building could fall down? How do you know all this?" Daniel looked at Harry as if he were a child.

"Harry, it's not the first bank I've blown up, if you remember."

"You do what you think we have to do. I'll go and make sure that bastard inside can't get out."

Harry slipped silently up the alley past the window and peeked around the corner. The halos of the gaslights were barely visible through the falling snow and there was no one to be seen on the main street. He was about to step onto the wooden sidewalk, but caught himself and slipped back around the corner, his heart racing. He remembered that the last time they'd walked past the front window and that they were silhouetted by the lamplight. Trying hard not to let the boards under him announce his presence, he got down on his knees and carefully crawled along the walkway below the lower edge of the iron barred window of the bank.

The bank's doors were made of heavy wood with large brass handles, and were bolted from the inside. Harry grinned at his inventiveness as he weaved the wire through and around the handles, making them impossible to open without wire cutters. He used all of the wire, twisted the ends and then hid the ends in the tangle of his knots. Satisfied that he had done the best he could, he crawled back along the side walk to the corner and ran down the alley, where Daniel was packing snow over the canvas that covered the dynamite.

"Give me a hand here, Harry. I can't do it all myself."

Harry stood back.

"For God's sake, Harry, get moving! We're not planning to stay for breakfast, are we?"

"Why are you doing all of that?"

"I covered the dynamite and the fuses. Now we're putting weight on it so that it will muffle the blast and make it go in towards the building, not out here into the street."

Harry looked at Daniel with new respect. "You really learned a lot from Sparky, didn't you?"

"And others."

They snuck up to the window and each in turn looked to see the shadow of the Sheriff, sitting in the stuffed chair with his feet up on the manager's desk, rocking back and forth on the rear legs, sipping coffee. Daniel reached out, grabbed Harry's arm and pointed to the side door of the building, where he and Red's men had loaded the money.

"Did you get that door?"

"Shit!"

"Then hurry, unless you want us to be permanent residents here in Leadville."

"I don't have any more wire." It was then that Harry remembered throwing away the telegraph wire.

"We've got to do something, or he'll come out of that door as soon as he gets his fat ass off the floor."

"If he comes out that door, we'll shoot him."

"Yeah, we'll just shoot the Sheriff. That would put everyone in the state after us."

"Shit!" Harry yelled, slapping his hip.

Daniel stood back and looked at him in dismay. "Don't tell me we came here to rob a bank and you forgot to bring a gun."

Harry's small Colt revolver was right where he had left it, under his bed. "Alright, so I'm not perfect."

"Not perfect?" Daniel shrieked in Harry's ear. "I'm surprised you remembered to bring the dynamite."

"Of course I remembered the dynamite! I wrote it down on my list."

Daniel threw his arms up in the air in frustration and turned away. "We've got to do something about the door." He looked about him and found a piece of wood to wedge the door closed. It was a pitiful gesture so he took off his belt and with some pulling, found that it was almost the right length to loop around the handle of the door, then through the iron railing. But, it was not quite long enough.

"Give me your belt, Harry."

"But my pants will fall down."

"Give it to me, Harry."

Harry reluctantly gave up his belt.

Daniel did his best to secure the door. It was a temporary thing at best, but if it gave them time to get to their horses and disappear into the night, then it was definitely better than nothing and well worth the inconvenience.

"Will it work?" Harry joined Daniel, placing anything that was weighty over the dynamite and covering the fuses.

"It'd better work or we might be staying right here in Leadville, permanently. I hope you brought matches?"

"Of course I did. Do you think I'm an idiot?" Harry searched for his matches, missing the look of fury in his partner's eyes. "Can I light the fuses?" he asked, out of character.

"You can light the fuses." Daniel laughed.

The first match broke, the second was wet. Daniel was near to the point of grabbing the matches from Harry when the third one flared brightly. They huddled close while Daniel held the fuse for Harry to light.

"Will they both go off at the same time?" Harry was suddenly concerned.

"I cut the fuses the same length so they should. But I'm only guessing." Harry had removed his gloves to light the matches and Daniel did the same.

"Here we go, partner." Harry said, smiling into Daniel's face.

The first fuse caught and ran towards the dynamite. The second fuse was more reluctant and took several seconds to catch. Daniel watched dispassionately at the sparks of fire as they sputtered and hissed on their way. They sputtered and stopped, then spurt forward, only to stop and pause and, at times, seemed to go completely out before running on again, impatient at their last delay.

"What if they go out?" Harry asked. The snow was falling heavily, threatening to extinguish the fuses.

"Cover that one with your hat and I'll cover this one."

Satisfied that the fuses were burning and now under the canvas, they ran back across the alley and crouched down behind some barrels and boxes, stacked between two buildings. Their fingers in their ears, they waited. They smiled at each other in anticipation.

No explosion came.

"It should've gone off by now, don't you think?" Harry asked.

"Give it a little more time." Seconds rolled by.

Impatient, Daniel jumped up from their safe place behind the barrels and ran across the road. Harry watched intently as Daniel lifted the canvas and poked around in the snow with his fingers, looking for the trail of burned fuses. He couldn't find them. His heart was racing. He held his hands up to his face to shield his eyes from the blowing snow and almost missed seeing the brief flash of light that sparked off to his right. It was almost at the wall of the bank. He spun around and raced for their shelter.

Harry saw Daniel turn back, head down racing towards him. Suddenly there was a burst of blinding light coming at him and Harry was flung backwards through the air like a doll, landing in a heap of snow and garbage. He lay helpless, curled up in a ball, his arm over his head in a futile attempt to protect himself from the pieces of timber, brick and mortar that fell on and about him.

Slowly the rain of rubble subsided.

After several breaths, when he was certain that it was safe, Harry cautiously raised his head and opened his eyes. The alley was a mass of strewn bricks, rubble and snow. Dust clouded and clogged the air. Pieces of the bank's rear walls were still falling and everything around him was enveloped in a ringing, smoky fog.

He crawled onto his knees, his eyes tearing from the brick dust that had been blasted at him. His head hurt inside and out and he was shaky on his feet. He stood painfully and stepped out into the alley, cupping his hands to his mouth.

"Daniel!" he called out.

The second explosion blew him backwards once more, tossing him into the air like a ball. This time everything went black.

It was silent when he opened his eyes. Nothing moved, except more pieces of the bank that rained down on him. He looked around, his hearing gone. He struggled to push himself up, disoriented and deaf.

He took several cautious steps over the rubble and was surprised when he tripped over Daniel, lying face down, covered in wreckage. He turned him over. Daniel opened his eyes and tried to speak, but nothing came out. Harry lifted him to his feet and supporting each other they stumbled to the wall of the bank, or where the wall used to be.

The building groaned, its timbers swinging back and forth eerily; what remained of the corner of the building was a skeleton. Smoke mixed with the falling snow swirled about them and they covered their heads as pieces of plaster and mortar fell like rain. Where once the sturdy walls of the bank had stood, solidly defying robbery, now the interior of its invulnerable vault was a gaping hole from which gold and silver coins spilled into the street. They looked about them at the destruction they had wrought and then at the dozens of boxes of coins and money bags littering the ground.

Harry laughed loudly and slapped Daniel on the shoulder, then reached down to lift a money box and realized in an instant that they had a new problem. The boxes weighed over one hundred pounds each and would be too heavy to take in the sleds. He stood stock-still, trying to grasp the fact that they'd robbed the bank and now could take barely anything with them.

⚜

The Sheriff had been dozing, quietly content to be away from his wife and her nagging. It was Christmas, for God's sake. All he'd heard for days was what they were going to eat and what things they needed to buy. It just went on and on and on so he didn't really mind volunteering to guard the bank on Christmas Eve. Ever since the robbery of the bank in Telluride and the nearby sighting of the robbers, the manager, Mr. Ebest, had insisted on having a deputy guard his bank every night. Though the Sheriff had imagined that Butch Cassidy was most probably in Utah, he had acquiesced to Mr. Ebest's request at the urging of the town council. He was rocking back in the manager's comfortable chair, enjoying a cup of coffee, when the first explosion went off.

The chair shot out from under him and he fell backwards heavily, hitting his head on the floor. Stunned and shaking his head to clear it, he clambered to his feet and stumbled to the front door of the bank but found it locked from the outside. Still groggy, he turned and was heading back towards the vault when the second explosion sent him crashing into the wall and back onto the floor. The building trembled and the floor gave an evil groan. He tried to stand, but he toppled forward on his face. Even getting up to his knees took all of his strength. The inside of the bank was dark, clouded with thick dust and the floor tilted awkwardly. When he moved his jaw, he felt chips of his teeth grinding in his mouth as if he was chewing sand.

Deaf to all but the ringing inside his head, he ran to the shattered window, but saw nothing.

Next he tried the side door into the alley but the door stayed closed. Rushing back to the window he smashed out the remaining glass with the butt of his pistol and pushed his face against the iron bars. Everything outside in the alley was still and silent and dark.

He was caught by surprise when he caught a glimpse of a man running through the rubble carrying heavy bags, then, he saw another one. For a moment he thought that his salvation was near. "Hey! You two men! Help me get out of here!" They ignored him. Then it dawned on him. The only logical reason they wouldn't come to help him was the thing he dreaded. Butch Cassidy was robbing his bank.

Harry was busily grabbing moneybags and attempting to carry them over the rubble. It was difficult, they were heavy and awkward to carry and the snow made the footing treacherous. He saw that Daniel was struggling with the bags.

"Are you OK?" Still dazed, Daniel nodded, his face taut with pain. "Get back to the horses and load the bags," he yelled. Daniel shook his head. "Go back to the horses," Harry yelled into his ear and pointed.

Daniel, dragging two bags, stumbled off. Harry looked about him at the ground littered with his newly appropriated wealth and, reluctant to leave it, decided that he was going to make the best of this opportunity.

The Sheriff reached his right arm through the window up to his shoulder, pushing his face against the bars to try to see around the corner. For a moment, he thought they'd gone. Then he glimpsed one of the robbers as he ran back behind the bank. The Sheriff's heart was pounding and he was breathing hard. The pain inside his head made him even angrier.

Suddenly, the man re-appeared and he was dragging moneybags. The sound of the pistol barely registered but in the muzzle flash he glimpsed a dark figure running. "Stop!" he yelled in frustrated anger. "I'll get you, you filthy robbing bastards. Get back here!" he yelled impotently into the night, then emptied his gun in their general direction.

He rushed to reload but his shaking hands defied him. Cartridges fell on the floor but he ignored them, pulling more from his belt. Finally reloaded, he stuck his pistol back out through the window again and emptied his gun into the night, pulling it back in to reload once more. Somebody must have heard all of his shooting. He hoped they didn't shoot him, thinking he was one of the robbers. He busied himself reloading his pistol once more.

Daniel had made it to where their horse was tethered but now the pain in his wrist forced him to hold his arm as he ran back for more bags. It was then that he heard the sound of gunfire.

It was eerily quiet as Harry made his way back across the narrow alley. He had a good grip on four of the heavy money bags and had turned downhill heading for the horses when out of the corner of his eye he saw something emerge from the window of the bank. Turning his head for a quick look he saw the flash, and it was lucky that he was looking that way. The flash of light surprised him and sent him stumbling face first onto the ground, probably saving his life. The sound of the gun had registered somewhere in Harry's brain, but the thing he'd always remember was the searing pain in his shoulder and the sound of the bullet that buzzed like a bee next to his ear.

The boom of the gun dissipated into the storm, the silence set in again. It was a tangible thing, as thick and heavy as the falling snow. Something had happened, but he didn't know what it was until he tried to push himself up from the ground. His right arm buckled under him as a sharp, searing pain shot through his brain. That was when the Sheriff decided to start shooting at him again.

The Sheriff was as mad as he'd ever been in his life. Not only had Butch Cassidy robbed his bank, it happened while he was guarding it. He would be the laughing stock of the town.

Boom! Boom! Boom!

He looked out again at the whiteness of the night. The robbers had disappeared into the storm. In frustration he stuck his arm back out through the window and emptied his last rounds into the storm. Somebody must have heard the noise, he thought.

The gunfire seemed to go on forever and Harry flinched at every shot, expecting the next one to finish him. The silence returned. He needed no more invitation to get going and hurled himself and his bags down the road. He'd gone but a few yards when his momentum carried him headlong into Daniel coming to find him.

"Grab these," Harry yelled, handing Daniel two of the bags. Daniel grabbed them and together they stumbled down the hill. Harry felt his arm grow weak and lost his grip on the bag he had in his right hand. He thought about bending down to pick it up, but the sounds of more pistol shots changed his mind. What he did see was the glistening of his blood on the bag and the dark drops falling from his sleeve onto the snow. He slumped to his knees.

Daniel saw Harry slumped over, cradling his arm.

"What's the matter, Harry?"

"Have a look for me, will ya'?" Harry pointed over his shoulder.

The snow accumulating on the coat made it difficult to see anything but a small patch that seemed to be free of snow. Daniel poked at it with his finger.

Harry screamed with pain and jumped to his feet clutching his shoulder.

Daniel looked at his finger and saw that there was something dark and wet glistening on his fingertip. Harry tried to reach around to feel it for himself, but gave up from the pain.

"Here Harry, let me help you." Daniel took him under his left arm and together they stumbled down to where their horse waited.

"Did we lose the bags?" Harry asked.

"I saved one of them."

"Well, that's better than none I guess. Come on. Let's get back home before someone in this town wakes up."

Daniel tied the moneybags to the horse's reins and, supporting Harry, they ran back and reattached the sled as before.

As they rode their sleds down the narrow street heading out of town, there were no more lights shining than when they'd arrived. It was as if the bank got robbed every Christmas. Their horses obediently picked up the pace and settled into a fast trot. It was the speed that the Morgans were most comfortable with, but with the Sheriff shooting up the night, Daniel wished that he could do something to make them go just a bit faster.

They joined the main road at the edge of town and nothing unusual was happening. No posse, no vigilantes, no angry peasants with flaming torches screaming for their blood. Daniel thought that for all they had done getting here and robbing the bank, it was a bit of a letdown. Harry was thinking the same thing. He looked in vain for the moon, but the snow was a blowing curtain inches from his face. The most important question came to his mind. What time was it?

Chapter 30

Why, after two explosions capable of blowing up a building, a dozen or more pistol shots and his screaming at the top of his lungs till he was hoarse, had not one of deputies appeared? Painfully frustrated, he walked to the side door and with determined hatred, fired the last of his bullets at the doorknob. The wood shattered, but the door still wouldn't open.

The Sheriff was over six-feet tall and thick of build. He enhanced that presence by being the most intolerant individual he'd ever met.

Clenching his jaw, he hurled himself at the door which splintered around the handle and gave way under the onslaught. His momentum carried him off the steps over the railing into the street below. He was writhing in pain, clutching his knee, when the first help arrived, his eldest son Hamlett, followed by a handful of curious drunks.

"Ham, get these people away from the money." The Sheriff said to his son.

"Are you alright, Pa?" Hamlett asked, helping his father to his feet.

"I'll be a lot better when I catch the bastards who robbed the bank. I'm not certain but I think there were only two of them."

A small crowd, drawn by the noise, was growing rapidly. More than a dozen people, mostly drunks, had arrived to gape at the hole in the bank and at the bags of money and coins scattered over the ground. Some were already scavenging the scattered coins.

"Get away from that money. Do you hear me?" he yelled.

"D'ya think it could've been Butch Cassidy and his gang?" said his son, showing a spark of deductive reasoning.

The Sheriff nodded his agreement, having considered that possibility when he first fell out of his chair. "Watch the money until you get some more help. I'm going to see which way they went," he said, stumbling off down the hill.

Though it was the middle of the night, following the robbers was easy. He just followed the furrows in the snow where they had dragged the bags and he hadn't gone far when something dark on the ground, partly covered by snow, caught his eye. Turning it over with his foot he saw it was one of the bank's money bags. Bending down, he wiped his finger across the dark smudge on the bag; he lit a match and smiled with satisfaction. It shone bright red in the glare of the match. "Gotcha," he said.

Fighting the wind and the blowing snow the Sheriff limped further down the hill and found two more money bags close by. Someone was running towards him so he quickly walked away from the bags and met his son, coming for him.

"Pa! Shouldn't we get after them fellers?" Hamlett asked.

"Here, take this bag back to the office, lock it up in a cell and cover it with a blanket. I don't want anyone else to see it just yet. Have the deputies guard the money in the street and tell someone to go and get the manager. He's probably asleep. Tell him his bank's been robbed. He'll know what to do." The Sheriff handed his son the bloody bag. "Wake up the telegraph operator too. Have him send a message to the Sheriff in Buena Vista telling him to be on the lookout for Butch Cassidy coming his way. Maybe we'll get lucky." The Sheriff took a deep breath. "Then hurry on over to the livery, I'll saddle our horses and we'll go after them fellers. OK?" Hamlett dashed off, excitedly.

When his son had left, the Sheriff gathered up the two money bags and placed them out of sight under a pile of timber in an abandoned shack. Satisfied that they would not be discovered until he returned for them he walked as quickly as he could manage to the livery where he and his son stabled their horses.

The Sheriff knew he'd have to chase after the robbers soon or he'd lose them in the storm. The snow was falling heavily, so rapidly that it was effectively covering whatever tracks the robbers might have left. His rage boiled when he arrived at the barn and found the doors tied shut with tightly knotted wire. He banged on them in frustration and tore at the wire.

Hamlett found him sitting on the ground with his back against the doors, his fingers torn, and his new Christmas gloves tattered.

"Get me some cutters. And hurry, Goddamn it."

꧁꧂

So far, so good, Harry thought, as he sped through the blizzard, letting the horse have its head. The storm had come at the right time and it had been heavy enough to both dampen the explosion and cover their getaway. All things considered, he was feeling pretty good about himself, in spite of the bullet which might still be in his shoulder.

His head came up with surprise as the moon burst on the night and pulled the storm behind them. Unfazed by the weather their horses trotted along at their steady gait putting more and more miles behind them. With difficulty, Harry turned his head and was pleased to see Daniel close behind. What was an even better sight was that there was no one following them.

They quickly and silently made the turn at Balltown and at the top of the hill, where on a sunny day they could've seen the lakes, Harry pulled his horse to a stop. He stood with effort and stretched his arm, shocked when dark liquid spilled from his sleeve onto the snow. He kicked at it with his feet before Daniel saw it—the last thing he needed was to scare the boy more. Harry handed the whiskey bottle to Daniel.

"What time do you think it is, Harry?"

Harry looked at the sky again, but the moon had disappeared.

"It's late. Put some more snow on my shoulder, will ya'?" Daniel packed the hole with as much snow as it would hold and said nothing when the snow came away black with blood.

He could see that Harry was in great pain but he knew that there was nothing they could do but to keep going and hope they could make it. There would be a lot of explaining to do if Harry failed to make it home.

The snow fell even more heavily as they headed up the valley to Twin Lakes. At times, the storm would ease, teasing them and in those fleeting moonlit moments, the far side of the valley became visible, floating just above the flat blackness of the lakes. Just as suddenly, the storm would overtake them and the blanket of snow would envelope them once more.

Harry pressed his eyes closed tightly, partly in pain, partly against the freezing wind that whipped his face. His shoulder throbbed, his hand was going numb and to make matters worse he could feel sticky, warm blood pooling in the elbow of his coat. When he opened his eyes he felt nauseous and light headed.

Lulled by the wind, Daniel dozed and realized that they were at Twin Lakes only when the sound of the howling wolves woke him up. They slowly and quietly passed the Lodge and Daniel opened the gate into the corral and began to untie the harnesses.

"Hear them wolves? I guess Gloria's getting some." Harry whispered. "That Frank is one lucky son of a bitch, ain't he?"

They hurried about their task finding the horses they had brought and were leading them from the corral when light from the door of the cabin illuminated them. Ducking down under their horses they saw Gloria emerge.

"Don't worry darling. He won't bother you, he's passed out drunk," Gloria said to someone inside, and then Newly appeared in the doorway. Harry and Daniel exchanged a look and watched closely as Gloria wrapped herself in her shawl and kissed Newly on the lips. "Besides, it's Christmas," she said to him. They watched her walk briskly across the road to the Lodge, cautiously open the door and disappear inside. Newly disappeared into his cabin also and both Daniel and Harry breathed a sigh of relief.

They were opening the corral gate when the piercing sound of a woman's screams split the stillness of the night. Suddenly, the door to the Lodge opened and light spilled out across the road silhouetting Frank holding a rifle in his hand and Gloria frantically trying to pull him back inside the Lodge.

Daniel and Harry crouched down even lower.

"No! Frank, no! Please! I promise I'll never do it again. I promise," Gloria wailed into the night. "Please Frank, don't do anything—please," she cried, trying to hold him back. He shook her off and punched her in the face with his fist. She fell back inside onto the floor, wailing.

"I'll be back to deal with you later!" Frank yelled. Levering a round into his rifle, he marched across the road towards them.

Frank was passing not more than thirty paces from them heading for the cabin. Harry's horse shied and moved leaving Harry exposed. Frank turned his head in their direction momentarily, but he continued on. Harry ducked under his horse again. They watched Frank barge into the cabin and then heard the sounds of a violent fight which sounded as if Frank was tearing the cabin apart board by board, using Newly as a hammer.

"Let's get the hell away from here before that asshole shoots us. For all he cares, we came over here for some Christmas treats, too," Harry said.

They led the horses away from the noise, then climbed back onto the sleds and headed up the Pass. They hadn't gone but a hundred yards when the sound of a gunshot reached them.

Daniel cringed when he heard the report of the rifle. He cringed once more when he heard the second shot. Harry also heard the shots.

⚍⚏

The Sheriff and his son had been riding hard through the deepening snow for more than an hour, but had seen nothing of the robbers who had a half-hour head start on them. His only consolation was that their horses laden with heavy money bags would be slower and would tire much sooner than his. Unfortunately it was impossible to see anything in the white-out and the men they were following could have turned off the road anywhere, or changed horses and he would not have known.

Though their faces were freezing, the Sheriff felt little discomfort. He was becoming increasingly concerned with what might happen if they actually caught up to Butch Cassidy and whomever was riding with him.

As they approached the mouth of the canyon, the storm came with a new ferocity and the snow swirled around them with stinging force. Their world closed in around them as the blizzard gathered its fury and their horses balked and tried to turn their tails to the force of the wind.

After minutes of struggling with the horses the Sheriff stopped and drew closer to his son. "Go back to town. Go take care of the bank." He yelled.

"What about you? Aren't you coming, too?" Hamlett yelled in reply.

"Go on back. I'm going to go up the canyon a ways. No use both of us freezin' to death. I want to see if they're holed up at Balltown."

Reluctantly but gratefully, his son headed back the way they'd come.

The Sheriff pulled his hat down further over his face and turned his horse back into the storm. It was difficult going for both he and his horse, but he knew the robbers were having the same difficulties, hopefully more.

Balltown was dark and deserted. Not even the saloon had a light on. He waded through the deep snow to the door of the bar and pounded on it until a lamp brightened from inside.

"It's me, Ted. The Sherriff. I got to stay here tonight. That OK with you?" he yelled through the door. The door opened to a sleepy, drunken bar owner. The Sheriff strode past him, shaking snow off his coat and hat. He pulled a chair up to the stove and put his boots against the hot iron.

"Sure, Sheriff, make yourself comfortable."

"Seen any strangers come through here tonight?"

Ted tossed the Sheriff a blanket. "Nope. Just you." Ted went back to his bed in the back room, hoping that it was all a dream. Waking up the Sheriff and making him breakfast was not his idea of a merry Christmas morning.

The fire was still hot in the potbellied stove that was the community center of Balltown. His feet were frozen numb, and for certain were going to hurt when the blood started flowing again. He listened to the whistling wind until he nodded off, hanging the robbers a dozen times in his mind.

Harry was worried about the weather and the time until dawn. Their horses were slowing down, struggling more as the road angled uphill more steeply and the snow became deeper. Because of their weight, the sleds were beginning to push snow in front of them and the more the snow piled up, the slower they went. He hoped he wouldn't have to get out and walk up the Pass. He tried to lift his arm and nearly blacked out from the surge of pain. He assumed from the pain that he must be mortally wounded.

Daniel's sled was becoming a problem so he stopped to see why it was slewing sideways. He yelled for Harry to stop, but he couldn't possibly have been heard over the storm. Daniel dug around the front of the sled until he discovered the problem; one of the runners was coming loose. The leather thong that held it together had broken and he saw that eventually the runner would break off completely, leaving him stranded.

He got back into the sled and continued uphill, following Harry's tracks as far as the steep, sharp turn that marked the last, long climb up to the summit. He knew where he was but there was no way to catch up to Harry, unless he decided to stop and wait for him.

Daniel's horse was breathing hard and he knew it was having a difficult time, but it was faster to ride than it was to walk up-hill. Incredibly, the great beast plodded forward, seldom losing its footing, taking step after step as they climbed and climbed. It was cruel to have to push the horses so much. Once again he thought of Gloria.

The storm surprised Daniel with its ferocity when he rose above the tree line. It tore at his clothing and his hat and found its way into every crack or vent in his clothing. Once again they had slowed to a stop so he climbed out to inspect his sled and was horrified to find that the runner had broken off completely.

Afraid to leave the sled and the money, knowing it could lead the Sheriff to them as directly as leaving a letter, he decided that he could help the horse if he did some pushing. Walking to the rear of the sled he grasped the rails tightly and pushed with all his remaining strength, but freed from the drag on the sled his horse bolted and raced off into the storm. He lunged for the sled, but fell and helplessly watched his horse disappear into the night, dragging the sled with it. Desperate and exhausted he could only pray that his horse would catch up to Harry and that he would see that Daniel was in trouble and would come back to rescue him.

For Daniel there was no alternative; if he was to survive he must keep going. He pushed himself to his feet and climbed the road following the trail left by the sled, knowing if he wandered too far to the right, he would walk off the cliff and disappear into the night in a tumbling ball of snow. Just the effort of breathing sapped his strength, but he lumbered on, trying to keep his head in front of his feet.

"Harry," he called out as loudly he could. The wind gave him his only answer. "Harry!" he called again. It was futile and he knew it.

He put his head down against the wind and walked upwards into the storm. Enveloped in the swirling snow, he was unknowingly walking out onto the narrow ledge that led to the Summer Mine. A steep drop of over one-thousand feet awaited him should he slip. He'd walked several yards blindly, when a gust of wind pushed him to his left. He put out his hand and the suddenness of the solid wall shocked him but he resisted his reaction to step back. In the gusting whiteout conditions, he would never have known that he'd stepped off the cliff and into oblivion until it was too late.

He held out his arm and rested against the wall. His mind labored to put this place into perspective and when he did, he almost fainted with terror. He dropped down on his hands and knees to feel for the edge and recoiled when he found it barely a foot away from his knee.

Keeping his arm on the wall, he backed along the trail until the rock wall was no more. By dragging his feet through the snow, he found the deep groove in the snow where the sled had been dragged and then turned uphill. Moments later, he ran into the sled which had broken loose and now lay across the road, gathering snow. He sat down on the broken sled and put his head in his hands to block out the blizzard.

Didn't he know in his heart that Harry's grand venture would be his folly? He was going to die and it was only partially Harry's fault that he would never see Kate or his family again. Anger arose in his heart and overcame his fear. If he was to survive, he would have to reach the top where Harry was, even if it meant leaving the money behind. He pushed himself off the sled, turned and was knocked over backwards by Harry coming downhill, leading Daniel's horse.

"What the hell you doin' sittin' there?" Harry was relieved, even if he was angry.

"The sled is broken," Daniel screamed.

Harry saw the problem. "Tie the bags together with these," he yelled. They hurriedly unloaded the four money-bags and tied them together using the horse's reins.

"Give me a hand!" Harry, obviously in pain, pointed towards the cliff. Daniel joined him and together they pushed the sled downhill a few feet at a time until it lurched out of their hands and toppled over the edge. It might be a problem explaining the loss of the sled, but it would be a much bigger problem for them if they died on the Pass.

"How're you doin'?" Harry yelled at Daniel's ear.

"OK," Daniel managed, with effort.

Harry's pain and discomfort had surged while he had waited at the top and had it not, he might have missed Daniel's snow-covered horse walking up to nuzzle his horse. He saw immediately that the sled had broken away and his first thoughts had not involved Daniel's fate, but finding the money and keeping it all if his partner was dead.

"Hold onto his tail and let him pull you up the hill," Harry yelled. "Don't fall down." Harry advised as he slapped the horse on the flank. It took several tentative steps forward and stopped. "God, don't tell me he's done for."

Harry's mind went blank momentarily, thinking their saga would end with the brave bank robbers dying on the Pass. Just as quickly the horse lifted his tail and let go a tremendous blast of hot gas into their faces. Moments later the horse resumed its slow trudge up the road.

At the summit, they found Harry's horse standing patiently where he had left it. They loaded the moneybags onto Harry's sled and tied the two remaining bags to the chest strap of his horse. It was going to be dangerous and painful for Harry, being that he would have to straddle the bags for the descent and falling off would be a possibility.

Daniel's plight remained a problem. There was no room for him on the sled and neither was it possible to ride since the Morgan's back was too broad for that. Grasping at straws Harry took the leather straps that had broken from Daniel's sled and knotted them together, several feet behind the horse.

"Get out of your coat," Harry yelled over the wind.

"No, Harry. I'll freeze."

"Just do it if you want to see your girlfriend again."

Daniel removed his gloves and fought with the buttons until he had them all undone and handed the coat over. Harry held the coat backwards so that Daniel could place his arms in the sleeves then he turned Daniel around roughly and buttoned the coat up the backside. It was difficult using just one hand and Harry only managed three buttons before he had to sit. Concerned but also exhausted, Daniel watched over Harry as he recovered his strength and then tied the reins around Daniel's wrists.

"What's this for, Harry?" Daniel had to yell. Harry was so exhausted, he didn't really care anymore.

"You're going sledding….and you're the sled." Harry was breathless, "I'll be behind you…..in case anything happens. Just keep your head down…. until the horse stops…. Got it?"

Daniel nodded. Harry pulled Daniel's hat down over his ears and covered his face with his scarf.

"Are you ready partner?" Daniel nodded. Harry smiled and slapped Daniel's horse on the flanks hard. He laughed when Daniel was pulled off his feet and disappeared into the storm being dragged down the mountain road and into the night. Still laughing at his ingenuity, Harry climbed into his sled as quickly as his condition allowed, and followed Daniel's horse into the storm.

Harry was delirious with his feeling of accomplishment and from his loss of blood. His attention returned when his horse slowed and tentatively made the first turn on the western slope of the mountain. Even though the storm whipped and pulled at every part of him and his shoulder felt like it had a burning poker in it, he felt successful, immortal and strangely grateful. For just that moment, he felt imbued with God's blessings.

⊰⊱

Daniel was being pulled and tossed from side to side. The torture of his wrist seemed interminable. Snowflakes of all sizes filled the air, swimming around his head; blotting out everything further than arm's length. When he lifted his head, he saw the huge hooves flicking clumps of snow at him, so he let his head fall down into his hat and prayed.

The last obstacle they faced was getting through the town of Independence without being seen. Harry was counting on the fact that at this time of the morning and in these conditions, with the snow falling so heavily, they would have to actually collide with someone before they would be seen. He was wondering if they had already passed the town when he heard a man singing. It was brief and stopped suddenly. The horses kept their pace.

A drunken miner stumbling home almost caught sight of the two bank robbers blanketed thickly in snow as they sped down the road. If he'd stepped a couple of feet more into the road before deciding to relieve himself, he might have been killed by them.

"Fucking reindeer," he mumbled as he closed his coat.

Harry was becoming increasingly nervous about the time they had left until daylight. He looked constantly up to where the sky should be, but saw only never-ending snow. The pain in his shoulder was draining him and though his eyes were weary and he craved sleep he fought to keep his eyes open, just as Daniel fought to keep his closed.

Harry felt the pace of his horse pick up and he realized they were close to the barn and now, just like he was, they were in a hurry to get home. It buoyed his spirit greatly because the eastern sky was becoming significantly lighter by the minute.

When they arrived at Red's barn it was still mostly dark. Harry helped Daniel to his feet amid groans from every movement, no matter how small. They unhitched the horses and led them into their corral barely disturbing the other Morgans asleep, still as statues. Their own horses were tied to the tree where they had left them and after leading them to the road and removing the blankets which had kept them warm and mostly dry; they hitched Harry's horse to the remaining sled and departed quietly.

The leaden sky was becoming much lighter when at last they entered town. Harry dragged the blankets behind the sled, hoping it would smooth their tracks that would then be covered by the falling snow. There was nothing more he could do but hope the old Indian trick would work.

When they reached their cabin they hurried the moneybags inside, and shoved them under the beds. Harry counted seven bags before they grabbed the buckets of whiskey mash from the storage room, placed them in the sled and headed for the stable.

Dawn was clearly arriving. Usually, at this time of day there would be traffic heading to and from the mines. But thankfully this was Christmas morning so it was more than likely that between the hangovers and the Christmas presents, the streets would stay mostly deserted till mid-morning. Their luck was holding but there was still one more task ahead of them before they could rest.

The stable was deathly quiet when they entered. Joe's door was closed and the other horses were slumbering. They unsaddled their horses and Daniel gave them a quick brushing so they didn't look as though they'd been ridden, while Harry spooned the sweet whiskey, salt and potato mash into some of the horses' feed buckets, but not all of them. He smiled watching his horse and the others devour it like hungry children. Harry wondered what kind of hangover it would produce in a horse.

With half of the horses in the barn enjoying their special breakfast, Harry and Daniel headed for the door but they ducked down behind a stall when they heard the door to Joe's room open. He rumbled a cough to clear his throat and then they were forced to listen as he relieved himself into a bucket, the sound of which went on and on, in stops and starts. Though it felt like it took forever, eventually they heard Joe close his door and go back to bed. Silently they opened the side door and quickly stepped out into the morning.

Too spent to pull the sled back to Harry's cabin, they left it by the side of the barn and threw a blanket over it. They were so completely exhausted that they stumbled repeatedly and drunkenly up the narrow path to their cabin. Harry reached for the door handle.

"Merry Christmas, Harry." Willy Tomb called from the outhouse. "Hey, you guys just getting home?" Both of their hearts stopped in unison. They felt the first of many waves of anxiety come over their depleted bodies.

"Yeah. We had a big night." Harry replied with false merriment.

"Merry Christmas, Willy," Daniel called to him, as they hurried inside and fell immediately onto their respective beds.

"What on earth was he doing, trying to be pleasant at this ungodly hour of the morning? That man should rightly be shot." Harry started laughing. He winced every time he laughed.

Daniel felt his own laughter come from the place where his tension and fears had held residence. For the first time in his life, he had triumphed. His joy was different from Harry's, but it resonated loudly and their laughter shook the cabin.

Chapter 31

The Sheriff was up early and out the door at first light. His boots were still wet. It was still snowing and the road was knee-deep with the snow that had fallen during the night. There were only two ways to go from where he was, south towards the next town of Buena Vista, or west towards Twin Lakes and Aspen. If they tried to make it to Buena Vista, the sheriff there would be on the lookout for them since the telegraph warning him about the robbers would be there soon, if not already.

He concluded that they would have had to have found shelter somewhere, or freeze to death during the night, so it was also possible that they could have holed up for the night in Twin Lakes. If that was the case, he figured he might run into them.

The visibility improved with the dawn, but the snow continued to fall as his horse waded through the already deep snow, leaving messy tracks in her path. They were both shivering with fatigue and cold when they reached Twin Lakes.

Under the blanket of new snow everything seemed quiet and peaceful. Judging from the tracks in the snow, someone or several people had walked from the Lodge to the bunkhouse; the tracks were fairly new. He could imagine the cowboy who lived there, or the robbers, walking over for a hot cup of coffee. He decided to check the bunkhouse first.

He pulled out his pistol and checked that it was loaded, though it always was. The cabin door was slightly ajar, but he heard no noise from inside. Certain that his approaching footsteps crunching the fresh dry snow would have given him away already; he approached the bunkhouse with caution. No sounds came from the small building, and there was drifted snow piled inside the door. Opening the door slowly, he felt the heat of the stove and saw the carnage.

⊰⊱

Daniel awoke to moans and groans. He had dozed, but not really slept. Part of him had stayed conscious in anticipation of the Sheriff barging in on them. Harry was trying to get his shirt off with one hand and struggling mightily. His back, where he'd pulled the shirt up, was brownish red with fresh and dried blood mingled together.

"Wait, Harry, let me help you." Harry's eyes were bloody red and sunken and his face had no color at all. Daniel poured some hot water into a pan and tried to hide his shock as he went behind Harry with the warm water and a not too filthy towel. He dabbed at the wound gently and Harry groaned at each touch. The wound was long and looked nasty.

Slowly, the undershirt released itself from the clotted blood and Daniel got his first good look at the wound. But as he washed away the remnants of Harry's shirt and hair from the bear skin coat, the more he cleaned it the less serious it appeared. The bullet had grazed the shoulder and not penetrated, leaving a straight groove just below the shoulder itself and over the top of it. Though the wound was ugly and messy, the bullet had missed hitting the shoulder bones by a whisker. It was not a life threatening wound unless infection set in.

"What's it look like?" Harry demanded. He had the whiskey bottle in his good hand and had been slugging from it while Daniel worked on his wound.

"I'll tell you something, Harry. You're a lucky man. If you'd been standing up, it would've gone through your lung, I think."

"But what's it look like?"

Daniel took down the small mirror they used for shaving and tried to show him the wound. Through much discomfort and various contortions, Harry got a glimpse. Satisfied, he relaxed and handed the whiskey bottle to Daniel. "Pour some of this on it."

Daniel took the whiskey bottle and poured some on the wound. Harry bit into the towel, barely muffling his screams as the whiskey and blood ran down his back.

"Hey, don't waste it." Harry snapped. "I bought that stuff special for Christmas." With some difficulty, he reached into his pants pocket and pulled out a small blue glass bottle. "Here, pour some of this on there, too." Daniel took the small blue bottle with the word "Cocaine" in raised letters on the side and poured some of the liquid on the wound. "Do you think you can bandage that up for me?"

"Sure. I'll put some honey on the wound to keep it clean. That's what my mother used to do. What can I use for a bandage?"

Harry went to his bed and pulled off one of the filthy sheets. "Here, use this. I think I can afford a new sheet now."

Daniel ripped the cloth and made a bandage that went around Harry's chest and another that went over his shoulder, then another strip for a sling.

They both jumped as the noon whistle sounded.

"You'd think that just one day of the year they could turn that damned thing off," Harry complained. "Hey, do you want to open some of our presents?"

The handle of one of the moneybags was visible under Harry's bed.

"I can't believe we did it." Daniel said. Harry poured more coffee, whiskey, and the rest of the cocaine into his cup.

"Well, partner, we did it." Harry opened the door a little and peeked out. The snow was still coming down, but not as hard. "I doubt if anyone could have followed us back here with all this snow." Harry jammed a chair under the door handle, pulled the bag from underneath his bed, lifted it painfully and set it on the table heavily. "Let's see if it was worth all that trouble."

They had no way to cut the heavy lock on the bag, so Harry set to it with his knife. The bag was made of sturdy canvas, but gave way to the knife quickly. Daniel picked it up by the bottom and emptied the contents onto the table. Stacks of money tumbled out, covering the table and falling onto the floor. There were bundles and bundles of five-dollar bills, in stacks of one hundred dollars. Daniel counted fifty stacks. There was five-thousand dollars in just one bag.

Excitement ran through them as they opened another, then another. One was full of tens, one had twenties, but most of them were fives; they had picked up a bag of ones too. There were seven bags and a total of fifty-one thousand dollars. Money covered the table and lay about their feet on the floor. For a long time they sat silently, looking at the piles of paper money. Occasionally, Harry would pick up a bundle, smell it and smile, savoring the aroma.

"Where are we going to put it all, Harry? I don't think it's all going to fit under there." Daniel pointed at the oven.

"It'll fit. We'll make it fit. Let's get it back under the beds. I don't want some thieving bastard to come in here and relieve us of our profit. I'd kill the scoundrel and not think about it a second." Harry was recovering at a miraculous rate; he was out of his sling and cradling stacks of money in his arms. He pulled back his straw mattress and laid the money on the bed, neatly covering it back up when he'd finished. Daniel did the same. When they were finished, their beds were half a foot thicker than they'd been. Most noticeable was that Harry's bed was actually made.

"Where can we put it all?" Daniel worried. The small burrow under the oven was hardly much bigger than a dent in the ground.

"Well, we can't dig a hole outside; the ground is frozen, and this paper stuff will just get wet and rot if we bury it in the snow. Other than hiding it in the mines, I can't think of any place safer than right here with us. Can you?" Daniel had to agree after considering the options. "Hey, isn't Wheeler's Christmas party tonight?" Harry said, as if suddenly remembering. Daniel looked up, surprised.

"Oh, I forgot about that." He fell back onto his bed and draped his arm over his eyes. "I'm too tired."

"You've got to go." Harry was thinking of his options, including taking the money while Daniel was out at the party and heading off into the night to God knows where.

"I'll go if you'll go," replied Daniel. It hadn't occurred to him that Harry had not been invited.

"That's an interesting idea." Harry was feeling no pain. He lowered himself gingerly onto his bed, lying on his good side, and drifted into a dreamless sleep.

⊲⊱

The Sheriff closed the door quickly on the mess inside the bunkhouse. He took a deep breath, steeled his stomach against the smell, pushed the door open again and walked inside. There was evidence of a fierce fight; things were scattered about the room and the bunk beds lay smashed or leaned awkwardly from their broken supports. Newly's body was draped over the table in the middle of the room. The Sheriff walked around it and examined it from all sides.

It became obvious that he'd taken a serious beating before he'd been killed. Blood was splattered on the bed frames and the walls and in small puddles around the room. His jaw was about as dislocated as the Sheriff could ever have imagined, his head lay back off the table and his tongue appeared to have been cut out. He'd probably bled to death or drowned in his own blood before his heart had been cut out, but perhaps not.

His pants were pulled down around his ankles, over his boots. Blood covered his white legs from groin to knee, and then drained downward to his shins. There was a gunshot wound in his groin and another in his knee that would have made the pain from all the other wounds tolerable by comparison. He was, by medical definition, neutered.

The air outside was fresher than he'd ever smelled. He looked at the tracks in the snow and followed them to the front door of the Lodge. He didn't bother knocking. When he entered, Frank grabbed for the rifle leaning next to his chair. He took one look at the Sheriff and sat back down.

"What're you doin' here?" Frank asked.

"Lookin' for whoever robbed the bank last night. I was wonderin' if you'd seen anyone come through here." He paused. "But I guess you've been kinda busy."

Frank said nothing.

"You havin' a merry Christmas, Frank?"

Frank remained silent. The Sheriff strolled over to the fireplace, where Frank was watching the fire intently, and sat in a big chair across from him. "Got any coffee?"

"Yeah, it's in the kitchen."

The Sheriff got up and walked towards the kitchen.

"Where's Gloria?"

"She's in the kitchen."

The Sheriff quickened his stride but stopped abruptly at the doorway to the kitchen. Gloria was all over the kitchen.

⊰⊱

Daniel made an effort to primp for the party. He went to Mr. Chin's for a bath and found that it was crowded with other men doing the same thing for the same reason. There was a general feeling of happiness in the air at the bathhouse and it lent itself wonderfully to the season of goodwill to all men. Daniel could hardly contain his elation, as gradually the magnitude of their feat entered his awareness.

The place where he saw himself in the great scheme of things was forever altered. He knew he would never again think like the boy he was yesterday. He looked down at himself and noticed for the first time that there were hairs growing from his nipples and a few dark strands on his chest.

Though bathing was not a particularly high priority on Harry's list of personal hygiene, Daniel knew that Harry couldn't be seen in the bathhouse where other men would notice the wound. Questions would be asked, word would spread. As he soaked in the warm bath, he decided that he would have to acquire a small tub of some sort. He smiled at the vision of Harry trying to sit in a tub not much bigger than a bucket.

Back at the cabin, he took out his one good white shirt and tied the best knot in his tie that he could manage. He did his best to clean his vest and hoped that he could leave his big smelly bearskin coat someplace it wouldn't be noticed. He looked at himself in the mirror and noted with pleasure that he did look as good as he felt. By all signs, it was going to be a merry Christmas; it was the coming new year that concerned him.

Harry was asleep and snoring loudly. Daniel wished the inert form "Merry Christmas" and headed out for what was potentially the best evening of his young life. He stepped with light feet and with an assurance in his gait that told the world he was a champion, at least for this one night. Though he could never tell a living soul what he'd done, he knew that he'd done it against all odds and the fury of nature.

⠀⠀⠀❧❧

The Hotel was lit from all angles. Every room was a source of illumination, shining so brightly that the road outside was as bright as daytime. Carriages and sleighs lined up outside the front doors, and Daniel could see men in uniforms greeting the people as they entered. He felt like he was walking on air as he crossed the street; it was dreamlike. The building looked like a palace.

At the front door he stood in line waiting his turn to enter, exchanging season's greetings with the other equally impressed guests. In the foyer, Jerome B. Wheeler had stationed himself to personally greet his guests. He was surrounded by well-wishers and some fawning wives of his less successful competitors, but he caught sight of Daniel as he entered and waved him over.

"How're you doing, young man? Merry Christmas to you." He clamped his arm around Daniel's shoulder, announcing to those around him that Daniel was going to join his company and make him even richer. Daniel was embarrassed at the attention; he smiled politely and shook all of the offered hands.

"Go on in and enjoy yourself, my boy," Jerome leaned close, "but don't go too far. There's someone I want you to meet." Daniel nodded and gave his coat to a girl who turned up her nose as she staggered away with it through the crowd.

The foyer and main salon leading into the ballroom were festooned with Christmas decorations. The hanging chandeliers sent sparkling slivers of prismatic light across the room in all directions. Everywhere he looked there were women "Oohing" and "Aahing" over each other's fashions. Daniel noticed that there were a number of young ladies around his age, some of whom were very attractive indeed. He wondered why he'd never seen them before. Some shyly looked his way.

There was a broad table in the center of the salon on which were small glass cups for the punch and plates of many types of small delicacies, including finger sandwiches and tiny meat-filled pastries. He hadn't realized how hungry he was and started stuffing the tiny sandwiches into his mouth.

"I didn't think you'd come."

He turned to see Kate at his shoulder, reaching for a glass of punch. Daniel began choking on his sandwich. He spluttered and coughed and made a mess, struggling to keep the food in his mouth as he convulsed. Eventually he regained a portion of his former dignity.

"I'm so sorry," he got out finally. He tried vainly to brush away the food that had escaped his mouth and landed on her dress, but she politely pushed his hand away. She was faintly laughing at his embarrassment and it seemed to make everything alright again.

"Come sit at our table. My mother wanted you to join us."

She did something that Daniel found wondrous: she linked her arm through his and guided him deftly through the crowd; he felt on top of the world. Kate's dress seemed to be of the latest fashion, judging from the glares of some of the older women present. It was made of deep green silk and the bodice was cleverly engineered of overlapping lace in such a way that encouraged the imagination of a young man. He felt proud that she was on his arm and that she was apparently pleased to be there with him.

The grand ballroom was even more spectacular than the other rooms they'd passed through. Filled with dazzling chandeliers and wall lighting displaying all manner of art, the room was spectacular. At the front of the room was a dais where a band played softly to the guests as they found their tables.

Impossible to ignore and commanding the attention of all, a colossal object, completely covered by a red satin sheath filled one whole corner of the ballroom. Whatever it was, it reached almost to the high ceiling. The lights from the electric lamps around the room shone on the richness of the covering, adding to the curiosity in whatever was underneath. A small crowd surrounded the object, drinking and filling the time by speculating on what might be under the deep red satin sheath.

Shirley's table, at the back corner of the room, was set for five and she was standing talking to another woman when they arrived.

"Oh, Daniel, I want you to meet someone. Mrs. Wheeler, I'd like you to meet Mister Daniel Carrington."

Mrs. Wheeler extended her hand. Daniel took the lifeless appendage, hoping that she didn't notice his reaction to the clamminess of her skin. She was a big woman with a large head, thick lips and several chins. When she shook Daniel's hand, he noticed that the pale skin on the underside of her bare, flabby arm wobbled.

"I'm pleased to meet you, young man. Are you the one Jerome's been on about these past weeks?"

"And you remember Kate, don't you?" Shirley continued with her introductions.

Mrs. Wheeler drew a deep breath as she appraised Shirley's daughter. "My, how you've grown. Chicago must be agreeing with you." She turned her attention back to Daniel. "It's nice to meet you, Mister Carrington. Now, if you'll all excuse me I must return to our guests. Please enjoy yourselves. I'll see you next Tuesday for luncheon, Shirley." She moved off.

Shirley looked at Daniel, appraising him. "My, my, aren't you a handsome young man this evening," she said, giving him a warm hug and smiling at him. "You've met my other daughter Rachelle, haven't you?"

Rachelle sat sullenly, ignoring him. Shirley and Kate shrugged to each other in a knowing gesture and ignored her, seating Daniel between them.

"Where's Harry? I was hoping he would join us," Shirley said. Kate looked away at the mention of Harry's name.

"He's not feeling well," Daniel lied. Shirley rolled her eyes. He was grateful that she chose not to pursue the subject.

"Well, if he's not coming and Red's not here, I think we should all go and get ourselves some of Jerome's fine cuisine before it gets eaten. Come on Rachelle, let's go eat."

Tables laden with food lined two walls of the giant room and were filled to overflowing with dozens of dishes in a feast for the eyes and the stomach. There was so much food, Daniel couldn't imagine where it had all come from. Along one table he saw platters of geese, duck and fowl of every description. Another table held roasted elk quarters, deer tenderloins, a carving station sporting a four foot tall haunch of beef, terrines of delicious smelling soups and stews, and a brazier, where skewers of meat and vegetables sizzled, giving off the most enticing aromas. One table held nothing but cakes and pies and other fancy desserts that made Daniel's mouth water.

Engrossed in consuming the delicious food they failed to see a tall well-dressed man approach their table.

"Good evening, everyone, Merry Christmas. May I join you?"

Red stood across the table from them, his plate also overflowing. Shirley brightened visibly. "Oh, Red, how lovely to see you, please sit down and have dinner with us."

She moved to get up, but Red held up his hand, pulled the open chair out from the table and sat next to Kate, directly across from Shirley.

"How's about we all toast this fine meal and the man who provided it." Red proposed, "to the health of Jerome Wheeler and his family." They clinked wine glasses and dove into the delicious-smelling food with ravenous appetites.

During dessert Daniel felt a hand rest on his right leg. He took in a sharp breath. Kate looked at him, her eyes narrow and mischievous. Casually wiping his mouth, he moved his hand under the table to hold hers, but she pulled it away.

"Are you enjoying your dessert, Daniel?" Shirley inquired, softly inclining her head towards him. "You don't seem to be eating much of it." Daniel took another spoonful and Kate's hand returned to his right leg once again.

"Oh, I like it very much, thank you." He wiped his mouth and pushed his chair away from the table. "Please excuse me, I have to go to the lavatory."

As he crossed the dance floor, he heard his name called and saw that Jerome Wheeler was gesturing for him to come over to his table, which was adjacent to the stage. The dance floor was crowded with guests in conversation, but they parted as if by magic as he approached Wheeler's table.

"There you are, young man." Jerome shook his hand again and guided Daniel towards his table with an arm around his shoulder. "Here, I want you to meet my family. This is my wife, Mrs. Wheeler." Daniel looked at the woman he'd met just before dinner at Shirley's table. He'd expected a similar welcome, but was surprised when she extended her hand straight from her shoulder

"It's nice to meet you. What did you say your name was again?"

"Daniel Carrington, my dear," Jerome said, deflecting the current of disdain that flowed between them. Daniel felt himself being gently guided away from Mrs. Wheeler and gratefully felt the release of her talons. "And this is my daughter Abigail. Lovely, isn't she?"

There was no doubt that Abigail ate well. In many regards, she looked like a female version of her father.

"I'm very pleased to meet you, Abigail." It came out like the bleating of a sheep being led to slaughter. Jerome looked from Daniel to Abigail, then to his wife, giving her a none too subtle wink and a look of shrewd satisfaction that was unreturned.

Abigail was not an unattractive young woman. She had a kind, if full face. She was about Daniel's age and her dress was designed to show her most flattering assets, while hiding the bulk of her figure.

"It's nice to meet you, Mr. Carrington."

What did capture Daniel's attention was the diamond necklace around Abigail's neck. The diamonds shimmered and glittered in the brilliant electric light. He found himself drawn to the necklace and at the same time, the shape and curve of Abigail's ample bosom. Both were spectacular to behold and to be held, he was sure; he blushed at the thought.

"Here, Daniel, I think you're embarrassing the girl," Jerome said with a laugh. "Why don't you come and sit with us young man? We'd love to have your company, wouldn't we, my dear?" Mrs. Wheeler stiffened at the suggestion.

"Ah, well thank you, Mr. Wheeler, but I was just on my way to the lavatory."

"As a matter of fact, I have to do the same. What say we go together? I've got a few folks I'd like to introduce you to anyway." Without looking back, Wheeler led the way across the room, smiling and shaking

hands as he did. Following Jerome, Daniel glanced back and caught
two important impressions. One was the smile from Abigail, the other
was the glare from her mother, looking far from pleased.

On their passage crossing the dance floor, Daniel met the judge,
Sheriff Hunter, Jerome's partner David Hyman, and their respective
families in a blurred slew of names and faces. He discovered that he
was somewhat known by most of the men he met.

There was a lot of, "So *you're* the young feller that Jerome's been
telling us about?" and the like. The feeling of celebrity found its way
into his demeanor. After so many unexpected friendly introductions,
he was feeling taller and prouder than he'd felt before. Though his
wrist throbbed with every handshake, he stoically took every offered
hand and smiled through the shooting pain.

Finally reaching the lavatory, Wheeler smiled at him before they
entered and held a finger to his lips. "Watch this," he said, as he reached
around the door and turned the switch on the wall back and forth,
sending the room into alternating darkness and brilliance, much to
the annoyance of the other men using the facilities. They complained
loudly when he opened the door, laughing at them. "Oh, stop your
whining, you ruffians. Haven't you ever seen the miracle of electric
light before?"

Daniel felt obliged to stay close to Wheeler and took the urinal
next to him. After some sounds of effort and discomfort, Wheeler let
out a sigh of satisfaction as he released the pressure on his bladder.

"What do you think of her, son?"

"I think your wife is a very beautiful woman, sir," he replied, not
smiling. "That's not who I mean and you know it." He paused, looked
around the room and whispered conspiratorially, "Abigail, my daughter. What do you think of her?"

Daniel finished his business and washed his hands in the wonderfully warm water that ran from the shiny brass faucets. Diplomacy was
on his mind. He was admiring the white marble basin and the polished
marble counter when Wheeler joined him.

"Well, what do you think of her? I know she's not the most beautiful girl in the world but she does have a, certain attractiveness, as I'm

sure you noticed." Daniel saw him admiring his reflection, sucking in his corpulent stomach as if to will it to disappear.

Daniel thought desperately to come up with an answer that would cover the obvious, but demonstrate his piety to his possible future employer. "She seems like a lovely girl, Mr. Wheeler."

Wheeler shook his head and said nothing more.

As they departed, the attendant handed them warm towels to dry their hands and sprinkled sweet-smelling water on their shoulders. Daniel smiled broadly and followed Wheeler back into the ballroom. Suddenly he felt faint. His hands became cold and clammy and he could feel the sweat trickle from under his arms. His vision blurred and his fingers tingled; his knees trembled. He stopped and leaned against the wall.

"Are you alright?" Wheeler asked, looking quite concerned.

Slowly, Daniel's vision returned, but his legs were weak and he felt unsure of his ability to walk. It was the fatigue, the pain, and the wine working on him. He would have to sit soon or risk the embarrassment of fainting.

Wheeler solicitously guided him over to his table and helped him sit in the vacant chair next to his daughter. Daniel sat heavily and instantly became aware of the glare that Mrs. Wheeler was impaling him with. After a few deep breaths, he regained his composure and attempted to stand, but Abigail placed her hand lightly on his arm and was looking at him with concern. He saw in her face a kindness that was deficient in her mother. He smiled at her without knowing why, and she blushed, but held his gaze.

"Please excuse me, Abigail, but I think I need some fresh air."

Nodding politely to Mrs. Wheeler he stood, but felt that Abigail let go of his hand reluctantly. He headed for the entrance, all the while feeling Kate's eyes follow him across the room.

The entryway beckoned, he was feeling faint but his path to the doors was blocked by a multitude of guests smoking, drinking and laughing boisterously. Leaning against a pillar for support he was ready to faint when he saw Red approaching. A wave of fear swept over him as he remembered what he had witnessed at Twin Lakes. He had an overwhelming desire to fall on his knees, confess his sins and be done with the burden of the knowledge that Red's man, Newly, was probably dead. He looked for the door; he had to get outside and breathe, but Red saw him.

Red was standing talking with Sparky Langford, Leafy Lane and a group of other men all drinking and laughing in festive humor. They signaled for him to join them but Daniel shook his head and clung onto the wall. Panic and guilt threatened to overcome him and he was struggling with the overpowering urge to run for the door, when Shirley came to his rescue.

"I was wondering where you were," she said, smiling. Taking him by the hand she led him through the crowd, which parted for her miraculously, over to join Red's group. Placing her hand on Red's arm, she smiled up at him and then at his friends. "Excuse me boys, but these two are mine." She laughed, as she linked her arm through Red's, drawing them out of the bar.

"Why don't you come back inside and I'll let you take turns dancing with me and my beautiful daughters?" she said, leading them both back into the main ballroom. Daniel allowed himself to be led, though all he wanted was to breathe fresh air.

As they trooped into the ballroom, the band struck their first chords and all heads turned to look towards the raised dais. Looking splendid and impressive in his tailored dark suit and fancy brocade waistcoat was Jerome B. Wheeler, holding his hands in the air to marshal the boisterous crowd's attention.

A round of friendly jeers came from the wide assortment of friends and associates who had been invited to the grand affair.

Jerome B. Wheeler was nothing if not genuinely committed to the growth and survival of his town. He was a great showman, and looked in every way to be the millionaire, major domo of the town. "Ladies and gentlemen, and I use the latter term loosely—"

There was a round of hoots and jeers.

"My family and I are glad to see you all here. We hope that you are all enjoying yourselves. There's plenty of food and plenty to drink and the band will play till the last man drops." The crowd applauded vigorously. "Let's have an Aspen party we'll all remember."

Another round of applause rose from the crowd.

"Now you're all probably wondering what I have hidden under the tent over here. But first things first," he held his hands up to quell the wave of guesses and crude suggestions that came at him from all angles. "How do you all like the electric lighting here in my hotel?"

At that signal, the lights went out, sending the room into total darkness. As the sounds of dismay rose, the lights came back on all over the room in a burst of brilliance. Seconds later, the lights turned off and on in sequence around the room to gasps of awe and the delight of all those present. There was a solid round of applause when they all came back on again. Then, one by one, the lights on the walls went off and only the chandeliers and those by the stage stayed on. Jerome B. Wheeler was in his element.

Daniel was intent on the entertainment and failed to notice that Kate had moved next to him, straining to see over the people in front of her. To Daniel's delight, she slipped her hand into his to steady herself. Daniel smiled. His heart raced with the pleasure of the contact.

"We now have the first electrically lighted hotel in the state of Colorado. Take that, Leadville." There followed a round of applause that ceased only when Wheeler held up his hands.

"This puts us on the map as far as mountain towns go and shows that pretentious town, Leadville, just which city is the best city in the whole state of Colorado." The crowd roared their agreement. He held up his hands and regained a semblance of order in the overcrowded room. "We're not a town anymore—we're a city. The city, of Aspen! In the new State of Colorado." The crowd applauded wildly, cheering for their fledgling state.

Daniel was surprised when Kate slipped her arm around his waist. He protectively draped his arm around her shoulder and she leaned into him, a small gesture, but wonderfully exciting.

"So, to celebrate this historic occasion, I thought it would be fitting to give you and the City of Aspen a Christmas present." Jerome continued on. "So, without further ado, I'm going to ask my lovely wife and daughter to come over here to unveil the Christmas gift from our family, to all of you."

There was a low hum of conversation as Mrs. Wheeler and Abigail walked around the stage and took their places on either side of the satin-covered mystery.

"Ladies and gentlemen, we present to you and to our wonderful little city—" He theatrically paused and was gratified to hear the room fall completely silent. "The Silver Queen!"

As they'd rehearsed, Wheeler's wife and daughter pulled away the satin cover, which slipped in slow motion from the front to the back as the lamps in the ballroom all came on at once, filling the room with blinding light. When the realization of what they were seeing came into their consciousness, a roar rose from the crowd. Daniel had never seen anything so beautiful in his whole life. It sounded as if he wasn't the only one having that thought.

The Silver Queen was an enormous silver and gold statue of a female goddess sculpted in the classic Grecian style. She was massive, she was splendid and her crown of gold and glass stellar beams radiated light, glittering with a multitude of precious gems of various colors, dancing their magic over the awestruck crowd.

Cast of solid silver the statue stood at least the height of three full-grown men. The queenly goddess sat regally under a delicate silver canopy in a boat-shaped chariot drawn by two small winged cherubs, each carrying a cornucopia overflowing with solid silver and gold nuggets. Enthroned and adorned in gold and gems her imperious bearing matched her enormous value.

The imposing object glistened and glowed with the magnificence of craftsmanship and detail. She seemed to radiate more than just the wealth of her surroundings; she seemed to draw the love from the room to her breast and symbolically held the heart of Aspen in her hand.

The crowd surged forward pushing Daniel and Kate towards the front of the room. Kate started to lose her balance and her walking stick fell from her hand. For a moment, she panicked; the crowd had turned her around so that she was facing Daniel and he could see the fear in her eyes. She was only slightly shorter than Daniel and she reached up to brace herself against him. It was a natural gesture to stop from falling, but in that fraction of a second, she found herself face to face with Daniel in what was her first embrace.

He looked down into her eyes and saw something he'd never noticed before; there were gold flecks in her green eyes and they reflected the light from the chandeliers and the Silver Queen. His heart felt like it had moved higher in his chest and its beating was enough to drown out any other sound. She lingered in his arms adjusting to the press of the crowd; she dropped her eyes and stepped backwards from him. He couldn't help himself—he kept his arm around her waist and drew her to him again. The warm rush of his emotions was so intoxicating, he felt like he'd fallen off a cliff into an abyss.

She felt warm all over. His hand, resting so lightly on her back, drifted down so that he could feel the curve of her body under the layers of material. She did the unexpected. She moved closer to him. It was the sweetest and most wonderful feeling of his life.

"Come on, you two, let's get closer and give it a good look." Red was shielding them from Shirley.

Daniel looked past Red and saw that Rachelle was not looking at the silver statue, but was looking directly at him. It was the same kind of look that he'd received from her the very first time they'd seen each other, that morning in Shirley's brothel. She was peering into his soul with disgust, pity, and with a touch of hatred. It was disturbing.

Shirley took Daniel's hand as the band struck up a jaunty tune and guests began flowing onto the dance floor. "How about you and me go for a spin around the dance floor, young man?"

"I'm not a very good dancer."

"You're just shy. I can teach you." Shirley smiled at Kate as she led him out onto the dance floor. Kate was laughing at her mother teaching Daniel to dance when Leafy walked up to her and offered her his hand.

"Would you like to dance, Kate?"

Daniel was watching, as was Shirley. They watched Kate lay her cane against a chair and take Leafy's arm and step onto the floor. Leafy looked as awkward as Daniel felt in his attempts to be graceful, but Shirley brought his attention back to her and with her guidance they began moving about the dance floor with the other dancers. They were passing the Wheelers' table, when Jerome excused himself from his admirers and pulled them aside.

"Well, what do you think of her, Shirley?"

"She's the most hideous thing I've ever seen, Jerome."

"I'm talking about the Silver Queen, you know. Not my wife." He let out a huge rumbling laugh which caught the attention of both his wife and his daughter. "She cost me over fifty thousand dollars. Not my wife, the Silver Queen." He laughed again. "There's over five tons of silver and gold in her, plus all those rubies, sapphires, emeralds and diamonds that she's wearing in her crown. She's worth a small fortune." He elbowed Daniel in the ribs. "Guess who I'm talking about now?" He bellowed laughter again. "Are you two having a merry Christmas?" he said conspiratorially. "Enjoying yourselves at my expense I hope?"

"We certainly are, Jerome. Thank you for having the balls to invite me and my family to your wonderful party." Shirley placed her hand on his arm fondly and he covered her hand with his.

"You're both very welcome." Wheeler said and turned to face his unsmiling wife. "Aren't they, my dearest?" Jerome took his wife's hand and hoisted her out of her chair. She smiled politely to Shirley. "How's about, you and me, take a spin around the dance floor, my dove?" Mrs. Wheeler took his hand and they swung gracefully into a dance which took them out into the center of the floor.

"He's a very good dancer." Daniel remarked watching the Wheelers twirl around the crowded floor.

"So is she, for someone her size," Shirley whispered, making them both laugh.

Shirley was also an excellent dancer and guided Daniel through several variations of dance compatible with the band's tempo. He was quite enjoying himself as was Shirley, when he felt a tap on his shoulder.

"I want to dance, too," Rachelle declared. A surprised Shirley smiled at her daughter and released Daniel with a raised eyebrow to

Rachelle. "Leafy is going to marry Kate. You know that, don't you?" Rachelle said as soon as her mother left.

Daniel looked at Leafy dancing with Kate and felt a pang of jealousy. "I wonder if Kate feels the same."

"She will, if she knows what's good for her," Rachelle replied venomously.

Observing her daughters, Shirley was impressed at how confidently Rachelle moved in time with the music. She wondered how she'd become so able, she also noticed how close they were dancing. Not so with Kate and Leafy, she noted.

Red took her hand. "Do you want'a go twirl around with an old cowboy?"

Shirley smiled at him. "You ain't old and you ain't a cowboy, so why not?" She allowed Red to guide her onto the floor but as Red took her in his arms she saw Kate walk away from Leafy, take her cane and hurry towards the ladies' powder room as Leafy marched off the dance floor in the opposite direction. Daniel also wanted to know what had transpired, but Rachelle had a grip on his arm and would not let him go. He saw Abigail wading through the crowd, following Kate.

"Dance with me!" Rachelle demanded.

⚜

Kate stood facing the mirror feeling ugly and betrayed. She wasn't ever going to be Leafy's girl. She hadn't even thought of him in that way since they were in school. Tears welled in her eyes.

The door to the powder room opened. Abigail entered and stood with Kate, looking at their reflections in the mirror. She placed her arm around Kate's shoulders as Kate brushed away her tears. The two other women using the facilities left, ignoring them, engaged in some private joke. Abigail took Kate by the shoulders and tenderly turned her to face her. She took out her kerchief from her sleeve and dabbed away Kate's tears. "You really like him, don't you?"

"Who? Leafy?" Kate cried. "He just told me that I had to marry him. That he was the only one who would marry a cripple like me." Kate looked imploringly at Abigail.

"That's not true, Kate." Abigail said, softly. "No, I meant that Daniel boy."

"I don't know." Kate replied.

A toilet flushed in one of the stalls behind them. Realizing that they were not alone Kate and Abigail hurried out of the bathroom.

The door to the toilet cubicle opened and Honey Bolon walked out smiling. She washed her hands, dried them and admired her reflection in the mirror. Reaching into her bodice she lifted her breasts higher, arranging them so as to better show off her charms.

"This truly is going to be an interesting Christmas, isn't it?" she said to her reflection, laughing.

Shirley wore a look of concern when Kate returned to the table. "Are you alright?" Kate nodded smiling bravely. "What was that all about, Kate?" Shirley placed a comforting hand on her knee. "Did Leafy say something to upset you?" Kate remained silent and unsmiling, her attention on Daniel and Rachelle. Red and Shirley exchanged knowing glances.

Rachelle had a tight grip on Daniel when Leafy and his sister approached them. Honey looked beautiful and her dress stressed the curves of her figure as she had planned. She swayed with ease and elegance as she walked towards them, smiling, her eyes on Daniel's the whole time. Leafy tapped Rachelle on the shoulder and pried her hands away from Daniel and they moved away in time to the music.

Daniel stood immobile. Honey moved closer, took his hand and wrapped his arm around her. She tightened her grip and began to sway him into the dance. Daniel followed, gliding with the rest of the crowd. None of this escaped Kate's attention, or Shirley's.

"Lost your new girlfriend, have you?" Honey teased.

"Who do you mean, Rachelle?"

"Kate."

"She's not my girlfriend."

"And she'd better not be, if you know what's good for you." She slipped her hand down and squeezed his groin while looking up at him. Daniel's look made her laugh.

Leafy was watching his sister intently, annoying Rachelle. She stepped on his foot to bring his attention back on her.

"I told him you were planning on marrying Kate," she said, "if that's what's worrying you."

"Thanks." Leafy said, barely paying attention to Rachelle. "She's crippled anyway. I'm the only one who would marry her." Leafy was intently watching his sister dancing with Daniel. "I have to go," Leafy said, and walked away leaving Rachelle standing alone amongst the swirling dancers. Honey saw this and excused herself.

"So, you did meet Honey Bolon, I noticed?" Shirley asked when he sat back down next to her.

"She's Leafy's sister," he said stiffly and became aware of the silence at the table.

Kate leaned over towards him and touched his hand. "Would you like to dance with me?" Daniel took her hand as she rested her cane against a chair. Together, they walked onto the dance floor.

Daniel was delighted to have his arm on Kate's narrow waist. She allowed him to take most of her weight. There was something familiar with the way she felt to him. She let her chin rest on his shoulder as they swayed to the rhythm of the waltz. She was an accomplished dancer, a credit to her schooling he supposed. Anyone observing would have been hard-pressed to notice her handicap while she was dancing.

Their cheeks brushed. He felt the light touch of her hair and smelled the fragrance of some flower. To all who took notice, they were a young couple familiar and enormously comfortable with each other. Shirley noticed it, as did Red. They smiled to each other as they let the music, the wine, and the happiness of the evening take doubts and fears away. Red guided Shirley over to where her daughter was dancing, nudging the youngsters as they glided past. Shirley noticed the bliss on her daughter's face.

Daniel swallowed hard and held her even closer.

"How does your mother know Mrs. Wheeler? he whispered.

"She's one of my mother's gambling friends, along with some of the other important women in town. They play cards on Tuesdays and my mother keeps them apprised of what their husbands are doing in town." Daniel looked at Kate in a whole different light.

The band was getting drunker and some of the guests had taken up instruments and were attempting to entertain the crowd with varying levels of success and musical ability.

"I think it's time we left," Shirley announced, as if reading Daniel's thoughts. The evening had gone by faster than Daniel would have liked. It was near midnight and the crowd was thinning.

"Daniel, what say you and I go and retrieve the ladies' coats?" Red said, inclining his head towards the door. They wandered past the bar which was full to the point of overflowing. Daniel stopped in his tracks.

"Something wrong?" In the midst of the drunken crowd was Harry, drunk and holding court. "Hey, it's Christmas. He's just letting off some steam. Come on lad, we don't want to keep the ladies waiting."

They retrieved the coats and said their goodnights to the Wheelers without incident. The storm had stopped and in front of them, up on the mountain, was one of the most beautiful scenes that Daniel could ever remember seeing.

Climbing the mountainside was a procession of lights, the lanterns of the miners climbing the mountain, returning to their respective mines for their shifts. The twinkling specks of light shone and blinked in the clear frozen air like fireflies. The full moon outlined the mountain, its light silhouetting the maiden of the mountain. The Silver Queen, as she was known, was clearly defined this night, lying on her side looking heavenwards, reclining on the richest silver veins in the known world. No wonder she seemed to be smiling.

The carriage came and their driver helped Shirley aboard. Kate leaned forward and kissed Daniel on the cheek, holding his gaze for a moment longer. Smiling blissfully he turned to help Rachelle into the carriage and was even more surprised when she launched herself up at him and landed a kiss squarely on his lips. Kate failed to notice and no one else seemed to have noticed but Red, who was smiling broadly and shaking his head.

"Goodnight gentlemen, and Merry Christmas," Shirley said. Red walked around to the far side of the carriage as she was tucking a blanket around her legs and handed Shirley a small box wrapped with a silver ribbon. Shirley leaned over and kissed him on his hairy cheek and smiled at him. "You're too sweet, you old fox."

"Merry Christmas," he said, as the driver flicked the reins and they drove off into the night. Daniel didn't move for a time as Red stood next to him. He placed one of his huge hands on Daniel's shoulder and guided him towards the bar where a piano was being abused loudly.

"What say you and I have ourselves a real drink to celebrate your success, young man?"

"What success?" Daniel thought everyone could read his thoughts.

"I think you've got what you wanted."

"What do you mean?"

"If I'm not mistaken, Kate seems to have set her eyes on you. Congratulations are in order, I think. Come on, let's save Harry from himself and get drunk on some of Jerome's free whiskey, shall we?"

They turned in time to see Harry stumble from the door of the bar, falling into the street. Red moved quickly and caught him by the arm. Harry yelled and dropped to his knees in pain.

"What's the matter, Harry?" Red asked laughing. "Is that old war wound acting up again?" From his knees, Harry looked up, and between the shooting pains stabbing his shoulder, the fatigue from the night before, and the half gallon of whiskey he'd consumed in the last few hours, he felt no inclination to rise. Red had other plans, and lifted him to his feet. Daniel was impressed at how Harry gathered himself up and allowed himself to be led back into the maelstrom of the Hotel Jerome Bar on its opening night.

Red pushed Harry through door ahead of him and announced to a round of applause, "Hey, everybody, Harry's back."

Chapter 32

The knock at the door startled them awake. They had both been asleep, wrestling with their own dreams and fears when the pounding began.

Harry tried to raise himself, but he fell back onto his bed, wincing in obvious pain. Daniel buckled his pants and went to the door, steeling himself for whatever might be on the other side.

"Who is it?" Daniel asked.

"It's me, Willy. Hey, open the door."

Daniel looked back at Harry and saw the same relief on his face he was feeling. He pulled the door open slightly and Willy pushed into the cabin. "You guys weren't up this morning, so I brought you the paper," he said.

Daniel had a quick look outside. It was the middle of the day, and not even the noon whistle had woken them. Willy was already inside, so there was no way of keeping him from following his natural curiosity. Daniel noticed that Harry casually slid his foot along the floor to push whatever might be there under the bed. Willy was walking around the room, excitedly reading them the headlines. "Butch Cassidy robbed the bank in Leadville," he crowed.

"What the hell are you talking about?" Harry was in pain and impatient. He snatched the paper out of Willy's hands.

"Joe has a message for you, Daniel, from Red. It's urgent." Willy opened the door and the light streamed into the cabin. "See you fellers later." The door closed behind him.

The information reported in the newspaper was mostly accurate as far as they remembered, including the fact that the Sheriff had reason to believe that he'd wounded one of the robbers as they escaped. The story went on to say that over seventy-thousand dollars was stolen. They had only fifty-one thousand. They looked at each other. Harry shrugged, but said nothing.

"Let me see how your shoulder looks today," Daniel said.

Harry groaned as his shirt was pulled off. The bandages were drenched with congealed blood that came away from the wound with warm water. The wound itself was nasty, but to Daniel's eye, it looked infection-free. He tore up what was left of Harry's old sheet and re-bound the wound. He left Harry with a full cup of whiskey then head-ed out to No Problem's stable. Harry lay back down to enjoy the story of the robbery. Butch Cassidy would be really pissed off when he found out that he'd been blamed for a robbery he didn't commit.

⊰⊱

Joe was with the horses out in the corral. He'd let Marigold out too, and she was enjoying the sunshine, with her head in a bucket of grain.

"Hi there, Joe. Willy told me that you wanted to see me," Daniel said as he approached.

"Did you hear about the robbery over there in Leadville on Christmas?" Joe asked with a wicked grin.

"I saw the headlines in the paper, but I didn't read any of it yet. Do you think it was Butch Cassidy?" Daniel felt uncomfortable and couldn't look at Joe.

"It might've been." Joe was inspecting the hoof of one of the horses. He let the foot drop and pulled himself upright, painfully. "Seems like whoever it was, was pretty damned lucky. It says in the paper that the Sheriff shot one of them." Joe looked at Daniel. "How's Harry feeling today?"

Daniel shuffled his feet. He knew that it would be the subject most talked about for some time. "He's feeling poorly, not surprising, con-sidering all of the free whiskey he poured into himself last night."

"Yeah, I heard he wasn't up to sellin' his spuds today. Them miners are goin' to be fit to be tied if he don't get his ass up there tonight. They count on you two fellers having something for them to eat up there. Thank him for my Christmas presents when you see him, will ya'."

Daniel nodded. He'd forgotten that they still had to get their pota-toes out to the miners or risk not only the loss of business, but raising suspicion if they failed to show up. It was dawning on him that even though they'd gotten away with the robbery, they were not out of danger by a long shot.

"Red wants to see you as soon as you can get out to his place," Joe was saying, though Daniel barely heard him.

"What was that?"

"I said that Red wants all you youngsters to head out to meet up with him, so's you all can get the Pass open." He laughed good naturedly. "Looks like you've got a few days of hard work ahead of you." Daniel stroked Marigold's head absently. "I had the vet come over yesterday." Daniel looked up, surprised. "Yeah, in the morning I found some of the horses down and thought I'd better have him come take a look. He was none too pleased to be coming out on Christmas, but he came over and checked on 'em." He looked at Marigold. "Your horse and Harry's and some of the others were down with something, but by the time the vet got here, they were back up on their feet and looking better."

Daniel remembered the concoction that Harry had fed them before they left the barn. "What was wrong with them?"

"I don't rightly know. They were all lying down and were a bit frothy around their mouths. They got up by themselves around noon and by the time the vet got here, they were fine. It scared me, though. There's nothing worse than having some sick animals while I'm supposed to be taking care of them. They're all OK now, but it was the damnedest thing. They were all sweaty and frothing at the mouth, then the next minute, they were up and drinking like camels. Just the damnedest thing I ever saw in horses."

"Well, thanks for your concern, Joe. Think she's well enough to go up the Pass?"

"I don't see why not." Joe looked at him intently. Daniel continued to saddle Marigold. Joe came over to him, holding an envelope in his hand.

"Give this to Red, will ya'? It must be pretty important. The telegraph operator brought it over himself."

Daniel stuffed the telegram into his pocket and mounted up, wondering if Joe already knew, as he did, the probable contents of the telegram he was carrying.

Marigold found the going tough, plowing through the knee-deep snow. Several other horses had gone ahead of them, but they'd only carved a narrow path that filled itself in again as soon as they had passed. When he reached Red's barn he found it deserted, so he followed the wagon tracks up the road.

He found Red and the other men several miles up the road, shoveling a path just wide enough for the wagon. It was hard work for the men at this high altitude, where the lungs strained to find the oxygen in the thin air. The men worked silently, conserving their energy. Red saw him coming.

"How's young Daniel feeling today?" Red greeted him merrily, leaning on his shovel, breathing deeply.

"Fair."

Red was resting his hand on the handle of his shovel and the other men followed his lead and took a break too.

"I don't know about Harry though."

That brought a smile to Red's face. Daniel recognized most of the men. Dutch and Pete waved to him.

Daniel dismounted. "Here, Red. Joe gave this to me. It's for you." He handed over the telegram. Though he'd been tempted to read it, he really didn't have to; it was not going to be good news. He watched as Red tore open the envelope and read the message.

Red's jaw clenched and unclenched a dozen times before he moved. Without saying a word, he picked up his shovel and attacked the drifts of snow with temper and vigor. The others took the cue from their leader and attacked the deep drifts with renewed energy.

Red remained silent and worked nonstop until he was the last man shoveling. They'd gone uphill another half a mile before he sat down in the snow and let his head fall into his hands. The men seemed to sense his anguish and rose to the occasion by holding their concern and curiosity in check. They leaned against the wagon or sat in the snow, not wanting to interrupt the thoughts of the man who was so much their leader and their friend.

Eventually Red lifted his head from his arms, stood up, and threw his shovel into the wagon; it was the signal that they should all do the same. He absently set the brake more securely on the wagon, even though it had been done not too long before, and set about detaching the team. Pete helped, while the others watched silently. When the team had been turned and were hitched facing downhill once more, he called them all over and broke out a bottle of whiskey. He took a deep drink and then passed the bottle to Pete.

"Fellers, I've got some bad news for you. The barn over in Twin Lakes burned down yesterday."

Everyone, including Daniel, gasped in shock.

"I bet that stupid ass Newly did it," said one of the men.

"He was always getting drunk," voiced another.

"That might be the case, but it seems that if he did, he paid a pretty high price." Red held up the telegram. "He died in the fire."

A ripple of gasps rolled through the men and they reflexively bowed their heads in tribute to a man's loss of life. Newly was far from the most liked cowboy in the bunch. He had a most disagreeable nature and a terrible temper when drunk. He would never be one of them, but he served a purpose, and so long as Red kept him busy, he kept up his part of the bargain. It was fortunate for him that Red permitted him to live in the bunkhouse at Twin Lakes, because trouble usually found him whenever he went into Leadville.

The bottle made it around in silence and when it passed back to Red, he corked it with a heavy hit, using the palm of his hand as effectively as a hammer. Following his lead they mounted up or rode in the wagon and wordlessly wound their way back down the valley. At the barn, the men from town continued on their way, while Daniel stayed with Red and Pete to put the team away and to keep Red company.

For his part, Red was dealing with the ramifications that would affect the business for the rest of the winter, at least. As if he didn't have enough on his mind. The railroad was almost through Glenwood

Canyon, linking Denver to the west coast. The Midland Railroad Company, coming in from the north through Haggerman's Tunnel would make the demise of his business a certainty. They sat around the iron potbellied stove, drinking coffee and whiskey silently and sullenly, each man engaged in his own thoughts.

Red stood and went into his room at the back of the barn, returning with another bottle of whiskey. Pete looked across at Daniel and raised his eyebrows in concern.

"Red, you know we don't need any more of that, don't you?" Pete said.

"You don't have to drink any of it, do you?" Red responded harshly.

"You don't have to snap at us, Red. We're just concerned. You know how you get when you drink too much."

"I know, Pete. I don't mean to growl. I know you're trying to help and I appreciate it." Red opened the bottle and looked at it. He poured whiskey into the glasses and raised his glass in a toast. "Here's to Newly." They clinked glasses and drank.

Daniel again remembered the sounds of the battle at the barn and the shots that he and Harry had heard.

"Pete, do you think we can get the road open in a week?" Red asked, bringing Daniel's attention back to the group.

"This is a pretty good snowfall, Red. But we've seen worse, I suppose. I cain't really remember since when, but if we don't get another big storm, we could have this side open in five days. At least up to the top of the Pass, but Lord knows how much snow fell up there. There could be as much as six feet on top."

Daniel found himself nodding in agreement, partly from the effects of the whiskey, but also because he had firsthand knowledge.

"I guess you fellers can imagine how anxious I am to get over there and see what happened. I hate being stuck here in this Godforsaken town sometimes."

"Red, you need to relax. We'll get there when we get there," said Pete. "You're right. We'll just have to do what we always do." Red finished off his whiskey in one gulp and slumped into his chair even deeper. "I just don't like not knowing what went on over there, especially with them two outlaws on the loose."

At the mention of the outlaws, Daniel's skin crawled up his spine and he shivered. Pete stood to go. Daniel rose too, glad that he was heading home.

"Look, we'll make another go of it tomorrow and we'll get the road open just as soon as we can. How's that sound to you?" Pete said, holding out his hand.

Red stood and gripped Pete's hand in real affection and clapped him on the back as he turned to leave. He walked them to the door of the barn and shook Daniel's hand as they went out into the dark of the evening.

"Thanks, fellers, I really do appreciate you coming and the help you're both giving me. I might not thank you as often as I should, but I don't want you to think that I don't appreciate it." He waved to them as they walked out to their horses and headed home.

❧

Harry almost had a heart attack when Daniel opened the door.

"God Almighty, don't you ever knock first?" Harry was holding the end of the chain with one hand and his chest with the other. "We've got to get the money hidden as soon as possible."

Daniel took off his coat and hat and with a few pulls, yanked the chain. The oven tilted backwards and slowly raised its front edge several inches from the floor.

"Shit," said Harry, frustration curdling his voice.

"What's the matter now?"

With the front of the steel base plate a foot off the floor, Daniel secured the chain and went around the front see what Harry was so unhappy about. The space under the oven was nowhere deep enough or long enough to hide all of the money. Daniel sat down on the floor next to Harry.

"Shit," he said softly. "What're we going to do now? Can't we just bury it in the ground somewhere?" Daniel asked, fatigue clouding his mind.

"No, we can't just bury it in the ground. I told you before. The ground is frozen solid and they call these the Rocky Mountains for a reason, too." Harry said, as if talking to a child. "And before you ask another stupid question, we can't just bury it in the snow, either." He looked at Daniel.

"What about putting it in one of the old mines up there on the mountain?" Daniel hoped aloud.

"Not a chance. Those miners are going back into them all the time, hoping against reason there's something there that they've missed. The last thing I want is to make some stupid miner a rich man on my money." Harry caught Daniel looking at him. "Our money," Harry corrected quickly.

"Did you know that the barn burned down over there in Twin Lakes?"

"Yeah, No Problem told me. I guess Frank got rid of that Newly fellow after all."

"Do you think Frank shot him?" Daniel whispered, though nobody could have heard him besides Harry.

"Knowing Frank, getting shot would've been a blessing to that poor bastard. He was probably still alive when Frank set the barn on fire." Daniel shuddered at the ghastly thought. "Look, someone has got to dig out a hole under there." Daniel shot him a look. "Well, you don't expect me to do it, do you?" Harry said, nursing his arm. "Just crawl under there and see if you can do it? I'll help if I can."

"What, you'll hold the candle while I chop the wood?" Daniel was tired and sarcasm came easy. Nevertheless, he crawled under the oven, sliding as far as he could without hitting his head on the hot steel above him. There was barely enough room to move his head. Along with the feeling of confinement, the possibility of being crushed by the heavy steel oven was as much as Daniel could tolerate without panicking.

Harry pushed a shovel into the hole. With a sigh, he took the shovel and started scraping at the dirt. At first he found little resistance and he dug several inches of soft soil out of the hole with little effort. He was just starting to think that the project had some merit to it, when he heard the first clang as the blade of the shovel hit rock. His back was already hurting from the position he was in and his knuckles were

scraped from the rough iron and the dirt that he had to pull out handful by handful.

He stopped digging to eat some dinner and took as much time as he
could before Harry impatiently urged him back into the hole. Daniel
was working in his undershirt, sweating from the hot oven above him
and he was now as filthy as one of the miners returning from a shift.
His respect for their lot in life had grown, now that he was actually
one of them in practice as well as spirit. Unsurprisingly, Harry was of
little help, but when they finally lowered the iron monster, Daniel was
pleased to see that had pulled out an impressive amount of soil and
rock. Not nearly enough to bury all of the money and keep it safe, but
if he kept at it, there might be a chance they could save their treasure
from discovery or destruction.

With the oven back in place, Harry removed the chains, returning
them to their original positions. The only giveaway to their alternate
purpose was the single eyebolt anchored in the heavy main beam of the
cabin. Daniel looked at it and Harry followed his eyes.

"We'll pull that bolt out of the rafter after we get all of the money
into the hole. Then no one will be able to lift the damned thing, unless
they pull the house down."

"Harry?" Daniel asked as Harry was struggling into his coat and
preparing to leave. Daniel had helped load up the cooked potatoes and
was resting on his bunk, bone weary.

"Yeah?" Harry responded with hesitation.

"What happened to the money in the box that was under the oven?"

Harry shuffled his feet as he wrestled himself into his coat, his arm
making it more difficult. "It got spent."

"Some of that was mine you know."

"Yeah, I know." Harry was anxious to leave. It was time, he
thought, to show this youngster who was boss here. It was, after all,
still his cabin.

Daniel had not really been surprised to find that the small mon-
eybox was not there, but he did feel that he deserved an explanation
about the whereabouts of his money. Harry was so self-absorbed, almost

nothing that didn't directly concern him was of much importance in these past few weeks.

"Is there a problem? I would imagine that the money we're sitting on would more than cover my borrowing some of yours." Daniel was too tired to argue and when he thought about it, Harry was right.

"I guess not. But, are you still going to go gambling every night? I thought we had an agreement." Harry's hand froze on the door handle.

"What do you mean?"

"It's your gambling that got us into this problem Harry, and I think there's too much for us to lose if you go on out and start gambling again. I mean, if you start losing big again and you have to pay off your debts with the money we've stolen, it might make people talk. You're poor, Harry. If you go out spending money like you've got a lot of it, then some people might want to know where it all came from all of a sudden." Daniel let his words hang.

"I'll give it some thought." Harry pulled the door open and went out into the night.

⋈

Out in the cold, Harry tried his best to keep his spirits up while he sold his potatoes. The pain from his shoulder kept nagging at him and he was grateful that few of the miners were interested in having conversation. Soon enough, the flow of miners dwindled and Harry packed up his gear before he'd sold everything, leaving a few stragglers disgruntled and chastened by their tardiness.

He was thirsty and needed a drink. He felt in his coat pocket for the money he'd collected for the evening's labor and found, to his surprise and delight, the thick sheaf of notes that he'd shoved into his coat pocket when Daniel wasn't looking. He heard the demons of his addiction calling out his name.

The door to The Paragon beckoned with its warm, inviting glow. Who could begrudge him the little pleasures of life, especially since he'd just ridden over one-hundred miles at night, robbed a bank, and gotten himself shot in the process? Surely he could indulge himself in some fine whiskey and the warmth of female companionship. The argument was all but won until he reached out to open the ornate glass door to the bar. It was too heavy for him to open and it reminded him that he was still wounded. Should one of the girls comment on the fresh bullet wound, it could be disastrous should they ever come under suspicion. Harry had no delusions about the loyalties of the prostitutes, but danger lurked between the sheets where paradise lay. He was standing looking at the door when it opened and Red came out.

"Howdy, Harry. You coming inside?" Red held the door open.

"Nah, I was thinking about it, but I guess I'll just go home instead." As soon as he said it, he felt better. He'd never been the type to pay much attention to the sane voices in his head, but now there was a greater need than he'd ever known to keep his wits about him. The sounds of women laughing from the floor above made them both look up, though the windows were closed.

"Walk with me to Joe's, then; that'll stop you from being tempted anymore this evening." They tucked their chins into their collars and headed west past the Ute City Bank, not talking until they were nearly to the stable.

"How's Daniel doin'?"

"What do you mean?"

"Things are going pretty fast for the youngster and I was wondering how you two were getting along." Red's pace had slowed and they stopped in the middle of the street under the bright moonlight. "Unless I'm mistaken, he's being courted by Jerome Wheeler in more ways than I could even guess." They walked along some more and Red stopped again, facing Harry. "You and I both know that we can't hold the boy back." Red paused and placed his hand on Harry's shoulder making Harry wince. "All we have to offer him are two broken-down men with worn-out dreams."

Why, Harry thought as he clenched his teeth and tolerated the surge of pain, did they always grab that shoulder?

"He's young, Red." It seemed that Harry's observation was correct, because Red went quiet.

"I'm a bit afraid for him," Red intoned.

"Why's that?" Harry was moving his shoulder gingerly, trying to settle the weight of his heavy coat more comfortably about him.

"Look, Harry, it's not that I don't like Wheeler. He's a reasonable man on one level. But I think that he's got too big a set of dreams and if he's not careful, he's going to bring down not only himself, but everyone around him. I don't know why I feel this, but I do, and I don't want that boy to get sucked in and sacrificed."

"I still don't get what you mean. Is Wheeler doing something illegal? I mean, something that we don't already know about?"

"Nope. I just have a feeling; it's nothing I can prove." They walked along, then Red stopped again. "You know, I've been looking for men to help us open the Pass." Harry had heard that from some of the miners just that evening. "I've never seen so much snow fall up there in one storm. I'm worried that if we can't get the Pass open and the wagons going again, this town of ours is going to run out of food and other things, too."

Harry stopped walking. "You don't think they'll run out of whiskey, do you?"

"No doubt, that too." Harry grabbed Red's sleeve.

"Oh my God! Red, please. You've got to get that Pass open."

Red laughed. "I can ski up to Independence and maybe hire some of them fellers up there to help clear the road. I'll have someone go talk to those Swedes and see if they'll help. Then we've got to get some more people from town here to help dig us out. If we get another storm right on top of this one, we'll be screwed for sure. This town can't last more than a week or two before these folks will be eating each other."

Harry knew this to be the truth.

"I guess we'll just have to get going tomorrow and try to get over the Pass. I can get some help from the other side in Leadville, if I can just get over there." Red was mainly talking to himself. "I'm sure there's been some avalanches and that'll slow us down some. Do you think you can give us a hand?"

Red laughed loudly, "I'm not serious. You'd be no use up there and I know it, Harry." Red slapped Harry on his bad shoulder again. Harry nearly passed out.

"You heard about Newly and the barn burning down, didn't you?" Red asked.

"Yeah. I heard from Joe. Sorry about Newly."

"I always hate to lose a man, you know that, but that trouble maker was no real loss. He's going to have to be replaced though and that might be tough. I do wonder how the fool happened to burn himself to death. We've never had an accident like that." Red walked on. "I'm going to have Daniel come over the Pass with us tomorrow. I just wanted you to know."

Harry shrugged, thinking that he could use the time alone without Daniel pestering him with guilt and imagined fears. The last thing in the world he needed was to have this kid threatening his lifestyle with such irrelevant things as his losing at poker. Harry would be glad to see him gone.

"Do you think he knows how to ski yet?" Red asked.

"I heard him say that the Swedes taught him."

"Tell him to pack his gear and meet me early. Tell him he'll likely be gone a week."

"You know what, Red? I'm going to miss him. I'm getting to like the little bastard." Harry laughed.

"You're a decent man sometimes Harry, no matter what others say about you."

He walked into the corral to fetch his horse, leaving Harry to walk the several hundred yards home by himself.

What "others" was Red talking about? He roused Daniel from his sleep roughly. "Come on, kid, we've got to dig that hole."

Daniel was so deep asleep he thought he heard Harry's voice in his dream. "What hole?" Daniel asked sleepily.

"The one we have to put the money in." Daniel realized immediately that he was not dreaming.

Harry set the chains and together they heaved until the oven was elevated as high it could go safely. Daniel excavated while Harry went out and sold his potatoes at midnight. The hole grew slowly and Harry piled the dirt into empty potato bags. Daniel was alternately shoveling and heaving, since the hole seemed to contain more rocks than dirt the deeper he went. He must have dug three feet into the earth before Harry let him rest, handing him a cup of warm coffee with whiskey and a hunk of bread dipped in honey. The honey dripped down his arm but it tasted wonderful and he drank and ate hungrily.

"How deep do you think we should go, Harry?"

"Deeper," Harry replied, sitting comfortably at the table, "and I'd get a move on. It'll be daylight before you know it and you have to ski over to Leadville today."

"What?" Daniel came up, hitting his head on the steel plate. "When was that decided?"

"Last night when we were walking home, I told Red you were a good skier," Harry laughed. "He said you should pack clothes for a week," he laughed again, "But you've got more hole to dig before that happens, so you'd better get on with it."

Daniel resigned himself to the task and heaved out more dirt, struggling mightily with the dense rocks that seemed to be the main components of the Rocky Mountains. Dawn was coming in the window under the curtains when he finally pulled himself out of the hole. Harry opened his eyes and deigned to walk the few paces over to the hole.

"Yeah, I'd say that's about right. Let's get the bags in there and fill the bastard back up."

They counted them as they pushed them into the hole as deeply as they could, seven bags total.

"It's not deep enough." Harry was right. The bags were bulky and took up too much room. It looked as though the steel base would sit too high and leave a space underneath that would be noticed.

"We have to take the money out of the bags. It should fit if we do that."

They pulled the money out of the bags and stacked it neatly into the hole. Daniel was pleased to see it fit with room to spare. They covered the money with the canvas and shoveled dirt on top.

Daniel failed to notice Harry remove several bundles of cash and slip them under his mattress.

Satisfied, they lowered the oven back into place. There'd be no potatoes for the shift today, but Harry knew that no matter how much grumbling he heard from the mob later in the day, he would be able to say to himself that he was now above selling potatoes to ungrateful miners.

Daniel hauled the two sacks of dirt into the small storage room, placing them behind other potato sacks, where no one would see them. The rocks he threw out into the snow. He was sweeping up the dirt around the oven plate when there was a knock on the door. Daniel opened it a fraction to find Red standing there.

"Oh good, you're up. Are you ready to go? I want you to come with us back over the Pass today." He saw Harry lying on his bed and said, "Harry, why don't you ever clean this place like Daniel does? I swear the place's never looked better."

"Yeah, I'm taking housecleaning lessons from the boy. I think I'll have the gist of it soon, but I need to watch some more."

"Listen, son, you look like you could use a scrub, so why don't you get yourself cleaned up. I'll be back for you in an hour, after I round up some more men." Without waiting for Daniel's reply, he opened the door to leave. "Thanks, son, I really need your help. Pack for a couple of days; we don't know how long we'll be gone. Have you got skis?"

Daniel was still reeling from the shock of having to go back over the Pass and could only shake his head stupidly.

"Never mind. I'll get Joe to rustle you up some. Harry, why don't you get some rest? You look like you could use it." Red said, smiling as he closed the door. Daniel was ready to collapse.

Harry jumped up from his bunk and quickly covered the few paces to where the chains from the overhead beam hung limply to the floor. They'd forgotten to replace them in their original position. Fortunately, Red had failed to notice. That was the second time they had not been careful. Leafy had noticed it.

Harry stood on the chair and tried to remove the eyebolt that carried the chain. The bolt was stuck. He turned to Daniel with such a piteous look that Daniel felt obligated to help, even though he could barely lift his arms. Harry steadied the chair as Daniel struggled with the iron bolt. With some difficulty and a short length of iron bar, he was able to lever the bolt to turn by placing the bar through the eye, letting his weight pull it downwards. With some wiggling, the pin came away from the beam, nearly hitting Harry on the head when it fell. Daniel deftly returned the bolt into its original hole.

"I don't think anyone's going to bother that money till we go about it ourselves, eh?" Harry had collapsed again on his bed and was looking at Daniel, satisfaction on his face. Daniel staggered over to his bunk to lie down.

"You'd better get washed up and packed. You've a long walk in front of you today." Daniel wished one of them would die. It didn't matter to him who. Either way, he would be relieved of a troublesome burden and he could sleep. He slowly got up, put some water on the stovetop to heat, and collapsed on his bed.

Two winks later, there was a loud knocking on the door and his new hell began.

Chapter 33

"Come on, lad. Time to go." It was Red again. Having only just left, he was somehow back at their door. Harry was nowhere to be seen. "Try to get a move on. We've a long way to go today. I'll see you out at the ranch."

Daniel gasped at his reflection in the mirror. His hair was filthy and matted and his face streaked with grime. He washed hurriedly and put on clean clothes, making sure that they were the warmest he possessed.

At the stable, he was saddling his horse when Joe came up to him with a small bundle. "Here, I think you might need these. I doubt I'll be using them again."

Daniel opened the bundle to find a pair of mittens made of soft fur and a furry hat with flaps that went down over the ears. "Thanks, Joe. Think I'll be needing them?"

"Let me tell you one thing about these mountains. It's better to have 'em and not need 'em than to be sorry you didn't bring 'em. No problem."

Daniel put the hat on his head and instantly felt the heat collect in the fur. His head started to sweat.

"It's marmot pelt," Joe informed him.

"Thanks, Joe," Daniel said and put the old gloves on. They were well worn, but the inside was lined with fur as well as the outside, and they were unbelievably warm.

"I got something else for ya', but don't go telling anyone, OK?"

Daniel saw that Joe had a two small glass bottles in his outstretched hands. One was blue, and the other red.

"This one, here," Joe held up the blue bottle, "this one here is for emergencies. If you run out'a steam and you have to make a run for it, put some of this under your tongue."

Daniel looked at the bottle skeptically.

"It'll give you some extra energy and you just never know in the mountains. Sometimes you can be only a few hundred yards from shelter and not know it. It might save your life, but use it only if you have to, OK?"

Daniel nodded in agreement. "OK, Joe. What's in the other one?"

Joe took the bottle and tilted it so that the red powder in it shifted like sand. The bottle itself was clear, the powder inside was a burnt red color. "This is the hottest pepper in the world. Mexicans use it for cooking, but we use it when our feet get frozen. You shake some of it into your socks if your feet start to freeze." Joe took the bottle back and held it up in front of Daniel's face for emphasis. "Now don't go putting too much in there, because it'll take the skin right off your feet and you'll be in worse shape. Just sprinkle some in there and shake it around. Then shake the rest out."

Daniel took the bottles and put them in his pack. Joe reached out and put a hand on Daniel's arm, gently but firmly holding onto him.

"Remember what I said. Only use them if you have to."

"OK, Joe. I'll remember."

"Good luck, son, and watch out for that Sheriff over there. I hear he's got it in for you." Joe watched him go, and closed the door behind him.

At Red's barn, Daniel was surprised to find many more men than he'd expected, perhaps twenty. Among them were the Swedes, loading their equipment onto a wagon.

"Hey, are you the vun coming skiing vis us over that goddamned Pass?" Nodding, Daniel shook their hands.

"Dis is good," Tomas said, smiling. They admired Daniel's gloves and hat.

"Hey, these are pretty good damned t'ings ever I seen." They were intrigued with the workmanship. "Vhere do you get some t'ings like zis, eh?"

"No Problem Joe gave them to me."

"Hey, dat's that old feller vith the stable, yes?" Tomas reluctantly gave them back.

"How you doin', Daniel?" Leafy was loaded down with shovels as he walked past, heading for the wagon. Daniel wanted to talk to Leafy more, but the Swedes had other plans.

"Hey, you come vith us now. Ve got some skis for you."

They led him towards the wagon. Daniel noticed a sled tied to the rear of the wagon filled with skis and long poles. They dug out two long skis and placed them on the ground next to him. Since he'd done this before, he knew to get the leather straps over his boots and tie them tightly around his ankles, then back through the loops next to his toes.

Bjorn handed him a pair of long poles with hooped baskets on the ends. Daniel had seen them use these poles to push themselves along, so he strapped them onto his hands and took a few tentative strides.

"You remember vat ve teach you, ya?" Bjorn asked. Daniel lied and nodded. They watched as he made it to the top of the small incline where the barn road reached the main road. He could feel their attention on him.

The hill was only a gentle incline, so Daniel pushed himself with the poles, expecting to have to push all the way back down through the deep snow. All eyes were on him as he began his glide downhill towards them. He started to fall backwards, but by using the poles for support, he regained his balance and all seemed quite under control again, for another few yards, at least. He was picking up speed and heading for the group of men and the wagon, but only when he saw the men scattering did he feel any alarm. He realized he couldn't stop and was gaining more speed. Out of desperation, he hopped his feet sideways and changed his course barely enough to miss the wagon. Bjorn yelled at him to fall down, but he was moving too fast for that, so he aimed himself approximately towards the open doors of the barn, hoping to end his ride in the pile of hay bales.

Suddenly Red appeared directly in front of him, a large pack on his back, his head down in thought.

"Look out! Look out!" Daniel yelled at the top of his lungs, then wrapped his arms around the big man and took him completely off his feet. They went down with a loud thump and a whoosh of expelled air.

The Swedes were the first to reach them and they quickly untangled the two bodies. Daniel found he wasn't so much hurt as embarrassed. His wrist was throbbing again, but that seemed to be the worst of the injuries.

Red seemed uninjured and if not angry, then definitely upset, though it had been far from intentional that they'd met with such force. The Swedes were more concerned about their precious skis than his well-being. Around him, the crowd of watchers had all but laughed themselves to tears. Red threw Daniel a dark look and held up his hand.

"Alright, you lot, let's get this circus up the road," Red said and picked up his gear. "Leafy, come over here a minute, will you?"

"Yes, Red." Leafy had been waiting for just this moment.

"Did you bring your skis?"

Leafy pointed to where they were leaning against the fence. "Sure did."

"Good, can you come over with us? I need some strong backs and you can give us a hand once we get over there."

"Sure, Red."

"I also need you to keep an eye on young Daniel here. Think you can do that for me?"

Leafy was all smiles. For once, Daniel was glad to have someone mind him.

"You'll come along in the wagon, boys. You won't be needin' your horses, so put them up in the barn." Red said.

The men mounted and headed up the road, while Red and Pete guided the wagon through the gate and followed them.

Daniel, Leafy and the Swedes dashed after the wagon and climbed over the backboard as it was turning the corner. The wagon was stacked mostly with shovels, but there were hampers and milk containers for the worker's lunches. They towed a sled behind the wagon and Daniel could see that their skis were strapped onto it.

When they reached the place where the road needed clearing, the men dismounted and took to shoveling the drifted snow while the Swedes unhitched the sled and unloaded the skis.

Pete came to wish them good luck and shook hands with each in turn, while the Swedes tied thin strips of animal skins to all of their skis to prevent them from sliding backwards when the road became steeper.

"Pete, I'm sorry that you have to stay behind, but I really need you to take care of things here and to get this group up to the top as soon as you can. I'll rustle up some men in Leadville and, with luck we'll reach the top from the other side about the same time as you. It all depends on what I find over in Twin Lakes when we get there."

"Sure enough, Red. I'll take care of it. Watch out for the youngsters and don't go starting any avalanches. Good luck, fellers."

With that, they started walking in single file up the road. The first man broke trail and the second person in their team dragged the sled, which held their supplies. In the event it became stuck, the man behind could push it over the obstruction.

They traded off pulling the sled and when it was Daniel's turn he was surprised at how heavy it was. He gamely trudged on and after a while, he didn't notice it behind him at all. The road had flattened out some, and it peacefully wound through the forest where the road gently climbed.

Red was hoping to reach the town of Independence before nightfall, then head over the Pass the following morning, if it was possible.

Passing above the timberline where the trees stopped growing and where the landscape was nude and open to the harsh winter winds, they heard someone calling Red's name. The man put down his fishing pole, came over to them, and shook their hands as old friends.

"They're like this in the winter," said Leafy quietly. "The rest of the year, they couldn't care less. They're a pretty strange bunch up here."

The man talked to Red at length and then mounted his skis and led them to a small log cabin. They found the cabin was neat and clean, almost as if they'd been expected, which in fact, they were. This type of weather was no stranger to these miners and no matter how much snow there was on the ground, they knew that Red and his men would be coming along in due course to open up the road.

They started a fire in the pot-bellied stove and soon were drinking hot coffee, gratefully warming their frozen fingers. One of the miners' wives, a smiling, weathered woman, brought them a pot of stew and a loaf of fresh hot bread which they accepted gratefully, being hungry enough to eat anything.

As they settled onto their bunks after the meal, Red returned the pot and visited with some of the miners to arrange a work crew for the following days. By the time he returned, he found them snoring peacefully. It was dark and bitterly cold outside, so he threw a few more logs on the fire and settled in a chair, thinking about the days ahead.

Red looked over at his team of men and felt pride in them. The Swedes were old friends. They were both master carpenters and if the lumber was available, they could build a house in a week. Not only build the house, but make all the furniture as well. He was glad to have them along, more importantly because their mountain skills on the frigid terrain they were about to cross tomorrow might just save all their lives.

He took a bottom bunk and collapsed onto it still clothed, waking before dawn to find the Swedes making coffee and pancakes on the stove top. It smelled wonderful.

They were on their way before the sun had caught the peaks of the mountains that loomed over the valley. It was the coldest temperature that Daniel could remember and according to Leafy, the coldest part of the winter was still ahead of them, come January. He was glad for the hat and mittens and he wished he'd had them when he and Harry had ridden over the Pass in the storm.

The going was tough on all but the Swedes, who insisted on breaking trail. They plowed through the deep snow relentlessly, charging through it as if they were machines, and Daniel gained enormous respect for the two friendly giants.

Red kept his head down and prayed with every breath that his heart would not give out. The sharp pains in his chest demanded his concentration to control but he spoke not a word of it as they ascended into the crystal clear morning.

They encountered several places where the snow had slid down, onto and over the road. Whenever they came to these places, the small party would cross separately, waiting till one was safely across before calling the next one to follow. The snow slides were many feet deep in places and Red gauged how much work it would take to clear the road. He didn't envy the men who would be doing the shoveling. They would earn every cent of their pay.

Red handed out lengths of rope and long sturdy poles from the sled and Daniel watched as the others tied the ropes around their waists. Bjorn tied one around himself, and then around Daniel.

"What are these for?" he asked when Bjorn was satisfied with the knot.

"It's just in case, OK?"

Daniel was still curious. "In case of what?"

"In case ve get caught in an avalanche."

"Then what happens?"

"Then whoever isn't dead, goes and finds ze others by following ze ropes." He said it so plainly that Daniel felt he would be unreasonable if he asked more questions.

Bjorn looped the rope attached to the sled over Daniel's shoulder and headed off towards the drop-off, where the slope went steeply down into the valley. Leafy followed Red and Tomas, with Daniel at the rear.

The snow had drifted along the ridges of the summit, but as soon as they started down, the going became much easier, though the snow was up to their waists in places. The heavier Bjorn broke a wide path and the others slid along easily, catching up after he'd gone ahead a ways.

Daniel found that the sled helped hold him back some and the forces of gravity helped, but still their progress was slower than he had expected. Daniel was gliding along with smooth strides, when he found Tomas alongside of him.

"This is how ve get around in Norway all vinter."

"I thought you said you were Swedes."

"No. Zat's vhat all the ozers call us. I zink it's easier for zem to say zat ve're Svedes. It doesn't matter to us, zough." He pulled ahead slightly. "Vatch this, Daniel."

Tomas turned his skis off the edge of the road and gracefully swooped down the hill, making long arcs in the perfectly smooth surface of the snow. Daniel watched in awe as Tomas came to a stop near to where Bjorn was pushing through on the road below them. Daniel had never seen anything like it. When Daniel reached him, he was smiling broadly.

"Vell, vhat do you zink?"

"Can you teach me to do that?" Daniel begged him, excitedly.

"Hey, sure I can. Maybe ve'll try it together a little later, eh?" Excited at the prospect, Daniel slid his skis along with new enthusiasm. He couldn't wait to get rid of the sled and skins and go sliding like Tomas.

They were crossing a wide open section of the descent and hurrying because of the danger of avalanche, when they heard the rumble of an explosion from deep inside the mountain. Above them a rush of dirt and smoke erupted from the mouth of the old mine. The miners had exploded dynamite somewhere within.

"Hurry! Zere could be avalanche!" Bjorn shouted from behind him. "Get in ze trees," he shouted. Then Daniel heard it, a sound approaching from above; a sickening whisper of rushing wind. The mountain was coming down on them.

"Hurry, Hurry!" Bjorn screamed. Aware that their lives were in danger Tomas and Red needed no urging. Leafy let go of the sled and raced for the trees with Bjorn close behind.

Tomas made the tree line first and pulled Red in. He screamed out to his brother, who was sliding as fast as he could, gaining on Leafy with every stride.

Daniel made it into the trees and was pulled to safety by Tomas's massive strength. He lay in the snow flat on his back, the sound of the avalanche becoming louder like a train coming down the mountain. He tried to get to his feet, but with a crash of falling trees and a whoosh of air, it was upon them. Briefly he caught the look of terror on Leafy's face as he and Bjorn were snatched away by the torrent of dirt, snow, rocks, and small trees. One moment they were there, the next, they were gone, as if they'd never been there at all.

Just as abruptly, he was pulled into the crushing noisy torrent as tons of snow cascaded all around him. He grabbed onto the closest tree but the rushing snow pulled his hands away and one of his gloves came off. The cascading snow hurled him up against another tree and it felt as if he was being torn apart at the waist by a force unlike anything he'd felt before.

As suddenly as it came, it stopped, leaving the air thick with ice crystals. He was covered with debris and couldn't get to his feet for the weight of the snow on his skis. He called out for help, but heard nothing except for his heart pounding in his chest. His feet were twisted under him, but slowly he felt the rope around his waist ease its tension. A hand appeared at his shoulder, pulling him up to his feet. Tomas at least had survived, and Daniel gripped his hand tightly. Red too had survived and was wading through the avalanche debris below them.

"Red, I see you!" Tomas yelled, pointing down the hill. "Look for my brozer and Leafy. You go over that way." Tomas yelled. "Come vis me, Daniel. Ve look over dere." Daniel was struggling with his skis, "Keep your skis on your feet or you will sink into ze snow." Climbing over broken tree branches and clumps of snow they hurried from the shelter of the trees onto the chaos of the avalanche, frantically searching the slope for their friends.

"I see one," Daniel yelled, and raced for the strand of rope trailing off into the snow. He was joined by Tomas and digging furiously they found a ski and then a leg and dug faster. Leafy's hand appeared and then his head came up and he gasped for air.

"Vhere's my brozer?" Tomas screamed. "Bjorn, Bjorn!" Tomas called again and again in fear and futility. "Qvick, ve don't have much time, look for ze rope."

Leaving Leafy to recover, they climbed further out onto the uneven slope which only moments before had looked pristine and beautiful. Filled with anger and frustration, calling his brother's name, Tomas slogged through the debris field, wading and stumbling over the uneven slabs of snow.

Higher up than either Tomas or Red, Daniel was the first to see the rope, fifty yards below him.

"There it is," he screamed and they raced like madmen towards the tail of rope. Tomas was the first one to it and he began digging furiously. The snow was hard and compacted and it tore at their naked fingers.

Red found Bjorn. "Here he is! I've got him!"

They pulled his head away from the snow and Tomas wailed when he saw what the avalanche had done to his brother. Bjorn was bloodied and beaten and it looked like part of the side of his head was bashed in. Through his tears, Tomas dug as if his brother's life depended on it. When they had most of his body uncovered, they pulled with all of their remaining strength until he came free. Tomas was beside himself with grief, but sanity returned to him when Red realized that Bjorn was not dead.

"Leafy," Red's voice came with the authority of a man used to the command of other men. "I want you and Daniel to go and find the sled. It's got to be down there. I need you to find it and hurry." Leafy and Daniel threw themselves out onto the slope littered with thick tilting slabs of compressed snow and ice.

"There it is." Leafy shouted, stumbling over the slabs of snow with Daniel in close pursuit. When they reached the sled, they were surprised to find it and its contents more or less intact. He wondered if Harry's sled was also buried here somewhere.

"Bring up those poles and a blanket," Red yelled from above.

Tomas was crippled from the thought of losing his brother and could neither think nor act until he'd digested the catastrophe. Red had inspected Bjorn and but for the head injury, he seemed intact, more or less.

"I think he'll live, but we need to get him to a doctor as soon as possible. I don't like the look of this." Red pointed to the visible dent in the side of the head, just above Bjorn's right ear. It was bleeding profusely and his breathing was shallow. "Let's get him down to the sled."

Daniel and Leafy carried the poles and blanket up to the others. By tying the ends of the rope together, looping them into coils, and then slipping the poles through the coils, they fashioned a stretcher in minutes. It took much longer for the four of them to carry Bjorn's unconscious body downhill, but they managed. While Red attended to Bjorn's head wound, the others went back uphill to retrieve what they could of their ski gear. Surprisingly, all of it was recovered and was still functional. Red arranged the contents of the sled into a bed of sorts and they placed Bjorn in it as gently as they could manage under the circumstances.

Tomas looked up the mountain and shook his fists at the sky. "You stupid miners, you nearly killed my brozer!"

"And us too, Tomas, don't forget that. We'll have a talk with them one day soon, eh? But let's get your brother taken care of first," said Red. Tomas shouldered the rope connected to the sled and started off downhill at a furious pace. They were all shaken and would have rather done nothing more than rest awhile, but the seriousness of Bjorn's injuries demanded that they push on without delay.

It was mid-afternoon when they reached Twin Lakes; the sun having dipped behind the mountains, the valley was darkening quickly. Red's bunkhouse was nothing but charred timber, but he was relieved to see that the barn was untouched by the fire and all of the horses seemed at ease. The burnt timbers of the bunkhouse stood in ugly, dark contrast to the freshly fallen snow. It was eerily quiet.

Red ran to the front door of the Lodge. When he tried to open the door, he found it locked. Though smoke rose from the chimney and light came from inside, no one came to the door when he knocked. For as long as he could remember, the door had always been open. He hurried around to the back of the Lodge and was surprised to find the wolves' pen empty and the door to the cage wide open.

He tried the back door. It was open, so he entered cautiously. The kitchen was dark and there was an unusual smell of decay. "Frank? Gloria?" Red called out. "Are you here?"

"Fuck off and get out," he heard from the main room.

"It's only me, Frank. Red Corcoran." Red closed the door behind him and walked into the main room.

Frank was half sitting, half lying in one of the large chairs, with a bottle in his hand and a rifle leaning up against his chair. The fireplace threw out little heat from the embers that glowed dimly in the grate.

"I thought I told you to get out." Frank was very drunk and Red detected his meanness almost as if it were radiating from the man.

"Frank, I need to put one of my men up here, then I need to go get the doctor. He's hurt bad and he needs a doctor quick."

"I told you, get the fuck out. The Lodge is closed. Closed for good. Now, get out before I have to shoot you."

"Where's Gloria?" Red looked about the room.

Frank rose clumsily, grabbed the rifle and pointed it at Red's chest.

"I told you to get the fuck out of here. The bitch's gone and she's never coming back, so there you have it. Get the fuck out of my place or I'll put a bullet in you, so help me God."

Red backed out of the room, not taking his eyes off Frank as he retreated, and a shudder ran up his spine as he passed through the kitchen.

Watching Red return, Daniel knew that something was terribly wrong without having to go inside.

"Sorry boys, I guess the Lodge is closed. Let's get one of the wagons hitched as fast as we can and get on into Leadville. I don't know about you fellers, but after we get Bjorn to the doctor, I think we could all use a drink."

With the wagon hitched, they loaded the unconscious Bjorn in the back and covered him with blankets and hay. Leafy and Tomas huddled in the back, looking over him. They started out for Leadville with Red driving, Daniel sitting beside him. Deep in thought, Red said not a word.

Chapter 34

Harry had never hated work so much. He felt as if he was locked into a hell of his own creation.

He lay on his bunk with a stack of stolen money on his chest. He was imagining that after the interest in the robbery died down, by the spring at the latest, he could dig up the money, skedaddle out of town, and no one would be the wiser. Perhaps he could return to Salt Lake City as a man of means; he could gain the respect of his wives and the fathers of the church. Maybe he could become an elder, or even a bishop. Bishop Rich sounded good to him. He'd have more women to take as his wives. Not a bad religion when compared to the competition.

A loud knock on the door startled him and he jumped up, spilling the money on the floor. Quickly, scooping up the bills he hurriedly pushed them under the blanket on his bed. He heard the knock again and headed to the door, his heart racing, hoping that it was not the Sheriff. After taking two deep breaths he opened the door. It was not the Sheriff.

"Is Daniel here?" Harry blocked the doorway.

"No, Honey. He's not here." Harry's instinct for self-preservation remained keen.

She pushed into the room, brushing Harry aside with surprising force and went directly to the back room, where the potatoes were kept.

"Where is he, Harry?"

"He's not here. I told you." Harry was wary now. This was exactly what he and the other men in town who knew her intimately were afraid of. She was nice enough when she wanted to be, actually very nice as he remembered, but the result of her affection could mean months of hiding from her wrath. Though she was smaller in size, Harry backed away from her and held his hands out in front of him defensively. "He's gone over the Pass with Red. They're going to open up the road."

"What was he doing with that whore's daughter at the Hotel?" It was the way she kept her right hand in her coat pocket that made Harry more respectful than usual.

"I have no idea who you mean, Honey." Harry was trying to think as quickly and clearly as possible, but the situation was looking less like it could be resolved by talk alone. Honey stepped closer, her eyes narrowed.

"You were there, Harry. I saw him first and I don't want that bitch, Kate sniffing around him again. You tell him that!" Honey backed away a pace but suddenly tears welled up in her eyes and ran down her cheek. Stunned, Harry reached out to her, as much for self-defense as to give comfort but she pulled away from him, turning her back on him. "Oh, Harry, I really love him," she sobbed.

Harry was shocked, but she shocked him even more by rushing to him, throwing her arms around him and sobbing into his chest.

Now Harry was just a man. Admittedly, a sometimes crazed and irresponsible man, but just a man. And, here was just a woman. Harry felt the weight of what could be a small pistol in her coat. He reached down to check. Honey was ahead of him. She reached for his hand and pulled it around behind her, then pulled his face to hers, her lips questing for his.

Her lips were as hot as a furnace, her mouth, moist and delicious. People could say what they liked about Honey, but she was a great kisser. He pushed her coat open and as he reached for her breast, she grabbed his ass with a grip of the drowning. They fumbled with each other's clothing and careened around the room until Harry had wrestled her close enough to the bed, where he pushed her willing body down and they fought each other to find the release they both required.

It was, to Harry, some of the wildest and most exciting sex he'd had in his life. Obviously in the years since they'd last fought this battle, she'd schooled herself in the sexual arts. In that morning, he learned things that at his age he'd never imagined. She was angry and needy and brought him to the edge time and time again before he allowed himself to float in the final burst of release.

Harry was reminded of his wound, as he felt Honey's hands reach under his undershirt to pull him one more time into her. In the last thrust of spurting, throbbing passion and the last trembling grip of her lips, she reached up behind him and sank her nails into his shoulders, the more to force him into her. Harry screamed in pain and pulled away from her, grabbing his shoulder. Honey looked at her hand and saw blood on it. She reached out to Harry, who pulled away.

"Harry, what's wrong with your shoulder?" She wiped off the blood on his blanket with obvious distaste.

"Nothing. It's nothing. I hurt my shoulder is all." He knew the next question and fumbled for an answer. "I-I fell down drunk and hurt it."

Honey was believing none of it. Having just allowed herself to be pummeled by this man, she felt the overwhelming need to minister to his wounds. Before he could react, she'd lifted his shirt and recoiled with her hand over her mouth. The bandages had come away from the wound and it had started bleeding again. He pulled the shirt back down and stood up, but when he bent forward to pull his pants up, he felt the blood rush from his head and he had to reach out for the bedpost for support.

"I think you should go now," he said, trying to sound gentle.

"You bastard, Harry Rich. You rape me and then tell me I should just go. I think I should tell the Sheriff what you did to me just now." She fumed as she dressed then stormed to the door. Harry could only watch, stupefied. "You just wait. I'll take care of you."

Harry reached under the blanket, took some of the money and pushed it into her hand. He saw in her eyes instantly that it was the wrong thing to do.

"If you think I'm a whore, then you'd better think I'm a good whore and you'd better pay me like one. If not, I'm going to the Sheriff right now." She stood with her hand outstretched.

Harry looked at her in disbelief. Honey found her well of tears and brought them up again, on call. Her lips trembled and the tears flowed.

"Alright, alright. Stop crying." He went back to the bed and took out more money, handing it over reluctantly.

Honey took it and pushed it into her coat pocket. "Thank you, Harry. You're a generous man when you have to be. Will you tell Daniel that I was over to see him and I want him to come to dinner when he is back? And I think this little visit," she moved to him and took his penis in her hand, squeezing it until he winced, "should stay between us. Don't you agree?" She kept her grip tight until Harry nodded. "Good boy, Harry. I'm glad I came to visit." She opened the door. "Let's visit again sometime," she said, with a wicked smile.

She closed the door and turned to find Kate standing there. "He's not there," she said as she brushed past Kate on the narrow path.

⊰⊱

It was brutally cold when they arrived in Leadville. Fortunately, the hospital there was by reputation the most modern in the state and the nursing staff, which were used to injuries coming from the mines at all hours of the night, went about their work with stern efficiency. Meanwhile, Red's crew waited nervously until a doctor approached them with news.

"He will probably live," the doctor said. "His constitution and his good health are working in his favor." But, the doctor explained that with all major injuries to the head, there was a certain amount of hope and wishful thinking in his forecast.

They drove the wagon into town, where Red booked them into the Grand Valley Hotel and wasted no time leading them into the bar. They found a quiet corner booth in the dining room and had just finished ordering their food when they saw the Sheriff enter the bar.

Red watched him talk to the bartender who subtly inclined his head in their direction. He stood at the bar and ordered a drink then swept the room with an experienced eye, a patient predator waiting for opportunity.

Their meals arrived and the Sheriff chose that moment to join them. Without being invited, he pulled up a chair and sat at the end of the table, next to Daniel. Daniel found that he was sitting elbow to elbow with the man who just a few days before had shot at him and Harry. Daniel's heart raced and his appetite faded mid-bite.

"Howdy, Red." The Sheriff looked around the table and made a point of glaring at Daniel. Red nodded to the Sheriff and continued eating. "I heard you boys had some trouble coming over the Pass today."

"Yeah, Sheriff, we got caught in a slide just this side of the summit. I'm guessing you've heard that Tomas's brother is in hospital." Red responded.

The Sheriff nodded and looked at Tomas. "I hope he's alright, Tomas," he said, oozing sincerity, "I always did like you two fellers. Not like the rest of the riffraff from over your way."

"He'll be glad to hear of your concern, I'm sure." Tomas had heard that the Sheriff hated everyone from Aspen.

The Sheriff turned to Daniel. "I thought I told you I didn't want to see you in my town again, young feller."

"Sheriff, you know there was a fire out at my place at Twin Lakes?" Red cut in.

The Sheriff took his eyes from Daniel and rocked back in his chair, looking down into his whiskey glass. "Yes, I sent you the telegram. Anything I can help you with?"

The table fell quiet; their chewing slowed to slow motion. Daniel had been working the same piece of beef for minutes, but it still wouldn't go down.

"As a matter of fact, yes there is. My man, Newly, he seems to have disappeared. We were too busy getting Bjorn to the hospital to do much searching." Red had stopped eating and was looking at the Sheriff, who was studiously considering his drink.

"My brother probably did the right thing and gave him a Christian burial."

"I didn't know you had a brother over there in Twin Lakes, Sheriff."

"He owns the Lodge."

They all stopped eating.

"Frank's my younger brother. Didn't happen to see him while you were there, did you?"

"As a matter of fact I did, Sheriff."

The Sheriff looked at Red, intently. The tension at the table swelled in the silence.

"He said his wife left him." Red resumed eating.

"Is that so?" Daniel could see the muscle in the Sheriff's jaw twitching.

"Funny thing though, Sheriff..." Red took another bite of steak and deliberately chewed it slowly. "How're your steaks, boys? Mine is delicious." The Sheriff shifted uncomfortably in his seat. They nodded their approval and followed their leader's direction, eating with new-found savor. "Tomas, is your steak OK?"

Tomas nodded appreciatively. "Hey, it's better than reindeer, but not so good as dressed elk I'm t'inking."

The Sheriff leaned forward, placing his hands flat on the table. "Red, I'm asking you a question."

"Oh. Sorry, Sheriff. It's probably nothing. After all, you've got a bank robbery to solve and I just bet that Butch Cassidy and his gang are still hereabouts, eh?"

The Sheriff's hand clenched and unclenched in time with the muscle in his jaw. Red played it like a poker hand. He was enjoying not being on the receiving end for a change and knew without looking up that Daniel would be enjoying it too.

Red finished his mouthful and dabbed at the corners of his mouth with his napkin before answering. He was the epitome of etiquette. "Well, Sheriff, Frank said that Gloria had left town, but when we drove out of town there were no wagon tracks. As a matter of fact, it looked like only one horse or perhaps two had ridden out of there." He paused theatrically. "Did she ride, Sheriff?"

"Well, she must've, Red." The Sheriff took out a small, thin cigar and took his time lighting it. He blew smoke over their food.

"Like I said before, Sheriff, I'd like to know what happened there and where my man Newly is. Whether he's a corpse or run off with your brother's wife, I'd still like to know."

"What are you suggesting, Red? If you've got some half-cocked idea of stirring up trouble over here, you'd better be careful what you say, and who you say it to. Do you get my drift?"

Red sat calmly, unruffled by the threat. The Sheriff stood to go as if he'd finished this exchange on his terms.

"I wish you luck, Sheriff." Red said.

"What's that supposed to mean?"

"I mean about catching the fellers who robbed your bank here."

"Oh, don't you go worrying about that, Red. When I do find them bastards, they'll wish they'd long gone from these parts, believe you me." He leaned close to Daniel. "And you! I don't ever want to see your skinny ass back here in my town, ever. Do you hear me?" He turned to face Red and leaned on the table, his knuckles turning white. "I don't care what business you say brought him here, I'll lock him up and ask questions later. And I guarantee it won't be a pleasant stay." The Sheriff pushed himself away from the table, causing their drinks to splash.

"What do you say there boys, another round of steaks?" Red asked them, his voice louder than necessary.

The Sheriff shot them a look of pure hatred as he headed away from the table towards the bar. He stopped and spoke to the bartender, who nodded and poured the Sheriff another drink. Doc Holliday came into the bar. He looked sick, but more drunk than infirm. The Sheriff caught his eye and motioned him to join him at the bar, where they huddled for a while before he tossed the bartender a coin and left.

The conversation at the table remained subdued. They declined to order more steak, though Red offered again. It was decided that in the morning, after visiting the hospital, they would purchase lumber and return to Twin Lakes to repair the bunkhouse as best they could.

They were heading towards the lobby, stomachs full and bone-weary, looking forward to a good night's sleep in clean beds with crisp linens, but were stopped by Doc, who lurched into their path. He was bleary-eyed and swayed slightly, but still had a menacing look. His long gray moustache was stained brown from the cigars and tobacco that had ruined his health and advanced his tuberculosis.

"I got a message for you Red, to take back over the Pass for me, if you'd be so kind to an old man."

If it weren't for the pistol in his coat pocket, they could have felt sorry for the old devil.

"I want you to tell that cheating, no good coward Harry Rich that he'd better run the other way if I see him again. He owes me money, and I plan to get it from him, and unless I do, you can tell him that the last notch on my gun is his, and I won't consider dying before I see that he gets what he deserves." He leaned close to Daniel. Daniel recoiled from the stench of his breath. "See that he gets the message or you'll be on my list too." He pulled himself back to a semblance of dignity and looked down his nose at Daniel. "I used to shoot brats like you for practice when I was young."

To Daniel's surprise, he held his hand out to Red, who took it like an old friend. "It's good to see you, Red."

"I see you're not dead, yet."

Doc laughed, his smile a mockery of humor. "Not yet—to the surprise of the doctors."

Red let the old man's hand go and patted him gently on the back. "Well, we got to get some shuteye and head out early tomorrow."

"Too bad about your man. I heard he got crisped at the barn." Doc looked at Red with one eyebrow raised.

"Yeah? Well, I don't rightly know about that yet, but I plan to look into it."

He was still smiling his horrid smile as they left him.

The hotel beds were as soft as clouds and they all slept well, except for Red, who had dreams of burning to death. The sounds of Newly's tortured screams startled him awake and left him sweating.

The morning dawned clear and cold, inviting the New Year to arrive. Red went off to organize the men he needed and went to the lumber yard for his building supplies.

Tomas visited Bjorn and found him awake and eating, with no memory of the near catastrophe he'd survived. Though they wanted to keep him in hospital, Bjorn could see no purpose. So wearing a large white bandage around his head and bandages around his chest, he joined them on the wagon for the trip out to Twin Lakes.

When they reached Twin Lakes, Frank was nowhere to be seen but there was a rough plank coffin in the barn containing Newly's body. Red used the butt of his pistol to raise the lid and, as familiar as he was with the sight of corpses, he was unprepared for what he saw. It took little skill to imagine the agony the man had suffered prior to the eventual relief his death had finally brought him.

For two days, Leafy and Daniel labored with the Swedes. In those short two days, they and several other men built the bunkhouse frame and roof. The small building still smelled of burned wood, but that would disappear in a few weeks, after they'd laid down a new floor. When the road crew arrived back after dark on the final evening and the men from town returned home, they sat around the small iron stove, which was the only item that Red had been able to salvage. The barn was their home until the cabin was rebuilt and they'd lined the stalls with fresh hay, and covered it with canvas for their bedding.

On this evening, there remained a small contingent of Red's workers who stayed with them in the barn to help open the final section of road. They all sat by the tiny stove and drank whiskey in the barn before turning in for the night. It would be less than half a day before they'd make it to the top of the Pass and "it will be all downhill from there," Red had said.

They reached the summit of the Pass in the afternoon. The sun was brilliant, but it had no real warmth and their work crew was glad to say their farewells, collect their hard-earned pay and head home again.

Red was pleased with their progress, but decided to wait for the Aspen team to reach them in the morning. They settled into their cabin in Independence and were greeted with hot food and fresh bread for their efforts. It seemed like a week since they'd left the cabin, but it had only been a few days. So many questions needed answering.

So many things had occurred over the past few days and now there was a suspicious death. At least one. Red was no stranger to death and though he'd had to use his hands, he found what killed Newly. Someone had broken most of the bones in the poor man's body. The ribs were crushed and both his legs had been broken. Someone, and Red had no doubt who, had tried to straighten them.

Then there was the mystery of the missing Gloria. Red had been very fond of her; over the years they'd shared stories and many years ago, after the death of his first wife, she'd come to him in the night. It had only been that one time and, though he'd never addressed the issue, he was hopeful it still was their secret.

He wondered if there would be an inquiry into Newly's death, but the revelation that Frank and the Sheriff were related seemed to make that prospect a dim possibility. The matter to be uncovered now was the whereabouts of the missing Gloria.

The arrival of the Aspen team mid-morning set them all to work, clearing the last part of the road to the summit. They didn't spend much time celebrating. After all, it was New Year's Eve and for bachelors and family men alike, it was temptingly filled with celebration. The bottle finished, and the men refreshed and slightly drunk, they packed up their shovels and gear and climbed aboard their wagons for their ride back down the valley and home.

Daniel, Leafy and Tomas climbed into their skis and took off down the road, ahead of the wagons. On the flat sections, they raced each other. The whiskey made it all the funnier when one or other fell into the snow banks on the side of the road. Daniel was best at going straight down the hill. He still had difficulty swooping and turning like the rest, but by the time they'd reached the bottom of the Pass and were heading to the barn, he felt more than a little accomplished and actually beat Leafy into the barn.

They were all very tired, but the brothers still had a ways to go home, so he and Leafy pulled them along behind their horses, 'jouring', down the valley to a point above their cabin by the river. There, they let go of the ropes and waved goodbye as they swung their skis off the road and gracefully fell out of sight in slow, swooping arcs through the trees.

Leafy and Daniel coiled the ropes, tied them to their saddles, and then headed back to town. There was a peace between them; perhaps it was that they had again shared another near disaster.

"Daniel," Leafy said after a while, "I'd like to ask you something."

"Sure, ask away."

"What do you think of Kate?"

"I think she's very nice. Why do you ask?"

"I thought I heard someone talking about how you liked her a lot," Leafy said frankly.

"I do like her a lot. I think she's smart and funny."

"Well, I like her a lot, too."

Daniel slowed his horse.

"I've been in love with her since we were kids. I plan on marrying her."

"I think you two would be great together," Daniel finally got out.

"So you don't mind?"

"Of course not, Leafy," he said with as much conviction and sincerity as he could manage.

Leafy stopped his horse and turned in his saddle, offering his hand to Daniel in friendship. "Will you be my best man at the wedding?"

"Of course I will."

They continued on in silence.

"Have you asked her yet?" Daniel asked after several minutes.

"I told her that we should get married in the spring. I think that's a good time to get married, don't you?" Daniel failed to answer.

They parted in town and Daniel made his way to No Problem's stable, leading his horse into the barn.

"Howdy there, stranger." At the far end of the barn, Joe sat in the shadows. "I thought you might be back tonight. I heard that you fellers nearly got yourselves killed."

"Well, it got a bit scary, but we made it OK." Daniel unbuckled his saddle and hung the tack on the wall.

"Which one of you got hurt?"

"It was Bjorn. He hurt his head and spent the night in hospital, but he seems OK now."

"I guess those Swedes are a pretty hard-headed lot."

"I lost one of your gloves."

"No problem, I'll make you another one." Daniel handed the remaining glove to Joe. "What did you fellers find over at Twin Lakes?"

Daniel told Joe about the run-in with the Sheriff and discovering that he was Frank's brother. Joe was most interested in their conversation with Doc Holliday and listened intently, asking for details.

"That Harry of yours had better take care of himself and stay out of Doc's way. Running into him could turn out bad." Daniel got to his feet and climbed into his coat to leave. "One thing, Daniel." He turned to listen. "Keep your eye on Harry."

"Why?"

"I hear he's been hitting the bottle pretty hard and flashing some money around."

Daniel felt his head start to pound. "Thanks for the advice, Joe."

"No problem. Hey—" Joe said. Daniel turned slowly. "Happy New Year, son."

"Thanks, Joe, same to you."

"No problem. Goodnight."

Daniel waved as he pushed the door open and walked out into the night. He pushed the door closed on his past and walked forward into his future.

Chapter 35

Harry came back from working on the mountain and roused Daniel out of bed. "Come on, get out of bed. We're heroes. I know at least a half a dozen women waiting to give us a special thank-you."

Daniel rolled over and tried to ignore him but Harry was already drunk by the sound of it and wouldn't be ignored.

"Honey was over here looking for you." Harry crowed, but Daniel was falling asleep. "Kate came over here looking for you, too."

Daniel rolled over and sat up, very awake. "When?"

"I don't remember exactly." Harry remembered exactly, because she'd arrived just as Honey was leaving. They had almost knocked each other over at his doorstep. He'd gone over to Honey's the day after while her son was at school and they'd fought each other to a draw on her bed again before she'd thrown him out. "Come on, boy. Get yourself dressed and we'll go on down to Shirley's and see what trouble we can get into. Send this year off with a bang. We haven't had a chance to celebrate our good fortune yet."

"I brought you the paper from Leadville." Daniel reached into his pack and pulled out the paper. Harry snatched it from him and sat at the table, reading the story. Daniel poured some warm water into the basin and washed as Harry read aloud. Harry's merriment soared as he read the quotes from the Sheriff. "'I will catch them, and I will bring them back here to face justice.'"

Harry was having a fine time reading about how the Sheriff chased the robbers and very nearly caught them at Balltown, according to his story; before the storm forced him to stop for the night. It was reported that he returned to Leadville the day after losing their trail. There was great speculation in the newspaper and in the bars about the identity of the culprits, who had so cleverly robbed the bank and managed to trap the Sheriff inside while doing so. It was little wonder the Sheriff was so angry at the robbers—he was the laughing stock of Leadville and, most probably, all over the state.

The public opinion was that it was Butch Cassidy, mainly because it was so brazen and their getaway so completely successful. The description of the damage to the bank, which they had caused, brought tears of joy to Harry's eyes. "I guess we really pissed off that Sheriff."

"You have no idea how much, Harry." Daniel said, with total conviction. "If he ever gets his hands on us, I don't want to be there." Daniel was shaving; he rinsed the blade in his bathwater and looked over at Harry. "You know that Frank killed Newly, don't you?"

Harry looked up from the paper. "You mean the cowboy, the one screwing Gloria?"

"Yeah. He was all burned up and Gloria is missing, too," Daniel said respectfully. The sadness in his voice was not lost on Harry.

"Well, that gives the Sheriff something else to work on after he finds Butch and his partner." Harry shifted in his chair.

"Harry, we know who killed Newly," Daniel whispered, "shouldn't we go and tell someone about it?" He hated the fact that they could do nothing about incriminating Frank without opening themselves up to suspicion.

Harry looked at Daniel from under his eyebrows.

"Yeah, I know we can't do anything about it," Daniel said in resignation, "I'm just afraid for Gloria is all. Frank told Red that she'd left him, but there were only horse tracks on the road. If she left him, I doubt that she'd leave without taking the wagon and her clothes, wouldn't you think?"

"Son, I've no doubt that she's alright and probably just went to cool off for a few days." Harry was unconvincing, even to himself.

"But she would've known about Newly being burned in the fire at the bunkhouse."

Harry rose and placed his hand on Daniel's shoulder. "Don't think about it. Come on! We've got some celebratin' to do. As long as that Sheriff is flying around the country looking for Butch Cassidy, we're safe as a church."

Daniel felt only slightly reassured. "OK, let's go get drunk."

"That's my boy." Harry patted the iron stove. "Hey, we're rich as soon as this thing blows over."

They grabbed their coats and headed out into the night.

"Harry, what if Butch Cassidy finds out that it was us that robbed the bank?"

"We won't be going to jail, I can tell you that."

⚜

Red and Joe sat by the potbellied stove at Joe's stable, enjoying the heat and peace as well as some of Red's whiskey. They were reading the paper from Leadville and relishing the story.

"Do you think it was Butch Cassidy and one of his boys that robbed that bank?"

"It makes some sense," Red replied, but he was thinking more about the situation at Twin Lakes and hadn't yet told Joe about the condition of Newly's body. "They robbed that bank in Telluride in August and Leadville isn't so far away. I have to admit, it was pretty smart how they locked the Sheriff in the bank while they robbed it."

"It says here that the Sheriff shot and wounded one of them." Joe was by nature a skeptical, practical man. "I wonder how he knows that. He says there was some blood on the snow, but it also says that it was snowing like a bitch."

"Well, if he's as good a shot as his brother Frank, I'm pretty damned sure he hit what he was shooting at." Red sipped at his whiskey.

"Yeah, I forgot they were brothers. That's a bad lot over there, isn't it? I'd sure hate to be Butch and whoever it was if they wound up in that jail of his." Joe clucked his gummy mouth and looked over at Red, who was lost in thought.

"What I'm wondering is why he didn't go on into Buena Vista after he followed them so far?" He paused, thinking. "And if the Sheriff had to hole up in Balltown because of the storm, where did the robbers hole up?" He lifted his eyes to Joe for some solution but there was none forthcoming. "Why don't we go into town and have us a few? What do you say, old man?"

"Sure, Red, let's go see what the kids are doing for fun these days."

For a man of his obvious years, he had remarkable agility and bounded out of his chair to fetch his coat. He even splashed on some cologne, which made Red laugh out loud.

"Them ladies seem to like it, Red." Red was still laughing as they left together, their hands deep in their pockets, their heads high.

◆

Shirley loved having a crowd around her. The bar was full of high-spirited miners, women, and girls of the sordid kind. She was buying as many drinks as she was selling. It was good for business and though she knew that some more than others were taking advantage of her generosity, she didn't mind too much.

She saw Harry and Daniel come through the front door and waved to them across the crowded bar. Daniel was slapped on the back repeatedly, accepted a drink that was offered and joined in toasting to anything and everything.

Red and Joe arrived to cheers and applause. They found rounds of drinks piling up in front of them as soon as they made it to the bar. Shirley came from behind the bar directly to Red and kissed him on the cheek.

Joe tapped Red on the shoulder. "What you got I don't got, Red? Where's my kiss, Shirley? I'm prettier than him."

She grabbed him, pulled him to her ample bosom and kissed him on the top of his head. "That's all you're getting tonight, Joe. You know how you tire me out, you tiger." Everyone around them laughed. Joe was red-faced to be the center of attention.

"What's it goin' to cost me to get into those panties of yours tonight, Shirley?" Joe offered loudly, it being an old joke between them.

"Thanks for asking Joe, but there's barely enough room in these bloomers for one ass," she patted her behind. She kissed him directly on the mouth to the hoots of everyone who'd overheard. "You're so sweet, I don't know why I didn't marry you the first time you asked me," she said.

"I don't remember ever asking, Shirley. You sure it was me?"

Shirley stood back a pace. "It could've been, Joe, but I remember you bein' much taller then." She hugged him again and let his hand stay around her waist.

It was shaping up to be a good party. A band of three was playing Irish music that had some merry miners dancing with anyone they could grab. The piano player was very good and the fiddle player was working up a good sweat, while the squeeze box player kept up a high paced rhythm. Daniel felt a tap on his shoulder and turned to find Kate looking up at him with a big smile.

"Would you like to dance with me, sir?"

Daniel was caught off guard and Shirley was smiling brightly.

"I've been wondering where you were," she said to Kate. "Where's Rachelle?"

"She's in the kitchen, helping the cook make sandwiches." Shirley looked at her daughter with obvious pride. "Then go out there and show us how it's done."

Kate gave her walking stick to Shirley, and leaning slightly on Daniel's arm, led him into a dance. The crowd clapped in time and some of the other girls caught men in their arms and followed in many variations of a reel.

Daniel was surprised that Kate showed almost no infirmity when she danced and he felt awkward as he tried to follow her steps. She looked up at him, her smile impish. "What kind of dance are you doing?"

"This is how we dance where I come from," he said, proudly.

"What, badly?" she laughed. But, she held onto him tighter and they fell into a rhythm with the other dancers.

There was no doubt they were the center of attention. Everyone, Harry included, was cheering and clapping them on as they circled the room, sometimes even dipping and swooping in time to the music. Shirley was smiling broadly and clapping to the tune and even Joe was clapping along with the beat. Out of the corner of his eye Daniel saw Leafy grab his coat and walk for the door.

"What's wrong?" Kate asked over the musical din.

Daniel hesitated and thought about telling her what Leafy had told him, but it would do no good and would only create more difficulties. He lost the enjoyment of the moment. Kate, seeing this as rejection, turned and walked off the dance floor into the kitchen, as he tried to catch her. Shirley took hold of his arm lightly.

"What's happened?" she asked of him.

"Leafy told me today that he wanted to marry Kate. And then..." He trailed off.

"Come with me, young man." Shirley took him by the hand and led him into the Parlor where it was less crowded. They sat at a table and when Glennis came towards them, she waved her off.

"Look, Daniel, I know that Leafy's had his heart set on Kate since they were children together in school. I know it, and so does she. If she wanted Leafy, don't you think that she would've asked him to dance with her?"

Daniel considered the information, his eyes full of sadness. "But I don't want to hurt Leafy. He's my friend."

"You can't stop that from happening. You know that, don't you? Kate is the only one who can do that." Feeling for Kate's young suitor, Shirley leaned back, looking deeply into him and saw his conviction and love. She'd made up her mind that of all the young men in this town looking for love or pleasure, he seemed the only one whom she trusted. And she knew from their conversations that Kate had feelings for him, too.

"Go on back in there and have another drink. I'll go and see what I can do." They stood and he allowed her to push him through the doors, back into the noisy bar.

Shirley marched into the kitchen, looking for Kate. Rachelle looked up as her mother entered and without speaking, pointed towards her office.

When she opened the door, Kate was sitting in the darkness, quietly crying. Shirley did what mothers throughout history have done when they see their daughters in pain. She knelt in front of her and tried her best to calm her. "What're you crying about?" Shirley reached her arms around her daughter and enveloped her, her heart filling with love.

"Oh, I don't know. I probably just needed a good cry is all." Kate let her head fall onto her mother's shoulder. "What's wrong with me? Is it because I'm a cripple?" She sobbed deep wracking sobs of romantic pain.

"Oh, Katey, it's not that."

"Then what is it?" Her sobs wrenched at Shirley's heart.

"Look at me," Shirley said with the stern authority of a parent. "Look at me," she repeated.

Kate looked up into her eyes.

"Leafy talked to Daniel today and told him that he planned to marry you." Shirley took Kate's hands in hers. "Daniel doesn't want to hurt either of you. He's just a bit confused and it's up to you to make it alright between them. Now, wash your face and go on out there and grab that boy and go dance with him until I tell you two to stop. OK?"

Kate dabbed at her eyes and had one of those waves of love for her mother that only mothers and daughters know.

Shirley became aware of Rachelle standing in the doorway. Before she could say anything more, Rachelle ran from the kitchen, out the back door and into the alleyway. By the time Shirley had reached the door, she was gone from sight. She waited. In a few moments, she saw a small head appear from a doorway, and then she saw Rachelle run away from her, down the alleyway.

"Rachelle, Rachelle, stop," she called out to no avail. "That girl will be the death of me," she said to herself as she went back inside.

Rachelle stopped running when she heard her mother close the kitchen door. She'd run out without her coat and would have to go back for it if she wanted to survive.

"What? You back again, you little mischief-maker?" the cook said to Rachelle when she slid back into the kitchen. She held her finger up to her lips and went up the back stairs to the landing, where she could look down on the bar from a slit in the curtains.

Daniel felt a nudge from Harry and turned to see Kate coming back into the room, holding her mother's hand. He couldn't imagine a more beautiful mother and daughter in the history of the world. Even in the moments since he'd last seen her, she seemed to have developed another ten degrees of beauty.

His heart skipped a beat at her approach. Even though the room was noisy, there seemed to be no sound except that of the blood rushing in his ears. She came to him, took his hand, and guided him to the dance floor. There was no music but she leaned against him and they heard the plaintive hum of the violin calling hearts to order. The crowd surrounded them, but they forgot about them, lost in the mood, invisible to all but Shirley, Red, Harry, and Joe, who'd never missed anything in this known life.

"They make a nice couple, don't they?" Joe said, to no one in particular.

"Yes, they do," said Red, who found that his hand was resting lightly on Shirley's hip. She looked up at him and touched his hand gently.

"I'd better get the sandwiches from the kitchen," Shirley said, hoping they wouldn't notice her emotion. She pushed her way through the crowd and soon returned, followed by her kitchen help, who were carrying heaping trays of sandwiches.

She had her bartender help her up onto the bar and whistled for the room to quiet. "Alright! Alright everyone, it's nearly midnight and you all know what that means."

A thunderous cheer of "free whiskey" rose from the crowd.

"Here's a toast to the New Year," she said and pointed to the wall clock, both hands nearly vertical. "To all of my friends and to you others out there, who aren't," she said, pointing to Jerome Wheeler, who had just come into the bar still wearing his fine fur coat and tall hat.

They all turned and laughed. Jerome saluted Shirley.

"Happy New Year! Drinks are on the house!" Shirley declared.

The roar was deafening. Shirley noted with pleasure that even Wheeler was cheering and shaking hands with everyone around. When Shirley tried to get down from the bar, she was hoisted onto the shoulders of several men and carried around the room like an empress on a palanquin.

Everyone was busy shaking hands and wishing each other well; a few, including Rachelle from her perch and Leafy from the outside looking through the window, watched as Kate and Daniel kissed.

"Happy New Year, Kate," he whispered.

"And a Happy New Year to you, Mr. Carrington."

They were swept up as the music wailed. Men danced with each other and passed the girls around, whirling them all over the room. Kate and Shirley were passed from man to man, delighting in the attention and dancing.

Leafy had recovered some of his composure. He was hurt and embarrassed that he'd confided his feelings to Daniel just that evening. Feeling betrayed, he'd watched them dance and kiss. It was like having a red hot poker plunged into his heart. Every time he thought about it, he felt stinging in his eyes.

As he walked home, he experienced a feeling he'd not often had before. Leafy was a kindly person and felt ill will towards no one, usually. In a sudden flash of understanding, he saw that Daniel had walked over him. He'd confided in him and what he'd done was not what friends did to friends. They'd gone through experiences that should have made them even closer than friends, but now he saw Daniel with the woman he loved, knowing full well that Kate was his reason for living.

And Kate, what was her reason for the betrayal? They'd talked about getting married for years. She might have gone away to some big school in the east, but that didn't make her any better than she'd been before she'd left. Plus, she was a cripple. He wandered home, depressed. The New Year wasn't starting well.

The party broke up around two o'clock. Shirley allowed Daniel to walk Kate home and watched them as he helped her into her coat and took her arm.

"They grow up so fast." Red said, putting his arm protectively around Shirley's shoulder.

"Yes, they do," Shirley sighed.

Shirley made sure that the bartender had help cleaning the bar-room, then led her friends into the Parlor where they all sat, including Jerome Wheeler, and ended the evening with a nightcap. Harry was on his best behavior but he excused himself, obviously to find a game. Jerome left with him.

⚜

Daniel had held Kate's hand the whole time walking her home. She'd leaned on his arm and they walked in step so that her limp was almost forgotten for once in her life. He was strong and his accent was delightful. He was very concerned with Leafy's feelings, which he knew he'd hurt. She was quiet about her feelings for Leafy, but that was a matter best reserved for a time when she and Leafy could talk about such things privately. She knew it would be difficult, but she wanted them all to be friends.

Kate couldn't have been happier when she finally closed the door, then headed upstairs to her bed. The taste of his kisses still lingered on her lips as she undressed and washed her face before she dropped into bed. She wanted to dream of the possibilities of her life with this young man and the wonder of having a family with him.

She heard the front door open and footsteps coming up the stairs, expecting to hear the door to her mother's room open. Instead, she heard the door to her room open and close. The sound of Rachelle crying softly subsided and Kate finally drifted off to sleep.

⚜

Daniel was pleasantly intoxicated both with the effects of the whiskey and with the bliss of his first true romance. As he walked from Shirley's home, involved with his thoughts, he didn't notice the figure waiting for him. A small woman stepped into his path. He stopped to make way for her. He was still smiling from Kate's kisses and was completely at peace with the world. When he looked up, he was surprised to see it was Rachelle.

The slap across his face came as a complete shock. It felt like he'd been hit with a brick. Daniel was completely taken off guard when the hand appeared, coming at him like a train in the night. When it connected with his cheek he found himself sitting on the ground, his sprained wrist taking the brunt of his weight in the fall. He grabbed it in pain and looked up at his assailant.

Rachelle stood over him, baring her teeth. "You're a bastard," she said, before she ran into the house.

Daniel picked himself up and felt his cheek. He was not hurt, but he was confused and mystified by what he'd done to deserve the attack. He couldn't wait to tell Harry and get the benefit of his prodigious experience on the matter, but the cabin was empty when he arrived.

⚞⚟

Harry and Jerome Wheeler were in his lavishly appointed and decorated suite on the second floor in the Hotel Jerome, relaxing in deep armchairs, smoking good cigars, sipping cognac from crystal goblets. Harry was admiring the room's décor and his dark amber liquid, which reflected the light from the new electric fixtures. He'd been quietly enjoying the comforting warmth and aroma of the pine logs crackling in the fireplace, when Jerome broke the silence.

"I'll get right to the point, Harry. I like you. I think that you have the wherewithal to be a good businessman like myself." Flattery was often more successful than raw aggression but he was not above using either, if necessary.

"I think that you're a fine judge of men, Jerome," Harry responded predictably.

Wheeler smiled to himself. "I've got a question for you."

Harry was listening, though he was considering the smoke curling from his cigar.

"What do you know about your young partner? Daniel Carrington's his name, isn't it?"

Harry exhaled cigar smoke, taking his time at it. "He's a good lad, Jerome. He's reliable and as far as I can tell trustworthy." He took another puff. "I'd trust him with my life, if it ever came down to it."

"Would you now, Harry?"

"Yes, I would, Jerome."

"Well, that's comforting to hear. But what do you really know about him? Where's he from? He's not one of these Irish troublemakers, is he?"

Harry was grateful when Carter and Boot Hill entered with several other men and three women. Jerome, being the consummate host, proclaimed the bar open and stood up to welcome his guests.

"Harry, I want to talk to you later about this. You wouldn't mind, would you?"

"No, not at all Jerome." Harry stood to leave.

"No, no. You're my guest, Harry. Why don't you stay and join us in a friendly game? You know Carter and Boot Hill," he said. Harry nodded to them. "And I'm sure you know the mayor and Sheriff Hunter? Gentlemen, this here is Harry Rich. He's an old friend of ours and I invited him to join us." They all shook hands and took seats.

The scantily dressed women were willing and observant and brought drinks to the men as they seated themselves around the mahogany card table. One sat on the Sheriff's lap as the other two led the mayor into the adjoining bedroom, closing the door behind them. Harry had not seen these particular girls before and was admiring them as they exited the room.

"Harry, I notice you're a ladies man, too," Jerome said, as he expertly shuffled a deck of cards. Harry nodded in a world-wise way.

"Good. Then I want you to avail yourself of our ladies' generosities." Harry nodded and smiled. "When the mayor is done, and I don't for the world think that it will be much longer, please be my guest. Choose any of them you want." Jerome winked at him. "I'm sure you'll find them charming and energetic."

Jerome pulled a small blue bottle out of his vest pocket and handed it to the girl sitting on the Sheriff's knee. She removed the stopper, poured some of the liquid into her whiskey, and passed the bottle around the table. It was mostly empty by the time it reached Harry. Jerome withdrew another, handing it to Harry.

"Go ahead; this is not one of those nights you want to go to sleep early."

Harry nodded, poured some onto his glass and quaffed the liquid in one gulp.

The door to the bedroom opened and a disheveled mayor emerged, tucking his shirt back into his pants over his ample stomach.

"Now what were you saying about a card game, Jerome?" the mayor said, patting one of the young women on her ample bottom.

"Well, you old stud, I thought you'd never get finished with your business in there." The girls who had been entertaining the mayor came back into the room wearing flimsy underclothes.

Jerome passed out cigars to all, including the women. Harry's mouth had become very dry and his tongue felt as thick as an elbow, but he felt in a wonderful mood and ready for another party. He looked with renewed vigor at the ladies lounging around the room.

"Better take off your clothes, girls. We men are about to have us a card game." The girls did as they were told, giggling as the men watched. They lounged about or sat in the men's laps, their white, lacy camisoles unbuttoned to their waists, leaning over provocatively whenever something was requested. Jerome shuffled the cards and encouraged them to come to the table for the game. Harry joined them at the table, a cigar in his mouth and money in his pocket, looking forward to a night of sex and successful gambling.

He'd never felt so good, or so lucky.

Chapter 36

"Wheeler wants to see you today," Harry said, as he entered the cabin. Daniel was lying in bed, his arm over his eyes. "Did you hear me?"

"Yeah, I heard you. Why does he want to see me?" Harry was pulling a sack of potatoes out from the back room. "Do you need a hand with that?"

"Well, if you think we're still partners..."

Daniel let it go. No use provoking an argument at this hour. He reluctantly got out of bed and helped Harry open the sack and load the potatoes. Harry put the coffee pot on the stove and Daniel got a strong smell of liquor coming from him.

"You need a bath, Harry."

Harry dropped the pot on the stove. "A dog always smells his own shit first."

"What's that supposed to mean then?"

"You're not the sweetest flower either, you know. And if I were going to meet with my future father-in-law this morning, I'd be scrubbing at my pits till they bled."

"What do you mean, father-in-law?"

During the long night, there had been varieties of sexual conduct befitting the richest man in town and a few of his closest allies. Harry had been privileged to be enjoined in one of the wildest nights of his life. He was sexually replete, physically exhausted and still inebriated enough to have no remorse about his gambling losses. That would come later.

He did remember that he'd become the bearer of a message to Daniel about his need to visit with Wheeler. As his synapses coalesced into memory, he also recalled borrowing money from several players at the table. This was altogether different from just owing money.

Borrowing cash money committed him to debt and he realized with a shock, that he'd borrowed money from influential players, with witnesses present. His stomach turned over and he had to concentrate not to vomit.

"Have you been gambling again, Harry?"

"A little bit, maybe." Harry hated being caught.

"Did you lose a lot?"

"A little bit."

"Who did you lose it to? Did you lose to Mr. Wheeler?"

"I don't remember." Harry was sobering up and the remorse was building. He absently looked at the oven, considering the money buried beneath. Daniel noted that Harry avoided his gaze.

Harry acted as if the previous conversation had never happened. "What were we talking about?"

"About me becoming Wheeler's son-in-law."

"Oh! We were having a quiet drink," Harry began, back to his old self, confident and beguiling, "and he mentioned just how impressed he was with you. He asked me what I thought about you, so I told him."

"Go on, Harry."

"He said he was hoping that you would decide to take his offer of employment. He said that he was looking for good workers."

"He's got plenty of them in the mines. What did he mean?"

"Truth be told; Jerome is looking for someone he can bring into his company. Someone special. Someone smart enough for him to take under his wing. He thinks you could be the one." Harry held Daniel's stare; he needed Daniel to believe that he had his best interests at heart. "Are you going to take the job?"

"Not if it includes marrying his daughter. Did he really say that?" Harry was beaming inside; Daniel had taken the bait. "I mean, is he expecting me to ask her or am I just supposed to accept it?" Harry had to stifle a laugh at Daniel walking around the room, self-involved. "Well, I'm not going to do it. "

"Now come on, Daniel, let's not go overboard here. You should at least listen to what the man has to say. This could be a golden opportunity for you to go in with a successful businessman and learn something." Harry was the voice of reason, even pensive for the moment. "You know, young man, it's only once or twice in a lifetime that an opportunity comes along that can open the door to a completely different world. I'm not saying that you should, but it seems that Jerome Wheeler is offering you a chance. It might be a world of fortune and fame like he has. Or, it could be an opportunity to go and screw up like you've done already." Harry paused for emphasis. "But you'll never know unless you give it a shot, will you?"

Daniel trusted his heart to tell him the correct road to take, but it seemed he'd lost touch with it since he'd partnered up with Harry. The only thing he knew for sure was that he truly wanted Kate in his life. No girl had ever made him feel the way he felt when he was with her. Perhaps she would be proud of him if he showed some ambition and potential. It would certainly make his mother proud. His heart turned over in his chest at what pain it would cause should she ever find out he'd robbed a bank. He shook his head to rid the thought from his mind.

"By the way, Honey wants to see you. Seems like you're one hell of a popular guy these days."

"What does she want?"

"Probably the same thing they all want." Daniel looked at him, not understanding. "You, son. They want you."

"What do they want me for?"

"Here, help me with this bandage, will you?" Harry removed his jacket, vest, shirt and undershirt. There was dried blood on his shirt. Daniel noticed it had a bad odor as he was pulling it off.

"You gotta keep this wound clean, Harry," Daniel said.

"Yeah, it's real easy to reach around my back to wash it while you're traipsing all over the Rockies. It would've been hard to explain down at Mr. Chins. 'Oh yeah, Mr. Chin, yes this is a new bullet hole in my back. Yes, I got it for Christmas. They were giving them away free the night I robbed the bank in Leadville.'"

"OK, Harry. I get it. We'll get a bathtub."

Daniel unwound the bandages tied around Harry's shoulder and put them into a bucket at his feet. He inspected the wound closely and except for some discharge, it looked like it was healing. It was still an open wound about four inches long, and though the edges that had been seared by the bullet were dark, there were some definite healing signs.

Harry moaned and whined as Daniel tended to the wound. With much complaining from Harry, the bandage was replaced and new cloth strips wound around his shoulder again.

"Why would they want me?" Daniel asked as he helped Harry into a clean shirt.

"God only knows. As soon as they get their hands on you, all they want to do is change you. Just ask Red or Joe if you don't believe me."

"Harry. Why would a woman hit you if you didn't do anything to hurt her?"

Harry looked at Daniel with a look of sympathy. "Son, there's a million known reasons for them to do that. There's probably a million more that don't even make sense to them either, but they do it anyway. Why do you ask? Did Kate slap you last night?"

Daniel was caught off guard; Harry smiled knowingly.

"No, she didn't hit me. Her sister Rachelle did."

"That's one hell of a crazy girl there. She's crazier'n seven hundred drunk Indians."

"Why's she crazy?"

"Listen, I gotta get goin' if I'm goin' to make any money. How about helping me with the potatoes and we'll go down and have us a drink after we're done?" Harry got up and started the loading, then turned to Daniel. "We gotta get that dirt out'a here soon; it doesn't look good to have bags of dirt in the house. Someone might think that we've been burying something in here."

"We could take it now."

"Nah, we'll wait till dark and then we'll drop it on the road."

At the base of the mountain, while he and Harry went about their business, they watched some of the miners take the road up the hill with their skis on, and some of the returning miners come sliding down with varying degrees of success. Bjorn and Tom came up the road wearing their skis, pushing hard and fast towards them.

"Hey there, Daniel, how are you? You are vell?" Bjorn asked, answering his own question. He still wore the bandages around his head wound but covered them with a woolen cap.

They shook hands enthusiastically. Harry barely paid them any notice.

"What are you boys doing up here?" Daniel asked.

"Ve're going up there to ski." Bjorn pointed up the hill. "Hey, ve vant to vin the ski race this year like ve did last year, eh, Tomas?"

"Ya, ya, sure, ve do. Now ve got some new competition here." Tomas laughed, pointing his gloved finger at Daniel.

"What race?" Daniel asked.

"Ze ski race down ze mountain. Vhat, did Harry not even tell you about zis races?" Daniel looked at Harry who returned his look with a shrug. "Ve race down zhe mountain, den zhere are some races vis horses troo town." Bjorn and Tomas exchanged looks. "Hey, you got a horse, Daniel. Vhy don't you go in this races vis us? Ve show you how to vin, you betcha."

"I don't know; I'm not very good at skiing yet." Daniel was remembering their faces at Red's barn and the ribbing he got from all present.

"Daniel, look up zere." He pointed up the hill. "None of zem is very good eizer." To Daniel, it did seem that most of the men trying to ski were either running into each other, or in various stages of righting themselves. "Hey, come vis us. It's just for fun, but if you vin, you get a hundred dollars."

That got Daniel's attention. Though he was sitting on a small fortune in his cabin, he still thought himself poor, and a hundred dollars was more than a month's wages in the mines.

"Go and get your skis and ve'll practice vis you."

"Harry, you don't mind if I go with Tom and Bjorn, do you?"

Harry looked sullen. "Go do whatever you want."

"Thanks, Harry."

Daniel rushed back to the cabin to get his skis. Harry watched him go and his mood darkened even more. Harry didn't want to admit it, but he was actually looking forward to spending some time with Daniel. He'd had the success of the robbery bottled up in him and he needed to relive the adventure. Even if it had to be done privately, he still needed his ego to be stroked.

All he'd heard around town was Butch Cassidy this, and Hole in the Wall Gang that. It was getting tedious. He wanted more than anything to jump up and announce to the world that he, Harry Rich, was the one they should be talking about in such glowing and admiring tones. All he wanted was some validation or recognition. Hadn't he taken a greater gamble than all others and come out of it with the greatest prize?

Harry was packing up his gear when Kate arrived. She limped along with her cane, struggling up the slight incline to where Harry had set up his stall.

"Hi, Harry, how are you?" she asked.

"I'm better, now that you've come to ask me to marry you." The world brightened around him as the peal of her laugh broke Harry's gloomy mood.

"I'm glad you've finally come to your senses, even though you are a bit old for me," he joked.

"Harry, you wouldn't know what to do with me." She paused. "Oh, I forgot, you've got one over there in Salt Lake, don't you?"

Nothing escaped Shirley's network of spies. It was probably as good as old No Problem Joe's, if the truth be known.

"Well, in the Mormon religion, it's actually expected that each man take as many wives as he can afford, for the good of the community. Life's tough over there by the Great Salt Lake; hard on women. It's good to have a few to spare." Harry was at his most congenial when he was around a woman. "Besides, I'm still a spring colt just waiting for another chance to run with the herd again."

Her smile vanished for a second. Harry remembered her crippled leg. He put his arm around her shoulders, ignoring the miner waiting to purchase his potatoes. "Oh, Katey, I'm sorry. You know I didn't mean anything by that. I'm just a stupid man."

"Ain't that the truth," said the miner who was still waiting. Harry gave him his most withering stare.

"You know you're beautiful, don't you?"

"Yeah, just like those potatoes," said the miner.

Harry petulantly sold the man his potatoes. The miner examined them. One was smaller than the other.

"These wouldn't feed a rabbit, Harry."

Harry reluctantly gave the man another potato. "Well? What are you waiting for now? Go on, git. You're late for your shift. Git goin'."

"Hi there." It was Daniel, carrying the two ten-foot long wooden skis over his shoulder, the long stick in his hand.

Kate beamed. "I didn't know you could ski."

"I can't really; I'm just learning. The Swedes asked me to join them. They said there were some races soon and I should go in the one with the horses."

Daniel was half speaking to Harry, but Harry was now intent on wrapping up his wares and seemed to be paying little attention to them. He was trying to lift the remaining potatoes into the sled. Daniel dropped his skis to help. Kate was surprised by Daniel's sudden move, but she saw the look of pain on Harry's face.

"Are you OK, Harry?" she asked. "Are you hurt?"

"I'll be alright," he said, pushing Daniel away. "I can get it."

"My mother was wondering if you and Harry would like to come over to have dinner with us on Saturday night?"

"Tell your mother thanks." Harry looped the sling to the sled over his good shoulder and headed towards the cabin. Daniel watched him go.

"Is he hurt?"

"No, it's just an old wound or something." Daniel watched Harry.

"Will he be alright?" Kate was concerned.

"He'll be fine; he just hasn't been to sleep yet." Daniel bent to pick up his skis as the Swedes glided to a stop near them.

"Ve thought you ver taking a long time, but I see you been busy doing other more important t'ings, eh?" Bjorn was smiling.

"Vell, are you coming or are you going to bore zis beautiful lady all ze day long?"

Kate touched her index finger to her chin and gave a small curtsy to Bjorn, who doffed his hat in return.

"I should go now and let you have some fun." She reached out to Daniel, passed him a note, and pushed it and his hand into the pocket of his coat. He smiled and she blushed and walked away as the boys watched appreciatively.

"Hey, is zis Big Shirley's daughter?" Bjorn asked.

"Yeah, that's one of them." Daniel answered.

"Vell done, my friend. I zink you have a vinner dere. Vhat do you zink, Tom?"

"I zink vell done, too." They watched her for a few moments more. "Hey, let's go skiing. The mountain is not getting any younger."

"And ve are not eizer," answered his brother.

Carrying their skis on their shoulders, they headed up the mountain again. Several hundred yards up the hill they strapped on their skis. One at a time, the brothers headed down. Others on the hill stopped to watch them swoop and curve their long wooden skis in long graceful arcs through the snow. The brothers stopped near the bottom of the hill. Daniel faced the fact that it was now his turn.

Gritting his teeth, he started down the hill. He'd only gone twenty feet before he fell into the snow. Undaunted, he struggled against gravity and pushed off at a gentle angle across the hill. The speed was more manageable, but when he realized he was heading over the edge of the hill and into the trees, he panicked and threw himself into the snow again. Riding the skis downhill was more of a challenge than he had thought, and it was taking much more effort to master than it had been the first time he'd done it.

Again he started off, pointed in the opposite direction across the hill. The results were the same and he went over the front of the skis. It took two more attempts before he was finally down at the bottom of the hill, where the brothers tackled him as he sped past. Adding to his embarrassment, Kate was laughing and waving to him from further down at bottom of the hill.

"I t'ink you need anozer lesson," said Tomas sincerely, trying not to laugh.

"What was I doing wrong?" Daniel's ego was bruised.

"You fall down too much," said Bjorn, who fell about laughing.

"Come on, I'll help you," said Tomas, the more patient of the two. This time, he was shown the correct position and how to steer by using the long pole they'd carried up the hill. When they eventually made it to the bottom again, Bjorn was watching and waiting for them.

"Zhat was much better," he announced to Daniel, who filled with pride at the compliment. "You didn't fall down so much."

Kate remained at the bottom, waving back to him whenever he waved at her. She seemed content to sit on a hay bale and to watch his follies. When the sun dropped behind Shadow Mountain, the temperature fell rapidly. Though Daniel was exhausted, he was the last one off the hill, and groaning at his injuries, assured the brothers that he would practice every chance he could get.

Harry was sleeping soundly when Daniel got home, so he filled the oven for the next shift. There was a knock on the door and when he opened it, he found Honey standing there, unsmiling and tight-lipped.

"Are you coming to dinner at my house or not?"

Daniel was surprised at her tone.

"Where's Harry? Is he in there?" She tried to peer around the door, so he stepped outside with her. Harry needed the rest.

"He's home, but he's sleeping."

"No doubt, after what he did last night." She clucked and rolled her eyes. "So, you don't have other plans?"

Daniel shook his head.

Her tone softened, as if by magic. "Then you'll come over for supper? Jackson's been asking about you."

"Should I bring something?" Daniel asked her back as she left.

"No, just yourself. Don't get drunk before you get there." She pulled him to her and kissed him passionately. "There'll be more of that later if you're a good boy."

Closing the door, he sat down on the edge of his bunk; Honey had confused him again. He thought about skipping dinner, but that would create problems. She was unpredictable, to say the least. He had Kate on his mind. It would not do to complicate matters if he was serious.

He cooked the potatoes, went out and sold them. When he returned, he put the money on the table. He washed, put on his cleanest shirt and headed out to an evening he'd rather not face. He knew well that he'd missed his meeting with Wheeler.

Daniel hesitated on the porch, considering the situation, but in the end he shrugged his shoulders and knocked. Honey opened the door and Daniel handed her the candy he'd bought for Jackson.

"Oh, Daniel, you didn't need to do that." She smiled widely, then leaned forward and kissed him. Daniel was barely in the door.

Jackson was glad to see him and immediately took Daniel on a tour of his Christmas presents. He explained that he'd eaten all of the candy that he'd been given and was excited that Daniel had brought him more.

Daniel could smell sage and garlic coming from the roast as it was placed on the table. It truly was a thing of beauty, roasted to a golden brown and glistening with the glaze of the basting juices. Daniel nearly fainted with hunger, saliva filled his mouth and his stomach began growling. Jack heard his stomach rumbling and started giggling.

"I like my men to have good appetites," Honey said.

Jackson nodded enthusiastically as Honey brought more plates of food to the table. Aromatic steam rose from the meat as she expertly shaved slices neatly onto their plates. Daniel was in heaven the moment the food touched his lips. The meat was tender, not like any elk he'd had before. The gravy of elk drippings, red wine, and raisins was delicious, when he slowed enough to taste.

"You were hungry, Mr. Daniel," Jackson announced with a certain amount of awe.

"This is the best meal I've ever eaten," and though somewhat embarrassed, he held his plate out for more food, which Honey replenished gladly.

After supper was over, at Jackson's urging, he told them about the trip over the Pass and how close they'd come to disaster in the snow slide. Jackson was fascinated by the whole story and had Daniel repeat it. The gruesome details of Bjorn's head wound receiving his full attention.

Honey eventually worked Jackson out of the room, against his desperate pleadings to stay up a little later. His protestations were theatrical, but had the same effect on his mother as on every mother.

She came back down the stairs and walked over to Daniel; his eyes followed her every step and he traced her form in his mind. She held out her hand and led him to the couch facing the fireplace. She took both of his hands in hers, and after looking at them as if to read what they would tell her, she took his left hand and held it against her cheek. He could feel the texture of the tiny soft hairs along the line from her ear to her jaw, the delicate softness of the skin around her mouth and chin.

Honey stood and went about the room turning down the lamps until the only light came from the fire. She walked to him, knowing his eyes would never leave her.

She slowly undid the top buttons on her blouse, the creamy whiteness of her breasts reflected in the fire's glow. Leaning forward, she kissed him softly, her mouth warm and inviting. He reached up for her and she slid onto his lap and into his embrace, his face buried in her bosom.

Smiling wickedly she knelt down in front of him and unbuttoned his pants, laughing in pleasure as he sprang to attention.

His eyes closed in ecstasy as the warm wetness of Honey's mouth engulfed him, all of him. He moaned so loudly, he thought he'd wake Jackson, but Honey's mouth kept the pace alive and he felt himself losing control. She squeezed him hard, then stroked him gently, and the combination instantly brought him to the edge of heaven. He came in torrents. Honey continued until Daniel could take no more and pushed her head back and away from him. She wiped her mouth on the tail of his shirt, then laid her head on his lap, blowing cool air on his twitching penis.

Honey smiled as she slipped her hand inside his shirt and felt the ripples of his stomach muscles as they twitched and trembled at her touch and kisses. Suddenly, she stopped. They both heard the creak of a board. Their breaths stopped and they looked at each other guiltily.

Daniel thought back to the first time he'd had sex this way. The similarities, the anger and the fear, the tension and the release, the fear of discovery. He tried to concentrate on the face in front of him, the mouth so willing to please, those beautiful soft breasts lying moist and expectant of some attention.

But, Gloria was in his mind, too. She'd followed her passion and it had led to her destruction, to which he was possibly a witness. Guilt swept over him. He needed to find out what had happened. He had to go back over there.

The board creaked again. He brought his head back up to find Honey's face close to his, holding her finger in front of her lips.

"Maybe you ought'a go," she said huskily.

Honey stood and straightened her clothes. Daniel lusted for her, illuminated by the glow of the embers in the fireplace. She felt angel but looked devil.

He lingered at the door, but she finally broke away and pushed him outside. "I want you to listen to me, Daniel." Her mood had turned suddenly cold. "I don't want you sniffing around that slut Kate, if you know what's good for you. She's Leafy's girl." Her smile returned and she took Daniel's hand in hers. "How about you come for dinner again Saturday night? I'd like that."

"No, I can't." Daniel countered, thinking as quickly as his sexually drugged mind would allow. "I'll be over the Pass then, I think," he lied.

"Goodnight then," she said and closed the door loudly.

With his head swimming and his pants chafing, he drifted down the hill and home, wondering what it was that he had gotten himself into.

Chapter 37

"Nice of you to drop by," Wheeler's sarcasm was undeniable. "Make yourself comfortable. I'll be with you in a minute." Wheeler went back into his office and closed the door. Daniel could hear muffled conversation. Carter opened the door and ushered him into the office. Wheeler pointed him to a chair.

"Sit down, Mr. Carrington." Wheeler seated himself behind his desk and considered the young man across from him. "It took you long enough to get over here. Was there a problem?"

"No, Mr. Wheeler. I just didn't get the message from Harry," Daniel said, hoping the lie would go unnoticed.

"Well, never mind. You're here now." He steepled his fingers on his burnished oak desk and looked at Daniel, not speaking. Daniel felt uncomfortable, but held Wheeler's stare. When he thought he was going to have to blink, Wheeler dropped his eyes to the papers on his desk. It seemed that he had arrived at some conclusion.

"I'll come right to the point. I'm offering you a job with my company."

"I've already got a job, Mr. Wheeler."

Wheeler held up his hand. "Yes, I know, son. But you have to look to the future. Now, I know you've done well for Red and even for Harry. They both speak highly of you."

"I try to work hard, that's all I know, Mr. Wheeler."

"I know you do, and that's why I'm giving you this opportunity."

Wheeler leaned back in his chair and considered Daniel in silence. To Wheeler it was more than a job that he was offering. With his physical health deteriorating, and the fact that he didn't have sons, he was looking out for his family's future as well as protecting all that he'd worked for. He knew that his daughter had noticed this young man and liked him. If he could bring him into the fold of his influence and show him some of the benefits of being a man of wealth and power, Daniel might eventually arrive at his way of thinking.

Wheeler had complete trust in Carter and shared almost everything with him, including his medical condition that was privy only to his doctor and his wife. Wheeler had convinced Carter that what he needed was someone joined by marriage to continue his businesses for the sake of both his family and the business. He'd assured Carter that his position as mine boss was never going to be in jeopardy.

"Well. Do you want the job?"

"I'd hate to leave Red in the lurch," Daniel said honestly. "He's been good to me. I can't leave him another man short, that wouldn't be right."

"What if I talked to Red and we worked something out? Maybe you could start working with Carter on some of your days off. How does that sound? Then in the spring you can come work full-time." He let the information sink in. "You do know that when the rail line reaches here from Glenwood Springs, Red's business will be finished for good, don't you?" Wheeler held up his hand. "Not to say that he won't be able to do something else. But with the rail line going all the way from here to Glenwood, then to each coast through Denver and Salt Lake, his little company will be the first victim of progress in this valley."

It seemed that both Red and Wheeler were somehow wrestling for the soul of this Daniel Carrington, if that was his real name. Harry had triggered some suspicion about this during one of his drunken bouts of losing at poker. It was unusual for Harry to be reluctant when pressed for gossip or information, but in the case of his partner, he was particularly hesitant. Jerome Wheeler was by nature a suspicious man. More than once his intuition about someone or something had either advanced his fortunes or had saved them.

"Look, I think I know how you feel, Daniel. You feel you'd let Red down, and I respect that. Let me talk to him and let's see if we can come up with a solution. Would you be happy with that?"

"Yes, sir. Red's been good to me and taught me a lot. I'd hate to let him down," Daniel said with some relief.

"So, let's get to the meat of the matter. Do you want to come work for me and Carter?"

Seconds ticked by.

"Yes, sir. If it doesn't put Red in a bad situation, I'd like to learn about the mining business."

Wheeler let out a long sigh of relief. "You had me going there for a moment, son." Even if Daniel didn't marry his daughter, he'd still be working alongside Carter, and that would only be a good thing for all concerned.

"That would be nice, sir. Thank you."

Wheeler guided him towards the door and Carter opened it for them. "Good."

Daniel left them, his mood buoyant and headed out into the bright, cold sunshine and breathed deeply in gratitude for blessings he felt he didn't deserve.

"Well, Carter, what do you think? Do you think he'll work out?" Wheeler was back at his desk and Carter was sitting in the chair where Daniel had sat.

"I think he's got some potential, just as you do, Mr. Wheeler."

"It's a pity that you're too old to marry my daughter. That would solve all my problems, wouldn't it?" Wheeler laughed. Carter smiled. Not for the first time did Carter think lustfully of Abigail, of those big, snow-white breasts heaving with passion. Then there was all that money. Fortunately, Wheeler was blithely unaware that there had already been an occasion for Abigail to traverse the boundaries of genteel behavior with Mr. Carter.

※

"Did you go see Wheeler?" Harry was in his usual mood: surly.

Daniel nodded in reply.

"What did you tell him?" Harry stopped piling potatoes in the oven and waited for the answer.

"I didn't tell him anything," Daniel said.

"You had to tell him something. What did you say to him?"

"About what, Harry?" Daniel turned to face him. "Why, is he so interested all of a sudden in where I come from?"

"I didn't tell him nothing about you," Harry protested. "That would be pretty damned stupid, wouldn't it? The last thing I need is for you to get into trouble with all that money of mine." Harry caught himself. "Of ours, I mean. Under the floor here."

"That's right, Harry, the money is ours, not yours."

"OK, OK, I know it's our money. You don't have to get all heated up about it. Are we still going to Shirley's tomorrow night?" Harry was desperate to change the subject. The sooner he was able to get the money out of the cabin and get himself out of town, the better. It was getting a little too complicated in Aspen these days.

"I'm going." Daniel replied.

After dinner he sat down at the table and under the wan light of the lantern, he wrote a long overdue letter to his mother.

He filled the letter with descriptions of his exploits since his last letter, avoiding the subject of robbing the bank, of course. He wrote how much he missed her and his sister and inquired about news from his brother. He sealed and addressed the letter, then fell back onto his bed and was instantly asleep.

Harry wasn't home when Daniel woke in the morning, so he sold the potatoes for him, knowing full well he'd never see a penny for his efforts. Harry was still not home when Daniel returned, so he went skiing up on the mountain again. Since it was Saturday, many other men were up there tuning their skills. He found a general camaraderie among them and learned how to use the long pole to change direction and for stopping.

He went to Mr. Chin's for a bath and found the place crowded. It was a Saturday routine for some of the miners, this weekly bath. One thing unsettled him; he overheard two men talking about Harry in some detail. One was the tall man whom Daniel recognized as the one who had passed him at Honey's place. The thing that disturbed him most was that they knew about Harry losing at poker to Jerome Wheeler.

⊰⊱

Kate greeted him at the door and led him into the dining room, where Red and Shirley were already seated at the dining table drinking wine.

"Come on in, Daniel. Where's Harry?" Shirley asked.

"I thought he'd be here." Daniel replied.

"Kate, will you go up and ask Rachelle to come down for dinner, please?"

Kate headed upstairs.

"I hear you had a talk with Mr. Wheeler yesterday, Daniel," Shirley inquired. "Did it go well?"

Daniel's face reddened. There was obviously nothing that wasn't immediately known to everyone. "He offered me a job again."

"What did you tell him?" Shirley asked.

The sound of a door slamming shook the house. They all looked as Kate came down the stairs, her head down and tears brimming in her eyes. There was an uncomfortable silence while she dried her eyes with her handkerchief.

"What happened, Kate?" Shirley asked softly.

Red and Daniel exchanged glances.

"Nothing. Rachelle's not coming down to dinner. She called me a bitch."

"Excuse me, gentlemen. I'll just be a moment."

Shirley placed her napkin on the table and headed upstairs.

⊰⊱

Rachelle was lying on her side, her head turned to the wall. Shirley sat on the edge of the bed and stroked her daughter's hair.

"What's the matter, baby?"

Rachelle pushed Shirley's hand away violently. "Nothing."

"Come on, tell me."

"She can't have him. She's already got Leafy, hasn't she?"

"Can't have who, Rachelle?" Shirley knew, but needed to hear it from her daughter.

"She can't have Daniel. I saw him first."

Rachelle was not the kind of girl who used tears as a weapon or as a way to achieve her desires. Actually, as an infant, she hardly ever cried.

Nothing could change what was growing between Kate and Daniel, of which Shirley approved. Her concern was with her youngest, but she felt unable to help. "There'll be someone for you one day, believe me."

"But I want *him!*" she screamed.

"But, Rachelle, my darling, that's up to him. Don't you see that?"

Rachelle flung herself back on the bed and covered her head with the pillow.

"Come on down for dinner when you feel better."

As Shirley came downstairs, there was a knock on the door. She opened the door and found Harry on her doorstep, drunk as usual.

"Nice of you to show up, Harry." She let him in and closed the door behind him.

"Am I late?"

"Yes, and you're drunk, too. I don't remember asking you to be drunk when I invited you over for supper." She followed Harry into the dining room and he took his place at the end of the table.

"I didn't think you'd be here, Red."

Red didn't answer.

"I invited the both of you since you're both my friends, Harry." Shirley went to the kitchen to help Maisie.

When she returned, Maisie brought in a platter of fried chicken and mashed potatoes, steaming in a large bowl, filling the air with the smell of roasted garlic and thick, rich gravy seasoned with herbs. Somehow, Maisie had managed to find vegetables other than carrots and potatoes, and served spinach in a cream sauce, and string beans with bacon. Harry was about to reach out for the food when Red announced that it would be nice to say a prayer in gratitude. Harry sent a nasty look to Red, but he ignored it and said grace elegantly.

"Do you think you're going to go and work for Mr. Wheeler, Daniel?" Kate asked as the food was passed around the table.

Daniel felt all eyes on him.

"I...I haven't made up my mind yet. I wanted to ask Red about some things, first."

Red looked over at Daniel with obvious pride and felt Shirley's hand touch his knee for an instant.

"Daniel, you know how much I appreciate the work you've done for me, let alone saving Harry's life." Red shot Harry a look. Harry was engrossed in eating. The table fell silent. Harry looked up. "We were just saying that we remember how Daniel here saved your life on the Pass."

"Don't you think it's about time we all dropped that subject?" Harry continued eating heartily.

"Why, Harry? It's true, isn't it?" Shirley asked.

Harry stopped chewing. "So what if it's true? I've taken care of him ever since, haven't I?"

"That's not the point, Harry. We were just saying that this is an opportunity that Wheeler wouldn't offer without some consideration, don't you agree? You know him better than we do."

"Hey, I don't know what Wheeler's thinking of doing. I'd just be careful if I was Daniel."

"What do you mean, Harry? Don't you trust Wheeler? You play poker with him almost every night, don't you?" Shirley teased. "You seem to be such good friends. You, and the sheriff, and the Mayor getting up to tricks every night upstairs at the Hotel."

"What the hell business is it of yours? Of any of you?" Harry gripped his knife and fork tightly. His smile had turned to a snarl. All sound at the table stopped.

"Harry, settle down. We're all your friends here, you know," Shirley replied sternly.

"No, I don't know." Harry pushed himself from the table and threw his napkin down. "It's none of your business how much I lose or win. I've got plenty of money, don't you worry about me." Harry abruptly stood and strode for the door, slamming it behind him.

The door to the kitchen opened and Maisie stuck her head in.

"You all ready for dessert yet?" She noticed they were all looking towards the front door. "What happened? Did Mr. Harry hate my cookin'?"

"No, Maisie, he's just drunk is all."

"Well, that's none different from any other time he eats here." She withdrew to the kitchen and they resumed eating, except Daniel.

Daniel pushed away from the table. "I'm sorry, Shirley, but I'm worried about Harry. I think I should go after him."

"Daniel, I don't know what's eating Harry, but it's none of your fault." Her eyes implored him to heed her advice. "He's just this way because...well, because he's losing pretty heavily to Wheeler and from what I hear, he's in trouble. But it's his fault and he's responsible for his own debts, not you. From what I've seen, you've more than done your share for the man. That's how I see it anyway." Daniel placed his napkin on the table and smiled at Kate.

"Thank you for dinner Shirley, but I have to go find him. He is my partner after all," Daniel said, rising.

"You should be able to find him easily enough," Shirley said. "He's probably in the Hotel Jerome. He doesn't stray far from that place these days."

"Before you go, Daniel, can you do one more trip over the Pass with me?" Red asked. I've a feeling that you're going to get an offer from Jerome that you should accept. But, if you could help me once more, I'd appreciate it. Monday?"

"Sure, Red."

Kate helped Daniel into his coat. It felt satisfying to think that she had a man of her own to take care of. "Will you let me ride your horse in the race next week?"

Daniel drew back. "What race?"

"The ski jouring race through town. I think we can win." Her eyes were alight with excitement.

Daniel smiled at her. "OK. If it's alright with your mother."

Kate hugged him through his many layers. He draped his arms around her and held her close. She kissed him and sent him through the door.

"What's ski jouring?"

"You'll see. I know we can win." The door closed, Kate pulled the curtains apart to blow him a last kiss.

Daniel felt lightheaded but returned to earth when he looked at the ground and saw Harry's departing footprints in the fresh snow. He wouldn't need to be an Indian to follow the tracks. Just as Shirley predicted, they led directly to the Hotel Jerome. Daniel pushed into the bar and joined Harry sitting at the end of the bar, sullen and drinking alone.

"You got any money?" Harry asked.

Daniel pulled out a roll of bills from his pocket and gave some to Harry.

"Look at these fools, still talking about Butch Cassidy." Harry was getting drunker. "The real bank robbers could be sitting right here under their noses." Daniel was getting nervous. Harry's voice was getting louder. The cowboys next to them turned their heads to listen as Harry wavered on his stool and bumped them needlessly.

"Sorry about that. He's just getting a bit drunk." Daniel shrugged and smiled at them and they went back to their conversation. "Harry, you've got to keep quiet. Someone's going to hear you," Daniel whispered in Harry's ear. Harry pushed him away sending Daniel into the men standing next to them. They were hostile, had the hard look of range riders and they wore guns on their belts.

"You know it's against the law to carry guns in this town?" Harry said loudly.

"We don't need permission, feller." The man opened his coat, revealing a badge. "We're looking for them fellers that robbed the Leadville Bank."

One of them reached over and punched his finger into Daniel's chest. "Wouldn't know anything about that, would you young feller?"

Harry gave Daniel a warning look. "So, you say you think some fools from over here robbed your precious bank in Leadville?" Harry said, loudly enough that more than a couple of locals heard and were paying casual interest.

"The Sheriff thinks he might just find them fellers over here, in your shithole of a town. Are you goin' to help us, old man?" The cowboy leaned into Harry, pushing Daniel to the side. Harry had two glasses of good quality whiskey in front of him on the bar. He casually turned the glasses in his hand while fingering a couple of matches in the other hand, under the rim of the bar.

"Did you hear that?" Harry said over his shoulder, to the men behind him. "This clown thinks someone from Aspen robbed their bank. And he called Aspen a shithole."

"Come to think on it," the huskier of the two said, leaning into Harry. "You two look just like the ones we're looking for."

"You mean you fellers think that Harry robbed that bank?" said one of Harry's drinking acquaintances. "You gotta be out'a your minds." The wag continued, "Harry couldn't rob himself, let alone a bank," which brought howls of laughter from the men who knew Harry.

"We should have a talk with you outside, anyway." The burley cowboy closest to Harry grabbed Harry's coat. With a flick of his wrist, Harry lit the matches he'd been holding and flamed the whiskey in his glass. It burned with a dull blue flame, almost invisible in the smoky light of the bar.

The gunfighter was unaware of the flame, until Harry tossed it onto the front of his coat and over his neck. He reached out for Harry's throat, but instantly reached for his own, slapping his hands at the invisible flames that were raging in his clothing. Suddenly, the room was a melee of thrown fists and falling men.

Harry ducked and grabbed Daniel by the arm and in a crouch, pushed and dragged him through the forest of swirling fists and shuffling feet. Harry gathered his coat around him and walked casually and soberly out into the foyer of the Hotel. They stood together looking into the bar and watched the mayhem inside through the leaded windows.

"What's going on in there?" A familiar voice asked from behind them.

"Oh, just another bar fight, by the looks of it," Daniel replied, surprised to find Jerome Wheeler standing behind them, looking over their shoulders at the riot in his precious bar.

"Damn. I thought I'd avoid this sort of thing, too. But boys will be boys."

"Sure looks that way, Jerome," Harry said.

"I'm glad to see that you don't get involved with this sort of thing. Not good for the reputation, is it?" He slapped Daniel and Harry on their backs, laughing. "Sure hope they don't break nothing." A glass flew at them from the melee inside, smashing the beautiful acid etched glass in the door next to them. "Damn, that thing cost me a bundle." He looked at the pieces on the floor. "It came all the way from New York."

They watched him walk up the stairs, Hotel staff and bellhops fawning over him as he passed. The sounds of the brawl seemed quieter now. The deputies had arrived and some order was returning to the bar.

"It's about time we were off I think, don't you?" Harry said.

They headed out the door and across the street. They watched the bar being emptied unceremoniously as men were heaved out the door and lay sprawled on the snowy sidewalk.

"See, Daniel. No one here thinks we could've gone over there and robbed that bank. We're in the clear, partner. Say, can I borrow some of your money for a few days?"

Chapter 38

Daniel saw nothing of Harry the next day. He cooked the potatoes for the miners and after he'd finished selling them, he brushed his hair, and put on the same clean clothes he'd worn to dinner the night before. He took his Bible and headed off to St. Mary's Church.

He saw Big Shirley and her daughters there. Rachelle turned her head and fixed him with her piercing green eyes. Kate smiled at him. Shirley nudged her daughters' attention back to the service. Kate reluctantly pulled her eyes away. It seemed like minutes before Rachelle turned away.

After the service, he waited outside the church to see Kate and was surprised to find that he recognized many of the parishioners.

"Good morning, Daniel."

"Good morning, Shirley, Kate, Rachelle. How are you all this morning?"

"Did you catch up with Harry last night?" Shirley asked.

"Yes, I found him at the Jerome Bar. Just like you said."

"Was that before or after the brawl?"

Daniel's jaw dropped. "Before."

"So, you two had no part in the fight, then." Shirley was smiling. Kate slipped her gloved hand into his and gave him a smile that would brighten any man's day. Rachelle glared at them.

"What was this ski jouring that you talked about last night?" Daniel asked Kate.

"I'll show you. Why don't you get your skis and I'll change clothes and meet you at No Problem's stable? It's fun. You'll like it. Won't he, Mom?"

Daniel had already made up his mind that he'd do almost anything to spend time with Kate, even risk bodily injury.

"Just be careful with my daughter," Shirley said.

"I want to know who's going to be taking care of me," Daniel replied.

"Now, Kate, you'll take care of Daniel, won't you? At least get a doctor," Shirley said in jest.

"I'll see you at Joe's then?" Kate said, smiling brightly. Daniel watched them walk away. Rachelle looked back at him angrily as they turned the corner.

⚒

Harry was asleep when Daniel got back to the cabin. There was money lying on the bed; the exact amount that Harry had borrowed. Daniel changed clothes, gathered his skis and headed to the stable, where he found No Problem sweeping out the stalls. "What's 'skijouring', Joe?"

Joe stopped his labor and sat down on a hay bale. "Son, it's a dangerous race, I got to tell you. You'll be getting dragged behind a horse as fast as a horse can go and you're going to be sliding along on them skis you got there."

"Kate's going to ride my horse."

Joe chuckled.

"You're going to trust that girl to drag your ass all around town, more than she's doing already?" Joe looked at Daniel's fallen face. "Now come on, son, I didn't mean it that way, you know that. I think the world of that young filly, and her mother, too. She's had more than her share of troubles in this life already and she's not as crazy as her sister, yet. That's the good part." Joe leaned forward. "The other good part is that I taught her to ride, so I guess you're in good hands." Joe stood up and shook Daniel's hand. "If she's got her hooks into you this far then I ought'a go along and help out. Don't you think?"

"That would be nice, Joe. I have no idea of what I'm supposed to do."

Joe heaved the saddle off the top rail of the stall as Daniel placed the saddle blanket over Marigold's back. She shuddered at the touch of the blanket, but her ears perked up and twitched, facing backwards trying to hear the conversation.

"I hear you're having dinner with Wheeler and his family tonight," Joe said casually as he threw the stirrup strap over Marigold's back.

"How is it that you know everything going on in this town, Joe?" Daniel had stopped cinching the belly strap.

Joe shrugged. "I don't rightly know that I know everything, I just listen is all. I look out for my friends, too. Maybe that helps. Like them fellers that Harry and you got into a fight with last night at the bar. Harry probably shouldn't have tried to burn them up. One of them was the deputy Sheriff of Leadville, and the Sheriff's son, to boot."

Daniel felt as if someone had kicked him between the legs.

"Them fellers were none too happy. But they got sent back home early this morning, so you shouldn't have any more trouble from them, unless they find you over there in Leadville. That deputy had a nasty burn on his neck and face, I hear. I don't believe he knows who Harry is, so Harry's probably pretty safe for the time being. I doubt if anyone would tell on him, but you never know in this town anymore. There's a lot'a strange things happening around here these days, I've noticed."

"Like what, Joe?"

Kate entered wearing a heavy riding dress, a sheepskin jacket and a scarf around her throat. "Did Daniel tell you that we're going to win this race next week?" she asked. Joe nodded and winked at her.

Kate let the horse smell her thoroughly and wrapped her arms around Marigold's neck and squeezed. Marigold nuzzled Kate's hair and took some of it in her mouth playfully.

"She likes you." Joe looked on, approvingly. He had known Kate since she was a little girl, when she and her mother had first arrived in town. Camille Doray, had acquired some money, by devious means it was rumored, and had made a shrewd investment when she bought Big Shirley out of the business. She and Joe had remained friends for all of these years and he knew Kate well, and loved her like a daughter.

On the other hand, Rachelle was a problem. Joe had his suspicions of who the father was, but Shirley would never let on. She had done her best to keep the stigma of her daughters' paternity at bay with absolute discretion. But the cruel taunting of the other children, especially compared to the sympathy that they showed to Kate, had turned the child into a cauldron of anger and spite.

Joe went to the back of the stable to find the lengths of leather strap he would use for the harness. They were tangled, and he remembered that Harry had used them over Christmas so he could drag the Christmas trees into town. He hadn't seen the old sled since then. He paused wondering where it had gotten to.

Outside, he fitted the harness to the ring in the chest strap and watched as Kate mounted up and took the reins in her hands, just as he'd shown her. Daniel took the ends of the straps and turned to Joe.

"Is there any trick to this, Joe?"

"Just try not to fall down. And if you do, let go of the straps." He went inside and came back quickly. "Made you another glove, son. I hope it fits."

Daniel pulled it on and smiled at the feel of the new fur inside. "Thanks, Joe, it fits fine."

He took the leather straps in his hands. Joe showed him the best way to hold them, so that he could both control his direction and potentially the direction of the horse. It was the job of the rider to control the speed and the general direction of the horse, but by pulling on the straps in his hand, he could help steer the horse as it turned. It sounded simple enough.

"Keep the straps tight. You get into trouble if you get too much slack in them. If that happens, you slow down. Then, when the horse takes up the slack, you get pulled off your feet. Be careful of that." Daniel nodded and shortened the reins. "Alright Kate, take him out for a run, but try to bring him back alive."

When they returned, Daniel was looking the worse for the wear. Kate was beaming with accomplishment.

"Well, how did it go?" Joe asked as he helped Kate dismount.

"If he can keep standing, I think we've got a chance, Joe."

"Well, what do you think of the sport of ski jouring?"

"Like Kate says, if I can stay upright, I think I can do it. But I'm glad I don't have to do it every day."

Chapter 39

Red's place was a hive of activity, though it was still dark.
"Good morning, Daniel. Ready for your last trip?" Red was leading horses into their harnesses.

"What do you mean?" Daniel helped him with the tack.

"I talked to Jerome yesterday. He told me he was going to make you an offer you'd be foolish to refuse."

"He didn't mention talking to you?"

Red laughed. "I guess he wouldn't, it's not his style. Here, hand me that strap. What did you tell him?"

"About what?" Daniel played dumb.

"You're getting to be as bad as old Jerome himself," said Red. "What do you think of Abigail?"

Daniel held his hands out in front of him mimicking her endowments. Pete and the others came in from the corral with the rest of the Morgans in tow.

"You two gotta' be talkin' about Wheeler's daughter," Pete said.

"Well, she's pretty aggressive. I can tell you that," Red joked.

"Just like her mother," Daniel added.

"You should ask Carter about that sometime," Pete added with a wink.

"Why?" Daniel asked. Red shot Pete a cautionary look.

"Oh, nothing. I just thought that he was the one that Wheeler wanted to take over from him when he died."

"That's enough talk, boys." Red saw where the conversation might lead. "We've a long way to go and a whole lot of silver to deliver, so let's stop the gum bumpin' and get the wagons hitched up."

It was an uneventful journey. Daniel rode with Red on the wagon and for the most part they were silent. At the summit the weather was clear and cold. They turned the wagons around for the downward journey on the eastern side of the Pass. When all was secured, Red pulled Daniel aside.

"I'm going to have you stay in Twin Lakes this trip. You're a little too unpopular for me over there right now."

"OK, Red. I'll do whatever you want me to do," Daniel responded, relieved.

"I knew you'd understand. Pity Gloria's not there. You look like you could do with some of her kindnesses."

Daniel held up his hands in front of him, defensively. "No thanks. Not while she's still married to Frank."

"Yeah, I can understand that," Red said good-naturedly.

"You two fellers planning to come along with us, or should we just pick you up on the way back?" said Pete, who was driving the first wagon.

With a slap on the back, Red mounted the second wagon and Daniel took his place at the front, ready to guide the axles when the time came. They passed the first turn, but couldn't tell if the miners were blasting or not. After the last incident, Red had devised a plan to place a red cloth on the entrance of the mine whenever he was going down the road. So far, the system had worked. During their descent, Daniel had a chance to look at the avalanche that had nearly swept them to their end and was relieved that he saw no sign of their old sled, yet.

When they reached Twin Lakes in mid-afternoon, the Lodge appeared deserted. Its windows were shuttered and only a thin wisp of smoke rose from the chimney.

Red had concerns about Frank, but was confident that Daniel could fend for himself with the pistol they'd left with him should Frank cause him problems. He was satisfied that Daniel appeared to be settling in for a comfortable, if cold night in the bunkhouse as he waved them off on their way to Leadville.

Daniel made himself useful after they'd left, filling the cracks and loose chinking in the walls and around the doors that allowed the freezing outside air to steal his heat. He was about to start cooking his supper when there was a knock at the door. He pulled his hat down on his head to cover his face and opened the door.

It was Frank. His eyes were bloodshot and he now wore a full beard blotched with patches of gray. His face was drawn and pallid. The effect made his appearance nightmarish. More disconcerting was the fact that he was casually holding his rifle in the crook of his arm.

"Where's Red?" His breath was vile and his teeth brown and rotten with stains. The cadaverous effect made it difficult to be friendly or cordial to the man. All this over and above the fact that Daniel knew him to be a cold-blooded killer.

"You the only one here?"

"Yes." Daniel cleared his throat. "Is there something that you wanted?"

Frank swept the cabin with his eyes. "I wanted to warn you that there're a couple of wolves hanging about. I wouldn't go walking around outside tonight if I was you."

"Thanks for the warning." Smiling for all he was worth, Daniel closed the door and waited for what seemed like minutes before he heard Frank turn and leave.

The rough new bunkhouse had no windows, which worked in Daniel's favor, if he couldn't see out, Frank couldn't see in. It would get much colder when the sun set and he hoped that the cold would keep Frank indoors.

After cleaning the pot he filled it with water from the lake and boiled it on the potbellied stove. He added some salt pork, cut potatoes, onion, added a little pepper, and tried to relax. It was impossible. He paced around the small room and made himself eat, even though his stomach was too nervous to enjoy it. Still, it tasted fair enough and it was filling. Feeling replete and comfortable he started to doze but was startled awake by a blood-chilling howl.

He jumped up and looked outside. Nothing moved. Only thin starlight and the pale light that glowed in the windows in the Lodge illuminated the scene outside his door. All was quiet again. He put on his bearskin coat and pulled the fur hat that Joe had given him down low on his head then stepped quickly outside and ran to the Lodge, trying to stay in whatever shadows he could find.

He heard a sound behind him and nearly soiled himself. Frank's presence was everywhere and he had to convince himself that Frank was inside the Lodge, hopefully, drunk. The silence was unearthly. Moving carefully, he crept along the side of the Lodge, staying close to the wall. Stepping up onto a pile of cut firewood he peeked in the window of the Lodge.

Frank sat in a chair across from the fireplace, his rifle across his lap, a bottle in his hand. Daniel moved to get a better view but the log he was standing on shifted, rattling the logs beneath it. Abruptly, Frank looked up at the window just as Daniel ducked his head. He held his breath and peeked inside again. Frank remained in his chair. Daniel moved on.

The wolves' pen was enclosed by the wire fence, but the gate was open. He was only a short distance from the back door of the Lodge and in the glim light he could see animal tracks going into the pen and there was something, or someone huddled in the rear.

He took a cautious step into the pen and heard the soft crushing sound again, this time definitely closer, but still he could see nothing. Crouching down, he crept further into the pen surrounded by the pungent odor of dog shit and the distinct presence of something even more foul smelling.

The confinement of the small space pushed in on him from all sides but he crawled further inside. Then he saw something strange, like a log against the wall. His fingers traced it and he felt the folds of some material, not frozen, but pliant in his gloved hand. He sat on his haunches, took off his glove and pulled out a couple of large matches from his pocket. The chill of the night immediately made his fingers as cold as icicles. The first match broke. He tried another. The match flared and he immediately threw it at the thing he saw in the flash of light. He screamed and tried to turn in the confined space. He tried to stand but hit his head and yelped again, falling back onto the filthy floor of the pen. He pushed himself back from the horror he'd seen. Calming down, he reached out for the glove he'd dropped. It would be difficult to explain to Red that he'd lost it in the bunkhouse, and Frank would surely find it at some point.

He lit another match, to be certain of what he'd seen. As it flared again, he was struck not only with the feeling of horror, but with an overwhelming sense of sadness for Gloria, and hatred for Frank. In the dying light, he saw the damage Frank had wrought on this gentle and generous woman. Even in her frozen form, as disfigured as she was, there was a serenity about her corpse.

Suddenly he felt, rather than smelled, hot breath on his neck. Half expecting to find Frank with his rifle pointed at him, he turned around slowly, his mind working out reasons for him to be where he was.

He was trapped. There were two of them. Their gleaming yellow eyes seemed to catch the light and drain his courage. He remembered the stories about how Gloria had raised the wolves, and he had no doubt they were protecting her corpse.

His face was but a foot from theirs and their noses sniffed him intently. Watchful and silent, they curled their lips and bared their fangs. Daniel put on his glove. Still on his hands and knees, he summoned the courage to get out of the tiny space. He didn't want to end up sharing the pen with Gloria. He blew his breath at the dogs and pushed his head out. They backed away. He moved forward some more. They pointed their faces to the sky and together howled so loudly, it almost deafened him. He wanted to grab them to shut them up. They howled again, a long, mournful wail. Intuitively, he understood their anguish and felt like joining them. His fear had changed to the inconsolable keening of a lover's loss. He was, for just that moment, one with them.

The door at the back of the Lodge burst open casting a long shaft of yellow light across the snow between the pen and the back door, outlining the shapes of the wolves clearly.

"I see you bastards!" Frank yelled.

Daniel was only partly out of the pen and retreated back inside quickly. The rifle boomed, then boomed again. Something plucked at the snow next to his hand. He pulled back reflexively. The rifle boomed again and a hole appeared in the wall in front of his face, showering him with splinters. Daniel held his breath. Frank was walking towards the pen, his footsteps crunching the snow. Daniel knew he'd be caught inside, defenseless. He realized he had forgotten to strap on his pistol. His heart beat so loudly, he thought Frank would hear it. The rifle barked, then night found its silence once more.

The door to the Lodge was still open. The light from the kitchen found its way into the pen, casting a ghastly glow on Gloria's body. Though she was frozen solid, Daniel could see that the poor woman's body had been horribly abused and mutilated.

The wait seemed interminable, but eventually the footsteps receded and the door to the Lodge closed. After several minutes, Daniel crept out and hurried back to the bunkhouse, looking back over his shoulder as he ran. He quickly took off his coat and hat and brushed the snow off them. He tried to brush off his boots, but they had too much snow on them. He took them off, slid them under his bunk, and lay down. He looked towards the floor, noticing that he'd left a trail of snow from the door. He jumped up and was using his book to sweep away the snow, when he heard the crunch of approaching footsteps.

Throwing himself onto the bunk, he opened up his book as the door opened. Frank looked at him, his eyes bloodshot from drink, his rifle firmly clutched in his hand. He wore no coat but looked comfortable, even though the temperature was below zero. He was breathing heavily.

"What can I do for you?" Daniel tried to slow his own breathing, to slow his pounding heart.

Frank looked around the room as if to discover someone hiding. "There are timber wolves roaming about. They're hungry. Maybe you should stay inside."

"That's kind of you. I'll just stay right here and read my book." Daniel hoped he wasn't stammering, but he couldn't tell for sure.

"You been outside tonight?" Frank's eyes narrowed to slits for a fraction of a second and a cold shudder ran through Daniel.

"Just went outside to relieve myself is all."

"Did you hear any shots then?"

"I thought I heard something, but I was doing the dishes." Daniel looked quickly to the table and breathed a sigh of relief that dirty dishes weren't lying in the tub. Frank followed his eyes and he looked back at Daniel, as if considering a problem.

"I was just trying to kill them wolves," said Frank. He tipped the barrel of his rifle in some form of salute as he closed the door behind him.

Daniel relaxed, the sound of his lungs releasing air in a whisper. He looked down to see that the book, which he'd been "reading," was upside-down. "Shit."

Daniel turned down the lamp to almost complete darkness. He switched to the other set of bunks, making his bed on the top bunk. If Frank did return with criminal intent, he would attack the wrong bunk. Daniel would be able to shoot him from above. He placed one of his boots against the door, so he would hopefully hear it fall if someone tried to open the door. He climbed onto his bunk and placed his pistol under the thin pillow. Satisfied that he'd done the best he could, he lay on his bunk, fully intending to stay awake all night. The thought of Frank stalking around the pen in the night and finding his footprints, leading into and obviously running away from the scene, was enough to keep him awake, but the sizzling of the coal in the stove dragged at his eyelids.

He woke with a start, it was not quite dawn but the eastern sky was showing its surrender of the night. He was still alive, which he found a little surprising. Carefully and reluctantly, he opened the door and went outside to relieve himself.

It had snowed a little during the night. At his feet there were many small prints made by a large dog, or a wolf, or worse, two wolves. Noting that one set of prints circled the bunkhouse and approached from the other side, the wolves had been checking the perimeter; Daniel gained a greater appreciation of their cunning and cleverness.

Frank's tracks he studied more closely, but realized he could be seen from the Lodge. Casually, he looked over at the upstairs windows of the Lodge. He thought he saw one of the curtains move, and quickly went back inside.

He kept his gun belt on and free of his coat as he went about rounding up the Morgans and buckling them to their harnesses. Still, he found himself looking over his shoulder every few seconds, though he never caught sight of either the wolves or Frank.

Red arrived around the time that Daniel was certain that he was in the sights of Frank's rifle. The relief that he felt as Red drove the lead wagon into the corral must have been telling.

"Everything alright lad? You look kinda nervous."

"The wolves are around here. I saw tracks around the door and I heard them howling last night."

"You say there are wolves around? They must be Gloria's. Maybe Frank will shoot 'em."

"I heard him shooting at something last night."

"Something, or someone?" Red looked at Daniel with a raised eyebrow. "You go help the boys load up while I go over and see what Frank's up to." Red headed off towards the lodge.

Daniel went back to work, moving the boxes of money and sliding the important supplies, whiskey mainly, onto the other wagons. Several minutes later, Red was back.

"That's the most disagreeable son of a bitch I've never had the pleasure of meeting." Red said on his return. He put his hands on his hips squinting in the glare. "Aren't those Gloria's wolves out there on the lake?"

Indeed the wolves were out on the frozen lake, their gray coats in contrast to the brilliant white of the snow. They were loping away, occasionally looking behind them at the wagons moving along the shoreline. Daniel vividly remembered their sharp teeth and low growls. The skin on the back of his neck crawled at the thought.

Daniel rode with Red, taking the reins for the climb up to the summit while Red sat silently for most of the trip.

"Have you thought any more about working for Wheeler?" The question surprised Daniel. Red caught his eye. "I'm not firing you. As a matter of fact, all the men seem to like and respect you, and that's unusual with this bunch." Red abruptly pointed below them. "Is that a sled down there?" He stood up in the wagon and shaded his eyes, peering down into the rubble left by the avalanche. Red sat back down. "Oh, well. I guess it'll just have to wait for the spring."

Daniel shifted in his seat cringing, wondering if the pieces of bent wood were the remains of the sled he and Harry had pushed over the side of the road.

"Look, I'm not telling you anything you don't know already, but that Sheriff's got a hard-on for you. Not for nothing, but I think it's best that you don't risk getting into his clutches and especially that you don't end up in that jail of his."

Daniel was silent. He really liked working for Red, even though it was cold and dangerous, but the benefits of staying away from Frank and the Sheriff couldn't be denied.

"Come on son, this isn't such a difficult decision to make, is it?" Red slapped him on the shoulder and Daniel brightened and smiled.

"Red, do you think it's the right thing to do? I mean work for Wheeler?"

"There's probably a hundred young fellers in Aspen who would give their right testicle for the opportunity he's offered you. Mind you now; he'll work you hard, but in the long run you'll come out on top. I guarantee it." Red was as paternal as he could be.

"You're right, Red. I don't think I should come this way again. But, I don't want to leave you and Pete shorthanded, so I won't go unless you're going to be alright."

"That's not your worry, son. We'll be alright. I just want you to watch out for yourself and that beautiful young woman that's got her eyes set on you."

"Who's that?".

"Kate. You idiot." Red laughed out loud.

⊰⊱

They got back to town in the early evening. Daniel was brushing Marigold when Joe emerged from his cell in the back. Harry's horse wasn't in the stall.

"How was the trip?"

"Pretty good, I guess. For my last trip."

Joe thought for a moment. "I think that's a wise decision, son. What did Red say when you told him?"

"Red suggested it. Where's Harry's horse?"

"Someone came by and took it."

Daniel stopped brushing. "He let someone borrow his horse?"

"Well, he didn't actually borrow it. He said he'd won it in a poker game."

Daniel finished brushing Marigold and quickly gathered his gear and saddlebags.

"By the way, Honey's looking for you," Joe said as Daniel reached the door.

"What does she want?"

"Impossible to tell but, I'd watch myself if I was you. That there's a wild mare, if you know what I mean."

"I'll see you later, Joe."

Daniel waved thanks and headed for home. By the time he made it to the door, he was sweating with fear. The cabin was dark and cold when he arrived, the stove had faint warmth to it. Harry must have been gone since yesterday. The miners would be very pissed off.

He tried to pull the log into the fire with the come-along chain, but it wouldn't budge. When he investigated, he found to his dismay that the eyebolt had been moved. It was now positioned where they had lifted the oven to hide the money underneath. His heart sank; someone had swept around the base of the oven.

Daniel gathered himself and repositioned the eyebolt. Then, when it was in the correct position, he hauled on the chain, pulling the log into the hearth to keep the fire going. It wouldn't do for people to see they were out of business. In addition it was imperative that he foil any chance that Harry could get at the money. He was as sure as ever that the money under the floor was their Achilles' heel.

When the fire was hot enough, he filled the oven with potatoes, hoping they'd be done by the time it came to sell them. He was determined to cover Harry's tracks. It would keep the illusion going that they were still partners.

Daniel busied himself unpacking his gear. He put the coffee pot on the fire and was delighted to find that there was still half a bottle of whiskey under the sink. Soon he felt fortified again and was preparing to take the potatoes out of the oven when there was a knock at the door.

Honey didn't wait to be invited inside; she pushed past him and turned on him as if continuing a previous conversation.

"Why haven't you been over to see me?" Her cheeks were flushed.

"I was over the Pass with Red. Why, did I say I was coming over?"

"No. But I thought that you'd found someone else." She came to him and pulled him to her with the fearsome strength of a drowning man.

Before he knew it, he was kissing her deeply. She responded ferociously and they found themselves bundled together, falling onto Harry's bed. Fighting with is belt buckle and unable to open his pants, she rode him wildly, her hips thrusting back and forth until she squealed in pleasure. Abruptly, at the height of her climax, she jumped up, pulling her dress back about her. Daniel was stunned.

"No! Not here. I can't. Not here!" She ran to the door and looked back at him, her face full of smiling tears. "It's not you, Daniel. I have to go. I'll see you after the race tomorrow. Good luck."

With that she was gone, leaving him dazed and confused, the sound of the slamming door ringing in his ears.

Chapter 40

Daniel was awakened by Harry humming a tune and pushing the frying pan around the stove. When he got out of bed to investigate, he saw pancakes stacked high on a tin plate and a dozen eggs cooking.

"What happened to your horse, Harry?"

"I tricked some yokel into taking it off my hands." He continued stirring the eggs.

"Why are you cooking so many eggs and pancakes?"

"It's for your big race today. You do remember the races?" Harry mocked him.

"Of course I do. But what's all this for?" Daniel was incredulous.

"You need plenty of energy if you're going to win," Harry said.

Daniel reached for the whiskey to add to his coffee. Harry pulled it from his reach.

"Not until you win the races, son. I'm just looking out for you. You need to be sober today."

After pushing a third plate on him, and satisfied that Daniel could eat no more, Harry set about readying his skis. He inspected them in detail, ensuring that the leather straps were sound and weren't going to let loose prematurely.

Harry rubbed a piece of candle wax over the bottom of the skis.

"What are you doing now?"

"This is my secret. You can walk uphill and not slip backwards and then when you want to come down, you just scrape it off with your knife, like this." Daniel watched as Harry carefully scraped the wax off the bottom of the ski, using the flat backside of his knife.

"No one does this anymore, you see. It's going to be our little secret." Harry winked at Daniel conspiratorially. They headed out for the hill. As they were leaving, they heard a voice from above calling to Daniel.

"Good luck, Daniel, but my money's on Leafy Lane today." It was Willy Tomb, sitting on the toilet with the door open to the world, as usual.

"Thanks, Willy." Daniel waved as they headed down the path. "What was that about, Harry?" Harry pointedly ignored the question.

"Here, let me help you with those." Harry took the long skis and hoisted them over his shoulder, marching in step with Daniel. "You need to keep fresh."

They arrived at the base of the hill to find a crowd assembled and a festive mood all around. People were chatting merrily, patting competitors on the back. Even the competitors were wishing each other good luck. Harry was in deep conversation with several men when there came a booming voice.

"I have an announcement to make," yelled the owner of the Mother Lode through a bullhorn. He was standing on a wagon dressed as a ringmaster of a circus, top hat and tails. "Welcome, one and all to our Mid-Winter Festival. All those who would be competitors, please get ready to head up the hill to the start area. Now for the rules." A groan rose from the crowd, then laughter. "The race will begin when you hear the noon whistle and not a second before. We have judges this year."

More laughter rose from the assemblage. "When you boys hear that whistle, you ski down as fast as you can. The first one down here to touch this wagon I'm standing on gets this one hundred dollars." He held up a bundle of paper money and waved it at them. "So off you go gentlemen, and good luck." He raised his voice, remembering a point he'd missed. "There's one more thing to tell you all," he cast a finger about the crowd, "there's to be no betting on this race."

"I'm taking wagers over here." Harry yelled out loudly. Laughter erupted from the crowd. Everyone near was pushing money into Harry's hands. Harry was writing down bets as fast as he could scratch numbers on paper.

"Harry, you aren't betting on me, are you?"

"Wouldn't do that Daniel, it wouldn't be prudent. You're not the fastest skier here."

Daniel watched, surprised that Harry could manage the money flowing through his hands and write down the bets so quickly.

"Who's going to win, then?"

"Oh, one of the Swedes," Harry said in a whisper. "I don't know which one; we haven't figured that out yet."

"What do you mean?"

Harry pushed one of his gloved hands over Daniel's mouth none too gently and shushed him to silence, looking over his shoulder as he did so. "Remember I told you that the Swedes and I had business in the past?"

Daniel nodded, people were looking at them.

"Well, this is the business. Now you, on the other hand," Daniel was still trying to understand. "All you have to do is beat Leafy in both of the races."

"I don't understand." Daniel felt like a dolt.

"Just do as I say and everything will be OK. Do you hear me?"

Someone wrapped a strong arm around his waist, lifting him completely off the snow. When he was finally released, he saw the great smiling faces of Bjorn and Tomas. He'd never seen so many white teeth.

"So you're here to vin ze race, my friend?" Bjorn playfully punched Daniel on the left shoulder, possibly dislocating the arm from the socket.

"Harry sure wants me to." They winked and nodded at Harry.

"Hey, ve must be very good teachers if he does this, eh, Tomas?" Daniel stood and rubbed his shoulder. "Come vis us den."

With Daniel in tow, they headed up the road.

"Daniel, wait." Kate was walking towards them. Both she and her mother were dressed in similar fashion. Kate handed him a handkerchief tied with a red ribbon, it smelled of lilacs.

"I brought this for you, for good luck." She tucked it inside his scarf and pushed it down into his collar further than was necessary. He felt invincible.

"Good luck young man," Joe said, appearing from the crowd and slapping him on the shoulder. "Watch out for the last turn," Joe whispered to him and left to stand with Shirley, who blew him a kiss.

Leafy was walking up ahead of them. Daniel hadn't spoken to him since the trip to Leadville.

The Swedes passed Leafy, their measured, relentless strides enough to humble the fittest man in town. Though his heart was pounding in his chest, Daniel caught up to Leafy.

"Hi there, Leafy."

"Hi," was all Leafy said. Daniel pushed on ahead.

There were more than twenty contestants climbing the hill, puffing and panting with the exertion of every step. When he finally reached the top, Daniel fell on the snow gasping for air. He was surprised to see that the Swedes had taken off their skis and were scraping the bottoms with their knives, just as Harry had done.

"Daniel, you had better do vhat ve are doing. If I know Harry, zen he put on candle vax and dat von't vork. Here, give me your skis." Tomas took the skis and shook his head. "Look, Bjorn, Harry nearly ruined your old skis."

"It looks like he vants you to go slow." Bjorn laughed.

"Why would he want to do that?"

The Swedes just shook their heads. Daniel sighed. The day was getting longer and longer and it wasn't even noon.

They took out a candle and lit it using just one match. It would have taken Daniel twenty. He watched as they heated the blades of their knives over the candle that they hooded with their coats. They scraped his skis clean of Harry's wax then took out a piece of bear pelt.

"Dis here is de secret to skiing fast," Bjorn showed him the fat on the skin.

"Vatch Daniel." They heated the skin over the candle and rubbed it along the bottoms of the skis rapidly, smoothing the surface to a satiny shine. They held the skis at arm's length and smiled approval to each other. Satisfied, they gave them back to Daniel.

"Bear grease, now zey are fast. But you have to keep zem moving on the snow until ze race starts. Zey will freeze to the snow if you don't keep dem moving like zis." The brothers slid their skis back and forth like they were running in place. Daniel did the same.

Finally, all of the contestants were at the top of the slope, anxiously waiting for the noon whistle to signal the start of the race. The town was laid out beneath his feet. When he stood on the edge of the road overlooking the town, he could see it between the fronts of his skis.

Without warning, Tomas and Bjorn started off down the hill. An instant later, the rest of the racers pushed over the edge and followed them. An instant later Daniel heard the whistle. Everyone had been watching for the steam from the whistles, everyone but him.

Things began to go wrong immediately. Daniel's speed was increasing at an alarming rate. He had absolutely no control; he was going way too fast for that. Two racers cartwheeled off to his left and those on his right were rapidly forming a cluster of speeding madmen, veering in front of him.

The first road he had to cross came at him at impressive speed. He tried his best to absorb the four-foot drop, and felt his knees come up about his ears, then his legs were extended out in front of him. Time seemed to slow to a creeping procession of thoughts and pictures of various possible deaths. He flailed the air with his arms to keep his balance and managed to get his legs back beneath him an instant before he landed on the snow again. To his amazement, he'd cleared the road and was still upright on his skis, a complete surprise to him and apparently to the spectators because he heard their screams and laughter as he sped past.

He was gaining on the main group quickly. He heard the roar from the crowd at the bottom of the hill as they caught their first glimpse of the melee as it came over the rise, speeding towards the finish.

The pack hurtled on, shedding unfortunates as it went, and Daniel was becoming quite proficient at dodging the fallen warriors. They went into the last dip in the terrain before cresting the final knoll.

Without intending to, he found himself in the middle of the pack. The leaders were slowing down and he was speeding up, and for a fleeting moment he thought he might win the race. Ahead of him, the Swedes were leading the pack with Leafy right behind them, crouching down to gain speed. Only yards separated them and he was gaining on them rapidly.

He was coming equal with Leafy and when he turned his head to look his eyes widened when he saw who was passing him. Leafy emphatically pointed at something ahead of them, and then stood up to slow down, as did the others.

The Swedes were in the lead and made a sharp left turn. The pack followed, but Daniel was going too fast and continued hurtling straight down the hill. At the last second, he saw the road coming up at him and realized why the others had turned away from it. It looked like a cliff to Daniel.

He hit the road hard and a whoosh of air escaped his lungs as he was bounced into the air, his legs extended high over his head, twisting. The people in the crowd appeared upside-down. He was beginning to enjoy the odd sensation when both gravity and the ground came up to meet him.

The fall seemed to go on and on as he spun like a runaway wheel into the crowd. His back took the brunt of the fall, his lungs collapsed and his breath exhaled in a rush. Vaguely, he remembered hearing the crowd screaming and felt people falling around him as he and his skis scythed through the spectators.

The sunlight dazzled him when he regained consciousness and he vaguely remembered many hands helping him to his feet.

"You're alright aren't you, pardner?" Harry was his affable but unconcerned self.

"Did I win?"

"No. You missed the finish line by a mile," Harry smiled broadly, "but you were fast. You scared me half to death. You nearly beat Leafy. I almost lost money."

"I thought that you wanted me to win, Harry. Why did you bet against me?"

Kate pushed through the crowd, concern creasing her pretty brow. "I saw you fall. Are you alright?"

Daniel nodded to reassure her. Joe and Shirley appeared, looking concerned. Joe pointed down and Daniel immediately saw what he was looking at. The front third of his ski was broken.

"I guess that takes care of the jouring race, then." Daniel's disappointment was only partly sincere. Harry looked crestfallen, his shoulders slumped in disappointment. The crowd around him dissipated and some patted him on the back in encouragement as they left. Bjorn and Tomas appeared with several young women linked arm in arm with them.

"Hey, Daniel, vhat happened to you?"

He pointed down at his broken ski.

"Your ski don't look so good."

"I didn't see the road coming."

"Don't feel too bad about it. Everyone makes that mistake once. Even Tomas here couldn't turn in time von year and he had a fall. Didn't you, little bruzzer?" Tomas smiled and punched Bjorn hard on his shoulder.

"Vhat can ve do about his skis?"

"Ve still have von hour to fix it."

"Can it be fixed?" asked Daniel.

"Maybe," Bjorn sounded doubtful.

"I'm sorry I broke your ski, Bjorn."

"Hey, dese t'ings happen vhen you race."

Daniel felt a hand on his shoulder, it was Joe. "Come on over to my place and we'll see what we can do for you," Joe said and led the way off the hill.

"We did pretty good this morning," Harry said to Daniel. "I got a hundred bucks at least. Are you going to be able to race this afternoon?" Harry tried to put his arm around Daniel's shoulder. "You're not still mad that I bet on you to lose, are you?"

"Yeah, Harry, I guess I am."

"Alright, I can see you're angry with me, but I did it for us, you know?" Harry hurried on.

Kate put her arm through Daniel's, and with Bjorn and Tomas urging him forward, he found himself falling in behind Joe, one painful step after the other.

"Who won the race?" Daniel asked.

"Hey, you won't believe it. Tomas won," said Harry. "Congratulations, Tomas." Harry passed Tomas a wad of money.

"It vas his turn, I von it last year," said Bjorn.

"But, your friend Leafy? He nearly beat my bruzzer." Tomas was laughing. "Bjorn, I t'ink you're getting too old to race, hey?" Tomas slapped his older brother on the back, good-naturedly. "Now ve help our friend to beat dis Leafy Lane."

⚔

Joe's stable was warm. The smell of the horses was a fond and familiar odor to Kate. She stroked Marigold's flanks and scratched her long nose. Marigold flared her nostrils and smelled Kate's hair, then dropped her head and nuzzled her, almost pushing her off her feet.

"What do you think?" Daniel looked over Tomas's shoulder.

"I'm sorry, Daniel, but dis ski is finished. I never vould've sought dat such a skinny boy could break von of my skis." He took the tip of the ski and pulled it back. It snapped off.

"Maybe you can use these old things." Joe held a pair of skis that had seen better days. They were small and dirty and looked like relics from an age gone by.

"Zey are too short," laughed Bjorn. "Dees look like little girl's skis."

"They are. I made them for Kate when she was a youngster." Joe took the skis and held them in his hand, appreciating the feel.

"But zey are not real skis. Zey must be long like ours, eh Tomas?"

"Maybe? Maybe not," said Tomas. "Zey vould be gut for turning corners I'm t'inkin'."

"Ja. Ja. You could be right, little bruzzer."

The skis were snatched out of Joe's hands and the brothers went about ripping off the old bindings and fitting new leather straps to them.

"There are six other teams in the race," Harry announced as he entered the barn. They all ignored him. "People are betting on Leafy to win."

"Who did you bet on?" Daniel asked.

"No one!" Harry said, and turned on his heels and walked out. Daniel appeared stunned.

"Daniel, look here." Joe called to him.

When Daniel turned, he saw they were all looking at him.

Joe spoke gently to him. "Son, that's just how he is." Joe held his hands in front of him, palms upturned in frustration. "He's always been that way and he most probably always will be that way. There's nothing you can do about it. No problem."

Daniel walked off, slamming the door. Kate followed and found him leaning on a rail, watching the horses. She stood quietly and placed her hand gently on his arm.

"Really, Daniel, Joe's right. I've known Harry most of my life and he's always been a selfish person. I don't know why you consider him such a good friend, anyway. All he ever does is talk down to you."

"You don't know him like I do. He's got a lot on his mind right now. He's my partner and my friend. Don't talk like that about him." Daniel turned away petulantly.

"I'm sorry, Daniel," Kate said sincerely. "I just think that you trust him too much."

"It's too late. I have to trust him now," Daniel said.

Bjorn held the door open for them to come inside. "Hey, come see vhat ve have done to your new skis."

The skis had been cleaned and the leather shone new and strong. They had also used their knives to sharpen the side edges. It was hard to recognize them as the ones Joe had resurrected. Joe took Daniel's old bearskin coat and held the inside skin to the hot steel of the stove. It hissed and smoked; the smell was putrid. He took the coat and rubbed the seared membrane along the bottom of the skis.

"This is pure bear fat, son," Joe said. "It's slicker'n dog snot on a brass doorknob." He handed the skis to Tomas, who rubbed the base furiously until he was pleased with the results. When both skis were done, Joe and Tomas ceremoniously handed them to Daniel. "Now let's see about this horse of yours, shall we?" Joe checked the chest and belly straps and gave the saddle a solid yank.

"Jump up on her, Kate." Joe boosted her into the saddle as he'd done hundreds of times before.

"Now son, I want you to listen to me." Joe ensured he had Daniel's full attention. "You gotta hold on tight to the reins. Remember that."

He slapped Marigold on the rump. Marigold leaped a step or two and nearly dragged Daniel off his feet. His wrist still hurt and he winced as searing pain shot up his arm.

His first impression was that the skis were bad. They kept skidding out from under him and it was very difficult to keep them pointed straight.

Kate slowed down and turned them back towards the barn.

"How are they?" Kate asked.

"I don't know yet. They're very slippery."

"Good." She lightly spurred Marigold and for the first time, Daniel noticed that she was wearing spurs. The acceleration was amazing. His eyes teared and his hat flew back on his head, only the strings under his chin kept it on. They passed the stable at a full gallop with Joe, Bjorn, and Tomas cheering and clapping from the fence.

When Kate pulled Marigold up, Daniel couldn't stop and ran into Marigold's rear end. Smiling all the while, she dragged him back to the barn.

Joe met them at the gate. "Well, what do you think, son? Think them skis are fast enough?"

"Can they be too fast?" he asked.

"Hey, not if you vant to vin a race zey are not," Bjorn said, slapping him hard on the back.

⚞⚟

Aspen was alive. There were hundreds of people lining the sidewalks throughout the town. The bars were filled to overflowing and children ran about, chasing each other in the streets which were clear of all traffic.

Daniel was surprised by the size of the crowds lining the streets.

"Why are there so many people down here?" he asked Joe.

"They're here to watch us win the race," Kate said.

"You mean we ride through the town?"

"We're going to race down to the Hotel Jerome along Main Street, then we have to make that corner there," Kate pointed towards the

Court House, "and come up here and head down Hyman Street, past the Paragon. Then we go past the Opera House, past the Mother Lode, around the Palace and back onto Main Street, past the Hotel again and that's the finish line. Almost a mile I guess, maybe shorter." Kate smiled her beautiful smile.

It was a happy, if slightly drunken crowd that greeted Jerome Wheeler and the ringmaster when they appeared on the balcony of the Hotel. He waited patiently till the heckling faded, dodging snowballs thrown in their general direction. Mrs. Wheeler and Abigail appeared on the balcony and the crowd quieted respectfully.

"Alright, everybody. Happy Winterskol!"

A cheer rose from the crowd.

"Now, who's racing today? Come up here in front and face the crowd."

They joined the group of other competitors. Daniel noted that all the riders were men.

"You'll all go down to Fourth Street and when my lovely wife fires this pistol, you all ride up past the Hotel here." There was a cheer from the crowd. "Then you go up Galena Street, past the Paragon, turn down Hyman Street, turn at the Palace and back here to the Hotel. The first one past here the second time wins the money." There was another cheer from the crowd. "Off you go and may the best team win."

Daniel remarked on the bales of hay that had been set out in a haphazard manner along the length of Main Street.

Joe laughed. "Oh, they're just there to make it interesting for the spectators. I advise you to avoid hitting them if you can." He tapped Kate on the leg. "Think you can miss the hay bales, dear?"

"No problem, Joe," she answered, laughing.

Daniel considered the course in front of them. Even if Leafy was not in the race, it still left five teams remaining and that was going to make it very dangerous if they all reached the first corner at the same time. Bjorn and Tomas gave him a pat on the back.

"Try to cut ze corners close," Tomas said and winked.

Daniel nodded.

Shirley came over to Kate and patted her daughter's hand, trying not to look worried. She looked beautiful and excited sitting atop Marigold. "Please be careful and don't hurt yourselves. I know you'll win." She leaned forward and kissed Daniel.

Daniel and Kate waved farewell to their little band of supporters as they rode the six blocks up the gradual incline of Main Street. They were almost at the starting point when they heard the sound of a running horse coming from behind them.

Rachelle reined up Leafy's horse as they came nearer and Daniel saw that it was Leafy on the skis.

"Congratulations on your race this morning." Daniel offered.

"Thanks, but I didn't win." Leafy smiled back.

"But you nearly did. Bjorn told me." Daniel felt relieved that they were at least talking.

"Still think you're goin' to win now?" Rachelle said harshly to Kate.

Kate smiled. "You like Daniel, don't you?"

"Why not?" Rachelle snapped back. "You've already got Leafy, haven't you?"

"I don't want Leafy." Kate shot back at her sister.

"I don't want him either," Rachelle said too loudly.

Leafy turned around, glaring at them.

"Racers. Get ready." The starter called, looking at his watch.

Kate and Rachelle pulled their horses next to each other. Kate leaned over and appeared to be whispering to Rachelle. Daniel and Leafy saw them shake hands. He skied up alongside Kate.

"What was that all about?" he asked.

"Oh, nothing, just a small wager."

"What did you bet?"

"I can't tell you until the finish. But I can tell you this," Kate looked down at him seriously, her smile now a frown, "I hope that you're better at this race than the one this morning, or you might not like the result."

"What do you mean?" They heard the report of the pistol fired from the Hotel. Daniel was nearly pulled off his feet when Kate used her spurs. Marigold dashed forward and took up the slack in the reins. He righted himself as they hurtled down Main Street amid a crowd of

galloping horses that kicked up blinding clumps of snow. Men of varying abilities jostled each other for position.

The horses and skiers were side by side when they came to the first
of the obstacles. They split, some going left, the others, right. Daniel
could see almost nothing ahead of them and almost ran into the first
of the hay bales.

He'd lost sight of Leafy but had no doubt he was ahead of them,
since Kate was at the back of their pack. They passed another of the
bales and this one caught one of the cowboys, ripping his ski out from
under him and sending him to the ground, hard. His rider pulled up to
help his fallen comrade. There were five teams remaining.

The hay bales were more numerous now and the horses in the lead
bumped each other to pass through the breaks. Another fallen skier
flashed past Daniel as they flew down the street. Now they were four.

He clearly heard the cheers of the crowd as they passed the Hotel
and headed into the first right hand turn. So far, the skis were working as expected and Marigold was running with little effort, being well
conditioned from her trips over the Pass.

He remembered his lesson from Tomas; 'go for the inside of the
corner', the corner was coming up quickly.

The result was another near catastrophe. He had turned his skis
before Kate had turned her horse and though the intention had merit,
laws of physics were nearly his undoing. Kate had Marigold heading to
the inside of the corner too, and he was catching up fast.

"Kate! Kate!" Daniel yelled.

Kate turned her head quickly and saw that Daniel had taken the
shorter line into the corner and was right up next to her. But Kate was
a skilled rider and guided Marigold into the turn with confidence,
yelling at the crowd to get out of their way. Daniel bounced off several
unwary spectators, ricocheting between his victims and the other competitors, but somehow managing to keep on his feet. When he opened
his eyes, there were only two teams ahead of them.

Emboldened, he maneuvered his skis to the left and to the outside
of the next corner, using the same technique as before and aiming for
the inside of the turn. This time he had much more room and took

a wider turn, trying not to be drawn to the outside like the others. He accelerated as he crossed astern of his horse and bumped into the horse coming up the inside. He risked a look up at the rider and saw Rachelle, lips drawn tight, her teeth clenched, trying to ride her mount into him. Her horse missed stepping on his skis by a miracle.

He felt the pull of the reins and more pain shot up his arm. Rachelle bumped Kate as she passed them. Marigold slipped, but held on. Again they shot forward. They were now neck and neck with one of the miners' teams, and Rachelle was closing in on the cowboys in front of them. They passed The Paragon and Daniel got a glimpse of the bare-breasted girls at the windows, cheering them on.

The thrill of the excitement of the race coursed through his body and a mysterious calm descended over him. Everything seemed to be going by more slowly now. He could see the rhythmic precision of the horse's hooves as they ran, and the precise amount that he and Kate were gaining on the leader.

He swung wide and looked around Marigold and the horses they were following into the turn. Fortunately, the spectators there had the good sense to step back. He intended to take the inside line, but as he began making his turn towards the corner, the horse in front moved to its left and into their path, causing Kate to slow down. It was luck and good horsemanship that saved them.

When the cowboys in front swung wide, Kate spurred Marigold into the corner and shot forward. The cowboy looked at Kate as she passed, disbelief written across his face. Daniel was bounced to the left and got his skis tangled under the hooves of the cowboy's horse. His ski was pulled out from under him and he almost fell as the horse lost its footing. In a panic, he turned to his right and closed his eyes once more. Amid a clatter and a great deal of screaming, he looked back to see that the horse had fallen and was skidding on its side across the snow, carrying its rider and skier with it into the crowd of spectators.

Leafy and Rachelle were just ahead of them. They had almost caught the cowboys who were in the lead. Kate was riding smoothly and intelligently, fast, but controlling her speed. All three teams were now racing at a full gallop, heading into the last turn onto Main Street. They were catching up to the leaders as they slowed down for the corner. He felt Kate slow Marigold slightly, then a little more. To his left, Leafy and the cowboy were bumping each other and though the cowboy was beefy and strong, Leafy was the better skier and had much more control. They were locked in a duel and were drifting to the left side of the road, preparing for the last big turn back onto Main Street. Suddenly Daniel realized what Kate was doing.

She was slowly pushing the two teams over to the left as she came up on the inside. Because they were slowing for the corner, the skiers were getting in each other's way. She nudged Marigold lightly with her spurs, so that the others could see her on the inside of them, taking the shorter line. A second later, Kate pulled back on the reins, pulling Marigold's head up and to the right. They had all come level with the corner house, starting into the final turn.

Rachelle and the cowboy's horse were locked together, trying to make the turn at the corner and their skiers were becoming entangled. Kate saw the finish line directly ahead of them and Marigold saw Joe standing in the middle of the road, waving an enormous bunch of carrots. Marigold found a youthful burst of speed and flew across the finish line to loud cheers from the crowd.

They were immediately enveloped by the crowd. So dense, even the Swedes had a hard time pushing through, dragging No Problem Joe with them. Kate looked around for Rachelle and Leafy but they appeared to be amongst the tangle of horses and skiers a block away by the drug store.

The ringmaster took Marigold's reins and led them back to the front of the Hotel, where Wheeler and his family awaited them. "Congratulations to you two, for the wonderful race you just won." There rose a great cheer and round of applause from the crowd.

Daniel helped Kate down from her horse. They held hands as they watched Wheeler, ever the showman, take out a large envelope from his vest pocket and wave it in the air.

"Here you are," he announced. "One hundred dollars! And a, 'Well Done!' from all of us. Isn't that right, folks?" The crowd cheered again.

He shook Kate's hand, then shook Daniel's, holding onto it fervently, pride showing all over his florid face. Wheeler handed them the envelope and together they held it high above their heads, so the crowd could see. Another round of applause came from the crowd milling around them.

Slowly the excitement died down. The crowd dissolved and either went about their business or filed back into the Jerome Bar to drink and to settle bets.

Flushed with excitement, Kate threw her arms around Daniel and jumped up and down. "This is the first anything I've won, ever."

Daniel was oblivious to other eyes on them. "It's the first thing I've ever won, too."

Their affections for each other swelled in the moment of triumph. Without thinking about the propriety of her actions, Kate grabbed the back of Daniel's head and pulled him to her. When their mouths reached each other's, a flash went off. They pulled apart, laughing at the surprise of having had their picture taken.

Someone tapped Daniel on the shoulder and he broke from their embrace, reluctantly drawing his eyes away from Kate. He caught sight of the Wheelers, watching them from the front steps of the Hotel. They wore a mixture of expressions: Jerome proud, his wife smug, and Abigail with tears in her eyes. Daniel saw her brush them away.

Still holding Kate's hand, he turned and was surprised to see Honey close behind him. She looked at him with the fire of her anger boiling in her eyes. She wound up with her hand behind her back and slapped him across his face so hard, it sounded like a gunshot.

"What was that for?" Daniel screamed with the same plaintive whimper of millions of men before him.

"I told you I didn't want you seeing this bitch again." She pointed at Kate.

Joe and the Swedes and even Red and Harry were near them, but none of them made a move to help him.

Shirley took Kate in her arms protectively.

"I can see anyone I want to, Honey," Daniel said.

Honey made a dash at him, arm cocked to hit again. One of the Swedes stepped in and steered her away.

She looked back with an expression of unveiled malevolence. "You heard me Daniel. I mean it!"

He turned back to Kate, shocked and stunned.

Kate threw the prize money at his feet, turned and walked away. Only Shirley cast a backward glance as they went, disappointment clearly written on her face.

Daniel began to tremble. He felt Red's hand on his shoulder and looked up at him uncomprehending. He felt his face flush in embarrassment.

He felt another tap on his shoulder and flinched reflexively. He turned to see Rachelle looking at him, just as mean as Honey. Leafy had hold of the reins of his horse, and he wasn't smiling either. The slap from Rachelle across Daniel's other cheek snapped his head around. He held his hand to his cheek, a look of pure astonishment on his face.

"What was that for?"

Rachelle planted her hands on her hips, defiantly sneering at him. There was a mounting feeling of discomfort in both himself and the crowd watching the incident. "That's for cutting us off," she yelled.

Leafy was shocked by Rachelle's outburst. He reached out his hand and Daniel took it gratefully. "Congratulations, Daniel." Leafy said. "You won fair and square." Rachelle stormed off through the crowd.

"I think this calls for a drink, don't you Red?" Harry said, smiling broadly, enjoying the free entertainment. "It's not every day you get slapped by two women and neither one of them are your wives."

"Here, here," said Red. "Harry should know all about that, shouldn't he, boys?" Joe and the Swedes joined Red and Harry in pushing Daniel into the Jerome Bar, where he was greeted by a loud round of cheers. Harry took the envelope from Daniel's hand, holding it up for the crowd to see.

"Drinks are on us, boys." He flourished the envelope.

Daniel snatched it from him. "Not with our winnings, Harry. You can buy the round if you want to, but this here, this belongs to Kate and me. By the way, I hope you didn't bet against me again."

"Not a chance. I told you I wouldn't do that, didn't I?" Harry reached into his pocket and pulled out a thick wad of bills. "This time, I bet on you to win and got six to one odds." He threw his arms around Daniel, hugging him tightly. "You were magnificent."

Someone reached through the crowd and handed Harry money.

"Thank you," he said, winking at the man.

The crowd was patting Daniel on the back from every direction. He began to feel the pressure all around him, surrounding him, pushing his emotions to the surface. Hot tears formed behind his eyes and he looked up at the ceiling to stem the flood. The lights, the noise, the crowd, the not knowing what Harry was up to, the loss of the woman he loved, and the crazy one, Honey, who started it all. It was getting to be too much for his brain to handle.

His vision hazed with his tears as he pushed his way through the crowd and into the large foyer of the Hotel. Exhausted, he fell into one of the plush red velvet couches. He tenderly ran his hand over the smooth carved arms of the couch.

He felt the presence of someone sitting next to him, someone warm, a presence that radiated into him. He snuffled back some of his tears and gathered strength. Joe would know what it was that he was feeling and what he should do.

But Abigail was sitting there, leaning forward, her elbows resting on her knees, looking into the fire. As Daniel watched, she seemed to transform into a painting. About her, the room was lit by the sunlight coming through the leaded glass doors and windows. The chandeliers and the beveled edges of the glass panes cast broken ribbons of spectral lights throughout the room. One of them happened to be lying across her forehead and her hair.

She said nothing. He was about to break the silence, but she lifted her finger and he was stilled as if turned to stone. She turned to face him and it was obvious she also had been crying.

"Congratulations," she said softly, the only emotion the slight quivering of her top lip. She truly was a beautiful woman in this light. A booming voice from behind broke their moment of communion.

"Are you coming, Abigail?" Jerome called, from the door to the dining room. She dabbed at her eyes and stood, sniffing back her tears. She held out her hand and Daniel rose and took it gently, tenderly. She looked down to collect herself, ready to say something of emotional weight, but then seemed to change her mind.

"Congratulations, Daniel, I wish you the best of everything." She affected her bravest smile, "be good to her."

She turned and walked with grace over to her father. Jerome waved to Daniel; he returned his wave and sat back down on the couch. He'd only started to fathom Abigail's last remark when Joe sat heavily into the couch, holding out two glasses of whiskey.

Daniel took one and downed it in one gulp, wincing as he swallowed the burning liquid. "Why're women so much trouble, Joe?"

"Rats, son," was all Joe said.

"Rats?"

"Yes. I'm sorry to say that all them ladies have rats in their heads." Joe turned to face Daniel to impress on him the absolute truth of his observation. "Some have bigger rats than others. Don't misunderstand me, son. I love 'em, but they all have them rodents in there somewhere, eating away at their common sense." Joe sighed and placed an old withered hand on Daniel's knee for emphasis. "Cranial rodents, we men call 'em."

Daniel half expected Joe to start his cackling, which he usually did at his own jokes, but that didn't happen.

"What did that Wheeler girl have to say?"

"Nothing, she just congratulated me is all."

"Oh?" Joe said, looking over at Daniel. "Just congratulations?" Joe paused a moment, considering this. "I guess you won." He paused again. "Well, you've almost won."

"Won what, Joe?"

Joe patted Daniel on the arm and stood. "I'm going back to your party in there. Do you want to come?"

"OK, but just for a while. I should get my gear home and Marigold brushed down."

"Don't worry about it son, we've taken care of it for ya'." He pulled Daniel out of the clutches of the couch with surprising strength. "Let's forget about women for a while and do some drinking. What do you say, champ?" Joe led him into the bar. He was again greeted by the cheers of the crowd.

It was indeed good to be a winner.

Chapter 41

"What is it with women? You can't live with 'em and there's no bounty on 'em." Harry was rambling on about his considerable experiences with women, sometimes drifting off in the middle of a sentence. No one seemed to notice, much less be bothered by it. His head dropped onto the back of the couch, one of the several facing the fireplace.

"Look, if it'll help, I'll go and talk to Shirley and explain what happened." Red offered.

"I knew it was the wrong thing to do, but I didn't think it was that wrong. It's not like we had intercourse or anything like that."

Joe came awake, as did Red. Harry sat up. They looked at each other.

"You mean you never laid a hand on Honey Lane?" Harry smiled broadly. "You mean to say that all those times you were over there at her house, you never got laid?" He looked at Daniel skeptically. "Not even once?"

"Not even once, I promise you." Daniel lifted his head and found them all watching him. "Really, I didn't."

"I don't believe it," Harry said. "I mean, I believe you, that you and she didn't, you know, do the dirty deed. I just mean that no one goes over to Honey's house and doesn't get laid by Honey."

"Don't worry, son. We were all young once, weren't we, boys?" Heads bobbed tiredly. "Give it a couple of days and we'll see what we can do for you," Red said. "I think it's time we all went home." Red stood and surveyed the vacant foyer. He saw that it was nearly three o'clock. He had a trip coming up and his team of wagons was returning later that day. He hoped that Pete had had a good trip and that Frank hadn't gone strange again.

As they were heading through the big front doors, Harry turned to Daniel. "You can make it home OK, can't you?"

"Yeah, don't you worry about me, Harry. My friends will make sure I get home OK."

With the whiskey doing most of the thinking and all of the talking, it just came out. The result was immediate. Harry stiffened his jaw and took a deep breath.

"Yeah, I guess they will." He swiveled on his heels, pushed back through the heavy doors and headed directly up the stairs.

"Perhaps that was a bit uncalled for, Daniel," said Red.

"I'm tired of doing all the work while he just does whatever he wants. I'm tired of it," Daniel lamented.

Joe took one arm and Red the other, and together they staggered homeward, arms linked together for mutual support.

"Screw Harry, I'm going to take that job with Wheeler. I'll show him." He closed one eye and looked up at Red. "That'll show him, won't it, Red?"

They carried Daniel inside his cabin and let him fall onto his bunk. The cabin was warm, but Red went over and gave the chain a pull to move the log enough to keep the fire going through the night. He admired the system that Harry had designed and built, but wondered about the purpose of the extra eyebolt at the end of the beam. He'd never noticed it before. Joe covered Daniel with his bearskin coat and headed for the door. Red followed.

"Do you think he'll really take that job with Wheeler?" Joe was navigating the path ahead of Red.

"He'd be a fool not to. No matter what trickery Wheeler's up to, I think he'll come out of it OK. And there's no doubt that he'll learn a thing or two. He's a bright lad." Red changed the subject abruptly. "What was Honey on about today? She wants to settle down with one man? That's not like her, Joe."

"Like I told the youngster, they've got rodents in their heads, nibbling away at their brains. You know, sometimes if you look deep into their eyes, you can see the little critters running back and forth. No problem."

⌗

Jerome B. Wheeler sat at his desk, smoking, drinking coffee, and trying to wake up. He'd barely made it into bed the previous evening
without waking his wife, when she rolled over on him and wanted to
play amorous. He was nothing if not sexually active and he'd never had
trouble making love to his wife. She complained as much as any other
wife, but as long as she had what she wanted, she pretty much left him
alone to do what he wanted to do. It was an expensive arrangement,
but as a wise man knows, all women get paid, no matter what the
circumstances.

There was a knock on his office door. Daniel entered, looking
well-scrubbed.

"Come on in here, my boy." Wheeler got up from his chair and
came around to the other side to welcome his young guest. "Come in
and sit down. I didn't expect to see you so early. After your victory, and
all that celebrating." Wheeler had a firm hold of Daniel's hand. "I must
say, your ski jouring was a vast improvement over your morning's performance." Wheeler laughed and Daniel blushed. "Sit down and we'll
have ourselves a little chit chat."

There was another knock on the door and Carter stuck his head in.

"Did you need to see me, Mr. Wheeler?"

"Not right now, Carter, but I'll need to see you in a while. Stick
around, will you?" Carter looked to see who was in the chair and raised
his eyebrows to Wheeler. Wheeler waved him out, and the door closed
behind him.

"Now where were we? Oh yes, you were looking for a job, weren't
you?"

"Actually, you wanted to offer me a job, Mr. Wheeler."

Wheeler exhaled his cigar smoke directly at him. Daniel leaned to
the side, dodging most of it.

"OK, Mr. Carrington. I want to put you to work learning how to
run one of the shifts."

"But I don't know anything about mining, Mr. Wheeler."

"Not a problem. I'll put you with Carter and he'll teach you the
ropes. I just want you to get the feel for the job. I'm not expecting to

find you with a pick and shovel. It's going to be your job to manage
these dumb miners we've got working for us."

Daniel felt the hair on his nape rising.

"We used to have decent crews here once," Wheeler sighed.
"They'd work from morning to night and bring up tons of silver, no
complaining. Now all we get are these Irish troublemakers, crying
and whining if they don't get their way. What do they want days off
for? They'll only end up in one of the whorehouses, blowing through
their money, and have nothing to show for it, ever. It's a good thing
I keep them working seven days a week. It forces them to save their
money."

Daniel gripped the arms of the chair so tightly he lost feeling in his
fingers. The door opened and Abigail came into the room, dressed in
a nurse's uniform.

"Oh, I'm sorry, Daddy, I didn't know you had someone with you."

She came into the room tentatively and sat in the chair that Daniel
had pulled over for her.

"Now, Abigail, I've just asked young Daniel here to come work for
us. Do you think he should accept?"

Wheeler loved this sort of thing; the way he played people was
masterful. He kept his eyes on Abigail.

"Yes, Daddy, I think he should take the job." She turned to face
Daniel squarely. She smiled at him and he returned the smile.

"Is that all you wanted me for, Daddy? I have to get over to the
hospital for my shift." She rose to leave.

"Perhaps Daniel here would do me the service of driving you over
to the hospital then." Wheeler walked them to the door without waiting for Daniel to answer.

"Come back when you're done and we'll send you down with the
noon shift to get you familiar. You'll report to Carter tomorrow one
hour before the morning shift starts and you'll be on the payroll as of
today." He held out his hand and Daniel shook it.

"Mr. Carter, did you hear that?" Carter nodded, he'd been standing just outside the office door.

"Good. Welcome to the Smuggler Mining Company, son." Carter and Wheeler watched the pair go, and then returned to the office, closing the door behind them.

"Nice boy, don't you think?"

"Yes, sir," Carter replied dryly.

"Come on, Carter, you know who's going to run this business when I'm gone, don't you?"

Carter said nothing.

"You are, of course. It'll be a long time before the boy's anywhere near ready; don't you think I know that?" They sat down and Wheeler offered his chief engineer a cigar and lit one for himself too. Jerome enjoyed cigars as much as winning.

⊣⊨

Outside, Daniel helped Abigail into the buggy and drove it across town, towards the hospital. The silence was strained.

"She loves you. You know that, don't you?"

"Who?" Daniel was taken by surprise.

"Kate. She loves you. I've known her a long time and I've never seen her look at anyone the way she looks at you." Abigail seemed to deflate as she said it. Daniel could think of nothing to say. "I want you to treat her well and be nice to her. Will you promise me that?" Daniel heard the tremor in her voice.

"I don't know what you're talking about."

"She doesn't love Leafy. She loves you, you idiot."

"She hates me."

They rode along in silence, past the smelters and up the hill towards the hospital. Abruptly, Abigail grabbed the reins, pulling the buggy to a stop behind some trees. She turned to face Daniel and took his hands in hers. Her eyes remained closed as if in a trance, her breast heaving.

"I'm glad you're going to work for my father," she said.

He took back his hand and saw that she was smiling at him. He flicked the reins and coaxed the horse up the small rise to the hospital.

As he helped her down from the buggy, she leaned forward, her ample bosom pressing against his chest. She searched his eyes.

"Perhaps we can all be good friends." She turned and walked into the hospital.

He drove back across town and found Carter waiting for him. As soon as he'd tied the buggy horse to a rail, Carter led him across the street and into the Smuggler Mining Company offices. Daniel met some of the other shift managers before being led into the mining office, where the ore totals were counted and the shift logs were kept. Later they went down into the mine with one of the foremen on a guided tour. Daniel was amazed at how far some of the mineshafts went under the ground. Not only did the shafts go down seventeen levels deep, but a person could walk from the north side of the valley, underneath the town and come up again on the south side of the valley, just above their cabin.

The whistle sounded for the end of the shift. Daniel was swept along with the others, up and out into the fresh air. Even though it was only four o'clock in the afternoon, the sun had already gone down behind Shadow Mountain. Daniel thanked Carter and Ed, the foreman, for the tour. They shook hands firmly as they parted. Tired and dirty, all he wanted was to be away from the noise and to sit quietly somewhere.

He was leaving the mine through the main gate when he saw Honey standing outside, holding tightly onto Jackson's hand. He held back behind the wall as other miners passed by him in their work-induced stupor. Looking around for a way out, he slipped to his left and followed the tin wall to the end. He dared a look back praying that she wouldn't follow him.

Over the rocks and piles of discarded lumber and machinery he scurried until he thought himself at a safe distance. He sneaked another quick look back. Honey was still standing outside of the mine, searching the faces. Daniel breathed a sigh of relief, dusted off his pants and coat and headed into town, though he did look behind several times, just to be sure.

Things were becoming a bit too complicated for him. There was the situation with Kate to explain, if she ever talked to him again. Then there was the Honey problem. He faced the fact that he was afraid of her; she was trouble for sure. He didn't like the idea of forever looking over his shoulder or carrying a gun to bed. Then there was Rachelle, who had taken it upon herself to be the administrator of punishment for unknown crimes. And, now, there was Abigail.

❧

Daniel wrote a letter to his mother that night; it was like the others, filled with optimism. Except for the part about winning the race, it was a lie. Kate was a topic. His mother was always hopeful that Daniel would find a soul mate sometime, somewhere; a born romantic, even by Irish standards. Secretly, she'd always hoped he would become a poet of renown and allow his grand imagination to infect generations to come, for the greatness of Ireland and Celtic pride. His head dropped onto his chest as he read the drivel he'd written.

He awoke from a bad dream in a sweat to find that Harry had not made it home again. It was still dark and he was alone, with only the soft, faint hissing of the fire smoldering. It being a work day, he washed quickly and was out the door before the sun had risen over the mountains.

His day was brutal and long, just as they all were, but he had kept to his schedule and was hardly drinking at all. He was usually so tired after his fourteen-hour day, he ate at a restaurant on the way home, had maybe a beer with dinner, then a quick wash of the armpits, and then went to bed. He'd gone by Kate's place almost every night after work, but hadn't worked up the nerve to knock on her door. He waited across the street, sometimes till he was almost frozen, watching to see if he could catch a glimpse of her crossing in front of the window. He nearly froze his toes off and left feeling stupid, every time.

❧

Each morning he woke up before dawn, now that his body was in the routine, and did it by habit. He made coffee, washed, dressed, gulped the coffee like milk, ran to work and was usually on time. The one time he was late, he was reminded of his tardiness all day from Mr. Bellows, his office boss. The fact that Mr. Wheeler had personally hired him gave him no special treatment.

In the mornings, he and Carter would inspect the maps of the tunnels, then allocate the shifts for the next twenty-four hours. After that, they would have a meeting with the head blaster, usually Sparky Langford, to discuss the daily explosives schedule. Most days, they would then head over to the coal yards to order coal for the smelters, then pay a visit to the smelters themselves.

This was really the most interesting part of the day for him, where the great furnaces transformed the crushed rock into billets of silver. Like a moth, he would lean as far forward as he could until his face felt like it was about to blister. He wanted to get as close as he could to the miracle of the creation of the glowing liquid silver as it was poured into the slugs that formed it as it cooled.

Lunch was usually over a table of maps and diagrams, just sandwiches and mugs of coffee. Boot Hill was the geologist of the company and continued to be a mystery to Daniel, though he respected him highly. Carter wouldn't make a decision to use dynamite until he and Boot had made a close inspection of the place to be blasted. Usually there were a dozen tunnels being mined, sometimes more, going in different directions and at different depths. The most critical danger was that other mining companies had shafts that came close to and at times crossed over or under their tunnels. It was Boot's job to coordinate with the other mines as to where and when they could blast and not cause a cave-in.

Daniel followed them around the mine like a dog trailing its master, always paying close attention to what they spoke about. Though he was enjoying the work, the long hours and abuse he had to suffer at the hands of Mr. Bellows held his bliss in check. Under the relentless scrutiny, he was understanding the accounting system better and had recently been put in charge of a shift. It was complicated and noisy in the mines, but it was this accounting that gave the men their wages. Mistakes in that department meant angry miners at his door. He was determined to be good at the job for that reason alone, if nothing else.

Days later, he gathered his courage and opened his last letter from his mother. Her handwriting was as beautiful as ever, but Daniel could see a difference in the shape of the letters, a slight wavering that had never been there before. She missed Daniel more than words could tell and wanted the best for him, of course. She was delighted that he'd met someone whom he liked and could tell that this girl was someone special by the way he'd talked about her in his last letter.

She told him of the winter in New York, that it was bitter and that they had very little heat, but they were getting enough to eat. She had not heard from his brother and she was worried about him. Something had fallen on the page and smudged the words. His heart surged in his chest and he was racked by tears that splashed on the table when they fell. The sorrow shook his body, it ebbed slowly as if his prayer had fulfilled its promise. He would see his mother again and it would be soon and she would be proud of him. That was his prayer that night, and every other night.

He climbed into his coat and walked the half-mile to Shirley's house, not really knowing what he was going to do once he got there. A tree across the street from her house had become a friend over the past weeks. A voice from behind him startled him.

"What're you doing here?"

He was shocked to find Rachelle standing there.

"You're not going to hit me again, are you?" Daniel pulled back slightly from her, even though she was much smaller than him.

"No." She pushed her chin deeper into her coat. "She doesn't like you anymore."

"Why not?"

"You fucked Honey."

"No, I didn't." His voice was shrill in denial.

"It doesn't matter, does it? You should go home and stop bothering us. Besides, she's going back East to school." Rachelle turned and strode across the street and into her house.

Like a fool Daniel watched the empty windows, hoping for his salvation to come running across the street into his open arms.

The air was colder than it had been just minutes before. His feet
took him downtown and he found himself standing outside of the
Paragon, looking in the picture windows like a hungry child outside a
bakery. He could hear the laughter and occasional shouts of the men
as they entertained themselves and the women of the house. Like a
bee drawn to a flower, he opened the door and pushed his way to the
bar.

Shirley waved him over and took both of his hands in hers.

"How're you doin' there, stranger?" She looked into his eyes and
saw the pain there. "Come on. Let's you and me have a little talk. You
look like you could use a friend." She came from around the bar and
took his hand, leading him to a quiet table. They sat for several minutes not speaking. "Do you want a drink?"

He shook his head. "No, I'm not going to drink anymore."

"I've never heard that before," she said, oozing sarcasm. "Daniel,
Kate's just as miserable about this as you are, believe me. I like you, and
I think that you'd be good to her."

Daniel looked up at Shirley like a drowning man, the glimmer of
hope buoying him. "But she hates me." He felt the tears welling up in
his eyes.

"She is disappointed in you." Kate wasn't the only one.

"But n.n.nothing h.h.happened," he stammered in his defense.
"Well, something happened, but not what she thinks, honestly." Daniel
was adamant.

"Do you mean to tell me that you and Honey didn't have sexual
intercourse any of the times you went over there for dinner?"

"No." His head fell and his chin rested on his chest. "I'm still a
virgin," he said softly.

Shirley nearly burst the buttons on her dress, trying not to explode
with both laughter and surprise. 'Virgin' was a word seldom heard in
the confines of her bar and the word rang out like a lone bell in a fog.

She looked around to see if anyone else had heard the confession.
Like a priest, she bestowed her admiration and at the same time, her

forgiveness. She looked at him with a new appraisal and decided he was the right man for her daughter. Once committed to a path of action, she was formidable, as most men in town knew well.

"I hear that you've been working hard every day. Why don't you go home and get some rest and I'll see what I can do."

"But she's going back East to school, isn't she?" Daniel let out.

"Who told you that?"

"Rachelle told me."

"Where did you see Rachelle?" Shirley leaned forward, her fists knuckled on the table.

Daniel knew he was in trouble. He hung his head as she asked again.

"Daniel, where did you see Rachelle?"

"I was across the street from your house."

"I thought that was you over there." Shirley laughed. "Have you seen Harry lately?" she asked.

Daniel shrugged. "No. Joe's worried about him."

She looked at Daniel, making up her mind to tell him what she'd heard. "I hear he's been at the Hotel every night, gambling. And he's been losing, is what I hear." She put her hand on his. "Now go home and get some rest. I'll have a little talk with Kate." She decided to take a gamble. "Why don't you come for dinner tomorrow night?" She touched his arm lightly. "Come over about seven and smell nice for her."

With a bounce in his step, he headed for the door just as Harry came barging in. Daniel held the door open as Harry collected himself. He was definitely drunk; Daniel could smell the sour breath.

"Oh. It's you. I want to talk to you." He grabbed Daniel's coat as he pushed past, heading for the bar.

"Not now, Harry. I have to get up in the morning."

"Come on, let's have a drink. We'll talk. Come on, just one?" Daniel looked over at Shirley and she quickly waved him to leave. "What? You're too fucking important now to drink with your old partner?"

"Look, Harry, I really am tired and I'm not drinking whiskey anymore."

"You're getting way too uppity these days." Harry waved his finger in front of his one open eye, then made a pistol gesture with it. "Well, if you won't drink with me, I'll just find someone else who will."

Harry looked at the people around the room. Daniel saw that they all avoided his gaze, but when he looked at Shirley, she stared him down. He turned back and looked Daniel up and down. "I think I'll just have to go back to the Hotel then. They're not all so uppity there."

He pushed out into the street. Daniel called out to him, but Harry kept on going, head down, shoulders hunched.

⊰⊱

Harry was pissed off, drunk and angry to boot. His mood darkened as he lost. By the time Jerome made it to the table after his evening diversions, Harry was well on his way to the worst night of gambling in his career. He'd lost everything he'd arrived with already and it was just midnight.

He made it to his bed, ungracefully, before dawn, and Daniel had pretended not to hear the bull in the china shop. Daniel wasn't the only one faking sleep. Harry waited a minute or two after Daniel left and checked outside to make sure that he was not coming back. When he was certain, he got up on the chair and moved the chain and eyebolt. He got the eyebolt into the new hole with some difficulty, being that he'd been drunk for most of the past two days. He pulled the chains through the bolt and gave a tug on them. The chains moved a fraction and he fell off the chair and flat onto his injured shoulder. He climbed the chains again and pulled again but the giant oven moved only slightly. He pulled with all his weight once more and got it to move a half an inch but the effort he'd expended was so great, he had to sit down before he threw up.

When the queasiness passed, he tried pulling on the chain again and the oven moved another inch. He didn't remember that it ever weighed this much before. By lunchtime, he had a space big enough to crawl in as far as his shoulders. He started to dig furiously, but made little headway. The dirt he excavated he pushed behind him or down his shirt, which is where most of it went. The dirt collected in his nose and he found a sneeze building. He panicked. What if the sneeze let the chain release and the oven crushed him? The skin on Harry's neck crawled and sweat chilled him.

He tried to back out, but his suspenders caught on a bolt under the oven. He felt caught like a rat in a trap. He pushed back harder and his face swelled with the exertion and panic as he tried to stop the sneeze from coming. The sneeze, when it came, was not the explosion he'd expected, but a snot-filled blast that blew up dirt and dust. He relaxed, but only for a second. Quite certain that the thing was going to fall on him eventually, he slipped his suspenders off the bolt over his ear and backed out of his tomb. He sat on the floor almost in tears from fear and frustration. So much money just a few feet away and he couldn't touch it.

He was becoming desperate. The rules of the poker game were that you had to pay your debts to leave the game. It was a good rule, Harry thought, at least while he was winning. He thought quite differently about it now. He'd had to borrow money as a direct loan from Jerome just to be allowed to go home and get more money. He promised them that he would be back at the table the next night, ready to play as always.

He searched Daniel's bag and looked where he usually kept his money. There was a note, but no money.

Went to the bank. Sorry.

He crumpled up the note and threw it at the oven.

⚔

Daniel stopped off at the bathhouse on the way home from work and scrubbed himself from head to toe. He felt light of heart but heavy with the burden of guilt about the incidents with Honey. She'd been at the mine entrance several nights after work, but he hadn't seen her for a few days. He just hoped that she would leave him alone. She was the main reason that he was going through this ordeal.

He'd just gotten his first full pay and he felt the weight of the money he'd earned. Admittedly, it wasn't a great deal of money, but

it meant something to him, different from the money he earned with
Red or Harry. It was not just payment for his effort, but his reward
for having made a decision about his future. The weather was getting
warmer and he had a potentially dramatic decision he was considering
for the coming spring. It all hinged on tonight. He said a small hope-
filled prayer before he entered the cabin.

As he closed the door he knew that something wasn't right. He
saw the crumpled piece of paper on the floor, read it, then pulled out
his pack from under his bed and saw that Harry had gone through
it. There were dirt footprints leading to the door, faint, but there. He
opened the door and saw the prints leading away from the cabin. He
reached up for the eyebolt that was usually tightly screwed into the
beam. It came out on the first twist.

Quickly, he arranged the eyebolt and chains. With furious energy,
he lifted the oven up and shone the lamp under the base. He could see
that Harry or someone else had attempted to unearth the money but,
except for a few grooves in the dirt, not much had changed. Relieved,
he smoothed the dirt under the base again and lowered the oven to
the floor before he sat down to take a breath. He was in a quandary.
Should he yell at Harry and accuse him of trying to steal their money
or should he pretend he never noticed? One thing was for sure—he
couldn't move out of the cabin and let Harry take his sweet time digging it up. And Daniel knew he would.

Donning a clean shirt he appraised himself in the small mirror.
Then he attempted to straighten his wavy hair; it fought him but he
slicked it down as best he could.

He was about to leave when he stopped and looked at the beam
again. An idea dawned on him. Standing on a chair, he took a small
branch and plugged the hole in the beam. When he was done, the hole
was filled and flush with the rest of the beam. Harry would have a
devil of a time digging it out or drilling another hole. It was the best he
could do on short notice.

It was truly late now, so he hurried along the road to Shirley's. As
he was passing Joe's stables, he heard someone calling his name. When
he stopped, he saw No Problem Joe coming towards him.

"You seen Harry?"

"No, why?"

"I hear he's gotten himself in some big trouble." Daniel could hear the concern in his voice.

"There's not too much I can do about that, Joe. He's a grown man, you know."

"But, son, it wouldn't do either of you any good to have people coming around asking questions, would it?"

Daniel considered the warning and nodded. "Thanks for the advice, Joe. I gotta hurry—I'm late to Shirley's for dinner."

"Good luck, son." He heard Joe call out.

Chapter 42

Shirley opened the door for Daniel with a devious smile. She helped him with his coat, took his hand and led him into the dining room. The table was beautifully set. Rachelle sat at the table, sullenly ignoring him. He felt the tension in the room.

"Daniel would you be a dear and open this bottle of wine for me? I have to go help Maisie in the kitchen," Shirley said, smiling.

Rachelle glared at Daniel, and he smiled back.

"Kate, dinner's ready! Our guest is here," Shirley called.

Daniel watched the stairs and heard the creaking of the boards above and the sound of a door being closed. With rapt attention, he watched Kate appear, descending slowly, apprehensively. He saw the delicate shape of her ankles as she lifted her skirt so slightly. Two more steps and her waist, narrow and flat, became visible. He felt his cheeks growing hotter.

Another few steps and there she was, standing in front of him, looking at him. Her eyes were the clearest and deepest things he'd seen since he crossed the ocean. Her hair was pulled loose and hung below her shoulders in waves of glisten and sheen. She wore silver earrings and around her neck was a thin black velvet and lace band with a cameo. Daniel couldn't speak. They looked at each other in silence.

Shirley entered and smiled. "Are you having trouble with the wine, Daniel?" she asked, trying not to laugh.

He looked at the half-opened bottle in his hand, then put it down and took an envelope from his vest. "I brought you something." He handed the envelope to Kate. "It's yours, really."

Kate counted the fifty dollars in the envelope and with no expression handed it back. "I can't take it."

"Please. You won it fair and square." He pressed it into her hands.

"Not fair and square," Rachelle yelled. "You weren't fair; you shouldn't have cut us off. We should've won. You cheated. The both of you cheated." Rachelle was up on her feet. "How could you do that? I'm your little sister. You're supposed to let me win."

The tension in the room thickened like gravy.

"Here, you take the money if it's so important." Kate held out the money. Rachelle slapped it out of her hand and headed for the front door.

"Rachelle, that's not nice, especially in front of Daniel. He's our guest." Shirley spoke through clenched teeth.

"I don't care, she can have him," Rachelle said in parting as she grabbed her coat and disappeared out the door.

Daniel bent down to pick up the money and bumped heads with Kate as she did the same. It broke the tension and they smiled at each other, friends again he hoped.

"Well. It must be time to eat. I'm sure that we'll have plenty of food now," Shirley said and helped Maisie with the dinner. Wanting to forget Rachelle's outburst they went about making the most of their dinner.

Kate and Daniel sat side by side. She kept her hands above the table and only when she was talking about the race in detail did she reach out and rest her hand on his. He stared at it as if his hand had been turned to gold.

They ate baked ham with potatoes and carrots. For dessert, Maisie had made a shoofly pie. Daniel thought the name was quite funny till they told him there were real flies in it. He ate two servings anyway.

After the meal, Shirley let Daniel and Kate clear the table and wash the dishes. They worked together well and except for Daniel dropping and breaking one of Shirley's good plates, it all went pretty much as she had hoped.

"Well, what do you think?" she asked Maisie.

"He the one that's been hanging out under the tree across the street every night?" Maisie smiled at Shirley, "he's crazy, but she could do worse." She loved the girls even though they were a handful, but she loved Shirley more. Shirley had saved her and her mother from a nasty fate and they had stuck it out as a team ever since. Her mother was simply called 'Mother' by everyone in Shirley's place. She ran the brothel with Shirley's complete authority and trust. Having had too much of men as a young black girl growing up in a brothel, Maisie had not yet married, but she always smiled coyly when asked about becoming someone's wife.

"I wish I knew what that little firebrand of mine is doing right now." Shirley was relaxing with her wine; she'd kicked off her shoes and was sitting in front of the fire, her legs stretched out, her ankles crossed. Daniel and Kate came into the sitting room and sat by the fire in the love seat. Their hips touched and their thighs pressed against each other's, and when Kate took his hand in hers and squeezed it, he almost had a climax. If this was love, he was going to die a happy man.

"Why don't we step outside for some fresh air?" Shirley suggested to Daniel. He took the hint and helped Shirley into her coat, then grabbed his own. They stepped out onto the front porch.

Shirley linked her arm through his. "Well, Daniel what do you think?"

"Think about what?"

"About Kate, you silly boy." She looked at him hard, then her face softened. "I'm not stupid, Daniel, no matter what they say about me." Daniel tried to object but she shushed him. "I'd like to know what you're going to do to stop my daughter from going to that school of hers back East." She faced him and held both of his hands in hers. He shifted from foot to foot nervously, his eyes avoiding hers until he finally gathered the courage to answer. She waited patiently for him to speak.

"Well, Mrs. Doray," he said finally. He heard someone running along the street and turned. Shirley pulled his hands to get his attention back. "If it would be alright with you, I'd like to ask Kate to marry me."

Shirley collected her thoughts before speaking again.

"I spoke to Honey. She's a little tramp, but she wouldn't dare lie to me. She vouched for the fact that you never had sex with her."

Daniel flushed with embarrassment, but she hadn't said no to his proposal to marry Kate. The sound of the running feet was getting closer. They turned to see two figures running down the middle of the street towards them; one was Rachelle. Shirley took her hands back.

"What's wrong?" she said as Rachelle raced up to her. She was out of breath. Leafy was close behind her coming through the front gate.

"You have to come quick," Leafy panted. He was breathing heavily from running in his heavy coat and his words came in spurts.

"What is it?" Daniel was scared that something bad had happened. He knew not what, but there were many possibilities—the cabin or the stable.

"It's Harry," Leafy blurted out.

"Is he hurt?" It wouldn't be too far from the realm of possibility that Harry could be shot or beaten.

"No, nothing like that—it's worse." Leafy was getting his breath back. "He's telling everyone that you two robbed the bank in Leadville."

Daniel's heart dropped to his boots. The blood drained from his face and his fingers tingled. He grabbed Leafy by his shoulders. "Where is he?"

"He's over at the Hotel, upstairs with Wheeler and he's really drunk."

Daniel ran to the street but stopped. "Thank you for dinner and tell Kate I'll see her tomorrow. I have to go."

She watched as Daniel and Leafy ran off towards town. Rachelle attempted to follow, but a stern call from her mother brought her back. The door behind them opened. Kate looked around for Daniel. Her smile faded.

"Where did Daniel go?"

"He had to leave. There's some trouble with Harry and Leafy came to get him. He said that he'd talk to you tomorrow." Kate tried to see past her mother at the two figures disappearing down the street. Shirley turned Kate back inside, "come on, let's go in and have some of that coffee." She stood aside to let Rachelle by and slapped her on her bottom as she passed her. "Little pest," she said to Rachelle's back.

"I'm going to bed." Rachelle announced. They watched as she bolted up the stairs two at a time. "Goodnight," she yelled, then slammed the bedroom door.

"I just don't know what I'm going to do with that girl," Shirley said.

─┅┋┅─

Harry had felt the tension at the table gathering weight, like wet snow on a roof. The cards were dealt around and his money had left him for all eternity, as had his luck, it seemed. He saw his right hand make a bet. It was not a good hand to bet on. Didn't he know that? It was a stupid bet.

The man across the table was the town's weasel; he was a lawyer. He had no friends and a bad complexion, but he took his poker seriously. And Harry was taunting him. Jerome had folded, as had Carter. The Mayor had also thrown in his hand and they were all watching the unfolding game intently. Only the Judge and the weasel across from him remained in the game.

It was Harry's call and he looked quickly at his cards, snapping them back on the table when his mind finally registered their values. He was drifting now, his mood subdued, he'd watched his hard-won winnings and more, move like a tide from his side of the table to the other. It was as if the money and the chips were taunting him to come and get them back. He began a conversation with his money and then realized that everyone was watching him.

The weasel had bet two hundred dollars, there was no limit at the table. With considerable effort, Harry pushed the remainder of his money out onto the pile in the center of the table. It totaled almost one thousand dollars.

"I'll call you." Harry said quietly.

"That's not enough," said the weasel.

"It's all I got," answered Harry.

"I don't care, it's not enough to make a call."

They stared at each other. Nobody else spoke.

"I can cover it if I lose." Harry said loudly, confidently.

"I don't think you can, Harry. I heard you sold your horse."

Harry dropped his eyes to the table, considering his reply. "Wasn't much of a horse." He looked up for some support, but everyone avoided his eyes. "I swear I can get you the money."

"Where? You got a stash buried under your bed or something?" The temperature at the table rose dramatically.

"Well, that's enough for me, fellers. I'm out." The Judge then rose from his chair, and after shaking Jerome's hand, politely tipped his hat and kissed the girls on the cheek as he left.

"Goodnight, Judge," they intoned as he went. The room fell quiet.

"I just got it is all you need to know." Harry insisted.

Leafy had been using the toilet when he'd overheard two men talking about some poor wretch losing a bunch of money upstairs in the gambling room. He went upstairs just to watch, and recognized Harry, sitting with his back to him. He saw that there was a lot of money in the middle of the table and that Harry was playing with the man they called "the weasel."

"And where will you get all this money, Harry?" he heard the lawyer ask.

"Did you rob that bank over in Leadville or something?" asked someone across the table.

"Maybe," Harry announced, and sat back, self-importantly. The room stilled like a church. "Maybe me and my partner did it." Harry boasted, fully enjoying this fleeting moment of attention, as he blithely committed both himself and Daniel to disaster.

Leafy had heard enough—he knew something very bad was happening and tried to do something about it. He approached Harry to get him out of there, but Harry brushed his hand away and continued on his self-destructive path.

"Are we going to play cards or not?" Harry said, belligerently.

"You mean to say that you and your partner robbed the bank in Leadville and you want us to think that it wasn't Butch Cassidy, but he got blamed for it?"

"Yeah, that's right," Harry said seriously.

Leafy decided he had to find Daniel before Harry got them both in big trouble. He hurried from the room and headed outside, grabbing his coat in the bar as he went. He almost ran into Rachelle, standing at the window outside the bar, looking in.

"What're you doing here?" he asked her.

"I was looking for you." She dropped her head.

"Do you know where Daniel is?"

"Why is everybody so worried about Daniel all of a sudden?" Hurt, she turned away, but he turned her around to face him.

"Rachelle, it's really important that you tell me if you know."

"He's over at my house. Why?"

"Come on, we've got to find him. Harry's blowing his mouth off and Daniel's got to get him out of there quick, before there's trouble." He dashed across the street between the carriages, pulling Rachelle along by the hand.

"This way, it's a short cut," she said, leading him through a hole in a fence between the buildings. He slipped and fell, but she grabbed his hand and they ran as fast as they could manage.

⚜

Daniel made it to the poker room in minutes. It was deathly quiet when he entered. Two men were holding Harry down at the table and the man across the table was pointing a small pistol at Harry's chest. Jerome Wheeler was looming over the table, not in charge of the situation, though he was trying.

"Now come on, boys," Jerome said good-naturedly. "We're all friends here, aren't we?" He looked from one to the other. The gun didn't waver from its mark. "Please, gentlemen, let's not end a friendly game on this note. Gunplay is the last thing we want here." Jerome was using all of his powers of persuasion to prevent bloodshed. His reputation would be sullied and his political aspirations would suffer. "Look here, I'll cover Harry's bet if he loses. Is that OK with you?"

"No," said the weasel firmly, putting the gun down on the table in clear view. Daniel saw that Harry only had one hand on the table. He watched him fidget with something underneath the table, closing his legs as he did. He placed both hands back on the table slowly. The room breathed again.

"What've you got?" Harry's eyes bored into the rat-faced man across from him.

"Three jacks." He laid down three cards. They were indeed jacks.

"Not good enough." Harry rose from his slouch like a phoenix and laid down his cards, three kings, a five and a three. He reached for the pot, encircling it with his arms as a lover would.

"Not good enough."

Harry, half out of his chair, his arms motionless, watched in horror as the rat-faced lawyer across from him laid down his other two cards, both aces, both black, giving him a full house. Harry let the air leak from his lungs slowly as he sat back down. The weasel gathered the money, arranging it carefully and as Harry watched intently he stuffed the money into his pocket.

"My name's Eugene Heber. I'm a lawyer as you know, and if you don't pay up by tomorrow, I'll take your cabin by Friday." He went over and shook Jerome's hand, but kept his pistol pointed at Harry as he backed out of the room. "Goodnight, gentlemen."

Daniel reached under Harry's good arm and lifted him out of his chair. He came up easily. He had nothing under the table. Just like Harry to try to bluff a man with a gun.

"Come on, Harry, let's go home. You need some sleep," Daniel said.

"I don't need no goddamned nursemaid. Get the hell away from me," he snarled. He pushed Daniel away falling back into his chair.

"Come on, Harry, you can't stay here." Daniel lifted him again. This time there was no resistance. He helped him into his coat and they headed out the door. Wheeler was nowhere in sight. The others in the room avoided looking at them. Leafy followed down the stairs and Daniel noticed that a number of men were watching them, both from the railing above and the floor below.

Harry was difficult to control, though drunkenly amiable to everyone. He shrugged Daniel off. At any other time, they would have laughed at his antics as he fought with the buttons on his coat.

"Can I help you get him home?" Leafy offered.

"No thanks, Leafy. I'll manage. No use both of us getting Harry's vomit all over us." Daniel tried to make light of the situation but he was afraid that Harry would start talking about the money buried under their floor. "Thanks for coming to get me, Leafy," Daniel said sincerely.

Leafy smiled and waved as he left them. They slipped and stumbled their way home, pausing several times for Harry to rest.

"I really did something stupid tonight, didn't I?" Harry leaned against an alley wall.

"Yes, you did, Harry," Daniel said with a resignation that he felt but couldn't yet acknowledge to himself. The grand game was over.

"Do you think we'll get into trouble?"

Daniel leaned his back against the wall. He had nobody to blame but himself for the piteous situation he was in. He roughly pushed Harry along the alley, with every step hating him more and more for what had done to his dreams.

"Maybe no one will tell the Sheriff, eh?" Harry said.

Daniel knew they were in serious trouble. Harry mumbled all the way home, falling often enough to make the job of hoisting him to his feet a tedious thing. Harry completed the journey to his cabin on his hands and knees.

"Damned gravity," he mumbled, laughing at his own humor as he fell through the door into the cabin. Daniel levered Harry into his bed with little effort. When he was settled, Daniel pulled the blanket over him and turned to go. A hand grabbed his belt.

"Thanks, partner. I'm sorry I talked too much. Sometimes, I just can't help it."

"God Almighty, Harry. You ask a lot of your friends. You really do," Daniel said, sincerely. "You could put us in jail for a long time, you and your big mouth."

"I'm sorry, Daniel. I screwed up and I'm sorry. Nothing will come of it, you'll see. I can trust all those fellers at the table—there's that unwritten rule."

"What unwritten rule?"

"I don't know, something sacred between gamblers and liars."

"And which one are you?" Daniel crawled into his bed.

"How am I going to get the money to pay that Heber weasel?" Harry turned over on his side and sighed deeply. "I can't let him have the cabin—it's the only thing I own." There was a pause of a couple of seconds. "That and there's all that money buried under the oven."

"How much did you lose tonight?"

"Goodnight." Harry drifted off to the place where this day never happened.

"Goodnight, Harry," Daniel said.

Harry was softly snoring already.

Daniel laid awake all night.

The knock came as he knew it would. He found Willy there instead of the Sheriff. Willy was brandishing a newspaper and talking excitedly.

"What's this all about, Willy, shouldn't you be in the shitter about now?" Daniel pointed uphill at their outhouse.

"Yeah, I was about to go, but I got the newspaper and then I got excited. You should see it."

Daniel opened the paper and as the shock hit him, he backed up into the cabin, closed the door in Willy's face, and nearly fainted.

Willy shrugged, looked up at the outhouse, turned, and went back downtown to get another newspaper.

"Harry." Daniel had read some of the story. "Harry, Harry, wake up." He shook Harry's corpse and kept reading. "Harry, you'd better wake up. We're about to be arrested."

Harry sat up and grabbed at the paper.

"'Aspen Men Rob Bank,'" Daniel continued reading, "'Two local men admit to robbing the Leadville bank. Witnesses state that the men bragged about their feat in a conversation with a credible citizen. The men, who are yet to be arrested, are of dubious reputations known to the Sheriff. It is expected that they will flee the county and join up with their partners, Butch Cassidy and the Hole in the Wall Gang, in Utah.'" Daniel fell onto his bed. Harry grabbed the paper out of his hands.

"I hope you're happy now that we're part of the Hole in the Wall Gang."

"Well, they don't mention us by name. Maybe we can get out of town."

"And go where, Harry? You don't think that our descriptions aren't going to be all over the state in a day?"

Harry lay back down on the bed as a second and much louder knock pounded on their door. Daniel opened it reluctantly.

It was Wally, the town's largest but nicest deputy. "I'm sorry, Harry, but the sheriff asked me to see if you wouldn't mind coming down to the office." Harry looked like a dead deer, his face frozen, his eyes glazed over. "You can come down whenever you like, as long as it's before he goes home for lunch. OK?" Harry closed the door on him and they heard him leave.

"What are we going to do about the money, Harry?"

"Which money?"

"The money you owe the lawyer. The one who's going to take away this cabin and…." Daniel pointed down at the floor beneath the oven. "That money."

"Hell, I don't know. Maybe we can dig it up and solve all of our problems."

"How much do you owe? It couldn't be that much, could it?" Harry was looking down at the floor, trying to stop the room from spinning. "No. Don't tell me, Harry. I don't want to know. Look, I've got some money. I'll lend it to you, OK?"

"It's not going to help."

"What do you mean it's not going to help? I've got nearly four hundred dollars."

"Where?"

"What do you mean where?" Then it dawned on him. "You went looking for it again, didn't you?"

Harry didn't look up. "It's not enough unless you've got four hundred more."

Daniel fell into the chair and looked at Harry as if he'd never met him before. "I don't believe you."

"Oh, it's true. That bastard did not have a full house. I dealt him his damned cards. Then I watched him cheat. Right there in front of me. God, I hate lawyers."

There was another knock on the door. They looked at each other. Daniel went and opened it.

A reporter from the *Aspen Times* stood, pencil poised over his notebook. "Is Harry Rich there?"

Daniel wasn't about to let anyone into the cabin.

"Hey, Harry, are you in there?" the reporter yelled over Daniel's shoulder.

"Who is it?" Harry asked, feigning illness.

"He wants to know who you are," Daniel sniped.

"Tell him I want to interview him about the robbery. I want to know how you fellers did it."

He must have fallen in the snow with the force of the door slamming in his face. Daniel stood, looking at the door, then opened it again. The reporter was sitting in the snow.

"Sorry about that. The wind must've blown it shut."

"I just want a statement, that's all. You his partner?"

"Yes, I am. But not like that," he tried to recover. "We sell potatoes to the miners. That's our business. Selling potatoes, not robbing banks." He slammed the door on him again. The reporter hurried off down the path.

"We have to do something about the money Harry, and fast."

"How long would it take to dig it up?" Harry was clutching at straws. "We would only have to take out some of it and we could leave the rest of it under there. You know, for later."

Daniel hung his head, thinking of the wooden plug he'd driven into the hole they used as the anchor for the eyebolt. He looked up at the beam. They could drill another hole, he supposed. What a way to spend his first day off. He looked down and thought about the money so near, then about spending years in jail. "Can you go to Wheeler for a loan?"

Harry shook his head. "He already loaned me money."

"Would he loan you another four-hundred dollars?"

"I don't think so." Harry paused, taking a deep breath. "That's how much I owe him already."

Daniel got up and walked to the door, turning to face Harry. "You've been trying to dig it up, haven't you?" Harry closed his eyes to ponder his splitting headache. "You'd already decided it would be easier to run. You would've just headed out of town without me, wouldn't you?" Daniel reached for his coat. "What kind of a friend are you?" Daniel yelled at Harry.

He reached for the door handle, but two loud knocks stopped him. He looked over at Harry, who shrugged. The banging came again, just two knocks, but loudly determined. Daniel opened the door to Sheriff Hunter and Wally, his deputy.

"Harry in there?" The sheriff had his hand on the butt of his gun. "Harry, come on out here, unarmed."

Harry came to the door and opened it enough so that the sheriff could see that he was unarmed. He stood there in his long johns, his pants unbuttoned and his shirt stained under the armpits. "God, but you're a sight in the morning, Harry." The sheriff shook his head, but Daniel noticed he kept his hand on his gun.

He motioned them inside, but Big Wally remained in the doorway. Harry went about absently trying to tidy up, but it was hopeless. He sat on his bunk, crossing his legs self-consciously. "What can I do for you, sheriff?"

The sheriff laughed out loud and slapped his thigh. "Harry, you are something, do you know that?"

Harry had known Bob Hunter for years, long before he'd been elected sheriff. He was a good man and fair. They'd been friends a long time.

"Harry, I got to take you in," Sheriff Hunter said sadly, holding his hands apart. "Get dressed and come on with me and Wally. You'd better come on down too, son, so I don't have to make two trips." He walked to the door. "We'll wait outside. You might want to bring another set of underwear, Harry. Those look like they could go wash themselves and I don't want you to go stinking up my new jail."

"Are we being arrested?" Harry inquired.

"Why, yes you are, Harry."

"And why, exactly, are we being arrested?"

"I've been told by the Judge, among others, that you and this kid here were part of the gang that robbed the Bank of Leadville on Christmas night, and he believed you." The businesslike, matter-of-fact tone of his voice thrust through Daniel like a cold sword.

"Good thing no one who knows you believes you." He smiled at Harry. "Go on, get dressed, so we can get this nonsense off my desk and I can get on with my life. Get moving or I'll have to charge you with resisting arrest and put you in handcuffs." He patted his pockets, but couldn't find them. "Lucky for me you're not real bank robbers, eh?" He laughed and closed the door.

"Well, that's not as bad as it could be," Harry said.

Daniel's fist landed directly on Harry's jaw. Harry crashed into the table and sprawled backwards over the fallen furniture, landing on his butt. The door opened and Sheriff Hunter stuck his head in.

"You fellers alright?" He grinned widely seeing Harry flat on his butt and Daniel rubbing his hand.

"Yeah, sheriff. I'm just doing some tidying up before you take us to *jail*!" Daniel screamed the final word with all the anger that had built up behind the dam of his frustration.

Harry got to his feet and stuck out his hand. "No hard feelings, then?"

Harry let it fall to his side and watched Daniel grab his Bible from his pack, his coat, gloves, and hat, and walk out the door.

For a moment, Harry filled with a flood of self-pity. He shrugged his shoulders and looked around the little cabin. He patted the cool oven and looked up at the beam. For the first time, he noticed that the hole in the beam had been filled.

Daniel must have realized that he was trying to steal the money, prompting him to fill the hole in the beam. That little bastard, he thought. Harry's face and mood were set as he closed the door on their little fortune, for what he hoped was not the last time.

⊰⊱

The cells were in the basement of the jail. They were clean and there were two bunks against the walls, just like in their cabin. The deputy asked them if they needed anything as he guided them in, then he locked their cell door, the sound of finality echoing about the room.

Daniel fumed silently, alternately sitting in despair and pacing in fury. He grew more anxious as the day wore on. Harry responded to the tension by going to sleep. Deputy Wally kept sticking his head in and asking if he could get him anything. He declined, but was heartened by the consideration. Dinner came, but he had no appetite. Harry ate and went back to sleep. Time crawled; eventually night came, but sleep didn't—not for him.

They were led into court the following morning. The courtroom was crowded. Daniel saw Shirley, Kate, and even Rachelle and Leafy seated near the front. They smiled and waved, except Rachelle. Kate blew him a kiss, making him smile self-consciously.

"All rise."

They stood and watched as the Judge took his chair. Stories that Daniel had heard regarding the courts of England and what he'd heard of justice on the American west gave him neither consolation nor hope.

"Will the accused stand?"

They did as they were told.

"Well, Harry Rich, what do you have to say for yourself now? It looks like your mouth has finally done what the sheriff and the courts have not been able to do all these years."

"What's that, Your Honor?" Harry asked in his politest voice.

"That, Mr. Rich, is to get rid of you, for once and for all." The judge looked over the rim of his glasses at the man who had relieved him of so much of his money over the past weeks. There was no sympathy in his eyes, and they focused on Harry, burning into him like a magnifying glass in the sunlight, murdering the hopes in his heart like ants.

The Judge sat back and rested his hands across his roundness. "It seems as though the Sheriff of Leadville has some unfinished business with you." He read from a telegram: "'You're both remanded in custody until such time as you are to be taken to Leadville for trial for the robbery of the Bank of Leadville.'" And, just for the record, I don't think you could possibly have done this, Harry. But for all the times robbers get away with it, I think it's only fair that once in a long while someone only slightly less guilty gets convicted of one."

The judge pounded his gavel with the finality and authority of the truly divinely ordained. "And this court is adjourned."

The sheriff beckoned for them to follow him. As they stood to go, Daniel saw that Kate was visibly upset and her mother had her arm around her shoulders. Rachelle was as impassively bored as ever, and Leafy looked sad. Shirley smiled at him and nodded.

Outside the courthouse as they were led back to the jailhouse, the same reporter was standing on the steps, his pencil and notebook at the ready.

"Did you two do it?" he yelled at them. "Where are Butch and the rest of them fellers? Did you two warn them before you got arrested?"

"Well, of course we did. They're our partners, aren't they?" Harry said.

Daniel pulled at Harry's sleeve, but he couldn't be stopped.

"The fact that we never left town and still rode over one-hundred miles through a snow storm proves that we're responsible, doesn't it?" Harry rambled on. "We didn't even have to rob the bank. They just rode over here the next day and dropped the money off to us."

"Where did you hide the money, Harry?" another voice called.

Harry was an anarchist if nothing else. "We hid it in one of the mines, of course. Where else?"

The reporter wrote furiously. As they were led away, a photographer rushed in front of them and took a picture of them being led away in handcuffs. When the paper came out, it had that picture on the front page with the caption: "We Hid the Money in a Mine." The picture was grainy in the newspapers across the country, but Harry could still be seen smiling broadly.

The town fathers and the mine owners never forgave Harry for that remark. It sent several thousand miners on a treasure hunt and brought the town to a standstill for a month.

Chapter 43

The Sheriff of Leadville was confused when he received the first telegraph message. He put it off to one side and forgot about it. The next morning, there was another from the same man. Something had to be done about the information, but he wanted to keep it quiet.

It had been a long night. With his new mistress demanding so much of his time, and his wife making the rest of his life miserable, it was a wonder he went home at all these days.

He called in one of his sons and showed him the telegram. "I seem to remember that name too, Dad." Hamlett smiled at a chance to return to Aspen, revenge on his mind.

"Why don't you go over there, pick 'em up and bring 'em back? The Mayor's been all over my ass to find them bastards, and even if they aren't the ones, it'll look like we're doin' somethin'." He waved Hamlett off.

After his son left, he thought more about the bags of money he had in his safe. He had given the bag with the bloodstains on it back to the bank, but had kept the two remaining moneybags. If anyone found the real robbers, he would just say that it was evidence he'd been saving. If Butch and his partner were never caught, which was possible, he'd be free and clear. He could leave town with the money safely in his valise and no one would be the wiser.

Harry Rich had an accomplice, according to the telegram in his hand. God Almighty, wouldn't it be just wonderful if it was that skinny little snot of a kid he hung around with, the one who worked for Red Corcoran? He smiled at the prospect.

He smiled more, at the thought of all of the praise that would be heaped on him. He might even get elected mayor because of it. He remembered the morning he would rather forget, when he had ridden out to the Lodge and found the grizzly scenes and had to take care of his younger brother's crimes. He squirmed uncomfortably in his chair.

His bowels shifted at the gruesome memory of what he'd seen and had to do that day.

He'd thought the problem was over. Newly was forgotten. And Gloria, well that was a potential problem, but since she was known to have loose moral values and was an ex-whore, she was easy to dismiss. No one had asked about her. He'd not been out there since Christmas, thinking that the less he knew of his brother's problems, the more distant his connection to him would be.

He looked again at the safe against the wall of his office and smiled the smile of the black-hearted. The bank robbery had been a blessing in disguise, so long as they didn't catch Butch Cassidy.

Oddly though, he'd only followed two men that night and the two over there in Aspen would have made it four men robbing his bank. Where were the other two and where did they go? It was sure that those two clowns over there in Aspen, no matter who they were, did not pull the robbery off alone. No one could have made it over that Pass on horseback that night. It was snowing too much and they would've gotten lost. He hadn't seen any tracks in the snow when he'd arrived in Twin Lakes that morning. Maybe Frank saw some tracks; he didn't remember if he'd asked him that question. Perhaps, just maybe, he and Frank could invent some evidence to convict those bastards anyway. Now that would be the icing on the cake.

⊰⊱

Shirley was having a difficult time. The town had gone mad and it was all Harry's fault. Since being quoted in the newspaper that he had hidden the stolen money in one of the mines, he'd released a frenzy of drunken miners dashing all over the place, digging everywhere. The Paragon Bar was empty. Even her girls were touched with the treasure fever. She felt like she was the only sane one left in town.

Admittedly, Harry was famous for his fanciful tales of how he was going to rob that bank. But he was no different from any of those other hopeless dreamers who would pour their hard-earned wages into their bellies and talk about the riches hidden in that vault. Harry might be guilty of talking about it more, but he was just another dreamer who had never had a successful idea in his life. It would be more than a miracle if this was his doing.

For Shirley, the fact that he was dragging poor Daniel into this mess was another strike against Harry. Kate was beside herself with worry, and who could blame her?

"Why don't you go over and see if Daniel's horse is being fed?" Kate looked up at her mother and smiled at the idea. "I'm sure she could use the company, too."

Kate brightened and Shirley held out her coat and hat to her. She opened the door for her and kissed her as she took her cane from the stand by the door and walked out to the street. Shirley watched her as far as she was able, pressing her face against the cold pane of glass long after she'd disappeared.

⊰⊱

Kate was busy brushing Marigold and didn't hear Joe come up behind her and was startled when he spoke.

"I do believe she likes that."

"Oh, it's you, Joe. You scared me." Kate looked at him, her eyes full of sadness. "Do you think they did it, Joe?"

He considered the question a long time. "Not a chance. Not Harry, he's just not capable. This is all happening because Harry shot his mouth off again and the wrong person heard it. They'll be out of jail tomorrow, no problem."

Kate returned to her brushing. "I hope so."

She brushed and thought and brushed and thought some more. She'd liked Daniel from the first time she'd met him. He was considerate and brave, according to the stories, and he wasn't bad looking either. The thing with Honey had been just a misunderstanding, and after all, he was just a man. He'd probably had plenty of women. She pushed the images of their passion out of her mind with effort.

This was all Harry's fault. Harry was, at times, the topic of gossip amongst her mother's friends when they came over to play cards and drink sherry on Wednesday afternoons. Shirley liked to play cards and let her hair down and swap gossip with the best of them. Owning the most popular whorehouse in town gave her some inside information about the comings and goings of their husbands, too. These were all frontier women—they could handle their men doing what men had to do, but when they came home, they had to do what their women wanted them to do. That was the rule. Kate thought it a practical rule. After all, she was a practical girl.

⚜

Joe had sent word of Harry and Daniel's arrest out to Red's place, but he was on a trip over the Pass and wouldn't return until the next day, if the weather held. For his part, Joe was confused at what had happened to the boys. Obviously it had been Harry's stupidity, but who in his right mind would have believed him in the first place? The Judge was a decent man as far as judges went and Joe doubted he was the source of the problem. Then there was the lawyer they called the 'weasel'. Though he'd never met the man, there were the rumors and the occasional bit about his business dealings in the local newspaper. He seemed to be the front wave of the new type of men coming to the western mining towns. They were a bad lot, these lawyers, they could steal with impunity.

Joe stoked the coals in his potbellied stove and wondered again about the boys robbing the bank, considering the distance involved, the terrain and how unforgiving a winter storm could be. He knew their horses and their fitness and thought it ludicrous that they could cover that many miles. To make it even more implausible, he knew Harry. "Stupid bastard," he said aloud to himself.

"Did you say something, Joe?"

He'd forgotten Kate was still there. "No problem. I was just muttering to myself."

He liked Daniel and he liked Kate, too. He'd known her since she was young, even before the accident that had crippled her. It had taken years for her to get over her fear of horses after the accident when Joe's horse had crushed her foot. It had never healed completely. Back then, there was no hospital and the only doctor in town had wanted to amputate. Shirley refused, and together she and her daughter suffered, but Kate made it through. It healed well enough, though the foot would never be right again.

Still, it didn't seem to bother her all that much. He watched her and smiled to himself as she brushed the horse with long fluid strokes. For a moment, he was completely mesmerized by her movements, the way she bent and swayed, following the contours of the animal's back and hind legs. He became aware that he was staring and went back to his chores. They would be a good match, he thought with a smile. The problem was that one of them was in jail.

⊰⊱

"Mind if I tag along with you over the Pass, Red?" Red's wagons were heading out of Twin Lakes and it was mountain courtesy to allow riders to tag along.

"Sure enough, Deputy. What happened to your face?"

The deputy was leading two horses, so he tied them to the back of one of the wagons. "Some feller threw lit whiskey on me." He touched the fresh pink skin tenderly. The deputy was named Hamlett—his mother had had a strange reaction to a play she once saw and the name was a constant burden. Not the brightest of the brothers, he was formidably strong, with a nasty temper to boot. Red was not surprised to hear that he'd been in a bar fight. He wondered at the fate of the one who threw the flaming whiskey.

"What you goin' over to Aspen for?"

"Some fellers over there said they robbed the bank."

"Is that so?" Red could think of no one he knew who would be so stupid.

"Yeah, some feller I think you might know. His name's Harry Rich."

Red let out a deep sigh. "Yeah, I know him. But you're goin' on a wild goose chase if you think he robbed the bank." Without realizing it, Red had flicked the reins and the team of Morgans had responded by picking up the pace. The deputy had to change his horse's gait to keep up.

"If it's the feller I'm thinking of, he's no bank robber." Red laughed.

It was Harry's best defense and his worst crime; he was a braggart and a liar. But still it was a serious thing and he hoped that Harry had the sense to keep Daniel out of his mess. The rest of the trip, Red was mostly silent, his mind working the immediate problems while wrestling with this new information. Joe's message was on a nail on his bedroom door when they arrived at the barn. He read it and his heart sank even more.

⊣⊢

The boys brightened when Shirley and Kate brought them their supper. Daniel had been sullen all day and had done his best to ignore Harry. Harry, for his part, was oblivious to the danger and bantered with the drunks as they surfaced and were released. He knew most of them. Though some of them felt sorry for Harry, most found his plight somewhat humorous, in that his big mouth had gotten him into jail. Most had little pity for him, but looked sadly on the hapless Daniel, sitting with his back to the wall, his head buried in his blanket.

Wally helped slide the plates of food under the cell door and Daniel thanked him. Wally was one of the good guys, and to date, had never arrested anyone and rarely wore his gun.

Shirley smiled at Daniel and scowled at Harry before she left Kate and Daniel holding hands through the bars, both looking sad. Unsurprisingly, Shirley noted, Harry had wolfed down his food with gusto and in the few minutes before they were politely asked to leave, he'd moved onto his dessert.

Daniel stood at the cell door long after Kate left. He briefly looked at his food, but left it untouched and retreated into his blanket. Harry ate it for him. It was the least he could do for his friend.

It was early morning when Deputy Hamlett arrived at the jail to pick them up for the trip back over the Pass. Daniel was finally dozing off when the door to the jail cells opened and they heard Sheriff Hunter's voice.

"Come on down, Deputy. They're down here in our deluxe accommodations. Ahh, there you are boys, all awake after your breakfast in bed?"

Harry's smile died the instant he saw the face of the man wearing the star and the gun. Ham recognized Harry just as quickly. His smile of pure satisfaction was alarming. For the first time in his life, Harry felt real fear. He'd been lucky and resourceful the first time they'd met in the bar, but his luck seemed to have run out.

Hamlett abruptly pushed Sheriff Hunter out of the way and reached through the bars for Harry. Sheriff Hunter reacted quickly and stepped between them.

"I see you've met Harry before."

Hamlett touched his face automatically. "That's right, Sheriff, we've met, but not formally."

"Well, this is Harry Rich, and this here is Daniel Carrington." Daniel turned over sleepily to face the sheriff, and moaned loudly when he recognized the deputy with the seared face.

Ham was enjoying himself, smiling broadly. "We've got a real nice cell waiting for you two when we get over to Leadville. My Daddy's going to treat you boys real well, I'd imagine."

"I'm mighty glad to hear that." The sheriff patted the deputy on the back and escorted him out.

"This is really bad, isn't it, Harry?" Daniel asked, rhetorically.

Harry banged his forehead against the bars slowly, with purpose. "Why him? Why did it have to be him?" Harry went to his bunk and dropped into a fetal position, not saying another word.

⊰⊱

"I've got a bad feeling about this, Red," Joe said. They were drinking coffee and sitting by the stove. "Did you know he's the feller that Harry threw the flames on?"

Red stopped mid-sip and looked over his cup at Joe in disbelief. "Then they're in more trouble than I thought." Red sipped his coffee. "When do you think he'll take them back over to Leadville?"

"Tomorrow is my guess. That Sheriff is probably licking his lips just thinking about getting his hands on Harry."

"We should find out. It wouldn't be good to have the boys shot on their way to jail." Red put down his empty cup and with Joe, headed directly to the Sheriff's office.

"Can we visit with the boys, sheriff?" Red asked.

"They're already gone." Red and Joe looked at each other, equally concerned. "Yeah. Ham thought he'd get a jump on the day and get home before dark. Said he'd just got married and missed his wife. He seems a nice feller, don't you think?"

Red didn't answer as he swept out the door with Joe trailing behind.

"I just can't see them getting there alive. You and I know they couldn't have robbed that bank, but I've got a feeling that deputy wants to hurt both of them real bad, and now he's got his chance. I'm worried, Joe. Once they're in jail, they should be alright, but on the way over, there are just too many things that could happen to them, and no one to witness it. I'm going after them."

They were walking quickly past the Smuggler Mine Land Offices when Jerome called out to them.

"Red, I gotta talk to you." Jerome's face was flushed.

"If it's about this mess that Harry's got himself into, I'm going after them. I want to make sure they get over to Leadville safely."

"Well, yes, that is one of the things that I wanted to talk about. But there's something else you should know, too." Jerome took several deep breaths. "Did you know I was there when Harry said that he robbed the bank?"

"No, I didn't, what happened?" Red asked.

Jerome told the story as briefly as time would allow and finished with the question that everyone was asking. "Do you think they actually did the robbery?"

"What do you think, Jerome? Harry's a fool. We all know that, but he could as much rob that bank as he could fly through the air."

"I'm glad to hear you think that, Red. I've taken a liking to young Daniel and I think he's a fine young man. I've sent off to Denver to have David Hyman's lawyer come on up and see if he can help them. It shouldn't be too hard for him to prove that they couldn't possibly have done it. It's too damned far to go there and back all in one night anyway, isn't it?"

Both Red and Joe had been thinking along the same line of thought. They were pretty sure that it couldn't be done, but with all of the other strange things going on, their certainty was wavering. Red had told Joe that he had seen what looked like a part of a sled sticking out of the snow. The sled was on Joe's mind too; he wondered why he hadn't seen Harry's old sled since Christmas.

"Look, here's the reason I wanted to talk to you, Red. Harry lost a considerable amount of the Judge's money to a Mr. Heber. He's one of the fine young lawyers new to this town. I don't think you've met him, have you?"

"No, but I've heard of him, Jerome. Not the kind of feller I'd play poker with, if you know what I mean."

"True, but a good payer if he loses. Anyway, Harry lost to him and owes him some money. If he doesn't pay up, he's going to get the judge to let him take Harry's house because of the debt."

"Can he do that?"

"Sure he can, if there were witnesses."

"No problem," Joe added.

"And the judge was one of the witnesses?" Red sighed. "Well then, how much does he owe this Heber fellow?"

"About four hundred and about the same to me," Jerome said.

"Harry's going to lose his house then," Red said.

"I can pay it for him. I've got the money of course, but that's not the problem," said Wheeler. "Heber won't take it from anyone except Harry. I think it's something personal between them."

"How long would it take for him to do this?"

"Not long with the Judge on his side."

"I think we've got a bigger problem right now if we want to keep those boys alive. Harry's house isn't going to be much of a matter to him if he's dead." Red shook hands with Jerome, as did Joe, and they hurried off. Shirley caught them on the next corner.

"Where are the boys, Red?" Her worry showed.

"The Sheriff's son came and took them back over the Pass. He just happens to be the one that Harry burned in that fight at the Hotel a while back. I'm going to try to tag along so's nothing untoward happens to them accidentally."

"Do you think you can catch up to them?"

"Not a problem if they're not in a hurry."

"Good luck." She kissed him on the lips. Joe raised an eyebrow, but said nothing. They walked the rest of the way to the stable quickly and Red mounted up.

"Joe, make sure they don't take his house, will you?"

"No problem, Red. You be careful—that Sheriff's just as likely to put you in jail with them. I can't believe he really thinks they robbed his bank."

"To tell you the truth, I don't think he really cares. So long Joe."

Red spurred his horse and took off. There were few travelers on the road and the few he did run across told the same tale: three men riding fast, one leading two men in handcuffs. They were several miles ahead of him.

⊰⊱

"Hey, Deputy, can we rest a minute? I have to take a leak."

Ham turned in his saddle and looked at Harry. "You should'a thought about that before we left."

"You didn't give us much time."

Ham was a sadistic man when he was in a good mood. Today, he was in a particularly good mood. They'd passed through Independence, where it wasn't every day they saw a Deputy leading two men in handcuffs. It gave them something for them to talk about.

When they reached the summit, Ham stopped to give their horses time to catch their breath. He let them dismount to relieve themselves and watched them closely as they went about their business. The day was more than half gone, but they would be in Leadville by dark if they kept moving. They mounted again, ready for the descent. Daniel looked back one last time out towards Aspen, at the love and the future happiness he was leaving behind. His eyes filled with tears.

"What's the matter, son? Afraid you won't be back for about ten years?" Ham laughed loudly at his own joke. Below them, in the distance, Daniel could see someone on the road, riding up the Pass.

They rode down the eastern side of the mountain, below where the avalanche had almost killed them. Daniel was shocked when he saw that the runner of their sled was becoming visible as the snow melted. He got Harry's attention and nodded in that direction. Ham didn't see the look of fear creep over their faces as they passed the remains of their sled. They stopped again at the bottom of the hill at the final turn in the road, where a small stream wandered through a meadow.

"What're we stopping for?" Daniel asked.

"This is where he's going to have his fun," Harry predicted.

"That's right, Mr. Rich. I think you and me have some unfinished business to attend to."

Ham dismounted and grabbed Harry by his coat, pulling him off his horse. Harry's foot stuck in the stirrup and he toppled, awkwardly suspended.

"Having some trouble there?" Ham pulled Harry's foot free and Harry fell heavily on his bad shoulder, wincing in pain. Ham was nothing if not fast with his feet. He kicked at Harry as he fell and caught him on the cheek with his boot.

"You know what? That felt really satisfying." He kicked Harry again, this time in the back. "That felt real good, too." Ham failed to notice that Daniel was edging closer. "I got me some firewater here in my pack for just this type of celebration." Ham went to his horse and came back with a bottle of whiskey. He tilted it back and forth in front of Harry's widening eyes. "How about a little drink then?"

Ham opened the bottle and poured the whiskey on Harry's head. Harry licked at it as it dripped over him and down into his shirt. "Now, what do you say to a little birthday celebration, eh? I got the matches. You can be the cake, Mr. Rich."

He drew a match across his gun belt and it flared, barely visible in the bright sunlight. Harry recoiled and tried to crawl away. He came closer with the flame and Harry whimpered loudly. "Not so brave now, are you?" Harry blew the match out. Ham struck another. Another wave of fear ran through Harry's bowels.

Ham tossed the match at Harry, but it went out and failed to catch. He threw another, then another. He drew his gun. "Get up, Mr. Rich."

Harry did as he was told. Ham grabbed him roughly by the coat and turned him around to face him. "Aren't you the lucky one? This is my last match." He held it up in Harry's face. "Well, here goes." He drew the match across the back of his belt and the match flared. Hamlett waved the flame close to the coat and Harry stepped backwards. Daniel nudged his horse closer, getting Harry's attention. Harry looked at Daniel. Ham followed his gaze and when he turned his head, Harry blew the match out. Ham angrily threw the match down on the ground. "We're wasting time here, Mr. Rich." He waved his pistol at Daniel as a warning. "Turn around."

Harry turned, passing a plaintive look to Daniel. Ham rested the barrel of the gun on Harry's right shoulder and leaned close to Harry's ear. "This is the last sound you'll ever hear from this ear, Mr. Rich."

He placed the muzzle next to Harry's ear and fired.

BOOM!

It was a large caliber pistol and the report from it was like thunder. Harry screamed at the searing pain inside of his head. He lifted his hands to his ear. Ham whacked him viciously with the barrel of his gun. Harry dropped to his knees, holding his hands up to the side of his head, whimpering in pain.

Ham dragged him back up to his feet. The barrel of the gun was pushed against his face. "This is what happens when you try to escape, Mr. Carrington."

Harry was in shock. His head screamed at him in pain so intense, he was nearly blind. He turned to face his executioner, his face stretched in fear and pain.

Ham pushed him with the barrel of his gun.

"It really would look better if you ran, Mr. Rich." The clicks of Hamlett pulling back the hammer on his pistol sounded unusually loud. Ham turned Harry to face away from him and lifted the gun to the back of Harry's head. Daniel nudged his horse forward. He was reaching out to loop the reins over the Deputy's head, when he felt something touch his leg. It was the barrel of a rifle. Red shook his head, No, and smiled.

"Hi there, Deputy. These criminals giving you some trouble, are they?" Red was slightly behind Daniel, his rifle casually resting across his saddle, pointed in Ham's direction. "I couldn't help hearing the gunshot. I thought there might be some problem here." Relief surged through Daniel. Red's horse was breathing hard.

Red hadn't taken his eyes from the Deputy, still pointing his pistol at Harry's head. Slowly, Hamlett lowered it, grabbing Harry as he did and pushing him towards his horse.

"No problem here, just a little disciplinary situation. It's all taken care of now though, isn't it, Mr. Rich?" Red saw the black burn mark on Harry's cheek and shook his head in pity. Harry lifted his cuffed hands to his face.

"What brings you over this way without your wagons, Red?" Hamlett asked with transparent innocence, angered that his fun had been spoiled.

"I got some problems in Twin Lakes and I got to go to the bank and straighten out some things."

Red had been taken by surprise when he heard the shot echo up the steep valley, but had little doubt about its meaning. His horse responded like the trooper she was and ran all the way down the road with effortless speed. She was just about the best horse he'd ever owned and they had been partners so long, he thought she knew what he wanted, even before he asked it of her. Such a horse comes along usually only once in a horseman's life. He patted her neck affectionately several times as they rode into Twin Lakes.

There was little chance that Ham would try anything untoward with Red present. It would be too hard to explain to his father how Red had tried to rescue his prisoners and he'd had to kill them all. Not even his father would believe that story.

⇥⇤

At Twin Lakes they all dismounted and stretched their legs. The horses drank and the men urinated. Frank was butchering some game when they arrived, looking slovenly. He hadn't shaved for weeks and his beard was growing in gray. He carried his rifle wherever he went these days, anxious about the wolves that kept him awake at night. His eyes were darkly circled and bloodshot to the point that they were hard to look into, let alone out from. He was a pitiful creature.

Red was shocked at his appearance; he'd not seen him in the past month. He never seemed to leave the Lodge when they were around.

"Hi there Ham," he said, intentionally ignoring Red. "What're you doin' with these fellers?" Frank stood a few feet away and looked past them at the expanse of frozen water of the lakes.

"I'm takin' them to jail, Uncle Frank. They're the ones that robbed the bank on Christmas, we think."

Frank looked at Harry and Daniel again. His mind had been rotting with disuse, whiskey, guilt, and fear, but it still had some traction to it. "Well, I recognize that one," he pointed to Daniel. "He might've been the one I spotted that night."

The blood in Harry's veins froze solid. Daniel remembered that when they were trying to exchange their horses, Frank had looked their way briefly, focused on his path to murder and mayhem, and Daniel and Harry were certain that he hadn't seen them in the dim light. It had been snowing heavily and, bundled up in their hats and coats, how could he have recognized them?

Whether he saw them or not, this was Frank's chance at revenge for the many betrayals of his deceased wife.

"Just keep your mouths shut, you two," Red said quietly.

Ham was considering this new information, his mind fumbling with the implications. He smiled when it finally occurred to him that they now had a witness.

"Well, that's pretty damned interesting, Uncle Frank. I guess you'd be willing to state that in court?"

Frank looked from Daniel to Harry and settled his painful gaze on Daniel. "Why yes, Ham. I believe I would."

"That's good, Uncle Frank. I'll bet my Dad is going to be very happy to hear that you saw them here after the robbery. It makes sense that they rode over the Pass after the storm and just holed up here in one of the cabins for the night." Ham was very pleased with his deductive powers. "Let's get going. I imagine my Dad has got some plans for you."

Daniel pretended to be having trouble mounting his horse when, with only one foot in the stirrup, he pulled on his reins. It was a good piece of horsemanship, Red thought later. Daniel was holding onto the pommel as his horse reared up and knocked Frank down. He leapt on top of Frank and pushed his handcuffed wrists down across Frank's throat with all his might. He had once heard that the look of fear is foreign to the bully until the day that man dies; he saw that look in Frank's eyes. He leaned down next to Frank's ear as he pushed on his throat harder as if trying to stand.

"I know about Gloria, Frank." Daniel whispered. "I know you killed her. The wolves told me."

The effect was instantaneous. Frank threw Daniel off and grabbed for his rifle. Daniel rolled away and stood to find Frank pointing his rifle at him. He levered a round into it clumsily, his eyes wild and angry.

"NO! They didn't! They couldn't." Frank was insane.

"Don't do it, Uncle Frank. It was an accident." Ham spurred his horse between them. "Dad would think harshly if you killed him before we got to convict him." The logic in the argument helped his decision to lower the rifle.

Red returned his pistol to its holster.

Frank backed away from Daniel and retreated into the Lodge, slamming the door. Ham took Daniel's horse by the reins and held it so that Daniel could mount. The nervous horse kept looking back at Daniel, its eyes wide and its feet moving constantly.

"You can ride a horse, can't you?" Ham asked sarcastically.

Daniel ignored him and allowed himself and his horse to be led all the way into Leadville. Red rode along with them, still giving the bank as the reason for his presence. It was after nightfall when they finally reached the jail, where the Sheriff was waiting for them at the door. It seemed that all of his deputies were there, too. It was a very severe reception, except that the Sheriff looked more than a little happy.

The Sheriff roughly pushed them into a cell and personally locked them in. It was only then that he spoke. "Well, Harry, and whatever your name is, I warned you two never to come back to my town." He looked at the sullen faces of his two new toys. "You're going to regret shooting your mouth off, Mr. Rich."

"Uncle Frank said that he saw him at the Lodge Christmas night," Ham hurried to add.

"Now, don't that just make my evening worthwhile?" He pushed the other deputies out of the cell room, but came back alone for one last word. "Sleep well, gentlemen. Tomorrow we're going to have a little talk, private like." He was laughing as he locked the door behind him.

The Sheriff noticed that Red was still in the office. "What can I do for you now, Red? It's a little bit late for you to be riding around town."

"Just happened to be riding this way and wanted to help your deputy bring these two dangerous criminals in is all."

"Well, thank you for your help." The Sheriff ushered Red out and closed the door behind him. "The rest of you get out of here too. I want to talk to my favorite son here." The deputies filed out, disappointed not to be part of the excitement. When they'd left, he looked at his son and held out his hands for an answer.

"Someone had to teach that Harry feller a lesson," Hamlett said, spitefully.

The Sheriff slapped Ham hard across the face.

"That's for not shooting them both for trying to escape. Now we gotta go through a trial, you idiot." He locked eyes on his son and reached out with his hand again. Ham flinched, but instead of hitting him, his father patted him gently on the reddened cheek. The Sheriff sat down behind his desk. He motioned his son to sit across from him. "Now. Tell me again exactly what Frank said."

Chapter 44

The jail in Leadville was cold. They were given one blanket each, and Daniel wore his around his shoulders to conserve his thin reserves of warmth. Hour after hour, he shivered from the cold. He was not only cold and tired, but lonely and scared as well. Everything that he'd feared when he committed himself to Harry's harebrained idea was happening. As angry as he was at Harry, he couldn't help but blame himself. After all, he was the one who decided to go back over the Pass that night.

"Harry? Are you awake?"

"NO! Go away. Let me sleep."

"I saw Gloria's body."

Harry rolled over and faced Daniel. "Where?"

"In the wolves' pen. I went looking around and I found her." The memory of his fright and the gore of her corpse threatened to overwhelm him. "That's what I told Frank. I told him that the wolves told me that he was the one who killed her." Daniel smiled at his deviousness.

"So that's why you did it?"

"I had to let him know that I knew where her body was."

"I was wondering what that was all about."

Harry had wondered what Daniel was trying to do when he wheeled his horse at Frank. The fact that Frank was willing to testify that he'd seen them late that night at Twin Lakes was a problem. But the threat of Daniel exposing the facts about what they'd observed that awful night might shake his commitment. They could possibly go to jail for robbing the bank, but they could then point their fingers at Frank for the murders. Therein lay some justice, for them and for Gloria, too.

Harry was not much in the way of good company. His face was swollen and he was on the verge of tears with the pain in his ear. He was miserable, but found solace by wrapping himself tightly in his bearskin coat and curling up in a fetal position, facing the wall. Daniel thought him a pitiful creature, reminding him more of a sleeping child than of the man who used to be his friend.

⊲⊳

The Sheriff was up early the next morning and riding south to Twin Lakes as the sun rose. He had a busy day ahead of him and wanted to be back in town to press the Judge for a speedy trial. The sooner they had the trial, the better his chance of a conviction. He was unsure that they actually were the culprits, though they seemed his best bet at the moment. That was definitely the case if Frank was going to stand up in court to testify that he'd seen them that night, but then, he hadn't talked to Frank yet.

By the time he reached the Lodge, his butt was sore and his face was near frozen. The days were getting longer as spring approached, but the nights and the mornings were still as cold as they ever were. He dismounted at the back of the Lodge and noted the silence; a complete stillness. It was broken by a long wailing howl coming from somewhere in the trees. The back door opened and Frank came out, firing his rifle into the trees behind the Lodge.

"What the hell are you shootin' at, Frank?" The Sheriff saw something move out of the corner of his eye and Frank fired again. "Goddamn it, Frank, will you stop doing that?"

Frank blocked the door, the rifle held tightly against his shoulder, his eyes sighting along the barrel. The Sheriff pushed the barrel aside and stepped past Frank. The Sheriff wrinkled his nose at the horrible stench in the kitchen.

"You could clean the place, Frank."

"Leave me alone, Clayton. Did you come all this way out here to criticize my housekeeping?"

"Actually, no. I'm interested in what you told my son yesterday."

Frank didn't remember much of the day after that kid told him he knew about him murdering Gloria—the empty whiskey bottles on the table mutely attested to the fact.

"What was it I said?" Frank fell into his chair, almost making it.

"Goddamn it, Frank." He helped his brother off the floor and back into his chair. "You told Ham you saw that young feller outside on Christmas. The night you massacred your wife and that cowboy! You do remember that, don't you?"

Frank closed his eyes.

His brother looked at him and sighed. "It doesn't really matter if it's a lie. All you have to do is tell the judge that you saw them and that'll be that. The case solved, me the hero, you coming back here to drink yourself to death."

An armistice had arrived between them and a semblance of peace settled in the room.

"That kid saw her body." The peace was broken.

"What did you say?" The Sheriff was sitting erect, his spine rigid. "Frank, what did you say just then?"

"I said the kid saw Gloria." Frank's voice was low and lethally soft.

"How do you know? Tell me everything you remember."

"I saw his tracks going from the bunkhouse to the wolves' pen when he was here last. I didn't find them until after he and Red and his men had left. I was planning on killing him the next time I saw him, but he never came back again."

"Why didn't you just get rid of her?"

"Don't you think I tried? I put it in their pen, hoping they'd eat it when they got hungry. But it was real strange; they just lay there looking at it, like it was going to get up and feed them again. It was frozen. Maybe they didn't eat frozen things I thought, but they ate old Billy Smith in a coupla' days. Nothing left to bury, bones all over the county." Frank's smile was full of wickedness as he remembered the scattered pieces of what used to be a man. The Sheriff listened with rapt interest; his brother was on the near edge of madness.

"Well, what happened?" he asked, but Frank was off, lost somewhere in what used to be his mind. "Frank, hey, I'm not here for my health or your company. Frank!" he yelled again.

Frank jerked back to the present. He looked off towards the frozen lakes. "She had sex with him, Clayton. I heard them."

"Frank, everybody had sex with your wife."

Frank festered. "You can't dig a grave in wintertime, d'you know that, Clayton?"

"Yes, I know that, Frank. Then what happened?"

"I took her out there." Frank pointed uphill behind the Lodge, away from the lakes. "She was frozen like a log, so I packed her on one of the mules and carted her out into the woods, left her there. I figured if the wolves and coyotes didn't eat her, then the crows and vultures would, come spring." Frank had brightened somewhat and was looking at his brother with fervent eyes. "You're not going to believe what happened." He leaned forward abruptly. "They brought her back."

"What exactly do you mean by 'They brought her back?'"

"Clayton, I promise you." He paused for a moment. "Somehow they dragged her body back and left it in the shed. So I took it further out." He looked close to tears. "They brought her back again. I nearly tripped over her one morning, outside the back door." He paused again. "God, Clayton. They're devils. They want to kill me." Frank sucked in air to stifle his rising panic. "They come sniffing and yappin' around every night. I saw them standing on their hind legs lookin' in the window one time. They were tryin' to find a way in, I betcha'."

"Why don't you kill them, then?"

"What the hell do you think I was shooting at when you came by?" Frank was red-faced. "They keep me up all night with their howling and yipping. Every night, every night they parade around the place, making the noise of the devil himself. Sometimes in the day, I see them walking across the lake, but I just can't hit them. It's like they're ghosts or something."

"Why not drop her in the lake?" It seemed an obvious solution to Frank's dilemma. "The ice is pretty good still, by the look of it. I would've thought that you might've thought of that yourself by now." The Sheriff walked slowly to the kitchen and looked at the dark stains that would have been Gloria's final legacy. The outlines of her bloody demise were barely evident, but they were still visible.

"You know how I feel about water, Clayton. I never was much good around water. It scares me, you know that."

The Sheriff looked at his younger brother with a mixture of pity and fear.

"Take care of the problem before you bring us both down."

Frank nodded lamely. "Sure, Clayton, I'll do it."

"Today, Frank. You'll do it today, won't you?"

"OK. Thanks, I owe you."

"Yes, you do, little brother."

Outside, his horse was wide-eyed and skittish when he went towards her. She stamped her feet and twisted her head. He had a devil of a time settling her down. He felt something behind him, watching him, but when he turned, he saw nothing, just a whispering in the trees. He had to admit, it gave him a creepy feeling knowing that he was being watched. Without thinking, he checked his pistol and tugged his rifle free before he mounted and rode away, holding his horse in check and fighting her until they were several miles away from the Lodge. By then, the feeling of being watched diminished.

He headed back to Leadville feeling little better about the situation that had started out so promising, and now had the potential of turning on him and biting him in the ass. If he could just trust Frank to get rid of the evidence in the lake, all would be well again. The thought of Harry in his jail drew him home.

The Sheriff was surprised when he turned the corner onto Main Street. Even from a distance, he could see the crowd outside his office. Immediately after he dismounted, he was accosted by at least a dozen reporters asking questions, while photographers exploded flash powder in his face from every direction.

"Do you have the men who robbed the bank, Sheriff?" one persistent fellow asked, as he tried to push past him and into the office.

"Is it Butch Cassidy in there, Sheriff?" asked another. That question stopped his forward rush to the door.

He turned to face the crowd. "No. I can honestly say that we don't have Butch Cassidy in my jail."

"Well, who are they, Sheriff? Are they part of their gang, then?"

"We don't know that yet, but we'll let you know when we do, OK?" He pushed the door open to his office and found his men edgy, some held rifles. "What's goin' on here, Ham? Put those damned rifles away, for God's sake. They're just reporters."

"Well, we saw the crowd and figured there might be trouble," Ham ventured.

"Goddamn it, Ham, we got a couple of drunks in there, not Robin Hood." The deputies looked at each other, confused. "Where did they all come from, Ham? We don't have but a couple of reporters and I didn't even see them in that crowd anywhere.

"They all came in on the morning train from Denver. Some say there's more coming from Salt Lake and Kansas City tomorrow. I guess they all heard about the story over the telegraph."

He grew up in simpler times and longed for their return, which if he became mayor, he would work for. These newfangled gadgets he didn't understand, and being the simple sort of man he was, he resented those who did.

"Sheriff, there's a lawyer in there with them fellers," said a young deputy.

"What was that you said?" the Sheriff's look made the deputy quail in fear.

"There's a lawyer in there." He ventured again. "He said he was hired to defend them. He arrived with the reporters. I guess he's from Denver, too."

"Alright." He used all his strength to calm himself. "You fellers tell the reporters that we'll tell 'em what's going on when we know something. Two of you stay outside the door, the rest of you, go on about your rounds. Get a move on."

He tore open the door to the cells. Looking at the lawyer, he was assured that his expectation would be justified. The man looked almost comical; tall and birdlike, young and eager-looking, not at all like the typical decrepit men of his profession. He locked eyes with the Sheriff, his eyes were keen.

"Sheriff, I'm wondering why there aren't any charges filed for the arrest of these men." His voice boomed in the confines of the room.

The Sheriff girded his authority about him. "I've been busy. Exactly who are you?"

"I'm here to help these two innocent unfortunates, Sheriff. I'm Mr. Greenberg, attorney at law."

"Good. Then, Mr. Greenberg, I don't want to see you here in my jail again." He pushed the lawyer out through the door and closed it behind him.

"I'll be back, Sheriff." Greenberg yelled from the other side of the door.

"Yeah I'm sure you will. Turd!" He turned back to face the cell with his hands on his hips, his fingers drumming on the butt of his pistol. "I think you two robbed that bank and I'm going to prove it, no matter how many lawyers you find. You're mine now, boys."

Daniel and Harry looked at each other, conveying their concern.

"After I finish with the charges, I'll come back and we'll have our little chat. How does that sound to you?" He turned to leave. "Can I get you boys anything?"

"How about some heat?" said Harry.

"Sorry, this ain't no hotel." He came back to the bars of their cell, his eyes bright with humor. "How about a steak?" He could see Harry brighten. "Dream on, fellers," he laughed loudly. "I have a feeling you two'll be here for a spell, so you might as well get comfortable. By the way, I got a reliable witness," he said as the door slammed shut behind him.

"It could be worse, you know." Harry forced a laugh. "He could've taken our blankets with him."

"Shut up, Harry."

"Come on, partner, you've got to cheer up. Look, we've got a lawyer, thanks to Jerome, and he's going to get us out of here."

"Shut your mouth for a while, will you, Harry?"

"That's not a nice thing to say to your partner."

"Partner, you say? If it wasn't for your big mouth, we wouldn't be in here."

"Can't you get over that for just a minute?"

"Not till we get out of here." Daniel got up and went to the window, where he could just see the tops of the mountains between the buildings across the alley. He looked south, knowing his heart lay in that direction.

⊰⊱

"How are they doing, Red?" Shirley was behind the bar when Red and Joe had arrived. Snow followed them, even though spring was just around the corner.

"They could be better, but then we could be younger." Red's humor did little to raise Shirley's spirits. She smiled thinly and continued polishing the glass in her hand. "The Sheriff's making a big deal about how they're definitely the ones who did the robbery. Says he has a witness that saw them over at Twin Lakes that night. Just so happens, the witness is his brother, Frank."

"They said in the paper that the trial's going to be next week. Is that what you heard?"

"Yes, I'm afraid it is. I spoke to the lawyer and he seems to think they're just going to railroad them so that the Sheriff can get elected Mayor. The boys are his ticket to becoming Mayor, as he sees it."

"What's their lawyer like?" she asked.

"Well, I wouldn't want to pick a fight with him in court. He's young, but seems a pretty tough customer, from what I could tell. He doesn't seem to think there's much of a case if they don't find the stolen money."

"Has anyone looked in on Harry's cabin?" Red asked.

"Willy Tomb was supposed to, but Leafy moved in there after he found some miners trying to dig up the place," Joe volunteered.

"I think we'd better go see what happened, Joe."

"No problem."

They left Shirley absently polishing glasses and headed to Harry's cabin. When they arrived, smoke was rising from the chimney vent. Inside, they found Leafy struggling with the log and having a difficult time getting the pulley system to work. He was reaching for his rifle as the door opened. He relaxed when he saw Red.

"That's right neighborly of you to take care of Harry's cabin for him, Leafy," Red said to him.

Leafy blushed at the praise. "Joe told my dad that he'd heard talk of digging up the place. I just thought that someone should mind it for them."

"You're a good boy, Leafy. It looks like you're having some trouble there." Red saw that the eyebolt that supported the pulley had been turned, so he straightened it. "There, that should work now." He then noticed that the other hole had been plugged. "Did you plug this hole, Leafy?"

"No. It was plugged when I got here."

He looked around the cabin and saw that someone had been messing with it, searching it. "Seems like you got here just in time, too."

"Yeah, there were two men I didn't recognize in here when I came last night. The rifle convinced them they should leave."

"I think one of us should stay here while they get this thing sorted out," Red suggested.

"I just can't believe they robbed that bank," said Leafy, pulling the log into the fire easily.

"That's because they didn't," Red said with authority. "Listen Leafy, there's something you can do for us. You might get a visit from a lawyer feller. Don't let him in, no matter what he says or does. OK?"

"Sure, Red." Leafy looked at Joe and Joe gave him the thumbs up sign of the blasters.

"No problem." Joe was confident that Leafy would hold off an army if need be. They shook hands and Joe promised to look in on him.

"We have to do something about that weasel lawyer, Joe," Red said as they walked down the path together.

"I have some money put away for emergencies."

"You'd do that for Harry?"

"It'd be more for the boy. No problem."

"You're a good friend, Joe. I have a little stashed away, too."

"Well, I guess we should go see a weasel then." Joe quickened his pace.

They walked in step like two old gunfighters, on their way to see Mr. Eugene Heber, the weasel and lawyer. Red was confident that he could convince Mr. Eugene Heber to accept his money to pay Harry's debts. He still had his gun on his hip, under his coat, as an extra hand in their negotiations.

"Red. Hold up a minute." Wheeler called out as they were passing his office. "How's it going over there?" Jerome asked. He was out of breath.

"Pretty well, I guess. We won't know till the trial, though. That Sheriff has it in for the boys."

"Did the lawyer get there?"

"Yeah, he arrived on the morning train."

"Good. He's the best in Denver. It would mean a lot to him to beat that Sheriff in his own town. They've crossed swords before, by the sounds of it. He's a mean son of a bitch, I've heard."

"Well, Joe and me, we've got another son of a bitch lawyer we've got to talk to now." They'd stopped outside the Brand Building and Red pointed at the sign above the door. 'Eugene Heber Esquire. Attorney at Law.' "Do you want to come in and lend some of your weight here?"

Wheeler smiled and shook his head. "Ah, no thanks Red. I don't like gunplay before I've had my lunch. Thanks all the same." He turned to go.

"Say, Jerome?"

Wheeler turned back. "I want to thank you for getting the lawyer. I don't think they're guilty, but a good lawyer couldn't hurt their case."

"Well, I'm not a big fan of lawyers either, but I trust judges less, if you know what I mean." Jerome laughed. "Good luck, boys."

They marched into Heber's office without knocking.

The Wild West wasn't so dead or gone after all.

⊰⊱

"I want you to get these boys some hot food in here, Sheriff," Mr. Greenberg bellowed. "Now, if you please."

The lawyer had marched into the Sheriff's office, angry. The judge had not seen his side of the case—that there was no real evidence, other than hearsay, to keep them in jail. The judge told him that the Sheriff had a witness and that was enough for them to be held for trial. Mr. Greenberg had stormed out of the courthouse, his fury rising as he marched down the street to where the reporters were pressing against the door of the Sheriff's office. He had to push his way through and was only allowed entrance when he brandished letters from both the courthouse and his employer, David Hyman, whose name opened most doors in this part of Colorado.

One of the deputies carried in a tray, on which were two cups of coffee and two pieces of dry bread. The lawyer watched as they wolfed it down and grasped the warm coffee cups in their shivering hands.

"Besides your idle boasting, Mr. Rich, is there anything I should know that would connect you two to the robbery? The Sheriff has told the reporters that he has a witness who could put you both over here the night of the robbery. What do you know about that?"

They looked at each other, but said nothing.

"OK, how about this, then? The Sheriff says that he wounded one of the robbers as they were getting away, and found blood tracks when he was following them. Do either of you have a gunshot wound?"

Harry closed his eyes for a fraction of a second, but it didn't escape the eagle eyes of Mr. Greenberg. He leaned closer and whispered, "Is there something I should know, Mr. Rich?"

"No, no. I just thought of something. I hurt my shoulder some time back, but it wasn't a bullet wound or anything like that."

"I hope not, Mr. Rich. That would not be a good thing to discover at the trial."

Harry reached up and felt his shoulder; Daniel looked at him, he shrugged and dropped his hand.

"Well, I don't think they've got much of a case here, gentlemen. No bullet wound, no evidence, and only hearsay evidence at that. I'd say you'll soon be back where you belong." He stood to leave. "I'll see about getting you some decent food. It's criminal what they're putting you

two boys through. I'll be back in a week—before the trial, to be sure."
He went to the door and banged on it. "Deputy, open the door here."

The door opened and he was gone.

"That went well, don't you think?" Harry was unrealistically buoyed.

"We're going to prison, I just know it." Daniel fell back on the bunk.

"What I'm worried about is the scar on my back." Harry took off his coat and his shirt. Daniel lifted his undershirt to expose the scar from the bullet wound. "What does it look like?" It still looked raw around the edges. There was some discharge on his undershirt.

"I think we have a big problem, Harry," he said, coming around to face him. "If they ask to see your back, it's going to be pretty obvious that you've been shot."

"How long did he say until the trial?" Harry asked quietly.

"I think he said a week or so."

Harry brightened. "I have an idea, but we need a candle or a lamp."

"What're you going to do?" Daniel grasped at a sliver of hope.

"I'll show you tonight. Let's just see if we can get a candle from the deputy—say you have to read the Bible or something."

Food arrived; it was hot and filling and their spirits brightened.

⁂

It had been several days since his brother had visited with him, and the pressing need to dispose of the body for good had been weighing on him. With spring approaching, he had to get it out on the lake before the ice thinned far from shore where it was deep enough that she would never be discovered. The daylight was ebbing and the road was deserted, so he mustered his courage by drinking a half a bottle of whiskey and set about his grizzly task.

Frank found that Gloria was difficult to deal with in death just as she was when she was alive. Her body was frozen solid, but it was still difficult to manage, just as it had been when she was alive. His intention was to drag her across the lake in his canoe. It would be risky, but he knew his brother was right, as he always was. Gloria needed to be at the bottom of the lake permanently. Still, simply thinking of being so far from shore loosened his bowels.

He had stitched two grain sacks together to stuff her body in, and he avoided looking at it as much as possible as he did. He'd tried to close her eyes, but they had been frozen open, so he gouged them from their sockets. The mutilated breasts that had given so much pleasure in life, hung frozen to her side. For the first time, he wished he'd just shot her and been done with it.

He placed several heavy stones in the bag and tied the top tightly, breaking her head off at the slashed neck as he stuffed her in. He laughed at the sound it made. His mood brightened when he rolled her out of the shed and put her in the canoe.

Usually the canoe slid easily along the snow, but the added weight made it much more difficult to pull and he was forced to rest several times to gather his strength while constantly looking out for the wolves, his rifle close by. His boots had gotten wet at the lake edge and he cursed at the numbing cold that seeped into his feet. Reluctantly he stepped onto the ice and slowly trudged across the frozen water, dragging the canoe behind him.

The going got tougher the further out onto the lake he went. The snow on the lake had been windblown into sharp ice ridges and they eventually tore a hole in the bottom of the canvas skin of the canoe. Frank discounted it as another inconvenience. The ice under his feet seemed solid and the canoe was working like it should. He thought he saw something moving out of the corner of his eye and grabbed his rifle from the canoe.

It could be the wolves, but if they came at him out on the lake, he'd have a clear shot. He wouldn't miss this time. The reassuring thought of being rid of them for good made him smile. He placed the rifle back in the canoe and pulled again. It was slow going, and the effort was exhausting. He was sweating, so he took off his heavy coat and threw it in the canoe. He labored on. Again he thought he saw something move on the ice. The wind blew loose snow over the surface of the lake, and the wolves were indistinct because of it. Their pale grey coats blending in with the terrain so that when they stopped moving and lay down they became invisible to Frank's watering eyes.

Frustrated and exhausted by the effort, Frank decided he'd gone far enough. Removing his axe he swung and chipped the ice. He swung again, and dented the ice some more. Again and again he beat the ice, and slowly the hole opened for him. The wind chilled him. He doubled his efforts, careful not to get too near the edge of the hole for fear of falling into the icy water.

His strength had almost gone, and he realized how much of it had been sucked away with all of the whiskey he'd been drinking. When he judged the hole to be big enough he reached into the canoe for the body. Again he was surprised at how weak he was. The sack with the body and rocks seemed to have doubled in weight. He couldn't get a decent grip, so he took off his gloves and threw them into the canoe with his rifle.

His strength gone, Frank had to tip the canoe on its side to wrestle the body out and, exhausted from the struggle, he fell on his rear when it finally emerged. With considerable effort, he regained his footing and dragged the weighted sack to the hole. For a moment he considered saying something over Gloria's body, but then with a shrug and a smile he kicked the corpse into the hole. It gurgled and disappeared immediately but he watched the hole for a time, thinking that perhaps she would come back up and pull him in with her. He laughed at the thought and turned in time to see one of the wolves crouching down. It suddenly jumped up and began running towards him.

Frank laughed at what he saw. The animal was fifty yards away. One shot would put him in the hole with his mistress. He turned to the canoe for his rifle and froze as he looked at the snarling white teeth of the other wolf. He snarled back and went for his rifle, but not before the animal snapped at his hand. Looking from side to side, he judged his chances of getting to his rifle. He advanced a foot, and both of the wolves did the same. He was surprised at how well they worked together. For a moment, he formed some respect at their hunting skills.

They smelled him; he could tell, because their nostrils flared and they growled low. What were they smelling, his fear? He'd heard that they could do that. He'd never liked the damned things. Why she kept them around, he had no idea, but now was the time to get rid of them, once and for all. He lunged for the rifle.

The wolf to his right leapt at him with amazing speed and grabbed his arm. He fell back, but he had the rifle. The wolf was snapping viciously, closer and closer to his neck. Frank slashed at it with the rifle and heard the yelp of the well-timed blow connecting; he smiled with superiority. He looked to his left to see the other wolf climbing over the canoe at him. He swung the rifle around. Point blank, he couldn't miss. The wolf stopped and moved back. Frank raised the rifle and smiled. Suddenly, he was savaged on the hand by the wolf he'd just hit. He let go of the rifle, grabbing his torn hand, backing up as he did.

His foot started to slip. Startled, he looked down and saw that he was on the edge of the hole he'd dug for Gloria. He recovered his balance and tried to step over the hole, but as he turned to look for his rifle, one of the wolves lunged at him and he lost his footing. His leg slipped into the hole, but he still had one foot out. He tried to stop falling into the hole by throwing his body sideways. He reached out for some purchase, but his body went further in.

Instinctively, he pulled his hand back to brace himself, but felt himself falling further into the freezing water. He was in up to his waist and could feel the drag of the water on his wet clothing. The wolves snapped at his hands.

He clutched again at the snow, and again they snapped at his hands. They made no effort to savage him now, as they most assuredly could have done. They just patiently waited, snarling happily at his dilemma. He hated them more than ever as his strength ebbed away with his body heat. His hatred for the wolves and for Gloria was the only thing to warm him.

They lay down in the snow next to the hole and watched with patient disinterest. Frank's fingers finally lost their grip on the edge of the hole and he slipped under the surface, cursing them loudly until his last gasp.

The wolves turned and trotted back across the deserted lake to the safety of the forest, satisfied.

Chapter 45

Harry shivered uncontrollably and convulsed, his teeth chattered loudly.

"Will you hurry up for God's sake? Do you want me to get pneumonia?" Harry was naked to the waist.

Daniel was busily working the bear grease onto Harry's back.

"How's it lookin'?" he asked.

"Put your coat on." Harry turned his coat inside out and climbed back into it gratefully. Daniel passed the candle over the inside membrane of the bearskin which made the membrane sweat oil. When he had sufficient grease on his hand, Harry removed his coat and Daniel wiped the grease onto Harry's back again.

"How's it looking?"

"I think it's going to look pretty good." Daniel was admiring his work.

"God Almighty, it stinks."

"That's not all bear you're smelling."

Harry reached around to scratch his back and Daniel slapped his hand away. It wasn't a vicious slap, but the tension between them had not eased much since they first arrived in jail. Harry looked at Daniel menacingly.

"Harry, if you don't let me do this, we're never going to get out of here. Keep your hands away from your back, OK?"

"Are you f-f-f-finished?" he demanded through chattering teeth.

"You can put your coat on again."

Daniel turned the heavy coat inside out and Harry slipped into it uncomfortably. He pulled his blanket around his shoulders and lay back down on his bunk, shivering.

"Do you think this'll work?" Harry asked when his shivering calmed down.

"It had better work, Harry." Daniel returned to the window and looked longingly at the wintry scene outside. He let the rough woolen curtain fall back and sat down on the edge of his bunk. He picked up the newspaper and read it by the candlelight. "The newspapers are saying we're guilty, but they can't figure how we did it."

"Unless they find our sled, they're not going to."

Their stay in the Leadville jail had not been too kind to Harry. They had decided to promote Harry's hairiness, upon which their defense rested. Harry was growing a beard; he was looking very scruffy and his odor polluted the whole room.

Since their arrival, they'd been mostly left alone, which had worked to their benefit. The only time they saw anyone was when they were brought their meager food or tormented by the Sheriff, who was taking a personal interest in their discomfort. Thoughtfully, he made sure they saw the newspapers daily. He'd threatened to beat them, but the fact that they had a bulldog of a lawyer curbed his enthusiasm. He was becoming more frustrated every day. They were now receiving less food and it was never hot.

Red visited whenever he was over that way. The information he brought raised their hopes every visit. According to Red, the rush to discover their buried money was losing steam. Aspen had settled down again to something close to normality. They heard that reporters from as far away as New York were planning to attend the trial. Thanks to the telegraph, newspapers far and wide had grabbed the story and fueled the debate.

Red brought Daniel letters from Kate at every visit, and Daniel had found in them his strength and his courage. The trial was set for two days hence and the only thing he found promising in that was that he would see her once again, and every night he prayed that it would not turn out to be the last time. He also prayed that the trick with the bearskin coat would work. He knew, as did Harry, that if the Sheriff convinced the court that Harry's wound was a bullet wound, it would be compelling evidence.

Shirley and his other friends back in Aspen had rallied around Daniel, according to what he read in Kate's letters. She also mentioned that even Honey had come over to their house to offer her support. He reread Kate's letters each night until he fell asleep. It was usually then that he worried himself sick, thinking that his mother would somehow see his picture in the paper and be disappointed in him again.

Red had brought pen and paper for Daniel to write back and he personally delivered those letters to Kate. Shirley, Kate, Joe, and even Jerome Wheeler had made plans to come over to Leadville for the trial to lend their support, and that filled them both with some hope. Someone, they didn't know whom, had taken care of Harry's gambling debt. The fact that Leafy was standing guard also gave them some assurance that their stolen money was still safe.

Red was leaving the Sheriff's office when the Sheriff caught up with him outside the building.

"Say there, Red. Wait up a minute, will you?" His politeness was toxic.

"Sure, Sheriff, what can I do for you?" Red was respectful, no matter what he thought of the man in private. He knew that he was going to be asked to do something for the man even before he spoke.

"Do you think you could deliver a message for me to my brother Frank in Twin Lakes?"

"Sure enough, Sheriff." The Sheriff handed him an envelope, official-looking and sealed with wax. "Haven't seen him for a while, a week maybe. Do you want me to put it under his door?"

"What do you mean you haven't seen him?"

"Just that I haven't seen him. I have seen his canoe out on the lake, though."

"Let me get this straight. You haven't seen my brother for days, but his canoe is out on the lake?"

"That's about it, Sheriff, that's as much as I can tell you."

"I think I'll go on out there and deliver this myself." The Sheriff took the envelope back and went inside his office. Red was at the bank when he saw the Sheriff riding out of town at a fast trot.

⊰⊱

As the Sheriff rode to Twin Lakes, the question of why the canoe was on the lake puzzled him. Frank was nothing if not careful of his hunting equipment. He wouldn't even loan his own brother the canoe to go fishing. A feeling of unease grew deep in his stomach.

At the Lodge, he walked around back and found the door to the kitchen unlocked and the Lodge dark and cold. He called to his brother, but received no answer. He called again, then went back outside. Walking across the road to where there was a better view of the lake, he saw what Red had seen. Not quite in the middle of the lake was the dark outline of the canoe.

The lake itself was still and serene. He tested the ice and found that it was not sound enough for him to walk on, so he walked along the edge to another place where the ice appeared to be thicker and ventured out. Having fished in the lake he knew that if the ice gave way it would probably be shallow enough where he was for him to make it back to shore. He was less confident the further out he went. Occasionally, he heard the ice creak underneath him and froze on the spot, his heart pounding.

The Sheriff stood on the ice, considering his predicament. He looked out at the canoe again. He took one more step and felt the ice crack again. He froze, still as a statue.

The Sheriff was quite a bit heavier than his brother Frank and had been since they were children. Frank would have made it further safely, just because he was lighter. He slowly moved his weight one step forward and a heart-stopping feeling ran up his body as he felt the ice give a little, it had a spongy feeling under his foot. He backed away, carefully making his way to the shore. The tension had sapped his strength so much he had to rest on a rock on the shore while he pondered his dilemma.

Out on the lake the canoe sat alone and kept its secrets, taunting him. He knew what Frank had been trying to do, but couldn't fathom what had happened on the ice. He was drawn to the object out there, so near but so unapproachable. There was something in the canoe. Perhaps it was just Frank's coat, but perhaps it was Frank. He walked back and forth in frustration like a tiger in a cage, then decided to head back to Leadville.

The Sheriff was furious as he rode back to town and his mood became worse by the mile. Something had happened to Frank and the answer lay in the canoe. He had to get out to it and hoped that it had something, no matter what it was, which would help him find his brother, so that they could convict those bastards in his jail.

Tomorrow he'd go out with Ham and that skinny new deputy and they'd get that canoe.

⊰⊱

Kate waited patiently for Red to arrive with the letters from Daniel. She often busied herself helping her mother or Maisie with the dinner, but on the days when Red came back from his trips over the Pass with Daniel's letters, she couldn't concentrate. She could hardly wait to see him again, even though she was going to be in court. She had no doubt they would be found not guilty, no doubt at all.

What buoyed her spirits was that several thousand miners had dug in or around every mineshaft on the mountain, used or forgotten, and had found no trace of the money. They had become folk heroes as long as people thought that they were guilty.

Red would usually stay for dinner, as he had each time he brought mail from Daniel. Her mother liked having him around. Maisie thought he was the cat's whiskers. She loved his manliness, especially his big man's laugh. She would roll about when he got going telling some story or other, and that just made them all catch the laughter. They'd all end up laughing and pointing at each other. He always had seconds of everything and if it wasn't for her mother, Kate had no doubt that Maisie would be in bed with him any chance she got; she was so in love with his appetite.

Kate must have drifted off; she didn't hear the knock on the door. She woke when her mother ushered Red in and helped him out of his coat.

"You'll stay for dinner, won't you, Red?"

Shirley paid more attention to her appearance whenever Red was expected. Kate liked that her mother had feelings for someone, and she approved of Red highly. Not like when she used to see Harry. Kate had never really been glad to see him there. He had not been very clean, either.

"Hi there, Kate, I think this is for you." Red handed her a letter and she retreated to her favorite chair to read it.

"How're the boys doing, Red?" Shirley asked, inviting Red to join her on the sofa.

"Not bad, considering everything that's going on. That town's turning into a circus. I had a hard time getting us all in at the hotel. Jerome's going to be staying with the Tabors, so he'll be fine."

Maisie came into the room, wiping flour from her face with her dishtowel. "Well, Mr. Red, aren't you just a sight for sore eyes? I sure hope you're hungry." He kissed her on the cheek and she quivered with delight. "Oh, stop it!" she said, pushing him away. "You men are all alike, aren't they, Miss Shirley? If we didn't feed them, they'd never come around."

Red liked Maisie and had known her since she was Kate's age. She'd always been with Shirley. Between her and Mother, they'd helped raise Kate and Rachelle. Red dutifully pulled the chairs out for Shirley and Kate when she finally arrived at the table, subdued but happy, still holding Daniel's letter.

"How's Daniel taking it, Kate?"

"He doesn't sound very confident and he says he's always cold. He hates Harry and they're not getting along well, it seems." Kate looked at her mother, who reached out and held her hand.

"We'll be seeing him soon enough, you shouldn't worry. Nobody's going to believe Harry did it."

A place had been set at the table for Rachelle, but she failed to make an appearance.

They enjoyed their meal in spite of Rachelle's absence, but the mood at the table was subdued and they ate quietly. The food was delicious as always, but there was a pall of tense apprehension that dampened the usual lively conversation. Red excused himself after dinner, saying that he had to attend to the teams and the equipment for the trip back over the Pass with passengers the next day. Red promised to be there early to pick them up. They all said goodnight and he reluctantly took the pie that Maisie had packed.

"In case you get hungry later, Mr. Red."

Kate retired almost immediately, still holding onto her letter. Shirley waited up for Rachelle. She stayed awake most of the night.

⊰⊱

The Sheriff was up early and had three cups of coffee and the same number of bowel movements before his deputies arrived. They found him pacing the floor, impatient to get going, knowing that their best chance to retrieve the canoe was to get out on the ice early, while it was still cold and the sun hadn't weakened it. He was in a sullen, dirty mood. The curious deputies had no idea where they were going until they turned off the main road at Balltown and headed up the valley to Twin Lakes.

He was concerned about his brother, as much for his being his star witness as for his safety. Should his brother be found dead; the inquiry that would be sure to follow could do him no good. He needed to find his brother and he needed to find him alive. Alternatively, if his brother was dead, the boys in his jail might get off and he could keep the money, not a totally unpleasant thought. His mood brightened until the lake came into view and he saw the dark spot out on the frozen surface that was his brother's canoe.

He stopped off at the Lodge and searched the building, but found no evidence of Frank having been there for what looked like several days. The Sheriff then led his team around the lake to the point closest to the canoe. He'd packed a horse with ropes and a grappling hook that he'd gotten from one of the blacksmiths, and snowshoes, figuring that they would spread the weight and give his deputy a better chance of making it to the canoe and back.

Lemley, the tall, thin, reluctant deputy was sent out onto the lake wearing the snowshoes and a rope tied around his waist. He made his way onto the ice stepping carefully and cautiously, following the groove the canoe had left. The deputy was not the bravest of men. He needed encouragement, and finally threats from the Sheriff for him even to get within a dozen yards of the canoe.

Now just twenty feet away, he could see into the canoe, but his view was not good. He yelled back at the Sheriff, but couldn't make himself heard clearly. The Sheriff motioned for him to go out further. He yelled and pointed, but the gestures and the encouragement did little to alleviate the mounting fear that gathered weight the further from shore the deputy ventured.

Ever more cautiously, he edged further towards the canoe, dragging the extra rope and the grappling hook. Crack! He heard the fracturing of the ice as its surface strength was tested again. Ahead of him he saw the hole that Frank had dug next to the canoe, a slightly bluer patch on the whiter than white surface of the ice. Closer he edged. He felt the slight movement of the ice under his feet. He froze, lest he fall through.

He regained his courage and shuffled slightly closer, the quivering under his feet happening again. He was not going any further. He looked back towards the shore at the Sheriff swinging the rope, demonstrating to him how to throw the hook. Cautiously, he gathered the rope and started the hook swinging. He lofted it and was disappointed that it didn't go even halfway to the canoe. He reeled it in and tried again. This time, he got it to go further and heard it fall into the hole and not in the canoe as he'd wanted. He pulled on the rope and the iron hook came up to the surface. He felt the prongs catch on the edge of the hole. He swore in frustration.

He tugged again, but nothing happened. If he couldn't get the hook back, it would not go down well with the Sheriff, of that he was sure. Frustrated, he pulled on the rope. It wouldn't budge. He got down on his hands and knees and crawled closer to the hole. He pulled on the rope and felt it come up some more, but then it sank back down out of his grasp, as if something heavy was at the end. He pulled it up again, to where he could get his hands on the end of the hook and gave it a long, hard pull. He felt the ice under him give way with a snap like breaking bones.

Alarmed, the Sheriff watched as the young deputy pushed up to his knees.

"Stop! Stop!" he yelled, but it was too late. In his haste, the deputy had climbed to his feet, but tripped on his snowshoes as he turned to run. There came a loud crack. For the deputy, the world tilted to one side and he was enveloped in icy water. He almost lost consciousness from the shock of the frigid water as it swarmed over his body, sucking the heat and the life from him instantly. He exhaled the only air he hadn't screamed from his lungs. He felt himself sinking fast then something bumped his feet under him. He screamed and kicked, then reached up to grab for the side of the canoe, pulling it towards him. For a moment he thought he might live, but the freezing water sapped his energy like water on fire.

Again he touched something solid under the surface, but whatever was under him moved away. His numb, frozen brain told him it was a big fish. He laughed in his mind at the size of it, he'd touched it, and it was huge. The canoe came sliding into the hole with him, filling with water from the gash in its skin. Numbed to the core, he felt the rope tug on him and slowly pull him to the surface, onto the ice.

The canoe slid slowly into the lake, but as it went under, he saw a black coat float on the surface after the boat had gone under. He reached for it weakly, but it was too far away. As quickly as they could pull on the rope, they dragged him to the shore, weak and shivering and scared out of his wits.

⊰⊱

Harry was reading from the **Salt Lake Sentinel**, looking concerned.

"What's the matter Harry? Are you afraid someone over in Salt Lake City will read this and come looking for you?"

"That's not so far away from the possible."

"Come on, Harry. Who over there gives a damn about you and me? We're just a couple of stupid bank robbers as far as they're concerned."

Harry nodded, intent on reading the paper.

The door clanged open and the Sheriff entered, enraged. He was losing control. Though they had searched for weeks in Aspen, there was no evidence of the stolen money, and now he'd lost his only witness. He still had one last hope.

"You can go now, Deputy."

"'You sure Sheriff?"

"Yeah, I'll be alright. I don't think these two dickless wonders would have the guts to try anything, do you?"

The door closed behind him and the Sheriff was alone with his prisoners, his pistol in his hand. He opened the cell door, pulled in a chair, and sat blocking the door, glaring at them, holding his colt loosely in his hand.

"Well, son," the Sheriff said, looking directly at Daniel. "I guess it's about time we had ourselves a little talk. What did you say to my brother Frank?"

"Nothing, Sheriff. What would I have to say to someone who kills people?" Daniel and Harry both saw the reaction this had on the Sheriff.

He forced a smile; a vile contortion of his face. He looked down, savoring the moment. "Son, you'd better listen to me and listen good. Do you remember the last time we met? I do believe that I specifically told you that I didn't ever want to see you here again. Do you remember that?"

"Sheriff, we wouldn't be here if your dolt of a son hadn't come over and dragged us here," Harry said.

"Shut up, Mr. Rich. I'll get to you in a minute. Son, do you remember the time I saw you groveling in the mud?"

"With Butch Cassidy and that other feller, you mean?"

The Sheriff looked up and sat shocked still. "What do you mean?"

"Do you remember when the papers had those pictures of Butch Cassidy and that feller after that bank in Telluride got robbed?" The Sheriff didn't bother to nod. "Well, Sheriff, I got a pretty good look at those men the night they robbed me over in Stringtown. Then I saw them the next day when you were pushing me around. They looked just like the men in the papers. I'd say that you had Butch Cassidy here in your town and you actually talked to him and sent him on his way."

The Sheriff punched Daniel in the face, sending him reeling back against the wall. Harry moved to get up, but the Sheriff pointed the pistol at him.

"I wouldn't mind killing you both while you attempted to escape, do you know that?" Daniel dabbed at his nose, smearing blood across his face. "I think you must've been mistaken there, son." The Sheriff sat back heavily on his wooden chair. "There could be a resemblance, but it definitely wasn't them."

"If you say so."

"Now, let's get friendly-like and see if we can't come to some understanding. I believe that you took that money from our bank." Daniel and Harry exchanged a look. "I know that those bags of money are over there in your valley someplace." The Sheriff looked at each of them in turn to check for comprehension. "If you two were to somehow find them for us, there might be some latitude that I could work out with our judge over here. He's not usually a friendly sort, you know, but I do have some sway with him, I do believe. What do you think about that?"

"Let me get this right, Sheriff. If we tell you where we hid the money from the robbery that we didn't commit, you might be able to get the judge to go lightly on us when he sentences us for being guilty?" Daniel said.

The Sheriff sat back, smiled and nodded. "You're a quick thinker, son."

"Then you're a bigger ass than everyone thinks you are, including your daughter."

"Stand up, son." The Sheriff pointed the gun at his eye. "You'll be resisting a sheriff and trying to escape. They'd believe me before Harry here." Daniel stood up. The Sheriff smiled. "This is for your education."

There was not an instant between the last word and the fist that lashed out and hit Daniel in the stomach, buckling his knees and sending him to the floor. The Sheriff's pistol was pointed at Harry's belly. "I wouldn't do that, Mr. Rich. Some of this might come your way too" Harry sat back down on his bunk.

The Sheriff picked Daniel up by the collar and threw him against the wall, then sat back down heavily, the effort draining him; sweat beading on his brow. Daniel got his breath back and wiped his chin on his sleeve, the remnants of his lunch on the floor. He sat on his bunk and considered the Sheriff.

"All you got on us, Sheriff, is that Harry got drunk and shot off his mouth. You don't have anything else. You don't even have a witness."

"Is that the case? That's not all I got, son. I do know I shot one of you two as you were getting away. I know that for sure."

"Yeah, Sheriff? How do you know that?" Harry asked, resisting the impulse to rub his shoulder where the bullet had hit him.

"Let's just say a little birdie told me."

"We didn't rob your bank, Sheriff," Harry interjected.

"Now what am I supposed to believe, Harry? That when you're drunk, you robbed the bank, but now you're sober, you didn't?" He held his pistol loosely in his hand, looking from the gun to Harry, to Daniel, to the gun.

"He's telling the truth, Sheriff." Daniel noticed that his voice didn't quaver.

"You," he said, pointing at Daniel. "I want you to keep your mouth shut till I get to you. Do you understand me?" Daniel decided to comply.

"I know you're a drunk, Harry. Doc Holliday says you owe him quite a bit of money." He paused for effect. "And the last time I spoke to him, he was very put out that you haven't paid him back. I think you should've kept your mouth shut and stayed where you were. Don't you?"

Harry looked the Sheriff directly in the eye, holding his gaze for what seemed like minutes. "I guess we'll have to leave it up to the jury, Sheriff."

"What I think is that you started believing your own bullshit."

"I don't think the jury is going to put me in jail for being a liar, do you, Sheriff?"

"Ah, but here's where it gets interesting, I think you had to rob the Bank to pay off your debts and you convinced this young feller to go along with you. I think he was the other robber."

"I don't know what it is you're talking about," Daniel said softly.

"Son, if you tell me where Harry hid the money, I can convince the judge that you didn't have anything to do with this affair. You could just walk out of here with your friends and go on with your life with that pretty cripple girl who's here with her whore mother."

Harry grabbed Daniel's sleeve.

"I just can't believe that you're allowing this here piece of shit," he said, casually pointing the barrel of his pistol at Harry again, "to put you in jail for what, at least ten years? Your girl will be gone off with some miner, she'll probably have a half-dozen snotty kids running around by then, and you'll just be a memory to her. Is that what you want?" Daniel remained silent, festering at the insults.

"Do you like whiskey, son?"

"I don't drink."

The Sheriff laughed loudly. "You're either a fool or a liar. I can see why you two get on so well together." He paused, entertaining a new thought. "Or perhaps you think I'm a fool, then?" He grabbed Daniel by the shoulder and held the pistol to the side of Daniel's nose. "She's a cripple and you'd have no nose. Wouldn't that make a nice wedding photograph?" He squeezed Daniel's shoulder harder.

"You'd let me go if I told you that Harry robbed the bank?"

"That's right, son. I would. You can trust me."

Harry's skin crawled.

"Of course, you'd also have to tell me where you hid the money. But that wouldn't be a problem, would it?" The Sheriff was onto a course that the boys hadn't seen coming. "It wouldn't matter whether you had Harry as a partner, or if you had me. Either way, you could have half of what you stole. That's a pretty good deal if you ask me." He smiled down at Harry. "Don't you think that's a good deal, Harry?"

"What's in it for me, then?" Harry whimpered.

"You're going to jail, Harry." The Sheriff laughed loudly. "That's what's in it for you. You'll be there alone. That should be a lot of fun."

Harry looked at Daniel and tried to divine his response. For the first time, he saw a look in Daniel's eyes, the growing anger that he had built up for him. A surge of fear ran through him.

"I might even let you see my lovely daughter." The Sheriff enjoyed his superiority. "You remember her? She seems to be a bit sweet on you, by the way." The Sheriff showed his rotten gums when he smiled. "Now that sounds pretty damned good to me. That is, compared to spending the best years of your life in some cold cell being buggered at night by all of them inmates." He let the gruesome image sink in. "You're good-looking, boy—I'm sure you would get all the affection you ever wanted in there. What do you think, Harry?"

The Sheriff had pulled Daniel closer and had his arm around his shoulders, squeezing him tightly. Harry was relieved to see Daniel relax, closing his eyes as if resolving some dilemma. The Sheriff waited patiently for Daniel's answer. He was a confident man.

"Sheriff, I think you're going to make a fool of yourself." Daniel smiled and pointed his finger at the Sheriff's face. "If you can't find the money, then you're out of luck. You lose."

The Sheriff reacted predictably. He shoved Daniel fiercely against the wall, the pistol pointed at his chest. The gruesome, gummy smile returned.

"Maybe you do have some gumption in there, boy. I don't think you used it wisely, but there you go." The Sheriff sat back down and through his clenched teeth breathed deeply, gathering his anger into a focus. "It's about time you found out about some of the justice we deal out around here."

The Sheriff casually flipped his pistol in his hand, catching it by the barrel. In one quick movement, he hammered the butt of the pistol onto Daniel's knee. Daniel screamed and fell to the floor clutching his knee, his mouth wide in agony. Just as deftly, the Sheriff reversed the gun and caught it by the handle, pointing it at Harry.

"I feel a lot better now, don't you? I'll be back again, after I've had my supper." He stood with the gun pointed at Harry, the contorted body of Daniel moaning and writhing on the floor. "Boys, I'm glad we had this little talk. I'm sure I'll be having the pleasure of your company until such time as I deem it fit to send you off to the state prison." Smiling, he closed and locked the cell door and left them.

"Let me have a look at it," Harry said.

Breathing shallowly through clenched teeth, Daniel let Harry pull up the leg of his pants. The knee was swelling and the bruise looked like it was going to be ugly. There was a dent in the kneecap and Harry touched it gently, causing Daniel to push him back violently.

"Leave me alone—haven't you done enough damage?"

Harry retreated to his bunk and watched his partner writhe in pain. He felt sorry for Daniel for the first time; an odd feeling. He woke when their dinner was pushed under their cell door. Daniel ignored the food and limped to the window, peering out deep in thought.

Harry was miserable and cold. He wrapped the bearskin coat around himself more tightly, pulling his knees up to his chest and his cap down over his ears. "Look, I can understand why you could feel this way and all, but I thought at least we could still be friends." Harry's voice was almost plaintive. "I know I've made some mistakes, but I'm not all bad, am I?"

He joined Daniel at the window and looked out at the snow-covered mountains in the distance, radiant in the moonlight. He tried to put a comforting arm around Daniel but he shrugged him off, pushed past him and fell onto his bunk. Harry pulled the rough blanket curtain back over the window and went back to sit and shiver on his bunk.

Daniel was still lost in his thoughts, but the sound of Harry's teeth chattering broke into them. Abruptly he stood up, wincing from the pain in his knee, and limped back to the window. "God Almighty, it's cold in here," he said.

Harry could barely hear the words but he noticed the lilt; occasionally the accent came through. "Sheriff, do you think we can trouble you for some coffee in here before we freeze to death?" Harry yelled.

"Go ahead and freeze to death," the Sheriff's voice boomed from the other room. "Your dicks could freeze off before I give a damn about you." The Sheriff slammed the door behind him as he went back into his warm office. Daniel pulled the blanket over his head. Harry sighed loudly.

"Come on now, let's be friends again like old times," said Harry.

"You know what, Harry?" Daniel looked at him with a stare just short of hatred. "We'd be a lot better friends if we weren't in this mess.

And, we wouldn't be in here if you would've just kept your mouth shut."

Harry couldn't help but feel humbled by this lad of a mere eighteen years whose life he had just ruined. They both understood with absolute clarity that there would never be the same trust between them again even if, by some slim chance, their scheme should work. Harry slowly and painfully got to his feet again and making sure that the Sheriff could not see them, he took off his bearskin coat and his undershirt and turned the coat inside out.

"Help me with this again, will ya?" Reluctantly, Daniel came over to Harry's bunk and passed the candle back and forth, melting the fat from the skin and smearing it on Harry's hairy shoulders. He worked quickly as Harry started to shiver violently in the frigid air of their cell.

"Jeez, you smell bad."

Harry ignored the comment. "Are you finished yet or are you getting aroused by my manly back?"

For the first time in days, Daniel allowed a small smile as he carefully smeared the grease onto Harry's hairy back. "That's about as good as it's going to get, I think." He slapped him gently on the shoulder that he'd been working on.

Harry winced in pain and turned around to face him. "Hey, you little shit, that hurt. You meant to do that, didn't you?" Harry reversed his coat and climbed into it gingerly without putting his undershirt back on. "Damn it, this thing's itchy."

Daniel ignored him and pulled his coat around himself as he lay back down on the bed, feeling miserable again.

"Don't be so down, partner. This is going to work—just you wait and see. Before you know it, we'll be free men again." He lowered his voice, "We'll be rich, too. Just you wait and see, my friend."

From inside his cocoon, Daniel let out a small laugh, filled with contempt. "Yeah Harry. We'll be free only if the jury is blind and lady justice takes a day off."

Harry opened his coat and took a smell of his odor. He recoiled. "You're right. I do smell some. I think I could use some of Big Shirley's fancy perfume."

"Harry, you always stink, if you'll excuse me for saying. A bucket of that perfume wouldn't help. Goodnight and good luck tomorrow." Daniel let out a heavy sigh. "For both of our sakes, I hope we pull this off." He retreated further into his shell, willing himself to sleep, knowing that sleep would never come. Not this night, anyway.

Chapter 46

The Sheriff was almost jovial as he shoved their coffee and bread at them through the floor slot in the bars. Usually one of his deputies did it.

"How'd you boys sleep?" He'd chosen a fine black suit for the trial, to reinforce his respectability. Better to make a statement if he looked the part of the politician. "I thought you boys might like to see today's papers." He held up the newspapers, "'GUILTY' Says Leadville Sheriff," and scattered them on the cell floor.

Harry got to his feet, wrapped in his bearskin coat and blanket. He could only barely stand the itching torment of the coat for a couple of hours before it drove him into near madness. This past night, he'd suffered it far longer, keeping in mind that his future and his freedom might depend on it. He reached for the coffee, but hesitated when he saw their faces on the front page of the **Salt Lake Sentinel**. The Sheriff kicked the tray, sending the coffee splashing over the papers.

"That wasn't very nice, Sheriff," Harry said.

"Oh, I'm so sorry, fellers." He turned to leave. "By the way, son," he looked at Daniel coldly, "I don't think anyone would believe you if you were to tell about how you hurt your leg. I wouldn't bother to mention it if I were you." He pointed his finger and thumb in a pistol gesture at Daniel. "You fellers might be here for a spell if this goes badly for you today, and I have a feeling it will." He stood at the door. "You can wash up before the trial, if you know how." That darkly gummy smile came again. "I'll see you two in court." His laugh sent chills up their spines.

"You know, I'm really getting to dislike that man." Harry was looking hard at the picture of them in the paper.

Daniel limped his way to the tray of slop on the floor, holding himself upright by supporting himself on the bars. His knee hurt like it was on fire and it wouldn't bend without excruciating pain shooting up to his brain. He sat back with his coffee and soggy bread.

"This is not good," Harry said, pointing to the picture showing him with a full beard. "This could be very bad."

"Harry, you're never going to be beautiful."

"But that's how I looked when I lived in Utah." Harry rubbed his beard that had grown out full and black, only a few patches of gray.

"Maybe you should shave."

"Nah."

The door opened and their lawyer came in with an older man.

"Good morning, boys. Are they treating you alright in here?" He was jovial. "This is my partner, Mr. Stanhope." They all shook hands.

"What happened to your leg?" Mr. Greenberg asked when he saw Daniel in pain.

"The Sheriff showed me a little taste of Wild West justice last night." He lifted his pant leg and showed them his bruised, swollen knee. "He tried to convince me to confess."

The lawyers looked at each other and shook their heads.

"Now, about your trial here this morning? I don't want you to worry too much about it," said Mr. Stanhope, "they've got no real evidence and everyone thinks you're just a liar, Mr. Rich."

Harry looked shocked.

"Well? Would you rather have us prove to the jury that you're the smartest criminal west of Kansas and go to jail for it, or would you like to go free as a fool and a liar?"

Harry considered the question.

"Mr. Rich, it's not a question you have to answer. The jury will make up its own mind," Greenberg said, smiling.

Harry lifted his head with a look of relief. He couldn't be sure he'd pick the correct answer anyway.

"Mr. Carrington, we'll be painting you as an unfortunate boy who got mixed up with a drunken liar. No one will dare convict you for stupidity alone, son." Mr. Stanhope nodded in agreement.

"Do you think anyone will believe you?" Harry asked.

"Don't you worry, Mr. Rich. We can make anyone look stupid if it will win our case," Mr. Stanhope said, confidently.

"I think Mr. Rich will just have to be himself to win his case," Greenberg said with equal conviction.

"Well, that's good to know," Harry said as the lawyers stood to leave. "And you say you're the best?"

"Yes, Mr. Rich. We're the best that Jerome Wheeler's money can buy. He appears to have a vested interest in this case." Douglas Greenberg was nothing if not brutally honest. It gained him few friends and more than enough enemies. He felt he'd only just begun his career.

"There's just one thing," Stanhope said. "The Sheriff seems convinced that one of you two is wounded, so he's going to ask to have you inspected by a doctor."

Harry blanched noticeably.

"I recommend you two clean yourselves up before court. I'll make sure they send you in some hot water so you can shave. It never hurts to make a good impression on the jury," Mr. Stanhope suggested.

Daniel rubbed his chin and found some stubble growing on his cheeks and chin.

"You should be free by sunset," Stanhope said. "Unless we lose," he muttered to Greenberg. They left, clutching their valises and walking the walk of the justified.

⚏

Kate hardly slept. Her tossing and turning kept Shirley awake, too. Eventually they sat up together till about two in the morning, silently listening to the steam clanging through the heating pipes in the room. Shirley was at a loss. She sat next to her daughter and held her. They hadn't been like this in the same bed for years. Smiling at her memories and running her fingers through her daughter's thick dark hair, she eventually drifted off and awoke around sunrise with a cramp in her neck.

The day dawned clear and bright but did little to lighten either Kate's or Shirley's mood. The hotel dining room was unusually busy, crowded with the influx of visiting reporters and those who had come to see the trial. To Kate's surprise, although dressed demurely for the occasion, they still drew some attention when they joined Red and Joe for breakfast.

Jerome Wheeler came rolling into the dining room a moment later, causing a commotion as he always did. Dressed in his finest regalia, his top hat shining brightly, he could have been going to either his daughter's wedding or a parade. The reporters at the next table watched his arrival with interest.

"Good morning, my friends," he said as he sat. "Are we all ready for a great triumph of jurisprudence?" The table failed to respond in kind. The reporters at the next table stopped eating, listening for gossip. "Come on, now. Cheer up all of you!" Jerome insisted. "When this debacle is over we'll all be going home over the Pass together. What do you say, Red? Are you ready to take our young man back home where he belongs?" Kate abruptly stood and rushed from the table. Shirley followed her. "Did I say something wrong?"

Red held his hand up. "No, Jerome, she's just worried is all. Let's give her a minute or two, shall we?"

Jerome took out a gold pocket watch from his vest and checked the time with the large standing hall clock in the corner of the dining room. They both told the time to be eight-thirty. Jerome noticed that the reporters were listening intently, trying to overhear something, but Jerome was no fool when the press was around. Shirley and Kate returned, both calm once again, and smiling bravely.

"I think we should move along and get our seats in the courthouse before the rabble arrives." They were heading outside when one of the reporters approached them.

"Mr. Wheeler, I do believe you have a personal interest in one of the accused bank robbers. Is that true?"

"Why yes, I do."

"Do you think they robbed the bank?"

Wheeler laughed loudly, and motioned Red to lead the little group to the court house." My dear sir, there's no chance that these two boys robbed any bank. They're simple men and they're hard working men too, but to be perfectly honest, they're too stupid."

"Is it true that one of them is a gambler over there in Ute City?"

"I wouldn't know anything about that, but I do know that the name of the town is Aspen, not Ute City."

"Is it true that you hired their lawyers, Mr. Wheeler?"

The reporter was well informed. Jerome took a closer look at him. He had dark, intelligent eyes and a look of determination. Jerome had seen the look before, and though it was a good thing in business, it could be a source of problems with this newspaper reporter. Jerome was instantly on guard.

"Now if you will excuse us? We have to go. Good day to you, sir."

They found a small crowd waiting outside the courthouse when they arrived and Jerome was immediately waylaid by admirers and reporters, neither of whom he avoided earnestly. Shirley artfully ignored questions about her business and her association with the men on trial as Red and Joe slowed their assault and allowed her and Kate to enter the courtroom relatively unmolested.

Jerome came in a while later and sat at the end of the row, nearest the defense table where he spoke quietly with Stanhope and Greenberg. He seemed unsurprised when Mr. Stanhope and Shirley exchanged smiles.

A door opened noisily and Harry and Daniel were led into the courtroom by the Sheriff and Kate almost fainted at their appearance. Even Shirley was shocked at the drawn features and shabby clothing. She took Kate's hands and held them firmly. If it was the Sheriff of Leadville's intent to show the boys in the worst possible light, he succeeded admirably. Daniel limped noticeably. Even though he was nervous and afraid, he visibly brightened when he saw Kate. She gave him her biggest smile and Daniel seemed to take life from this small gesture.

Harry, on the other hand, was somber and morose. He looked at the court and the jury and forced on them his best smile, but it had an alarming effect. They whispered amongst themselves until the Judge was ushered in and announced that the court was in session. Daniel and Harry sat, but didn't look at each other.

They all listened intently as the charges were read and the lawyers for both sides made their opening statements. For their first witness the prosecuting attorney called the Sheriff's brother, Frank, to the stand.

"He's not here, Your Honor," the Sheriff said to the Judge.

"Why not, Sheriff? Isn't it your job to see that your witnesses are present and on time?"

"I don't know where he is, Your Honor. He hasn't been seen for a week or more."

"You don't have a witness then; is that what you're trying to tell me, Sheriff?"

"He might come later, Your Honor."

"Then it will do you no good, Sheriff."

The Sheriff smarted at the rebuke. He was hopeful that his brother could be found before the end of the trial. He had sent his son Ham out to the Lodge and told him to stay there on the chance that Frank might show up in time to be brought in for the trial. It was a thin chance, but he had to take it.

Witnesses came and went in procession. The jury listened intently. Harry scratched. Greenberg asked questions of the deputies and the bank manager, and wrote in detail the answer to each question.

Red was called as an expert on the geography of the area between Leadville and Aspen. "They tell me that it's well known in these parts that you have the most experience at traveling over Independence Pass in the winter. Is that true, Mr. Corcoran?" the prosecutor asked.

"I've lived the longest of any of the men traveling that route. So, I guess it's fair to say that."

"Mr. Corcoran, how long does it take you to make the trip on average, and how far is it from Aspen to here would you say?"

"Well, it's about sixty miles going from here to there. About the same coming back too, I'd say." The laughter died down slowly. "It takes us most of a day to make the trip one way."

"Do you think that you could ride over and back in one day?"

"Not on any horse I've ever heard of."

"What if a person had several horses at his disposal?"

"It would still be next to impossible even then. I've got the best mountain horses in the state and I don't think that even they could make the trip. That's why we have so many teams. They get tired. It takes a lot out of horses and men just being up there, let alone riding like Paul Revere both ways. You'd need at least a half a dozen horses. A dozen, if there were two men."

"Could a man ride one of your horses, Mr. Corcoran?"

"Not with any saddle I've seen. Their backs are this wide." Red held his arms out wide. "It would take a large man to sit on one of them for any length of time, and he wouldn't be walking for some time after."

"Could you do it, Mr. Corcoran?" The prosecutor turned to face the jury for effect.

"Well…" Red thought carefully, measuring the effects of his words. He, of all people, could find a way, if one was to be found. He thought about the avalanche and the piece of sled sticking out of the snow in a place it shouldn't be. Then there was the mysterious illness of the horses, and the disappearance of Gloria and then her husband, Frank. There was a lot to this matter that he didn't know and wondered he ever would.

"If the conditions were perfect and it was the middle of summer, perhaps I could. But not at night in a storm like we had over Christmas; it couldn't be done."

No Problem Joe was called to the stand.

"Can you say for certain the horses that these men owned were in your stable all night?" The prosecutor asked him with gravity.

"I can say that they were there in the morning, and that was before sunup," Joe replied.

"When was the last time you saw these men and their horses?"

"Before I went to sleep," Joe replied.

"And what time was that?"

"I don't rightly remember, but I do know it was before sunup," Joe replied, a ripple of laughter passing through the courtroom. The Judge could see that the prosecutor was going to need a strong drink at the end of this day.

"Alright then, Mr. Bolon, when was the last time you saw the accused men on Christmas Eve?" The prosecutor was becoming frustrated.

"I saw them when they were delivering Christmas trees." This got another round of laughter.

"Were they on their horses then?"

"How would they deliver Christmas trees without them?" Another murmur of laughter rolled around the courtroom.

"And approximately what time was that, Mr. Bolon?"

"Sometime between sundown and when I went to sleep."

"Can you be more specific, Mr. Bolon?" The prosecutor's frustration was getting to him.

"No, I can't. What do I look like, a clock?" That got more laughs.

The prosecutor looked flustered. "Can you remember what time it was that you went to bed?"

"No, I can't."

"Can you give me an approximate time?"

"No, I can't."

"Why not, Mr. Bolon?"

"Because it was Christmas. Because I was shit-faced drunk. That's why I went to bed." The Judge had to hammer his gavel a half a dozen times before the room calmed and quieted.

"What time was it that you first saw their horses on Christmas Day?"

"I told you, when I woke up and that was..." Joe looked at the lawyer with his toothless grin.

"Before sunup," the prosecutor finished for him. "Yes, you told us, Mr. Bolon. No more questions, Mr. Bolon. Thank you." The prosecutor returned to his chair and Mr. Greenberg took over.

"Now, Mr. Bolon, do you remember seeing the horses in question on Christmas morning?"

"Yes, sir." Joe nodded to emphasize the point.

"Why is that?"

"Because them horses and some of the others was sick, that's why."

"How sick?"

"Sick enough to call out the vet on Christmas morning." Joe said it as a statement of fact, and both the audience and the jury murmured in agreement at the implications.

"Could these horses have been ridden to Leadville and back the night before?" Greenberg was leaning on the rail next to Joe, looking at the jury.

"Not laying down like they were, they couldn't."

"Thank you, Mr. Bolon."

Joe was excused. He winked at Harry and Daniel in his mischievous way as he passed them. The wink was so overdone that the room erupted into another round of laughter.

The prosecutor called Eugene Heber to the stand.

"You've stated that you heard Mr. Rich state that he robbed the bank here in Leadville. Is that true?"

"Yes, it is."

"Where were you at the time?" Heber looked up at Wheeler who shook his head at him.

"We were playing poker."

"Did you lose money to Mr. Rich?"

"No. I took everything he had."

"Would you say that Mr. Rich was drunk when he told you this story?"

"Yes, I would say that."

Harry felt the venom coming from the man, but he kept looking directly at him until he stepped down from the witness stand.

The prosecutor then called the Sheriff. The room stilled as all eyes watched him take the stand. He had the look of concentrated dedication and he knew that he looked the part of the professional lawman. He acknowledged his wife, but was troubled to see that his daughter was looking at Daniel. His fury rose again and he tugged at the collar of his new shirt, fighting the constriction.

The prosecutor asked rudimentary questions about the robbery, such as the time and place of the explosion. The Sheriff told how he was caught inside the bank as it was being robbed. He noticed there was snickering while he told of the dreadful time he had been locked inside the bank, unable to defend it. The reporters recorded every word.

"Did you shoot at the robbers, Sheriff?" he asked.

"Hell yes, I shot at them. I hit one of them, too." He looked directly at Harry when he said this.

"How did you know you hit one of them?"

"I found some blood on this money bag." The Sheriff held up the empty money bag for the jury to see. The brown stains were clear.

"Do you know which one you hit?" The room was watching the Sheriff closely. He was concentrating hard on Harry, and the jury followed his stare. Harry scratched at himself unconsciously, looking down at the floor.

"I'm not sure, but I hope it was that one." The Sheriff pointed at Harry. The court murmured again and the reporters wrote feverishly.

"I ask the court to allow me to have a doctor examine the defendants, Your Honor."

Mr. Stanhope rose. The sound of his chair scraping the wooden floor boomed loudly in the stillness of the courtroom. "Whoa, there." He cleared his throat noisily and adjusted his glasses. "Your Honor, I would like to ask the Sheriff to clarify a point for the jury, if I may?" The Sheriff visibly stiffened. He looked at Mr. Stanhope with barely veiled contempt. Stanhope smiled back at him, the picture of civility.

"Do you have any more questions, Mr. Prosecutor?" the judge asked.

"No, not at present, Your Honor."

The Judge nodded and sat back; enjoying the show. He knew, as did everyone, that these two fools couldn't possibly have crossed over the Pass and back in one night. He'd thought from the start that the case against them was flimsy at best. But the political pressure forced him to go along with the bullying and whining of the Sheriff, who had never been popular with him or the court. His opinion of the man was mediocre at best.

Mr. Stanhope spoke with surprising force; his age was not his undoing by any measure. "Sheriff, could you show the court how it was that you think you shot the escaping robber while you were still locked in the bank? Did he come out and show himself so that you could get a clear shot at him?"

"No, I had to lean out the window and fire down the street like this." The Sheriff stood and demonstrated how he'd had to reach out and turn his wrist to affect the shot.

"I'm not quite sure that I can see what you did exactly, Sheriff," said Stanhope. He looked intently at the Sheriff and pointed at the bars on the front of the witness stand made of ornately carved wood balusters spaced six inches apart. "Do these bars here look about the same distance apart as the bars in the bank to you, Sheriff?"

The Sheriff nodded, bemused by the question.

"Would you reach through the bars and show us how you could shoot at the robbers, Sheriff?"

The prosecutor stood to object, but was waved back into his seat by the judge.

The Sheriff was a big man and had difficulty getting down on his knees. Finally in position, after much huffing and puffing, he reached his arm through the bars and turned his hand, holding the pistol as far as it would bend towards the jury. The jury ducked for cover.

"It's not loaded," the Sheriff contended loudly.

The jurors relaxed and climbed back into their seats. The Sheriff's face, which was pressed against the bars, was flushed red from the exertion and the force with which he was attempting to show the court his best shooting angle. Daniel noticed an artist dashing off lines on a page in a book, his hand working quickly as he smiled to himself.

"It doesn't look like a good shot if the men were standing down the street, does it, Sheriff?" He paused for effect. "Do you still think you hit one of the robbers, Sheriff? You can stand up now."

Flushed with both the exertion and the embarrassment at being ridiculed, the Sheriff gratefully stood up and sat back on the witness chair. "I got a decent look at one of them, so I took my best shot."

"How many shots did you fire?"

"I reloaded a couple of times, so probably a dozen or more." The Sheriff was still holding his pistol and looked at it carefully as he returned it to its holster.

"Are you a good shot with that pistol?"

"I'm not bad, I guess. I usually hit what I aim at."

"So you think you shot one of these men?"

"Yes, I do."

"Can you tell me for certain which one it was?" Stanhope walked over to where the boys were sitting, bordered by the deputies. The courtroom was deathly silent. "Was it this one Sheriff?" He pointed at Daniel. "Or was it this one?" He stood behind Harry.

"I don't know which one, but I do know that I shot one of 'em."

"Now, Sheriff, you said you had a witness that would put these boys at Twin Lakes on the night of the robbery. Is that true?"

"Yes, it is." The Sheriff felt his heart sinking like a stone in water.

"And where is this witness?"

"I don't know."

Stanhope took off his glasses and polished them with a clean white handkerchief. He replaced his glasses and took great care refolding the handkerchief. He faced the jury, smiling.

"So all we have here is that you think you shot someone robbing the bank and you think it was one of these two men over here? Is that correct?"

"I know I shot one of them two, if that's what you're asking."

"But you don't have any other witnesses, Sheriff?"

"No, I told you that." The Sheriff was losing his temper.

"Let me ask you this, Sheriff. Do you think that you could ride over the Pass from Leadville to Aspen and back here to Leadville in one day?"

The Sheriff thought deeply; the courtroom watched with keen interest. It was upon this point that the charges were founded.

"I don't know if it's ever been tried before." The Sheriff was quite pleased with himself at his detour around the question. He sat back and gloated behind Mr. Stanhope's back. Most people in the room could see that he was playing with the old lawyer. Douglas Stanhope didn't seem to mind; in fact he didn't seem to register the fact. He gave Daniel a tiny wink.

"That's nice to know, Sheriff, but the question was whether you think that you could do it. Please answer the question put to you. Or don't you understand the question?"

"Goddamn it, yes, I understand the question."

"Well, could you do it, Sheriff?"

The Sheriff squirmed in his seat and pressed his weight against the arms of the chair, his anger rising, his face changing color, darkening visibly.

"I might if I had plenty of horses and the weather was good."

"Let's say for argument that you had the horses. Do you think you could do it in bad weather, then?" Stanhope wheeled on the Sheriff, coming to the rail of the witness box and fixing him with his coldest stare. "What if it was the biggest storm of the year, and it happened the same night you were going to go over the Pass. Do you think you'd want to try it then, Sheriff?"

The Sheriff looked hard at Stanhope and appraised him anew. He was not the drunken lawyer he remembered who had hung out in the saloons and drank himself stupid each day. "No, I wouldn't."

"Sheriff, do you think that anyone in his right mind would attempt such a trip? Such a person would have to be crazy, wouldn't he, Sheriff?" He held up his hand before either the Sheriff or the prosecutor could object. "I'm sorry, Sheriff, what would you know about being crazy?"

There was a smattering of laughter through the room. The judge banged his gavel for order, but was really quite enjoying the show.

"Let me rephrase the question, then. Do you think, under the stormy conditions that existed on Christmas Eve, that such a trip could be possible?"

"Well, yes, possibly. Anything's possible these days, isn't it?"

"Sheriff, we're not talking about 'anything' here. We're talking about riding one hundred and twenty miles over the highest pass in the Rocky Mountains, robbing your bank, and riding back over that pass through the biggest snowstorm of the year. And you would have us believe that you, in your professional capacity, think that you could do it?"

"I didn't say I could do it."

"That's right, Sheriff, but you did say that you thought that it could be done. Is that right, Sheriff?"

"Well, yes and no."

Douglas Stanhope loved this kind of thing; he lived for it. He knew the Sheriff couldn't very well say that he could do it, when all the others giving evidence doubted it could be done. Red had been adamant when he gave testimony, that it was impossible to do.

"Well then, Sheriff, since we've proven that riding over the Pass and back would not be feasible, then may we ask how you think these two men did it?"

"I don't know." The Sheriff sounded more defeated.

"And unless I'm mistaken, you still can't find the money the robbers stole."

The courtroom collectively held its breath.

"That's right. We haven't found the stolen money yet."

"Then you have no witness and no evidence for this court to convict these men, do you, Sheriff?" Stanhope was as magnificent as Shirley knew he would be. She'd trusted herself to his skill before and he'd risen to the challenge like a knight of old.

"But I shot one of them. I know it!" The Sheriff jumped out of his chair and bellowed the statement, making half the room jump with shock. "Judge, you got to have a doctor look at them. You'll see what I mean. These two robbed the bank and one of them has a bullet wound in the back. I can prove what I say."

Doug Stanhope turned to the Judge, his hands splayed in question. "You can't allow this, Your Honor. The Sheriff has no proof and we've heard from credible witnesses that nobody could ride from Aspen to Leadville and back in one night through a storm, no matter how many horses they had."

The Judge rubbed his stubbled chin, looking from the accused robbers to the Sheriff, to the lawyer.

"Alright, Sheriff, I know you've gotten quite involved with this case, so I'll let a doctor look at their backs."

The Sheriff beamed. Harry and Daniel moaned softly. Stanhope took a step towards the Judge's bench to object, but the Judge held up his hand for him to stop.

"Let the Sheriff have this one, Mr. Stanhope, will you?" It was more a statement than it sounded to Douglas Stanhope. "Do you have a doctor here, Sheriff?" the Judge continued.

"I'd like to call Doc Holliday to do the examination, Your Honor," the Sheriff announced with swollen civic pride.

"I'm right here, Your Honor," graveled a voice from the back of the room.

The assembly turned towards the decrepit visage of the dying old gunfighter. He made his way to the front of the room to be sworn in. In passing, he grinned wickedly at Harry.

"You're a doctor of medicine, aren't you?" the prosecutor asked him.

"More of a dentist by training, but yes I am a doctor, though I don't practice much these days." He punctuated his statement with a convulsive coughing spasm that gurgled and wheezed for what seemed like minutes.

"And in your life, you've had some experience with bullet wounds, have you?" The prosecutor asked, after the good doctor had reclaimed his composure somewhat.

"Yes, sir, I have. Both ways."

"What do you mean, both ways, doctor?"

"Well, both in their treatment and in causing them." The good doctor announced proudly. The court laughed in discomfort at the aging killer.

There wasn't a soul in Leadville who hadn't seen this decrepit old man around town and there was not one young boy in town that hadn't followed him around at some point in their lives. The reporters wrote down every word and the artist sketched at a rapid pace as if the man were about to drop dead in front of them.

"The Sheriff has stated that he shot one of these men in the back. Would you do us the service of inspecting them for us, doctor?"

Doc Holliday controlled his delight as best he could, but couldn't help looking at Harry with a wry smile. Harry withered under his gaze. Even if he didn't have a gunshot wound on his back, the good doctor could still put him in jail if he went along with the Sheriff. The Judge called them forward.

Reluctantly, Harry and Daniel went forward to the front of the room and stood near the jury. Daniel looked back and tried to smile at Kate. Harry was far less positive; his demeanor that of a defeated man, shoulders slumped, looking down at the floor. Doc Holliday came near Harry and tapped him on the shoulder. Harry jumped at the touch.

"Don't worry there, Harry, this'll all be over soon," he whispered in his ear, laughing as he did. Harry considered the cadaverous face of Doc Holliday and did his best to raise a smile.

"Would you gentlemen take off your shirts for the doctor, please?" the Judge asked them politely.

Daniel was the first to bare his back, to the giggles of the young women in the room. The doctor inspected it closely, turning it towards the jury before announcing that there was no evidence of a wound. Daniel replaced his shirt and looked at Kate. She was smiling.

"Alright. Now you, Mr. Rich," Holliday wheezed phlegm into Harry's ear. "Let's get down to it, shall we?"

The spectators sat quietly in anticipation and watched intently as Harry slowly took off his clothes. He stopped at his undershirt; it was filthy and caused muttering through the room.

"Now, now, Mr. Rich, would you do us the honor of removing your undershirt?" Harry froze for a moment.

"I realize you're not used to an audience." Doc Holliday turned to the courtroom. "Would you all cover your eyes for the sake of Mr. Rich's modesty please?" he announced. The crowded room pretended to cover their eyes, laughing. Most of the women were covering their eyes theatrically, with their fingers splayed and laughing to each other. The Judge hammered his gavel to bring the room to order.

Harry turned and pulled his shirt up so that Doc was the only one who could actually see his shoulder. Doc pulled a face, pinching his nose.

"You could have at least washed for the court, you know. Justice might be blind, but I'm certain she can smell. Turn around for the jury, if you would. That is, if your sense of modesty allows?"

Harry turned his back to the jury and to the courtroom so that all in the room could see his back. From a distance, it looked completely covered by the thick black hair. It was an exceptionally hairy back, almost unnatural. Shirley squeezed Kate's hand so hard, she looked at her mother. Shirley let her head fall onto her chest and started to shake. Her mouth was clenched, her eyes tightly shut, but still tears ran down her cheek. Red looked from her to Kate and then to Joe, but Shirley wouldn't look up until she'd regained her poise and wiped the tears from her cheek.

In the front of the courtroom, Doc Holliday was making a close inspection of Harry's back and shoulder. He leaned close to Harry's ear.

"Now, Harry, this could go badly for you." For emphasis, he poked a finger into the inflamed wound under the thick matting of hair and a small amount of the hair came off on his fingers. "This is pretty good, Harry, I have to admit," he whispered.

Harry forced a wan smile to Doc and the suspense-filled courtroom.

"You still owe me some money, Harry." Harry's knees trembled, but he stayed standing as the doctor poked around some more. Sharp pain seared his brain at every touch, but he clenched his teeth and smiled through it all.

"The way I see it Harry, is that I can let you get away with this, or I can put you and your little friend in jail for a long, long time. You do know that, don't you?" Another poke at the wound and beads of sweat popped out on Harry's forehead. "So, I'll make you a deal. You give me half of the money you stole and you go free."

Doc squeezed Harry's right shoulder for emphasis. The old warrior had an iron grip. Harry felt his pain overwhelming him. His vision blurred, but Doc released the shoulder and Harry breathed again. Doc leaned closer. "Is it a deal, Harry?"

Harry turned and looked into the ice cold eyes of his executioner. "It's a deal," he said, without moving his lips.

Doc patted Harry on the sore shoulder again. "Thank you, Mr. Rich, you can put your shirt back on."

Harry and Daniel walked slowly back to their seats as if descending from the gallows after being pardoned. Doc Holliday returned to the witness chair, facing the courtroom and the jury.

"Your conclusion, doctor?" asked the judge.

A whisper of speculation ran through the room, but it died as Doc Holliday considered his opinion. Harry and Daniel waited, hardly daring to breathe. The good doctor took his time; he looked at the Sheriff several times, seemingly burdened by his decision. With a loud, phlegmatic, wheezing sigh, he sat up in his chair and faced the Judge.

"Though I'd like to inflict one on Mr. Rich, and I may still yet, I can't see any evidence of a bullet wound on either of them, Your Honor."

The Sheriff jumped out of his chair and rushed towards the Judge. "That's not true, Judge. I can prove it!" he shouted.

The Judge hammered with his gavel for order in his courtroom. "Sheriff, you're out of order." His voice was loud and his message clear, but the Sheriff couldn't be mollified. "Sit down, Sheriff."

"That hair on his back is fake!"

"I said sit down, Sheriff."

Humiliated, the Sheriff reluctantly sat back down.

Shirley, who was the only one who knew the truth, held her breath. She watched the Sheriff then turned her attention to Harry, who looked directly at her and quickly looked away. Shirley now knew their secret.

⊰⊱

The jury was sent out and the gallery moved around the room or wandered outside to stretch their legs.

Stanhope and Greenberg smiled confidently as Harry and Daniel were led to a small cell behind the courtroom to await the jury's decision. The Sheriff came and stood silently, pouring pure menace into the cell.

"I know you did it, Harry. That hair on your back didn't fool me one bit."

"You did look pretty funny trying to push your face through those bars, Sheriff." Harry felt his courage rising like a sleeping tiger. "I was surprised you got a shot off at all."

The Sheriff came closer. "I'm going to dog your days until I find where you hid that money."

"I'm pretty sure I know where those other moneybags are. They're probably right there in that safe in your office."

The Sheriff made a lunge quicker than Harry could retreat. He held Harry by the neck and pulled his gun, pointing it at Daniel.

"It's loaded, now. So, don't even think of trying anything."

"We know about Frank killing Gloria. And Newly, too." Daniel pressed on. "We saw what he did to Newly and heard the shots." He moved closer, now less than an arm's length away. "I saw what he did to Gloria. I saw what your brother did to that poor woman. He cut out her heart and you saw it, didn't you? How would it look if we came up with that story? I guess your political future would be in jeopardy wouldn't it, Sheriff? Let Harry go."

The Sheriff withered as memories of the scene at the Lodge ran through his head.

"I said, let him go. Now! Do you hear me, Sheriff?" Daniel stepped closer and forced the Sheriff's arm away from Harry's throat. Harry slid to the floor, gasping for air.

The Sheriff backed away and raised his pistol, a twisted smile grew on his mottled face. Daniel hoped that his last memory of this earth wouldn't be the disgusting sight of the Sheriff's teeth. He looked at the dark hole at the end of the barrel, expecting to see the bullet as it flew from the hole and embedded itself in his chest. The courtroom door slammed open.

"The jury's back, Sheriff," the deputy announced. He noticed the Sheriff's gun in his hand. The Sheriff turned and replaced his pistol in its holster. He climbed the stairs two at a time without saying another word.

The jury was a mixed group and typical of the men who were the core of any community. They had rugged, haggard faces with deep lines of relentless work and failed dreams. Daniel looked along the rows of them, seeking some cognition of their decision, but finding none.

The reporters and court artist worked at collecting impressions as the Judge brought the room to order. The air tensed like a string straining to cope with a heavy weight.

"Have you reached your verdict?"

"Yes, we have, Your Honor."

"What say you, then?"

"Your Honor, we find them not guilty, on the grounds that we just can't believe they robbed the bank. We don't believe that anyone could travel from Aspen to Leadville and back in one day, let alone one night, Your Honor."

The crowd erupted in cheering and hoots. The Judge banged his gavel and called the room to order. When it finally settled down, he spoke to Harry and Daniel sternly. "Gentlemen, it would appear that this court finds you not guilty. You are free to go."

The assembled gallery cheered. Harry sighed with relief. It had only cost him Daniel's half of the stolen money to be free again.

Daniel grabbed Harry and hugged him until he cried out in pain from his shoulder wound. They were surrounded by a crowd of reporters and well-wishers. It seemed they'd gathered quite a reputation from all of the publicity. Harry was pressed by some of the women and Daniel was the focus of some unwanted but flattering attention. He fought them away and found Kate and Shirley waiting for him. Kate threw her arms around him and he hugged her until she thought she'd break.

"Congratulations," she whispered softly into his ear.

"Will you marry me Kate?" he whispered into hers.

"What took you so long?" Shirley heard Kate reply.

Jerome tapped Daniel on his shoulder. "Will you excuse us for a moment, ladies?" Jerome said, and guided Daniel away from Kate and Shirley. "I knew you were innocent all the time," Jerome said, leading him back towards the lawyer's table. Douglas Stanhope and his partner were packing their papers.

"I can't thank you enough, Mr. Stanhope, and you too, Mr. Greenberg. I don't know where I'd be if you hadn't been here to help me and Harry." They both shook his hand and Jerome Wheeler's as well.

"Well, Mr. Carrington, as Mr. Wheeler here knows, I would've taken your case for free as long as I got the chance to ream out our least favorite Sheriff here one more time. As Mr. Wheeler is aware, the Sheriff drove me out of Leadville some time ago. It was my pleasure to come on back and rub his nose in the dirt again."

Wheeler smiled. "Go on Douglas. Tell him the rest of the story. I'm sure the boy will enjoy it as much as I do," encouraging Stanhope to continue.

"It's nothing to be proud of really. But back when I was a younger man, I was far more interested in the whiskey and the women here

than I was in defending the rights of the unjustly aggrieved. I had a
friend, a young whore who asked me to help her get some back-pay
from a man she had worked for that wouldn't pay her. She'd arrived
in Leadville with a travelling gambler, and when she got pregnant he
deserted her. He left her penniless. She took the only work she could
find and she was forced to live with a brothel keeper because she was
young and already had a baby to support.

Anyway, this brothel keeper made her clean his brothel, service
him sexually and keep house for him. Eventually, she became pregnant
by him and when he found out, he kicked her out into the street. That's
where we became friends. We sued the miserable bastard, and we won.
She got four thousand dollars for her unpaid services. Unfortunately
for me, the bar owner gave up the brothel and whiskey business, got
himself elected Sheriff, and proceeded to run me out of town." He
looked at Daniel in the most pleasant way, satisfied. "So, this here was
my revenge. I can't thank you fellers enough."

"Who was the woman?" Daniel asked. He looked at the lawyer
who looked at Wheeler questioningly.

"Your friend, Big Shirley," he answered, as if to an idiot.

"You mean…you mean to tell me…that…"

Wheeler put his hand on his shoulder. "Yes, Daniel. The Sheriff is
Rachelle's father."

Chapter 47

"Oh my God, Harry, look what they did to your cabin." Daniel's shock finally found words.

Harry was sitting in a chair just inside the door, surveying the damage. Their bunks had been broken into splinters and their clothes had been scattered about. The floorboards had been pulled up and the floor dug into. It looked like a new mining venture. Harry got down on his haunches and inspected the base of the oven. It was clear that whoever had destroyed his place wanted to check under the heavy metal oven, though it appeared that its sheer weight had foiled them. He touched the places where they had tried steel bars to shift the beast.

They were alone in the cabin. Harry had left them when the wagon came closest to where he lived, but Daniel had stayed with the wagon all the way to Shirley's house. After they'd let Joe off at his stable, the four of them continued to her house. Shirley and Red rode up on the driving bench, their shoulders and hips touching as the wagon rolled and swayed along the muddy, rutted road.

Daniel and Kate rode in the back of the wagon, keeping warm under the tarps and blankets they'd brought for the trip. They'd eventually run out of the wild enthusiasm that had flowed over them as they left Leadville, and had settled down to quiet contemplation for the majority of the journey. Passing through Stringtown, he'd thumbed his nose at the owner of the hotel, standing at the front door, broom in hand, dumb-looking.

Harry talked incessantly the whole way. He was as happy as a man could be, but after a dozen miles his enthusiastic banter grated on the rest of them. Red and Joe took turns pretending to listen to Harry. Naturally, he failed to notice their lack of interest in his ramblings. At the very least, he was somewhat entertaining.

Jerome had gone back to Denver on the train with the lawyers, after announcing his intention to have a fine party for them at his Hotel on his return. He'd even told Daniel to take some time off and to come back to work when he felt up to it.

Their arrival back in Aspen changed it all. For Daniel and Harry, the shock of seeing their home ransacked had brought them both back to the harshness of their existence. Having been acquitted of the bank robbery, they had felt that one of their main burdens had been lifted, but that passed as soon as they saw the remnants of their possessions scattered about the cabin.

They realigned the oven and started a fire. They were almost too tired to move, but went out to eat at the White Kitchen. As they walked through town, their heads down, they weren't recognized by a soul. It was as if the town they knew had changed while they'd been away. Things that looked familiar now had a dreamlike quality to them.

The restaurant was almost full with the usual crowd of miners having their dinner after their shifts. Hardly anyone paid them any attention when they walked in, except Hickory, who came rushing over to them to give them big hugs.

"I told everyone that you two were too stupid to do the robbery and do you know what? Almost everyone in town believed me."

Harry had learned to keep his mouth shut. They saw Joe waving at them. He was sitting with Red.

"Nice to see you boys again," Red said as they sat. Hickory placed two steaming bowls of stew in front of them. They looked up at her and she shrugged.

"Sorry, boys, that's all we got left." She looked over at Joe. "How's it, Joe?"

Joe was struggling with some tobacco in his gummy mouth and he managed to swallow it before he answered. "Do you know what kind of meat this is?"

"Sorry, Joe, it's a mystery to me. All I know is it's something that died."

"No problem." He went on pummeling another piece of meat with his gums, smiling all the while.

Red looked serious. "Joe told me that someone went through your cabin while we were over in Leadville." They'd barely arrived back, and even without seeing the cabin, Joe knew all that had happened.

"Leafy said it happened when he was at work, and I believe him," Joe said.

"Did they take anything?" Red asked, watching Harry closely.

"Not that I could tell. They even left my whiskey." Harry paused. "Who did it, Joe?" he asked.

"Someone who thinks you two boys robbed the bank."

"And who might that be?" Harry's voice was softer and lower now.

"I don't know, Harry," Joe answered before taking another mouthful.

"By the way, congratulations Daniel," Red said, relieving the tension.

Daniel blushed, and looked around the table at the faces of the men who had become his closest friends.

"Congratulations for what? I got off too, you know," Harry said, his mouth half full of food.

"Not that, Harry. Daniel here's about to get married."

"Is that right?" Harry asked incredulously. "Who to?"

Red and Joe burst out laughing. "There were people who actually thought you robbed the bank, and here you are, too slow to see that Daniel has proposed to Kate," Red laughed.

"You did? When?" Harry's look was one of shock and disappointment.

"When you were busy talking to all those reporters after the trial."

"I'm sorry to hear that." Harry smirked.

"I still have to ask Shirley if I can marry her." Daniel felt his throat constrict. It had been hard enough to bring up the subject the first time, before they were interrupted.

"No problem," said Joe.

Red sat back and leaned his chair against the wall. "By the way, she asked me to invite you over tomorrow evening for dinner. I'm sure you can have your little chat then."

"That calls for a celebration, then," Harry said enthusiastically, swiping his bread around his bowl. He pushed it away, belched with satisfaction, and patted his pockets. "I don't have any money." Harry pulled his pants pockets inside out to emphasize his poverty.

Red shook his head and rolled his eyes, then called Hickory over and handed her some money. She smiled and kissed him on the cheek. She sneered at Harry as they headed for the door, but caught Daniel by the hand.

"Congratulations, Daniel, you're a lucky man." She kissed him on the cheek and his embarrassment flared.

"Does everyone here in this town know everything?"

"Well, not everything," said Red sagely as he opened the door for him.

⊰⊱

Daniel woke the next morning slowly, painfully. His head was fuzzy, his mouth as dry as a desert, his tongue tasted like he'd licked a cat, and his head pounded with every beat of his heart. He was lying face down in the stall next to Marigold. He had no recollection of how he got where he was, but as he picked stray bits of sharp hay out of his face and clothing, he remembered a few glimpses, like pictures shown out of order. He got to his feet with difficulty and went outside to relieve himself, only to be beaten back inside by the brightness of the sunlight reflected off the snow.

He heard the shuffling of feet. When he opened his eyes again he found Joe holding a cup of coffee out to him.

"No problem, son. The hair of the dog that bit you."

"How did I get here, Joe?"

"You might say that you weren't goin' no place else. No problem. You talked to your horse a while, then just fell down. Good a place as any, I'd say." Joe reached into his pocket, pulled out an envelope, and handed it to Daniel. "Here, this is from Red. He said it's yours. You probably need it."

Daniel opened it and found two hundred dollars. He was speechless.

"He said you needed some things."

Daniel thought of the money hidden under the cabin floor. "Who did it, Joe?" Daniel was as serious as a cave-in. He fixed his steel-blue eyes on Joe.

"Someone who thinks he knows something I don't." With that, he walked back to his room and closed the door behind him.

Daniel held the money tightly in his hand, and looking at it, considered again what the money under the cabin floor meant to him and his future. He had a desperate need to write to his mother, but what would he tell her? What could he tell her?

⁂

Kate and Shirley spent the day together, mostly talking. Rachelle had left the house early. As was her wont, she failed to inform anyone of her destination or intentions.

Dinner had gone smoothly and Maisie was becoming fond of Daniel and obviously approved of him—he was a good eater. Shirley had been impressed at Daniel's resolve to give up drinking and had easily forgiven his lapse of discipline the previous night. She'd heard about it at the Paragon and was not the least surprised when Daniel worked his confession into the conversation, followed, as it must be, by his reiteration of his commitment to the avoidance of alcohol.

Shirley found that she was looking at this young man differently. Not so much as her daughter's suitor, but as her future son-in-law. The man who would keep her daughter safe and happy. She reveled at the thought of grandchildren in her house, surrounding her with the laughter she missed during her own daughter's childhood. Kate's happiness would be the reward for all the pain and effort; more than enough reward.

She knew it was coming when Daniel cleared his throat and took Kate's hand in his. He shuffled uncomfortably in his chair and composed himself in such an endearing manner that she was ready to do the asking for him. Finally, with a gentle, encouraging squeeze of his hand, an anxious Kate prodded him into action.

"Mrs. Doray, I wanted to know if…" Daniel's resolve failed him for a moment.

Shirley waited, trying not to seem impatient. Kate turned her eyes to the ceiling and squeezed his hand again, this time with considerably more urgency. Daniel looked at Kate, drawing strength.

"I wanted to know if you would allow me to marry your daughter." He exhaled for the first time in minutes. He looked at Kate. They both turned and looked at Shirley, their young eyes gleaming.

"I suggest the first day of spring."

"I beg your pardon?" Daniel wondered if the question had been answered.

"I said I think we should have the wedding on the first day of spring. Don't you?"

Kate launched herself across the room, wrapping her arms around her mother, who held her just as tightly. "Did you know?" she asked slyly.

"Of course I knew. Do you think I got to be this old and haggard without knowing what you're up to?" She stood up and gave Daniel a hug. It was a different hug than he'd gotten from Shirley before; more formal, proper and wholly natural. He had a new family and it felt good.

"I'm going to leave you two alone for a few minutes, but I would like a word with you privately before you go, Daniel, if I may. We have many things to discuss between now and the wedding." Shirley went out into the kitchen, where she found Maisie sitting at the table, trying to look unknowing and uninterested.

"Come on, Maisie, I know you were listening at the door—I could see your shadow. What do you think?"

"Oh, Miss Shirley, I think they're going to make a beautiful bride and groom. I really do."

Shirley sat heavily in the chair, her eyes filled with tears of fear, loss, and joy. "Do you think he'll make her happy?"

"Oh, it'll be alright, don't you worry none. It always seems to work itself out, doesn't it?"

"Maisie, I'm only worrying about one thing, really."

"What's that Miss Shirley?"

"Our boy out there's a virgin."

"Oh Lordy. Whatch'a goin' to do about dat?"

"I'm not quite sure yet, Maisie. Short of teaching him myself, I mean."

"Oh, Miss Shirley." There was a pause. "You was just foolin' wit' me, wasn't you?"

"I'm not sure, Maisie." She slid up to the door where she could look through the crack. It was a beautiful scene; they were illuminated by the soft yellow glow of the lamp and the flickering flashes from the fireplace. Shirley sighed and squared her shoulders. She rejoined Maisie at the table where a cup of tea now sat in front of her.

"Well, here we go. I guess I'll have to train another man." Maisie covered her uneven teeth when she laughed. Shirley slowly opened the door. "Kate, it's time you went to bed. Kiss Daniel goodnight and tell him you'll see him at dinner tomorrow night."

Daniel looked blankly at Shirley.

"You'll be coming here to dinner regularly I hope, Daniel. I wouldn't want you to be out there getting yourself into trouble every night with Harry Rich. Kiss her goodnight and let her get her beauty sleep."

Shirley took her coat from the rack and went out onto the porch. After a lingering kiss that she could see clearly through the lace curtains, Daniel opened the door and let go of Kate's hand. Kate looked at her mother suspiciously, but Shirley shooed her inside.

There was a moment of awkwardness until Shirley contrived the most innocent way to ask the question that had begged the asking.

"Do you think Kate's a virgin?" She watched as her question struck home.

"I'd never thought about it, really. She has spent a lot of time in your brothel."

Shirley didn't really mean to slap him as hard as she did. The poor boy flew backwards off the porch to the snowy ground like he'd been hit with a ton of rocks. She hurriedly bent down and helped him back to his feet as he rubbed his face with his hand to smooth his ego and his cheek.

"Why are women always hitting me?"

"You'll get used to it." She turned and linked her arm in his as they walked towards the corner of the street. "I'm sorry that I slapped you, but you have to realize that I love my daughters. I won't have anyone saying or thinking bad things about them. Do you accept my apology?"

"Yes, but please don't hit me again."

She stopped, took him by his shoulders, and turned him to face her. "Will you promise to take care of her and do your absolute best to make her happy?" She searched Daniel's face.

"Yes, I do," he said with heartfelt sincerity.

"Then call me Shirley. You'll come for dinner then?"

"Yes, Mrs. Dor—" he caught himself. "Yes, Shirley. I'd like that."

"Good. Then go home and help Harry get his cabin in order." Daniel nodded and turned to go. "Goodnight, Daniel."

"Goodnight, Shirley."

She watched him as he walked away under the new electric street-light. It cast its yellowish glare over him, making his shadow move from behind him to lead him as he passed under the light. It was chilly so she went back inside and turned down the lamps and climbed the stairs.

Kate's door was open and she stood for a moment watching her daughter brushing out her long shiny hair. Shirley knocked softly and came in and sat down next to her daughter smiling. "Are you happy, Kate?"

Kate stopped her brushing and watched her mother's reflection in the mirror. "Yes, Mother. I think I love him very much," the pause was long and heavy, "and, I think he loves me, too." Shirley was taken by the maturity of her daughter's statement.

"Kate, I've a question that I have to ask you."

"Yes, Mother, I'm still a virgin." The look on Shirley's face made Kate burst out laughing. "You shouldn't look so shocked." Shirley hugged her daughter and left her room.

"More problems," she said quietly to herself. She'd moved Rachelle into the spare room and went to her door and knocked. She opened the door and looked in to find the room empty.

"More problems," she said as she went to her own room and un-dressed for bed.

⊰▷⊱

Over the next few days, Harry and Daniel worked at rebuilding their cabin. All thoughts of selling potatoes took second place. Together they levered the giant oven back into its original spot, but Harry found that he was often looking at the plugged hole in the beam where the eyebolt used to go. Daniel caught him looking several times. He could see the effect the temptation of the buried money was having on Harry.

⊰▷⊱

"Listen here, sweetie, I got nothing against men." Maybelle was probably the most portly, buxom, and popular of all the women working for Big Shirley. "As a matter of fact, I wouldn't press these here titties against them all hours of the day and night if I didn't like it." She turned herself around, admiring her reflection in the mirror. It was her favorite mirror because it had some flaw in it that made them all look thinner. "But you gotta understand what they want from us and what you wanna get from them. Do you understand, sweetie? Can you pull this a little bit tighter for me?"

Kate came behind Maybelle and pulled on the strings and cords that pulled her large frame into the semblance of an hourglass figure. Kate thought that there must be at least as much rigging on her corset as on a sailing boat. Maybelle backed away from the mirror and watched the magic of the illusion make her into the epitome of the fashion of the times. She adjusted her ample breasts so that the dark aureole around her nipples made an appearance, slightly peeking over the top of the black lace prisons of her corset.

"All these men we see here are just grown-up boys. Some of them aren't even very grown-up, are they, girls?" She made a measuring gesture with her thumb and forefinger. The girls laughed and so did Kate, in a demure way. She'd heard from the girls of the disappointing size of some men, but also had heard the stories of the surprisingly well-endowed ones. Apparently size did matter, but it was an unpredictable occurrence in the nature of men. "Listen, sweetie, it don't really matter how big he is if he treats you nice. That's right, isn't it, girls?" There was a round of agreement.

"Not if you like a great big one, it's not." The small voice brought them to tears of laughter; it came from Kim Ellen, one of the three sisters. She was the youngest and the most timid of the girls in the room and in the house. At least on the surface she appeared that way. There were stories of her customers running out of her room, dragging their pants behind them with her in hot pursuit, seeking more of them than they could deliver.

They were sitting in the small reception area where the girls would wait for their customers. Mother was knitting, she was always knitting, but nobody ever found out what it was that she knitted. The folds of the material piled up over the years and went from one color to the next with random regularity.

Shirley appeared from downstairs carrying a covered basket which she placed on the card table. "You're not trying to scare my daughter, are you, ladies?" She went to Kate and touched her cheek gently. "Don't listen to them. They're just a beastly lot of money-hungry whores." As the groans of denial rose, Shirley pulled out a pair of bottles of champagne from the basket and platters of food that she had laid out on the table.

"Ladies, how about we all have a drink and tell my little girl about some of the things that she should expect to experience tomorrow when she gets married."

The women looked from one to the other acknowledging the strict ban on girls drinking on the job. "Come on, girls, let's close the place for the night and have ourselves' a little party. Go put on some clothes, Maybelle."

"Is it going to be that kind of party, Shirley?"

"It would be a nice change, don't you think?"

Kate sat on the couch near the fireplace, Shirley sat next to her.

"Now, Kate, you mustn't believe everything these old wagon wheels tell you. There hasn't been one husband in Maybelle's life that she hasn't driven away or badgered to death." She held up the bottles of champagne for Kate to see. "Look here, baby, real French champagne.

I've been saving it for just this occasion." Shirley stepped back and held a bottle at arm's length, carefully removing the wire from the neck. She slowly twisted the cork, easing it out until it popped. The glasses were filled and the girls gathered around Kate. On Shirley's cue, they lifted their glasses. Kate rose gracefully and hugged her mother.

"Kate," Shirley proposed the toast, "to a good husband, many children, and a happy marriage." They giggled as the wine tickled their noses. Maybelle drank hers in one gulp, belching loudly when she'd finished it. Their laughter filled the room and Shirley refilled the glasses. Even Mother had a second glass.

"Now let's talk turkey, girls. What can we tell my daughter that's going to keep her husband happy and at home at night?" There was a pause while they all looked at each other.

"Good sex," they loudly chorused.

⊰⊱

"Why are the women here always slapping me, Red? You never get hit."

"Rats," said Joe, slowly sinking lower into the high-backed chair.

"Well, that's one reason." Red waxed philosophical. "They're just different from us. They think differently."

"Does it change when you get married?"

"Yeah, it gets a whole lot worse," said Harry, wading into the conversation with the weight of his multiple experiences. They laughed. "I've got three wives. I think it's three, and they all get along with each other quite well. It's me they can't get along with."

"I can understand that," said Red.

"How does that work, Harry? When I was young, people weren't so forgiving as to tolerate two wives alive at the same time, let alone three of them," Joe said.

"Ah, it's a Mormon thing. They need kids, so they cooked up this religious thing that allows a man as many wives as he can afford."

"Why did you do it, then?" Daniel asked.

"There's something to love about every woman who walks the earth. It's up to each man to find it and fondle it as much as they'll let you." Harry extended his hands in front of him, fondling a pair of imaginary breasts. "My advice; wait till they're asleep and keep your boots close by."

⊰⊱

Kate was feeling more than a little drunk, as were the other women in the room. She was curled up with her mother's arm around her shoulder, looking pensively at each of the girls around the room.

"Kate, you don't have to do this," Kim Ellen said, "but your mother's right. You don't want to live the rest of your life wonderin' if there's a better lover out there. Least of all one of them smooth-talking gamblers that'll take from you what he wants, and leave you behind without even a goodbye. And they're out there, aren't they, Shirley?"

"But what about Daniel? Who's going to teach him?" Kate wasn't following the conversation all that well, but part of it had sunk in.

"Just like your mother suggested," said Kim Ellen, "let one of us teach him how to touch you and how to please you. Better now than four years and four kids from now, wouldn't you say?"

Kate looked up at her mother.

"She's got a point there, Kate."

"Who should I choose, then?" Shirley leaned closer to Kate and whispered in her ear. Kate smiled.

"One thing," said Kate. All the girls were sitting more erect than they'd been a moment before. "You have to do it in the dark and he can't ever know that I was in on it." The girls were very alert now. "And whomever I pick has to be my bridesmaid tomorrow." They all nodded their agreement, smiling hopefully. "Now, who'll volunteer?"

Shirley had to put out her hand to stop them all from rushing Kate. "Back up girls!"

"I know what you're up to," Kate said smiling a knowing smile. "You all just want to sleep with my future husband, don't you?"

The girls all laughed.

"OK. Let's make it fair. I have to see what we're offering my poor Daniel." Like a stampede, the girls ran to their rooms and quickly returned in their most provocative undergarments.

⊲⊳

The nights were still cold, but the days were warming. Shirley had always loved this time of year; the spring temperatures were pleasant with the promise of summer to come, but still there was some of the bite of winter in the night air. She made for the private room that she knew the boys were dining in and was unsurprised to find a naked girl dancing provocatively in front of Daniel.

"Jerome Wheeler, I'm shocked," she announced, as she swept into the room. "And don't go looking at me that way either, Red Corcoran. I wouldn't put it past you to be at the bottom of this, too." She pointed a finger at Harry.

"And you, Harry Rich, here you are, trying to sully the reputation of the man who's going to marry my daughter tomorrow. You have no idea what kinds of diseases this little whore might be carrying. If something happened and my daughter got sick, I swear to God, I'd kill the lot of you, and no court in the state would convict me." She turned her attention on Wheeler, who looked like a stunned deer.

"Jerome, I want to have a word with you, please. And Daniel! Keep your hands in your pockets." She and Jerome left the room together.

Jerome Wheeler was used to giving orders, had been most of his adult life, but an order from Big Shirley was equal to an order from God or his mother. Shirley turned to face him.

"Jerome, I want to borrow your best parlor room for the night. Do you mind?" Shirley was her beguiling self again.

"What's this about, Shirley? You come in here ordering me about like I don't matter to you. I still own the Paragon, you know."

Shirley took his hand in hers. "You're still coming to the wedding tomorrow, aren't you?"

"Of course I am. I'm not too sure how happy my wife and daughter are about it, but I'll make sure they're there. You can count on it. I've ordered the best of everything for the party, and that Chinese fellow Mr. Chin is having his wife make up those little dim sum things too, for good luck."

Jerome was glad that he could be a part of the wedding plans. He'd grown quite fond of his young protégé and was looking forward to the wedding, almost as much as if it were his own daughter he was marrying.

"Why do you want my parlor, Shirley?"

She leaned close and told him her purpose.

He laughed heartily and slapped his belly. "Sure enough, I like the idea. You can be sure I'll hold him here until you get the room ready. Say a half-hour then?" They shook hands and Shirley went to finish her arrangements.

❈

Harry was resting his cheek on the breast of the nude girl sitting on his lap when Jerome returned.

"Well, lad, I guess you were lucky that she didn't come in here a while back, aren't you?" Jerome laughed and went to the table, opening a new deck of cards and a fresh box of cigars. "What say we all have a friendly game of poker, fellers? And, no cheating this one time, Harry. You've cost me too much as it is."

They sat around the table and started playing. They played several hands, when Shirley came back into the room looking all business.

"Do you boys mind if I borrow Daniel? I promise I'll get him back before the wedding."

The men around the table looked at each other silently. Daniel obediently followed Shirley out the door, looking back at them plaintively. She led him up the stairs to the top floor, where she opened a door to a plush salon and invited him in.

"Would you open that for me please, Daniel?" Shirley handed Daniel a bottle of champagne. She walked around the parlor, inspecting the sheets, and then the bathroom. Daniel was wrestling with the bottle, looking for something to use to take off the top when he heard water running into the bathtub and walked over to investigate. Shirley stood at the door, blocking his way with formidable ease.

"Let me give you a hand with that. This is how you do it." Shirley took the bottle from him and opened it, then went to the cabinet where the crystal cut glasses and champagne flutes were displayed and removed two of them.

"Sit down, Daniel." He did as he was told. She poured the champagne, handing him one of the glasses. He was slightly drunk already, against both his wishes and his better judgment, but his friends had been insistent. "I want you to promise me something." She raised Daniel's chin and looked at him seriously. "I want you to promise me this. Whatever happens in this room tonight, you'll never tell a soul about it. Not anyone, ever, especially not Kate. Is that a understood, Daniel?"

"What's going to happen?"

"Never you mind. Just do as you're told, pay attention, and remember what you learn here. After tomorrow, there's only going to be one woman in your life till the day you die." She took his hands in hers, "Daniel, this is my little gift to you tonight. You could say that it's my wedding present to the both of you. I want nothing more than to see you two happy, and raising a great big family of grandchildren for me to spoil."

Daniel smiled.

Shirley walked into the bathroom and turned off the water, then poured sweet-smelling bath salts into the water and tested the temperature. She found Daniel, still as stone, standing where she'd left him. "I expect you to bathe tonight and again tomorrow, before the wedding. Do you have some new clothes?"

"Yes, Red picked them out."

"Do they fit you?"

"Mrs. Chin is fixing them."

"I'll have to thank her." She came around the table and took Daniel's hand, leading him into the bathroom. "I want you to get into the bath and wait."

"What's going to happen?"

"Just do as you're told, and remember as much as you can. This is the last night that you are a single man, so have fun and don't drink too much, OK?" She smiled at him and inspected his broad young chest and flat stomach. She smiled again at the thought that her daughter had chosen her man well.

"Get clean and I'll see you at the church at noon tomorrow." She pushed him into the bathroom and put his champagne flute on the small table next to the tub. "Go on, get in. You've a long night ahead of you."

Daniel did as he was told, unbuckling his belt and pulling off his boots.

"Remember what I told you about bathing tomorrow. If you don't, I'll cut that little pecker of yours off myself. Goodnight, Daniel." She blew him a kiss as she left.

The bath was luxury itself. He let himself slide down till the water touched his chin. He heard the tinkle of glasses coming from the other room and was suddenly alert. He hadn't heard the door open.

"Who's there? Shirley, is that you?" The lights in the main room began to dim and he started to panic. "Shirley, is that you?" he asked again. "Who's there?" he called out and reached for his pants but stopped.

He saw a hand reach around the corner and turn the light switch on the wall. The room fell into darkness. His eyes couldn't adapt fast enough, but he felt the presence of someone and saw a silhouette enter the room. The lights outside the Hotel in the street were just barely enough to outline the hourglass figure of whoever was entering the room.

"No more talking. Close your eyes," the disembodied voice said. Daniel complied. Whoever it was, took his face and kissed him gently. He panicked from the surprise and the guilt, his heart beating a tattoo in his chest.

"Shh," the voice said as she placed a silk blindfold over his eyes.

She took his hand and washed it gently. She rubbed soap between his fingers and up his arm. She washed his chest lazily, her hand stroking the skin around his shoulders, sliding around to the back of his neck to massage the tension away. He leaned forward in unasked compliance and felt his muscles relax all the way down to his toes.

He reached out for her, but she stopped him.

"Shh," she whispered again. "Not yet."

She took his hand and placed it on her chest, over her heart. He could feel the heart beating quickly and strongly as she guided it over her full, firm breasts. His hand slid with the water and soap and he felt again the excitement of her nipple, hard and round between his fingers. She rubbed the back of his hand over it and he heard her gasp softly. She slid her hand down into the water, over his tight muscles, further and further, deeper and deeper, until he felt her take his manhood in her hand and give a gentle squeeze. The reaction was instantaneous. Every muscle quivered in his body as if he'd been shocked by lightning.

"Shh," the voice lulled again. She withdrew her hand. Even though it was a disappointment, it allowed him to breathe again and to regain some of his self-control.

She soaped his back and scrubbed the skin with a rough cloth, rinsing him off when she was done. "Stand up," she whispered.

"Now? Here?" he asked, his voice constricted like he was a child again.

"Do as you're told."

He stood and she rinsed him off, cupping the water in her hands. She dried him with a soft warm towel took his hand and led him to the bed. She took scented cream and smoothed it over the hard muscles of his back and massaged his neck until his body finally surrendered to her will. Her hands pushed at the long muscles of his legs, and her fingers spread over the firm taut roundness of his buttocks. He quivered again at her touch.

"Why are you doing this?" he asked into the pillow, not really caring about the answer.

"Turn over," she demanded, he complied. She rubbed the lotion over his chest and slowly stroked his penis with the warm lotion until it pulsed in her hand. He felt her swing her leg over his hips and straddle him, then took his hands to her breasts. He was almost crazy with desire. He felt the wetness of her as she slid back and forth over his stomach, making his muscles twitch and his penis throb.

She kissed him lightly and stood up from the bed. "Come with me," she said and took his hand and led him back to the bath. Through the sound of the rushing water she whispered in his ear; "Relax, you've a long night ahead of you." It was the second time he'd heard that said. She held his hand as he got back into the bath. He sank into the liquid bliss, and she kissed him as she left him alone again to soak.

He heard the door close behind her.

"Would you like some more champagne?"

Suddenly, he was awake again. It was a different voice. Not so soft, not so young.

"Yes, please," he replied.

"Come with me," the voice advised, and he let himself be led from the bath into the bedroom again.

Next he was tossed onto the bed and forcibly held down. His hands were tied together before he could defend himself, and then they were tied to the brass headpiece of the bed. Whoever it was surprised him totally, and pinched his nipples so hard, he cried out.

"Be quiet," the voice told him. "Or I might hurt you."

Daniel got hard, then he was wrenched away from his orgasm by her application of sweet pain. He cried out for her to stop but she laughed deeply, at times plugging his mouth with her breasts, smothering him until he almost gagged. She would pull away from him and he would suck in air, then it would happen again, those soft deadly breasts covering his mouth and his nose.

She slowly rubbed his erection, alternately squeezing it and kissing it.

He came and groaned and arched his back in ecstasy. He heard her sigh as if she'd broken her toy. She took a warm cloth from the bath and washed him while he lay on the bed, gasping for air.

"Do you like this?" she asked.

He gave up a long moan while the ecstasy took him. He whimpered at every stroke of the warm wet cloth. "Very much," he growled into the darkness.

Her face was close to his ear. "Well, women like this too." It was like a whispered warning. "Now I'm going to show you what a woman likes." She untied his hands but not the blindfold. "Give me your hands," she took his hands and massaged the fingers and the palms. He began to relax. "Do you like this?" she whispered in his ear.

Daniel could only groan in pleasure.

"And this is how we like to be touched." His hands had never been so wonderfully employed and he smiled into the darkness at the sublime pleasure of her body. She took his hands and placed them on her hips as she rocked back and forth. "Gently now," she whispered. She guided his hands along her thighs up to a woven field of warm moistures that brought groans from his persecutor. Her breath came in gasps and she gripped him tightly with her thighs. Her weight lifted from the bed and he heard her dressing, the swish of silk as her clothing rustled over her body. She kissed him lightly.

"Give me your hands," she demanded, he obliged, hoping to have more tactile instruction, but his hands were once again tied to the bed head. He felt the warmth of her breath and the brush of her hair across his face as she came closer. "Kate's a very lucky girl," she whispered. The next thing he heard was the door closing.

Daniel relaxed, feeling he was finally alone, but he still had his hands tied to the bed. He struggled against the silk knots but they wouldn't give. Just as he was about to panic, he felt fingers moving up his arms and to his bonds above his head.

"No, no more, I can't take it. Let me go, please."

"Shh." It was a different voice.

He froze. He could have sworn that his heart stopped dead.

"Shh," the sound came again. The voice was calming, warming, sensual. He felt his body relax and he felt the warm cloth over his body again. The knots above his head slowly released their grip and he took his arms down painfully.

"Leave the blindfold on. Give me your hands," the voice softly commanded.

He allowed her to guide his hands between her legs. He felt the tuft of her pubic hair and she guided his hand around her hips, along her thighs, and between her legs. Her hands moved his slowly but continuously.

He tried to help.

She took his hands in hers. "Let me show you how."

He could feel and hear the pleasure he was giving her.

She relaxed her grip and let him experiment while her hips moved slowly from side to side. The muscles of her stomach tensed and quivered rhythmically before shuddering to climax. Daniel had no idea what was happening, but kept up with her motions. She arched her back and pressed herself against him. He tried to pull his hand away but she held it tightly against her, guiding his fingers inside of her, groaning with pleasure. He felt her relax and she released his hand to gently roam over her shoulders and breasts. Her nipples were taut but tender, she continued to have small quakes as the waves of her pleasure ebbed and flowed through her. He was slipping into sleep when he felt her stir.

His body cried out for sleep, but she took some of the cold champagne and allowed him to drink from her breasts slowly, just a sip at a time. He fell back on the bed. He felt her move her head down between his legs. Her mouth was slightly chilled from the champagne as she took his penis between her lips and sucked it into her mouth. It was the most exquisite feeling of his life.

"Oh, God." He moaned loudly and tried to sit up. He sensed that she was smiling at him, holding his limp penis gently in her small hand. She pushed him back down on the bed gently, but with firm pressure. She massaged his penis using warm cream and the cool champagne until he was hard. She slid into the bed beside him and pulled him on top of her. He tried to push his way into her, but she backed away.

"Slowly now." Her encouragement was what he needed. Ever so slowly, he felt the divine wonder as she guided him into her. He entered her, a little at a time. It was slow and wonderful.

She'd only moved but a little when she felt the sudden rush of his explosion inside her. He moaned and then groaned as she quickened her pace, thrusting against him, trying to get the most out of him she could. He came in a gasping explosion. Again and again she pushed against him and then she slowed and became still, breathing deeply, resting her hand on his sweaty chest, feeling his heartbeat like a train going full speed.

For the first time since all of this had begun, he thought of Kate, and his imagination ran away into the fields of pleasure he would share with her. The specter of his guilt then abruptly rose to torment him and threatened to overwhelm the sweet memory of his pleasure.

"Just hold me," she said, and he felt the wetness on her cheeks as she lay with her head on his chest. He did as she asked and shortly felt her tremble underneath him. He tried to roll off, but she gripped him tightly, her nails pressing painfully into his back. "I'm alright, just hold me." It was in that manner and at that moment that he learned the most important secret of pleasing a woman. He held her tightly, lovingly, until the tremor had passed. She kissed him one last time and pushed him off her. The swish of her clothing as she dressed filled Daniel with a feeling of desertion and desolation. He trembled.

She came to him and kissed him gently on the cheek. "Just remember to take a bath. Women always like a man to smell nice. Now get some sleep." She went to the door. Before she opened it, she softly said, "Kate is the luckiest girl in the world."

Chapter 48

There was a loud knocking at the door. At least, Daniel thought it was at the door. He got up and answered the noise in his head. He wasn't ready for what he saw, could never be ready, really. There stood a maid, dressed in a frilly apron with a cup of coffee and rolls on a tray. She handed it to him, then looked downward and smiled. He realized that he was dressed in his undershirt and nothing else. She smiled and was still standing at the door looking down at him when he closed it. He heard her footsteps recede.

A small envelope was on the tray. He picked it up and went to open the drapes, allowing the sunlight to throw itself into the room. Looking at the ornate clock on the mantle, he saw that it was already nine o'clock. He opened the envelope and read the note that said simply: *Take a bath. Get dressed. Get to Church.* There was no signature, but there was a faint scent of perfume on the note that he held under his nose. It had a wondrous effect on him almost instantly. His nostrils flared at the exotic fragrance and he felt his blood surge through him. He was alive. He knew that his whole future lay ahead of him.

There came another knock on the door, and this time he pulled on his pants, which he eventually found underneath the bed. He could see only one of his boots. As he went to answer the door, his cup of coffee in his hand, random memories of the night rampaged through his swampy brain. He was smiling broadly when he opened the door and found the same maid standing there, trying to hold back a smile. She held out his suit of clothes with a fresh white carnation tucked into the lapel buttonhole, and presented a crisp white shirt wrapped in thin paper. He thanked the maid and went back inside, laying the black suit on the chair by the window as he headed for the bathroom.

He was in the bath no more than a few minutes when there was another knock at the door. Wrapping the towel around him and dripping water through the room over the expensive carpets, he was surprised to find Harry, a bottle of whiskey in his hand. His eyes were bleary and he smelled to high heaven.

"God Almighty, Harry, you look awful."

He staggered into the room. Closing the drapes against the bright morning light and covering his eyes, he collapsed onto one of the couches.

"If you're going to be my best man, you'd better go take a bath. We only have a couple of hours."

Daniel pulled him to his feet, pushing him towards the bathroom. He heard the water splash and the sigh of pleasure that he'd uttered himself, just minutes before.

"Where are your clothes?"

"They're on the floor where I left them."

"Harry, you wait here and I'll go get you some clean clothes. Yours are filthy. I'm not going to have the best man looking like he just came from the mines." Daniel headed out, hurrying to their cabin. When he arrived, he waved to Willy Tomb, who was sitting on his throne.

"Today's the day, eh?" Willy said over the top of his paper. Daniel stopped with his hand on the door.

"Yep." Daniel's mood had roamed on his walk to the cabin. His eyes filled with the pure joy he felt. "Today's the day."

"Good luck, I hope it turns out alright for you."

"Thanks."

"You movin' out then?" Willy inquired.

"We're moving in with Big Shirley for a while until we can find a place."

Shirley had suggested it. It was probably her way of hanging onto her daughter for just a few more moments. He pushed his way through the door, but noticed new footprints around his doorstep, smaller than either his or Harry's. He went inside, but nothing seemed to have changed. He looked around closely and checked his meager possessions, but all seemed to be in order.

He was just about to leave, having gathered as many clean clothes for Harry as he could find, when he noticed some small wood chips on the top of the oven. Looking up, he noticed that someone had been digging into the plugged hole in the beam. He stood on the chair and found to his consternation that indeed someone had been trying to reopen the hole where the eyebolt used to go. He brushed them off and made sure that the oven had plenty of timber to burn. The oven was their only protection.

Harry had gotten back into the potato business. They'd rarely discussed the robbery and the implications of the money buried under the oven. It was just something they didn't want to discuss until it became safe to retrieve the money.

"Congratulations," Willy called out from his throne as Daniel left and headed back down the path to the road. He was not yet at the road and was considering the wood chips, when he suddenly froze. He threw Harry's clothes into the snow and ducked behind a narrow tree.

His movement caught the eye of one of the riders, who turned his way to look, but kept his horse moving. The other rider was tall and thin, bent over at the shoulders, wearing a large black hat. He turned his head, searching the trees with the keen eyes of a hunter. Daniel's heart stopped. It only started again when he saw the rider turn back and continue on. He clutched the tree with both hands and tried to think.

He recognized the rider who had looked directly at him. How could he ever forget him? It was the Sheriff's son, Hamlett. The other rider could only be Doc Holliday. He watched and waited until he could see them no longer, then he picked up Harry's clothes from the snow. Daniel hurried back to the hotel, taking the alleys and looking around every corner before dashing across the streets.

Out of breath by the time he reached the Hotel, he found Red and Joe sitting in the foyer by the fireplace.

"What're you two doing here?" They both looked up at him in surprise.

"What're you doing down here? Why aren't you up there, getting dressed? We knocked on the door, but nobody answered," said Red.

"So we came down here for a drink," Joe added, sipping his coffee and wrinkling his nose slightly.

"Harry's in the bath." He turned to head upstairs, but Red stopped him.

"Is anything wrong, Daniel?"

"No, I'm just nervous."

Red slapped him on the back. "That's normal the first couple of times." He winked at Daniel. "The next one will be easier, I promise you." He slapped Daniel on the back hard and pushed him up the stairs.

⊀⊱

"Harry?"

No answer. Daniel rushed into the bathroom, dreading finding that Harry had drowned on his wedding day. Harry was in the tub, a face cloth covering his head, a whiskey bottle lying on the floor. Daniel reached out and removed the cloth.

"I thought you'd never get here."

Daniel picked up the empty bottle and tried to hit Harry with it. Red grabbed his arm.

"Steady on, son. It's bad luck to kill a drunk on your wedding day." Red handed the bottle to Joe. "Here, Joe, you do it for him."

"No problem," said Joe, advancing towards Harry.

"Hand me a towel, for God's sake."

"Shave your face while you're in there, Harry." Red reached out and grabbed Daniel's chin, looking at him sternly. "And you'd better do the same thing or you'll go to your wedding looking like you spent last night with a bunch of whores." Red smiled broadly and picked up the empty champagne bottle, tipping it upside down. Red looked at Joe and smiled.

"I sure could use a drink," Joe said.

"You fellers better get a move on. We'll meet you downstairs."

Joe took a quick roll in the soft bed.

"Come on, Joe, I'll get you this room the next time you get married. I promise." Daniel laughed as they left.

"Come here, Daniel. Help me with this, will you?"

Daniel went into the bathroom and found Harry with small pieces of white paper stuck to several cuts on his face.

"What did you do?" There was a particularly nasty nick under his chin, leaking blood down his neck.

"Hey, I'm nervous."

"Harry, you'd think you were the one getting married. Look at your hands."

Harry held out his hands and they shook noticeably.

He stopped dabbing at the cuts on his face and put on his shirt. Daniel was almost dressed when he heard Harry swearing. He emerged from the bathroom, his tie knotted vaguely around his neck. Daniel pulled him in front of the big mirror over the fireplace and reached around him to tie his tie from behind. Finished, they put on their coats and checked their appearance in the mirror. They looked good side by side, their faces tanned and shiny, the color of their skin contrasting with the whiteness of their shirts and the dark color of the jackets.

"I'm sorry I spent all of your money."

"It's alright, Harry," Daniel replied. "I know where there's plenty more." Harry didn't laugh, which gave Daniel pause.

"I'm sorry that I got you into all that trouble, too."

"That's OK, Harry."

"I'm glad we're still friends after all the trouble I caused you."

"It's alright."

"And all the money I stole from you."

"Yes, I know all about that and I forgive you." Daniel turned to face Harry, placing his hand on Harry's shoulder. "We're still friends."

"And always will be," said Harry, opening the door for Daniel.

"After you, my friend. Let's go and get you hitched."

"Have you got the ring, Harry?"

Harry blanched patting his pockets.

꜒꜖

Shirley had her carriage decked out in ribbons of pink and lilac, with fresh flowers sitting in small vases, front and rear. The day was warm and springtime sunny, the sky a robin's egg blue and cloudless. Dix, her manager, was dressed immaculately for the occasion, with his best coat and tails. He helped the girls into the carriage and took his seat on the driver's bench. When they were all settled, blankets tucked around their feet, he gently slapped the horse with the reins and they headed to the church.

Outside the church, Jerome Wheeler and his family greeted them warmly; even Mrs. Wheeler was almost smiling, as was Abigail, who hugged Kate. Kate and Abigail held each other at arm's length and Abigail admired her dress with genuine approval and envy. Shirley was directing Rachelle to enter the church when Wheeler approached and handed her an envelope.

"This is a little something for you and the kids." Shirley took the envelope and kissed Jerome on the cheek.

"Thank you, Jerome." He smiled at her warmly, then turned and ushered his family inside. She opened the envelope and gasped, her hand coming up to her mouth to stifle the words.

"Oh my God." She held the deed to the Paragon building.

"What is it? Is something wrong?" Kate came to her mother. Shirley threw her arms around her. Jerome smiled at them. She was now a wealthy woman in her own right.

"No, my darlings, everything is just fine." With a smile of gratitude for Jerome, Shirley directed her attention back on her daughters. "Is he in there?" Shirley called to Rachelle, who looked into the church and nodded. They were standing just inside the front door, about to make their walk down the aisle.

"Kate," Shirley said softly to her daughter as she arranged the veil under her tiara of flowers. "I want you to know you can always come to me, no matter what the problem. Do you understand that?" Kate nodded, too overwhelmed with emotion to speak. Her eyes were glistening. With that, Shirley let the veil fall over her daughter's lovely face, and they entered the church arm in arm to the strains of the wedding march, played by a lone organist.

Kate's bridesmaids, Kim Ellen, Lauralee and Cindy, turned and led the way; Rachelle was the last in line. Shirley held onto Kate's arm to steady her daughter. With a practiced gait, they gracefully walked towards the altar. The church was crowded, and all eyes turned.

To Shirley, it was the most beautiful scene she'd ever witnessed. Daniel and the men were splendidly dressed in their dark suits and snowy white shirts. Their carnations shone like stars on their chests. Even Red looked dashing and freshly shaved.

The priest stood regally in his simple vestments, the church was decorated all over with flowers. It truly looked like spring with the bright sunlight shining through the colored glass of the window above the altar. She, Kate, and the bridesmaids passed through a brilliant shaft of sunlight that fell on them halfway down the aisle.

Daniel could not take his eyes off his bride-to-be as she entered the church and slowly walked towards him. Her dress was simple but elegant, dazzling white, with a short train of satin and lace.

Harry was the best man in name only, Red and Leafy stood alongside him. Harry fidgeted, feeling his pockets repeatedly, pulling them out or peering into them. Red elbowed him. The bridesmaids came forward to stand opposite them, smiling and looking radiant.

The nearer Kate came, the more Daniel could feel his attraction to her. He had to cross his hands in front of him, which made the bridesmaids giggle. They were enjoying his discomfort. Harry nudged him from behind; Daniel ignored him. Harry nudged him again.

"What?" he hissed under his voice.

"Don't go passing out on me. You'll miss the best parts."

Daniel looked back at his bride coming nearer, gliding down the aisle. He felt his heart increase speed and sweat run from his armpits under his shirt. He felt another nudge from Harry again.

"What is it now, Harry?"

"I can't find the ring."

Daniel rolled his eyes to the heavens.

Shirley led Kate up to the altar, where she stood next to Daniel. The ceremony began. Daniel's feet wouldn't keep still; he had to go to the toilet again, though he'd gone not long before. He was very much dreading the moment when the priest asked for the ring, his anxiety getting the best of him. He couldn't concentrate on what the priest was saying. Kate looked over at him with concern. He smiled to reassure her.

"May I please have the ring?" the priest asked, unaware of the problem.

Daniel held out his hand to Harry. Harry looked at the waiting hand and fidgeted in his pockets again.

"I can't find it," he announced in a murmur that rolled through the room. As the dismay rose at the news, Shirley stepped forward and passed something to Harry. Mystified, he looked at her.

"Maybelle found it in her bed this morning," Shirley whispered. His face lit up and he held the ring up for everyone to see. There was an audible sigh of relief throughout the church.

The priest made a clucking noise with his tongue. He took the ring and handed it to Daniel, who placed it on Kate's finger. It slid into place easily, a perfect fit. The smile of hope and optimism that lit her face was like a brilliant light, shining from within. It seemed as though everyone in the room smiled and glowed along with her.

"I now pronounce you man and wife. You may kiss your bride."

Daniel raised the veil from Kate's face, took her face gently in his hands, and kissed her tenderly. There was a long round of applause and cheers from all around them.

The priest shook hands with them and they walked back down the aisle towards the sunlight and their future life together.

Shirley and Red walked together. He smiled as she passed her arm through his. He covered her forearm with his large hand and they walked together down the aisle as one. Harry linked arms with the bridesmaids and they turned to follow. Leafy walked over to Rachelle, solemnly and deliberately took her hand, and they followed along behind.

Shirley noticed a large woman at the back of the church whom she didn't know. Most of the guests were simple folk, but dressed well; this woman was dressed for travel. Her coat was heavy and she had the well-worn look of a woman who'd had a difficult life. The woman seemed to have some definite purpose. She was peering over and around the heads of the congregation. Shirley saw her dart out the front door.

"On behalf of my family, everybody's invited over to my Hotel for a small celebration and lots to drink." Jerome Wheeler was applauded and cheered by all.

Jerome guided Daniel and Kate off to the side, taking Daniel by the hand in a warm handshake. He forced an envelope into Daniel's hands and guided it into his breast pocket.

"Don't lose that. It's so you can have a nice place to live." Kate kissed Jerome hard on the cheek as Daniel pumped his hand. "I think you'll be my partner someday, young man," Jerome said with pride. "I want you to have a big family. Now, let's go over to the Hotel and get the festivities started."

An arm reached over Shirley's shoulder, pushing her out of the way. Shirley saw that it was the woman from the back of the church. The woman grabbed Harry by the collar of his coat. Harry, with a look of abject terror on his face, spun around and pulled away from the woman, tearing his coat in the process, and ran down the aisle of the church.

"Come back here, Harry!" the woman screamed as she tried to push past Shirley. The crowd at the door blocked her way.

"Can I help you?" Shirley asked politely.

The woman halted her assault. "Not unless you're married to that spineless worm." The woman kept furtively looking past her at Harry's back, which was disappearing into the church, knocking people off their feet as he went.

"There's a wedding going on here."

The woman stopped momentarily and speared Shirley with an icicle stare.

"Yes, I know, I'm quite familiar with them. I had one with that little weasel there." She pointed past Shirley at Harry's back. "Come back here, Harry Rich!" she screamed over Shirley's head. Harry darted towards the front of the church, looking over his shoulder as he flew past. Daniel rushed after him, heading back into the church.

Daniel caught him at the side of the altar. Harry's eyes were wide and he pulled away, full of fear, reaching for the door handle.

"There's someone out there I don't want to see."

"Yeah, I know. He's got a big horse, a big hat, and a big gun."

"Who're you talking about?" Harry asked, as if Daniel were speaking a foreign language.

"Doc Holliday and that deputy that tried to kill us. You do remember them, don't you?"

Harry turned to face the altar, piously lifting his face to the wooden crucifix on the wall. "Oh God, please don't desert me now."

"God will never desert you, my son," the priest said from the side door.

"Can he find me a fast horse then, padre?"

The priest saw a large woman coming down the aisle of his church, with nothing but the devil's own mayhem in her mind.

"No, but he can show you the side door." He headed into the sacristy. "Through here, quickly." He ushered them through the door and bolted it behind them, then pointed at the door to the street behind the church. Harry needed no written directions; he turned quickly and shook Daniel's hand.

"I gotta get out'a here."

"Who is that, Harry? The woman with the gun." They jumped at a loud banging on the door. The priest was also looking for an answer.

"Oh. Just one of my lovely wives."

"Just one?" asked the priest, in astonishment.

"She's the mean one, too. I really got to get going. I'd love to stay, really I would. But…" The pounding of the pistol butt on the door reverberated through the small cold room like the pounding of coffin nails.

"When will you be back?" Daniel felt a surge of worry and concern for his friend.

"If they get their hands on me; probably not till the second coming."

"What about your cabin?"

Again the door rocked with malicious intent. They watched as the door started a rhythmical banging as someone's full weight was slamming against it. "She seems like a capable woman, Harry." Daniel was beginning to enjoy Harry's predicament.

"Look, Daniel, I have to get away from here. I'm more afraid of my wife than I am of Doc Holliday. The cabin's yours and Kate's, my wedding gift to you both."

The door ground inward, the wall crumbling around the hinges. Harry grabbed Daniel, hugged him quickly, and headed for the door.

"I'll hold her here," Daniel yelled as the door gave way.

"I doubt it, but thanks anyway." And he was gone.

Harry went through the side door as fast as a rabbit, fully appreciating the determination of the woman he'd married. He made it outside as the door to the altar behind him gave way and he crashed into the side of a wagon drawn up outside the door. He held his head, ducked under the wagon and found himself looking down the barrel of a shotgun held by a young girl not much bigger than the gun itself.

"Going somewhere, Harry?"

Harry had to wonder if all this was not just a bad dream. He turned the other way, pushing off the wall to get a running start, then ran into his other wife, holding a pistol expertly.

Harry smiled disarmingly. "Well, Beth, I was thinking of you the other day, but I have to get going now, you see. Important stuff I gotta do." Harry held up both his hands in surrender to the overwhelming firepower. "You know how it is, but thanks for dropping by." He slapped at the shotgun, knocking it out of her hand and reached down quickly to pick it up. He pointed it at Beth's chest. "Sorry, Beth, I really must be going."

He turned to find the barrel of a pistol looking him right between the eyes. "Come on back home, Harry. We all miss you."

"Yeah, Harry, we miss you," Beth said. "The children miss you, too." She knocked on the side of the wagon and three little heads popped up from under the blankets.

"Daddy," they chorused. The older woman burst from the church.

"Get under them blankets before that skinny old man in the black hat shoots you. Go on. Get in, Harry," she advised. "I wouldn't mind that old man doin' it, but I think we girls will enjoy working you to death more."

Harry looked around and saw Daniel and the priest standing at the door. "I'll be back," he said to Daniel.

"Not in this life, you won't," the older woman said, jabbing him in the side with her pistol.

He waved to Daniel weakly as he climbed into the wagon and joined the little ones under the blankets. The older woman jumped lithely into the driver's seat and took up the reins, slapping the horses expertly. The wagon rolled down the alley and turned towards Main Street. Daniel saw that Doc Holliday and Hamlett had placed their horses across the alley to block the road.

Daniel raced back inside, through the splintered door to where Kate stood with Shirley and the rest, grouped around the front door of the church, looking baffled. He grabbed Red, pointing to where Doc and Hamlett were sitting on their mounts, looking down the alley at the approaching wagon. He hurriedly told Red what had happened. Red called the sheriff over and spoke to him quietly. The crowd was quietly following every move of the drama.

In silence, they watched the wagon come down the alley. Doc Holliday stepped his horse into its path and locked eyes on the burly woman holding the reins. He looked over the wagon and saw only the small children. "Howdy, ma'am," he said and she nodded back politely. Harry recognized the voice and held his breath. The kids playfully sat all over him. Ham rode around the wagon and the two women kept their guns close at hand.

"You all wouldn't know a feller named Harry Rich by any chance, would you?"

"No, sir, we don't. I'd appreciate you moving your damned horse so's we can pass, if it's all the same to you."

Doc warmed to the woman. "Where might you be headin', ma'am, if you don't mind my askin'? You don't seem to have a husband to protect you and all this brood. Or do you?"

"I'd say that's none of your business. And I'll ask you again to get out'a my way." She reached for the pistol. Doc held up his hands, but Ham continued inspecting the wagon and its contents. The children grew quiet.

The sheriff approached the two men. "Howdy, Ham, Doc. Everything here alright with you fellers?"

"Howdy, sheriff," Doc wheezed. "We were just looking for that Harry Rich feller. He owes me some money." The young woman banged the shotgun butt into the heap of clothing in the wagon. There was a faint groan. "We was wonderin' if he might be at this here wedding. You haven't seen him, have you?" The sheriff looked around at the guests who had gathered about them.

"Any of you folks here seen Harry Rich?" he asked loudly. The people in the crowd looked at each other, shaking their heads. Nobody spoke a word.

"No, not today," Daniel answered, moving to the front of the crowd. "As a matter of fact, he was supposed to be my best man." He looked at Kate and smiled.

"Best man, eh? Now that's a laugh, ain't it, Ham?" The deputy smiled a crinkly smile that contorted his disfigured face.

"We're all disappointed that he didn't show up." Daniel added.

The crowd all murmured their combined disappointment. The kids in the wagon were fidgeting all over Harry's inert body. Doc rode over to the youngest woman sitting on the buckboard of the wagon, holding tightly to her shotgun. He touched the brim of his hat formally. "He wouldn't be your daddy, would he, miss?"

"You could be my daddy, mister. We're looking for one."

The older woman sneered at Doc, slapped at the horses, and clicked for them to move. Doc and Ham let them by, closely checking the back of the wagon again as it passed. The kids in the back waved.

Jerome broke through the crowd. He looked at Red and at the sheriff and then at Daniel, who tilted his head towards the wagon that was slowly moving away.

"Say there, Doc, this here's a celebration. What say we all go back to the Hotel and have ourselves a drink? You look like you could use one there too, deputy. Come on over. Be my guests."

Doc looked from the wagon to Daniel, then back at the wagon. The women didn't turn around. The wagon slowly crept down Main Street.

"That's mighty generous of you, Mr. Wheeler." Doc looked at Daniel. "That is, if young Mr. Carrington don't hold a grudge?"

Daniel looked from Doc Holliday to the wagon leaving town and saw Harry lift his head and wave, only to have one of his wives swipe at him. "Grudges are bad business I think, Mr. Holliday," said Daniel.

"That's right neighborly of you," Doc had a phlegmatic spasm. It subsided after what seemed like minutes. "But we're heading down valley towards Glenwood Springs. My guess is that Mr. Rich has used some of his weak mind to clear out'a here. I guess we'll just move on along and try to catch up with him." Doc's lips curved in a tiny pained smile as he looked at the departing wagon. One of the children waved at him.

"I feel that widow woman and her brood could use some protection. I think she might like to get to know me. If you get my drift, Mr. Wheeler?" Doc smiled as he and the deputy turned their horses and with not a backward glance, followed after the wagon carrying Harry and his wives to the promised land of Utah.

Shirley took Red's hand. No Problem Joe appeared and was swamped by Maybelle's breasts in a joyous embrace. Bjorn and Tomas linked arms with the three bridesmaids, as happy as a pair of bachelors could be in the state of Colorado.

"Kate, there's something that happened last night that I have to tell you about." Daniel looked at Kate with pleading eyes. "I didn't mean for it to happen. It just did. And I'm sorry."

Kate touched his cheek and looked deeply into his eyes. She leaned into him and he felt the inviting warmth of her body.

"Shhh," she whispered in his ear. "It's OK. I know all about it, I was there," she said softly, mischievously smiling, and Daniel's eyes grew wide as sudden realization dawned on him that it was Kate who was in bed with him last night.

Daniel laughed, and hugged his new bride to him in absolute love and wonder. He was truly the luckiest man.

"Well, I guess we're really married then," he said, laughing. "We even have our own cabin to live in. I'm sure, with a woman's touch, it could look very nice."

Kate looked into his eyes, a shadow passing over her lovely face.

"That oven will have to go."

"I guess I can do that." They fell into an embrace and as they kissed long and passionately, a cheer arose from the crowd.

"Well folks. Let's all go and have ourselves a party," Wheeler announced loudly.

To a huge round of applause, Jerome B. Wheeler flamboyantly led the guests off to enjoy the finest celebration possible at the new Hotel Jerome.

Rachelle pulled at her mother's sleeve.

"What is it now, Rachelle?"

Rachelle was holding onto Leafy's hand, looking deceptively innocent. "I've got something to tell you."

Shirley and Red waited while Rachelle and Leafy looked to each other for courage.

"I think I'm pregnant," Rachelle announced.

"Oh my God, Red," Shirley held her hands to her cheeks. "Tell me this is not happening?" Red put his arm around Shirley's shoulder and laughed his great big laugh.

Daniel put his arm around his new wife and wondered if they might have their own children someday. With a sense of pride, he thought about being able to support his family and his thoughts turned to the money that Harry had left behind under the oven in the cabin. He sighed.

He knew that someday Harry would show up again...

... to be continued in ...
The Silver Queen.

Made in the USA
Charleston, SC
13 March 2016